JANE
AUSTEN

JANE
AUSTEN

PRIDE AND PREJUDICE

SENSE AND SENSIBILITY

LONGMEADOW PRESS

Published exclusively for Marks and Spencer p.l.c. in 1983 by
Octopus Books Limited
59 Grosvenor Street
London W1

Pride and Prejudice was first published in Great Britain in 1813
Sense and Sensibility was first published in Great Britain in 1811

Published exclusively for Waldenbooks in 1984 by

Octopus Books Limited
59 Grosvenor Street
London W1

ISBN 0 681 28766 7

Printed by Kingsport Press, USA

CONTENTS

PRIDE AND PREJUDICE

Chapter One

IT IS A TRUTH UNIVERSALLY ACKNOWLEDGED, that a single man in possession of a good fortune, must be in want of a wife.

However little known the feelings or views of such a man may be on his first entering a neighbourhood, this truth is so well fixed in the minds of the surrounding families, that he is considered as the rightful property of some one or other of their daughters.

'My dear Mr Bennet,' said his lady to him one day, 'have you heard that Netherfield Park is let at last?'

Mr Bennet replied that he had not.

'But it is,' returned she; 'for Mrs Long has just been here, and she told me all about it.'

Mr Bennet made no answer.

'Do not you want to know who has taken it?' cried his wife impatiently.

'*You* want to tell me, and I have no objection to hearing it.'

This was invitation enough.

'Why, my dear, you must know, Mrs Long says that Netherfield is taken by a young man of large fortune from the north of England; that he came down on Monday in a chaise and four to see the place, and was so much delighted with it that he agreed with Mr Morris immediately; that he is to take possession before Michaelmas, and some of his servants are to be in the house by the end of next week.'

'What is his name?'

'Bingley.'

'Is he married or single?'

'Oh! single, my dear, to be sure! A single man of large fortune; four or five thousand a year. What a fine thing for our girls!'

'How so? how can it affect them?'

'My dear Mr Bennet,' replied his wife, 'how can you be so tiresome! You must know that I am thinking of his marrying one of them.'

'Is that his design in settling here?'

'Design! nonsense, how can you talk so! But it is very likely that he *may* fall in love with one of them, and therefore you must visit him as soon as he comes.'

'I see no occasion for that. You and the girls may go, or you may send them by themselves, which perhaps will be still better, for as you are as handsome as any of them, Mr Bingley might like you the best of the party.'

'My dear, you flatter me. I certainly *have* had my share of beauty, but I do not pretend to be any thing extraordinary now. When a woman has five grown up daughters, she ought to give over thinking of her own beauty.'

'In such cases, a woman has not often much beauty to think of.'

'But, my dear, you must indeed go and see Mr Bingley when he comes into the neighbourhood.'

'It is more than I engage for, I assure you.'

'But consider your daughters. Only think what an establishment it would be for one of them. Sir William and Lady Lucas are determined to go, merely on that account, for in general you know they visit no new comers. Indeed you must go, for it will be impossible for *us* to visit him, if you do not.'

'You are over scrupulous surely. I dare say Mr Bingley will be very glad to see you; and I will send a few lines by you to assure him of my hearty consent to his marrying which ever he chuses of the girls; though I must throw in a good word for my little Lizzy.'

'I desire you will do no such thing. Lizzy is not a bit better than the others; and I am sure she is not half so handsome as Jane, nor half so good humoured as Lydia. But you are always giving *her* the preference.'

'They have none of them much to recommend them,' replied he; 'they are all silly and ignorant like other girls; but Lizzy has something more of quickness than her sisters.'

'Mr Bennet, how can you abuse your own children in such a way? You take delight in vexing me. You have no compassion on my poor nerves.'

'You mistake me, my dear. I have a high respect for your nerves. They are my old friends. I have heard you mention them with consideration these twenty years at least.'

'Ah! you do not know what I suffer.'

'But I hope you will get over it, and live to see many young men of four thousand a year come into the neighbourhood.'

'It will be no use to us, if twenty such should come since you will not visit them.'

'Depend upon it, my dear, that when there are twenty, I will visit them all.'

Mr Bennet was so odd a mixture of quick parts, sarcastic humour, reserve, and caprice, that the experience of three and twenty years had been insufficient to make his wife understand his character. *Her* mind was less difficult to develope. She was a woman of mean understanding, little information, and uncertain temper. When she was discontented she fancied herself nervous. The business of her life was to get her daughters married; its solace was visiting and news.

Chapter Two

MR BENNET WAS AMONG THE EARLIEST of those who waited on Mr Bingley. He had always intended to visit him, though to the last always assuring his wife that he should not go; and till the evening after the visit was paid, she had no knowledge of it. It was then disclosed in the following manner. Observing his second daughter employed in trimming a hat, he suddenly addressed her with,

'I hope Mr Bingley will like it Lizzy.'

'We are not in a way to know *what* Mr Bingley likes,' said her mother resentfully, 'since we are not to visit.'

'But you forget, mama,' said Elizabeth, 'that we shall meet him at the assemblies, and that Mrs Long has promised to introduce him.'

'I do not believe Mrs Long will do any such thing. She has two nieces of her own. She is a selfish, hypocritical woman, and I have no opinion of her.'

'No more have I,' said Mr Bennet; 'and I am glad to find that you do not depend on her serving you.'

Mrs Bennet deigned not to make any reply; but unable to contain herself, began scolding one of her daughters.

'Don't keep coughing so, Kitty, for heaven's sake! Have a little compassion on my nerves. You tear them to pieces.'

'Kitty has no discretion in her coughs,' said her father; 'she times them ill.'

'I do not cough for my own amusement,' replied Kitty fretfully.

'When is your next ball to be, Lizzy?'

'To-morrow fortnight.'

'Aye, so it is,' cried her mother, 'and Mrs Long does not come back till the day before; so, it will be impossible for her to introduce him, for she will not know him herself.'

'Then, my dear, you may have the advantage of your friend, and introduce Mr Bingley to *her*.'

'Impossible, Mr Bennet, impossible, when I am not acquainted with him myself; how can you be so teazing?'

'I honour your circumspection. A fortnight's acquaintance is certainly very little. One cannot know what a man really is by the end of a fortnight. But if *we* do not venture, somebody else will; and after all, Mrs Long and her nieces must stand their chance; and therefore, as she will think it an act of kindness, if you decline the office, I will take it on myself.'

The girls stared at their father. Mrs Bennet said only, 'Nonsense, nonsense!'

'What can be the meaning of that emphatic exclamation?' cried he. 'Do you consider the forms of introduction, and the stress that is laid on them, as nonsense? I cannot quite agree with you *there*. What say you, Mary? for you are a young lady of deep reflection I know, and read great books, and make extracts.'

Mary wished to say something very sensible, but knew not how.

'While Mary is adjusting her ideas,' he continued, 'let us return to Mr Bingley.'

'I am sick of Mr Bingley,' cried his wife.

'I am sorry to hear *that*; but why did not you tell me so before? If I had known as much this morning, I certainly would not have called on him. It is very unlucky; but as I have actually paid the visit, we cannot escape the acquaintance now.'

The astonishment of the ladies was just what he wished; that of Mrs Bennet perhaps surpassing the rest; though when the first tumult of joy was over, she began to declare that it was what she had expected all the while.

'How good it was in you, my dear Mr Bennet! But I knew I should persuade you at last. I was sure you loved your girls too well to neglect such an acquaintance. Well, how pleased I am! and it is such a good joke, too, that you should have gone this morning, and never said a word about it till now.'

'Now, Kitty, you may cough as much as you chuse,' said Mr Bennet; and, as he spoke, he left the room, fatigued with the raptures of his wife.

'What an excellent father you have, girls,' said she, when the door was shut. 'I do not know how you will ever make him amends for his kindness; or me either, for that matter. At our time of life, it is not so pleasant I can tell you, to be making new acquaintance every day; but for your sakes, we would do any thing. Lydia, my love, though you *are* the youngest, I dare say Mr Bingley will dance with you at the next ball.'

'Oh!' said Lydia stoutly, 'I am not afraid; for though I *am* the youngest, I'm the tallest.'

The rest of the evening was spent in conjecturing how soon he would return Mr Bennet's visit, and determining when they should ask him to dinner.

Chapter Three

NOT ALL THAT MRS BENNET, HOWEVER, with the assistance of her five daughters, could ask on the subject was sufficient to draw from her husband any satisfactory description of Mr Bingley. They attacked him in various ways; with barefaced questions, ingenious suppositions, and distant surmises; but he eluded the skill of them all; and they were at last obliged to accept the second-hand intelligence of their neighbour Lady Lucas. Her report was highly favourable. Sir William had been delighted with him. He was quite young, wonderfully handsome, extremely agreeable, and to crown the whole, he meant to be at the next assembly with a large party. Nothing could be more delightful! To be fond of dancing was a certain step towards falling in love; and very lively hopes of Mr Bingley's heart were entertained.

'If I can but see one of my daughters happily settled at Netherfield,' said Mrs Bennet to her husband, 'and all the others equally well married, I shall have nothing to wish for.'

In a few days Mr Bingley returned Mr Bennet's visit, and sat about ten mintues with him in his library. He had entertained hopes of being admitted to a sight of the young ladies, of whose beauty he had heard much; but he saw only the father. The ladies were somewhat more fortunate, for they had the advantage of ascertaining from an upper window, that he wore a blue coat and rode a black horse.

An invitation to dinner was soon afterwards despatched; and already had Mrs Bennet planned the courses that were to do credit to her house-keeping, when an answer arrived which deferred it all. Mr Bingley was obliged to be in town the following day, and consequently unable to accept the honour of their invitation, &c. Mrs Bennet was quite disconcerted. She could not imagine what business he could have in town so soon after his arrival in Hertfordshire; and she began to fear that he might be always flying about from one place to another, and never settled at Netherfield as he ought to be. Lady Lucas quieted her fears a little by starting the idea of his being gone to London only to get a large party for the ball; and a report soon followed that Mr Bingley was to bring twelve ladies and seven gentlemen with him to the assembly. The girls grieved over such a number of ladies; but were comforted the day before the ball by hearing, that instead of twelve, he had brought only six with him from London, his five sisters and a cousin. And when the party entered the assembly room, it consisted of only five altogether; Mr Bingley, his two sisters, the husband of the eldest, and another young man.

Mr Bingley was good looking and gentlemanlike; he had a pleasant countenance, and easy, unaffected manners. His sisters were fine women, with an air of decided fashion. His brother-in-law, Mr Hurst, merely looked the gentleman; but his friend Mr Darcy soon drew the attention of the room by his fine, tall person, handsome features, noble mien; and the report which was in general circulation within five minutes after his entrance, of his having ten thousand a year. The gentlemen pronounced him to be a fine figure of a man, the ladies declared he was much handsomer than Mr Bingley, and he was looked at with great admiration for about half the evening, till his manners gave a disgust which turned the tide of his popularity; for he was discovered to be proud, to be above his company, and above being pleased; and not all his large estate in Derbyshire could then save him from having a most forbidding, disagreeable countenance, and being unworthy to be compared with his friend.

Mr Bingley had soon made himself acquainted with all the principal people in the room; he was lively and unreserved, danced every dance, was angry that the ball closed so early, and talked of giving one himself at Netherfield. Such amiable qualities must speak for themselves. What a contrast between him and his friend! Mr Darcy danced only once with Mrs Hurst and once with Miss Bingley, declined being introduced to any other lady, and spent the rest of the evening in walking about the room, speaking occasionally to one of his own party. His character was decided. He was the proudest, most disagreeable man in the world, and every body hoped that he would never come there again. Amongst the most violent against him was Mrs Bennet, whose dislike of his general behaviour, was sharpened into particular resentment, by his having slighted one of her daughters.

Elizabeth Bennet had been obliged, by the scarcity of gentlemen, to sit down for two dances; and during part of that time, Mr Darcy had been standing near enough for her to overhear a conversation between him and Mr Bingley, who came from the dance for a few minutes, to press his friend to join it.

'Come, Darcy,' said he, 'I must have you dance. I hate to see you standing about by yourself in this stupid manner. You had much better dance.'

'I certainly shall not. You know how I detest it, unless I am particularly acquainted with my partner. At such an assembly as this, it would be insupportable. Your sisters are engaged, and there is not another woman in the room, whom it would not be a punishment to me to stand up with.'

'I would not be so fastidious as you are,' cried Bingley, 'for a kingdom! Upon my honour, I never met with so many pleasant girls in my life, as I have this evening; and there are several of them you see uncommonly pretty.'

'You are dancing with the only handsome girl in the room,' said Mr Darcy, looking at the eldest Miss Bennet.

'Oh! she is the most beautiful creature I ever beheld! But there is one of her sisters sitting down just behind you, who is very pretty, and I dare say, very agreeable. Do let me ask my partner to introduce you.'

'Which do you mean?' and turning round, he looked for a moment at Elizabeth, till catching her eye, he withdrew his own and coldly said, 'She is tolerable; but not handsome enough to tempt *me*; and I am in no humour at present to give consequence to young ladies who are slighted by other men. You had better return to your partner and enjoy her smiles, for you are wasting your time with me.'

Mr Bingley followed his advice. Mr Darcy walked off; and Elizabeth remained with no very cordial feelings towards him. She told the story however with great spirit among her friends; for she had a lively, playful disposition, which delighted in any thing ridiculous.

The evening altogether passed off pleasantly to the whole family. Mrs Bennet had seen her eldest daughter much admired by the Netherfield party. Mr Bingley had danced with her twice, and she had been distinguished by his sisters. Jane was as much gratified by this, as her mother could be, though in a quieter way. Elizabeth felt Jane's pleasure. Mary had heard herself mentioned to Miss Bingley as the most accomplished girl in the neighbour-hood; and Catherine and Lydia had been fortunate enough to be never without partners, which was all that they had yet learnt to care for at a ball. They returned therefore in good spirits to Longbourn, the village where they lived, and of which they were the principal inhabitants. They found Mr Bennet still up. With a book he was regardless of time; and on the present occasion he had a good deal of curiosity as to the event of an evening which had raised such splendid expectations. He had rather hoped that all his wife's views on the stranger would be disappointed; but he soon found that he had a very different story to hear.

'Oh! my dear Mr Bennet,' as she entered the room, 'we have had a most delightful evening, a most excellent ball. I wish you had been there. Jane was so admired, nothing could be like it. Every body said how well she looked; and Mr Bingley thought her quite beautiful, and danced with her twice. Only think of *that* my dear; he actually danced with her twice; and she was the only creature in the room that he asked a second time. First of all, he asked Miss Lucas. I was so vexed to see him stand up with her; but, however, he did not admire her at all; indeed, nobody can, you know; and he seemed quite struck with Jane as she was going down the dance. So, he enquired who she was, and got introduced, and asked her for the two next. Then, the two third he danced with Miss King, and the two fourth with Maria Lucas, and the two fifth with Jane again, and the two sixth with Lizzy, and the Boulanger –'

'If he had had any compassion for *me*,' cried her husband impatiently, 'he would not have danced half so much! For God's sake, say no more of his partners. Oh! that he had sprained his ankle in the first dance!'

'Oh! my dear,' continued Mrs Bennet, 'I am quite delighted with him. He is so excessively handsome! and his sisters are charming women. I never in my life saw any thing more elegant than their dresses. I dare say the lace upon Mrs Hurst's gown –'

Here she was interrupted again. Mr Bennet protested against any descrip-tion of finery. She was therefore obliged to seek another branch of the subject, and related, with much bitterness of spirit and some exaggeration, the shocking rudeness of Mr Darcy.

'But I can assure you,' she added, 'that Lizzy does not lose much by not suiting *his* fancy; for he is a most disagreeable, horrid man, not at all worth pleasing. So high and so conceited that there was no enduring him! He walked here, and he walked there, fancying himself so very great! Not handsome enough to dance with! I wish you had been there, my dear, to have given him one of your set downs. I quite detest the man.'

Chapter Four

WHEN JANE AND ELIZABETH WERE alone, the former, who had been cautious in her praise of Mr Bingley before, expressed to her sister how very much she admired him.

'He is just what a young man ought to be,' said she, 'sensible, good humoured, lively; and I never saw such happy manners! – so much ease, with such perfect good breeding!'

'He is also handsome,' replied Elizabeth, 'which a young man ought likewise to be, if he possibly can. His character is thereby complete.'

'I was very much flattered by his asking me to dance a second time. I did not expect such a compliment.'

'Did not you? *I* did for you. But that is one great difference between us. Compliments always take *you* by surprise, and *me* never. What could be more natural than his asking you again? He could not help seeing that you were about five times as pretty as every other woman in the room. No thanks to his gallantry for that. Well, he certainly is very agreeable, and I give you leave to like him. You have liked many a stupider person.'

'Dear Lizzy!'

'Oh! you are a great deal too apt you know, to like people in general. You never see a fault in any body. All the world are good and agreeable in your eyes. I never heard you speak ill of a human being in my life.'

'I would wish not to be hasty in censuring any one; but I always speak what I think.'

'I know you do; and it is *that* which makes the wonder. With *your* good sense, to be so honestly blind to the follies and nonsense of others! Affectation of candour is common enough; – one meets it every where. But to be candid without ostentation or design – to take the good of every body's character and make it still better, and say nothing of the bad – belongs to you alone. And so, you like this man's sisters too, do you? Their manners are not equal to his.'

'Certainly not; at first. But they are very pleasing women when you converse with them. Miss Bingley is to live with her brother and keep his house; and I am much mistaken if we shall not find a very charming neighbour in her.'

Elizabeth listened in silence, but was not convinced; their behaviour at the assembly had not been calculated to please in general; and with more quickness of observation and less pliancy of temper than her sister, and with a judgment too unassailed by any attention to herself, she was very little disposed to approve them. They were in fact very fine ladies; not deficient in good humour when they were pleased, nor in the power of being agreeable where they chose it; but proud and conceited. They were rather handsome, had been educated in one of the first private seminaries in town, had a fortune of twenty thousand pounds, were in the habit of spending more than they ought, and of associating with people of rank; and were therefore in every respect entitled to think well of themselves, and meanly of others. They were of a respectable family in the north of England; a circumstance more deeply impressed on their memories than that their brother's fortune and their own had been acquired by trade.

Mr Bingley inherited property to the amount of nearly an hundred thousand pounds from his father, who had intended to purchase an estate, but did not live to do it. – Mr Bingley intended it likewise, and sometimes made choice of his county; but as he was now provided with a good house and the liberty of a manor, it was doubtful to many of those who best knew the easiness of his temper, whether he might not spend the remainder of his days at Netherfield, and leave the next generation to purchase.

His sisters were very anxious for his having an estate of his own; but though he was now established only as a tenant, Miss Bingley was by no means unwilling to preside at his table, nor was Mrs Hurst, who had married a man of more fashion than fortune, less disposed to consider his house as her home when it suited her. Mr Bingley had not been of age two years, when he was tempted by an accidental recommendation to look at Netherfield House. He did look at it and into it for half an hour, was pleased with the situation and the principal rooms, satisfied with what the owner said in its praise, and took it immediately.

Between him and Darcy there was a very steady friendship, in spite of a great opposition of character. – Bingley was endeared to Darcy by the easiness, openness, ductility of his temper, though no disposition could offer a greater contrast to his own, and though with his own he never appeared dissatisfied. On the strength of Darcy's regard Bingley had the firmest reliance, and of his judgment the highest opinion. In understanding Darcy was the superior. Bingley was by no means deficient, but Darcy was clever. He was at the same time haughty, reserved, and fastidious, and his manners, though well bred, were not inviting. In that respect his friend had greatly the advantage. Bingley was sure of being liked wherever he appeared, Darcy was continually giving offence.

The manner in which they spoke of the Meryton assembly was sufficiently characteristic. Bingley had never met with pleasanter people or prettier girls in his life; every body had been most kind and attentive to him, there had been no formality, no stiffness, he had soon felt acquainted with all the room; and as to Miss Bennet, he could not conceive an angel more beautiful. Darcy, on the contrary, had seen a collection of people in whom there was little beauty and no fashion; for none of whom he had felt the smallest interest, and from none received either attention or pleasure. Miss Bennet he acknowledged to be pretty, but she smiled too much.

Mrs Hurst and her sister allowed it to be so – but still they admired her and liked her, and pronounced her to be a sweet girl, and one whom they should not object to know more of. Miss Bennet was therefore established as a sweet girl, and their brother felt authorised by such commendation to think of her as he chose.

Chapter Five

WITHIN A SHORT WALK OF LONGBOURN lived a family with whom the Bennets were particularly intimate. Sir William Lucas had been formerly in trade in Meryton, where he had made a tolerable fortune and risen to the honour of knighthood by an address to the King, during his mayoralty. The distinction had perhaps been felt too strongly. It had given him a disgust to his business and to his residence in a small market town; and quitting them both, he had removed with his family to a house about a mile from Meryton, denominated from that period Lucas Lodge, where he could think with pleasure of his own importance, and unshackled by business, occupy himself solely in being civil to all the world. For though elated by his rank, it did not render him supercilious; on the contrary, he was all attention to every body. By nature inoffensive, friendly and obliging, his presentation at St James's had made him courteous.

Lady Lucas was a very good kind of woman, not too clever to be a valuable neighbour to Mrs Bennet. – They had several children. The eldest of them, a sensible, intelligent young woman, about twenty-seven, was Elizabeth's intimate friend.

That the Miss Lucases and the Miss Bennets should meet to talk over a ball was absolutely necessary; and the morning after the assembly brought the former to Longbourn to hear and to communicate.

'You began the evening well, Charlotte,' said Mrs Bennet with civil self-command to Miss Lucas. 'You were Mr Bingley's first choice.'

'Yes; – but he seemed to like his second better.'

'Oh! – you mean Jane, I suppose – because he danced with her twice. To be sure that *did* seem as if he admired her – indeed I rather believe he *did* – I heard something about it – but I hardly know what – something about Mr Robinson.'

'Perhaps you mean what I overheard between him and Mr Robinson; did not I mention it to you? Mr Robinson's asking him how he liked our Meryton assemblies, and whether he did not think there were a great many pretty women in the room, and *which* he thought the prettiest? and his answering immediately to the last question – Oh! the eldest Miss Bennet beyond a doubt, there cannot be two opinions on that point.'

'Upon my word! – Well, that was very decided indeed – that does seem as if – but however, it may all come to nothing you know.'

'*My* overhearings were more to the purpose than *yours*, Eliza,' said Charlotte. 'Mr Darcy is not so well worth listening to as his friend, is he? – Poor Eliza! – to be only just *tolerable*.'

'I beg you would not put it into Lizzy's head to be vexed by his ill-treatment; for he is such a disagreeable man that it would be quite a misfortune to be liked by him. Mrs Long told me last night that he sat close to her for half an hour without once opening his lips.'

'Are you quite sure, Ma'am? – is not there a little mistake?' said Jane. – 'I certainly saw Mr Darcy speaking to her.'

'Aye – because she asked him at last how he liked Netherfield, and he could not help answering her; – but she said he seemed very angry at being spoke to.'

'Mis Bingley told me,' said Jane, 'that he never speaks much unless among his intimate acquaintance. With *them* he is remarkably agreeable.'

'I do not believe a word of it, my dear. If he had been so very agreeable he would have talked to Mrs Long. But I can guess how it was; every body says that he is ate up with pride, and I dare say he had heard somehow that Mrs Long does not keep a carriage, and had come to the ball in a hack chaise.'

'I do not mind his not talking to Mrs Long,' said Miss Lucas, 'but I wish he had danced with Eliza.'

'Another time, Lizzy,' said her mother, 'I would not dance with *him*, if I were you.'

'I believe, Ma'am, I may safely promise you *never* to dance with him.'

'His pride,' said Miss Lucas, 'does not offend *me* so much as pride often does, because there is an excuse for it. One cannot wonder that so very a fine young man, with family, fortune, every thing in his favour, should think highly of himself. If I may so express it, he has a *right* to be proud.'

'That is very true,' replied Elizabeth, 'and I could easily forgive *his* pride, if he had not mortified *mine*.'

'Pride,' observed Mary, who piqued herself upon the solidity of her reflections, 'is a very common failing I believe. By all that I have ever read, I am convinced that it is very common indeed, that human nature is particularly prone to it, and that there are very few of us who do not cherish a feeling of self-complacency on the score of some quality or other, real or imaginary. Vanity and pride are different things, though the words are often used synonymously. A person may be proud without being vain. Pride relates more to our opinion of ourselves, vanity to what we would have others think of us.'

'If I were as rich as Mr Darcy,' cried a young Lucas who came with his sisters, 'I should not care how proud I was. I would keep a pack of foxhounds, and drink a bottle of wine every day.'

'Then you would drink a great deal more than you ought,' said Mrs Bennet; 'and if I were to see you at it I should take away your bottle directly.'

The boy protested that she should not; she continued to declare that she would, and the argument ended only with the visit.

Chapter Six

THE LADIES OF LONGBOURN SOON WAITED on those of Netherfield. The visit was returned in due form. Miss Bennet's pleasing manners grew on the good will of Mrs Hurst and Miss Bingley; and though the mother was found to be intolerable and the younger sisters not worth speaking to, a wish of being better acquainted with *them*, was expressed towards the two eldest. By Jane this attention was received with the greatest pleasure; but Elizabeth still saw superciliousness in their treatment of every body, hardly excepting even her sister, and could not like them; though their kindness to Jane, such as it was, had a value as arising in all probability from the influence of their brother's admiration. It was generally evident whenever they met, that he *did* admire her; and to *her* it was equally evident that Jane was yielding to the preference which she had begun to entertain for him from the first, and was in a way to be very much in love; but she considered with pleasure that it was not likely to be discovered by the world in general, since Jane united with great strength of feeling, a composure of temper and a uniform cheerfulness of manner, which would guard her from the suspicions of the impertinent. She mentioned this to her friend Miss Lucas.

'It may perhaps be pleasant,' replied Charlotte, 'to be able to impose on the public in such a case; but it is sometimes a disadvantage to be so very guarded. If a woman conceals her affection with the same skill from the object of it, she may lose the opportunity of fixing him, and it will then be but poor consolation to believe the world equally in the dark. There is so much of gratitude or vanity in almost every attachment, that it is not safe to leave any to itself. We can all *begin* freely – a slight preference is natural enough; but there are very few of us who have heart enough to be really in love without encouragement. In nine cases out of ten, a woman had better shew *more* affection than she feels. Bingley likes your sister undoubtedly; but he may never do more than like her, if she does not help him on.'

'But she does help him on, as much as her nature will allow. If *I* can perceive her regard for him, he must be a simpleton indeed not to discover it too.'

'Remember, Eliza, that he does not know Jane's disposition as you do.'

'But if a woman is partial to a man, and does not endeavour to conceal it, he must find it out.'

'Perhaps he must, if he sees enough of her. But though Bingley and Jane meet tolerably often, it is never for many hours together; and as they always see each other in large mixed parties, it is impossible that every moment should be employed in conversing together. Jane should therefore make the most of every half hour in which she can command his attention. When she is secure of him, there will be leisure for falling in love as much as she chuses.'

'Your plan is a good one,' replied Elizabeth, 'where nothing is in question but the desire of being well married; and if I were determined to get a rich husband, or any husband, I dare say I should adopt it. But these are not Jane's feelings; she is not acting by design. As yet, she cannot even be certain of the degree of her own regard, nor of its reasonableness. She has known him only a fortnight. She danced four dances with him at Meryton; she saw him one morning at his own house, and has since dined in company with him four times. This is not quite enough to make her understand his character.'

'Not as you represent it. Had she merely *dined* with him, she might only have discovered whether he had a good appetite; but you must remember that four evenings have been also spent together – and four evenings may do a great deal.'

'Yes; these four evenings have enabled them to ascertain that they both like Vingt-un better than Commerce; but with respect to any other leading characteristic, I do not imagine that much has been unfolded.'

'Well,' said Charlotte, 'I wish Jane success with all my heart; and if she were married to him tomorrow, I should think she had as good a chance of happiness, as if she were to be studying his character for a twelve-month. Happiness in marriage is entirely a matter of chance. If the dispositions of the parties are ever so well known to each other, or ever so similar beforehand, it does not advance their felicity in the least. They always continue to grow sufficiently unlike afterwards to have their share of vexation; and it is better to know as little as possible of the defects of the person with whom you are to pass your life.'

'You make me laugh, Charlotte; but it is not sound. You know it is not sound, and that you would never act in this way yourself.'

Occupied in observing Mr Bingley's attentions to her sister, Elizabeth was far from suspecting that she was herself becoming an object of some interest in the eyes of his friend. Mr Darcy had at first scarcely allowed her to be pretty; he had looked at her without admiration at the ball; and when they next met, he looked at her only to criticise. But no sooner had he made it clear to himself and his friends that she had hardly a good feature in her face, than he began to find it was rendered uncommonly intelligent by the beautiful expression of her dark eyes. To this discovery succeeded some others equally mortifying. Though he had detected with a critical eye more than one failure of perfect symmetry in her form, he was forced to acknowledge her figure to be light and pleasing; and in spite of his asserting that her manners were not those of the fashionable world, he was caught by their easy playfulness. Of this she was perfectly unaware; – to her he was only the man who made himself agreeable no where, and who had not thought her handsome enough to dance with.

He began to wish to know more of her, and as a step towards conversing with her himself, attended to her conversation with others. His doing so drew her notice. It was at Sir William Lucas's, where a large party were assembled.

'What does Mr Darcy mean,' said she to Charlotte, 'by listening to my conversation with Colonel Forster?'

'That is a question which Mr Darcy only can answer.'

'But if he does it any more I shall certainly let him know that I see what he is about. He has a very satirical eye, and if I do not begin by being impertinent myself, I shall soon grow afraid of him.'

On his approaching them soon afterwards, though without seeming to have any intention of speaking, Miss Lucas defied her friend to mention such a subject to him, which immediately provoking Elizabeth to do it, she turned to him and said,

'Did not you think, Mr Darcy, that I expressed myself uncommonly well just now, when I was teazing Colonel Forster to give us a ball at Maryton?'

'With great energy; – but it is a subject which always makes a lady energetic.'

'You are severe on us.'

'It will be *her* turn soon to be teazed,' said Miss Lucas. 'I am going to open the instrument, Eliza, and you know what follows.'

'You are a very strange creature by way of a friend! – always wanting me to play and sing before any body and every body! – If my vanity had taken a musical turn, you would have been invaluable, but as it is, I would really rather not sit down before those who must be in the habit of hearing the very best performers.' On Miss Lucas's persevering, however, she added, 'Very well; if it must be so, it must.' And gravely glancing at Mr Darcy. 'There is a fine old saying, which every body here is of course familiar with – "Keep your breath to cool your porridge," – and I shall keep mine to swell my song.'

Her performance was pleasing, though by no means capital. After a song or two, and before she could reply to the entreaties of several that she would sing again, she was eagerly succeeded at the instrument by her sister Mary, who having, in consequence of being the only plain one in the family, worked hard for knowledge and accomplishments, was always impatient for display.

Mary had neither genius nor taste; and though vanity had given her application, it had given her likewise a pedantic air and conceited manner, which would have injured a higher degree of excellence than she had reached. Elizabeth, easy and unaffected, had been listened to with much more pleasure, though not playing half so well; and Mary, at the end of a long concerto, was glad to purchase praise and gratitude by Scotch and Irish airs, at the request of her younger sisters, who with some of the Lucases and two or three officers joined eagerly in dancing at one end of the room.

Mr Darcy stood near them in silent indignation at such a mode of passing the evening, to the exclusion of all conversation, and was too much engrossed by his own thoughts to perceive that Sir William Lucas was his neighbour, till Sir William thus began.

'What a charming amusement for young people this is, Mr Darcy! – There is nothing like dancing after all. – I consider it as one of the first refinements of polished societies.'

'Certainly, Sir; – and it has the advantage also of being in vogue amongst the less polished societies of the world. – Every savage can dance.'

Sir William only smiled. 'Your friend performs delightfully;' he continued after a pause, on seeing Bingley join the group; – 'and I doubt not that you are an adept in the science yourself, Mr Darcy.'

'You saw me dance at Meryton, I believe, Sir.'

'Yes, indeed, and received no inconsiderable pleasure from the sight. Do you often dance at St James's?'

'Never, sir.'

'Do you not think it would be a proper compliment to the place?'

'It is a compliment which I never pay to any place if I can avoid it.'

'You have a house in town, I conclude?'

Mr Darcy bowed.

'I had once some thoughts of fixing in town myself – for I am fond of superior society; but I did not feel quite certain that the air of London would agree with Lady Lucas.'

He paused in hopes of an answer; but his companion was not disposed to make any; and Elizabeth at that instant moving towards them, he was struck with the notion of doing a very gallant thing, and called out to her,

'My dear Miss Eliza, why are not you dancing? – Mr Darcy, you must allow me to present this young lady to you as a very desirable partner. – You cannot refuse to dance, I am sure, when so much beauty is before you.' And taking her hand, he would have given it to Mr Darcy, who, though extremely surprised, was not unwilling to receive it, when she instantly drew back, and said with some discomposure to Sir William,

'Indeed, Sir, I have not the least intention of dancing. – I entreat you not to suppose that I moved this way in order to beg for a partner.'

Mr Darcy with grave propriety requested to be allowed the honour of her hand; but in vain. Elizabeth was determined; nor did Sir William at all shake her purpose by his attempt at persuasion.

'You excel so much in the dance, Miss Eliza, that it is cruel to deny me the happiness of seeing you; and though this gentleman dislikes the amusement in general, he can have no objection, I am sure, to oblige us for one half hour.'

'Mr Darcy is all politeness,' said Elizabeth, smiling.

'He is indeed – but considering the inducement, my dear Miss Eliza, we cannot wonder at his complaisance; for who would object to such a partner?'

Elizabeth looked archly, and turned away. Her resistance had not injured her with the gentleman, and he was thinking of her with some complacency, when thus accosted by Miss Bingley.

'I can guess the subject of your reverie.'

'I should imagine not.'

'You are considering how insupportable it would be to pass many evenings in this manner – in such society; and indeed I am quite of your opinion. I was never more annoyed! The insipidity and yet the noise; the nothingness and yet the self-importance of all these people! – What would I give to hear your strictures on them!'

'Your conjecture is totally wrong, I assure you. My mind was more agreeably engaged. I have been meditating on the very great pleasure which a pair of fine eyes in the face of a pretty woman can bestow.'

Miss Bingley immediately fixed her eyes on his face, and desired he would tell her what lady had the credit of inspiring such reflections. Mr Darcy replied with great intrepidity,

'Miss Elizabeth Bennet.'

'Miss Elizabeth Bennet!' repeated Miss Bingley. 'I am all astonishment. How long has she been such a favourite? – and pray when am I to wish you joy?'

'That is exactly the question which I expected you to ask. A lady's imagination is very rapid; it jumps from admiration to love, from love to matrimony in a moment. I knew you would be wishing me joy.'

'Nay, if you are so serious about it, I shall consider the matter as absolutely settled. You will have a charming mother-in-law, indeed, and of course she will be always at Pemberley with you.'

He listened to her with perfect indifference, while she chose to entertain herself in this manner, and as his composure convinced her that all was safe, her wit flowed long.

Chapter Seven

MR BENNET'S PROPERTY CONSISTED ALMOST entirely in an estate of two thousand a year, which, unfortunately for his daughters, was entailed in default of heirs male, on a distant relation; and their mother's fortune, though ample for her situation in life, could but ill supply the deficiency of his. Her father had been an attorney in Meryton, and had left her four thousand pounds.

She had a sister married to a Mr Philips, who had been a clerk to their father, and succeeded him in the business, and a brother settled in London in a respectable line of trade.

The village of Longbourn was only one mile from Meryton; a most convenient distance for the young ladies, who were usually tempted thither three or four times a week, to pay their duty to their aunt and to a milliner's shop just over the way. The two youngest of the family, Catherine and Lydia, were particularly frequent in these attentions; their minds were more vacant than their sisters', and when nothing better offered, a walk to Meryton was necessary to amuse their morning hours and furnish conversation for the evening; and however bare of news the country in general might be, they always contrived to learn some from their aunt. At present, indeed, they were well supplied both with news and happiness by the recent arrival of a militia regiment in the neighbourhood; it was to remain the whole winter, and Meryton was the head quarters.

Their visits to Mrs Philips were now productive of the most interesting intelligence. Every day added something to their knowledge of the officers' names and connections. Their lodgings were not long a secret, and at length they began to know the officers themselves. Mr Philips visited them all, and this opened to his nieces a source of felicity unknown before. They could talk of nothing but officers; and Mr Bingley's large fortune, the mention of which gave animation to their mother, was worthless in their eyes when opposed to the regimentals of an ensign.

After listening one morning to their effusions on this subject, Mr Bennet coolly observed,

'From all that I can collect by your manner of talking, you must be two of the silliest girls in the country. I have suspected it some time, but I am now convinced.'

Catherine was disconcerted, and made no answer; but Lydia, with perfect indifference, continued to express her admiration of Captain Carter, and her hope of seeing him in the course of the day, as he was going the next morning to London.

'I am astonished, my dear,' said Mrs Bennet, 'that you should be so ready to think your own children silly. If I wished to think slightingly of any body's children, it should not be of my own however.'

'If my children are silly I must hope to be always sensible of it.'

'Yes – but as it happens, they are all of them very clever.'

'This is the only point, I flatter myself, on which we do not agree. I had hoped that our sentiments coincided in every particular, but I must so far differ from you as to think our two youngest daughters uncommonly foolish.'

'My dear Mr Bennet, you must not expect such girls to have the sense of their father and mother. – When they get to our age I dare say they will not think about officers any more than we do. I remember the time when I liked a red coat myself very well – and indeed so I do still at my heart; and if a smart young colonel, with five or six thousand a year, should want one of my girls, I shall not say nay to him; and I thought Colonel Forster looked very becoming the other night at Sir William's in his regimentals.'

'Mama,' cried Lydia, 'my aunt says that Colonel Forster and Captain Carter do not go so often to Miss Watson's as they did when they first came; she sees them now very often standing in Clarke's library.'

Mrs Bennet was prevented replying by the entrance of the footman with a note for Miss Bennet; it came from Netherfield, and the servant waited for an answer. Mrs Bennet's eyes sparkled with pleasure and she was eagerly calling out, while her daughter read,

'Well, Jane, who is it from? what is it about? what does he say? Well Jane, make haste and tell us; make haste, my love.'

'It is from Miss Bingley,' said Jane, and then read it aloud.

'My dear Friend,

'If you are not so compassionate as to dine to-day with Louisa and me, we shall be in danger of hating each other for the rest of our lives, for a whole day's tête-à-tête between two women can never end without a quarrel. Come as soon as you can on the receipt of this. My brother and the gentlemen are to dine with the officers. Your ever,

'Caroline Bingley.'

'With the officers!' cried Lydia. 'I wonder my aunt did not tell us of that.'

'Dining out', said Mrs Bennet, 'that is very unlucky.'

'Can I have the carriage?' said Jane.

'No, my dear, you had better go on horseback, because it seems likely to rain; and then you must stay all night.'

'That would be a good scheme,' said Elizabeth, 'if you were sure that they would not offer to send her home.'

'Oh! but the gentlemen will have Mr Bingley's chaise to go to Meryton; and the Hursts have no horses to theirs.'

'I had much rather go in the coach.'

'But, my dear, your father cannot spare the horses, I am sure. They are wanted in the farm Mr Bennet, are not they?'

'They are wanted in the farm much oftener than I can get them.'

'But if you have got them to day,' said Elizabeth, 'my mother's purpose will be answered.'

She did at last extort from her father an acknowledgment that the horses were engaged. Jane was therefore obliged to go on horseback, and her mother attended her to the door with many cheerful prognostics of a bad day. Her hopes were answered; Jane had not been gone long before it rained hard. Her sisters were uneasy for her, but her mother was delighted. The rain continued the whole evening without intermission; Jane certainly could not come back.

'This was a lucky idea of mine, indeed!' said Mrs Bennet, more than once, as if the credit of making it rain were all her own. Till the next morning, however, she was not aware of all the felicity of her contrivance. Breakfast was scarcely over when a servant from Netherfield brought the following note for Elizabeth:

'My dearest Lizzy,

'I find myself very unwell this morning, which, I suppose, is to be imputed to my getting wet through yesterday. My kind friends will not hear of my returning home till I am better. They insist also on my seeing Mr Jones – therefore do not be alarmed if you should hear of his having been to me – and excepting a sore-throat and head-ache there is not much the matter with me.

'Yours, &c.'

'Well, my dear,' said Mr Bennet, when Elizabeth had read the note aloud, 'if your daughter should have a dangerous fit of illness, if she should die, it would be a comfort to know that it was all in pursuit of Mr Bingley, and under your orders.'

'Oh! I am not at all afraid of her dying. People do not die of little trifling colds. She will be taken good care of. As long as she stays there, it is all very well. I would go and see her, if I could have the carriage.'

Elizabeth, feeling really anxious, was determined to go to her, though the carriage was not to be had; and as she was no horse-woman, walking was her only alternative. She declared her resolution.

'How can you be so silly,' cried her mother, 'as to think of such a thing, in all this dirt! You will not be fit to be seen when you get there.'

'I shall be very fit to see Jane – which is all I want.'

'Is this a hint to me, Lizzy,' said her father, 'to send for the horses?'

'No, indeed. I do not wish to avoid the walk. The distance is nothing, when one has a motive; only three miles. I shall be back by dinner.'

'I admire the activity of your benevolence,' observed Mary, 'but every impulse of feeling should be guided by reason; and, in my opinion, exertion should always be in proportion to what is required.'

'We will go as far as Meryton with you,' said Catherine and Lydia. – Elizabeth accepted their company, and the three young ladies set off together.

'If we make haste,' said Lydia, as they walked along, 'perhaps we may see something of Captain Carter before he goes.'

In Meryton they parted; the two youngest repaired to the lodgings of one of the officers' wives, and Elizabeth continued her walk alone, crossing field after field at a quick pace, jumping over stiles and springing over puddles with impatient activity, and finding herself at last within view of the house, with weary ancles, dirty stockings, and a face glowing with the warmth of exercise.

She was shewn into the breakfast-parlour, where all but Jane were assembled, and where her appearance created but a great deal of surprise. – That she should have walked three miles so early in the day, in such dirty weather, and by herself, was almost incredible to Mrs Hurst and Miss Bingley; and Elizabeth was convinced that they held her in contempt for it. She was received, however, very politely by them; and in their brother's manners there was something better than politeness; there was good humour and kindness. – Mr Darcy said very little, and Mr Hurst nothing at all. The former was divided between admiration of the brilliancy which exercise had given to her complexion, and doubt as to the occasion's justifying her coming so far alone. The latter was thinking only of his breakfast.

Her enquiries after her sister were not very favourably answered. Miss Bennet had slept ill, and though up, was very feverish and not well enough to leave her room. Elizabeth was glad to be taken to her immediately; and Jane, who had only been withheld by the fear of giving alarm or inconvenience, from expressing in her note how much she longed for such a visit, was delighted at her entrance. She was not equal, however, to much conversation, and when Miss Bingley left them together, could attempt little beside expressions of gratitude for the extraordinary kindness she was treated with. Elizabeth silently attended her.

When breakfast was over, they were joined by the sisters; and Elizabeth began to like them herself, when she saw how much affection and solicitude they shewed for Jane. The apothecary came, and having examined his patient, said, as might be supposed, that she had caught a violent cold, and that they must endeavour to get the better of it; advised her to return to bed, and promised her some draughts. The advice was followed readily, for the feverish symptoms increased, and her head ached acutely. Elizabeth did not quit her room for a moment, nor were the other ladies often absent; the gentlemen being out, they had in fact nothing to do elsewhere.

When the clock struck three. Elizabeth felt that she must go; and very unwillingly said so. Miss Bingley offered her the carriage, and she only wanted a little pressing to accept it, when Jane testified such concern in parting with her, that Miss Bingley was obliged to convert the offer of the chaise into an invitation to remain at Netherfield for the present. Elizabeth most thankfully consented, and a servant was dispatched to Longbourn to acquaint the family with her stay, and bring back a supply of clothes.

Chapter Eight

AT FIVE O'CLOCK THE TWO LADIES retired to dress, and at half past six Elizabeth was summoned to dinner. To the civil enquiries which then poured in, and amongst which she had the pleasure of distinguishing the much superior solicitude of Mr Bingley's, she could not make a very favourable answer. Jane was by no means better. The sisters, on hearing this, repeated three or four times how much they were grieved, how shocking it was to have a bad cold, and how excessively they disliked being ill themselves; and then thought no more of the matter: and their indifference towards Jane when not immediately before them, restored Elizabeth to the enjoyment of all her original dislike.

Their brother, indeed, was the only one of the party whom she could regard with any complacency. His anxiety for Jane was evident, and his attentions to herself most pleasing, and they prevented her feeling herself so much an intruder as she believed she was considered by the others. She had very little notice from any but him. Miss Bingley was engrossed by Mr

Darcy, her sister scarcely less so; and as for Mr Hurst, by whom Elizabeth sat, he was an indolent man, who lived only to eat, drink, and play at cards, who when he found her prefer a plain dish to a ragout, had nothing to say to her.

When dinner was over, she returned directly to Jane, and Miss Bingley began abusing her as soon as she was out of the room. Her manners were pronounced to be very bad indeed, a mixture of pride and impertinence; and she had no conversation, no stile, no taste, no beauty. Mrs Hurst thought the same, and added,

'She has nothing, in short, to recommend her, but being an excellent walker. I shall never forget her appearance this morning. She really looked almost wild.'

'She did indeed, Louisa. I could hardly keep my countenance. Very nonsensical to come at all! Why must *she* be scampering about the country, because her sister has a cold? Her hair so untidy, so blowsy!'

'Yes, and her petticoat; I hope you saw her petticoat, six inches deep in mud, I am absolutely certain; and the gown which had been let down to hide it, not doing its office.'

'Your picture may be very exact, Louisa,' said Bingley; 'but this was all lost upon me. I thought Miss Elizabeth Bennet looked remarkably well, when she came into the room this morning. Her dirty petticoat quite escaped my notice.'

'*You* observed it, Mr Darcy, I am sure,' said Miss Bingley; 'and I am inclined to think that you would not wish to see *your sister* make such an exhibition.'

'Certainly not.'

'To walk three miles, or four miles, or five miles, or whatever it is, above her ancles in dirt, and alone, quite alone! what could she mean by it? It seems to me to shew an abominable sort of conceited independence, a most country town indifference to decorum.'

'It shews an affection for her sister that is very pleasing,' said Bingley.

'I am afraid, Mr Darcy,' observed Miss Bingley, in a half whisper, 'that this adventure has rather affected your admiration of her fine eyes.'

'Not at all,' he replied; 'they were brightened by the exercise.' – A short pause followed this speech, and Mrs Hurst began again.

'I have an excessive regard for Jane Bennet, she is really a very sweet girl, and I wish with all my heart she were well settled. But with such a father and mother, and such low connections, I am afraid there is no chance of it.'

'I think I have heard you say, that their uncle is an attorney in Meryton.'

'Yes; and they have another, who lives somewhere near Cheapside.'

'That is capital,' added her sister, and they both laughed heartily.

'If they had uncles enough to fill *all* Cheapside,' cried Bingley, 'it would not make them one jot less agreeable.'

'But it must very materially lessen their chance of marrying men of any consideration in the world,' replied Darcy.

To this speech Bingley made no answer; but his sisters gave it their hearty assent, and indulged their mirth for some time at the expense of their dear friend's vulgar relations.

With a renewal of tenderness, however, they repaired to her room on leaving the dining-parlour, and sat with her till summoned to coffee. She was still very poorly, and Elizabeth would not quit her at all, till late in the evening, when she had the comfort of seeing her asleep, and when it appeared to her rather right than pleasant that she should go down stairs herself. On entering the drawing-room she found the whole party at loo, and was immediately invited to join them; but suspecting them to be playing high she declined it, and making her sister the excuse, said she would amuse herself for the short time she could stay below with a book. Mr Hurst looked at her with astonishment.

'Do you prefer reading to cards?' said he; 'that is rather singular.'

'Miss Eliza Bennet', said Miss Bingley, 'despises cards. She is a great reader and has no pleasure in anything else.'

'I deserve neither such praise nor such censure,' cried Elizabeth; 'I am *not* a great reader, and I have pleasure in many things.'

'In nursing your sister I am sure you have pleasure,' said Bingley; 'and I hope it will soon be increased by seeing her quite well.'

Elizabeth thanked him from her heart, and then walked towards a table where a few books were lying. He immediately offered to fetch her others; all that his library afforded.

'And I wish my collection were larger for your benefit and my own credit; but I am an idle fellow, and though I have not many, I have more than I ever look into.'

Elizabeth assured him that she could suit herself perfectly with those in the room.

'I am astonished,' said Miss Bingley, 'that my father should have left so small a collection of books. – What a delightful library you have at Pemberley, Mr Darcy!'

'It ought to be good,' he replied, 'it has been the work of many generations.'

'And then you have added so much to it yourself, you are always buying books.'

'I cannot comprehend the neglect of a family library in such days as these.'

'Neglect! I am sure you neglect nothing that can add to the beauties of that noble place. Charles, when you build *your* house, I wish it may be half as delightful as Pemberley.'

'I wish it may.'

'But I would really advise you to make your purchase in that neighbourhood, and take Pemberley for a kind of model. There is not a finer county in England than Derbyshire.'

'With all my heart; I will buy Pemberley itself if Darcy will sell it.'

'I am talking of possibilities, Charles.'

'Upon my word, Caroline, I should think it more possible to get Pemberley by purchase than by imitation.'

Elizabeth was so much caught by what passed, as to leave her very little attention for her book; and soon laying it wholly aside, she drew near the card-table, and stationed herself between Mr Bingley and his eldest sister, to observe the game.

'Is Miss Darcy much grown since the spring?' said Miss Bingley; 'will she be as tall as I am?'

'I think she will. She is now about Miss Elizabeth Bennet's height or rather taller.'

'How I long to see her again! I never met with anybody who delighted me so much. Such a countenance, such manners! and so extremely accomplished for her age! Her performance on the piano-forte is exquisite.'

'It is amazing to me,' said Bingley, 'how young ladies can have patience to be so very accomplished, as they all are.'

'All young ladies accomplished! My dear Charles, what do you mean?'

'Yes, all of them, I think. They all paint tables, cover skreens and net purse's. I scarcely know any one who cannot do all this, and I am sure I never heard a young lady spoken of for the first time, without being informed that she was very accomplished.'

'Your list of the common extent of accomplishments,' said Darcy, 'has too much truth. The word is applied to many a woman who deserves it no otherwise than by netting a purse, or covering a skreen. But I am very far from agreeing with you in your estimation of ladies in general. I cannot boast of knowing more than half a dozen, in the whole range of my acquaintance, that are really accomplished.'

'Nor I, I am sure,' said Miss Bingley.

'Then,' observed Elizabeth, 'you must comprehend a great deal in your idea of an accomplished woman.'

'Yes; I do comprehend a great deal in it.'

'Oh! certainly,' cried his faithful assistant, 'no one can be really esteemed accomplished, who does not greatly surpass what is usually met with. A woman must have a thorough knowledge of music, singing, drawing, dancing, and the modern languages, to deserve the word; and besides all this, she must possess a certain something in her air and manner of walking, the tone of her voice, her address and expressions, or the word will be but half deserved.'

'All this she must possess,' added Darcy, 'and to all this she must yet add something more substantial, in the improvement of her mind by extensive reading.'

'I am no longer surprised at your knowing *only* six accomplished women. I rather wonder now at your knowing *any*.'

'Are you so severe upon your own sex, as to doubt the possibility of all this?'

'I never saw such a woman. I never saw such capacity, and taste, and application, and elegance, as you describe, united.'

Mrs Hurst and Miss Bingley both cried out against the injustice of her implied doubt, and were both protesting that they knew many women who answered this description, when Mr Hurst called them to order, with bitter complaints of their inattention to what was going forward. As all conversation was thereby at an end, Elizabeth soon afterwards left the room.

'Eliza Bennet,' said Miss Bingley, when the door was closed on her, 'is one of those young ladies who seek to recommend themselves to the other sex, by undervaluing their own; and with many men, I dare say, it succeeds. But, in my opinion, it is a paltry device, a very mean art.'

'Undoubtedly,' replied Darcy, to whom this remark was chiefly addressed, 'there is meanness in *all* the arts which ladies sometimes condescend to employ for captivation. Whatever bears affinity to cunning is despicable.'

Miss Bingley was not so entirely satisfied with this reply as to continue the subject.

Elizabeth joined them again only to say that her sister was worse, and that she could not leave her. Bingley urged Mr Jones's being sent for immediately; while his sisters, convinced that no country advice could be of any service, recommended an express to town for one of the most eminent physicians. This, she would not hear of; but she was not so unwilling to comply with their brother's proposal; and it was settled that Mr Jones should be sent for early in the morning, if Miss Bennet were not decidedly better. Bingley was quite uncomfortable; his sisters declared that they were miserable. They solaced their wretchedness, however, by duets after supper, while he could find no better relief to his feelings than by giving his housekeeper directions that every possible attention might be paid to the sick lady and her sister.

Chapter Nine

ELIZABETH PASSED THE CHIEF OF THE night in her sister's room, and in the morning had the pleasure of being able to send a tolerable answer to the enquiries which she very early received from Mr Bingley by a housemaid, and some time afterwards from the two elegant ladies who waited on his sisters. In spite of this amendment, however, she requested to have a note sent to Longbourn, desiring her mother to visit Jane, and form her own judgment of her situation. The note was immediately dispatched, and its contents as quickly complied with. Mrs Bennet, accompanied by her two youngest girls, reached Netherfield soon after the family breakfast.

Had she found Jane in any apparent danger, Mrs Bennet would have been very miserable; but being satisfied on seeing her that her illness was not alarming, she had no wish of her recovering immediately, as her restoration to health would probably remove her from Netherfield. She would not listen therefore to her daughter's proposal of being carried home; neither did the apothecary, who arrived about the same time, think it at all advisable. After sitting a little while with Jane, on Miss Bingley's appearance and invitation, the mother and three daughters all attended her into the breakfast parlour. Bingley met them with hopes that Mrs Bennet had not found Miss Bennet worse than she expected.

'Indeed I have, Sir,' was her answer. 'She is a great deal too ill to be moved. Mr Jones says we must not think of moving her. We must trespass a little longer on your kindness.'

'Removed!' cried Bingley. 'It must not be thought of. My sister, I am sure, will not hear of her removal.'

'You may depend upon it, Madam,' said Miss Bingley, with cold civility, 'that Miss Bennet shall receive every possible attention while she remains with us.'

Mrs Bennet was profuse in her acknowledgments.

'I am sure,' she added, 'if it was not for such good friends I do not know what would become of her, for she is very ill indeed, and suffers a vast deal, though with the greatest patience in the world, which is always the way with her, for she has, without exception, the sweetest temper I ever met with. I often tell my other girls they are nothing to *her*. You have a sweet room here, Mr Bingley, and a charming prospect over that gravel walk. I do not know a place in the country that is equal to Netherfield. You will not think of quitting it in a hurry I hope, though you have but a short lease.'

'Whatever I do is done in a hurry,' replied he; 'and therefore if I should resolve to quit Netherfield, I should probably be off in five minutes. At present, however, I consider myself as quite fixed here.'

'That is exactly what I should have supposed of you,' said Elizabeth.

'You begin to comprehend me, do you?' cried he, turning towards her.

'Oh! yes – I understand you perfectly.'

'I wish I might take this for a compliment; but to be so easily seen through I am afraid is pitiful.'

'That is as it happens. It does not necessarily follow that a deep, intricate character is more or less estimable than such a one as yours.'

'Lizzy,' cried her mother, 'remember where you are, and do not run on in the wild manner that you are suffered to do at home.'

'I did not know before,' continued Bingley immediately, 'that you were a studier of character. It must be an amusing study.'

'Yes; but intricate characters are the *most* amusing. They have at least that advantage.'

'The country,' said Darcy, 'can in general supply but few subjects for such a study. In a country neighbourhood you move in a very confined and unvarying society.'

'But people themselves alter so much, that there is something new to be observed in them for ever.'

'Yes, indeed,' cried Mrs Bennet, offended by his manner of mentioning a country neighbourhood. 'I assure you there is quite as much of *that* going on in the country as in town.'

Every body was surprised; and Darcy, after looking at her for a moment, turned silently away. Mrs Bennet, who fancied she had gained a complete victory over him, continued her triumph.

'I cannot see that London has any great advantage over the country for my part, except the shops and public places. The country is a vast deal pleasanter, is not it, Mr Bingley?'

'When I am in the country,' he replied, 'I never wish to leave it; and when I am in town it is pretty much the same. They have each their advantages, and I can be equally happy in either.'

'Aye – that is because you have the right disposition. But that gentleman,' looking at Darcy, 'seemed to think the country was nothing at all.'

'Indeed, Mama, you are mistaken,' said Elizabeth, blushing for her mother. 'You quite mistook Mr Darcy. He only meant that there were not such a variety of people to be met with in the country as in town, which you must acknowledge to be true.'

'Certainly, my dear, nobody said there were; but as to not meeting with many people in this neighbourhood, I believe there are few neighbourhoods larger. I know we dine with four and twenty families.'

Nothing but concern for Elizabeth could enable Bingley to keep his countenance. His sister was less delicate, and directed her eye towards Mr Darcy with a very expressive smile. Elizabeth, for the sake of saying something that might turn her mother's thoughts, now asked her if Charlotte Lucas had been at Longbourn since *her* coming away.

'Yes, she called yesterday with her father. What an agreeable man Sir William is, Mr Bingley – is not he? so much the man of fashion! so genteel and so easy! – He has always something to say to every body. – *That* is my idea of good breeding; and those persons who fancy themselves very important and never open their mouths, quite mistake the matter.'

'Did Charlotte dine with you?'

'No, she would go home. I fancy she was wanted about the mince pies. For my part, Mr Bingley, *I* always keep servants that can do their own work; *my* daughters are brought up differently. But every body is to judge for themselves, and the Lucases are very good sort of girls, I assure you. It is a pity they are not handsome! Not that *I* think Charlotte so *very* plain – but then she is our particular friend.'

'She seems a very pleasant young woman,' said Bingley.

'Oh! dear, yes; – but you must own she is very plain. Lady Lucas herself has often said so, and envied me Jane's beauty. I do not like to boast of my own child, but to be sure, Jane – one does not often see any body better looking. It is what every body says. I do not trust my own partiality. When she was only fifteen, there was a gentleman at my brother Gardiner's in town, so much in love with her, that my sister-in-law was sure he would make her an offer before we came away. But however he did not. Perhaps he thought her too young. However, he wrote some verses on her, and very pretty they were.'

'And so ended his affection,' said Elizabeth impatiently. 'There has been many a one, I fancy, overcome in the same way. I wonder who first discovered the efficacy of poetry in driving away love!'

'I have been used to consider poetry as the *food* of love,' said Darcy.

'Of a fine, stout, healthy love it may. Every thing nourishes what is strong already. But if it be only a slight, thin sort of inclination, I am convinced that one good sonnet will starve it entirely away.'

Darcy only smiled; and the general pause which ensued made Elizabeth tremble lest her mother should be exposing herself again. She longed to speak, but could think of nothing to say; and after a short silence Mrs Bennet began repeating her thanks to Mr Bingley for his kindness to Jane, with an apology for troubling him also with Lizzy. Mr Bingley was unaffectedly civil in his answer, and forced his younger sister to be civil also, and say what the occasion required. She performed her part indeed without much graciousness, but Mrs Bennet was satisfied, and soon afterwards ordered her carriage. Upon this signal, the youngest of her daughters put herself forward. The two girls had been whispering to each other during the whole visit, and the result of it was, that the youngest should tax Mr Bingley with having promised on his first coming into the country to give a ball at Netherfield.

Lydia was a stout, well-grown girl of fifteen, with a fine complexion and good-humoured countenance; a favourite with her mother, whose affection had brought her into public at an early age. She had high animal spirits, and a sort of natural self-consequence, which the attentions of the officers, to whom her uncle's good dinners and her own easy manners recommended her, had increased into assurance. She was very equal therefore to address Mr Bingley on the subject of the ball, and abruptly reminded him of his promise; adding, that it would be the most shameful thing in the world if he did not keep it. His answer to this sudden attack was delightful to their mother's ear.

'I am perfectly ready, I assure you, to keep my engagement; and when your sister is recovered, you shall if you please name the very day of the ball. But you would not wish to be dancing while she is ill.'

Lydia declared herself satisfied. 'Oh! yes – it would be much better to wait till Jane was well, and by that time most likely Captain Carter would be at Meryton again. And when you have given *your* ball,' she added, 'I shall insist on their giving one also. I shall tell Colonel Forster it will be quite a shame if he does not.'

Mrs Bennet and her daughters then departed, and Elizabeth returned instantly to Jane, leaving her own and her relations' behaviour to the remarks of the two ladies and Mr Darcy; the latter of whom, however, could not be prevailed on to join in their censure of *her*, in spite of all Miss Bingley's witticisms on *fine eyes*.

Chapter Ten

THE DAY PASSED MUCH AS THE DAY before had done. Mrs Hurst and Miss Bingley had spent some hours of the morning with the invalid, who continued, though slowly, to mend; and in the evening Elizabeth joined their party in the drawing-room. The loo table, however, did not appear. Mr Darcy was writing, and Miss Bingley, seated near him, was watching the progress of his letter, and repeatedly calling off his attention by messages to his sister. Mr Hurst and Mr Bingley were at piquet, and Mrs Hurst was observing their game.

Elizabeth took up some needlework, and was sufficiently amused in attending to what passed between Darcy and his companion. The perpetual commendations of the lady either on his hand-writing, or on the evenness of his lines, or on the length of his letter, with the perfect unconcern with which her praises were received, formed a curious dialogue, and was exactly in unison with her opinion of each.

'How delighted Miss Darcy will be to receive such a letter!'

He made no answer.

'You write uncommonly fast.'

'You are mistaken. I write rather slowly.'

'How many letters you must have occasion to write in the course of the year! Letters of business too! How odious I should think them!'

'It is fortunate, then, that they fall to my lot instead of to yours.'

'Pray tell your sister that I long to see her.'

'I have already told her so once, by your desire.'

'I am afraid you do not like your pen. Let me mend it for you. I mend pens remarkably well.'

'Thank you – but I always mend my own.'

'How can you contrive to write so even?'

He was silent.

'Tell your sister I am delighted to hear of her improvement on the harp, and pray let her know that I am quite in raptures with her beautiful little design for a table, and I think it infinitely superior to Miss Grantley's.'

'Will you give me leave to defer your raptures till I write again? – At present I have not room to do them justice.'

'Oh! it is of no consequence. I shall see her in January. But do you always write such charming long letters to her, Mr Darcy?'

'They are generally long; but whether always charming, it is not for me to determine.'

'It is a rule with me, that a person who can write a long letter, with ease, cannot write ill.'

'That will not do for a compliment to Darcy, Caroline,' cried her brother – 'because he does *not* write with ease. He studies too much for words of four syllables. – Do not you, Darcy?'

'My stile of writing is very different from yours.'

'Oh!' cried Miss Bingley, 'Charles writes in the most careless way imaginable. He leaves out half his words, and blots the rest.'

'My ideas flow so rapidly that I have not time to express them – by which means my letters sometimes convey no ideas at all to my correspondents.'

'Your humility, Mr Bingley,' said Elizabeth, 'must disarm reproof.'

'Nothing is more deceitful,' said Darcy, 'than the appearance of humility. It is often only carelessness of opinion, and sometimes an indirect boast.'

'And which of the two do you call *my* little recent piece of modesty?'

'The indirect boast; – for you are really proud of your defects in writing, because you consider them as proceeding from a rapidity of thought and carelessness of execution, which if not estimable, you think at least highly interesting. The power of doing any thing with quickness is always much prized by the possessor, and often without any attention to the imperfection of the performance. When you told Mrs Bennet this morning that if you ever resolved on quitting Netherfield you should be gone in five minutes, you meant it to be a sort of panegyric, of compliment to yourself – and yet what is there so very laudable in a precipitance which must leave very necessary business undone, and can be of no real advantage to yourself or any one else?'

'Nay,' cried Bingley, 'this is too much, to remember at night all the foolish things that were said in the morning. And yet, upon my honour, I believed what I said of myself to be true, and I believe it at this moment. At least, therefore, I did not assume the character of needless precipitance merely to shew off before the ladies.'

'I dare say you believed it; but I am by no means convinced that you would be gone with such celerity. Your conduct would be quite as dependant on chance as that of any man I know; and if, as you were mounting your horse, a friend were to say, "Bingley, you had better stay till next week," you would probably do it, you would probably not go – and, at another word, might stay a month.'

'You have only proved by this,' cried Elizabeth, 'that Mr Bingley did not do justice to his own disposition. You have shewn him off now much more than he did himself.'

'I am exceedingly gratified,' said Bingley, 'by your converting what my friend says into a compliment on the sweetness of my temper. But I am afraid you are giving it a turn which that gentleman did by no means intend; for he would certainly think the better of me, if under such a circumstance I were to give a flat denial, and ride off as fast as I could.'

'Would Mr Darcy then consider the rashness of your original intention as atoned for by your obstinacy in adhering to it?'

'Upon my word I cannot exactly explain the matter, Darcy must speak for himself.'

'You expect me to account for opinions which you chuse to call mine, but which I have never acknowledged. Allowing the case, however, to stand according to your representation, you must remember, Miss Bennet, that the friend who is supposed to desire his return to the house, and the delay of his plan, has merely desired it, asked it without offering one argument in favour of its propriety.'

'To yield readily – easily – to the *persuasion* of a friend is no merit with you.'

'To yield without conviction is no compliment to the understanding of either.'

'You appear to me, Mr Darcy, to allow nothing for the influence of friendship and affection. A regard for the requester would often make one readily yield to a request, without waiting for arguments to reason one into it. I am not particularly speaking of such a case as you have supposed about Mr Bingley. We may as well wait, perhaps, till the circumstance occurs, before we discuss the discretion of his behaviour thereupon. But in general and ordinary cases between friend and friend, where one of them is desired by the other to change a resolution of no very great moment, should you think ill of that person for complying with the desire, without waiting to be argued into it?'

'Will it not be advisable, before we proceed on this subject, to arrange with rather more precision the degree of importance which is to appertain to this request, as well as the degree of intimacy subsisting between the parties?'

'By all means,' cried Bingley; 'let us hear all the particulars, not forgetting their comparative height and size; for that will have more weight in the argument, Miss Bennet, than you may be aware of. I assure you that if Darcy were not such a great tall fellow, in comparison with myself, I should not pay him half so much deference. I declare I do not know a more aweful object than Darcy, on particular occasions, and in particular places; at his own house especially, and of a Sunday evening when he has nothing to do.'

Mr Darcy smiled; but Elizabeth thought she could perceive that he was rather offended; and therefore checked her laugh. Miss Bingley warmly resented the indignity he had received, in an expostulation with her brother for talking such nonsense.

'I see your design, Bingley,' said his friend. – 'You dislike an argument, and want to silence this.'

'Perhaps I do. Arguments are too much like disputes. If you and Miss Bennet will defer yours till I am out of the room, I shall be very thankful; and then you may say whatever you like of me.'

'What you ask,' said Elizabeth, 'is no sacrifice on my side; and Mr Darcy had much better finish his letter.'

Mr Darcy took her advice, and did finish his letter.

When that business was over, he applied to Miss Bingley and Elizabeth for the indulgence of some music. Miss Bingley moved with alacrity to the piano-forte, and after a polite request that Elizabeth would lead the way, which the other as politely and more earnestly negatived, she seated herself.

Mrs Hurst sang with her sister, and while they were thus employed Elizabeth could not help observing as she turned over some music books that lay on the instrument, how frequently Mr Darcy's eyes were fixed on her. She hardly knew how to suppose that she could be an object of admiration to so great a man; and yet that he should look at her because he disliked her, was still more strange. She could only imagine however at last, that she drew his notice because there was a something about her more wrong and reprehensible, according to his ideas of right, than in any other person present. The supposition did not pain her. She liked him too little to care for his approbation.

After playing some Italian songs, Miss Bingley varied the charm by a lively Scotch air; and soon afterwards Mr Darcy, drawing near Elizabeth, said to her –

'Do not you feel a great inclination, Miss Bennet, to seize such an opportunity of dancing a reel?'

She smiled, but made no answer. He repeated the question, with some surprise at her silence.

'Oh!' said she, 'I heard you before; but I could not immediately determine what to say in reply. You wanted me, I know, to say "Yes," that you might have the pleasure of despising my taste; but I always delight in overthrowing those kind of schemes, and cheating a person of their premeditated contempt. I have therefore made up my mind to tell you, that I do not want to dance a reel at all – and now despise me if you dare.'

'Indeed I do not dare.'

Elizabeth, having rather expected to affront him, was amazed at his gallantry; but there was a mixture of sweetness and archness in her manner which made it difficult for her to affront anybody; and Darcy had never been so bewitched by any woman as he was by her. He really believed, that were it not for the inferiority of her connections, he should be in some danger.

Miss Bingley saw, or suspected enough to be jealous; and her great anxiety for the recovery of her dear friend Jane, received some assistance from her desire of getting rid of Elizabeth.

She often tried to provoke Darcy into disliking her guest, by talking of their supposed marriage, and planning his happiness in such an alliance.

'I hope,' said she, as they were walking together in the shrubbery the next day, 'you will give your mother-in-law a few hints, when this desirable event takes place, as to the advantage of holding her tongue; and if you can compass it, do cure the younger girls of running after the officers. – And, if I may mention so delicate a subject, endeavour to check that little something, bordering on conceit and impertinence, which your lady possesses.'

'Have you any thing else to propose for my domestic felicity?'

'Oh! yes. – Do let the portraits of your uncle and aunt Philips be placed in the gallery at Pemberley. Put them next to your great uncle the judge. They are in the same profession, you know; only in different lines. As for your Elizabeth's picture, you must not attempt to have it taken, for what painter could do justice to those beautiful eyes?'

'It would not be easy, indeed, to catch their expression, but their colour and shape, and the eye-lashes, so remarkably fine, might be copied.'

At that moment they were met from another walk, by Mrs Hurst and Elizabeth herself.

'I did not know that you intended to walk,' said Miss Bingley, in some confusion, lest they had been overheard.

'You used us abominably ill,' answered Mrs Hurst, 'in running away without telling us that you were coming out.'

Then taking the disengaged arm of Mr Darcy, she left Elizabeth to walk by herself. The path just admitted three. Mr Darcy felt their rudeness and immediately said, –

'This walk is not wide enough for our party. We had better go into the avenue.'

But Elizabeth, who had not the least inclination to remain with them, laughingly answered,

'No no; stay where you are. – You are charmingly group'd, and appear to uncommon advantage. The picturesque would be spoilt by admitting a fourth. Good bye.'

She then ran gaily off, rejoicing as she rambled about, in the hope of being at home again in a day or two. Jane was already so much recovered as to intend leaving her room for a couple of hours that evening.

Chapter Eleven

WHEN THE LADIES REMOVED AFTER dinner, Elizabeth ran up to her sister, and seeing her well guarded from cold, attended her into the drawing-room; where she was welcomed by her two friends with many professions of pleasure; and Elizabeth had never seen them so agreeable as they were during the hour which passed before the gentlemen appeared. Their powers of conversation were considerable. They could describe an entertainment with accuracy, relate an anecdote with humour, and laugh at their acquaintance with spirit.

But when the gentlemen entered, Jane was no longer the first object. Miss Bingley's eyes were instantly turned towards Darcy, and she had something to say to him before he had advanced many steps. He addressed himself directly to Miss Bennet, with a polite congratulation; Mr Hurst also made her a slight bow, and said he was 'very glad'; but diffuseness and warmth remained for Bingley's salutation. He was full of joy and attention. The first half hour was spent in piling up the fire, lest she should suffer from the change of room; and she removed at his desire to the other side of the fire-place, that she might be farther from the door. He then sat down by her, and talked scarcely to any one else. Elizabeth, at work in the opposite corner, saw it all with great delight.

When tea was over, Mr Hurst reminded his sister-in-law of the card-table – but in vain. She had obtained private intelligence that Mr Darcy did not wish for cards; and Mr Hurst soon found even his open petition rejected.

She assured him that no one intended to play, and the silence of the whole party on the subject, seemed to justify her. Mr Hurst had therefore nothing to do, but to stretch himself on one of the sophas and go to sleep. Darcy took up a book; Miss Bingley did the same; and Mrs Hurst, principally occupied in playing with her bracelets and rings, joined now and then in her brother's conversation with Miss Bennet.

Miss Bingley's attention was quite as much engaged in watching Mr Darcy's progress through *his* book, as in reading her own; and she was perpetually either making some inquiry, or looking at his page. She could not win him, however, to any conversation; he merely answered her question, and read on. At length, quite exhausted by the attempt to be amused with her own book, which she had only chosen because it was the second volume of his, she gave a great yawn and said, 'How pleasant it is to spend an evening in this way! I declare after all there is no enjoyment like reading! How much sooner one tires of any thing than of a book! – When I have a house of my own, I shall be miserable if I have not an excellent library.'

No one made any reply. She then yawned again, threw aside her book, and cast her eyes round the room in quest of some amusement; when hearing her brother mentioning a ball to Miss Bennet, she turned suddenly towards him and said,

'By the bye, Charles, are you really serious in meditating a dance at Netherfield? – I would advise you, before you determine on it, to consult the wishes of the present party; I am much mistaken if there are not some among us to whom a ball would be rather a punishment than a pleasure.'

'If you mean Darcy,' cried her brother, 'he may go to bed, if he chuses, before it begins – but as for the ball, it is quite a settled thing; and as soon as Nicholls has made white soup enough I shall send round my cards.'

'I should like balls infinitely better,' she replied, 'if they were carried on in a different manner; but there is something insufferably tedious in the usual process of such a meeting. It would surely be much more rational if conversation instead of dancing made the order of the day.'

'Much more rational, my dear Caroline, I dare say but it would not be near so much like a ball.'

Miss Bingley made no answer; and soon afterwards got up and walked about the room. Her figure was elegant, and she walked well; – but Darcy, at whom it was all aimed, was still inflexibly studious. In the desperation of her feelings she resolved on one effort more; and, turning to Elizabeth, said,

'Miss Eliza Bennet, let me persuade you to follow my example, and take a turn about the room. – I assure you it is very refreshing after sitting so long in one attitude.'

Elizabeth was surprised, but agreed to it immediately. Miss Bingley succeeded no less in the real object of her civility; Mr Darcy looked up. He was as much awake to the novelty of attention in that quarter as Elizabeth herself could be, and unconsciously closed his book. He was directly invited to join their party, but he declined it, observing, that he could imagine but two motives for their chusing to walk up and down the room together, with either of which motives his joining them would interfere. 'What could he mean? she was dying to know what could be his meaning' – and asked Elizabeth whether she could at all understand him?

'Not at all,' was her answer; 'but depend upon it, he means to be severe on us, and our surest way of disappointing him, will be to ask nothing about it.'

Miss Bingley, however, was incapable of disappointing Mr Darcy in any thing, and persevered therefore in requiring an explanation of his two motives.

'I have not the smallest objection to explaining them,' said he, as soon as she allowed him to speak. 'You either chuse this method of passing the evening because you are in each other's confidence and have secret affairs to discuss, or because you are conscious that your figures appear to the greatest advantage in walking; – if the first, I should be completely in your way; – and if the second, I can admire you much better as I sit by the fire.'

'Oh! shocking!' cried Miss Bingley. 'I never heard any thing so abominable. How shall we punish him for such a speech?'

'Nothing so easy, if you have but the inclination,' said Elizabeth. 'We can all plague and punish one another. Teaze him – laugh at him. – Intimate as you are, you must know how it is to be done.'

'But upon my honour I do *not*. I do assure you that my intimacy has not yet taught me *that*. Teaze calmness of temper and presence of mind! No, no – I feel he may defy us there. And as to laughter, we will not expose ourselves, if you please, by attempting to laugh without a subject. Mr Darcy may hug himself.'

'Mr Darcy is not to be laughed at!' cried Elizabeth. 'That is an uncommon advantage, and uncommon I hope it will continue, for it would be a great loss to *me* to have many such acquaintance. I dearly love a laugh.'

'Miss Bingley,' said he, 'has given me credit for more than can be. The wisest and the best of men, nay, the wisest and best of their actions, may be rendered ridiculous by a person whose first object in life is a joke.'

'Certainly,' replied Elizabeth – 'there are such people, but I hope I am not one of *them*. I hope I never ridicule what is wise or good. Follies and nonsense, whims and inconsistencies *do* divert me, I own, and I laugh at them whenever I can. – But these, I suppose, are precisely what you are without.'

'Perhaps that is not possible for any one. But it has been the study of my life to avoid those weaknesses which often expose a strong understanding to ridicule.'

'Such as vanity and pride.'

'Yes, vanity is a weakness indeed. But pride – where there is a real superiority of mind, pride will be always under good regulation.'

Elizabeth turned away to hide a smile.

'Your examination of Mr Darcy is over, I presume,' said Miss Bingley; – 'and pray what is the result?'

'I am perfectly convinced by it that Mr Darcy has no defect. He owns it himself without disguise.'

'No' – said Darcy, 'I have made no such pretension. I have faults enough, but they are not, I hope, of understanding. My temper I dare not vouch for. – It is I believe too little yielding – certainly too little for the convenience of the world. I cannot forget the follies and vices of others so soon as I ought, nor their offences against myself. My feelings are not puffed about with every attempt to move them. My temper would perhaps be called resentful. – My good opinion once lost is lost for ever.'

'*That* is a failing indeed!' – cried Elizabeth. 'Implacable resentment *is* a shade in a character. But you have chosen your fault well. – I really cannot *laugh* at it. You are safe from me.'

'There is, I believe, in every disposition a tendency to some particular evil, a natural defect, which not even the best education can overcome.'

'And *your* defect is a propensity to hate every body.'

'And yours,' he replied with a smile, 'is wilfully to misunderstand them.'

'Do let us have a little music,' – cried Miss Bingley, tired of a conversation in which she had no share. – 'Louisa, you will not mind my waking Mr Hurst.'

Her sister made not the smallest objection, and the piano-forte was opened, and Darcy, after a few moments recollection, was not sorry for it. He began to feel the danger of paying Elizabeth too much attention.

Chapter Twelve

IN CONSEQUENCE OF AN AGREEMENT BETWEEN the sisters, Elizabeth wrote the next morning to her mother, to beg that the carriage might be sent for them in the course of the day. But Mrs Bennet, who had calculated on her daughters remaining at Netherfield till the following Tuesday, which would exactly finish Jane's week, could not bring herself to receive them with pleasure before. Her answer, therefore, was not propitious, at least not to Elizabeth's wishes, for she was impatient to get home. Mrs Bennet sent them word that they could not possibly have the carriage before Tuesday; and in her postscript it was added, that if Mr Bingley and his sister pressed them to stay longer, she could spare them very well. – Against staying longer, however, Elizabeth was positively resolved – nor did she much expect it would be asked; and fearful, on the contrary, as being considered as intruding themselves need-lessly long, she urged Jane to borrow Mr Bingley's carriage immediately, and at length it was settled that their original design of leaving Netherfield that morning should be mentioned, and the request made.

The communication excited many professions of concern; and enough was said of wishing them to stay at least till the following day to work on Jane; and till the morrow, their going was deferred. Miss Bingley was then sorry that she had proposed the delay, for her jealousy and dislike of one sister much exceeded her affection for the other.

The master of the house heard with real sorrow that they were to go so soon, and repeatedly tried to persuade Miss Bennet that it would not be safe for her – that she was not enough recovered; but Jane was firm where she felt herself to be right.

To Mr Darcy it was welcome intelligence – Elizabeth had been at Netherfield long enough. She attracted him more than he liked – and Miss Bingley was uncivil to *her*, and more teazing than usual to himself. He wisely resolved to be particularly careful that no sign of admiration should *now* escape him, nothing that could elevate her with the hope of influencing his felicity; sensible that if such an idea had been suggested, his behaviour during the last day must have material weight in confirming or crushing it. Steady to his purpose, he scarcely spoke ten words to her through the whole of Saturday, and though they were at one time left by themselves for half an hour, he adhered most conscientiously to his book, and would not even look at her.

On Sunday, after morning service, the separation, so agreeable to almost all, took place. Miss Bingley's civility to Elizabeth increased at last very rapidly, as well as her affection for Jane; and when they parted, after assuring the latter of the pleasure it would always give her to see her either at Longbourn or Netherfield, and embracing her most tenderly, she even shook hands with the former. – Elizabeth took leave of the whole party in the liveliest spirits.

They were not welcomed home very cordially by their mother. Mrs Bennet wondered at their coming, and thought them very wrong to give so much trouble, and was sure Jane would have caught cold again. – But their father, though very laconic in his expressions of pleasure, was really glad to see them; he had felt their importance in the family circle. The evening conversation, when they were all assembled, had lost much of its animation, and almost all its sense, by the absence of Jane and Elizabeth.

They found Mary, as usual, deep in the study of thorough bass and human nature; and had some new extracts to admire, and some new observations of thread-bare morality to listen to. Catherine and Lydia had information for them of a different sort. Much had been done, and much had been said in the regiment since the preceding Wednesday; several of the officers had dined lately with their uncle, a private had been flogged, and it had actually been hinted that Colonel Forster was going to be married.

Chapter Thirteen

'I HOPE, MY DEAR,' SAID MR BENNET to his wife, as they were at breakfast the next morning, 'that you have ordered a good dinner to-day, because I have reason to expect an addition to our family party.'

'Who do you mean, my dear? I know of nobody that is coming I am sure, unless Charlotte Lucas should happen to call in, and I hope *my* dinners are good enough for her. I do not believe she often sees such at home.'

'The person of whom I speak, is a gentleman and a stranger.' Mrs Bennet's eyes sparkled. – 'A gentleman and a stranger! It is Mr Bingley I am sure. Why Jane – you never dropt a word of this; you sly thing! Well, I am sure I shall be extremely glad to see Mr Bingley. – But – good lord! how unlucky! there is not a bit of fish to be got to-day. Lydia, my love, ring the bell. I must speak to Hill, this moment.'

'It is *not* Mr Bingley,' said her husband; 'it is a person whom I never saw in the whole course of my life.'

This roused a general astonishment; and he had the pleasure of being eagerly questioned by his wife and five daughters at once.

After amusing himself some time with their curiosity, he thus explained.

'About a month ago I received this letter, and about a fortnight ago I answered it, for I thought it a case of some delicacy, and required early attention. It is from my cousin, Mr Collins, who, when I am dead, may turn you all out of this house as soon as he pleases.'

'Oh! my dear,' cried his wife, 'I cannot bear to hear that mentioned. Pray do not talk of that odious man. I do think it is the hardest thing in the world, that your estate should be entailed away from your own children; and I am sure if I had been you, I should have tried long ago to do something or other about it.'

Jane and Elizabeth attempted to explain to her the nature of an entail. They had often attempted it before, but it was a subject on which Mrs Bennet was beyond the reach of reason; and she continued to rail bitterly against the cruelty of settling an estate away from a family of five daughters, in favour of a man whom nobody cared anything about.

'It certainly is a most iniquitous affair,' said Mr Bennet, 'and nothing can clear Mr Collins from the guilt of inheriting Longbourn. But if you will listen to his letter, you may perhaps be a little softened by his manner of expressing himself.'

'No, that I am sure I shall not; and I think it was very impertinent of him to write to you at all, and very hypocritical. I hate such false friends. Why could not he keep on quarrelling with you, as his father did before him?'

'Why, indeed, he does seem to have had some filial scruples on that head, as you will hear.'

> Hunsford, near Westerham, Kent.
> 15th October.

Dear Sir,

The disagreement subsisting between yourself and my late honoured father, always gave me much uneasiness, and since I have had the misfortune to lose him, I have frequently wished to heal the breach; but for some time I was kept back by my own doubts, fearing lest it might seem disrespectful to his memory for me to be on good terms with any one, with whom it had always pleased him to be at variance. - "There, Mrs Bennet." - My mind however is now made up on the subject, for having received ordination at Easter, I have been so fortunate as to be distinguished by the patronage of the Right Honourable Lady Catherine de Bourgh, widow of Sir Lewis de Bourgh, whose bounty and beneficence has preferred me to the valuable rectory of this parish, where it shall be my earnest endeavour to demean myself with grateful respect towards her Ladyship, and be ever ready to perform those rites and ceremonies which are instituted by the Church of England. As a clergyman, moreover, I feel it my duty to promote and establish the blessing of peace in all families within the reach of my influence; and on these grounds I flatter myself that my present overtures of good-will are highly commendable, and that the circumstance of my being next in the entail of Longbourn estate, will be kindly overlooked on your side, and not lead you to reject the offered olive branch. I cannot be otherwise than concerned at being the means of injuring your amiable daughters, and beg leave to apologise for it, as well as to assure you of my readiness to make them every possible amends, - but of this hereafter. If you should have no objection to receive me into your house, I propose myself the satisfaction of waiting on you and your *family, Monday, November 18th, by four o'clock, and shall probably trespass on your hospitality till the Saturday se'night following, which I can do without any inconvenience, as Lady Catherine is far from objecting to my occasional absence on a Sunday, provided that some other clergyman is engaged to do the duty of the day. I remain, dear sir, with respectful compliments to your lady and daughters, your well-wisher and friend,*

WILLIAM COLLINS.

'At four o'clock, therefore, we may expect this peace-making gentleman,' said Mr Bennet, as he folded up the letter. 'He seems to be a most conscientious and polite young man, upon my word; and I doubt not will prove a valuable acquaintance, especially if Lady Catherine should be so indulgent as to let him come to us again.'

'There is some sense in what he says about the girls however; and if he is disposed to make them any amends, I shall not be the person to discourage him.'

'Though it is difficult,' said Jane, 'to guess in what way he can mean to make us the atonement he thinks our due, the wish is certainly to his credit.'

Elizabeth was chiefly struck with his extraordinary deference for Lady Catherine, and his kind intention of christening, marrying, and burying his parishioners whenever it were required.

'He must be an oddity, I think,' said she. 'I cannot make him out. – There is something very pompous in his stile. – And what can he mean by apologizing for being next in the entail? – We cannot suppose he would help it, if he could. – Can he be a sensible man, sir?'

'No, my dear; I think not. I have great hopes of finding him quite the reverse. There is a mixture of servility and self-importance in his letter, which promises well. I am impatient to see him.'

'In point of composition,' said Mary, 'his letter does not seem defective. The idea of the olive branch perhaps is not wholly new, yet I think it is well expressed.'

To Catherine and Lydia, neither the letter nor its writer were in any degree interesting. It was next to impossible that their cousin should come in a scarlet coat; and it was now some weeks since they had received pleasure from the society of a man in any other colour. As for their mother, Mr Collins's letter had done away much of her ill-will, and she was preparing to see him with a degree of composure, which astonished her husband and daughters.

Mr Collins was punctual to his time, and was received with great politeness by the whole family. Mr Bennet indeed said little; but the ladies were ready enough to talk, and Mr Collins seemed neither in need of encouragement, nor inclined to be silent himself. He was a tall, heavy looking young man of five and twenty. His air was grave and stately, and his manners were very formal. He had not been long seated before he complimented Mrs Bennet on having so fine a family of daughters, said he had heard much of their beauty, but that, in this instance, fame had fallen short of the truth; and added, that he did not doubt her seeing them all in due time well disposed of in marriage. This gallantry was not much to the taste of some of his hearers, but Mrs Bennet, who quarrelled with no compliments, answered most readily,

'You are very kind, sir, I am sure; and I wish with all my heart it may prove so; for else they will be destitute enough. Things are settled so oddly.'

'You allude perhaps to the entail of this estate.'

'Ah! sir, I do indeed. It is a grevious affair to my poor girls, you must confess. Not that I mean to find fault with *you*, for such things I know are all chance in this world. There is no knowing how estates will go when once they come to be entailed.'

'I am very sensible, madam, of the hardship to my fair cousins, – and could say much on the subject, but that I am cautious of appearing forward and precipitate. But I can assure the young ladies that I come prepared to admire them. At present I will not say more, but perhaps when we are better acquainted –'

He was interrupted by a summons to dinner; and the girls smiled on each other. They were not the only objects of Mr Collins's admiration. The hall, the dining-room, and all its furniture were examined and praised; and his commendation of every thing would have touched Mrs Bennet's heart, but for the mortifying supposition of his viewing it all as his own future property. The dinner too in its turn was highly admired; and he begged to know to which of his fair cousins, the excellence of its cookery was owing. But here he was set right by Mrs Bennet, who assured him with some asperity that they were very well able to keep a good cook, and that her daughters had nothing to do in the kitchen. He begged pardon for having displeased her. In a softened tone she declared herself not at all offended; but he continued to apologise for about a quarter of an hour.

Chapter Fourteen

DURING DINNER, MR BENNET SCARCELY spoke at all; but when the servants were withdrawn, he thought it time to have some conversation with his guest, and therefore started a subject in which he expected him to shine, by observing that he seemed very fortunate in his patroness. Lady Catherine de Bourgh's attention to his wishes, and consideration for his comfort, appeared very remarkable. Mr Bennet could not have chosen better. Mr Collins was eloquent in her praise. The subject elevated him to more than usual solemnity of manner, and with a most important aspect he protested that he had never in his life witnessed such behaviour in a person of rank – such affability and condescension, as he had himself experienced from Lady Catherine. She had been graciously pleased to approve of both the discourses, which he had already had the honour of preaching before her. She had also asked him twice to dine at Rosings; and had sent for him only the Saturday before, to make up her pool of quadrille in the evening. Lady Catherine was reckoned proud by many people he knew, but *he* had never seen any thing but affability in her. She had always spoken to him as she would to any other gentleman; she made not the smallest objection to his joining in the society of the neighbourhood, nor to his leaving his parish occasionally for a week or two, to visit his relations. She had even condescended to advise him to marry as soon as he could, provided he chose with discretion; and had once paid him a visit in his humble parsonage; where she had perfectly approved all the alterations he had been making, and had even vouchsafed to suggest some herself, – some shelves in the closets up stairs.

'That is all very proper and civil, I am sure,' said Mrs Bennet, 'and I dare say she is a very agreeable woman. It is a pity that great ladies in general are not more like her. Does she live near you, sir?'

'The garden in which stands my humble abode, is separated only by a lane from Rosings Park, her ladyship's residence.'

'I think you said she was a widow, sir? has she any family?'

'She has only one daughter, the heiress of Rosings, and of very extensive property.'

'Ah!' cried Mrs Bennet, shaking her head, 'then she is better off than many girls. And what sort of young lady is she? is she handsome?'

'She is a most charming young lady indeed. Lady Catherine herself says that in point of true beauty, Miss de Bourgh is far superior to the handsomest of her sex; because there is that in her features which marks the young woman of distinguished birth. She is unfortunately of a sickly constitution, which has prevented her making that progress in many accomplishments, which she could not otherwise have failed of; as I am informed by the lady who superintended her education, and who still resides with them. But she is perfectly amiable, and often condescends to drive by my humble abode in her little phaeton and ponies.'

'Has she been presented? I do not remember her name among the ladies at court.'

'Her indifferent state of health unhappily prevents her being in town; and by that means, as I told Lady Catherine myself one day, has deprived the British court of its brightest ornament. Her ladyship seemed pleased with the idea, and you may imagine that I am happy on every occasion to offer those little delicate compliments which are always acceptable to ladies. I have more than once observed to Lady Catherine, that her charming daughter seemed born to be a duchess, and that the most elevated rank, instead of giving her consequence, would be adorned by her. – These are the kind of little things which please her ladyship, and it is a sort of attention which I conceive myself peculiarly bound to pay.'

'You judge very properly,' said Mr Bennet, 'and it is happy for you that you possess the talent of flattering with delicacy. May I ask whether these pleasing attentions proceed from the impulse of the moment, or are the result of previous study?'

'They arise chiefly from what is passing at the time, and though I sometimes amuse myself with suggesting and arranging such little elegant compliments as may be adapted to ordinary occasions, I always wish to give them as unstudied an air as possible.'

Mr Bennet's expectations were fully answered. His cousin was as absurd as he had hoped, and he listened to him with the keenest enjoyment, maintaining at the same time the most resolute composure of countenance, and except in an occasional glance at Elizabeth, requiring no partner in his pleasure.

By tea-time however the dose had been enough, and Mr Bennet was glad to take his guest into the drawing-room again, and when tea was over, glad to invite him to read aloud to the ladies. Mr Collins readily assented, and a book was produced; but on beholding it, (for every thing announced it to be from a circulating library,) he started back, and begging pardon, protested that he never read novels. – Kitty started at him, and Lydia exclaimed. – Other books were produced, and after some deliberation he chose Fordyce's Sermons. Lydia gaped as he opened the volume, and before he had, with very monotonous solemnity, read three pages, she interrupted him with,

'Do you know, mama, that my uncle Philips talks of turning away Richard, and if he does, Colonel Forster will hire him. My aunt told me so herself on Saturday. I shall walk to Meryton to-morrow to hear more about it, and to ask when Mr Denny comes back from town.'

Lydia was bid by her two eldest sisters to hold her tongue; but Mr Collins, much offended, laid aside his book, and said,

'I have often observed how little young ladies are interested by books of a serious stamp, though written solely for their benefit. It amazes me, I confess; – for certainly, there can be nothing so advantageous to them as instruction. But I will no longer importune my young cousin.'

Then turning to Mr Bennet, he offered himself as his antagonist at backgammon. Mr Bennet accepted the challenge, observing that he acted very wisely in leaving the girls to their own trifling amusements. Mrs Bennet and her daughters apologized most civilly for Lydia's interruption, and promised that it should not occur again, if he would resume his book; but Mr Collins, after assuring them that he bore his young cousin no ill will, and should never resent her behaviour as any affront, seated himself at another table with Mr Bennet, and prepared for backgammon.

Chapter Fifteen

MR COLLINS WAS NOT A SENSIBLE man, and the deficiency of nature had been but little assisted by education or society; the greatest part of his life having been spent under the guidance of an illiterate and miserly father; and though he belonged to one of the universities, he had merely kept the necessary terms, without forming at it any useful acquaintance. The subjection in which his father had brought him up, had given him originally great humility of manner, but it was now a good deal counteracted by the self-conceit of a weak head, living in retirement, and the consequential feelings of early and unexpected prosperity. A fortunate chance had recommended him to Lady Catherine de Bourgh when the living of Hunsford was vacant; and the respect which he felt for her high rank, and his veneration for her as his patroness, mingling with a very good opinion of himself, of his authority as a clergyman, and his rights as a rector, made him altogether a mixture of pride and obsequiousness, self-importance and humility.

Having now a good house and very sufficient income, he intended to marry; and in seeking a reconciliation with the Longbourn family he had a wife in view, as he meant to chuse one of the daughters, if he found them as handsome and amiable as they were represented by common report. This was his plan of amends – of atonement – for inheriting their father's estate; and he thought it an excellent one, full of eligibility and suitableness, and excessively generous and disinterested on his own part.

His plan did not vary on seeing them. – Miss Bennet's lovely face confirmed his views, and established all his strictest notions of what was due to seniority; and for the first evening *she* was his settled choice. The next morning, however, made an alteration; for in a quarter of an hour's tête-à-tête with Mrs Bennet before breakfast, a conversation beginning with his parsonage-house, and leading naturally to the avowal of his hopes, that a mistress for it might be found at Longbourn, produced from her, amid very complaisant smiles and general encouragement, a caution against the very Jane he had fixed on. – 'As to her *younger* daughters she could not take upon her to say – she could not positively answer – but she did not *know* of any prepossession; – her *eldest* daughter, she must just mention – she felt incumbent on her to hint, was likely to be very soon engaged.'

Mr Collins had only to change from Jane to Elizabeth – and it was soon done – done while Mrs Bennet was stirring the fire. Elizabeth, equally next to Jane in birth and beauty, succeeded her of course.

Mrs Bennet treasured up the hint, and trusted that she might soon have two daughters married; and the man whom she could not bear to speak of the day before, was now high in her good graces.

Lydia's intention of walking to Meryton was not forgotten; every sister except Mary agreed to go with her; and Mr Collins was to attend them, at the request of Mr Bennet, who was most anxious to get rid of him, and have his library to himself; for thither Mr Collins had followed him after breakfast, and there he would continue, nominally engaged with one of the largest folios in the collection, but really talking to Mr Bennet, with little cessation, of his house and garden at Hunsford. Such doings discomposed Mr Bennet exceedingly. In his library he had been always sure of leisure and tranquillity; and though prepared, as he told Elizabeth, to meet with folly and conceit in every other room in the house, he was used to be free from them there; his civility, therefore, was most prompt in inviting Mr Collins to join his daughters in their walk; and Mr Collins, being in fact much better fitted for a walker than a reader, was extremely well pleased to close his large book, and go.

In pompous nothings on his side, and civil assents on that of his cousins, their time passed till they entered Meryton. The attention of the younger ones was then no longer to be gained by *him*. Their eyes were immediately wandering up in the street in quest of the officers, and nothing less than a very smart bonnet indeed, or a really new muslin in a shop window, could recall them.

But the attention of every young lady was soon caught by a young man, whom they had never seen before, of most gentlemanlike appearance, walking with an officer on the other side of the way. The officer was the very Mr Denny, concerning whose return from London Lydia came to enquire, and he bowed as they passed. All were struck with the stranger's air, all wondered who he could be, and Kitty and Lydia, determined if possible to find out, led the way across the street, under pretence of wanting something in an opposite shop, and fortunately had just gained the pavement when the two gentlemen turning back had reached the same spot. Mr Denny addressed them directly, and entreated permission to introduce his friend, Mr Wickham, who had returned with him the day before from town, and he was happy to say had accepted a commission in their corps. This was exactly as it should be; for the young man wanted only regimentals to make him completely charming. His appearance was greatly in his favour; he had all the best part of beauty, a fine countenance, a good figure, and very pleasing address. The introduction was followed up on his side by a happy readiness of conversation – a readiness at the same time perfectly correct and unassuming; and the whole party were still standing and talking together very agreeably, when the sound of horses drew their notice, and Darcy and Bingley were seen riding down the street. On distinguishing the ladies of the group, the two gentlemen came directly towards them, and began the usual civilities. Bingley was the principal spokesman, and Miss Bennet the principal object. He was then, he said, on his way to Longbourn on purpose to enquire after her. Mr Darcy corroborated it with a bow, and was beginning to determine not to fix his eyes on Elizabeth, when they were suddenly arrested by the sight of the stranger, and Elizabeth happening to see the countenance of both as they looked at each other, was all astonishment at the effect of the meeting. Both changed colour, one looked white, the other red. Mr Wickham, after a few moments, touched his hat – a salutation which Mr Darcy just deigned to return. What could be the meaning of it? – It was impossible to imagine; it was impossible not to long to know.

In another minute Mr Bingley, but without seeming to have noticed what passed, took leave and rode on with his friend.

Mr Denny and Mr Wickham walked with the young ladies to the door of Mr Philip's house, and then made their bows, in spite of Miss Lydia's pressing entreaties that they would come in, and even in spite of Mrs Philips' throwing up the parlour window, and loudly seconding the invitation.

Mrs Philips was always glad to see her nieces, and the two eldest, from their recent absence, were particularly welcome, and she was eagerly express-ing her surprise at their sudden return home, which, as their own carriage had not fetched them, she should have known nothing about, if she had not happened to see Mr Jones's shop boy in the street, who had told her that they were not to send any more draughts to Netherfield because the Miss Bennets were come away, when her civility was claimed towards Mr Collins by Jane's introduction of him. She received him with her very best politeness, which he returned with as much more, apologising for his intrusion, without any previous acquaintance with her, which he could not help flattering himself however might be justified by his relationship to the young ladies who introduced him to her notice. Mrs Philips was quite awed by such an excess of good breeding; but her contemplation of one stranger was soon put an end to by exclamations and inquiries about the other, of whom, however, she could only tell her nieces what they already knew, that Mr Denny had brought him from London, and that he was to have a lieutenant's commission in the —shire. She had been watching him the last hour, she said, as he walked up and down the street, and had Mr Wickham appeared Kitty and Lydia would certainly have continued the occupation, but unluckily no one passed the windows now except a few of the officers, who in comparison with the stranger, were become 'stupid, disagreeable fellows'. Some of them were to dine with the Philipses the next day, and their aunt promised to make her husband call on Mr Wickham, and give him an invitation also, if the family from Longbourn would come in the evening. This was agreed to, and Mrs Philips protested that they would have a nice comfortable noisy game of lottery tickets, and a little bit of hot supper afterwards. The prospect of such delights was very cheering, and they parted in mutual good spirits. Mr Collins repeated his apologies in quitting the room, and was assured with unwearying civility that they were perfectly needless.

As they walked home, Elizabeth related to Jane what she had seen pass between the two gentlemen; but though Jane would have defended either or both, had they appeared to be wrong, she could no more explain such behaviour than her sister.

Mr Collins on his return highly gratified Mrs Bennet by admiring Mrs Philips's manners and politeness. He protested that except Lady Catherine and her daughter, he had never seen a more elegant woman; for she had not only received him with the utmost civility, but had even pointedly included him in her invitation for the next evening, although utterly unknown to her before. Something he supposed might be attributed to his connection with them, but yet he had never met with so much attention in the whole course of his life.

Chapter Sixteen

AS NO OBJECTION WAS MADE TO THE young people's engagement with their aunt, and all Mr Collins's scruples of leaving Mr and Mrs Bennet for a single evening during his visit were most steadily resisted, the coach conveyed him and his five cousins at a suitable hour to Meryton; and the girls had the pleasure of hearing, as they entered the drawing-room, that Mr Wickham had accepted their uncle's invitation, and was then in the house.

When this information was given, and they had all taken their seats, Mr Collins was at leisure to look around him and admire, and he was so much struck with the size and furniture of the apartment, that he declared he might almost have supposed himself in the smaller summer breakfast parlour at Rosings; a comparison that did not at first convey much gratification; but when Mrs Philips understood from him what Rosings was, and who was its proprietor, when she had listened to the description of only one of Lady Catherine's drawing-rooms, and found that the chimney-piece alone had cost eight hundred pounds, she felt all the force of the compliment, and would hardly have resented a comparison with the housekeeper's room.

In describing to her all the grandeur of Lady Catherine and her mansion, with occasional digressions in praise of his own humble abode, and the improvements it was receiving, he was happily employed until the gentlemen joined them; and he found in Mrs Philips a very attentive listener, whose opinion of his consequence increased with what she heard, and who was resolving to retail it all among her neighbours as soon as she could. To the girls, who could not listen to their cousin, and who had nothing to do but wish for an instrument, and examine their own indifferent imitations of china on the mantelpiece, the interval of waiting appeared very long. It was over at last however. The gentlemen did approach; and when Mr Wickham walked into the room, Elizabeth felt that she had neither been seeing him before, nor thinking of him since, with the smallest degree of unreasonable admiration. The officers of the —shire were in general a very creditable, gentlemanlike set, and the best of them were of the present party; but Mr Wickham was as far beyond them all in person, countenance, air, and walk, as *they* were superior to the broad-faced stuffy uncle Philips, breathing port wine, who followed them into the room.

Mr Wickham was the happy man towards whom almost every female eye was turned, and Elizabeth was the happy woman by whom he finally seated himself; and the agreeable manner in which he immediately fell into conversation, though it was only on its being a wet night, and on the probability of a rainy season, made her feel that the commonest, dullest, most threadbare topic might be rendered interesting by the skill of the speaker.

With such rivals for the notice of the fair, as Mr Wickham and the officers, Mr Collins seemed likely to sink into insignificance; to the young ladies he certainly was nothing; but he had still at intervals a kind listener in Mrs Philips, and was, by her watchfulness, most abundantly supplied with coffee and muffin.

When the card tables were placed, he had an opportunity of obliging her in return, by sitting down to whist.

'I know little of the game, at present,' said he, 'but I shall be glad to improve myself, for in my situation of life –' Mrs Philips was very thankful of his compliance, but could not wait for his reason.

Mr Wickham did not play at whist, and with ready delight was he received at the other table between Elizabeth and Lydia. At first there seemed danger of Lydia's engrossing him entirely, for she was a most determined talker; but being likewise extremely fond of lottery tickets, she soon grew too much interested in the game, too eager in making bets and exclaiming after prizes, to have attention for any one in particular. Allowing for the common demands of the game, Mr Wickham was therefore at leisure to talk to Elizabeth, and she was very willing to hear him, though what she chiefly wished to hear she could not hope to be told, the history of his acquaintance with Mr Darcy. She dared not even mention that gentleman. Her curiosity however was unexpectedly relieved. Mr Wickham began the subject himself. He inquired how far Netherfield was from Meryton; and, after receiving her answer, asked in an hesitating manner how long Mr Darcy had been staying there.

'About a month,' said Elizabeth; and then, unwilling to let the subject drop, added, 'He is a man of very large property in Derbyshire, I understand.'

'Yes,' replied Wickham; – 'his estate there is a noble one. A clear ten thousand per annum. You could not have met with a person more capable of giving you certain information on that head than myself – for I have been connected with his family in a particular manner from my infancy.'

Elizabeth could not but look surprised.

'You may well be surprised, Miss Bennet, at such an assertion, after seeing, as you probably might, the very cold manner of our meeting yesterday. – Are you much acquainted with Mr Darcy?'

'As much as I ever wish to be,' cried Elizabeth warmly, – 'I have spent four days in the same house with him, and I think him very disagreeable.'

'I have no right to give *my* opinion,' said Wickham, 'as to his being agreeable or otherwise. I am not qualified to form one. I have known him too long and too well to be a fair judge. It is impossible for *me* to be impartial. But I believe your opinion of him would in general astonish – and perhaps you would not express it quite so strongly anywhere else. – Here you are in your own family.'

'Upon my word I say no more *here* than I might say in any house in the neighbourhood, except Netherfield. He is not at all liked in Hertfordshire. Every body is disgusted with his pride. You will not find him more favourably spoken of by any one.'

'I cannot pretend to be sorry,' said Wickham, after a short interruption, 'that he or that any man should not be estimated beyond their deserts; but with *him* I believe it does not often happen. The world is blinded by his fortune and consequence, or frightened by his high and imposing manners, and sees him only as he chuses to be seen.'

'I should take him, even on *my* slight acquaintance, to be an ill-tempered man.' Wickham only shook his head.

'I wonder,' said he, at the next opportunity of speaking, 'whether he is likely to be in this country much longer.'

'I do not at all know; but I *heard* nothing of his going away when I was at Netherfield. I hope your plans in favour of the —shire will not be affected by his being in the neighbourhood.'

'Oh! no – it is not for *me* to be driven away by Mr Darcy. If *he* wishes to avoid seeing *me*, he must go. We are not on friendly terms, and it always gives me pain to meet him, but I have no reason for avoiding *him* but what I might proclaim to all the world; a sense of very great ill usage, and most painful regrets at his being what he is. His father, Miss Bennet, the late Mr Darcy, was one of the best men that ever breathed, and the truest friend I ever had; and I can never be in company with this Mr Darcy without being grieved to the soul by a thousand tender recollections. His behaviour to myself has been scandalous; but I verily believe I could forgive him any thing and every thing, rather than his disappointing the hopes and disgracing the memory of his father.'

Elizabeth found the interest of the subject increase, and listened with all her heart; but the delicacy of it prevented farther enquiry.

Mr Wickham began to speak on more general topics, Meryton, the neighbourhood, the society, appearing highly pleased with all that he had yet seen, and speaking of the latter especially, with gentle but very intelligible gallantry.

'It was the prospect of constant society, and good society,' he added, 'which was my chief inducement to enter the —shire. I knew it to be a most respectable, agreeable corps, and my friend Denny tempted me farther by his account of their present quarters, and the very great attentions and excellent acquaintance Meryton had procured them. Society, I own, is necessary to me. I have been a disappointed man, and my spirits will not bear solitude. I *must* have employment and society. A military life is not what I was intended for, but circumstances have now made it eligible. The church *ought* to have been my profession – I was brought up for the church, and I should at this time have been in possession of a most valuable living, had it pleased the gentleman we were speaking of just now.'

'Indeed!'

'Yes – the late Mr Darcy bequeathed me the next presentation of the best living in his gift. He was my godfather, and excessively attached to me. I cannot do justice to his kindness. He meant to provide for me amply, and thought he had done it; but when the living fell, it was given elsewhere.'

'Good heavens!' cried Elizabeth; 'but how could *that* be? – How could his will be disregarded? – Why did not you seek legal redress?'

'There was just such an informality in the terms of the bequest as to give me no hope from law. A man of honour could not have doubted the intention, but Mr Darcy chose to doubt it – or to treat it as a merely conditional recommendation, and to assert that I had forfeited all claim to it by extravagance, imprudence, in short any thing or nothing. Certain it is, that the living became vacant two years ago, exactly as I was of an age to hold it, and that it was given to another man; and no less certain is it, that I cannot accuse myself of having really done any thing to deserve to lose it. I have a warm, unguarded temper, and I may perhaps have sometimes spoken my opinion *of* him, and *to* him, too freely. I can recall nothing worse. But the fact is, that we are very different sort of men, and that he hates me.'

'This is quite shocking! – He deserves to be publicly disgraced.'

'Some time or other he *will* be – but it shall not be by *me*. Till I can forget his father, I can never defy or expose *him*.'

Elizabeth honoured him for such feelings, and thought him handsomer than ever as he expressed them.

'But what,' said she, after a pause, 'can have been his motive? – what can have induced him to behave so cruelly?'

'A thorough, determined dislike of me – a dislike which I cannot but attribute in some measure to jealousy. Had the late Mr Darcy liked me less, his son might have borne with me better; but his father's uncommon attachment to me, irritated him I believe very early in life. He had not a temper to bear the sort of competition in which we stood – the sort of preference which was often given me.'

'I had not thought Mr Darcy so bad as this – though I have never liked him, I had not thought so very ill of him – I had supposed him to be despising his fellow-creatures in general, but did not suspect him of descending to such malicious revenge, such injustice, such inhumanity as this!'

After a few minutes reflection, however, she continued, 'I *do* remember his boasting one day, at Netherfield, of the implacability of his resentments, of his having an unforgiving temper. His disposition must be dreadful.'

'I will not trust myself on the subject,' replied Wickham, '*I* can hardly be just to him.'

Elizabeth was again deep in thought, and after a time exclaimed, 'To treat in such a manner, the godson, the friend, the favourite of his father!' – She could have added, 'A young man too, like *you*, whose very countenance may vouch for your being amiable' – but she contented herself with 'And one, too, who had probably been his own companion from childhood, connected together, as I think you said, in the closest manner!'

'We were born in the same parish, within the same park, the greatest part of our youth was passed together; inmates of the same house, sharing the same amusements, objects of the same parental care. *My* father began life in the profession which your uncle, Mr Philips, appears to do so much credit to – but he gave up every thing to be of use to the late Mr Darcy, and devoted all his time to the care of the Pemberley property. He was most highly esteemed by Mr Darcy, a most intimate, confidential friend. Mr

Darcy often acknowledged himself to be under the greatest obligations to my father's active superintendance, and when immediately before my father's death, Mr Darcy gave him a voluntary promise of providing for me, I am convinced that he felt it to be as much a debt of gratitude to *him*, as of affection to myself.'

'How strange!' cried Elizabeth. 'How abominable! – I wonder that the very pride of this Mr Darcy has not made him just to you! – If from no better motive, that he should not have been too proud to be dishonest, – for dishonesty I must call it.'

'It *is* wonderful,' – replied Wickham, – 'for almost all his actions may be traced to pride; – and pride has often been his best friend. It has connected him nearer with virtue than any other feeling. But we are none of us consistent; and in his behaviour to me, there were stronger impulses even than pride.'

'Can such abominable pride as his, have ever done him good?'

'Yes. It has often led him to be liberal and generous, – to give his money freely, to display hospitality, to assist his tenants, and relieve the poor. Family pride, and *filial* pride, for he is very proud of what his father was, have done this. Not to appear to disgrace his family, to degenerate from the popular qualities, or lose the influence of the Pemberley House, is a powerful motive. He has also *brotherly* pride, which with *some* brotherly affection, makes him a very kind and careful guardian of his sister; and you will hear him generally cried up as the most attentive and best of brothers.'

'What sort of a girl is Miss Darcy?'

He shook his head. – 'I wish I could call her amiable. It gives me pain to speak ill of a Darcy. But she is too much like her brother, – very, very proud. – As a child, she was affectionate and pleasing, and extremely fond of me; and I have devoted hours and hours to her amusement. But she is nothing to me now. She is a handsome girl, about fifteen or sixteen, and I understand highly accomplished. Since her father's death, her home has been London, where a lady lives with her, and superintends her education.'

After many pauses and many trials of other subjects, Elizabeth could not help reverting once more to the first, and saying,

'I am astonished at his intimacy with Mr Bingley! How can Mr Bingley, who seems good humour itself, and is, I really believe, truly amiable, be in friendship with such a man? How can they suit each other? – Do you know Mr Bingley?'

'Not at all.'

'He is a sweet tempered, amiable, charming man. He cannot know what Mr Darcy is.'

'Probably not; – but Mr Darcy can please where he chuses. He does not want abilities. He can be a conversible companion if he thinks it worth his while. Among those who are at all his equals in consequence, he is a very different man from what he is to the less prosperous. His pride never deserts him; but with the rich, he is liberal-minded, just, sincere, rational, honourable, and perhaps agreeable, – allowing something for fortune and figure.'

The whist party soon afterwards breaking up, the players gathered round the other table, and Mr Collins took his station between his cousin Elizabeth and Mrs Philips. – The usual inquiries as to his success were made by the latter. It had not been very great; he had lost every point; but when Mrs Philips began to express her concern thereupon, he assured her with much earnest gravity that it was not of the least importance, that he considered the money as a mere trifle, and begged she would not make herself uneasy.

'I know very well, madam,' said he, 'that when persons sit down to a card table, they must take their chance of these things, – and happily I am not in such circumstances as to make five shillings any object. There are undoubtedly many who could not say the same, but thanks to Lady Catherine de Bourgh, I am removed far beyond the necessity of regarding little matters.'

Mr Wickham's attention was caught; and after observing Mr Collins for a few moments, he asked Elizabeth in a low voice whether her relation were very intimately acquainted with the family of de Bourgh.

'Lady Catherine de Bourgh,' she replied, 'has very lately given him a living. I hardly know how Mr Collins was first introduced to her notice, but he certainly has not known her long.'

'You know of course that Lady Catherine de Bourgh and Lady Anne Darcy were sisters; consequently that she is aunt to the present Mr Darcy.'

'No, indeed, I did not. – I knew nothing at all of Lady Catherine's connections. I never heard of her existence till the day before yesterday.'

'Her daughter, Miss de Bourgh, will have a very large fortune, and it is believed that she and her cousin will unite the two estates.'

This information made Elizabeth smile, as she thought of poor Miss Bingley. Vain indeed must be all her attentions, vain and useless her affection for his sister and her praise of himself, if he were already self-destined to another.

'Mr Collins,' said she, 'speaks highly both of Lady Catherine and her daughter; but from some particulars that he has related of her ladyship, I suspect his gratitude misleads him, and that in spite of her being his patroness, she is an arrogant, conceited woman.'

'I believe her to be both in a great degree,' replied Wickham; 'I have not seen her for many years, but I very well remember that I never liked her, and that her manners were dictatorial and insolent. She has the reputation of being remarkably sensible and clever; but I rather believe she derives part of her abilities from her rank and fortune, part from her authoritative manner, and the rest from the pride of her nephew, who chuses that every one connected with him should have an understanding of the first class.'

Elizabeth allowed that he had given a very rational account of it, and they continued talking together with mutual satisfaction till supper put an end to cards; and gave the rest of the ladies their share of Mr Wickham's attentions. There could be no conversation in the noise of Mrs Philips's supper party, but his manners recommended him to every body. Whatever he said, was said well; and whatever he did, done gracefully. Elizabeth went away with her head full of him. She could think of nothing but of Mr Wickham, and of what he had told her, all the way home; but there was not time for her even to mention his name as they went, for neither Lydia nor Mr Collins were once silent. Lydia talked incessantly of lottery tickets, of the fish she had lost and the fish she had won, and Mr Collins, in describing the civility of Mr and Mrs Philips, protesting that he did not in the least regard his losses at whist, enumerating all the dishes at supper, and repeatedly fearing that he crouded his cousins, had more to say than he could well manage before the carriage stopped at Longbourn House.

Chapter Seventeen

ELIZABETH RELATED TO JANE THE NEXT day, what had passed between Mr Wickham and herself. Jane listened with astonishment and concern; – she knew not how to believe that Mr Darcy could be so unworthy of Mr Bingley's regard; and yet, it was not in her nature to question the veracity of a young man of such amiable appearance as Wickham. – The possibility of his having really endured such unkindness, was enough to interest all her tender feelings; and nothing therefore remained to be done, but to think well of them both, to defend the conduct of each, and throw into the account of accident or mistake, whatever could not be otherwise explained.

'They have both,' said she, 'been deceived, I dare say, in some way or other, of which we can form no idea. Interested people have perhaps misrepresented each to the other. It is, in short, impossible for us to conjecture the causes or circumstances which may have alienated them, without actual blame on either side.'

'Very true, indeed; – and now, my dear Jane, what have you got to say in behalf of the interested people who have probably been concerned in the business? – Do clear *them* too, or we shall be obliged to think ill of somebody.'

'Laugh as much as you chuse, but you will not laugh me out of my opinion. My dearest Lizzy, do but consider in what a disgraceful light it places Mr Darcy, to be treating his father's favourite in such a manner, – one, whom his father had promised to provide for. – It is impossible. No man of common humanity, no man who had any value for his character, could be capable of it. Can his most intimate friends be so excessively deceived in him? oh! no.'

'I can much more easily believe Mr Bingley's being imposed on, than that Mr Wickham should invent such a history of himself as he gave me last night; names, facts, every thing mentioned without ceremony. – If it be not so, let Mr Darcy contradict it. Besides, there was truth in his looks.'

'It is difficult indeed – it is distressing. – One does not know what to think.'

'I beg your pardon; – one knows exactly what to think.'

But Jane could think with certainty on only one point, – that Mr Bingley, if he *had been* imposed on, would have much to suffer when the affair became public.

The two young ladies were summoned from the shrubbery where this conversation passed, by the arrival of some of the very persons of whom they had been speaking; Mr Bingley and his sisters came to give their personal invitation for the long expected ball at Netherfield, which was fixed for the following Tuesday. The two ladies were delighted to see their dear friend again, called it an age since they had met, and repeatedly asked what she had been doing with herself since their separation. To the rest of the family they paid little attention; avoiding Mrs Bennet as much as possible, saying not much to Elizabeth, and nothing at all to the others. They were soon gone again, rising from their seats with an activity which took their brother by surprise, and hurrying off as if eager to escape from Mrs Bennet's civilities.

The prospect of the Netherfield ball was extremely agreeable to every female of the family. Mrs Bennet chose to consider it as given in compliment to her eldest daughter, and was particularly flattered by receiving the invitation from Mr Bingley himself, instead of a ceremonious card. Jane pictured to herself a happy evening in the society of her two friends, and the attentions of their brother; and Elizabeth thought with pleasure of dancing a great deal with Mr Wickham, and of seeing a confirmation of every thing in Mr Darcy's looks and behaviour. The happiness anticipated by Catherine and Lydia, depended less on any single event, or any particular person, for though they each, like Elizabeth, meant to dance half the evening with Mr Wickham, he was by no means the only partner who could satisfy them, and a ball was at any rate, a ball. And even Mary could assure her family that she had no disinclination for it.

'While I can have my mornings to myself,' said she, 'it is enough. – I think it no sacrifice to join occasionally in evening engagements. Society has claims on us all; and I profess myself one of those who consider intervals of recreation and amusement as desirable for every body.'

Elizabeth's spirits were so high on the occasion, that though she did not often speak unnecessarily to Mr Collins, she could not help asking him whether he intended to accept Mr Bingley's invitation, and if he did, whether he would think it proper to join in the evening's amusement; and she was rather surprised to find that he entertained no scruple whatever on that head, and was very far from dreading a rebuke either from the Archbishop, or Lady Catherine de Bourgh, by venturing to dance.

'I am by no means of opinion, I assure you,' said he, 'that a ball of this kind, given by a young man of character, to respectable people, can have any evil tendency; and I am so far from objecting to dancing myself that I shall hope to be honoured with the hands of all my fair cousins in the course of the evening, and I take this opportunity of soliciting yours, Miss Elizabeth, for the two first dances especially, – a preference which I trust my cousin Jane will attribute to the right cause, and not to any disrespect for her.'

Elizabeth felt herself completely taken in. She had fully proposed being engaged by Wickham for those very dances: – and to have Mr Collins instead! her liveliness had been never worse timed. There was no help for it however. Mr Wickham's happiness and her own was per force delayed a little longer, and Mr Collins's proposal accepted with as good a grace as she could. She was not the better pleased with his gallantry, from the idea it suggested of something more. – It now first struck her, that *she* was selected from among her sisters as worthy of being the mistress of Hunsford Parsonage, and of assisting to form a quadrille table at Rosings, in the absence of more eligible visitors. The idea soon reached to conviction, as she observed his increasing civilities toward herself, and heard his frequent attempt at a compliment on her wit and vivacity; and though more astonished than gratified herself, by this effect of her charms, it was not long before her mother gave her to understand that the probability of their marriage was exceedingly agreeable to *her*. Elizabeth however did not chuse to take the hint, being well aware that a serious dispute must be the consequence of any reply. Mr Collins might never make the offer, and till he did, it was useless to quarrel about him.

If there had not been a Netherfield ball to prepare for and talk of, the younger Miss Bennets would have been in a pitiable state at this time, for from the day of the invitation, to the day of the ball, there was such a succession of rain as prevented their walking to Meryton once. No aunt, no officers, no news could be sought after; – the very shoe-roses for Netherfield were got by proxy. Even Elizabeth might have found some trial of her patience in weather, which totally suspended the improvement of her acquaintance with Mr Wickham; and nothing less than a dance on Tuesday, could have made such a Friday, Saturday, Sunday and Monday, endurable to Kitty and Lydia.

Chapter Eighteen

TILL ELIZABETH ENTERED THE DRAWING-ROOM at Netherfield and looked in vain for Mr Wickham among the cluster of red coats there assembled, a doubt of his being present had never occurred to her. The certainty of meeting him had not been checked by any of those recollections that might not unreasonably have alarmed her. She had dressed with more than usual care, and prepared in the highest spirits for the conquest of all that remained unsubdued of his heart, trusting that it was not more than might be won in the course of the evening. But in an instant arose the dreadful suspicion of his being purposely omitted for Mr Darcy's pleasure in the Bingleys' invitation to the officers; and though this was not exactly the case, the absolute fact of his absence was pronounced by his friend Mr Denny, to whom Lydia eagerly applied, and who told them that Wickham had been obliged to go to town on business the day before, and was not yet returned; adding, with a significant smile,

'I do not imagine his business would have called him away just now, if he had not wished to avoid a certain gentleman here.'

This part of his intelligence, though unheard by Lydia, was caught by Elizabeth, and as it assured her that Darcy was not less answerable for Wickham's absence than if her first surmise had been just, every feeling of displeasure against the former was so sharpened by immediate disappointment, that she could hardly reply with tolerable civility to the polite inquiries which he directly afterwards approached to make. – Attention, forbearance, patience with Darcy, was injury to Wickham. She was resolved against any sort of conversation with him, and turned away with a degree of ill humour, which she could not wholly surmount even in speaking to Mr Bingley, whose blind partiality provoked her.

But Elizabeth was not formed for ill-humour; and though every prospect of her own was destroyed for the evening, it could not dwell long on her spirits; and having told all her griefs to Charlotte Lucas, whom she had not seen for a week, she was soon able to make a voluntary transition to the oddities of her cousin, and to point him out to her particular notice. The two first dances, however, brought a return of distress; they were dances of mortification. Mr Collins, awkward and solemn, apologising instead of attending, and often moving wrong without being aware of it, gave her all the shame and misery which a disagreeable partner for a couple of dances can give. The moment of her release from him was ecstasy.

She danced next with an officer, and had the refreshment of talking of Wickham, and of hearing that he was universally liked. When those dances were over she returned to Charlotte Lucas, and was in conversation with her, when she found herself suddenly addressed by Mr Darcy, who took her so much by surprise in his application for her hand, that, without knowing what she did, she accepted him. He walked away again immediately, and she was left to fret over her own want of presence of mind; Charlotte tried to console her.

'I dare say you will find him very agreeable.'

'Heaven forbid! – *That* would be the greatest misfortune of all! – To find a man agreeable whom one is determined to hate! – Do not wish me such an evil.'

When the dancing recommenced, however, and Dary approached to claim her hand, Charlotte could not help cautioning her in a whisper not to be a simpleton and allow her fancy for Wickham to make her appear unpleasant in the eyes of a man of ten times his consequence. Elizabeth made no answer, and took her place in the set, amazed at the dignity to which she was arrived in being allowed to stand opposite to Mr Darcy, and reading in her neighbours' looks their equal amazement in beholding it. They stood for some time without speaking a word; and she began to imagine that their silence was to last through the two dances, and at first was resolved not to break it; till suddenly fancying that it would be the greater punishment to her partner to oblige him to talk, she made some slight observation on the dance. He replied, and was again silent. After a pause of some minutes she addressed him a second time with

'It is *your* turn to say something now, Mr Darcy. – *I* talked about the dance, and *you* ought to make some kind of remark on the size of the room, or the number of couples.'

He smiled, and assured her that whatever she wished him to say should be said.

'Very well. – That reply will do for the present. – Perhaps by and bye I may observe that private balls are much pleasanter than public ones. – But *now* we may be silent.'

'Do you talk by rule then, while you are dancing?'

'Sometimes. One must speak a little, you know. It would look odd to be entirely silent for half an hour together, and yet for the advantage of *some*, conversation ought to be so arranged as that they may have the trouble of saying as little as possible.'

'Are you consulting your own feelings in the present case, or do you imagine that you are gratifying mine?'

'Both,' replied Elizabeth archly; 'for I have always seen a great similarity in the turn of our minds. – We are each of an unsocial, taciturn disposition, unwilling to speak, unless we expect to say something that will amaze the whole room, and be handed down to posterity with all the eclat of a proverb.'

'This is no very striking resemblance of your own character, I am sure,' said he. 'How near it may be to *mine*, I cannot pretend to say. – *You* think it a faithful portrait undoubtedly.'

'I must not decide on my own performance.'

He made no answer, and they were again silent till they had gone down the dance, when he asked her if she and her sisters did not very often walk to Meryton. She answered in the affirmative, and, unable to resist the temptation, added, 'When you met us there the other day, we had just been forming a new acquaintance.'

The effect was immediate. A deeper shade of hauteur overspread his features, but he said not a word, and Elizabeth, though blaming herself for her own weakness, could not go on. At length Darcy spoke, and in a constrained manner said,

'Mr Wickham is blessed with such happy manners as may ensure his *making* friends – whether he may be equally capable of *retaining* them, is less certain.'

'He has been so unlucky as to lose *your* friendship,' replied Elizabeth with emphasis, 'and in a manner which he is likely to suffer from all his life.'

Darcy made no answer, and seemed desirous of changing the subject. At that moment Sir William Lucas appeared close to them, meaning to pass through the set to the other side of the room; but on perceiving Mr Darcy he stopt with a bow of superior courtesy to compliment him on his dancing and his partner.

'I have been most highly gratified indeed, my dear Sir. Such very superior dancing is not often seen. It is evident that you belong to the first circles. Allow me to say, however, that your fair partner does not disgrace you, and that I must hope to have this pleasure often repeated, especially when a certain desirable event, my dear Miss Eliza, (glancing at her sister and Bingley,) shall take place. What congratulations will then flow in! I appeal to Mr Darcy: – but let me not interrupt you, Sir. – You will not thank me for detaining you from the bewitching converse of that young lady, whose bright eyes are also upbraiding me.'

The latter part of this address was scarcely heard by Darcy; but Sir William's allusion to his friend seemed to strike him forcibly, and his eyes were directed with a very serious expression towards Bingley and Jane, who were dancing together. Recovering himself, however, shortly, he turned to his partner, and said,

'Sir William's interruption has made me forget what we were talking of.'

'I do not think we were speaking at all. Sir William could not have interrupted any two people in the room who had less to say for themselves. – We have tried two or three subjects already without success, and what we are to talk of next I cannot imagine.'

'What think you of books?' said he, smiling.

'Books – Oh! no. – I am sure we never read the same, or not with the same feelings.'

'I am sorry you think so; but if that be the case, there can at least be no want of subject. – We may compare our different opinions.'

'No – I cannot talk of books in a ball-room; my head is always full of something else.'

'The *present* always occupies you in such scenes – does it?' said he, with a look of doubt.

'Yes, always,' she replied, without knowing what she said, for her thoughts had wandered far from the subject, as soon afterwards appeared by her suddenly exclaiming, 'I remember hearing you once say, Mr Darcy, that you hardly ever forgave, that your resentment once created was unappeasable. You are very cautious, I suppose, as to its *being created*.'

'I am,' said he, with a firm voice.

'And never allow yourself to be blinded by prejudice?'

'I hope not.'

'It is particularly incumbent on those who never change their opinion, to be secure of judging properly at first.'

'May I ask to what these questions tend?'

'Merely to the illustration of *your* character,' said she, endeavouring to shake off her gravity. 'I am trying to make it out.'

'And what is your success?'

She shook her head. 'I do not get on at all. I hear such different accounts of you as puzzle me exceedingly.'

'I can readily believe,' answered he gravely, 'that report may vary greatly with respect to me; and I could wish, Miss Bennet, that you were not to sketch my character at the present moment, as there is reason to fear that the performance would reflect no credit on either.'

'But if I do not take your likeness now, I may never have another opportunity.'

'I would by no means suspend any pleasure of yours,' he coldly replied. She said no more, and they went down the other dance and parted in silence; on each side dissatisfied, though not to an equal degree, for in Darcy's breast there was a tolerable powerful feeling towards her, which soon procured her pardon, and directed all his anger against another.

They had not long separated when Miss Bingley came towards her, and with an expression of civil disdain thus accosted her,

'So, Miss Eliza, I hear you are quite delighted with George Wickham! – Your sister has been talking to me about him, and asking me a thousand questions; and I find that the young man forgot to tell you, among his other communications, that he was the son of old Wickham, the late Mr Darcy's steward. Let me recommend you, however, as a friend, not to give implicit confidence to all his assertions; for as to Mr Darcy's using him ill, it is perfectly false; for, on the contrary, he has been always remarkably kind to him, though George Wickham has treated Mr Darcy in a most infamous manner. I do not know the particulars, but I know very well that Mr Darcy is not in the least to blame, that he cannot bear to hear George Wickham mentioned, and that though my brother thought he could not well avoid including him in his invitation to the officers, he was excessively glad to find that he had taken himself out of the way. His coming into the country at all, is a most insolent thing indeed, and I wonder how he could presume to do it. I pity you, Miss Eliza, for this discovery of your favourite's guilt; but really considering his descent, one could not expect much better.'

'His guilt and his descent appear by your account to be the same,' said Elizabeth angrily; 'for I have heard you accuse him of nothing worse than of being the son of Mr Darcy's steward, and of *that*, I can assure you, he informed me himself.'

'I beg your pardon,' replied Miss Bingley, turning away with a sneer. 'Excuse my interference. – It was kindly meant.'

'Insolent girl!' said Elizabeth to herself. – 'You are much mistaken if you expect to influence me by such a paltry attack as this. I see nothing in it but your own wilful ignorance and the malice of Mr Darcy.' She then sought her eldest sister, who had undertaken to make inquiries on the same subject of Bingley. Jane met her with a smile of such sweet complacency, a glow of such happy expression, as sufficiently marked how well she was satisfied with the occurrences of the evening. – Elizabeth instantly read her feelings, and at that moment solicitude for Wickham, resentment against his enemies, and every thing else gave way before the hope of Jane's being in the fairest way for happiness.

'I want to know,' said she, with a countenance no less smiling than her sister's, 'what you have learnt about Mr Wickham. But perhaps you have been too pleasantly engaged to think of any third person; in which case you may be sure of my pardon.'

'No,' replied Jane, 'I have not forgotten him; but I have nothing satisfactory to tell you. Mr Bingley does not know the whole of his history, and is quite ignorant of the circumstances which have principally offended Mr Darcy; but he will vouch for the good conduct, the probity and honour of his friend, and is perfectly convinced that Mr Wickham has deserved much less attention from Mr Darcy than he has received; and I am sorry to say that by his account as well as his sister's, Mr Wickham is by no means a respectable young man. I am afraid he has been very imprudent, and has deserved to lose Mr Darcy's regard.'

'Mr Bingley does not know Mr Wickham himself?'

'No; he never saw him till the other morning at Meryton.'

'This account then is what he has received from Mr Darcy. I am perfectly satisfied. But what does he say of the living?'

'He does not exactly recollect the circumstances, though he has heard them from Mr Darcy more than once, but he believes that it was left to him *conditionally* only.'

'I have not a doubt of Mr Bingley's sincerity,' said Elizabeth warmly; 'but you must excuse my not being convinced by assurances only. Mr Bingley's defence of his friend was a very able one I dare say, but since he is unacquainted with several parts of the story, and has learnt the rest from that friend himself, I shall venture still to think of both gentlemen as I did before.'

She then changed the discourse to one more gratifying to each, and on which there could be no difference of sentiment. Elizabeth listened with delight to the happy, though modest hopes which Jane entertained of Bingley's regard, and said all in her power to heighten her confidence in it. On their being joined by Mr Bingley himself, Elizabeth withdrew to Miss Lucas; to whose inquiry after the pleasantness of her last partner she had scarcely replied, before Mr Collins came up to them and told her with great exultation that he had just been so fortunate as to make a most important discovery.

'I have found out,' said he, 'by a singular accident, that there is now in the room a near relation of my patroness. I happened to overhear the gentleman himself mentioning to the young lady who does the honours of this house the names of his cousin Miss de Bourgh, and of her mother Lady Catherine. How wonderfully these sort of things occur! Who would have thought of my meeting with – perhaps – a nephew of Lady Catherine de Bourgh in this assembly! – I am most thankful that the discovery is made in time for me to pay my respects to him, which I am now going to do, and trust he will excuse my not having done it before. My total ignorance of the connection must plead my apology.'

'You are not going to introduce yourself to Mr Darcy?'

'Indeed I am. I shall intreat his pardon for not having done it earlier. I believe him to be Lady Catherine's *nephew*. It will be in my power to assure him that her ladyship was quite well yesterday se'nnight.'

Elizabeth tried hard to dissuade him from such a scheme; assuring him that Mr Darcy would consider his addressing him without introduction as an impertinent freedom, rather than a compliment to his aunt; that it was not in the least necessary there should be any notice on either side, and that if it were, it must belong to Mr Darcy, the superior in consequence, to begin the acquaintance. – Mr Collins listened to her with the determined air of following his own inclination, and when she ceased speaking, replied thus,

'My dear Miss Elizabeth, I have the highest opinion in the world of your excellent judgment in all matters within the scope of your understanding, but permit me to say that there must be a wide difference between the established forms of ceremony amongst the laity, and those which regulate the clergy; for give me leave to observe that I consider the clerical office as equal in point of dignity with the highest rank in the kingdom – provided that a proper humility of behaviour is at the same time maintained. You must therefore allow me to follow the dictates of my conscience on this occasion, which leads me to perform what I look on as a point of duty. Pardon me for neglecting to profit by your advice, which on every other subject shall be my constant guide, though in the case before us I consider myself more fitted by education and habitual study to decide on what is right than a young lady like yourself.' And with a low bow he left her to attack Mr Darcy, whose reception of his advances she eagerly watched, and whose astonishment at being so addressed was very evident. Her cousin prefaced his speech with a solemn bow, and though she could not hear a word of it, she felt as if hearing it all, and saw in the motion of his lips the words 'apology,' 'Hunsford' and 'Lady Catherine de Bourgh.' – It vexed her to see him expose himself to such a man. Mr Darcy was eyeing him with unrestrained wonder, and when at last Mr Collins allowed him time to speak, replied with an air of distant civility. Mr Collins, however, was not discouraged from speaking again, and Mr Darcy's contempt seemed abundantly increasing with the length of his second speech, and at the end of it he only made him a slight bow, and moved another way. Mr Collins then returned to Elizabeth.

'I have no reason, I assure you,' said he, 'to be dissatisfied with my reception. Mr Darcy seemed much pleased with the attention. He answered me with the utmost civility, and even paid me the compliment of saying, that he was so well convinced of Lady Catherine's discernment as to be certain she could never bestow a favour unworthily. It was really a very handsome thought. Upon the whole, I am much pleased with him.'

As Elizabeth had no longer any interest of her own to pursue, she turned her attention almost entirely on her sister and Mr Bingley, and the train of agreeable reflections which her observations gave birth to, made her perhaps almost as happy as Jane. She saw her in idea settled in that very house in all the felicity which a marriage of true affection could bestow; and she felt capable under such circumstances, of endeavouring even to like Bingley's two sisters. Her mother's thoughts she plainly saw were bent the same way, and she determined not to venture near her, lest she might hear too much.

When they sat down to supper, therefore, she considered it a most unlucky perverseness which placed them within one of each other; and deeply was she vexed to find that her mother was talking to that one person (Lady Lucas) freely, openly, and of nothing else but of her expectation that Jane would be soon married to Mr. Bingley. – It was an animating subject, and Mrs Bennet seemed incapable of fatigue while enumerating the advantages of the match. His being such a charming young man, and so rich, and living but three miles from them, were the first points of self-congratulation; and then it was such a comfort to think how fond the two sisters were of Jane, and to be certain that they must desire the connection as much as she could do. It was, moreover, such a promising thing for her younger daughters, as Jane's marrying so greatly must throw them in the way of other rich men; and lastly, it was so pleasant at her time of life to be able to consign her single daughters to the care of their sister, that she might not be obliged to go into company more than she liked. It was necessary to make this circumstance a matter of pleasure, because on such occasions it is the etiquette; but no one was less likely than Mrs Bennet to find comfort in staying at home at any period of her life. She concluded with many good wishes that Lady Lucas might soon be equally fortunate, though evidently and triumphantly believing there was no chance of it.

In vain did Elizabeth endeavour to check the rapidity of her mother's words, or persuade her to describe her felicity in a less audible whisper; for to her inexpressible vexation, she could perceive that the chief of it was overheard by Mr Darcy, who sat opposite to them. Her mother only scolded her for being nonsensical.

'What is Mr Darcy to me, pray, that I should be afraid of him? I am sure we owe him no such particular civility as to be obliged to say nothing *he* may not like to hear.'

'For heaven's sake, madam, speak lower. – What advantage can it be to you to offend Mr Darcy? – You will never recommend yourself to his friend by so doing.'

Nothing that she could say, however, had any influence. Her mother would talk of her views in the same intelligible tone. Elizabeth blushed and blushed again with shame and vexation. She could not help frequently glancing her eye at Mr Darcy, though every glance convinced her of what she dreaded; for though he was not always looking at her mother, she was convinced that his attention was invariably fixed by her. The expression of his face changed gradually from indignant contempt to a composed and steady gravity.

At length however Mrs Bennet had no more to say; and Lady Lucas, who had been long yawning at the repetition of delights which she saw no likelihood of sharing, was left to the comforts of cold ham and chicken. Elizabeth now began to revive. But not long was the interval of tranquillity; for when supper was over, singing was talked of, and she had the mortification of seeing Mary, after very little entreaty, preparing to oblige the company. By many significant looks and silent entreaties, did she endeavour to prevent such a proof of complaisance, – but in vain; Mary would not understand them; such an opportunity of exhibiting was delightful to her, and she began her song. Elizabeth's eyes were fixed on her with most painful sensations; and she watched her progress through the several stanzas with an impatience which was very ill rewarded at their close; for Mary, on receiving amongst the thanks of the table, the hint of a hope that she might be prevailed on to favour them again, after the pause of half a minute began another. Mary's powers were by no means fitted for such a display; her voice was weak, and her manner affected. – Elizabeth was in agonies. She looked at Jane, to see how she bore it; but Jane was very composedly talking to Bingley. She looked at his two sisters, and saw them making signs of derision at each other, and at Darcy, who continued however impenetrably grave. She looked at her father to entreat his interference, lest Mary should be singing all night. He took the hint, and when Mary had finished her second song, said aloud,

'That will do extremely well, child. You have delighted us long enough. Let the other young ladies have time to exhibit.'

Mary, though pretending not to hear, was somewhat disconcerted; and Elizabeth sorry for her, and sorry for her father's speech, was afraid her anxiety had done no good. – Others of the party were now applied to.

'If I,' said Mr Collins, 'were so fortunate as to be able to sing, I should have great pleasure, I am sure, in obliging the company with an air; for I consider music as a very innocent diversion, and perfectly compatible with the profession of a clergyman. – I do not mean however to assert that we can be justified in devoting too much of our time to music, for there are certainly other things to be attended to. The rector of a parish has much to do. – In the first place, he must make such an agreement for tythes as may be beneficial to himself and not offensive to his patron. He must write his own sermons; and the time that remains will not be too much for his parish duties, and the care and improvement of his dwelling, which he cannot be excused from making as comfortable as possible. And I do not think it of light importance that he should have attentive and conciliatory manners towards every body, especially towards those to whom he owes his preferment. I cannot acquit him of that duty; nor could I think well of the man who should omit an occasion of testifying his respect towards any body connected with the family.' And with a bow to Mr Darcy, he concluded his speech, which had been spoken so loud as to be heard by half the room. – Many stared. – Many smiled; but no one looked more amused than Mr Bennet himself, while his wife seriously commended Mr Collins for having spoken so sensibly, and observed in a half-whisper to Lady Lucas, that he was a remarkably clever, good kind of young man.

To Elizabeth it appeared, that had her family made an agreement to expose themselves as much as they could during the evening, it would have been impossible for them to play their parts with more spirit, or finer success; and happy did she think it for Bingley and her sister that some of the exhibition had escaped his notice, and that his feelings were not of a sort to be much distressed by the folly which he must have witnessed. That his two sisters and Mr Darcy, however, should have such an opportunity of ridiculing her relations was bad enough, and she could not determine whether the silent contempt of the gentleman, or the insolent smiles of the ladies, were more intolerable.

The rest of the evening brought her little amusement. She was teased by Mr Collins, who continued most perseveringly by her side, and though he could not prevail with her to dance with him again, put it out of her power to dance with others. In vain did she entreat him to stand up with somebody else, and offer to introduce him to any young lady in the room. He assured her that as to dancing, he was perfectly indifferent to it; that his chief object was by delicate attentions to recommend himself to her, and that he should therefore make a point of remaining close to her the whole evening. There was no arguing upon such a project. She owed her greatest relief to her friend Miss Lucas, who often joined them, and good-naturedly engaged Mr Collins's conversation to herself.

She was at least free from the offence of Mr Darcy's farther notice; though often standing within a very short distance of her, quite disengaged, he never came near enough to speak. She felt it to be the probable consequence of her allusions to Mr Wickham, and rejoiced in it.

The Longbourn party were the last of all the company to depart; and by a manoeuvre of Mrs Bennet had to wait for their carriages a quarter of an hour after every body else was gone, which gave them time to see how heartily they were wished away by some of the family. Mrs Hurst and her sister scarcely opened their mouths except to complain of fatigue, and were evidently impatient to have the house to themselves. They repulsed every attempt of Mrs Bennet at conversation, and by so doing, threw a langour over the whole party, which was very little relieved by the long speeches of Mr Collins, who was complimenting Mr Bingley and his sisters on the elegance of their entertainment, and the hospitality and politeness which had marked their behaviour to their guests. Darcy said nothing at all. Mr Bennet, in equal silence, was enjoying the scene. Mr Bingley and Jane were standing together, a little detached from the rest, and talked only to each other. Elizabeth preserved as steady a silence as either Mrs Hurst or Miss Bingley; and even Lydia was too much fatigued to utter more than the occasional exclamation of 'Lord, how tired I am!' accompanied by a violent yawn.

When at length they arose to take leave, Mrs Bennet was most pressingly civil in her hope of seeing the whole family soon at Longbourn; and addressed herself particularly to Mr Bingley, to assure him how happy he would make them, by eating a family dinner with them at any time, without the ceremony of a formal invitation. Bingley was all grateful pleasure, and he readily engaged for taking the earliest opportunity of waiting on her, after his return from London, whither he was obliged to go the next day for a short time.

Mrs Bennet was perfectly satisfied; and quitted the house under the delightful persuasion that, allowing for the necessary preparations of settlements, new carriages and wedding clothes, she should undoubtedly see her daughter settled at Netherfield, in the course of three or four months. Of having another daughter married to Mr Collins, she thought with equal certainty, and with considerable, though not equal, pleasure. Elizabeth was the least dear to her of all her children; and though the man and the match were quite good enough for *her*, the worth of each was eclipsed by Mr Bingley and Netherfield.

Chapter Nineteen

THE NEXT DAY OPENED A NEW SCENE at Longbourn. Mr Collins made his declaration in form. Having resolved to do it without loss of time, as his leave of absence extended only to the following Saturday, and having no feelings of diffidence to make it distressing to himself even at the moment, he set about it in a very orderly manner, with all the observances which he supposed a regular part of the business. On finding Mrs Bennet, Elizabeth, and one of the younger girls together, soon after breakfast, he addressed the mother in these words,

'May I hope, Madam, for your interest with your fair daughter Elizabeth, when I solicit for the honour of a private audience with her in the course of this morning?'

Before Elizabeth had time for any thing but a blush of surprise, Mrs Bennet instantly answered,

'Oh dear! – Yes – certainly. – I am sure Lizzy will be very happy – I am sure she can have no objection. – Come, Kitty, I want you up stairs.' And gathering her work together, she was hastening away, when Elizabeth called out,

'Dear Ma'am, do not go. – I beg you will not go. – Mr Collins must excuse me. – He can have nothing to say to me that any body need not hear. I am going away myself.'

'No, no, nonsense, Lizzy. – I desire you will stay where you are.' – And upon Elizabeth's seeming really, with vexed and embarrassed looks, about to escape, she added, 'Lizzy, I *insist* upon your staying and hearing Mr Collins.'

Elizabeth would not oppose such an injunction – and a moment's consideration making her also sensible that it would be wisest to get it over as soon and as quietly as possible, she sat down again, and tried to conceal by incessant employment the feelings which were divided between distress and diversion. Mrs Bennet and Kitty walked off, and as soon as they were gone Mr Collins began.

'Believe me, my dear Miss Elizabeth, that your modesty, so far from doing you any disservice, rather adds to your other perfections. You would have been less amiable in my eyes had there *not* been this little unwillingness; but allow me to assure you that I have your respected mother's permission for this address. You can hardly doubt the purport of my discourse, however your natural delicacy may lead you to dissemble; my attentions have been too marked to be mistaken. Almost as soon as I entered the house I singled you out as the companion of my future life. But before I am run away with by my feelings on this subject, perhaps it will be advisable for me to state my reasons for marrying – and moreover for coming into Hertfordshire with the design of selecting a wife, as I certainly did.'

The idea of Mr Collins, with all his solemn composure, being run away with by his feelings, made Elizabeth so near laughing that she could not use the short pause he allowed in any attempt to stop him farther, and he continued:

'My reasons for marrying are, first, that I think it a right thing for every clergyman in easy circumstances (like myself) to set the example of matrimony in his parish. Secondly, that I am convinced it will add very greatly to my happiness; and thirdly – which perhaps I ought to have mentioned earlier, that it is the particular advice and recommendation of the very noble lady whom I have the honour of calling patroness. Twice has she condescended to give me her opinion (unasked too!) on this subject; and it was but the very Saturday night before I left Hunsford – between our pools at quadrille, while Mrs Jenkinson was arranging Miss de Bourgh's foot-stool, that she said, "Mr Collins, you must marry. A clergyman like you must marry. – Chuse properly, chuse a gentlewoman for *my* sake; and for your *own*, let her be an active, useful sort of person, not brought up high, but able to make a small income go a good way. This is my advice. Find such a woman as soon as you can, bring her to Hunsford, and I will visit her." Allow me, by the way, to observe, my fair cousin, that I do not reckon the notice and kindness of Lady Catherine de Bourgh as among the least of the advantages in my power to offer. You will find her manners beyond any thing I can describe; and your wit and vivacity I think must be acceptable to her, especially when tempered with the silence and respect which her rank will inevitably excite. Thus much for my general intention in favour of matrimony; it remains to be told why my views were directed to Longbourn instead of my own neighbourhood, where I assure you there are many amiable young women. But the fact is, that being, as I am, to inherit this estate after the death of your honoured father, (who, however, may live many years longer), I could not satisfy myself without resolving to chuse a wife from among his daughters, that the loss to them might be as little as possible, when the melancholy event takes place – which, however, as I have already said, may not be for several years. This has been my motive, my fair cousin, and I flatter myself it will not sink me in your esteem. And now nothing remains for me but to assure you in the most animated language of the violence of my affection. To fortune I am perfectly indifferent, and shall make no demand of that nature on your father, since I am well aware that it could not be complied with; and that one thousand pounds in the 4 per cents. which will not be yours till after your mother's decease, is all that you may ever be entitled to. On that head, therefore, I shall be uniformly silent; and you may assure yourself that no ungenerous reproach shall ever pass my lips when we are married.'

It was absolutely necessary to interrupt him now.

'You are too hasty, Sir,' she cried. 'You forget that I have made no answer. Let me do it without farther loss of time. Accept my thanks for the compliment you are paying me. I am very sensible of the honour of your proposals, but it is impossible for me to do otherwise than decline them.'

'I am not now to learn,' replied Mr Collins, with a formal wave of the hand, 'that it is usual with young ladies to reject the addresses of the man whom they secretly mean to accept, when he first applies for their favour; and that sometimes the refusal is repeated a second or even a third time. I am therefore by no means discouraged by what you have just said, and shall hope to lead you to the altar ere long.'

'Upon my word, Sir,' cried Elizabeth, 'your hope is rather an extraordinary one after my declaration. I do assure you that I am not one of those young ladies (if such young ladies there are) who are so daring as to risk their happiness on the chance of being asked a second time. I am perfectly serious in my refusal. – You could not make *me* happy, and I am convinced that I am the last woman in the world who would make *you* so. – Nay, were your friend Lady Catherine to know me, I am persuaded she would find me in every respect ill qualified for the situation.'

'Were it certain that Lady Catherine would think so,' said Mr Collins very gravely – 'but I cannot imagine that her ladyship would at all disapprove of you. And you may be certain that when I have the honour of seeing her again I shall speak in the highest terms of your modesty, economy, and other amiable qualifications.'

'Indeed, Mr Collins, all praise of me will be unnecessary. You must give me leave to judge for myself, and pay me the compliment of believing what I say. I wish you very happy and very rich, and by refusing your hand, do all in my power to prevent your being otherwise. In making me the offer, you must have satisfied the delicacy of your feelings with regard to my family, and may take possession of Longbourn estate whenever it falls, without any self-reproach. This matter may be considered, therefore, as finally settled.' And rising as she thus spoke, she would have quitted the room, had not Mr Collins thus addressed her.

'When I do myself the honour of speaking to you next in this subject I shall hope to receive a more favourable answer than you have now given me; though I am far from accusing you of cruelty at present, because I know it to be the established custom of your sex to reject a man on the first application, and perhaps you have even now said as much to encourage my suit as would be consistent with the true delicacy of the female character.'

'Really, Mr Collins,' cried Elizabeth with some warmth, 'you puzzle me exceedingly. If what I have hitherto said can appear to you in the form of encouragement, I know not how to express my refusal in such a way as may convince you of its being one.'

'You must give me leave to flatter myself, my dear cousin, that your refusal of my addresses is merely words of course. My reasons for believing it are briefly these: – It does not appear to me that my hand is unworthy your acceptance, or that the establishment I can offer would be any other than highly desirable. My situation in life, my connections with the family of de Bourgh, and my relationship to your own, are circumstances highly in my favour; and you should take it into farther consideration that in spite of your manifold attractions, it is by no means certain that another offer of marriage may ever be made you. Your portion is unhappily so small that it will in all likelihood undo the effects of your loveliness and amiable qualifications. As I must therefore conclude that you are not serious in your rejection of me, I shall chuse to attribute it to your wish of increasing my love by suspense, according to the usual practice of elegant females.'

'I do assure you, Sir, that I have no pretension whatever to that kind of elegance which consists in tormenting a respectable man. I would rather be paid the compliment of being believed. I thank you again and again for the honour you have done me in your proposals, but to accept them is absolutely impossible. My feelings in every respect forbid it. Can I speak plainer? Do not consider me now as an elegant female intending to plague you, but as a rational creature speaking the truth from her heart.'

'You are uniformly charming!' cried he, with an air of awkward gallantry; 'and I am persuaded that when sanctioned by the express authority of both your excellent parents, my proposals will not fail of being acceptable.'

To such perseverance in wilful self-deception Elizabeth would make no reply, and immediately and in silence withdrew; determined, if he persisted in considering her repeated refusals as flattering encouragement, to apply to her father, whose negative might be uttered in such a manner as must be decisive, and whose behaviour at least could not be mistaken for the affectation and coquetry of an elegant female.

Chapter Twenty

MR COLLINS WAS NOT LEFT LONG to the silent contemplation of his successful love; for Mrs Bennet, having dawdled about in the vestibule to watch for the end of the conference, no sooner saw Elizabeth open the door and with quick step pass her towards the staircase, than she entered the breakfast-room, and congratulated both him and herself in warm terms on the happy prospect of their nearer connection. Mr Collins received and returned these felicitations with equal pleasure, and then proceeded to relate the particulars of their interview, with the result of which he trusted he had every reason to be satisfied, since the refusal which his cousin had steadfastly given him would naturally flow from her bashful modesty and the genuine delicacy of her character.

This information, however, startled Mrs Bennet; – she would have been glad to be equally satisfied that her daughter had meant to encourage him by protesting against his proposals, but she dared not to believe it, and could not help saying so.

'But depend upon it, Mr Collins,' she added, 'that Lizzy shall be brought to reason. I will speak to her about it myself directly. She is a very headstrong foolish girl, and does not know her own interest; but I will *make* her know it.'

'Pardon me for interrupting you, Madam,' cried Mr Collins; 'but if she is really headstrong and foolish, I know not whether she would altogether be a very desirable wife to a man in my situation, who naturally looks for happiness in the marriage state. If therefore she actually persists in rejecting my suit, perhaps it were better not to force her into accepting me, because if liable to such defects of temper, she could not contribute much to my felicity.'

'Sir, you quite misunderstand me,' said Mrs Bennet, alarmed. 'Lizzy is only headstrong in such matters as these. In every thing else she is as good natured a girl as ever lived. I will go directly to Mr Bennet, and we shall very soon settle it with her, I am sure.'

She would not give him time to reply, but hurrying instantly to her husband, called out as she entered the library,

'Oh! Mr Bennet, you are wanted immediately; we are all in an uproar. You must come and make Lizzy marry Mr Collins, for she vows she will not have him, and if you do not make haste he will change his mind and not have *her*.'

Mr Bennet raised his eyes from his book as she entered, and fixed them on her face with a calm unconcern which was not in the least altered by her communication.

'I have not the pleasure of understanding you,' said he, when she had finished her speech. 'Of what are you talking?'

'Of Mr Collins and Lizzy. Lizzy declares she will not have Mr Collins, and Mr Collins begins to say that he will not have Lizzy.'

'And what am I to do on the occasion? – It seems an hopeless business.'

'Speak to Lizzy about it yourself. Tell her that you insist upon her marrying him.'

'Let her be called down. She shall hear my opinion.'

Mrs Bennet rang the bell, and Miss Elizabeth was summoned to the library.

'Come here, child,' cried her father as she appeared. 'I have sent for you on an affair of importance. I understand that Mr Collins has made you an offer of marriage. Is it true?' Elizabeth replied that it was. 'Very well – and this offer of marriage you have refused?'

'I have, Sir.'

'Very well. We now come to the point. Your mother insists upon your accepting it. Is not it so, Mrs Bennet?'

'Yes, or I will never see her again.'

'An unhappy alternative is before you, Elizabeth. From this day you must be a stranger to one of your parents. – Your mother will never see you again if you do *not* marry Mr Collins, and I will never see you again if you *do*.'

Elizabeth could not but smile at such a conclusion of such a beginning; but Mrs Bennet, who had persuaded herself that her husband regarded the affair as she wished, was excessively disappointed.

'What do you mean, Mr Bennet, by talking in this way. You promised me to *insist* upon her marrying him.'

'My dear,' replied her husband. 'I have two small favours to request. First, that you will allow me the free use of my understanding on the present occasion; and secondly, of my room. I shall be glad to have the library to myself as soon as may be.'

Not yet, however, in spite of her disappointment in her husband, did Mrs Bennet give up the point. She talked to Elizabeth again and again; coaxed and threatened her by turns. She endeavoured to secure Jane in her interest, but Jane with all possible mildness declined interfering; – and Elizabeth sometimes with real earnestness and sometimes with playful gaiety replied to her attacks. Though her manner varied however, her determination never did.

Mr Collins, meanwhile, was meditating in solitude on what had passed. He thought too well of himself to comprehend on what motives his cousin could refuse him; and though his pride was hurt, he suffered in no other way. His regard for her was quite imaginary; and the possibility of her deserving her mother's reproach prevented his feeling any regret.

While the family were in this confusion, Charlotte Lucas came to spend the day with them. She was met in the vestibule by Lydia, who, flying to her, cried in a half whisper, 'I am glad you are come, for there is such fun here! – What do you think has happened this morning? – Mr Collins has made an offer to Lizzy, and she will not have him.'

Charlotte had hardly time to answer, before they were joined by Kitty, who came to tell the same news, and no sooner had they entered the breakfast-room, where Mrs Bennet was alone, than she likewise began on the subject, calling on Miss Lucas for her compassion, and entreating her to persuade her friend Lizzy to comply with the wishes of all her family. 'Pray do, my dear Miss Lucas,' she added in a melancholy tone, 'for nobody is on my side, nobody takes part with me, I am cruelly used, nobody feels for my poor nerves.'

Charlotte's reply was spared by the entrance of Jane and Elizabeth.

'Aye, there she comes,' continued Mrs Bennet, 'looking as unconcerned as may be, and caring no more for us than if we were at York, provided she can have her own way. – But I tell you what, Miss Lizzy, if you take it into your head to go on refusing every offer of marriage in this way, you will never get a husband at all – and I am sure I do not know who is to maintain you when your father is dead. – I shall not be able to keep you – and so I warn you. – I have done with you from this very day. – I told you in the library, you know, that I should never speak to you again, and you will find me as good as my word. I have no pleasure in talking to undutiful children. – Not that I have much pleasure indeed in talking to any body. People who suffer as I do from nervous complaints can have no great inclination for talking. Nobody can tell what I suffer! – But it is always so. Those who do not complain are never pitied.'

Her daughters listened in silence to this effusion, sensible that any attempt to reason with or sooth her would only increase the irritation. She talked on, therefore, without interruption from any of them till they were joined by Mr Collins, who entered with an air more stately than usual, and on perceiving whom, she said to the girls,

'Now, I do insist upon it, that you, all of you, hold your tongues, and let Mr Collins and me have a little conversation together.'

Elizabeth passed quietly out of the room, Jane and Kitty followed, but Lydia stood her ground, determined to hear all she could; and Charlotte, detained first by the civility of Mr Collins, whose inquiries after herself and all her family were very minute, and then by a little curiosity, satisfied herself with walking to the window and pretending not to hear. In a doleful voice Mrs Bennet thus began the projected conversation. – 'Oh! Mr Collins!' –

'My dear Madam,' replied he, 'let us be for ever silent on this point. Far be it from me,' he presently continued in a voice that marked his displeasure, 'to resent the behaviour of your daughter. Resignation to inevitable evils is the duty of us all; the peculiar duty of a young man who has been so fortunate as I have been in early preferment; and I trust I am resigned. Perhaps not the less so from feeling a doubt of my positive happiness had my fair cousin honoured me with her hand; for I have often observed that resignation is never so perfect as when the blessing denied begins to lose somewhat of its value in our estimation. You will not, I hope, consider me as shewing any disrespect to your family, my dear Madam, by thus withdrawing my pretensions to your daughter's favour, without having paid yourself and Mr Bennet the compliment of requesting you to interpose your authority in my behalf. My conduct may I fear be objectionable in having accepted my dismission from your daughter's lips instead of your own. But we are all liable to error. I have certainly meant well through the whole affair. My object has been to secure an amiable companion for myself, with due consideration for the advantage of all your family, and if my *manner* has been at all reprehensible, I here beg leave to apologise.'

Chapter Twenty One

THE DISCUSSION OF MR COLLINS'S offer was now nearly at an end, and Elizabeth had only to suffer from the uncomfortable feelings necessarily attending it, and occasionally from some peevish allusion of her mother. As for the gentleman himself, *his* feelings were chiefly expressed, not by embarrassment, or dejection, or by trying to avoid her, but by stiffness of manner and resentful silence. He scarcely ever spoke to her, and the assiduous attentions which he had been so sensible of himself, were transferred for the rest of the day to Miss Lucas, whose civility in listening to him, was a seasonable relief to them all, and especially to her friend.

The morrow produced no abatement of Mrs Bennet's ill humour or ill health. Mr Collins was also in the same state of angry pride. Elizabeth had hoped that his resentment might shorten his visit, but his plan did not appear in the least affected by it. He was always to have gone on Saturday, and to Saturday he still meant to stay.

After breakfast, the girls walked to Meryton to inquire if Mr Wickham were returned, and to lament over his absence from the Netherfield ball. He joined them on their entering the town and attended them to their aunt's where his regret and vexation, and the concern of every body was well talked over. – To Elizabeth, however, he voluntarily acknowledged that the necessity of his absence *had* been self imposed.

'I found,' said he, 'as the time drew near, that I had better not meet Mr Darcy; – that to be in the same room, the same party with him for so many hours together, might be more than I could bear, and that scenes might arise unpleasant to more than myself.'

She highly approved his forbearance, and they had leisure for a full discussion of it, and for all the commendation which they civilly bestowed on each other, as Wickham and another officer walked back with them to Longbourn, and during the walk, he particularly attended to her. His accompanying them was a double advantage; she felt all the compliment it offered to herself, and it was most acceptable as an occasion of introducing him to her father and mother.

Soon after their return, a letter was delivered to Miss Bennet; it came from Netherfield, and was opened immediately. The envelope contained a sheet of elegant, little, hot pressed paper, well covered with a lady's fair, flowing hand; and Elizabeth saw her sister's countenance change as she read it, and saw her dwelling intently on some particular passages. Jane recollected herself soon, and putting the letter away, tried to join with her usual cheerfulness in the general conversation; but Elizabeth felt an anxiety on the subject which drew off her attention even from Wickham; and no sooner had he and his companion taken leave, than a glance from Jane invited her to follow her up stairs. When they had gained their own room, Jane taking out the letter said,

'This is from Caroline Bingley; what it contains, has surprised me a good deal. The whole party have left Netherfield by this time, and are on their way to town; and without any intention of coming back again. You shall hear what she says.'

She then read the first sentence aloud, which comprised the information of their having just resolved to follow their brother to town directly, and of their meaning to dine that day in Grosvenor Street, where Mr Hurst had a house. The next was in these words. 'I do not pretend to regret any thing I shall leave in Hertfordshire, except your society, my dearest friend; but we will hope at some future period, to enjoy many returns of the delightful intercourse we have known, and in the mean while may lessen the pain of separation by a very frequent and most unreserved correspondence. I depend on you for that.' To these high flown expressions, Elizabeth listened with all the insensibility of distrust; and though the suddenness of their removal surprised her, she saw nothing in it really to lament; it was not to be supposed that their absence from Netherfield would prevent Mr Bingley's being there; and as to the loss of their society, she was persuaded that Jane must soon cease to regard it, in the enjoyment of his.

'It is unlucky,' she said, after a short pause, 'that you should not be able to see your friends before they leave the country. But may we not hope that the period of future happiness to which Miss Bingley looks forward, may arrive earlier than she is aware, and that the delightful intercourse you have known as friends, will be renewed with yet greater satisfaction as sisters? – Mr Bingley will not be detained in London by them.'

'Caroline decidedly says that none of the party will return into Hertfordshire this winter. I will read it to you –

'When my brother left us yesterday, he imagined that the business which took him to London, might be concluded in three or four days, but as we are certain it cannot be so, and at the same time convinced that when Charles gets to town, he will be in no hurry to leave it again, we have determined on following him thither, that he may not be obliged to spend his vacant hours in a comfortless hotel. Many of my acquaintance are already there for the winter; I wish I could hear that you, my dearest friend, had any intention of making one in the croud, but of that I despair. I sincerely hope your Christmas in Hertfordshire may abound in the gaieties which that season generally brings, and that your beaux will be so numerous as to prevent your feeling the loss of the three, of whom, we shall deprive you.'

'It is evident by this,' added Jane, 'that he comes back no more this winter.'

'It is only evident that Miss Bingley does not mean he *should*.'

'Why will you think so? It must be his own doing. – He is his own master. But you do not know *all*. I *will* read you the passage which particularly hurts me. I will have no reserves from *you*.' 'Mr Darcy is impatient to see his sister, and to confess the truth, *we* are scarcely less eager to meet her again. I really do not think Georgiana Darcy has her equal for beauty, elegance, and accomplishments; and the affection she inspires in Louisa and myself, is heightened into something still more interesting, from the hope we dare to entertain of her being hereafter our sister. I do not know whether I ever before mentioned to you my feelings on this subject, but I will not leave the country without confiding them, and I trust you will not esteem them unreasonable. My brother admires her greatly already, he will have frequent opportunity now of seeing her on the most intimate footing, her relations all wish the connection as much as his own, and a sister's partiality is not misleading me, I think, when I call Charles most capable of engaging any woman's heart. With all these circumstances to favour an attachment and nothing to prevent it, am I wrong, my dearest Jane, in indulging the hope of an event which will secure the happiness of so many?'

'What think you of *this* sentence, my dear Lizzy?' – said Jane as she finished it. 'Is it not clear enough? – Does it not expressly declare that Caroline neither expects nor wishes me to be her sister; that she is perfectly convinced of her brother's indifference, and that if she suspects the nature of my feelings for him, she means (most kindly!) to put me on my guard? Can there be any other opinion on the subject?'

'Yes, there can; for mine is totally different. – Will you hear it?'

'Most willingly.'

'You shall have it in few words. Miss Bingley sees that her brother is in love with you, and wants him to marry Miss Darcy. She follows him to town in the hope of keeping him there, and tries to persuade you that he does not care about you.'

Jane shook her head.

'Indeed, Jane, you ought to believe me. – No one who has ever seen you together, can doubt his affection. Miss Bingley I am sure cannot. She is not such a simpleton. Could she have seen half as much love in Mr Darcy for herself, she would have ordered her wedding clothes. But the case is this. We are not rich enough, or grand enough for them; and she is the more anxious to get Miss Darcy for her brother, from the notion that when there has been *one* intermarriage, she may have less trouble in achieving a second; in which there is certainly some ingenuity, and I dare say it would succeed, if Miss de Bourgh were out of the way. But, my dearest Jane, you cannot seriously imagine that because Miss Bingley tells you her brother greatly admires Miss Darcy, he is in the smallest degree less sensible of *your* merit than when he took leave of you on Tuesday, or that it will be in her power to persuade him that instead of being in love with you, he is very much in love with her friend.'

'If we thought alike of Miss Bingley,' replied Jane, 'your representation of all this, might make me quite easy. But I know the foundation is unjust. Caroline is incapable of wilfully deceiving any one; and all that I can hope in this case, is that she is deceived herself.'

'That is right. – You could not have started a more happy idea, since you will not take comfort in mine. Believe her to be deceived by all means. You have now done your duty by her, and must fret no longer.'

'But, my dear sister, can I be happy, even supposing the best, in accepting a man whose sisters and friends are all wishing him to marry elsewhere?'

'You must decide for yourself,' said Elizabeth, 'and if upon mature deliberation, you find that the misery of disobliging his two sisters is more than equivalent to the happiness of being his wife, I advise you by all means to refuse him.'

'How can you talk so?' – said Jane faintly smiling, – 'You must know that though I should be exceedingly grieved at this disapprobation, I could not hesitate.'

'I did not think you would; – and that being the case, I cannot consider your situation with much compassion.'

'But if he returns no more this winter, my choice will never be required. A thousand things may arise in six months!'

The idea of his returning no more Elizabeth treated with the utmost contempt. It appeared to her merely the suggestion of Caroline's interested wishes, and she could not for a moment suppose that those wishes, however openly or artfully spoken, could influence a young man so totally independent of every one.

She represented to her sister as forcibly as possible what she felt on the subject, and had soon the pleasure of seeing its happy effect. Jane's temper was not desponding, and she was gradually led to hope, though the diffidence of affection sometimes overcame the hope, that Bingley would return to Netherfield and answer every wish of her heart.

They agreed that Mrs Bennet should only hear of the departure of the family, without being alarmed on the score of the gentleman's conduct; but even this partial communication gave her a good deal of concern, and she bewailed it as exceedingly unlucky that the ladies should happen to go away, just as they were all getting so intimate together. After lamenting it however at some length, she had the consolation of thinking that Mr Bingley would be soon down again and soon dining at Longbourn, and the conclusion of all was the comfortable declaration that, though he had been invited only to a family dinner, she would take care to have two full courses.

Chapter Twenty Two

THE BENNETS WERE ENGAGED TO dine with the Lucases, and again during the chief of the day, was Miss Lucas so kind as to listen to Mr Collins. Elizabeth took an opportunity of thanking her. 'It keeps him in good humour,' said she, 'and I am more obliged to you than I can express.' Charlotte assured her friend of her satisfaction in being useful, and that it amply repaid her for the little sacrifice of her time. This was very amiable, but Charlotte's kindness extended farther than Elizabeth had any conception of; – its object was nothing less, than to secure her from any return of Mr Collins's addresses, by engaging them towards herself. Such was Miss Lucas's scheme; and appearances were so favourable that when they parted at night, she would have felt almost sure of success if he had not been to leave Hertfordshire so very soon. But here, she did injustice to the fire and independence of his character, for it led him to escape out of Longbourn House the next morning with admirable slyness, and hasten to Lucas Lodge to throw himself at her feet. He was anxious to avoid the notice of his cousins, from a conviction that if they saw him depart, they could not fail to conjecture his design, and he was not willing to have the attempt known till its success could be known likewise; for though feeling almost secure, and with reason, for Charlotte had been tolerably encouraging, he was comparatively diffident since the adventure of Wednesday. His reception however was of the most flattering kind. Miss Lucas perceived him from an upper window as he walked towards the house, and instantly set out to meet him accidentally in the lane. But little had she dared to hope that so much love and eloquence awaited her there.

In as short a time as Mr Collins's long speeches would allow, every thing was settled between them to the satisfaction of both; and as they entered the house, he earnestly entreated her to name the day that was to make him the happiest of men; and though such a solicitation must be waved for the present, the lady felt no inclination to trifle with his happiness. The stupidity with which he was favoured by nature, must guard his courtship from any charm that could make a woman wish for its continuance; and Miss Lucas, who accepted him solely from the pure and disinterested desire of an establishment, cared not how soon that establishment were gained.

Sir William and Lady Lucas were speedily applied to for their consent; and it was bestowed with a most joyful alacrity. Mr Collins's present circumstances made it a most eligible match for their daughter, to whom they could give little fortune; and his prospects of future wealth were exceedingly fair. Lady Lucas began directly to calculate with more interest than the matter had ever excited before, how many years longer Mr Bennet was likely to live; and Sir William gave it as his decided opinion, that whenever Mr Collins should be in possession of the Longbourn estate, it would be highly expedient that both he and his wife should make their appearance at St James's. The whole family in short were properly overjoyed on the occasion. The younger girls formed hopes of *coming out* a year or two sooner than they might otherwise have done; and the boys were relieved from their apprehension of Charlotte's dying an old maid. Charlotte herself was tolerably composed. She had gained her point, and had time to consider of it. Her reflections were in general satisfactory. Mr Collins to be sure was neither sensible nor agreeable; his society was irksome, and his attachment to her must be imaginary. But still he would be her husband. – Without thinking highly either of men or of matrimony, marriage had always been her object; it was the only honourable provision for well-educated young women of small fortune, and however uncertain of giving happiness, must be their pleasantest preservative from want. This preservative she had now obtained; and at the age of twenty-seven, without having ever been handsome, she felt all the good luck of it. The least agreeable circumstance in the business, was the surprise it must occasion to Elizabeth Bennet, whose friendship she valued beyond that of any other person. Elizabeth would wonder, and probably would blame her; and though her resolution was not to be shaken, her feelings must be hurt by such disapprobation. She resolved to give her the information herself, and therefore charged Mr Collins when he returned to Longbourn to dinner, to drop no hint of what had passed before any of the family. A promise of secrecy was of course very dutifully given, but it could not be kept without difficulty; for the curiosity excited by his long absence, burst forth in such very direct questions on his return, as required some ingenuity to evade, and he was at the same time exercising great self-denial, for he was longing to publish his prosperous love.

As he was to begin his journey too early on the morrow to see any of the family, the ceremony of leave-taking was performed when the ladies moved for the night; and Mrs Bennet with great politeness and cordiality said how happy they should be to see him at Longbourn again, whenever his other engagements might allow him to visit them.

'My dear Madam,' he replied, 'this invitation is particularly gratifying, because it is what I have been hoping to receive; and you may be very certain that I shall avail myself of it as soon as possible.'

They were all astonished; and Mr Bennet, who could by no means wish for so speedy a return, immediately said,

'But is there not danger of Lady Catherine's disapprobation here, my good sir? – You had better neglect your relations, than run the risk of offending your patroness.'

'My dear sir,' replied Mr Collins, ' I am particularly obliged to you for this friendly caution, and you may depend upon my not taking so material a step without her ladyship's concurrence.'

'You cannot be too much on your guard. Risk any thing rather than her displeasure; and if you find it likely to be raised by your coming to us again, which I should think exceedingly probable, stay quietly at home, and be satisfied that we shall take no offence.'

'Believe me, my dear sir, my gratitude is warmly excited by such affectionate attention; and depend upon it, you will speedily receive from me a letter of thanks for this, as well as for every other mark of your regard during my stay in Hertfordshire. As for my fair cousins, though my absence may not be long enough to render it necessary, I shall now take the liberty of wishing them health and happiness, not excepting my cousin Elizabeth.'

With proper civilities the ladies then withdrew; all of them equally surprised to find that he meditated a quick return. Mrs Bennet wished to understand by it that he thought of paying his addresses to one of her younger girls, and Mary might have been prevailed on to accept him. She rated his abilities much higher than any of the others; there was a solidity in his reflections which often struck her, and though by no means so clever as herself, she thought that if encouraged to read and improve himself by such an example as her's, he might become a very agreeable companion. But on the following morning, every hope of this kind was done away. Miss Lucas called soon after breakfast, and in a private conference with Elizabeth related the event of the day before.

The possibility of Mr Collins's fancying himself in love with her friend had once occurred to Elizabeth within the last day or two; but that Charlotte could encourage him, seemed almost as far from possibility as that she could encourage him herself, and her astonishment was consequently so great as to overcome at first the bounds of decorum, and she could not help crying out,

'Engaged to Mr Collins! my dear Charlotte, – impossible!'

The steady countenance which Miss Lucas had commanded in telling her story, gave way to a momentary confusion here on receiving so direct a reproach; though, as it was no more than she expected, she soon regained her composure, and calmly replied,

'Why should you be surprised, my dear Eliza? – Do you think it incredible that Mr Collins should be able to procure any woman's good opinion, because he was not so happy as to succeed with you?'

But Elizabeth had now recollected herself, and making a strong effort for it, was able to assure her with tolerable firmness that the prospect of their relationship was highly grateful to her, and that she wished her all imaginable happiness.

'I see what you are feeling,' replied Charlotte, – 'you must be surprised, very much surprised, – so lately as Mr Collins was wishing to marry you. But when you have had time to think it all over, I hope you will be satisfied with what I have done. I am not romantic you know. I never was. I ask only a comfortable home; and considering Mr Collins's character, connections, and situation in life, I am convinced that my chance of happiness with him is as fair, as most people can boast on entering the marriage state.'

Elizabeth quietly answered, 'Undoubtedly;' – and after an awkward pause, they returned to the rest of the family. Charlotte did not stay much longer, and Elizabeth was then left to reflect on what she had heard. It was a long time before she became at all reconciled to the idea of so unsuitable a match. The strangeness of Mr Collins's making two offers of marriage within three days, was nothing in comparison of his being now accepted. She had always felt that Charlotte's opinion of matrimony was not exactly like her own, but she could not have supposed it possible that when called into action, she would have sacrificed every better feeling to worldly advantage. Charlotte the wife of Mr Collins, was a most humiliating picture! – And to the pang of a friend disgracing herself and sunk in her esteem, was added the distressing conviction that it was impossible for that friend to be tolerably happy in the lot she had chosen.

Chapter Twenty Three

ELIZABETH WAS SITTING WITH HER mother and sisters, reflecting on what she had heard, and doubting whether she were authorised to mention it, when Sir William Lucas himself appeared, sent by his daughter to announce her engagement to the family. With many compliments to them, and much self-gratulation on the prospect of a connection between the houses, he unfolded the matter, – to an audience not merely wondering, but incredulous; for Mrs Bennet, with more perseverance than politeness, protested he must be entirely mistaken, and Lydia, always unguarded and often uncivil, boisterously exclaimed,

'Good Lord! Sir William, how can you tell such a story? – Do not you know that Mr Collins wants to marry Lizzy?'

Nothing less than the complaisance of a courtier could have borne without anger such treatment; but Sir William's good breeding carried him through it all; and though he begged leave to be positive as to the truth of his information, he listened to all their impertinence with the most forbearing courtesy.

Elizabeth, feeling it incumbent on her to relieve him from so unpleasant a situation, now put herself forward to confirm his account, by mentioning her prior knowledge of it from Charlotte herself; and endeavoured to put a stop to the exclamations of her mother and sisters, by the earnestness of her congratulations to Sir William, in which she was readily joined by Jane, and by making a variety of remarks on the happiness that might be expected from the match, the excellent character of Mr Collins, and the convenient distance of Hunsford from London.

Mrs Bennet was in fact too much overpowered to say a great deal while Sir William remained; but no sooner had he left them her feelings found a rapid vent. In the first place, she persisted in disbelieving the whole of the matter; secondly, she was very sure that Mr Collins had been taken in; thirdly, she trusted that they would never be happy together; and fourthly, that the match might be broken off. Two inferences, however, were plainly deduced from the whole; one, that Elizabeth was the real cause of all the mischief; and the other, that she herself had been barbarously used by them all; and on these two points she principally dwelt during the rest of the day. Nothing could console and nothing appease her. – Nor did that day wear out her resentment. A week elapsed before she could see Elizabeth without scolding her, a month passed away before she could speak to Sir William or Lady Lucas without being rude, and many months were gone before she could at all forgive their daughter.

Mr Bennet's emotions were much more tranquil on the occasion, and such as he did experience he pronounced to be of a most agreeable sort; for it gratified him, he said, to discover that Charlotte Lucas, whom he had been used to think tolerably sensible, was as foolish as his wife, and more foolish than his daughter!

Jane confessed herself a little surprised at the match; but she said less of her astonishment than of her earnest desire for their happiness; nor could Elizabeth persuade her to consider it as improbable. Kitty and Lydia were far from envying Miss Lucas, for Mr Collins was only a clergyman; and it affected them in no other way than as a piece of news to spread at Meryton.

Lady Lucas could not be insensible of triumph on being able to retort on Mrs Bennet the comfort of having a daughter well married; and she called at Longbourn rather oftener than usual to say how happy she was, though Mrs Bennet's sour looks and ill-natured remarks might have been enough to drive happiness away.

Between Elizabeth and Charlotte there was a restraint which kept them mutually silent on the subject; and Elizabeth felt persuaded that no real confidence could ever subsist between them again. Her disappointment in Charlotte made her turn with fonder regard to her sister, of whose rectitude and delicacy she was sure her opinion could never be shaken, and for whose happiness she grew daily more anxious, as Bingley had now been gone a week, and nothing was heard of his return.

Jane had sent Caroline an early answer to her letter, and was counting the days till she might reasonably hope to hear again. The promised letter of thanks from Mr Collins arrived on Tuesday, addressed to their father, and written with all the solemnity of gratitude which a twelvemonth's abode in the family might have prompted. After discharging his conscience on that head, he proceeded to inform them, with many rapturous expressions, of his happiness in having obtained the affection of their amiable neighbour, Miss Lucas, and then explained that it was merely with the view of enjoying her society that he had been so ready to close with their kind wish of seeing him again at Longbourn, whither he hoped to be able to return on Monday fortnight; for Lady Catherine, he added, so heartily approved his marriage, that she wished it to take place as soon as possible, which he trusted would be an unanswerable argument with his amiable Charlotte to name an early day for making him the happiest of men.

Mr Collins's return into Hertfordshire was no longer a matter of pleasure to Mrs Bennet. On the contrary she was as much disposed to complain of it as her husband. – It was very strange that he should come to Longbourn instead of to Lucas Lodge; it was also very inconvenient and exceedingly troublesome. – She hated having visitors in the house while her health was so indifferent, and lovers were of all people the most disagreeable. Such were the gentle murmurs of Mrs Bennet, and they gave way only to the greater distress of Mr Bingley's continued absence.

Neither Jane nor Elizabeth were comfortable on this subject. Day after day passed away without bringing any other tidings of him than the report which shortly prevailed in Meryton of his coming no more to Netherfield the whole winter; a report which highly incensed Mrs Bennet, and which she never failed to contradict as a most scandalous falsehood.

Even Elizabeth began to fear – not that Bingley was indifferent – but that his sisters would be successful in keeping him away. Unwilling as she was to admit an idea so destructive of Jane's happiness, and so dishonourable to the stability of her lover, she could not prevent its frequently recurring. The united efforts of his two unfeeling sisters and of his overpowering friend, assisted by the attractions of Miss Darcy and the amusements of London, might be too much, she feared, for the strength of his attachment.

As for Jane, *her* anxiety under this suspense was, of course, more painful than Elizabeth's; but whatever she felt she was desirous of concealing, and between herself and Elizabeth, therefore, the subject was never alluded to. But as no such delicacy restrained her mother, an hour seldom passed in which she did not talk of Bingley, express her impatience for his arrival, or even require Jane to confess that if he did not come back, she should think herself very ill used. It needed all Jane's steady mildness to bear these attacks with tolerable tranquillity.

Mr Collins returned most punctually on the Monday fortnight, but his reception at Longbourn was not quite so gracious as it had been on his first introduction. He was too happy, however, to need much attention; and luckily for the others, the business of love-making relieved them from a great deal of his company. The chief of every day was spent by him at Lucas Lodge, and he sometimes returned to Longbourn only in time to make an apology for his absence before the family went to bed.

Mrs Bennet was really in a most pitiable state. The very mention of any thing concerning the match threw her into an agony of ill humour, and wherever she went she was sure of hearing it talked of. The sight of Miss Lucas was odious to her. As her successor in that house, she regarded her with jealous abhorrence. Whenever Charlotte came to see them she concluded her to be anticipating the hour of possession; and whenever she spoke in a low voice to Mr Collins, was convinced that they were talking of the Longbourn estate, and resolving to turn herself and her daughters out of the house, as soon as Mr Bennet were dead. She complained bitterly of all this to her husband.

'Indeed, Mr Bennet,' said she, 'it is very hard to think that Charlotte Lucas should ever be mistress of this house, that *I* should be forced to make way for *her*, and live to see her take my place in it!'

'My dear, do not give way to such gloomy thoughts. Let us hope for better things. Let us flatter ourselves that I may be the survivor.'

This was not very consoling to Mrs Bennet, and, therefore, instead of making any answer, she went on as before,

'I cannot bear to think that they should have all this estate. If it was not for the entail I should not mind it.'

'What should not you mind?'

'I should not mind any thing at all.'

'Let us be thankful that you are preserved from a state of such insensibility.'

'I never can be thankful, Mr Bennet, for any thing about the entail. How any one could have the conscience to entail away an estate from one's own daughters I cannot understand; and all for the sake of Mr Collins too! – Why should *he* have it more than anybody else?'

'I leave it to yourself to determine,' said Mr Bennet.

Chapter Twenty Four

MISS BINGLEY'S LETTER ARRIVED, AND put an end to doubt. The very first sentence conveyed the assurance of their being all settled in London for the winter, and concluded with her brother's regret at not having had time to pay his respects to his friends in Hertfordshire before he left the country.

Hope was over, entirely over; and when Jane could attend to the rest of the letter, she found little, except the professed affection of the writer, that could give her any comfort. Miss Darcy's praise occupied the chief of it. Her many attractions were again dwelt on, and Caroline boasted joyfully of their increasing intimacy, and ventured to predict the accomplishment of the wishes which had been unfolded in her former letter. She wrote also with great pleasure of her brother's being an inmate of Mr Darcy's house, and mentioned with raptures, some plans of the latter with regard to new furniture.

Elizabeth, to whom Jane very soon communicated the chief of all this, heard it in silent indignation. Her heart was divided between concern for her sister, and resentment against all the others. To Caroline's assertion of her brother's being partial to Miss Darcy she paid no credit. That he was really fond of Jane, she doubted no more than she had ever done; and much as she had always been disposed to like him, she could not think without anger, hardly without contempt, on that easiness of temper, that want of proper resolution which now made him the slave of his designing friends, and led him to sacrifice his own happiness to the caprice of their inclinations. Had his own happiness, however, been the only sacrifice, he might have been allowed to sport with it in what ever manner he thought best; but her sister's was involved in it, as she thought he must be sensible himself. It was a subject, in short, on which reflection would be long indulged, and must be unavailing. She could think of nothing else, and yet whether Bingley's regard had really died away, or were suppressed by his friends' interference; whether he had been aware of Jane's attachment, or whether it had escaped his observation; whichever were the case, though her opinion of him must be materially affected by the difference, her sister's situation remained the same, her peace equally wounded.

A day or two passed before Jane had courage to speak of her feelings to Elizabeth; but at last on Mrs Bennet's leaving them together, after a longer irritation than usual about Netherfield and its master, she could not help saying,

'Oh! that my dear mother had more command over herself; she can have no idea of the pain she gives me by her continual reflections on him. But I will not repine. It cannot last long. He will be forgot, and we shall all be as we are before.'

Elizabeth looked at her sister with incredulous solicitude, but said nothing.

'You doubt me,' cried Jane, slightly colouring; 'indeed you have no reason. He may live in my memory as the most amiable man of my acquaintance, but that is all. I have nothing either to hope or fear, and nothing to reproach him with. Thank God! I have not *that* pain. A little time therefore. – I shall certainly try to get the better.'

With a stronger voice she soon added, 'I have this comfort immediately, that it has not been more than an error of fancy on my side, and that it has done no harm to any one but myself.'

'My dear Jane!' exclaimed Elizabeth, 'you are too good. Your sweetness and disinterestedness are really angelic; I do not know what to say to you. I feel as if I had never done you justice, or loved you as you deserve.'

Miss Bennet eagerly disclaimed all extraordinary merit, and threw back the praise on her sister's warm affection.

'Nay,' said Elizabeth, 'this is not fair. *You* wish to think all the world respectable, and are hurt if I speak ill of any body. *I* only want to think *you* perfect, and you set yourself against it. Do not be afraid of my running into any excess, of my encroaching on your privilege of universal good will. You need not. There are few people whom I really love, and still fewer of whom I think well. The more I see of the world, the more am I dissatisfied with it; and every day confirms my belief of the inconsistency of all human characters, and of the little dependence that can be placed on the appearance of either merit or sense. I have met with two instances lately; one I will not mention; the other is Charlotte's marriage. It is unaccountable! in every view it is unaccountable!'

'My dear Lizzy, do not give way to such feelings as these. They will ruin your happiness. You do not make allowance enough for difference of situation and temper. Consider Mr Collins's respectability, and Charlotte's prudent, steady character. Remember that she is one of a large family; that as to fortune, it is a most eligible match; and be ready to believe, for every body's sake, that she may feel something like regard and esteem for our cousin.'

'To oblige you, I would try to believe almost any thing, but no one else could be benefited by such a belief as this; for were I persuaded that Charlotte had any regard for him, I should only think worse of her understanding, than I now do of her heart. My dear Jane, Mr Collins is a conceited, pompous, narrow-minded, silly man; you know he is, as well as I do; and you must feel, as well as I do, that the woman who marries him, cannot have a proper way of thinking. You shall not defend her, though it is Charlotte Lucas. You shall not, for the sake of one individual, change the meaning of principle and integrity, nor endeavour to persuade yourself or me, that selfishness is prudence, and insensibility of danger, security for happiness.'

'I must think your language too strong in speaking of both,' replied Jane, 'and I hope you will be convinced of it, by seeing them happy together. But enough of this. You alluded to something else. You mentioned *two* instances. I cannot misunderstand you, but I intreat you, dear Lizzy, not to pain me by thinking *that person* to blame, and saying your opinion of him is sunk. We must not be so ready to fancy ourselves intentionally injured. We must not expect a lively young man to be always so guarded and circumspect. It is very often nothing but our own vanity that deceives us. Women fancy admiration means more than it does.'

'And men take care that they should.'

'If it is designedly done, they cannot be justified; but I have no idea of there being so much design in the world as some persons imagine.'

'I am far from attributing any part of Mr Bingley's conduct to design,' said Elizabeth; 'but without scheming to do wrong, or to make others unhappy, there may be error, and there may be misery. Thoughtlessness, want of attention to other people's feelings, and want of resolution, will do the business.'

'And do you impute it to either of those?'

'Yes; to the last. But if I go on, I shall displease you by saying what I think of persons you esteem. Stop me whilst you can.'

'You persist, then, in supposing his sisters influence him.'

'Yes, in conjunction with his friend.'

'I cannot believe it. Why should they try to influence him? They can only wish his happiness, and if he is attached to me, no other woman can secure it.'

'Your first position is false. They may wish many things besides his happiness; they may wish his increase of wealth and consequence; they may wish him to marry a girl who has all the importance of money, great connections, and pride.'

'Beyond a doubt, they *do* wish him to chuse Miss Darcy,' replied Jane; 'but this may be from better feelings than you are supposing. They have known her much longer than they have known me; no wonder if they love her better. But, whatever may be their own wishes, it is very unlikely they should have opposed their brother's. What sister would think herself at liberty to do it, unless there were something very objectionable? If they believed him attached to me, they would not try to part us; if he were so, they could not succeed. By supposing such an affection, you make every body acting unnaturally and wrong, and me most unhappy. Do not distress me by the idea. I am not ashamed of having been mistaken – or, at least, it is slight, it is nothing in comparison of what I should feel in thinking ill of him or his sisters. Let me take it in the best light, in the light in which it may be understood.'

Elizabeth could not oppose such a wish; and from this time Mr Bingley's name was scarcely ever mentioned between them.

Mrs Bennet still continued to wonder and repine at his returning no more, and though a day seldom passed in which Elizabeth did not account for it clearly, there seemed little chance of her ever considering it with less perplexity. Her daughter endeavoured to convince her of what she did not believe herself, that his attentions to Jane had been merely the effect of a common and transient liking, which ceased when he saw her no more; but though the probability of the statement was admitted at the time, she had the same story to repeat every day. Mrs Bennet's best comfort was, that Mr Bingley must be down again in the summer.

Mr Bennet treated the matter differently. 'So, Lizzy,' said he one day, 'your sister is crossed in love I find. I congratulate her. Next to being married, a girl likes to be crossed in love a little now and then. It is something to think of, and gives her a sort of distinction among her companions. When is your turn to come? You will hardly bear to be long outdone by Jane. Now is your time. Here are officers enough at Meryton to disappoint all the young ladies in the country. Let Wickham be *your* man. He is a pleasant fellow, and would jilt you creditably.'

'Thank you, Sir, but a less agreeable man would satisfy me. We must not all expect Jane's good fortune.'

'True,' said Mr Bennet, 'but it is a comfort to think that, whatever of that kind may befall you, you have an affectionate mother who will always make the most of it.'

Mr Wickham's society was of material service in dispelling the gloom, which the late perverse occurrences had thrown on many of the Longbourn family. They saw him often, and to his other recommendations was now added that of general unreserve. The whole of what Elizabeth had already heard, his claims on Mr Darcy, and all that he had suffered from him, was now openly acknowledged and publicly canvassed; and every body was pleased to think how much they had always disliked Mr Darcy before they had known any thing of the matter.

Miss Bennet was the only creature who could suppose there might be any extenuating circumstances in the case, unknown to the society of Hertfordshire; her mild and steady candour always pleaded for allowances, and urged the possibility of mistakes – but by everybody else Mr Darcy was condemned as the worst of men.

Chapter Twenty Five

AFTER A WEEK SPENT IN PROFESSIONS OF love and schemes of felicity, Mr Collins was called from his amiable Charlotte by the arrival of Saturday. The pain of separation, however, might be alleviated on his side, by preparations for the reception of his bride, as he had reason to hope, that shortly after his next return into Hertfordshire, the day would be fixed that was to make him the happiest of men. He took leave of his relations at Longbourn with as much solemnity as before; wished his fair cousins health and happiness again, and promised their father another letter of thanks.

On the following Monday, Mrs Bennet had the pleasure of receiving her brother and his wife, who came as usual to spend the Christmas at Longbourn. Mr Gardiner was a sensible, gentlemanlike man, greatly superior to his sister as well by nature as education. The Netherfield ladies would have had difficulty in believing that a man who lived by trade, and within view of his own warehouses, could have been so well bred and agreeable. Mrs Gardiner, who was several years younger than Mrs Bennet and Mrs Philips, was an amiable, intelligent, elegant woman, and a great favourite with all her Longbourn nieces. Between the two eldest and herself especially, there subsisted a very particular regard. They had frequently been staying with her in town.

The first part of Mrs Gardiner's business on her arrival, was to distribute her presents and describe the newest fashions. When this was done, she had a less active part to play. It became her turn to listen. Mrs Bennet had many grievances to relate, and much to complain of. They had all been ill-used since she last saw her sister. Two of her girls had been on the point of marriage, and after all there was nothing in it.

'I do not blame Jane,' she continued, 'for Jane would have got Mr Bingley, if she could. But Lizzy! Oh, sister! it is very hard to think that she might have been Mr Collins' wife by this time, had not it been for her own perverseness. He made her an offer in this very room, and she refused him. The consequence of it is that Lady Lucas will have a daughter married before I have, and that Longbourn estate is just as much entailed as ever. The Lucases are very artful people indeed, sister. They are all for what they can get. I am sorry to say it of them, but so it is. It makes me very nervous and poorly, to be thwarted so in my own family, and to have neighbours who think of themselves before anybody else. However, your coming just at this time is the greatest of comforts, and I am very glad to hear what you tell us, of long sleeves.'

Mrs Gardiner, to whom the chief of this news had been given before, in the course of Jane and Elizabeth's correspondence with her, made her sister a slight answer, and in compassion to her nieces turned the conversation.

When alone with Elizabeth afterwards, she spoke more on the subject. 'It seems likely to have been a desirable match for Jane,' said she, 'I am sorry it went off. But these things happen so often! A young man, such as you describe Mr Bingley, so easily falls in love with a pretty girl for a few weeks, and when accident separates them, so easily forgets her, that these sort of inconstancies are very frequent.'

'An excellent consolation in its way,' said Elizabeth, 'but it will not do for *us*. We do not suffer by *accident*. It does not often happen that the interference of friends will persuade a young man of independent fortune to think no more of a girl, whom he was violently in love with only a few days before.'

'But that expression of "violently in love" is so hackneyed, so doubtful, so indefinite, that it gives me very little idea. It is as often applied to feelings which arise from an half-hour's acquaintance, as to a real, strong attachment. Pray, how *violent was* Mr Bingley's love?'

'I never saw a more promising inclination. He was growing quite inattentive to other people, and wholly engrossed by her. Every time they met, it was more decided and remarkable. At his own ball he offended two or three young ladies, by not asking them to dance, and I spoke to him twice myself, without receiving an answer. Could there be finer symptoms? Is not general incivility the very essence of love?'

'Oh, yes! – of that kind of love which I suppose him to have felt. Poor

Jane! I am sorry for her, because, with her disposition, she may not get over it immediately. It had better have happened to *you*, Lizzy; you would have laughed yourself out of it sooner. But do you think she would be prevailed on to go back with us? Change of scene might be of service – and perhaps a little relief from home, may be as useful as anything.'

Elizabeth was exceedingly pleased with this proposal, and felt persuaded of her sister's ready acquiesence.

'I hope,' added Mrs Gardiner, 'that no consideration with regard to this young man will influence her. We live in so different a part of town, all our connections are so different, and, as you well know, we go out so little, that it is very improbable they should meet at all, unless he really comes to see her.'

'And *that* is quite impossible; for he is now in the custody of his friend, and Mr Darcy would no more suffer him to call on Jane in such a part of London! My dear aunt, how could you think of it? Mr Darcy may perhaps have *heard* of such a place as Gracechurch Street, but he would hardly think a month's ablution enough to cleanse him from its impurities, were he once to enter it; and depend upon it, Mr Bingley never stirs without him.'

'So much the better. I hope they will not meet at all. But does not Jane correspond with the sister? *She* will not be able to help calling.'

'She will drop the acquaintance entirely.'

But in spite of the certainty in which Elizabeth affected to place this point, as well as the still more interesting one of Bingley's being withheld from seeing Jane, she felt a solicitude on the subject which convinced her, on examination, that she did not consider it entirely hopeless. It was possible, and sometimes she thought it profitable, that his affection might be re-animated, and the influence of his friends successfully combated by the more natural influence of Jane's attractions.

Miss Bennet accepted her aunt's invitation with pleasure; and the Bingley's were no otherwise in her thoughts at the time, than as she hoped that, by Caroline's not living in the same house with her brother, she might occasionally spend a morning with her, without any danger of seeing him.

The Gardiners staid a week at Longbourn; and what with the Philipses, the Lucases, and the officers, there was not a day without its engagement. Mrs Bennet had so carefully provided for the entertainment of her brother and sister, that they did not once sit down to a family dinner. When the engagement was for home, some of the officers always made part of it, of which officers Mr Wickham was sure to be one; and on these occasions, Mrs Gardiner, rendered suspicious by Elizabeth's warm commendation of him, narrowly observed them both. Without supposing them, from what she saw, to be very seriously in love, their preference of each other was plain enough to make her a little uneasy; and she resolved to speak to Elizabeth on the subject before she left Hertfordshire, and represented to her the imprudence of encouraging such an attachment.

To Mrs Gardiner, Wickham had one means of affording pleasure, unconnected with his general powers. About ten or a dozen years ago, before her marriage, she had spent a considerable time in that very part of Derbyshire, to which he belonged. They had, therefore, many acquaintances in common; and, though Wickham had been little there since the death of Darcy's father, five years before, it was yet in his power to give her fresher intelligence of her former friends, than she had been in the way of procuring.

Mrs Gardiner had seen Pemberley, and known the late Mr Darcy by character perfectly well. Here consequently was an inexhaustible subject of discourse. In comparing her recollection of Pemberley, with the minute description which Wickham could give, and in bestowing her tribute of praise on the character of its late possessor, she was delighting both him and herself. On being made acquainted with the present Mr Darcy's treatment of him, she tried to remember something of that gentleman's reputed disposition when quite a lad, which might agree with it, and was confident at last, that she recollected having heard Mr Fitzwilliam Darcy formerly spoken of as a very proud, ill-natured boy.

Chapter Twenty Six

MRS GARDINER'S CAUTION TO ELIZABETH was punctually and kindly given on the first favourable opportunity of speaking to her alone; after honestly telling her what she thought, she thus went on:

'You are too sensible a girl, Lizzy, to fall in love merely because you are warned against it; and, therefore, I am not afraid of speaking openly. Seriously, I would have you be on your guard. Do not involve yourself, or endeavour to involve him in an affection which the want of fortune would make so very imprudent. I have nothing to say against *him*; he is a most interesting young man; and if he had the fortune he ought to have, I should think you could not do better. But as it is – you must not let your fancy run away with you. You have sense, and we all expect you to use it. Your father would depend on *your* resolution and good conduct, I am sure. You must not disappoint your father.'

'My dear aunt, this is being serious indeed.'

'Yes, and I hope to engage you to be serious likewise.'

'Well, then, you need not be under any alarm. I will take care of myself, and of Mr Wickham too. He shall not be in love with me, if I can prevent it.'

'Elizabeth, you are not serious now.'

'I beg your pardon. I will try again. At present I am not in love with Mr Wickham; no, I certainly am not. But he is, beyond all comparison, the most agreeable man I ever saw – and if he becomes really attached to me – I believe it will be better that he should not. I see the imprudence of it. – Oh! *that* abominable Mr Darcy! – My father's opinion of me does me the greatest honour; and I should be miserable to forfeit it. My father, however, is partial to Mr Wickham. In short, my dear aunt, I should be very sorry to be the means of making any of you unhappy; but since we see every day that where there is affection, young people are seldom withheld by immediate want of fortune, from entering into engagements with each other, how can I promise to be wiser than so many of my fellow creatures if I am tempted, or how am I even to know that it would be wisdom to resist? All that I can promise you, therefore, is not to be in a hurry. I will not be in a hurry to believe myself his first object. When I am in company with him, I will not be wishing. In short, I will do my best.'

'Perhaps it will be as well, if you discourage his coming here so very often. At least, you should not *remind* your Mother of inviting him.'

'As I did the other day,' said Elizabeth, with a conscious smile; 'very true, it will be wise in me to refrain from *that*. But do not imagine that he is always here so often. It is on your account that he has been so frequently invited this week. You know my mother's ideas as to the necessity of constant company for her friends. But really, and upon my honour, I will try to do what I think to be wisest; and now, I hope you are satisfied.'

Her aunt assured her that she was; and Elizabeth having thanked her for the kindness of her hints, they parted; a wonderful instance of advice being given on such a point, without being resented.

Mr Collins returned into Hertfordshire soon after it had been quitted by the Gardiners and Jane; but as he took up his abode with the Lucases, his arrival was no great inconvenience to Mrs Bennet. His marriage was now fast approaching, and she was at length so far resigned as to think it inevitable, and even repeatedly to say in an ill-natured tone that she 'wished they might be happy.' Thursday was to be the wedding day, and on Wednesday Miss Lucas paid her farewell visit; and when she rose to take leave, Elizabeth, ashamed of her mother's ungracious and reluctant good wishes, and sincerely affected herself, accompanied her out of the room. As they went down stairs together, Charlotte said,

'I shall depend on hearing from you very often, Eliza.'

'*That* you certainly shall.'

'And I have another favour to ask. Will you come and see me?'

'We shall often meet, I hope, in Hertfordshire.'

'I am not likely to leave Kent for some time. Promise me, therefore, to come to Hunsford.'

Elizabeth could not refuse, though she foresaw little pleasure in the visit.

'My father and Maria are to come to me in March,' added Charlotte, 'and I hope you will consent to be of the party. Indeed, Eliza, you will be as welcome to me as either of them.'

The wedding took place; the bride and bridegroom set off for Kent from the church door, and every body had as much to say or to hear on the subject as usual. Elizabeth soon heard from her friend; and their correspondence was as regular and frequent as it had ever been; that it should be equally unreserved was impossible. Elizabeth could never address her without feeling that all the comfort of intimacy was over, and, though determined not to slacken as a correspondent, it was for the sake of what had been, rather than what was. Charlotte's first letters were received with a good deal of eagerness; there could not but be curiosity to know how she would speak of her new home, how she would like Lady Catherine, and how happy she would dare pronounce herself to be; though, when the letters were read, Elizabeth felt that Charlotte expressed herself on every point exactly as she might have foreseen. She wrote cheerfully, seemed surrounded with comforts, and mentioned nothing which she could not praise. The house, furniture, neighbourhood, and roads, were all to her taste, and Lady Catherine's behaviour was most friendly and obliging. It was Mr Collins's picture of

Hunsford and Rosings rationally softened; and Elizabeth perceived that she must wait for her own visit there, to know the rest.

Jane had already written a few lines to her sister to announce their safe arrival in London; and when she wrote again, Elizabeth hoped it would be in her power to say something of the Bingleys.

Her impatience for this second letter was as well rewarded as impatience generally is. Jane had been a week in town, without either seeing or hearing from Caroline. She accounted for it, however, by supposing that her last letter to her friend from Longbourn, had by some accident been lost.

'My aunt,' she continued, 'is going to-morrow into that part of the town, and I shall take the opportunity of calling in Grosvenor-street.'

She wrote again when the visit was paid, and she had seen Miss Bingley. 'I did not think Caroline in spirits,' were her words, 'but she was very glad to see me, and reproached me for giving her no notice of my coming to London. I was right, therefore; my last letter had never reached her. I enquired after their brother, of course. He was well, but so much engaged with Mr Darcy, that they scarcely ever saw him. I found that Miss Darcy was expected to dinner. I wish I could see her. My visit was not long, as Caroline and Mrs Hurst were going out. I dare say I shall soon see them here.'

Elizabeth shook her head over this letter. It convinced her, that accident only could discover to Mr Bingley her sister's being in town.

Four weeks passed away, and Jane saw nothing of him. She endeavoured to persuade herself that she did not regret it; but she could no longer be blind to Miss Bingley's inattention. After waiting at home every morning for a fortnight, and inventing every evening a fresh excuse for her, the visitor did at last appear; but the shortness of her stay, and yet more, the alteration of her manner, would allow Jane to deceive herself no longer. The letter which she wrote on this occasion to her sister, will prove what she felt.

My dearest Lizzy, will, I am sure, be incapable of triumphing in her better judgement, at my expence, when I confess myself to have been entirely deceived in Miss Bingley's regard for me. But, my dear sister, though the event has proved you right, do not think me obstinate if I still assert, that, considering what her behaviour was, my confidence was as natural as your suspicion. I do not at all comprehend her reason for wishing to be intimate with me, but if the same circumstances were to happen again, I am sure I should be deceived again. Caroline did not return my visit till yesterday; and not a note, not a line, did I receive in the mean time. When she did come, it was evident that she had no pleasure in it; she made a slight, formal apology, for not calling before, said not a word of wishing to see me again, and was in every respect so altered a creature, that when she went away, I was perfectly resolved to continue the acquaintance no longer. I pity, though I cannot help blaming her. She was very wrong in singling me out as she did; I can safely say, that every advance to intimacy began on her side. But I pity her, because she must feel that she has been acting wrong, and because I am very sure that anxiety for her brother is the cause of it. I need not explain myself farther: and though we know this anxiety to be quite needless, yet if she feels it, it will easily account for her behaviour to me; and so deservedly dear as he is to his sister, whatever anxiety she may feel on his behalf, is natural and amiable. I cannot but wonder, however, at her having any such fears now, because, if he had at all cared about me, we must have met long, long ago. He knows of my being in town, I am certain, from something she said herself; and yet it should seem by her manner of talking, as if she wanted to persuade herself that he is really partial to Miss Darcy. I cannot understand it. If I were not afraid of judging harshly, I should be almost tempted to say, that there is a strong appearance of duplicity in all this. But I will endeavour to banish every painful thought, and think only of what will make me happy, your affection, and the invariable kindness of my dear uncle and aunt. Let me hear from you very soon. Miss Bingley said something of his never returning to Netherfield again, of giving up the house, but not with any certainty. We had better not mention it. I am extremely glad that you have such pleasant accounts from our friends at Hunsford. Pray go to see them, with Sir William and Maria. I am sure you will be very comfortable there.

Yours, &c.

This letter gave Elizabeth some pain; but her spirits returned as she considered that Jane would no longer be duped, by the sister at least. All expectation from the brother was now absolutely over. She would not even wish for any renewal of his attentions. His character sunk on every review of it; and as a punishment for him, as well as a possible advantage to Jane, she seriously hoped he might really soon marry Mr Darcy's sister, as, by Wickham's account, she would make him abundantly regret what he had thrown away.

Mrs Gardiner about this time reminded Elizabeth of her promise concerning that gentleman, and required information; and Elizabeth had such to send as might rather give contentment to her aunt than to herself. His apparent partiality had subsided, his attentions were over, he was the admirer of some one else. Elizabeth was watchful enough to see it all, but she could see it and write of it without material pain. Her heart had been but slightly touched, and her vanity was satisfied with believing that *she* would have been his only choice, had fortune permitted it. The sudden acquisition of ten thousand pounds was the most remarkable charm, of the young lady, to whom he was now rendering himself agreeable; but Elizabeth, less clear-sighted perhaps in his case than in Charlotte's, did not quarrel with him for his wish of independence. Nothing, on the contrary, could be more natural; and while able to suppose that it cost him a few struggles to relinquish her, she was ready to allow it a wise and desirable measure for both, and could very sincerely wish him happy.

All this was acknowledged to Mrs Gardiner; and after relating the circumstances, she thus went on: – 'I am now convinced, my dear aunt, that I have never been much in love; for had I really experienced that pure and elevating passion, I should at present detest his very name, and wish him all manner of evil. But my feelings are not only cordial towards *him*; they are even impartial towards Miss King. I cannot find out that I hate her at all, or that I am in the least unwilling to think her a very good sort of girl. There can be no love in all this. My watchfulness has been effectual; and though I should certainly be a more interesting object to all my acquaintance, were I distractedly in love with him, I cannot say that I regret my comparative insignificance. Importance may sometimes be purchased too dearly. Kitty and Lydia take his defection much more to heart than I do. They are young in the ways of the world, and not yet open to the mortifying conviction that handsome men must have something to live on, as well as the plain.'

Chapter Twenty Seven

WITH NO GREATER EVENTS THAN THESE in the Longbourn family, and otherwise diversified by little beyond the walks to Meryton, sometimes dirty and sometimes cold, did January and February pass away. March was to take Elizabeth to Hunsford. She had not at first thought very seriously of going thither; but Charlotte, she soon found, was depending on the plan, and she gradually learned to consider it herself with greater pleasure as well as greater certainty. Absence had increased her desire of seeing Charlotte again, and weakened her disgust of Mr Collins. There was novelty in the scheme, and as, with such a mother and such uncompanionable sisters, home could not be faultless, a little change was not unwelcome for its own sake. The journey would moreover give her a peep at Jane; and, in short, as the time drew near, she would have been very sorry for any delay. Every thing, however, went on smoothly, and was finally settled according to Charlotte's first sketch. She was to accompany Sir William and his second daughter. The improvement of spending a night in London was added in time, and the plan became perfect as plan could be.

The only pain was in leaving her father, who would certainly miss her, and who, when it came to the point, so little liked her going, that he told her to write to him, and almost promised to answer her letter.

The farewell between herself and Mr Wickham was perfectly friendly; on his side even more. His present pursuit could not make him forget that Elizabeth had been the first to excite and to deserve his attention, the first to listen and to pity, the first to be admired; and in his manner of bidding her adieu, wishing her every enjoyment, reminding her of what she was to expect in Lady Catherine de Bourgh, and trusting their opinion of her – their opinion of every body – would always coincide, there was a solicitude, an interest which she felt must ever attach her to him with a most sincere regard; and she parted from him convinced, that whether married or single, he must always be her model of the amiable and pleasing.

Her fellow-travellers the next day, were not of a kind to make her think them less agreeable. Sir William Lucas, and his daughter Maria, a good humoured girl, but as empty-headed as himself, had nothing to say that could be worth hearing, and were listened to with about as much delight as the rattle of the chaise. Elizabeth loved absurdities, but she had known Sir William's too long. He could tell her nothing new of the wonders of his presentation and knighthood; and his civilities were worn out like his information.

It was a journey of only twenty-four miles, and they began it so early as to be in Gracechurch-street by noon. As they drove to Mr Gardiner's door, Jane was at a drawing-room window watching their arrival; when they entered the passage she was there to welcome them, and Elizabeth, looking earnestly in her face, was pleased to see it healthful and lovely as ever. On the stairs were a troop of little boys and girls, whose eagerness for their cousin's appearance would not allow them to wait in the drawing-room, and whose shyness, as they had not seen her for a twelvemonth, prevented their coming lower. All was joy and kindness. They day passed most pleasantly away; the morning in bustle and shopping, and the evening at one of the theatres.

Elizabeth then contrived to sit by her aunt. Their first subject was her sister; and she was more grieved than astonished to hear, in reply to her minute enquiries, that though Jane always struggled to support her spirits, there were periods of dejection. It was reasonable, however, to hope, that they would not continue long. Mrs Gardiner gave her the particulars also of Miss Bingley's visit to Gracechurch-street, and repeated conversations occurring at different times between Jane and herself, which proved that the former had, from her heart, given up the acquaintance.

Mrs Gardiner then rallied her niece on Wickham's desertion, and complimented her on bearing it so well.

'But, my dear Elizabeth,' she added, 'what sort of girl is Miss King? I should be sorry indeed to think our friend mercenary.'

'Pray, my dear aunt, what is the difference in matrimonial affairs, between the mercenary and the prudent motive? Where does discretion end, and avarice begin? Last Christmas you were afraid of his marrying me, because it would be imprudent; and now, because he is trying to get a girl with only ten thousand pounds, you want to find out that he is mercenary.'

'If you will only tell me what sort of girl Miss King is, I shall know what to think.'

'She is a very good kind of girl, I believe. I know no harm of her.'

'But he paid her not the smallest attention, till her grandfather's death made her mistress of this fortune.'

'No – why should he? If it was not allowable for him to gain *my* affections, because I had no money, what occasion could there be for making love to a girl whom he did not care about, and who was equally poor?'

'But there seems indelicacy in directing his attentions towards her, so soon after this event.'

'A man in distressed circumstances has not time for all those elegant decorums which other people may observe. If *she* does not object to it, why should *we?*'

'*Her* not objecting does not justify *him*. It only shews her being deficient in something herself – sense or feeling.'

'Well,' cried Elizabeth, 'have it as you choose. *He* shall be mercenary, and *she* shall be foolish.'

'No, Lizzy, that is what I do *not* choose. I should be sorry, you know, to think ill of a young man who has lived so long in Derbyshire.'

'Oh! if that is all, I have a very poor opinion of young men who live in Derbyshire; and their intimate friends who live in Hertfordshire are not much better. I am sick of them all. Thank Heaven! I am going to-morrow where I shall find a man who has not one agreeable quality, who has neither manner nor sense to recommend him. Stupid men are the only ones worth knowing, after all.'

'Take care, Lizzy; that speech savours strongly of disappointment.'

Before they were separated by the conclusion of the play, she had the unexpected happiness of an invitation to accompany her uncle and aunt in a tour of pleasure which they proposed taking in the summer.

'We have not quite determined how far it shall carry us,' said Mrs Gardiner, 'but perhaps to the Lakes.'

No scheme could have been more agreeable to Elizabeth, and her acceptance of the invitation was most ready and grateful. 'My dear, dear aunt,' she rapturously cried, 'what delight! what felicity! You give me fresh life and vigour. Adieu to disappointment and spleen. What are men to rocks and mountains? Oh! what hours of transport we shall spend! And when we *do* return, it shall not be like other travellers, without being able to give one accurate idea of any thing. We *will* know where we have gone – we *will* recollect what we have seen. Lakes, mountains, and rivers, shall not be jumbled together in our imaginations; nor, when we attempt to describe any particular scene, will we begin quarrelling about its relative situation. Let *our* first effusions be less insupportable than those of the generality of travellers.'

Chapter Twenty Eight

EVERY OBJECT IN THE NEXT DAY'S journey was new and interesting to Elizabeth; and her spirits were in a state for enjoyment; for she had seen her sister looking so well as to banish all fear for her health, and the prospect of her northern tour was a constant source of delight.

When they left the high road for the lane to Hunsford, every eye was in search of the Parsonage, and every turning expected to bring it in view. The paling of Rosings Park was their boundary on one side. Elizabeth smiled at the recollection of all that she had heard of its inhabitants.

At length the Parsonage was discernible. The garden sloping to the road, the house standing in it, the green pales and the laurel hedge, every thing declared they were arriving. Mr Collins and Charlotte appeared at the door, and the carriage stopped at the small gate, which led by a short gravel walk to the house, amidst the nods and smiles of the whole party. In a moment they were all out of the chaise, rejoicing at the sight of each other. Mrs Collins welcomed her friend with the liveliest pleasure, and Elizabeth was more and more satisfied with coming, when she found herself so affectionately received. She saw instantly that her cousin's manners were not altered by his marriage; his formal civility was just what it had been, and he detained her some minutes at the gate to hear and satisfy his enquiries after all her family. They were then, with no other delay than his pointing out the neatness of the entrance, taken into the house; and as soon as they were in the parlour, he welcomed them a second time with ostentatious formality to his humble abode, and punctually repeated all his wife's offers of refreshment.

Elizabeth was prepared to see him in his glory; and she could not help fancying that in displaying the good proportion of the room, its aspect and its furniture, he addressed himself particularly to her, as if wishing to make her feel what she had lost in refusing him. But though every thing seemed neat and comfortable, she was not able to gratify him by any sigh of repentance; and rather looked with wonder at her friend that she could have so cheerful an air, with such a companion. When Mr Collins said any thing of which his wife might reasonably be ashamed, which certainly was not unseldom, she involuntarily turned her eye on Charlotte. Once or twice she could discern a faint blush; but in general Charlotte wisely did not hear. After sitting long enough to admire every article of furniture in the room, from the sideboard to the fender, to give an account of their journey and of all that had happened in London, Mr Collins invited them to take a stroll in the garden, which was large and well laid out, and to the cultivation of which he attended himself. To work in his garden was one of his most respectable pleasures; and Elizabeth admired the command of countenance with which Charlotte talked of the healthfulness of the exercise, and owned she encouraged it as much as possible. Here, leading the way through every walk and cross walk, and scarcely allowing them an interval to utter the praises he asked for, every view was pointed out with a minuteness which left beauty entirely behind. He could number the fields in every direction, and could tell how many trees there were in the most distant clump. But of all the views which his garden, or which the country, or the kingdom could boast, none were to be compared with the prospect of Rosings, afforded by an opening in the trees that bordered the park nearly opposite the front of his house. It was a handsome modern building, well situated on rising ground.

From his garden, Mr Collins would have led them round his two meadows, but the ladies not having shoes to encounter the remains of a white frost, turned back; and while Sir William accompanied him, Charlotte took her sister and friend over the house, extremely well pleased, probably, to have the opportunity of shewing it without her husband's help. It was rather small, but well built and convenient; and every thing was fitted up and arranged with a neatness and consistency of which Elizabeth gave Charlotte all the credit. When Mr Collins could be forgotten, there was really a great air of comfort throughout, and by Charlotte's evident enjoyment of it, Elizabeth supposed he must be often forgotten.

She had already learnt that Lady Catherine was still in the country. It was spoken of again while they were at dinner, when Mr Collins, joining in, observed.

'Yes, Miss Elizabeth, you will have the honour of seeing Lady Catherine de Bourgh on the ensuing Sunday at church, and I need not say you will be delighted with her. She is all affability and condescension, and I doubt not but you will be honoured by some portion of her notice when service is over. I have scarcely any hesitation in saying that she will include you and my sister Maria in every invitation with which she honours us during your stay here. Her behaviour to my dear Charlotte is charming. We dine at Rosings twice every week, and are never allowed to walk home. Her ladyship's carriage is regularly ordered for us. I *should* say, one of her ladyship's carriages, for she has several.'

'Lady Catherine is a very respectable, sensible woman indeed,' added Charlotte, 'and a most attentive neighbour.'

'Very true, my dear, that is exactly what I say. She is the sort of woman whom one cannot regard with too much deference.'

The evening was spent chiefly in talking over Hertfordshire news, and telling again what had been already written; and when it closed, Elizabeth in the solitude of her chamber had to meditate upon Charlotte's degree of contentment, to understand her address in guiding, and composure in bearing with her husband, and to acknowledge that it was all done very well. She had also to anticipate how her visit would pass, the quiet tenor of their usual employments, the vexatious interruptions of Mr Collins, and the gaieties of their intercourse with Rosings. A lively imagination soon settled it all.

About the middle of the next day, as she was in her room getting ready for a walk, a sudden noise below seemed to speak the whole house in confusion; and after listening a moment, she heard somebody running up stairs in a violent hurry, and calling loudly after her. She opened the door, and met Maria in the landing place, who, breathless with agitation, cried out,

'Oh, my dear Eliza! pray make haste and come into the dining-room, for there is such a sight to be seen! I will not tell you what it is. Make haste, and come down this moment.'

Elizabeth asked questions in vain; Maria would tell her nothing more, and down they ran into the dining-room, which fronted the lane, in quest of this wonder; it was two ladies stopping in a low phaeton at the garden gate.

'And is that all?' cried Elizabeth, 'I expected at least that the pigs were got into the garden, and here is nothing but Lady Catherine and her daughter!'

'La! my dear,' said Maria quite shocked at the mistake, 'it is not Lady Catherine. The old lady is Mrs Jenkinson, who lives with them. The other is Miss de Bourgh. Only look at her. She is quite a little creature. Who would have thought she could be so thin and small!'

'She is abominably rude to keep Charlotte out of doors in all this wind. Why does she not come in?'

'Oh! Charlotte says, she hardly ever does. It is the greatest of favours when Miss de Bourgh comes in.'

'I like her appearance,' said Elizabeth, struck with other ideas. 'She looks sickly and cross. – Yes, she will do for him very well. She will make him a very proper wife.'

Mr Collins and Charlotte were both standing at the gate in conversation with the ladies; and Sir William to Elizabeth's high diversion, was stationed in the doorway, in earnest contemplation of the greatness before him, and constantly bowing whenever Miss de Bourgh looked that way.

At length there was nothing more to be said; the ladies drove on, and the others returned into the house. Mr Collins no sooner saw the two girls than he began to congratulate them on their good fortune, which Charlotte explained by letting them know that the whole party was asked to dine at Rosings the next day.

Chapter Twenty Nine

MR COLLINS'S TRIUMPH IN CONSEQUENCE of this invitation was complete. The power of displaying the grandeur of his patroness to his wondering visitors, and of letting them see her civility towards himself and his wife, was exactly what he had wished for; and that an opportunity of doing it should be given so soon, was such an instance of Lady Catherine's condescension as he knew not how to admire enough.

'I confess,' said he, 'that I should not have been at all surprised by her Ladyship's asking us on Sunday to drink tea and spend the evening at Rosings. I rather expected, from my knowledge of her affability, that it would happen. But who could have foreseen such an attention as this? Who could have imagined that we should receive an invitation to dine there (an invitation moreover including the whole party) so immediately after your arrival!'

'I am the less surprised at what has happened,' replied Sir William, 'from that knowledge of what the manners of the great really are, which my situation in life has allowed me to acquire. About the Court, such instances of elegant breeding are not uncommon.'

Scarcely any thing was talked of the whole day or next morning, but their visit to Rosings. Mr Collins was carefully instructing them in what they were to expect, that the sight of such rooms, so many servants, and so splendid a dinner might not wholly overpower them.

When the ladies were separating for the toilette, he said to Elizabeth,

'Do not make yourself uneasy, my dear cousin, about your apparel. Lady Catherine is far from requiring that elegance of dress in us, which becomes herself and daughter. I would advise you merely to put on whatever of your clothes is superior to the rest, there is no occasion for any thing more. Lady Catherine will not think the worse of you for being simply dressed. She likes to have the distinction of rank preserved.'

While they were dressing, he came two or three times to their different doors, to recommend their being quick, as Lady Catherine very much objected to be kept waiting for her dinner. – Such formidable accounts of her Ladyship, and her manner of living, quite frightened Maria Lucas, who had been little used to company, and she looked forward to her introduction at Rosings, with as much apprehension, as her father had done to his presentation at St James's.

As the weather was fine, they had a pleasant walk of about half a mile across the park. – Every park has its beauty and its prospects; and Elizabeth saw much to be pleased with, though she could not be in such raptures as Mr Collins expected the scene to inspire, and was but slightly affected by his enumeration of the windows in front of the house, and his relation of what the glazing altogether had originally cost Sir Lewis de Bourgh.

When they ascended the steps to the hall, Maria's alarm was every moment increasing, and even Sir William did not look perfectly calm. – Elizabeth's courage did not fail her. She had heard nothing of Lady Catherine that spoke her awful from any extraordinary talents or miraculous virtue, and the mere stateliness of money and rank, she thought she could witness without trepidation.

From the entrance hall, of which Mr Collins pointed out, with a rapturous air, the fine proportion and finished ornaments, they followed the servants through an antichamber, to the room where Lady Catherine, her daughter, and Mrs Jenkinson were sitting. – Her Ladyship, with great condescension, arose to receive them; and as Mrs Collins had settled it with her husband that the office of introduction should be her's, it was performed in a proper manner, without any of those apologies and thanks which he would have thought necessary.

In spite of having been at St James's, Sir William was so completely awed, by the grandeur surrounding him, that he had but just courage enough to make a very low bow, and take his seat without saying a word; and his daughter, frightened almost out of her senses, sat on the edge of her chair, not knowing which way to look. Elizabeth found herself quite equal to the scene, and could observe the three ladies before her composedly. – Lady Catherine was a tall, large woman, with strongly-marked features, which might once have been handsome. Her air was not conciliating, nor was her manner of receiving them, such as to make her visitors forget their inferior rank. She was not rendered formidable by silence; but whatever she said, was spoken in so authoritative a tone, as marked her self-importance, and brought Mr Wickham immediately to Elizabeth's mind; and from the observation of the day altogether, she believed Lady Catherine to be exactly what he had represented.

When, after examining the mother, in whose countenance and deport-ment she soon found some resemblance to Mr Darcy, she turned her eyes on the daughter, she could almost have joined in Maria's astonishment, at her being so thin, and so small. There was neither in figure nor face, any likeness between the ladies. Miss de Bourgh was pale and sickly; her features, though not plain, were insignificant; and she spoke very little, except in a low voice, to Mrs Jenkinson, in whose appearance there was nothing remarkable, and who was entirely engaged in listening to what she said, and placing a screen in the proper direction before her eyes.

After sitting a few minutes, they were all sent to one of the windows, to admire the view, Mr Collins attending them to point out its beauties, and Lady Catherine kindly informing them that it was much better worth looking at in the summer.

The dinner was exceedingly handsome, and there were all the servants, and all the articles of plate which Mr Collins had promised; and, as he had likewise foretold, he took his seat at the bottom of the table, by her ladyship's desire, and looked as if he felt that life could furnish nothing greater. – He carved, and ate, and praised with delighted alacrity; and every dish was commended, first by him, and then by Sir William, who was now enough recovered to echo whatever his son in law said, in a manner which Elizabeth wondered Lady Catherine could bear. But Lady Catherine seemed gratified by their excessive admiration, and gave most gracious smiles, especially when any dish on the table proved a novelty to them. The party did not supply much conversation. Elizabeth was ready to speak whenever there was an opening, but she was seated between Charlotte and Miss de Bourgh – the former of whom was engaged in listening to Lady Catherine, and the latter said not a word to her all dinner time. Mrs Jenkinson was chiefly employed in watching how little Miss de Bourgh ate, pressing her to try some other dish, and fearing she were indisposed. Maria thought speaking out of the question, and the gentlemen did nothing but eat and admire.

When the ladies returned to the drawing room, there was little to be done but to hear Lady Catherine talk, which she did without any intermission till coffee came in, delivering her opinion on every subject in so decisive a manner as proved that she was not used to have her judgment controverted. She enquired into Charlotte's domestic concerns familiarly and minutely, and gave her a great deal of advice, as to the management of them all; told her how every thing ought to be regulated in so small a family as her's, and instructed her as to the care of her cows and her poultry. Elizabeth found that nothing was beneath this great Lady's attention, which could furnish her with an occasion of dictating to others. In the intervals of her discourse with Mrs Collins, she addressed a variety of questions to Maria and Elizabeth, but especially to the latter, of whose connections she knew the least, and who she observed to Mrs Collins, was a very genteel, pretty kind of girl. She asked her at different times, how many sisters she had, whether they were older or younger than herself, whether any of them were likely to be married, whether they were handsome, where they had been educated, what carriage her father kept, and what had been her mother's maiden name? – Elizabeth felt all the impertinence of her questions, but answered them very composedly. – Lady Catherine then observed,

'Your father's estate is entailed on Mr Collins, I think. For your sake,' turning to Charlotte, 'I am glad of it; but otherwise I see no occasion for entailing estates from the female line. – It was not thought necessary in Sir Lewis de Bourgh's family. – Do you play and sing, Miss Bennet?'

'A little.'

'Oh! then – some time or other we shall be happy to hear you. Our instrument is a capable one, probably superior to – You shall try it some day. – Do your sisters play and sing?'

'One of them does.'

'Why did not you all learn? – You ought all to have learned. The Miss Webbs all play, and their father has not so good an income as your's. – Do you draw?'

'No, not at all.'

'What, none of you?'

'Not one.'

'That is very strange. But I suppose you had no opportunity. Your mother should have taken you to town every spring for the benefit of masters.'

'My mother would have had no objection, but my father hates London.'

'Has your governess left you?'

'We never had any governess.'

'No governess! How was that possible? Five daughters brought up at home without a governess! – I never heard of such a thing. Your mother must have been quite a slave to your education.'

Elizabeth could hardly help smiling, as she assured her that had not been the case.

'Then, who taught you? who attended to you? Without a governess you must have been neglected.'

'Compared with some families, I believe we were; but such of us as wished to learn, never wanted the means. We were always encouraged to read, and had all the masters that were necessary. Those who chose to be idle, certainly might.'

'Aye, no doubt; but that is what a governess will prevent, and if I had known your mother, I should have advised her most strenuously to engage one. I always say that nothing is to be done in education without steady and regular instruction, and nobody but a governess can give it. It is wonderful how many families I have been the means of supplying in that way. I am always glad to get a young person well placed out. Four nieces of Mrs Jenkinson are most delightfully situated through my means; and it was but the other day, that I recommended another young person, who was merely accidentally mentioned to me, and the family are quite delighted with her. Mrs Collins, did I tell you of Lady Metcalfe's calling yesterday to thank me? She finds Miss Pope a treasure. "Lady Catherine," said she, "you have given me a treasure." Are any of your younger sisters out, Miss Bennet?'

"Yes, Ma'am, all.'

'All! – What, all five out at once? Very odd! – And you only the second. – The younger ones out before the elder are married! – Your younger sisters must be very young?'

'Yes, my youngest is not sixteen. Perhaps *she* is full young to be much in company. But really, Ma'am, I think it would be very hard upon younger sisters, that they should not have their share of society and amusement because the elder may not have the means or inclination to marry early. – The last born has as good a right to the pleasures of youth, as the first. And to be kept back on *such* a motive! – I think it would not be very likely to promote sisterly affection or delicacy of mind.'

'Upon my word,' said her Ladyship, 'you give your opinion very decidedly for so young a person. – Pray, what is your age?'

'With three younger sisters grown up,' replied Elizabeth smiling, 'your Ladyship can hardly expect me to own it.'

Lady Catherine seemed quite astonished at not receiving a direct answer; and Elizabeth suspected herself to be the first creature who had ever dared to trifle with so much dignified impertinence.

'You cannot be more than twenty, I am sure, – therefore you need not conceal your age.'

'I am not one and twenty.'

When the gentlemen had joined them, and tea was over, the card tables were placed. Lady Catherine, Sir William, and Mr and Mrs Collins sat down to quadrille; and as Miss de Bourgh chose to play at cassino, the two girls had the honour of assisting Mrs Jenkinson to make up her party. Their table was superlatively stupid. Scarcely a syllable was uttered that did not relate to the game, except when Mrs Jenkinson expressed her fears of Miss de Bourgh's being too hot or too cold, or having too much or too little light. A great deal more passed at the other table. Lady Catherine was generally speaking – stating the mistakes of the three others, or relating some anecdote of herself. Mr Collins was employed in agreeing to every thing her Ladyship said, thanking her for every fish he won, and apologising if he thought he won too many. Sir William did not say much. He was storing his memory with anecdotes and noble names.

When Lady Catherine and her daughter had played as long as they chose, the tables were broke up, the carriage was offered to Mrs Collins, gratefully accepted, and immediately ordered. The party then gathered round the fire to hear Lady Catherine determine what weather they were to have on the morrow. From these instructions they were summoned by the arrival of the coach, and with many speeches of thankfulness on Mr Collins's side, and as many bows on Sir William's, they departed. As soon as they had driven from the door, Elizabeth was called on by her cousin, to give her opinion of all that she had seen at Rosings, which, for Charlotte's sake, she made more favourable than it really was. But her commendation, though costing her some trouble, could by no means satisfy Mr Collins, and he was very soon obliged to take her Ladyship's praise into his own hands.

Chapter Thirty

SIR WILLIAM STAID ONLY A WEEK at Hunsford; but his visit was long enough to convince him of his daughter's being most comfortably settled, and of her possessing such a husband and such a neighbour as were not often met with. While Sir William was with them, Mr Collins devoted his mornings to driving him out in his gig, and shewing him the country; but when he went away, the whole family returned to their usual employments, and Elizabeth was thankful to find that they did not see more of her cousin by the alteration, for the chief of the time between breakfast and dinner was now passed by him either at work in the garden, or in reading and writing, and looking out of window in his own book room, which fronted the road. The room in which the ladies sat was backwards. Elizabeth at first had rather wondered that Charlotte should not prefer the dining parlour for common use; it was a better sized room, and had a pleasanter aspect; but she soon saw that her friend had an excellent reason for what she did, for Mr Collins would undoubtedly have been much less in his own apartment, had they sat in one equally lively; and she gave Charlotte credit for the arrangement.

From the drawing room they could distinguish nothing in the lane, and were indebted to Mr Collins for the knowledge of what carriages went along, and how often especially Miss de Bourgh drove by in her phaeton, which he never failed coming to inform them of, though it happened almost every day. She not unfrequently stopped at the Parsonage, and had a few minutes' conversation with Charlotte, but was scarcely ever prevailed on to get out.

Very few days passed in which Mr Collins did not walk to Rosings, and not many in which his wife did not think it necessary to go likewise; and till Elizabeth recollected that there might be other family livings to be disposed of, she could not understand the sacrifice of so many hours. Now and then, they were honoured with a call from her Ladyship, and nothing escaped her observation that was passing in the room during these visits. She examined into their employments, looked at their work, and advised them to do it differently; found fault with the arrangement of the furniture, or detected the housemaid in negligence; and if she accepted any refreshment, seemed to do it only for the sake of finding out that Mrs Collins's joints of meat were too large for her family.

Elizabeth soon perceived that though this great lady was not in the commission of the peace for the county, she was a most active magistrate in her own parish, the minutest concerns of which were carried to her by Mr Collins; and whenever any of the cottagers were disposed to be quarrelsome, discontented or too poor, she sallied forth into the village to settle their differences, silence their complaints, and scold them into harmony and plenty.

The entertainment of dining at Rosings was repeated about twice a week; and, allowing for the loss of Sir William, and there being only one card table in the evening, every such entertainment was the counterpart of the first. Their other engagements were few; as the style of living of the neighbourhood in general, was beyond the Collinses' reach. This however was no evil to Elizabeth, and upon the whole she spent her time comfortably enough; there were half hours of pleasant conversation with Charlotte, and the weather was so fine for the time of year, that she had often great enjoyment out of doors. Her favourite walk, and where she frequently went while the others were calling on Lady Catherine, was along the open grove which edged that side of the park, where there was a nice sheltered path, which no one seemed to value but herself, and where she felt beyond the reach of Lady Catherine's curiosity.

In this quiet way, the first fortnight of her visit soon passed away. Easter was approaching, and the week preceding it, was to bring an addition to the family at Rosings, which in so small a circle must be important. Elizabeth had heard soon after her arrival, that Mr Darcy was expected there in the course of a few weeks, and though there were not many of her acquaintance whom she did not prefer, his coming would furnish one comparatively new to look at in their Rosings parties, and she might be amused in seeing how hopeless Miss Bingley's designs on him were, by his behaviour to his cousin, for whom he was evidently destined by Lady Catherine; who talked of his coming with the greatest satisfaction, spoke of him in terms of the highest admiration, and seemed almost angry to find that he had already been frequently seen by Miss Lucas and herself.

His arrival was soon known at the Parsonage, for Mr Collins was walking the whole morning within view of the lodges opening into Hunsford Lane, in order to have the earliest assurance of it; and after making his bow as the carriage turned into the Park, hurried home with the great intelligence. On the following morning he hastened to Rosings to pay his respects. There were two nephews of Lady Catherine to require them, for Mr Darcy had brought with him a Colonel Fitzwilliam, the younger son of his uncle, Lord — and to the great surprise of all the party, when Mr Collins returned the gentlemen accompanied him. Charlotte had seen them from her husband's room, crossing the road, and immediately running into the other, told the girls what an honour they might expect, adding,

'I may thank you, Eliza, for this piece of civility. Mr Darcy would never have come so soon to wait upon me.'

Elizabeth had scarcely time to disclaim all right to the compliment, before their approach was announced by the door-bell, and shortly afterwards the three gentlemen entered the room. Colonel Fitzwilliam, who led the way, was about thirty, not handsome, but in person and address most truly the gentleman. Mr Darcy looked just as he had been used to look in Hertfordshire, paid his compliments, with his usual reserve, to Mrs Collins; and whatever might be his feelings towards her friend, met her with every appearance of composure. Elizabeth merely curtseyed to him, without saying a word.

Colonel Fitzwilliam entered into conversation directly with the readiness and ease of a well-bred man, and talked very pleasantly; but his cousin, after having addressed a slight observation on the house and garden to Mrs Collins, sat for some time without speaking to any body. At length, however, his civility was so far awakened as to enquire of Elizabeth after the health of her family. She answered him in the usual way, and after a moment's pause, added,

'My eldest sister has been in town these three months. Have you never happened to see her there?'

She was perfectly sensible that he never had; but she wished to see whether he would betray any consciousness of what had passed between the Bingleys and Jane; and she thought he looked a little confused as he answered that he had never been so fortunate as to meet Miss Bennet. The subject was pursued no farther, and the gentlemen soon afterwards went away.

Chapter Thirty One

COLONEL FITZWILLIAM'S MANNERS WERE very much admired at the parsonage, and the ladies all felt that he must add considerably to the pleasure of their engagements at Rosings. It was some days, however, before they received any invitation thither, for while there were visitors in the house, they could not be necessary; and it was not till Easter-day, almost a week after the gentlemen's arrival, that they were honoured by such an attention, and then they were merely asked on leaving church to come there in the evening. For the last week they had seen very little of either Lady Catherine or her daughter. Colonel Fitzwilliam had called at the parsonage more than once during the time, but Mr Darcy they had only seen at church.

The invitation was accepted of course, and at a proper hour they joined the party in Lady Catherine's drawing room. Her ladyship received them civilly, but it was plain that their company was by no means so acceptable as when she could get nobody else; and she was, in fact, almost engrossed by her nephews, speaking to them, especially to Darcy, much more than to any other person in the room.

Colonel Fitzwilliam seemed really glad to see them; any thing was a welcome relief to him at Rosings; and Mrs Collins's pretty friend had moreover caught his fancy very much. He now seated himself by her, and talked so agreeably of Kent and Hertfordshire, of travelling and staying at home, of new books and music, that Elizabeth had never been half so well entertained in that room before; and they conversed with so much spirit and flow, as to draw the attention of Lady Catherine herself, as well as of Mr Darcy. *His* eyes had been soon and repeatedly turned towards them with a look of curiosity; and that her ladyship after a while shared the feeling, was more openly acknowledged, for she did not scruple to call out,

'What is that you are saying, Fitzwilliam? What is it you are talking of? What are you telling Miss Bennet? Let me hear what it is.'

'We are speaking of music, Madam,' said he, when no longer able to avoid a reply.

'Of music! Then pray speak aloud. It is of all subjects my delight. I must have my share in the conversation, if you are speaking of music. There are few people in England, I suppose, who have more true enjoyment of music than myself, or a better natural taste. If I had ever learnt, I should have been a great proficient. And so would Anne, if her health had allowed her to apply. I am confident that she would have performed delightfully. How does Georgiana get on, Darcy?'

Mr Darcy spoke with affectionate praise of his sister's proficiency.

'I am very glad to hear such a good account of her,' said Lady Catherine; 'and pray tell her from me, that she cannot expect to excel, if she does not practise a great deal.'

'I assure you, Madam,' he replied, 'that she does not need such advice. She practises very constantly.'

'So much the better. It cannot be done too much; and when I next write to her, I shall charge her not to neglect it on any account. I often tell young ladies, that no excellence in music is to be acquired, without constant practice. I have told Miss Bennet several times, that she will never play really well, unless she practises more; and though Mrs Collins has no instrument, she is very welcome, as I have often told her, to come to Rosings every day, and play on the piano-forte in Mrs Jenkinson's room. She would be in nobody's way, you know, in that part of the house.'

Mr Darcy looked a little ashamed of his aunt's ill breeding, and made no answer.

When coffee was over, Colonel Fitzwilliam reminded Elizabeth of having promised to play for him; and she sat down directly to the instrument. He drew a chair near her. Lady Catherine listened to half a song, and then talked, as before, to her other nephew; till the latter walked away from her, and moving with his usual deliberation towards the piano-forte, stationed himself so as to command a full view of the fair performer's countenance. Elizabeth saw what he was doing, and at the first convenient pause, turned to him with an arch smile, and said,

'You mean to frighten me, Mr Darcy, by coming in all this state to hear me? But I will not be alarmed though your sister *does* play so well. There is a stubbornness about me that never can bear to be frightened at the will of others. My courage always rises with every attempt to intimidate me.'

'I shall not say that you are mistaken,' he replied, 'because you could not really believe me to entertain any design of alarming you; and I have had the pleasure of your acquaintance long enough to know, that you find great enjoyment in occasionally professing opinions which in fact are not your own.'

Elizabeth laughed heartily at this picture of herself, and said to Colonel Fitzwilliam, 'Your cousin will give you a very pretty notion of me, and teach you not to believe a word I say. I am particularly unlucky in meeting with a person so well able to expose my real character, in a part of the world, where I had hoped to pass myself off with some degree of credit. Indeed, Mr

Darcy, it is very ungenerous in you to mention all that you knew to my disadvantage in Hertfordshire – and, give me leave to say, very impolitic too – for it is provoking me to retaliate, and such things may come out, as will shock your relations to hear.'

'I am not afraid of you,' said he, smilingly.

'Pray let me hear what you have to accuse him of,' cried Colonel Fitzwilliam. 'I should like to know how he behaves among strangers.'

'You shall hear then – but prepare yourself for something very dreadful. The first time of my ever seeing him in Hertfordshire, you must know, was at a ball – and at this ball, what do you think he did? He danced only four dances! I am sorry to pain you – but so it was. He danced only four dances, though gentlemen were scarce; and, to my certain knowledge, more than one young lady was sitting down in want of a partner. Mr Darcy, you cannot deny the fact.'

'I had not at that time the honour of knowing any lady in the assembly beyond my own party.'

'True; and nobody can ever be introduced in a ball room. Well, Colonel Fitzwilliam, what do I play next? My fingers wait your orders.'

'Perhaps,' said Darcy, 'I should have judged better, had I sought an introduction, but I am ill qualified to recommend myself to strangers.'

'Shall we ask your cousin the reason of this?' said Elizabeth, still addressing Colonel Fitzwilliam. 'Shall we ask him why a man of sense and education, and who has lived in the world, is ill qualified to recommend himself to strangers?'

'I can answer your question,' said Fitzwilliam, 'without applying to him. It is because he will not give himself the trouble.'

'I certainly have not the talent which some people possess,' said Darcy, 'of conversing easily with those I have never seen before. I cannot catch their tone of conversation, or appear interested in their concerns, as I often see done.'

'My fingers,' said Elizabeth, 'do not move over this instrument in the masterly manner which I see so many women's do. They have not the same force or rapidity, and do not produce the same expression. But then I have always supposed it to be my own fault – because I would not take the trouble of practising. It is not that I do not believe *my* fingers as capable as any other woman's of superior execution.'

Darcy smiled and said, 'You are perfectly right. You have employed your time much better. No one admitted to the privilege of hearing you, can think any thing wanting. We neither of us perform to strangers.'

Here they were interrupted by Lady Catherine, who called out to know what they were talking of. Elizabeth immediately began playing again. Lady Catherine approached, and, after listening for a few minutes, said to Darcy,

'Miss Bennet would not play at all amiss, if she practised more, and could have the advantage of a London master. She has a very good notion of fingering, though her taste is not equal to Anne's. Anne would have been a delightful performer, had her health allowed her to learn.'

Elizabeth looked at Darcy to see how cordially he assented to his cousin's praise; but neither at that moment nor at any other could she discern any symptom of love; and from the whole of his behaviour to Miss de Bourgh she derived this comfort for Miss Bingley, that he might have been just as likely to marry *her*, had she been his relation.

Lady Catherine continued her remarks on Elizabeth's performance, mixing with them many instructions on execution and taste. Elizabeth received them with all the forbearance of civility; and at the request of the gentlemen remained at the instrument till her Ladyship's carriage was ready to take them all home.

Chapter Thirty Two

ELIZABETH WAS SITTING BY HERSELF the next morning, and writing to Jane, while Mrs Collins and Maria were gone on business into the village, when she was startled by a ring at the door, the certain signal of a visitor. As she had heard no carriage, she thought it not unlikely to be Lady Catherine, and under that apprehension was putting away her half-finished letter that she might escape all impertinent questions, when the door opened, and to her very great surprise, Mr Darcy, and Mr Darcy only, entered the room.

He seemed astonished too on finding her alone, and apologised for his intrusion, by letting her know that he had understood all the ladies to be within.

They then sat down, and when her enquiries after Rosings were made, seemed in danger of sinking into total silence. It was absolutely necessary, therefore, to think of something, and in this emergence recollecting *when* she had seen him last in Hertfordshire, and feeling curious to know what he would say on the subject of their hasty departure, she observed,

'How very suddenly you all quitted Netherfield last November, Mr Darcy! It must have been a most agreeable surprise to Mr Bingley to see you all after him so soon; for, if I recollect right, he went but the day before. He and his sisters were well, I hope, when you left London.'

'Perfectly so – I thank you.'

She found that she was to receive no other answer – and, after a short pause, added,

'I think I have understood that Mr Bingley has not much idea of ever returning to Netherfield again?'

'I have never heard him say so; but it is probable that he may spend very little of his time there in future. He has many friends, and he is at a time of life when friends and engagements are continually increasing.'

'If he means to be but little at Netherfield, it would be better for the neighbourhood that he should give up the place entirely, for then we might possibly get a settled family there. But perhaps Mr Bingley did not take the house so much for the convenience of the neighbourhood as for his own, and we must expect him to keep or quit it on the same principle.'

'I should not be surprised,' said Darcy, 'if he were to give it up, as soon as any eligible purchase offers.'

Elizabeth made no answer. She was afraid of talking longer of his friend; and, having nothing else to say, was now determined to leave the trouble of finding a subject to him.

He took the hint, and soon began with, 'This seems a very comfortable house. Lady Catherine, I believe, did a great deal to it when Mr Collins first came to Hunsford.'

'I believe she did – and I am sure she could not have bestowed her kindness on a more grateful object.'

'Mr Collins appears very fortunate in his choice of a wife.'

'Yes, indeed; his friends may well rejoice in his having met with one of the very few sensible women who would have accepted him, or have made him happy if they had. My friend has an excellent understanding – though I am not certain that I consider her marrying Mr Collins as the wisest thing she ever did. She seems perfectly happy, however, and in a prudential light, it is certainly a very good match for her.'

'It must be very agreeable to her to be settled within so easy a distance of her own family and friends.'

'An easy distance do you call it? It is nearly fifty miles.'

'And what is fifty miles of good road? Little more than half a day's journey. Yes, I call it a *very* easy distance.'

'I should never have considered the distance as one of the *advantages* of the match,' cried Elizabeth. 'I should never have said Mrs Collins was settled *near* her family.'

'It is a proof of your own attachment to Hertfordshire. Any thing beyond the very neighbourhood of Longbourn, I suppose, would appear far.'

As he spoke there was a sort of smile, which Elizabeth fancied she understood; he must be supposing her to be thinking of Jane and Netherfield, and she blushed as she answered,

'I do not mean to say that a woman may not be settled too near her family. The far and the near must be relative, and depend on many varying circumstances. Where there is fortune to make the expence of travelling unimportant, distance becomes no evil. But that is not the case *here*. Mr and Mrs Collins have a comfortable income, but not such a one as will allow of frequent journeys – and I am persuaded my friend would not call herself *near* her family under less than *half* the present distance.'

Mr Darcy drew his chair a little towards her, and said, '*You* cannot have a right to such very strong local attachment. *You* cannot have been always at Longbourn.'

Elizabeth looked surprised. The gentleman experienced some change of feeling; he drew back his chair, took a newspaper from the table, and, glancing over it, said, in a colder voice,

'Are you pleased with Kent?'

A short dialogue on the subject of the country ensued, on either side calm and concise – and soon put an end to by the entrance of Charlotte and her sister, just returned from their walk. The tête-à-tête surprised them. Mr Darcy related the mistake which had occasioned his intruding on Miss Bennet, and after sitting a few minutes longer without saying much to any body, went away.

'What can be the meaning of this!' said Charlotte, as soon as he was gone. 'My dear Eliza he must be in love with you, or he would never have called on us in this familiar way.'

But when Elizabeth told of his silence, it did not seem very likely, even to Charlotte's wishes, to be the case; and after various conjectures, they could at last only suppose his visit to proceed from the difficulty of finding any thing to do, which was the more probable from the time of year. All field sports were over. Within doors there was Lady Catherine, books, and a billiard table, but gentlemen cannot be always within doors; and in the nearness of the Parsonage, or the pleasantness of the walk to it, or of the people who lived in it, the two cousins found a temptation from this period of walking thither almost every day. They called at various times of the morning, sometimes separately, sometimes together, and now and then accompanied by their aunt. It was plain to them all that Colonel Fitzwilliam came because he had pleasure in their society, a persuasion which of course recommended him still more; and Elizabeth was reminded by her own satisfaction in being with him, as well as by his evident admiration of her, of her former favourite George Wickham; and though, in comparing them, she saw there was less captivating softness in Colonel Fitzwilliam's manners, she believed he might have the best informed mind.

But why Mr Darcy came so often to the Parsonage, it was more difficult to understand. It could not be for society, as he frequently sat there ten minutes together without opening his lips; and when he did speak, it seemed the effect of necessity rather than of choice – a sacrifice to propriety, not a pleasure to himself. He seldom appeared really animated. Mrs Collins knew not what to make of him. Colonel Fitzwilliam's occasionally laughing at his stupidity, proved that he was generally different, which her own knowledge of him could not have told her; and as she would have liked to believe this change the effect of love, and the object of that love, her friend Eliza, she sat herself seriously to work to find it out. – She watched him whenever they were at Rosings, and whenever he came to Hunsford; but without much success. He certainly looked at her friend a great deal, but the expression of that look was disputable. It was an earnest, steadfast gaze, but she often doubted whether there were much admiration in it, and sometimes it seemed nothing but absence of mind.

She had once or twice suggested to Elizabeth the possibility of his being partial to her, but Elizabeth always laughed at the idea; and Mrs Collins did not think it right to press the subject, from the danger of raising expectations which might only end in disappointment; for in her opinion it admitted not of a doubt, that all her friend's dislike would vanish, if she could suppose him to be in her power.

In her kind schemes for Elizabeth, she sometimes planned her marrying Colonel Fitzwilliam. He was beyond comparison the pleasantest man; he certainly admired her, and his situation in life was most eligible; but, to counterbalance these advantages, Mr Darcy had considerable patronage in the church, and his cousin could have none at all.

Chapter Thirty Three

MORE THAN ONCE DID ELIZABETH IN her ramble within the Park, unexpectedly meet Mr Darcy. – She felt all the perverseness of the mischance that should bring him where no one else was brought; and to prevent its ever happening again, took care to inform him at first, that it was a favourite haunt of hers.

– How it could occur a second time therefore was very odd! – Yet it did, and even a third. It seemed like wilful ill-nature, or a voluntary penance, for on these occasions it was not merely a few formal enquiries and an awkward pause and then away, but he actually thought it necessary to turn back and walk with her. He never said a great deal, nor did she give herself the trouble of talking or of listening much; but it struck her in the course of their third rencontre that he was asking some odd unconnected questions – about her pleasure in being at Hunsford, her love of solitary walks, and her opinion of Mr and Mrs Collins's happiness; and that in speaking of Rosings and her not perfectly understanding the house, he seemed to expect that whenever she came into Kent again she would be staying *there* too. His words seemed to imply it. Could he have Colonel Fitzwilliam in his thoughts? She supposed, if he meant any thing, he must mean an allusion to what might arise in that quarter. It distressed her a little, and she was quite glad to find herself at the gate in the pales opposite the Parsonage.

She was engaged one day as she walked, in re-perusing Jane's last letter, and dwelling on some passages which proved that Jane had not written in spirits, when, instead of being again surprised by Mr Darcy, she saw on looking up that Colonel Fitzwilliam was meeting her. Putting away the letter immediately and forcing a smile, she said,

'I did not know before that you ever walked this way.'

'I have been making the tour of the Park,' he replied, 'as I generally do every year, and intend to close it with a call at the Parsonage. Are you going much farther?'

'No, I should have turned in a moment.'

And accordingly she did turn, and they walked towards the Parsonage together.

'Do you certainly leave Kent on Saturday?' said she.

'Yes – if Darcy does not put it off again. But I am at his disposal. He arranges the business just as he pleases.'

'And if not able to please himself in the arrangement, he has at least great pleasure in the power of choice. I do not know any body who seems more to enjoy the power of doing what he like than Mr Darcy.'

'He likes to have his own way very well,' replied Colonel Fitzwilliam. 'But so we all do. It is only that he has better means of having it than many others, because he is rich, and many others are poor. I speak feelingly. A younger son, you know, must be inured to self-denial and dependence.'

'In my opinion, the younger son of an Earl can know very little of either. Now, seriously, what have you ever known of self-denial and dependence? When have you been prevented by want of money from going wherever you chose, or procuring any thing you had a fancy for?'

'These are home questions – and perhaps I cannot say that I have experienced many hardships of that nature. But in matters of greater weight, I may suffer from the want of money. Younger sons cannot marry where they like.'

'Unless where they like women of fortune, which I think they very often do.'

'Our habits of expence make us too dependant, and there are not many in my rank of life who can afford to marry without some attention to money.'

'Is this,' thought Elizabeth, 'meant for me?' and she coloured at the idea; but, recovering herself, said in a lively tone, 'And pray, what is the usual price of an Earl's younger son? Unless the elder brother is very sickly, I suppose you would not ask above fifty thousand pounds.'

He answered her in the same style, and the subject dropped. To interrupt a silence which might make him fancy her affected with what had passed, she soon afterwards said,

'I imagine your cousin brought you down with him chiefly for the sake of having somebody at his disposal. I wonder he does not marry, to secure a lasting convenience of that kind. But, perhaps his sister does as well for the present, and, as she is under his sole care, he may do what he likes with her.'

'No,' said Colonel Fitzwilliam, 'that is an advantage which he must divide with me. I am joined with him in the guardianship of Miss Darcy.'

'Are you, indeed? And pray what sort of guardians do you make? Does your charge give you much trouble? Young ladies of her age, are sometimes a little difficult to manage, and if she has the true Darcy spirit, she may like to have her own way.'

As she spoke, she observed him looking at her earnestly, and the manner in which he immediately asked her why she supposed Miss Darcy likely to give them any uneasiness, convinced her that she had somehow or other got pretty near the truth. She directly replied,

'You need not be frightened. I never heard any harm of her; and I dare say she is one of the most tractable creatures in the world. She is a very great favourite with some ladies of my acquaintance, Mrs Hurst and Miss Bingley. I think I have heard you say that you know them.'

'I know them a little. Their brother is a pleasant gentleman-like man – he is a great friend of Darcy's.'

'Oh! yes,' said Elizabeth drily – 'Mr Darcy is uncommonly kind to Mr Bingley, and takes a prodigious deal of care of him.'

'Care of him! – Yes, I really believe Darcy *does* take care of him in those points where he most wants care. From something that he told me in our journey hither, I have reason to think Bingley very much indebted to him. But I ought to beg his pardon, for I have no right to suppose that Bingley was the person meant. It was all conjecture.'

'What is it you mean?'

'It is a circumstance which Darcy of course would not wish to be generally known, because if it were to get round to the lady's family, it would be an unpleasant thing.'

'You may depend upon my not mentioning it.'

'And remember that I have not much reason for supposing it to be Bingley. What he told me was merely this; that he congratulated himself on having lately saved a friend from the inconveniences of a most imprudent marriage, but without mentioning names or any other particulars, and I only suspected it to be Bingley from believing him the kind of young man to get into a scrape of that sort, and from knowing them to have been together the whole of last summer.

'Did Mr Darcy give you his reasons for this interference?'

'I understood that there were some very strong objections against the lady.'

'And what arts did he use to separate them?'

'He did not talk to me of his own arts,' said Fitzwilliam smiling. 'He only told me, what I have now told you.'

Elizabeth made no answer, and walked on, her heart swelling with indignation. After watching her a little, Fitzwilliam asked her why she was so thoughtful.

'I am thinking of what you have been telling me,' said she. 'Your cousin's conduct does not suit my feelings. Why was he to be the judge?'

'You are rather disposed to call his interference officious?'

'I do not see what right Mr Darcy had to decide on the propriety of his friend's inclination, or why, upon his own judgment alone, he was to determine and direct in what manner that friend was to be happy.' 'But,' she continued, recollecting herself, 'as we know none of the particulars, it is not fair to condemn him. It is not to be supposed that there was much affection in the case.'

'That is not an unnatural surmise,' said Fitzwilliam, 'but it is lessening the honour of my cousin's triumph very sadly.'

This was spoken jestingly, but it appeared to her so just a picture of Mr Darcy, that she would not trust herself with an answer; and, therefore, abruptly changing the conversation, talked on indifferent matters till they reached the parsonage. There, shut into her own room, as soon as their visitor left them, she could think without interruption of all that she had heard. It was not to be supposed that any other people could be meant than those with whom she was connected. There could not exist in the world two men, over whom Mr Darcy could have such boundless influence. That he had been concerned in the measures taken to separate Mr Bingley and Jane, she had never doubted; but she had always attributed to Miss Bingley the principal design and arrangement of them. If his own vanity, however, did not mislead him, he was the cause, his pride and caprice were the cause of all that Jane had suffered, and still continued to suffer. He had ruined for a while every hope of happiness for the most affectionate, generous heart in the world; and no one could say how lasting an evil he might have inflicted.

'There were some very strong objections against the lady,' were Colonel Fitzwilliams's words, and these strong objections probably were, her having one uncle who was a country attorney, and another who was in business in London.

'To Jane herself,' she exclaimed, 'there could be no possibility of objection. All loveliness and goodness as she is! Her understanding excellent, her mind improved, and her manners captivating. Neither could any thing be urged against my father, who, though with some peculiarities, has abilities which Mr Darcy himself need not disdain, and respectability which he will probably never reach.' When she thought of her mother indeed, her confidence gave way a little, but she would not allow that any objections there had material weight with Mr Darcy, whose pride, she was convinced, would receive a deeper wound from the want of importance in his friend's connections, than from their want of sense; and she was quite decided at last, that he had been partly governed by this worst kind of pride, and partly by the wish of retaining Mr Bingley for his sister.

The agitation and tears which the subject occasioned, brought on a headache; and it grew so much worse towards the evening that, added to her unwillingness to see Mr Darcy, it determined her not to attend her cousins to Rosings, where they were engaged to drink tea. Mrs Collins, seeing that she was really unwell, did not press her to go, and as much as possible prevented her husband from pressing her, but Mr Collins could not conceal his apprehension of Lady Catherine's being rather displeased by her staying at home.

Chapter Thirty Four

WHEN THEY WERE GONE, ELIZABETH, as if intending to exasperate herself as much as possible against Mr Darcy, chose for her employment the examination of all the letters which Jane had written to her since her being in Kent. They contained no actual complaint, nor was there any revival of past occurrences, or any communication of present suffering. But in all, and in almost every line of each, there was a want of that cheerfulness which had been used to characterize her style, and which, proceeding from the serenity of a mind at ease with itself, and kindly disposed towards every one, had been scarcely ever clouded. Elizabeth noticed every sentence conveying the idea of uneasiness, with an attention which it had hardly received on the first perusal. Mr Darcy's shameful boast of what misery he had been able to inflict, gave her a keener sense of her sister's sufferings. It was some consolation to think that his visit to Rosings was to end on the day after the next, and a still greater, that in less than a fortnight she should herself be with Jane again, and enabled to contribute to the recovery of her spirits, by all that affection could do.

She could not think of Darcy's leaving Kent, without remembering that his cousin was to go with him; but Colonel Fitzwilliam had made it clear that he had no intentions at all, and agreeable as he was, she did not mean to be unhappy about him.

While settling this point, she was suddenly roused by the sound of the door bell, and her spirits were a little fluttered by the idea of its being Colonel Fitzwilliam himself, who had once before called late in the evening, and might now come to enquire particularly after her. But this idea was soon banished, and her spirits were very differently affected, when, to her utter amazement, she saw Mr Darcy walk into the room. In an hurried manner he immediately began an enquiry after her health, imputing his visit to a wish of hearing that she were better. She answered him with cold civility. He sat down for a few moments, and then getting up walked about the room. Elizabeth was surprised, but said not a word. After a silence of several minutes he came towards her in an agitated manner, and thus began.

'In vain have I struggled. It will not do. My feelings will not be repressed. You must allow me to tell you how ardently I admire and love you.'

Elizabeth's astonishment was beyond expression. She stared, coloured, doubted, and was silent. This he considered sufficient encouragement, and the avowal of all that he felt and had long felt for her, immediately followed. He spoke well, but there were feelings besides those of the heart to be detailed, and he was not more eloquent on the subject of tenderness than of pride. His sense of her inferiority – of its being a degradation – of the family obstacles which judgment had always opposed to inclination, were dwelt on with a warmth which seemed due to the consequence he was wounding, but was very unlikely to recommend his suit.

In spite of her deeply-rooted dislike, she could not be insensible to the compliment of such a man's affection, and though her intentions did not vary for an instant, she was at first sorry for the pain he was to receive; till, roused to resentment by his subsequent language, she lost all compassion in anger. She tried, however, to compose herself to answer him with patience, when he should have done. He concluded with representing to her the strength of that attachment which, in spite of all his endeavours, he had found impossible to conquer; and with expressing his hope that it would now be rewarded by her acceptance of his hand. As he said this, she could easily see that he had no doubt of a favourable answer. He *spoke* of apprehension and anxiety, but his countenance expressed real security. Such a circumstance could only exasperate farther, and when he ceased, the colour rose into her cheeks, and she said,

'In such cases as this, it is, I believe, the established mode to express a sense of obligation for the sentiments avowed, however unequally they may be returned. It is natural that obligation should be felt, and if I could *feel* gratitude, I would now thank you. But I cannot – I have never desired your good opinion, and you have certainly bestowed it most unwillingly. I am sorry to have occasioned pain to any one. It has been most unconsciously done, however, and I hope will be of short duration. The feelings which, you tell me, have long prevented the acknowledgment of your regard, can have little difficulty in overcoming it after this explanation.'

Mr Darcy, who was leaning against the mantel-piece with his eyes fixed on her face, seemed to catch her words with no less resentment than surprise. His complexion became pale with anger, and the disturbance of his mind was visible in every feature. He was struggling for the appearance of composure, and would not open his lips, till he believed himself to have attained it. The pause was to Elizabeth's feelings dreadful. At length, in a voice of forced calmness, he said,

'And this is all the reply which I am to have the honour of expecting! I might, perhaps, wish to be informed why, with so little *endeavour* at civility, I am thus rejected. But it is of small importance.'

'I might as well enquire,' replied she, 'why with so evident a design of offending and insulting me, you chose to tell me that you liked me against your will, against your reason, and even against your character? Was not this some excuse for incivility, if I *was* uncivil? But I have other provocations. You know I have. Had not my own feelings decided against you, had they been indifferent, or had they even been favourable, do you think that any consideration would tempt me to accept the man, who has been the means of ruining, perhaps for ever, the happiness of a most beloved sister?'

As she pronounced these words, Mr Darcy changed colour; but the emotion was short, and he listened without attempting to interrupt her while she continued.

'I have every reason in the world to think ill of you. No motive can excuse the unjust and ungenerous part you acted *there*. You dare not, you cannot deny that you have been the principal, if not the only means of dividing them from each other, of exposing one to the censure of the world for caprice and instability, the other to its derision for disappointed hopes, and involving them both in misery of the acutest kind.'

She paused, and saw with no slight indignation that he was listening with an air which proved him wholly unmoved by any feeling of remorse. He even looked at her with a smile of affected incredulity.

'Can you deny that you have done it?' she repeated.

With assumed tranquillity he then replied, 'I have no wish of denying that I did every thing in my power to separate my friend from your sister, or that I rejoice in my success. Towards *him* I have been kinder than towards myself.'

Elizabeth disdained the appearance of noticing this civil reflection, but its meaning did not escape, nor was it likely to conciliate her.

'But it is not merely this affair,' she continued, 'on which my dislike is founded. Long before it had taken place, my opinion of you was decided. Your character was unfolded in the recital which I received many months ago from Mr Wickham. On this subject, what can you have to say? In what imaginary act of friendship can you here defend yourself? or under what misrepresentation, can you here impose upon others?'

'You take an eager interest in that gentleman's concerns,' said Darcy in a less tranquil tone, and with a heightened colour.

'Who that knows what his misfortunes have been, can help feeling an interest in him?'

'His misfortunes!' repeated Darcy contemptuously; 'yes, his misfortunes have been great indeed.'

'And of your infliction,' cried Elizabeth with energy. 'You have reduced him to his present state of poverty, comparative poverty. You have withheld the advantages, which you must know to have been designed for him. You have deprived the best years of his life, of that independence which was no less his due than his desert. You have done all this! and yet you can treat the mention of his misfortunes with contempt and ridicule.'

'And this,' cried Darcy, as he walked with quick steps across the room, 'is your opinion of me! This is the estimation in which you hold me! I thank you for explaining it so fully. My faults, according to this calculation, are heavy indeed! But perhaps,' added he, stopping in his walk, and turning towards her, 'these offences might have been overlooked, had not your pride been hurt by my honest confession of the scruples that had long prevented my forming any serious design. These bitter accusations might have been suppressed, had I with greater policy concealed my struggles, and flattered you into the belief of my being impelled by unqualified, unalloyed inclination; by reason, by reflection, by every thing. But disguise of every sort is my abhorrence. Nor am I ashamed of the feelings I related. They were natural and just. Could you expect me to rejoice in the inferiority of your connections? To congratulate myself on the hope of relations, whose condition in life is so decidedly beneath my own?'

Elizabeth felt herself growing more angry every moment; yet she tried to the utmost to speak with composure when she said,

'You are mistaken, Mr Darcy, if you suppose that the mode of your declaration affected me in any other way, than as it spared me the concern which I might have felt in refusing you, had you behaved in a more gentleman-like manner.'

She saw him start at this, but he said nothing, and she continued,

'You could not have made me the offer of your hand in any possible way that would have tempted me to accept it.'

Again his astonishment was obvious; and he looked at her with an expression of mingled incredulity and mortification. She went on.

'From the very beginning, from the first moment I may almost say, of my acquaintance with you, your manners impressing me with the fullest belief of your arrogance, your conceit, and your selfish disdain of the feelings of others, were such as to form that ground-work of disapprobation, on which succeeding events have built so immovable a dislike; and I had not known you a month before I felt that you were the last man in the world whom I could ever be prevailed on to marry.'

'You have said quite enough, madam. I perfectly comprehend your feelings, and have now only to be ashamed of what my own have been. Forgive me for having taken up so much of your time, and accept my best wishes for your health and happiness.'   And with these words he hastily left the room, and Elizabeth heard him the next moment open the front door and quit the house.

The tumult of her mind was now painfully great. She knew not how to support herself, and from actual weakness sat down and cried for half an hour. Her astonishment, as she reflected on what had passed, was increased by every review of it. That she should receive an offer of marriage from Mr Darcy! that he should have been in love with her for so many months! so much in love as to wish to marry her in spite of all the objections which had made him prevent his friend's marrying her sister, and which must appear at least with equal force in his own case, was almost incredible! it was gratifying to have inspired unconsciously so strong an affection. But his pride, his abominable pride, his shameless avowal of what he had done with respect to Jane, his unpardonable assurance in acknowledging, though he could not justify it, and the unfeeling manner in which he had mentioned Mr Wickham, his cruelty towards whom he had not attempted to deny, soon overcame the pity which the consideration of his attachment had for a moment excited.

She continued in very agitating reflections till the sound of Lady Catherine's carriage made her feel how unequal she was to encounter Charlotte's observation, and hurried her away to her room.

Chapter Thirty Five

ELIZABETH AWOKE THE NEXT MORNING to the same thoughts and meditations which had at length closed her eyes. She could not yet recover from the surprise of what had happened; it was impossible to think of any thing else, and totally indisposed for employment, she resolved soon after breakfast to indulge herself in air and exercise. She was proceeding directly to her favourite walk, when the recollection of Mr Darcy's sometimes coming there stopped her, and instead of entering the park, she turned up the lane, which led her farther from the turnpike road. The park paling was still the boundary on one side, and she soon passed one of the gates into the ground.

After walking two or three times along that part of the lane, she was tempted, by the pleasantness of the morning, to stop at the gates and look into the park. The five weeks which she had now passed in Kent, had made a great difference in the country, and every day was adding to the verdure of the early trees. She was on the point of continuing her walk, when she caught a glimpse of a gentleman within the sort of grove which edged the park; he was moving that way; and fearful of its being Mr Darcy, she was directly retreating. But the person who advanced, was now near enough to see her, and stepping forward with eagerness, pronounced her name. She had turned away, but on hearing herself called, though in a voice which proved it to be Mr Darcy, she moved again towards the gate. He had by that time reached it also, and holding out a letter, which she instinctively took, said with a look of haughty composure, 'I have been walking in the grove some time in the hope of meeting you. Will you do me the honour of reading that letter? – And then, with a slight bow, turned again into the plantation, and was soon out of sight.

With no expectation of pleasure, but with the strongest curiosity, Elizabeth opened the letter, and to her still increasing wonder, perceived an envelope containing two sheets of letter paper, written quite through, in a very close hand. – The envelope itself was likewise full. – Pursuing her way along the lane, she then began it. It was dated from Rosings, at eight o'clock in the morning, and was as follows: –

Be not alarmed, Madam, on receiving this letter, by the apprehension of its containing any repetition of those sentiments, or renewal of those offers, which were last night so disgusting to you. I write without any intention of paining you, or humbling myself, by dwelling on wishes, which, for the happiness of both, cannot be too soon forgotten; and the effort which the formation, and the perusal of this letter must occasion, should have been spared, had not my character required it to be written and read. You must, therefore, pardon the freedom with which I demand your attention; your feelings, I know, will bestow it unwillingly, but I demand it of your justice.

Two offences of a very different nature, and by no means of equal magnitude, you last night laid to my charge. The first mentioned was that, regardless of the sentiments of either, I had detached Mr Bingley from your sister, – and the other, that I had, in defiance of various claims, in defiance of honour and humanity, ruined the immediate prosperity, and blasted the prospects of Mr Wickham. – Wilfully and wantonly to have thrown off the companion of my youth, the acknowledged favourite of my father, a young man who had scarcely any other dependence than on our patronage, and who had been brought up to expect its exertion, would be a depravity, to which the separation of two young persons, whose affection could be the growth of only a few weeks, could bear no comparison. – But from the severity of that blame which was last night so liberally bestowed, respecting each circumstance, I shall hope to be in future secured, when the following account of my actions and their motives has been read. – If, in the explanation of them which is due to myself, I am under the necessity of relating feelings which may be offensive to your's, I can only say that I am sorry. – The necessity must be obeyed – and farther apology would be absurd. – I had not been long in Hertfordshire, before I saw, in common with others, that Bingley preferred your eldest sister, to any other young woman in the country. – But it was not till the evening of the dance at Netherfield that I had any apprehension of his feeling a serious attachment. – I had often seen him in love before. – At that ball, while I had the honour of dancing with you, I was first made acquainted, by Sir William Lucas's accidental information, that Bingley's attentions to your sister had given rise to a general expectation of their marriage. He spoke of it as a certain event, of which the time alone could be undecided. From that moment I observed my friend's behaviour attentively; and I could then perceive that his partiality for Miss Bennet was beyond what I had ever witnessed in him. Your sister I also watched. – Her look and manners were open, cheerful and engaging as ever, but without any symptom of peculiar regard, and I remained convinced from the evening's scrutiny, that though she received his attentions with pleasure, she did not invite them by any participation of sentiment. – If you have not been mistaken here, I must have been in an error. Your superior knowledge of your sister must make the latter probable. – If it be so, if I have been misled by such error, to inflict pain on her, your resentment has not been unreasonable. But I shall not scruple to assert, that the serenity of your sister's countenance and air was such, as might have given the most acute observer, a conviction that, however amiable her temper, her heart was not likely to be easily touched. – That I was desirous of believing her indifferent is certain, – but I will venture to say that my investigations and decisions are not usually influenced by my hopes or fears. – I did not believe her to be indifferent because I wished it; – I believed it on impartial conviction, as truly as I wished it in reason. – My objections to the marriage were not merely those, which I last night acknowledged to have required the utmost force of passion to put aside, in my own case; the want of connection could not be so great an evil to my friend as to me. – But there were other causes of repugnance; – causes which, though still existing, and existing to an equal degree in both instances, I had myself endeavoured to forget, because they were not immediately before me. – These causes must be stated, though briefly. – The situation of your mother's family, though objectionable, was nothing in comparison of that total want of propriety so frequently, so almost uniformly betrayed by herself, by your three younger sisters, and occasionally even by your father. – Pardon me. – It pains me to offend you. But amidst your concern for the defects of your nearest relations, and your displeasure at this representation of them, let it give you consolation to consider that, to have conducted yourselves so as to avoid any share of the like censure, is praise no less generally bestowed on you and your eldest sister, than it is honourable to the sense and disposition of both. – I will only say farther, that from what passed that evening, my opinion of all parties was confirmed, and every inducement heightened, which could have led me before, to preserve my friend from what I esteemed a most unhappy connection. – He left Netherfield for London, on the day following, as you, I am certain, remember, with the design of soon returning. – The part which I acted, is now to be explained. – His sisters' uneasiness had been equally excited with my own; our coincidence of feeling was soon discovered; and, alike sensible that no time was to be lost in detaching their brother, we shortly resolved on joining him directly in London. – We accordingly went – and there I readily engaged in the office of pointing out to my friend, the certain evils of such a choice. – I described, and enforced them earnestly. – But, however, this remonstrance might have staggered or delayed his determination, I do not suppose that it would ultimately have prevented the marriage, had it not been seconded by the assurance which I hesitated not in giving, of your sister's indifference. He had before believed her to return his affection with sincere, if not with equal regard. - But Bingley has great natural modesty, with a stronger dependence on my judgment than on his own. - To convince him, therefore, that he had deceived himself, was no very difficult point. To persuade him against returning into Hertfordshire, when that conviction had been given, was scarcely the work of a moment. - I cannot blame myself for having done thus much. There is but one part of my conduct in the whole affair, on which I do not reflect with satisfaction; it is that I condescended to adopt the measures of art so far as to conceal from him your sister's being in town. I knew it myself, as it was known to Miss Bingley, but her brother is even yet ignorant of it. - That they might have met without ill consequence, is perhaps probable; - but his regard did not appear to me enough extinguished for him to see her without some danger. - Perhaps this concealment, this disguise, was beneath me. - It is done, however, and it was done for the best. - On this subject I have nothing more to say, no other apology to offer. If I have wounded your sister's feelings, it was unknowingly done; and though the motives which governed me may to you very naturally appear insufficient, I have not yet learnt to condemn them. - With respect to that other, more weighty accusation, of having injured Mr Wickham, I can only refute it by laying before you the whole of his connection with my family. Of what he has particularly accused me I am ignorant; but of the truth of what I shall relate, I can summon more than one witness of undoubted veracity. Mr Wickham is the son of a very respectable man, who had for many years the management of all the Pemberley estates; and whose good conduct in the discharge of his trust, naturally inclined my father to be of service to him, and on George Wickham, who was his god-son, his kindness was therefore liberally bestowed. My father supported him at school, and afterwards at Cambridge; - most important assistance, as his own father, always poor from the extravagance of his wife, would have been unable to give him a gentleman's education. My father was not only fond of this young man's society, whose manners were always engaging; he had also the highest opinion of him, and hoping the church would be his profession, intended to provide for him in it. As for myself, it is many, many years since I first began to think of him in a very different manner. The vicious propensities - the want of principle which he was careful to guard from the knowledge of his best friend, could not escape the observation of a young man of nearly the same age with himself, and who had opportunities of seeing him in unguarded moments, which Mr Darcy could not have. Here again I shall give you pain - to what degree you only can tell. But whatever may be the sentiments which Mr Wickham has created, a suspicion of their nature shall not prevent me from unfolding his real character. It adds even another motive. My excellent father died about five years ago; and his attachment to Mr Wickham was to the last so steady, that in his will he particularly recommended it to me, to promote his advancement in the best manner that his profession might allow, and if he took orders, desired that a valuable family living might be his as soon as it became vacant. There was also a legacy of one thousand pounds. His own father did not long survive mine, and within half a year from these events, Mr Wickham wrote to inform me that, having finally resolved against taking orders, he hoped I should not think it unreasonable for him to expect some more immediate pecuniary advantage, in lieu of the preferment, by which he could not be benefited. He had some intention, he added, of studying the law, and I must be aware that the interest of one thousand pounds would be a very insufficient support therein. I rather wished, than believed him to be sincere; but at any rate, was perfectly ready to accede to his proposal. I knew that Mr Wickham ought not to be a clergyman. The business was therefore soon settled. He resigned all claim to assistance in the church, were it possible that he could ever be in a situation to receive it, and accepted in return three thousand pounds. All connection between us seemed now dissolved. I thought too ill of him, to invite him to Pemberley, or admit his society in town. In town I belive he chiefly lived, but his studying the law was a mere pretence, and being now free from all restraint, his life was a life of idleness and dissipation. For about three years I heard little of him; but on the decease of the incumbent of the living which had been designed for him, he applied to me again by letter for the presentation. His circumstances, he assured me, and I had no difficulty in believing it, were exceedingly bad. He had found the law a most unprofitable study, and was now absolutely resolved on being ordained, if I would present him to the living in question – of which he trusted there could be little doubt, as he was well assured that I had no other person to provide for, and I could not have forgotten my revered father's intentions. You will hardly blame me for refusing to comply with this entreaty, or for resisting every repetition of it. His resentment was in proportion to the distress of his circumstances – and he was doubtless as violent in his abuse of me to others, as in his reproaches to myself. After this period, every appearance of acquaintance was dropt. How he lived I know not. But last summer he was again most painfully obtruded on my notice. I must now mention a circumstance which I would wish to forget myself, and which no obligation less than the present should induce me to unfold to any human being. Having said thus much. I feel no doubt of your secrecy. My sister, who is more than ten years my junior, was left to the guardianship of my mother's nephew, Colonel Fitzwilliam, and myself. About a year ago, she was taken from school, and an establishment formed for her in London; and last summer she went with the lady who presided over it, to Ramsgate; and thither also went Mr Wickham, undoubtedly by design; for there proved to have been a prior acquaintance between him and Mrs Younge, in whose character we were most unhappily deceived; and by her connivance and aid, he so far recommended himself to Georgiana, whose affectionate heart retained a strong impression of his kindness to her as a child, that she was persuaded to believe herself in love, and to consent to an elopement. She was then but fifteen, which must be her excuse; and after stating her imprudence, I am happy to add, that I owed the knowledge of it to herself. I joined them unexpectedly a day or two before the intended elopement, and then Georgiana, unable to support the idea of grieving and offending a brother whom she almost looked up to as a father, acknowledged the whole to me. You may imagine what I felt and how I acted. Regard for my sister's credit and feelings prevented any public exposure, but I wrote to Mr Wickham, who left the place immediately, and Mrs Younge was of course removed from her charge. Mr Wickham's chief object was unquestionably my sister's fortune, which is thirty thousand pounds; but I cannot help supposing that the hope of revenging himself on me, was a strong inducement. His revenge would have been complete indeed. This, madam, is a faithful narrative of every event in which we have been concerned together; and if you do not absolutely reject it as false, you will, I hope, acquit me henceforth of cruelty towards Mr Wickham.

I know not in what manner, under what form of falsehood he has imposed on you; but his success is not perhaps to be wondered at, ignorant as you previously were of every thing concerning either. Detection could not be in your power, and suspicion certainly not in your inclination. You may possibly wonder why all this was not told you last night. But I was not then master enough of myself to know what could or ought to be revealed. For the truth of every thing here related, I can appeal more particularly to the testimony of Colonel Fitzwilliam, who from our near relationship and constant intimacy, and still more as one of the executors of my father's will, has been unavoidably acquainted with every particular of these transactions. If your abhorrence of me should make my assertions valueless, you cannot be prevented by the same cause from confiding in my cousin; and that there may be the possibility of consulting him, I shall endeavour to find some opportunity of putting this letter in your hands in the course of the morning. I will only add, God bless you.

FITZWILLIAM DARCY.

Chapter Thirty Six

IF ELIZABETH, WHEN MR DARCY GAVE her the letter, did not expect it to contain a renewal of his offers, she had formed no expectation at all of its contents. But such as they were, it may be well supposed how eagerly she went through them, and what a contrariety of emotion they excited. Her feelings as she read were scarcely to be defined. With amazement did she first understand that he believed any apology to be in his power; and steadfastly was she persuaded that he could have no explanation to give, which a just sense of shame would not conceal. With a strong prejudice against every thing he might say, she began his account of what had happened at Netherfield. She read, with an eagerness which hardly left her power of comprehension, and from impatience of knowing what the next sentence might bring, was incapable of attending to the sense of the one before her eyes. His belief of her sister's insensibility, she instantly resolved to be false, and his account of the real, the worst objections to the match, made her too angry to have any wish of doing him justice. He expressed no regret for what he had done which satisfied her; his style was not penitent, but haughty. It was all pride and insolence.

But when this subject was succeeded by his account of Mr Wickham, when she read with somewhat clearer attention, a relation of events, which, if true, must overthrow every cherished opinion of his worth, and which bore so alarming an affinity to his own history of himself, her feelings were yet more acutely painful and more difficult of definition. Astonishment, apprehension, and even horror, oppressed her. She wished to discredit it entirely, repeatedly exclaiming, 'This must be false! This cannot be! This must be the grossest falsehood!' – and when she had gone through the whole letter, though scarcely knowing any thing of the last page or two, put it hastily away, protesting that she would not regard it, that she would never look in it again.

In this perturbed state of mind, with thoughts that could rest on nothing, she walked on; but it would not do; in half a minute the letter was unfolded again, and collecting herself as well as she could, she again began the mortifying perusal of all that related to Wickham, and commanded herself so far as to examine the meaning of every sentence. The account of his connection with the Pemberley family, was exactly what he had related himself; and the kindness of the late Mr Darcy, though she had not before known its extent, agreed equally well with his own words. So far each recital confirmed the other: but when she came to the will, the difference was great. What Wickham had said of the living was fresh in her memory, and as she recalled his very words, it was impossible not to feel that there was gross duplicity on one side or the other; and, for a few moments, she flattered herself that her wishes did not err. But when she read, and re-read with the closest attention, the particulars immediately following of Wickham's resign-ing all pretensions to the living, of his receiving in lieu, so considerable a sum as three thousand pounds, again was she forced to hesitate. She put down the letter, weighed every circumstance with what she meant to be impartiality – deliberated on the probability of each statement – but with little success. On both sides it was only assertion. Again she read on. But every line proved more clearly that the affair, which she had believed it impossible that any contrivance could so represent, as to render Mr Darcy's conduct in it less than infamous, was capable of a turn which must make him entirely blameless throughout the whole.

The extravagance and general profligacy which he scrupled not to lay to Mr Wickham's charge, exceedingly shocked her; the more so, as she could bring no proof of its injustice. She had never heard of him before his entrance into the —shire Militia, in which he had engaged at the persuasion of the young man, who, on meeting him accidentally in town, had there renewed a slight acquaintance. Of his former way of life, nothing had been known in Hertfordshire but what he told himself. As to his real character, had information been in her power, she had never felt a wish of enquiring. His countenance, voice, and manner, had established him at once in the possession of every virtue. She tried to recollect some instance of goodness, some distinguished trait of integrity or benevolence, that might rescue him from the attacks of Mr Darcy; or at least, by the predominance of virtue, atone for those casual errors, under which she would endeavour to class, what Mr Darcy had described as the idleness and vice of many years continuance. But no such recollection befriended her. She could see him instantly before her, in every charm of air and address; but she could remember no more substantial good than the general approbation of the neighbourhood, and the regard which his social powers had gained him in the mess. After pausing on this point a considerable while, she once more continued to read. But, alas! the story which followed of his designs on Miss Darcy, received some confirmation from what had passed between Colonel Fitzwilliam and herself only the morning before; and at last she was referred for the truth of every particular to Colonel Fitzwilliam himself – from whom she had previously received the information of his near concern in all his cousin's affairs, and whose character she had no reason to question. At one time she had almost resolved on applying to him, but the idea was checked by the awkwardness of the application, and at length wholly banished by the conviction that Mr Darcy would never have hazarded such a proposal, if he had not been well assured of his cousin's corroboration.

She perfectly remembered every thing that had passed in conversation between Wickham and herself, in their first evening at Mr Philip's. Many of his expressions were still fresh in her memory. She was *now* struck with the impropriety of such communications to a stranger, and wondered it had escaped her before. She saw the indelicacy of putting himself forward as he had done, and the inconsistency of his professions with his conduct. She remembered that he had boasted of having no fear of seeing Mr Darcy – that Mr Darcy might leave the country, but that *he* should stand his ground; yet he had avoided the Netherfield ball the very next week. She remembered also, that till the Netherfield family had quitted the country, he had told his story to no one but herself; but that after their removal, it had been every where discussed; that he had then no reserves, no scruples in sinking Mr Darcy's character, though he had assured her that respect for the father, would always prevent his exposing the son.

How differently did every thing now appear in which he was concerned! His attentions to Miss King were now the consequence of views solely and hatefully mercenary; and the mediocrity of her fortune proved no longer the moderation of his wishes, but his eagerness to grasp at any thing. His behaviour to herself could now have had no tolerable motive; he had either been deceived with regard to her fortune, or had been gratifying his vanity by encouraging the preference which she believed she had most incautiously shewn. Every lingering struggle in his favour grew fainter and fainter; and in farther justification of Mr Darcy, she could not but allow that Mr Bingley, when questioned by Jane, had long ago asserted his blamelessness in the affair; that proud and repulsive as were his manners, she had never, in the whole course of their acquaintance, an acquaintance which had latterly brought them much together, and given her a sort of intimacy with his ways, seen any thing that betrayed him to be unprincipled or unjust – any thing that spoke him of irreligious or immoral habits. That among his own connections he was esteemed and valued – that even Wickham had allowed him merit as a brother, and that she had often heard him speak so affection-ately of his sister as to prove him capable of *some* amiable feeling. That had his actions been what Wickham represented them, so gross a violation of every thing right could hardly have been concealed from the world; and that friendship between a person capable of it, and such an amiable man as Mr Bingley, was incomprehensible.

She grew absolutely ashamed of herself. – Of neither Darcy nor Wickham could she think, without feeling that she had been blind, partial, prejudiced, absurd.

'How despicably have I acted!' she cried. – 'I, who have prided myself on my discernment! – I, who have valued myself on my abilities! who have often disdained the generous candour of my sister, and gratified my vanity, in useless or blameable distrust. – How humiliating is this discovery! – Yet, how just a humiliation! – Had I been in love, I could not have been more wretchedly blind. But vanity, not love, has been my folly. – Pleased with the preference of one, and offended by the neglect of the other, on the very beginning of our acquaintance, I have courted prepossession and ignorance, and driven reason away, where either were concerned. Till this moment, I never knew myself.'

From herself to Jane – from Jane to Bingley, her thoughts were in a line which soon brought to her recollection that Mr Darcy's explanation *there*, had appeared very insufficient; and she read it again. Widely different was the effect of a second perusal. – How could she deny that credit to his assertions, in one instance, which she had been obliged to give in the other? – He declared himself to have been totally unsuspicious of her sister's attachment; – and she could not help remembering what Charlotte's opinion had always been. – Neither could she deny the justice of his description of Jane. – She felt that Jane's feelings, though fervent, were little displayed, and that there was a constant complacency in her air and manner, not often united with great sensibility.

When she came to that part of the letter in which her family were mentioned, in terms of such mortifying, yet merited reproach, her sense of shame was severe. The justice of the charge struck her too forcibly for denial, and the circumstances to which he particularly alluded, as having passed at the Netherfield ball, and as confirming all his first disapprobation, could not have made a stronger impression on his mind than on hers.

The compliment to herself and her sister, was not unfelt. It soothed, but it could not console her for the contempt which had been thus self-attracted by the rest of her family; – and as she considered that Jane's disappointment had in fact been the work of her nearest relations, and reflected how materially the credit of both must be hurt by such impropriety of conduct, she felt depressed beyond any thing she had ever known before.

After wandering along the lane for two hours, giving way to every variety of thought; re-considering events, determining probabilities, and reconciling herself as well as she could, to a change so sudden and so important, fatigue, and a recollection of her long absence, made her at length return home; and she entered the house with the wish of appearing cheerful as usual, and the resolution of repressing such reflections as must make her unfit for conversation.

She was immediately told, that the two gentlemen from Rosings had each called during her absence; Mr Darcy, only for a few minutes to take leave, but that Colonel Fitzwilliam had been sitting with them at least an hour, hoping for her return, and almost resolving to walk after her till she could be found. – Elizabeth could but just *affect* concern in missing him; she really rejoiced at it. Colonel Fitzwilliam was no longer an object. She could think only of her letter.

Chapter Thirty Seven

THE TWO GENTLEMEN LEFT ROSINGS the next morning; and Mr Collins having been in waiting near the lodges, to make them his parting obeisance, was able to bring home the pleasing intelligence, of their appearing in very good health, and in as tolerable spirits as could be expected, after the melancholy scene so lately gone through at Rosings. To Rosings he then hastened to console Lady Catherine, and her daughter; and on his return, brought back, with great satisfaction, a message from her Ladyship, importing that she felt herself so dull as to make her very desirous of having them all to dine with her.

Elizabeth could not see Lady Catherine without recollecting, that had she chosen it, she might by this time have been presented to her, as her future niece; nor could she think, without a smile, of what her ladyship's indignation would have been. 'What would she have said? – how would she have behaved?' were questions with which she amused herself.

Their first subject was the diminution of the Rosings party. – 'I assure you, I feel it exceedingly,' said Lady Catherine; 'I believe nobody feels the loss of friends so much as I do. But I am particularly attached to these young men; and know them to be so much attached to me! – They were excessively sorry to go! But so they always are. The dear colonel rallied his spirits tolerably till just at last; but Darcy seemed to feel it most acutely, more I think than last year. His attachment to Rosings, certainly increases.'

Mr Collins had a compliment, and an allusion to throw in here, which were kindly smiled on by the mother and daughter.

Lady Catherine observed, after dinner, that Miss Bennet seemed out of spirits, and immediately accounting for it herself, by supposing that she did not like to go home again so soon, she added,

'But if that is the case, you must write to your mother to beg that you may stay a little longer. Mrs Collins will be very glad of your company, I am sure.'

'I am much obliged to your ladyship for your kind invitation,' replied Elizabeth, 'but it is not in my power to accept it. – I must be in town next Saturday.'

'Why, at that rate, you will have been here only six weeks. I expected you to stay two months. I told Mrs Collins so before you came. There can be no occasion for your going so soon. Mrs Bennet could certainly spare you for another fortnight.'

'But my father cannot. – He wrote last week to hurry my return.'

'Oh! your father of course may spare you, if your mother can. – Daughters are never of so much consequence to a father. And if you will stay another *month* complete, it will be in my power to take one of you as far as London, for I am going there early in June, for a week; and as Dawson does not object to the Barouche box, there will be very good room for one of you – and indeed, if the weather should happen to be cool, I should not object to taking you both, as you are neither of you large.'

'You are all kindness, Madam; but I believe we must abide by our original plan.'

Lady Catherine seemed resigned.

'Mrs Collins, you must send a servant with them. You know I always speak my mind, and I cannot bear the idea of two young women travelling post by themselves. It is highly improper. You must contrive to send somebody. I have the greatest dislike in the world to that sort of thing. – Young women should always be properly guarded and attended, according to their situation in life. When my niece Georgiana went to Ramsgate last summer, I made a point of her having two men servants go with her. – Miss Darcy, the daughter of Mr Darcy, of Pemberley, and Lady Anne, could not have appeared with propriety in a different manner. – I am excessively attentive to all those things. You must send John with the young ladies, Mrs Collins. I am glad it occurred to me to mention it; for it would really be discreditable to *you* to let them go alone.'

'My uncle is to send a servant for us.'

'Oh! – Your uncle! – He keeps a man-servant, does he? – I am very glad you have somebody who thinks of those things. Where shall you change horses? – Oh! Bromley, of course. – If you mention my name at the Bell, you will be attended to.'

Lady Catherine had many other questions to ask respecting their journey, and as she did not answer them all herself, attention was necessary, which Elizabeth believed to be lucky for her; or, with a mind so occupied, she might have forgotten where she was. Reflection must be reserved for solitary hours; whenever she was alone, she gave way to it as the greatest relief; and not a day went by without a solitary walk, in which she might indulge in all the delight of unpleasant recollections.

Mr Darcy's letter, she was in a fair way of soon knowing by heart. She studied every sentence: and her feelings towards its writer were at times widely different. When she remembered the style of his address, she was still full of indignation; but when she considered how unjustly she had condemned and upbraided him, her anger was turned against herself; and his disappointed feelings became the object of compassion. His attachment excited gratitude, his general character respect; but she could not approve him; nor could she for a moment repent her refusal, or feel the slightest inclination ever to see him again. In her own past behaviour, there was a constant source of vexation and regret; and in the unhappy defects of her family a subject of yet heavier chagrin. They were hopeless of remedy. Her father, contented with laughing at them, would never exert himself to restrain the wild giddiness of his youngest daughters; and her mother, with manners so far from right herself, was entirely insensible of the evil. Elizabeth had frequently united with Jane in an endeavour to check the imprudence of Catherine and Lydia; but while they were supported by their mother's indulgence, what chance could there be of improvement? Catherine, weak-spirited, irritable, and completely under Lydia's guidance, had been always affronted by their advice; and Lydia, self-willed and careless, would scarcely give them a hearing. They were ignorant, idle, and vain. While there was an officer in Meryton, they would flirt with him; and while Meryton was within a walk of Longbourn, they would be going there for ever.

Anxiety on Jane's behalf, was another prevailing concern, and Mr Darcy's explanation, by restoring Bingley to all her former good opinion, heightened the sense of what Jane had lost. His affection was proved to have been sincere, and his conduct cleared of all blame, unless any could attach to the implicitness of his confidence in his friend. How grievous then was the thought that, of a situation so desirable in every respect, so replete with advantage, so promising for happiness, Jane had been deprived, by the folly and indecorum of her own family!

When to these recollections was added the development of Wickham's character, it may be easily believed that the happy spirits which had seldon been depressed before, were now so much affected as to make it almost impossible for her to appear tolerably cheerful.

Their engagements at Rosings were as frequent during the last week of her stay, as they had been at first. The very last evening was spent there; and her Ladyship again enquired minutely into the particulars of their journey, gave them directions as to the best methods of packing, and was so urgent on the necessity of placing gowns in the only right way, that Maria thought herself obliged, on her return, to undo all the work of the morning, and pack her trunk afresh.

When they parted, Lady Catherine, with great condescension, wished them a good journey, and invited them to come to Hunsford again next year; and Miss de Bourgh exerted herself so far as to curtsey and hold out her hand to both.

Chapter Thirty Eight

ON SATURDAY MORNING ELIZABETH and Mr Collins met for breakfast a few minutes before the others appeared; and he took the opportunity of paying the parting civilities which he deemed indispensably necessary.

'I know not, Miss Elizabeth,' said he, 'whether Mrs Collins has yet expressed her sense of your kindness in coming to us, but I am very certain you will not leave the house without receiving her thanks for it. The favour of your company has been much felt, I assure you. We know how little there is to tempt any one to our humble abode. Our plain manner of living, our small rooms, and few domestics, and the little we see of the world, must make Hunsford extremely dull to a young lady like yourself; but I hope you will believe us grateful for the condescension, and that we have done every thing in our power to prevent your spending your time unpleasantly.'

Elizabeth was eager with her thanks and assurances of happiness. She had spent six weeks with great enjoyment; and the pleasure of being with Charlotte, and the kind attentions she had received, must make *her* feel the obliged. Mr Collins was gratified; and with a more smiling solemnity replied,

'It gives me the greatest pleasure to hear that you have passed your time not disagreeably. We have certainly done our best; and most fortunately having it in our power to introduce you to very superior society, and from our connection with Rosings, the frequent means of varying the humble home scene, I think we may flatter ourselves that your Hunsford visit cannot have been entirely irksome. Our situation with regard to Lady Catherine's family is indeed the sort of extraordinary advantage and blessing which few can boast. You see on what a footing we are. You see how continually we are engaged there. In truth I must acknowledge that, with all the disadvantages of this humble parsonage, I should not think any one abiding in it an object of compassion, while they are sharers of our intimacy at Rosings.'

Words were insufficient for the elevation of his feelings; and he was obliged to walk about the room, while Elizabeth tried to unite civility and truth in a few short sentences.

'You may, in fact, carry a very favourable report of us into Hertfordshire, my dear cousin. I flatter myself at least that you will be able to do so. Lady Catherine's great attentions to Mrs Collins you have been a daily witness of;

and altogether I trust it does not appear that your friend has drawn an unfortunate – but on this point it will be as well to be silent. Only let me assure you, my dear Miss Elizabeth, that I can from my heart most cordially wish you equal felicity in marriage. My dear Charlotte and I have but one mind and one way of thinking. There is in every thing a most remarkable resemblance of character and ideas between us. We seem to have been designed for each other.'

Elizabeth could safely say that it was a great happiness where that was the case, and with equal sincerity could add that she firmly believed and rejoiced in his domestic comforts. She was not sorry, however, to have the recital of them interrupted by the entrance of the lady from whom they sprung. Poor Charlotte! – it was melancholy to leave her to such society! – But she had chosen it with her eyes open; and though evidently regretting that her visitors were to go, she did not seem to ask for compassion. Her home and her housekeeping, her parish and her poultry, and all their dependent concerns, had not yet lost their charms.

At length the chaise arrived, the trunks were fastened on, the parcels placed within, and it was pronounced to be ready. After an affectionate parting between the friends, Elizabeth was attended to the carriage by Mr Collins, and as they walked down the garden, he was commissioning her with his best respects to all her family, not forgetting his thanks for the kindness he had received at Longbourn in the winter, and his compliments to Mr and Mrs Gardiner, though unknown. He then handed her in, Maria followed, and the door was on the point of being closed, when he suddenly reminded them, with some consternation, that they had hitherto forgotten to leave any message for the ladies of Rosings.

'But,' he added, 'you will of course wish to have your humble respects delivered to them, with your grateful thanks for their kindness to you while you have been here.'

Elizabeth made no objection; – the door was then allowed to be shut, and the carriage drove off.

'Good gracious!' cried Maria, after a few minutes silence, 'it seems but a day or two since we first came! – and yet how many things have happened!'

'A great many indeed,' said her companion with a sigh.

'We have dined nine times at Rosings, besides drinking tea there twice! – How much I shall have to tell!'

Elizabeth privately added, 'And how much I shall have to conceal.'

Their journey was performed without much conversation, or any alarm; and within four hours of their leaving Hunsford, they reached Mr Gardiner's house, where they were to remain a few days.

Jane looked well, and Elizabeth had little opportunity of studying her spirits, amidst the various engagements which the kindness of her aunt had reserved for them. But Jane was to go home with her, and at Longbourn there would be leisure enough for observation.

It was not without an effort meanwhile that she could wait even for Longbourn, before she told her sister of Mr Darcy's proposals. To know that she had the power of revealing what would so exceedingly astonish Jane, and must, at the same time, so highly gratify whatever of her own vanity she had not yet been able to reason away, was such a temptation to openness as nothing could have conquered, but the state of indecision in which she remained, as to the extent of what she should communicate; and her fear, if she once entered on the subject, of being hurried into repeating something of Bingley, which might only grieve her sister farther.

Chapter Thirty Nine

IT WAS THE SECOND WEEK IN MAY, in which the three young ladies set out together from Gracechurch-street, for the town of — in Hertfordshire; and, as they drew near the appointed inn where Mr Bennet's carriage was to meet them, they quickly perceived, in token of the coachman's punctuality, both Kitty and Lydia looking out of a dining room up stairs. These two girls had been above an hour in the place, happily employed in visiting an opposite milliner, watching the sentinel on guard, and dressing a salad and cucumber.

After welcoming their sisters, they triumphantly displayed a table set out with such cold meat as an inn larder usually affords, exclaiming, 'Is not this nice? is not this an agreeable surprise?'

'And we mean to treat you all,' added Lydia; 'but you must lend us the money, for we have just spent ours at the shop out there.' Then shewing her purchases: 'Look here, I have bought this bonnet. I do not think it is very pretty; but I thought I might as well buy it as not. I shall pull it to pieces as soon as I get home, and see if I can make it up any better.'

And when her sisters abused it as ugly, she added, with perfect uncon-cern, 'Oh! but there were two or three much uglier in the shop; and when I have bought some prettier-coloured satin to trim it with fresh, I think it will be very tolerable. Besides, it will not much signify what one wears this summer, after the —shire have left Meryton, and they are going in a fortnight.'

'Are they indeed?' cried Elizabeth, with the greatest satisfaction.

'They are going to be encamped near Brighton; and I do so want papa to take us all there for the summer! It would be such a delicious scheme, and I dare say would hardly cost any thing at all. Mamma would like to go too of all things! Only think what a miserable summer else we shall have!'

'Yes,' thought Elizabeth, 'that would be a delightful scheme, indeed, and completely do for us at once. Good Heaven! Brighton, and a whole campful of soldiers, to us, who have been overset already by one poor regiment of militia, and the monthly balls of Meryton.'

'Now I have got some news for you,' said Lydia, as they sat down to table. 'What do you think? It is excellent news, capital news, and about a certain person that we all like.'

Jane and Elizabeth looked at each other, and the waiter was told that he need not stay. Lydia laughed, and said,

'Aye, that is just like your formality and discretion. You thought the waiter must not hear, as if he cared! I dare say he often hears worse things said than I am going to say. But he is an ugly fellow! I am glad he is gone. I never saw such a long chin in my life. Well, but now for my news: it is about dear Wickham; too good for the waiter, is not it? There is no danger

of Wickham's marrying Mary King. There's for you! She is gone down to
her uncle at Liverpool; gone to stay. Wickham is safe.'

'And Mary King is safe!' added Elizabeth; 'safe from a connection
imprudent as to fortune.'

'She is a great fool for going away, if she liked him.'

'But I hope there is no strong attachment on either side,' said Jane.

'I am sure there is not on *his*. I will answer for it he never cared three
straws about her. Who *could* about such a nasty little freckled thing?'

Elizabeth was shocked to think that, however incapable of such coarseness of *expression* herself, the coarseness of the *sentiment* was little other
than her own breast had formerly harboured and fancied liberal!

As soon as all had ate, and the elder ones paid, the carriage was ordered;
and after some contrivance, the whole party, with all their boxes, workbags,
and parcels, and the unwelcome addition of Kitty's and Lydia's purchases,
were seated in it.

'How nicely we are crammed in!' cried Lydia. 'I am glad I bought my
bonnet, if it is only for the fun of having another bandbox! Well, now let us
be quite comfortable and snug, and talk and laugh all the way home. And
in the first place, let us hear what has happened to you all, since you went
away. Have you seen any pleasant men? Have you had any flirting? I was in
great hopes that one of you would have got a husband before you came back.
Jane will be quite an old maid soon, I declare. She is almost three and twenty!
Lord, how ashamed I should be of not being married before three and twenty!
My aunt Philips wants you so to get husbands, you can't think. She says
Lizzy had better have taken Mr Collins; but I do not think there would have
been any fun in it. Lord! how I should like to be married before any of you;
and then I would chaperon you about to all the balls. Dear me! we had such
a good piece of fun the other day at Colonel Forster's. Kitty and me were to
spend the day there, and Mrs Forster promised to have a little dance in the
evening; (by the bye, Mrs Forster and me are *such* friends!) and so she asked
the two Harringtons to come, but Harriet was ill, and so Pen was forced to
come by herself; and then, what do you think we did? We dressed up
Chamberlayne in woman's clothes, on purpose to pass for a lady, – only
think what fun! Not a soul knew of it, but Col and Mrs Forster, and Kitty
and me, except my aunt, for we were forced to borrow one of her gowns; and
you cannot imagine how well he looked! When Denny, and Wickham, and
Pratt, and two or three more of the men came in, they did not know him in
the least. Lord! how I laughed! and so did Mrs Forster. I thought I should
have died. And *that* made the men suspect something, and then they soon
found out what was the matter.'

With such kind of histories of their parties and good jokes, did Lydia,
assisted by Kitty's hints and additions, endeavour to amuse her companions
all the way to Longbourn. Elizabeth listened as little as she could, but there
was no escaping the frequent mention of Wickham's name.

Their reception at home was most kind. Mrs Bennet rejoiced to see Jane
in undiminished beauty; and more than once during dinner did Mr Bennet
say voluntarily to Elizabeth,

'I am glad you are come back, Lizzy.'

Their party in the dining-room was large, for almost all the Lucases
came to meet Maria and hear the news: and various were the subjects which
occupied them; Lady Lucas was enquiring of Maria across the table, after the

welfare and poultry of her eldest daughter; Mrs Bennet was doubly engaged, on one hand collecting an account of the present fashions from Jane, who sat some way below her, and on the other, retailing them all to the younger Miss Lucases; and Lydia, in a voice rather louder than any other person's was enumerating the various pleasures of the morning to any body who would hear her.

'Oh! Mary,' said she, 'I wish you had gone with us, for we had such fun! as we went along, Kitty and me drew up all the blinds, and pretended there was nobody in the coach; and I should have gone so all the way, if Kitty had not been sick; and when we got to the George, I do think we behaved very handsomely, for we treated the other three with the nicest cold luncheon in the world, and if you would have gone, we would have treated you too. And then when we came away it was such fun! I thought we never should have got into the coach. I was ready to die of laughter. And then we were so merry all the way home! we talked and laughed so loud, that any body might have heard us ten miles off!'

To this, Mary very gravely replied, 'Far be it from me, my dear sister, to depreciate such pleasures. They would doubtless be congenial with the generality of female minds. But I confess they would have no charms for *me*. I should infinitely prefer a book.'

But of this answer Lydia heard not a word. She seldom listened to any body for more than half a minute, and never attended to Mary at all.

In the afternoon Lydia was urgent with the rest of the girls to walk to Meryton and see how every body went on; but Elizabeth steadily opposed the scheme. It should not be said, that the Miss Bennets could not be at home half a day before they were in pursuit of the officers. There was another reason too for her opposition. She dreaded seeing Wickham again, and was resolved to avoid it as long as possible. The comfort to *her*, of the regiment's approaching removal, was indeed beyond expression. In a fortnight they were to go, and once gone, she hoped there could be nothing more to plague her on his account.

She had not been many hours at home, before she found that the Brighton scheme, of which Lydia had given them a hint at the inn, was under frequent discussion between her parents. Elizabeth saw directly that her father had not the smallest intention of yielding; but his answers were at the same time so vague and equivocal, that her mother, though often disheartened, had never yet despaired of succeeding at last.

Chapter Forty

ELIZABETH'S IMPATIENCE TO ACQUAINT Jane with what had happened could no longer be overcome; and at length resolving to suppress every particular in which her sister was concerned, and preparing her to be surprised, she related to her the next morning the chief of the scene between Mr Darcy and herself.

Miss Bennet's astonishment was soon lessened by the strong sisterly partiality which made any admiration of Elizabeth appear perfectly natural; and all surprise was shortly lost in other feelings. She was sorry that Mr Darcy should have delivered his sentiments in a manner so little suited to recommend them; but still more was she grieved for the unhappiness which her sister's refusal must have given him.

'His being so sure of succeeding, was wrong,' said she; 'and certainly ought not to have appeared; but consider how much it must increase his disappointment.'

'Indeed,' replied Elizabeth, 'I am heartily sorry for him; but he has other feelings which will probably soon drive away his regard for me. You do not blame me, however, for refusing him?'

'Blame you! Oh, no.'

'But you blame me for having spoken so warmly of Wickham.'

'No – I do not know that you were wrong in saying what you did.'

'But you *will* know it, when I have told you what happened the very next day.'

She then spoke of the letter, repeating the whole of its contents as far as they concerned George Wickham. What a stroke was this for poor Jane! who would willingly have gone through the world without believing that so much wickedness existed in the whole race of mankind, as was here collected in one individual. Nor was Darcy's vindication, though grateful to her feelings, capable of consoling her for such discovery. Most earnestly did she labour to prove the probability of error, and seek to clear one, without involving the other.

'This will not do,' said Elizabeth. 'You never will be able to make both of them good for any thing. Take your choice, but you must be satisfied with only one. There is but such a quantity of merit between tham; just enough to make one good sort of man; and of late it has been shifting about pretty much. For my part, I am inclined to believe it all Mr Darcy's, but you shall do as you chuse.'

It was some time, however, before a smile could be extorted from Jane.

'I do not know when I have been more shocked,' said she. 'Wickham so very bad! It is almost past belief. And poor Mr Darcy! dear Lizzy, only consider what he must have suffered. Such a disappointment! and with the knowledge of your ill opinion too! and having to relate such a thing of his sister! It is really too distressing. I am sure you must feel it so.'

'Oh! no, my regret and compassion are all done away by seeing you so full of both. I know you will do him such ample justice, that I am growing every moment more unconcerned and indifferent. Your profusion makes me saving; and if you lament over him much longer, my heart will be as light as a feather.'

'Poor Wickham; there is such an expression of goodness in his countenance! such an openness and gentleness in his manner.'

'There certainly was some great mismanagement in the education of those two young men. One has got all the goodness, and the other all the appearance of it.'

'I never thought Mr Darcy so deficient in the *appearance* of it as you used to do.'

'And yet I meant to be uncommonly clever in taking so decided a dislike to him, without any reason. It is such a spur to one's genius, such an opening for wit to have a dislike of that kind. One may be continually abusive without saying any thing just; but one cannot be always laughing at a man without now and then stumbling on something witty.'

'Lizzy, when you first read that letter, I am sure you could not treat the matter as you do now.'

'Indeed I could not. I was uncomfortable enough. I was very uncomfortable, I may say unhappy. And with no one to speak to, of what I felt, no Jane to comfort me and say that I had not been so very weak and vain and nonsensical as I knew I had! Oh! how I wanted you!'

'How unfortunate that you should have used such very strong expressions in speaking of Wickham to Mr Darcy, for now they *do* appear wholly undeserved.'

'Certainly. But the misfortune of speaking with bitterness, is a most natural consequence of the prejudices I had been encouraging. There is one point, on which I want your advice. I want to be told whether I ought, or ought not to make our acquaintance in general understand Wickham's character.'

Miss Bennet paused a little and then replied, 'Surely there can be no occasion for exposing him so dreadfully. What is your own opinion?'

'That it ought not to be attempted. Mr Darcy has not authorised me to make his communication public. On the contrary every particular relative to his sister, was meant to be kept as much as possible to myself; and if I endeavour to undeceive people as to the rest of his conduct, who will believe me? The general prejudice against Mr Darcy is so violent, that it would be the death of half the good people in Meryton, to attempt to place him in an amiable light. I am not equal to it. Wickham will soon be gone; and therefore it will not signify to anybody here, what he really is. Sometime hence it will be all found out, and then we may laugh at their stupidity in not knowing it before. At present I will say nothing about it.'

'You are quite right. To have his errors made public might ruin him for ever. He is now perhaps sorry for what he has done, and anxious to re-establish a character. We must not make him desperate.'

The tumult of Elizabeth's mind was allayed by this conversation. She had got rid of two of the secrets which had weighed on her for a fortnight, and was certain of a willing listener in Jane, whenever she might wish to talk again of either. But there was still something lurking behind, of which prudence forbad the disclosure. She dared not relate the other half of Mr Darcy's letter, nor explain to her sister how sincerely she had been valued by his friend. Here was knowledge in which no one could partake; and she was sensible that nothing less than a perfect understanding between the parties could justify her in throwing off this last incumbrance of mystery. 'And then,' said she, 'if that very improbable event should ever take place, I shall merely be able to tell what Bingley may tell in a much more agreeable manner himself. The liberty of communication cannot be mine till it has lost all its value!'

She was now, on being settled a home, at leisure to observe the real state of her sister's spirits. Jane was not happy. She still cherished a very tender affection for Bingley. Having never even fancied herself in love before, her regard had all the warmth of first attachment, and from her age and disposition, greater steadiness than first attachments often boast; and so fervently did she value his remembrance, and prefer him to every other man, that all her good sense, and all her attention to the feelings of her friends, were requisite to check the indulgence of those regrets, which must have been injurious to her own health and their tranquillity.

'Well Lizzy,' said Mrs Bennet one day, 'what is your opinion *now* of this sad business of Jane's? For my part, I am determined never to speak of it again to anybody. I told my sister Philips so the other day. But I cannot find out that Jane saw any thing of him in London. Well, he is a very undeserving young man – and I do not suppose there is the least chance in the world of her ever getting him now. There is no talk of his coming to Netherfield again in the summer; and I have enquired of every body too, who is likely to know.'

'I do not believe that he will ever live at Netherfield any more.'

'Oh, well! it is just as he chooses. Nobody wants him to come. Though I shall always say that he used my daughter extremely ill; and if I was her, I would not have put up with it. Well, my comfort is, I am sure Jane will die of a broken heart, and then he will be sorry for what he has done.'

But as Elizabeth could not receive comfort from any such expectation, she made no answer.

'Well, Lizzy,' continued her mother soon afterwards, 'and so the Collinses live very comfortable, do they? Well, well, I only hope it will last. And what sort of table do they keep? Charlotte is an excellent manager, I dare say. If she is half as sharp as her mother, she is saving enough. There is nothing extravagant in *their* housekeeping, I dare say.'

'No, nothing at all.'

'A great deal of good management, depend upon it. Yes, yes. *They* will take care not to outrun their income. *They* will never be distressed for money. Well, much good may it do them! And so, I suppose, they often talk of having Longbourn when your father is dead. They look upon it quite as their own, I dare say, whenever that happens.'

'It was a subject which they could not mention before me.'

'No. It would have been strange if they had. But I make no doubt, they often talk of it between themselves. Well, if they can be easy with an estate that is not lawfully their own, so much the better. I should be ashamed of having one that was only entailed on me.'

Chapter Forty One

THE FIRST WEEK OF THEIR RETURN was soon gone. The second began. It was the last of the regiment's stay in Meryton, and all the young ladies in the neighbourhood were drooping apace. The dejection was almost universal. The elder Miss Bennets alone were still able to eat, drink, and sleep, and pursue the usual course of their employments. Very frequently were they reproached for this insensibility by Kitty and Lydia, whose own misery was extreme, and who could not comprehend such hard-heartedness in any of the family.

'Good Heaven! What is to become of us! What are we to do!' would they often exclaim in the bitterness of woe. 'How can you be smiling so, Lizzy?'

Their affectionate mother shared all their grief; she remembered what she had herself endured on a similar occasion, five and twenty years ago.

'I am sure,' said she, 'I cried for two days together when Colonel Millar's regiment went away. I thought I should have broke my heart.'

'I am sure I shall break *mine*,' said Lydia.

'If one could but go to Brighton!' observed Mrs Bennet.

'Oh, yes! – if one could but go to Brighton! But papa is so disagreeable.'

'A little sea-bathing would set me up for ever.'

'And my aunt Philips is sure it would do *me* a great deal of good,' added Kitty.

Such were the kind of lamentations resounding perpetually through Longbourn-house. Elizabeth tried to be diverted by them; but all sense of pleasure was lost in shame. She felt anew the justice of Mr Darcy's objections; and never had she before been so much disposed to pardon his interference in the views of his friend.

But the gloom of Lydia's prospect was shortly cleared away; for she received an invitation from Mrs Forster, the wife of the Colonel of the regiment, to accompany her to Brighton. This invaluable friend was a very young woman, and very lately married. A resemblance in good humour and good spirits had recommended her and Lydia to each other, and out of their *three* months' acquaintance they had been intimate *two*.

The rapture of Lydia on this occasion, her adoration of Mrs Forster, the delight of Mrs Bennet, and the mortification of Kitty, are scarcely to be described. Wholly inattentive to her sister's feelings, Lydia flew about the house in restless ecstasy, calling for every one's congratulations, and laughing and talking with more violence than ever; whilst the luckless Kitty continued in the parlour repining at her fate in terms as unreasonable as her accent was peevish.

'I cannot see why Mrs Forster should not ask *me* as well as Lydia,' said she, 'though I am *not* her particular friend. I have just as much right to be asked as she has, and more too, for I am two years older.'

In vain did Elizabeth attempt to make her reasonable, and Jane to make her resigned. As for Elizabeth herself, this invitation was so far from exciting in her the same feelings as in her mother and Lydia, that she considered it as the death-warrant of all possibility of common sense for the latter; and detestable as such a step must make her were it known, she could not help secretly advising her father not to let her go. She represented to him all the improprieties of Lydia's general behaviour, the little advantage she could derive from the friendship of such a woman as Mrs Forster, and the probability of her being yet more imprudent with such a companion at Brighton, where the temptations must be greater than at home. He heard her attentively, and then said,

'Lydia will never be easy till she has exposed herself in some public place or other, and we can never expect her to do it with so little expense or inconvenience to her family as under the present circumstances.'

'If you were aware,' said Elizabeth, 'of the very great disadvantage to us all, which must arise from the public notice of Lydia's unguarded and imprudent manner; nay, which has already arisen from it, I am sure you would judge differently in the affair.'

'Already arisen!' repeated Mr Bennet. 'What, has she frightened away some of your lovers? Poor little Lizzy! But do not be cast down. Such squeamish youths as cannot bear to be connected with a little absurdity, are not worth a regret. Come, let me see the list of the pitiful fellows who have been kept aloof by Lydia's folly.'

'Indeed you are mistaken. I have no such injuries to resent. It is not of peculiar, but of general evils, which I am now complaining. Our importance, our respectability in the world, must be affected by the wild volatility, the assurance and disdain of all restraint which mark Lydia's character. Execuse me – for I must speak plainly. If you, my dear father, will not take the trouble of checking her exuberant spirits, and of teaching her that her present pursuits are not to be the business of her life, she will soon be beyond the reach of amendment. Her character will be fixed, and she will, at sixteen, be the most determined flirt that ever made herself and her family ridiculous. A flirt too, in the worst and meanest degree of flirtation; without any attraction beyond youth and a tolerable person; and from the ignorance and emptiness of her mind, wholly unable to ward off any portion of that universal contempt which her rage for admiration will excite. In this danger Kitty is also comprehended. She will follow wherever Lydia leads. Vain, ignorant, idle, and absolutely uncontrolled! Oh! my dear father, can you suppose it possible that they will not be censured and despised wherever they are known, and that their sister will not be often involved in the disgrace?'

Mr Bennet saw that her whole heart was in the subject; and affectionately taking her hand, said in reply,

'Do not make yourself uneasy, my love. Wherever you and Jane are known, you must be respected and valued; and you will not appear to less advantage for having a couple of – or I may say, three very silly sisters. We shall have no peace at Longbourn if Lydia does not go to Brighton. Let her go then. Colonel Forster is a sensible man, and will keep her out of any real mischief; and she is luckily too poor to be an object of prey to any body. At Brighton she will be of less importance even as a common flirt than she has been here. The officers will find women better worth their notice. Let us hope, therefore, that her being there may teach her her own insignificance. At any rate, she cannot grow many degrees worse, without authorizing us to lock her up for the rest of her life.'

With this answer Elizabeth was forced to be content; but her own opinion continued the same, and she left him disappointed and sorry. It was not in her nature, however, to increase her vexations, by dwelling on them. She was confident of having performed her duty, and to fret over unavoidable evils, or augment them by anxiety, was no part of her disposition.

Had Lydia and her mother known the substance of her conference with her father, their indignation would hardly have found expression in their united volubility. In Lydia's imagination, a visit to Brighton comprised every possibility of earthly happiness. She saw with the creative eye of fancy, the streets of that gay bathing place covered with officers. She saw herself the object of attention, to tens and to scores of them at present unknown. She saw all the glories of the camp; its tents stretched forth in beauteous uniformity of lines, crowded with the young and the gay, and dazzling with scarlet; and to complete the view, she saw herself seated beneath a tent, tenderly flirting with at least six officers at once.

Had she known that her sister sought to tear her from such prospects and such realities as these, what would have been her sensations? They could have been understood only by her mother, who might have felt nearly the same. Lydia's going to Brighton was all that consoled her from the melancholy conviction of her husband's never intending to go there himself.

But they were entirely ignorant of what had passed; and their raptures continued with little intermission to the very day of Lydia's leaving home.

Elizabeth was now to see Mr Wickham for the last time. Having been frequently in company with him since her return, agitation was pretty well over; the agitations of former partiality entirely so. She had even learnt to detect, in the very gentleness which had first delighted her, an affectation and a sameness to disgust and weary. In his present behaviour to herself, moreover, she had a fresh source of displeasure, for the inclination he soon testified of renewing those attentions which had marked the early part of their acquaintance, could only serve, after what had since passed, to provoke her. She lost all concern for him in finding herself thus selected as the object of such idle and frivolous gallantry; and while she steadily repressed it, could not but feel the reproof contained in his believing, that however long, and for whatever cause, his attentions had been withdrawn, her vanity would be gratified and her preference secured at any time by their renewal.

On the very last day of the regiment's remaining in Meryton, he dined with others of the officers at Longbourn; and so little was Elizabeth disposed to part from him in good humour, that on his making some enquiry as to the manner in which her time had passed at Hunsford, she mentioned Colonel Fitzwilliam's and Mr Darcy's having both spent three weeks at Rosings, and asked him if he were acquainted with the former.

He looked surprised, displeased, alarmed; but with a moment's recollection and a returning smile, replied, that he had formerly seen him often; and after observing that he was a very gentleman-like man, asked her how she had liked him. Her answer was warmly in his favour. With an air of indifference he soon afterwards added, 'How long did you say that he was at Rosings?'

'Nearly three weeks.'

'And you saw him frequently?'

'Yes, almost every day.'

'His manners are very different from his cousin's.'

'Yes, very different. But I think Mr Darcy improves on acquaintance.'

'Indeed!' cried Wickham with a look which did not escape her. 'And pray may I ask?' but checking himself, he added in a gayer tone, 'Is it in address that he improves? Has he deigned to add ought of civility to his ordinary style? for I dare not hope,' he continued in a lower and more serious tone, 'that he is improved in essentials.'

'Oh, no!' said Elizabeth. 'In essentials, I believe, he is very much what he ever was.'

While she spoke, Wickham looked as if scarcely knowing whether to rejoice over her words, or to distrust their meaning. There was a something in her countenance which made him listen with an apprehensive and anxious attention, while she added,

'When I said that he improved on acquaintance, I did not mean that either his mind or manners were in a state of improvement, but that from knowing him better, his disposition was better understood.'

Wickham's alarm now appeared in a heightened complexion and agitated look; for a few minutes he was silent; till, shaking off his embarrassment, he turned to her again, and said in the gentlest of accents,

'You, who so well know my feelings towards Mr Darcy, will readily comprehend how sincerely I must rejoice that he is wise enough to assume even the *appearance* of what is right. His pride, in that direction, may be of service, if not to himself, to many others, for it must deter him from such foul misconduct as I have suffered by. I only fear that the sort of cautiousness, to which you, I imagine, have been alluding, is merely adopted on his visits to his aunt, of whose good opinion and judgment he stands much in awe. His fear of her, has always operated, I know, when they were together; and a good deal is to be imputed to his wish of forwarding the match with Miss de Bourgh, which I am certain he has very much at heart.'

Elizabeth could not repress a smile at this, but she answered only by a slight inclination of the head. She saw that he wanted to engage her on the old subject of his grievances, and she was in no humour to indulge him. The rest of the evening passed with the *appearance*, on his side, of usual cheerfulness, but with no farther attempt to distinguish Elizabeth; and they parted at last with mutual civility, and possibly a mutual desire of never meeting again.

When the party broke up, Lydia returned with Mrs Forster to Meryton, from whence they were to set out early the next morning. The separation between her and her family was rather noisy than pathetic. Kitty was the only one who shed tears; but she did weep from vexation and envy. Mrs Bennet was diffuse in her good wishes for the felicity of her daughter, and impressive in her injunctions that she would not miss the opportunity of enjoying herself as much as possible; advice, which there was every reason to believe would be attended to; and in the clamorous happiness of Lydia herself in bidding farewell, the more gentle adieus of her sisters were uttered without being heard.

Chapter Forty Two

HAD ELIZABETH'S OPINION BEEN ALL drawn from her own family, she could not have formed a very pleasing picture of conjugal felicity or domestic comfort. Her father captivated by youth and beauty, and that appearance of good humour, which youth and beauty generally give, had married a woman whose weak understanding and illiberal mind, had very early in their marriage put an end to all real affection for her. Respect, esteem, and confidence, had vanished for ever; and all his views of domestic happiness were overthrown. But Mr Bennet was not of a disposition to seek comfort for the disappointment which his own imprudence had brought on, in any of those pleasures which too often console the unfortunate for their folly or their vice. He was fond of the country and of books; and from these tastes had arisen his principal enjoyments. To his wife he was very little otherwise indebted, than as her ignorance and folly had contributed to his amusement. This is not the sort of happiness which a man would in general wish to owe to his wife; but where other powers of entertainment are wanting, the true philosopher will derive benefit from such as are given.

Elizabeth, however, had never been blind to the impropriety of her father's behaviour as a husband. She had always seen it with pain; but respecting his abilities, and grateful for his affectionate treatment of herself, she endeavoured to forget what she could not overlook, and to banish from her thoughts that continual breach of conjugal obligation and decorum which, in exposing his wife to the contempt of her own children, was so highly reprehensible. But she had never felt so strongly as now, the disadvantages which must attend the children of so unsuitable a marriage, nor ever been so fully aware of the evils arising from so ill-judged a direction of talents; talents which rightly used, might at least have preserved the respectability of his daughters, even if incapable of enlarging the mind of his wife.

When Elizabeth had rejoiced over Wickham's departure, she found little other cause for satisfaction in the loss of the regiment. Their parties abroad were less varied than before; and at home she had a mother and sister whose constant repinings at the dulness of every thing around them, threw a real gloom over their domestic circle; and, though Kitty might in time regain her natural degree of sense, since the disturbers of her brain were removed, her other sister, from whose disposition greater evil might be apprehended, was likely to be hardened in all her folly and assurance, by a situation of such double danger as a watering place and a camp. Upon the whole, therefore, she found, what has been sometimes found before, that an event to which she had looked forward with impatient desire, did not in taking place, bring all the satisfaction she had promised herself. It was consequently necessary to name some other period for the commencement of actual felicity; to have some other point on which her wishes and hopes might be fixed, and by again enjoying the pleasure of anticipation, console herself for the present, and prepare for another disappointment. Her tour to the Lakes was now the object of her happiest thoughts; it was her best consolation for all the uncomfortable hours, which the discontentedness of her mother and Kitty made inevitable; and could she have included Jane in the scheme, every part of it would have been perfect.

'But it is fortunate,' thought she, 'that I have something to wish for. Were the whole arrangement complete, my disappointment would be certain. But here, by carrying with me one ceaseless source of regret in my sister's absence, I may reasonably hope to have all my expectations of pleasure realized. A scheme of which every part promises delight, can never be successful; and general disappointment is only warded off by the defence of some little peculiar vexation.'

When Lydia went away, she promised to write very often and very minutely to her mother and Kitty; but her letters were always long expected, and always very short. Those to her mother, contained little else, than that they were just returned from the library, where such and such officers had attended them, and where she had seen such beautiful ornaments as made her quite wild; that she had a new gown, or a new parasol, which she would have described more fully, but was obliged to leave off in a violent hurry, as Mrs Forster called her, and they were going to the camp; – and from her correspondence with her sister, there was still less to be learnt – for her letters to Kitty, though rather longer, were much too full of lines under the words to be made public.

After the first fortnight or three weeks of her absence, health, good humour and cheerfulness began to re-appear at Longbourn. Everything wore a happier aspect. The families who had been in town for the winter came back again and summer finery and summer engagements arose. Mrs Bennet was restored to her usual querulous serenity, and by the middle of June Kitty was so much recovered as to be able to enter Meryton without tears; an event of such happy promise as to make Elizabeth hope, that by the following Christmas, she might be so tolerably reasonable as not to mention an officer above once a day, unless by some cruel and malicious arrangement at the war-office, another regiment should be quartered in Meryton.

The time fixed for the beginning of their Northern tour was now fast approaching; and a fortnight only was wanting of it, when a letter arrived from Mrs Gardiner, which at once delayed its commencement and curtailed its extent. Mr Gardiner would be prevented by business from setting out till a fortnight later in July, and must be in London again within a month; and as that left too short a period for them to go so far, and see so much as they had proposed, or at least to see it with the leisure and comfort they had built on, they were obliged to give up the Lakes, and substitute a more contracted tour; and according to the present plan, were to go no farther northward than Derbyshire. In that county, there was enough to be seen, to occupy the chief of their three weeks; and to Mrs Gardiner it had a peculiarly strong attraction. The town where she had formerly passed some years of her life, and where they were now to spend a few days, was probably as great an object of her curiosity, as all the celebrated beauties of Matlock, Chatsworth, Dovedale, or the Peak.

Elizabeth was excessively disappointed; she had set her heart on seeing the Lakes; and still thought there might have been time enough. But it was her business to be satisfied – and certainly her temper to be happy; and all was soon right again.

With the mention of Derbyshire, there were many ideas connected. It was impossible for her to see the word without thinking of Pemberley and its owner. 'But surely,' said she, 'I may enter his county with impunity, and rob it of a few petrified spars without his perceiving me.'

The period of expectation was now doubled. Four weeks were to pass away before her uncle and aunt's arrival. But they did pass away, and Mr and Mrs Gardiner, with their four children, did at length appear at Longbourn. The children, two girls of six and eight years old, and two younger boys, were to be left under the particular care of their cousin Jane, who was the general favourite, and whose steady sense and sweetness of temper exactly adapted her for attending to them in every way – teaching them, playing with them, and loving them.

The Gardiners staid only one night at Longbourn, and set off the next morning with Elizabeth in pursuit of novelty and amusement. One enjoyment was certain – that of suitableness as companions; a suitableness which comprehended health and temper to bear inconveniences – cheerfulness to enhance every pleasure – and affection and intelligence, which might supply it among themselves if there were disappointments abroad.

It is not the object of this work to give a description of Derbyshire, nor of any of the remarkable places through which their route thither lay; Oxford, Blenheim, Warwick, Kenelworth, Birmingham, &c. are sufficiently known. A small part of Derbyshire is all the present concern. To the little town of Lambton, the scene of Mrs Gardiner's former residence, and where she had lately learned that some acquaintance still remained, they bent their steps, after having seen all the principal wonders of the country; and within five miles of Lambton, Elizabeth found from her aunt, that Pemberley was situated. It was not in their direct road, nor more than a mile or two out of it. In talking over their route the evening before, Mrs Gardiner expressed an inclination to see the place again. Mr Gardiner declared his willingness, and Elizabeth was applied to for her approbation.

'My love, should not you like to see a place of which you have heard so much?' said her aunt. 'A place too, with which so many of your acquaintance are connected. Wickham passed all his youth there, you know.'

Elizabeth was distressed. She felt that she had no business at Pemberley, and was obliged to assume a disinclination for seeing it. She must own that she was tired of great houses; after going over so many, she really had no pleasure in fine carpets or satin curtains.

Mrs Gardiner abused her stupidity. 'If it were merely a fine house richly furnished,' said she, 'I should not care about it myself; but the grounds are delightful. They have some of the finest woods in the country.'

Elizabeth said no more – but her mind could not acquiesce. The possibility of meeting Mr Darcy, while viewing the place, instantly occurred. It would be dreadful! She blushed at the very idea; and thought it would be better to speak openly to her aunt, than to run such a risk. But against this, there were objections; and she finally resolved that it could be the last resource, if her private enquiries as to the absence of the family, were unfavourably answered.

Accordingly, when she retired at night, she asked the chambermaid whether Pemberley were not a very fine place, what was the name of its proprietor, and with no little alarm, whether the family were down for the summer. A most welcome negative followed the last question – and her alarms being now removed, she was at leisure to feel a great deal of curiosity to see the house herself; and when the subject was revived the next morning, and she was again applied to, could readily answer, and with a proper air of indifference, that she had not really any dislike to the scheme.

To Pemberley, therefore, they were to go.

Chapter Forty Three

ELIZABETH, AS THEY DROVE ALONG, watched for the first appearance of Pemberley Woods with some perturbation; and when at length they turned in at the lodge, her spirits were in a high flutter.

The park was very large, and contained great variety of ground. They entered it in one of its lowest points, and drove for some time through a beautiful wood, stretching over a wide extent.

Elizabeth's mind was too full for conversation, but she saw and admired every remarkable spot and point of view. They gradually ascended for half a mile, and then found themselves at the top of a considerable eminence, where the wood ceased, and the eye was instantly caught by Pemberley House, situated on the opposite side of a valley, into which the road with some abruptness wound. It was a large, handsome, stone building, standing well on rising ground, and backed by a ridge of high woody hills; – and in front, a stream of some natural importance was swelled into greater, but without any artificial appearance. Its banks were neither formal, nor falsely adorned. Elizabeth was delighted. She had never seen a place for which nature had done more, or where natural beauty had been so little counteracted by an awkward taste. They were all of them warm in their admiration; and at that moment she felt, that to be mistress of Pemberley might be something!

They descended the hill, crossed the bridge, and drove to the door; and, while examining the nearer aspect of the house, all her apprehensions of meeting its owner returned. She dreaded lest the chambermaid had been mistaken. On applying to see the place, they were admitted into the hall; and Elizabeth, as they waited for the housekeeper, had leisure to wonder at her being where she was.

The housekeeper came; a respectable-looking, elderly woman, much less fine, and more civil, than she had any notion of finding her. They followed her into the dining-parlour. It was a large, well-proportioned room, handsomely fitted up. Elizabeth, after slightly surveying it, went to a window to enjoy its prospect. The hill, crowned with wood, from which they had descended, receiving increased abruptness from the distance, was a beautiful object. Every disposition of the ground was good; and she looked on the whole scene, the river, the trees scattered on its banks, and the winding of the valley, as far as she could trace it, with delight. As they passed into other rooms, these objects were taking different positions; but from every window there were beauties to be seen. The rooms were lofty and handsome, and their furniture suitable to the fortune of their proprietor; but Elizabeth saw, with admiration of his taste, that it was neither gaudy nor uselessly fine; with less of splendor, and more real elegance, than the furniture of Rosings.

'And of this place,' thought she, 'I might have been mistress! With these rooms I might now have been familiarly acquainted! Instead of viewing them as a stranger, I might have rejoiced in them as my own, and welcomed to them as visitors my uncle and aunt. – But no,' – recollecting herself, – 'that could never be: my uncle and aunt would have been lost to me: I should not have been allowed to invite them.'

This was a lucky recollection – it saved her from something like regret.

She longed to enquire of the housekeeper, whether her master were really absent, but had not courage for it. At length, however, the question was asked by her uncle; and she turned away with alarm, while Mrs Reynolds replied, that he was, adding, 'but we expect him to-morrow, with a large party of friends.' How rejoiced was Elizabeth that their own journey had not by any circumstance been delayed a day!

Her aunt now called her to look at a picture. She approached, and saw the likeness of Mr Wickham suspended, amongst several other miniatures, over the mantlepiece. Her aunt asked her, smilingly, how she liked it. The housekeeper came forward, and told them it was the picture of a young gentleman, the son of her late master's steward, who had been brought up by him at his own expence. – 'He is now gone into the army,' she added, 'but I am afraid he has turned out very wild.'

Mrs Gardiner looked at her niece with a smile, but Elizabeth could not return it.

'And that,' said Mrs Reynolds, pointing to another of the miniatures, 'is my master – and very like him. It was drawn at the same time as the other – about eight years ago.'

'I have heard much of your master's fine person,' said Mrs Gardiner, looking at the picture; 'it is a handsome face. But, Lizzy, you can tell us whether it is like or not.'

Mrs Reynolds's respect for Elizabeth seemed to increase on this intimation of her knowing her master.

'Does that young lady know Mr Darcy?'

Elizabeth coloured, and said – 'A little.'

'And do not you think him a very handsome gentleman, Ma'am?'

'Yes, very handsome.'

'I am sure I know none so handsome; but in the gallery up stairs you will see a finer, larger picture of him than this. This room was my late master's favourite room, and these miniatures are just as they used to be then. He was very fond of them.'

This accounted to Elizabeth for Mr Wickham's being among them.

Mrs Reynolds then directed their attention to one of Miss Darcy, drawn when she was only eight years old.

'And is Miss Darcy as handsome as her brother?' said Mr Gardiner.

'Oh! yes – the handsomest young lady that ever was seen; and so accomplished! – She plays and sings all day long. In the next room is a new instrument just come down for her – a present from my master; she comes here to-morrow with him.'

Mr Gardiner, whose manners were easy and pleasant, encouraged her communicativeness by his questions and remarks; Mrs Reynolds, either from pride or attachment, had evidently great pleasure in talking of her master and his sister.

'Is your master much at Pemberley in the course of the year?'

'Not so much as I could wish, Sir; but I dare say he may spend half his time here; and Miss Darcy is always down for the summer months.'

'Except,' thought Elizabeth, 'when she goes to Ramsgate.'

'If your master would marry, you might see more of him.'

'Yes, Sir; but I do not know when that will be. I do not know who is good enough for him.'

Mr and Mrs Gardiner smiled. Elizabeth could not help saying, 'It is very much to his credit, I am sure, that you should think so.'

'I say no more than the truth, and what every body will say that knows him,' replied the other. Elizabeth thought this was going pretty far; and she listened with increasing astonishment as the housekeeper added, 'I have never had a cross word from him in my life, and I have known him every since he was four years old.'

This was praise, of all others most extraordinary, most opposite to her ideas. That he was not a good-tempered man, had been her firmest opinion. Her keenest attention was awakened; she longed to hear more, and was grateful to her uncle for saying,

'There are very few people of whom so much can be said. You are lucky in having such a master.'

'Yes, Sir, I know I am. If I was to go through the world, I could not meet with a better. But I have always observed, that they who are good-natured when children, are good-natured when they grow up; and he was always the sweetest-tempered, most generous-hearted, boy in the world.'

Elizabeth almost stared at her. – 'Can this be Mr Darcy!' thought she.

'His father was an excellent man,' said Mrs Gardiner.

'Yes, Ma'am, that he was indeed; and his son will be just like him – just as affable to the poor.'

Elizabeth listened, wondered, doubted, and was impatient for more. Mrs Reynolds could interest her on no other point. She related the subject of the pictures, the dimensions of the rooms, and the price of the furniture, in vain. Mr Gardiner, highly amused by the kind of family prejudice, to which he attributed her excessive commendation of her master, soon led again to the subject; and she dwelt with energy on his many merits, as they proceeded together up the great staircase.

'He is the best landlord, and the best master,' said she, 'that ever lived. Not like the wild young men now-a-days, who think of nothing but themselves. There is not one of his tenants or servants but what will give him a good name. Some people call him proud; but I am sure I never saw any thing of it. To my fancy, it is only because he does not rattle away like other young men.'

'In what an amiable light does this place him!' thought Elizabeth.

'This fine account of him,' whispered her aunt, as they walked, 'is not quite consistent with his behaviour to our poor friend.'

'Perhaps we might be deceived.'

'That is not very likely; our authority was too good.'

On reaching the spacious lobby above, they were shewn into a very pretty sitting-room, lately fitted up with greater elegance and lightness than the apartments below; and were informed that it was but just done, to give pleasure to Miss Darcy, who had taken a liking to the room, when last at Pemberley.

'He is certainly a good brother,' said Elizabeth, as she walked towards one of the windows.

Mrs Reynolds anticipated Miss Darcy's delight, when she should enter the room. 'And this is always the way with him,' she added. – 'Whatever can give his sister any pleasure, is sure to be done in a moment. There is nothing he would not do for her.'

The picture gallery, and two or three of the principal bedrooms, were all that remained to be shewn. In the former were many good paintings; but Elizabeth knew nothing of the art; and from such as had been already visible below, she had willingly turned to look at some drawings of Miss Darcy's, in crayons, whose subjects were usually more interesting, and also more intelligible.

In the gallery there were many family portraits, but they could have little to fix the attention of a stranger. Elizabeth walked on in quest of the only face whose features would be known to her. At last it arrested her – and she beheld a striking resemblance of Mr Darcy, with such a smile over the face, as she remembered to have sometimes seen, when he looked at her. She stood several minutes before the picture in earnest contemplation, and returned to it again before they quitted the gallery. Mrs Reynolds informed them, that it had been taken in his father's life time.

There was certainly at this moment, in Elizabeth's mind, a more gentle sensation towards the original, than she had ever felt in the height of their acquaintance. The commendation bestowed on him by Mrs Reynolds was of no trifling nature. What praise is more valuable than the praise of an intelligent servant? As a brother, a landlord, a master, she considered how many people's happiness were in his guardianship! – How much of pleasure or pain it was in his power to bestow! – How much of good or evil must be done by him! Every idea that had been brought forward by the housekeeper was favourable to his character, and as she stood before the canvas, on which he was represented, and fixed his eyes upon herself, she thought of his regard with a deeper sentiment of gratitude than it had ever raised before; she remembered its warmth, and softened its impropriety of expression.

When all of the house that was open to general inspection had been seen, they returned down stairs, and taking leave of the housekeeper, were consigned over to the gardener, who met them at the hall door.

As they walked across the lawn towards the river, Elizabeth turned back to look again; her uncle and aunt stopped also, and while the former was conjecturing as to the date of the building, the owner of it himself suddenly came forward from the road, which led behind it to the stables.

They were within twenty yards of each other, and so abrupt was his appearance, that it was impossible to avoid his sight. Their eyes instantly met, and the cheeks of each were overspread with the deepest blush. He absolutely started, and for a moment seemed immoveable from surprise; but shortly recovering himself, advanced towards the party, and spoke to Elizabeth, if not in terms of perfect composure, at least of perfect civility.

She had instinctively turned away; but, stopping on his approach, received his compliments with an embarrassment impossible to be overcome. Had his first appearance, or his resemblance to the picture they had just been examining, been insufficient to assure the other two that they now saw Mr Darcy, the gardener's expression of surprise, on beholding his master, must immediately have told it. They stood a little aloof while he was talking to their niece, who, astonished and confused, scarcely dared lift her eyes to his face, and knew not what answer she returned to his civil enquiries after her family. Amazed at the alteration in his manner since they last parted, every sentence that he uttered was increasing her embarrassment; and every idea of the impropriety of her being found there, recurring to her mind, the few minutes in which they continued together, were some of the most uncomfortable of her life. Nor did he seem much more at ease; when he spoke, his accent had none of its usual sedateness; and he repeated his enquiries as to the time of her having left Longbourn, and of her stay in Derbyshire, so often, and in so hurried a way, as plainly spoke the distraction of his thoughts.

At length, every idea seemed to fail him; and, after standing a few moments without saying a word, he suddenly recollected himself, and took leave.

The others then joined her, and expressed their admiration of his figure; but Elizabeth heard not a word, and, wholly engrossed by her own feelings, followed them in silence. She was overpowered by shame and vexation. Her coming there was the most unfortunate, the most ill-judged thing in the world! How strange must it appear to him! In what a disgraceful light might it not strike so vain a man! It might seem as if she had purposely thrown herself in his way again! Oh! why did she come? or, why did he thus come a day before he was expected? Had they been only ten minutes sooner, they should have been beyond the reach of his discrimination, for it was plain that he was that moment arrived, that moment alighted from his horse or his carriage. She blushed again and again over the perverseness of the meeting. And his behaviour, so strikingly altered, – what could it mean? That he should even speak to her was amazing! – but to speak with such civility, to enquire after her family! Never in her life had she seen his manners so little dignified, never had he spoken with such gentleness as on this unexpected meeting. What a contrast did it offer to his last address in Rosing's Park, when he put his letter into her hand! She knew not what to think, nor how to account for it.

They had now entered a beautiful walk by the side of the water, and every step was bringing forward a nobler fall of ground, or a finer reach of the woods to which they were approaching; but it was some time before Elizabeth was sensible of any of it; and, though she answered mechanically to the repeated appeals of her uncle and aunt, and seemed to direct her eyes to such objects as they pointed out, she distinguished no part of the scene. Her thoughts were all fixed on that one spot of Pemberley House, whichever it might be, where Mr Darcy then was. She longed to know what at that moment was passing in his mind; in what manner he thought of her, and whether, in defiance of every thing, she was still dear to him. Perhaps he had been civil, only because he felt himself at ease; yet there had been *that* in his voice, which was not like ease. Whether he had felt more of pain or of pleasure in seeing her, she could not tell, but he certainly had not seen her with composure.

At length, however, the remarks of her companions on her absence of mind roused her, and she felt the necessity of appearing more like herself.

They entered the woods, and bidding adieu to the river for a while, ascended some of the higher grounds; whence, in spots where the opening of the trees gave the eye power to wander, were many charming views of the valley, the opposite hills, with the long range of woods overspreading many, and occasionally part of the stream. Mr Gardiner expressed a wish of going round the whole Park, but feared it might be beyond a walk. With a triumphant smile, they were told, that it was ten miles round. It settled the matter; and they pursued the accustomed circuit; which brought them again, after some time, in a descent among hanging woods, to the edge of the water, in one of its narrowest parts. They crossed it by a simple bridge, in character with the general air of the scene; it was a spot less adorned than any they had yet visited; and the valley, here contracted into a glen, allowed room only for the stream, and a narrow walk amidst the rough coppice-wood which bordered it. Elizabeth longed to explore its windings; but when they had crossed the bridge, and perceived their distance from the house, Mrs Gardiner, who was not a great walker, could go no farther, and thought only of returning to the carriage as quickly as possible. Her niece was, therefore, obliged to submit, and they took their way towards the house on the opposite side of the river, in the nearest direction; but their progress was slow, for Mr Gardiner, though seldom able to indulge the taste, was very fond of fishing, and was so much engaged in watching the occasional appearance of some trout in the water, and talking to the man about them, that he advanced but little. Whilst wandering on in this slow manner, they were again surprised, and Elizabeth's astonishment was quite equal to what it had been at first, by the sight of Mr Darcy approaching them, and at no great distance. The walk being here less sheltered than on the other side, allowed them to see him before they met. Elizabeth, however astonished, was at least more prepared for an interview than before, and resolved to appear and to speak with calmness, if he really intended to meet them. For a few moments, indeed, she felt that he would probably strike into some other path. This idea lasted while a turning in the walk concealed him from their view; the turning past, he was immediately before them. With a glance she saw, that he had lost none of his recent civility; and, to imitate his politeness, she began, as they met, to admire the beauty of the place; but she had not got beyond the words 'delightful,' and 'charming,' when some unlucky recollections obtruded, and she fancied that praise of Pemberley from her, might be mischievously construed. Her colour changed, and she said no more.

Mrs Gardiner was standing a little behind; and on her pausing, he asked her, if she would do him the honour of introducing him to her friends. This was a stroke of civility for which she was quite unprepared; and she could hardly suppress a smile, at his being now seeking the acquaintance of some of those very people, against whom his pride had revolted, in his offer to herself. 'What will be his surprise,' thought she, 'when he knows who they are! He takes them now for people of fashion.'

The introduction, however, was immediately made; and as she named their relationship to herself, she stole a sly look at him, to see how he bore it; and was not without the expectation of his decamping as fast as he could from such disgraceful companions. That he was *surprised* by the connexion was evident; he sustained it however with fortitude, and so far from going away, turned back with them, and entered into conversation with Mr Gardiner. Elizabeth could not but be pleased, could not but triumph. It was consoling, that he should know she had some relations for whom there was no need to blush. She listened most attentively to all that passed between them, and gloried in every expression, every sentence of her uncle, which marked his intelligence, his taste, or his good manners.

The conversation soon turned upon fishing, and she heard Mr Darcy invite him, with the greatest civility, to fish there as often as he chose, while he continued in the neighbourhood, offering at the same time to supply him with fishing tackle, and pointing out those parts of the stream where there was usually most sport. Mrs Gardiner, who was walking arm in arm with Elizabeth, gave her a look expressive of her wonder. Elizabeth said nothing, but it gratified her exceedingly; the compliment must be all for herself. Her astonishment, however, was extreme; and continually was she repeating, 'Why is he so altered? From what can it proceed? It cannot be for *me*, it cannot be for *my* sake that his manners are thus softened. My reproofs at Hunsford could not work such a change as this. It is impossible that he should still love me.'

After walking some time in this way, the two ladies in front, the two gentlemen behind, on resuming their places, after descending to the brink of the river for the better inspection of some curious water-plant, there chanced to be a little alteration. It originated in Mrs Gardiner, who, fatigued by the exercise of the morning, found Elizabeth's arm inadequate to her support, and consequently preferred her husband's. Mr Darcy took her place by her niece, and they walked on together. After a short silence, the lady first spoke. She wished him to know that she had been assured of his absence before she came to the place, and accordingly began by observing, that his arrival had been very unexpected – 'for your housekeeper,' she added, 'informed us that you would certainly not be here till to-morrow; and indeed, before we left Bakewell, we understood that you were not immediately expected in the country.' He acknowledged the truth of it all; and said that business with his steward had occasioned his coming forward a few hours before the rest of the party with whom he had been travelling. 'They will join me early to-morrow,' he continued, 'and among them are some who will claim an acquaintance with you, – Mr Bingley and his sisters.'

Elizabeth answered only by a slight bow. Her thoughts were instantly driven back to the time when Mr Bingley's name had been last mentioned between them; and if she might judge from his complexion, *his* mind was not very differently engaged.

'There is also one other person in the party,' he continued after a pause, 'who more particularly wishes to be known to you, – Will you allow me, or do I ask too much, to introduce my sister to your acquaintance during your stay at Lambton?'

The surprise of such an application was great indeed; it was too great for her to know in what manner she acceded to it. She immediately felt that whatever desire Miss Darcy might have of being acquainted with her, must be the work of her brother, and without looking farther, it was satisfactory; it was gratifying to know that his resentment had not made him think really ill of her.

They now walked on in silence; each of them deep in thought. Elizabeth was not comfortable; that was impossible; but she was flattered and pleased. His wish of introducing his sister to her, was a compliment of the highest kind. They soon outstripped the others, and when they had reached the carriage, Mr and Mrs Gardiner were half a quarter of a mile behind.

He then asked her to walk into the house – but she declared herself not tired, and they stood together on the lawn. At such a time, much might have been said, and silence was very awkward. She wanted to talk, but there seemed an embargo on every subject. At last she recollected that she had been travelling, and they talked of Matlock and Dove Dale with great perseverance. Yet time and her aunt moved slowly – and her patience and her ideas were nearly worn out before the tête-à-tête was over. On Mr and Mrs Gardiner's coming up, they were all pressed to go into the house and take some refreshment; but this was declined, and they parted on each side with the utmost politeness. Mr Darcy handed the ladies into the carriage, and when it drove off Elizabeth saw him walking slowly towards the house.

The observations of her uncle and aunt now began; and each of them pronounced him to be infinitely superior to any thing they had expected. 'He is perfectly well behaved, polite, and unassuming,' said her uncle.

'There is something a little stately in him to be sure,' replied her aunt, 'but it is confined to his air, and is not unbecoming. I can now say with the housekeeper, that though some people may call him proud, *I* have seen nothing of it.'

'I was never more surprised than by his behaviour to us. It was more than civil; it was really attentive; and there was no necessity for such attention. His acquaintance with Elizabeth was very trifling.'

'To be sure, Lizzy,' said her aunt, 'he is not so handsome as Wickham; or rather he has not Wickham's countenance, for his features are perfectly good. But how came you to tell us that he was so disagreeable?'

Elizabeth excused herself as well as she could; said that she had liked him better when they met in Kent than before, and that she had never seen him so pleasant as this morning.

'But perhaps he may be a little whimsical in his civilities,' replied her uncle. 'Your great men often are; and therefore I shall not take him at his word about fishing, as he might change his mind another day, and warn me off his grounds.'

Elizabeth felt that they had entirely mistaken his character, but said nothing.

'From what we have seen of him,' continued Mrs Gardiner, 'I really should not have thought that he could have behaved in so cruel a way by any body, as he has done by poor Wickham. He has not an ill-natured look. On the contrary, there is something pleasing about his mouth when he speaks. And there is something of dignity in his countenance, that would not give one an unfavourable idea of his heart. But to be sure, the good lady who shewed us the house, did give him a most flaming character! I could hardly help laughing aloud sometimes. But he is a liberal master, I suppose, and *that* in the eye of a servant comprehends every virtue.'

Elizabeth here felt herself called on to say something in vindication of his behaviour to Wickham; and therefore gave them to understand, in as guarded a manner as she could, that by what she had heard from his relations in Kent, his actions were capable of a very different construction; and that his character was by no means so faulty, nor Wickham's so amiable, as they had been considered in Hertfordshire. In confirmation of this, she related the particulars of all the pecuniary transactions in which they had been connected, without actually naming her authority, but stating it to be such as might be relied on.

Mrs Gardiner was surprised and concerned; but as they were now approaching the scene of her former pleasures, every idea gave way to the charm of recollection; and she was too much engaged in pointing out to her husband all the interesting spots in its environs, to think of any thing else. Fatigued as she had been by the morning's walk, they had no sooner dined than she set off again in quest of her former acquaintance, and the evening was spent in the satisfactions of an intercourse renewed after many years discontinuance.

The occurrences of the day were too full of interest to leave Elizabeth much attention for any of these new friends; and she could do nothing but think, and think with wonder, of Mr Darcy's civility, and above all, of his wishing her to be acquainted with his sister.

Chapter Forty Four

ELIZABETH HAD SETTLED IT THAT Mr Darcy would bring his sister to visit her, the very day after her reaching Pemberley; and was consequently resolved not to be out of sight of the inn the whole of that morning. But her conclusion was false; for on the very morning after their own arrival at Lambton, these visitors came. They had been walking about the place with some of their new friends, and were just returned to the inn to dress themselves for dining with the same family, when the sound of a carriage drew them to a window, and they saw a gentleman and lady in a curricle, driving up the street. Elizabeth immediately recognizing the livery, guessed what it meant, and imparted no small degree of surprise to her relations, by acquainting them with the honour which she expected. Her uncle and aunt were all amazement; and the embarrassment of her manner as she spoke, joined to the circumstance itself, and many of the circumstances of the preceding day, opened to them a new idea on the business. Nothing had ever suggested it before, but they now felt that there was no other way of accounting for such attentions from such a quarter, than by supposing a partiality for their niece. While these newlyborn notions were passing in their heads, the perturbation of Elizabeth's feelings was every moment increasing. She was quite amazed at her own discomposure; but amongst other causes of disquiet, she dreaded lest the partiality of the brother should have said too much in her favour; and more than commonly anxious to please, she naturally suspected that every power of pleasing would fail her.

She retreated from the window, fearful of being seen; and as she walked up and down the room, endeavouring to compose herself, saw such looks of enquiring surprise in her uncle and aunt, as made every thing worse.

Miss Darcy and her brother appeared, and this formidable introduction took place. With astonishment did Elizabeth see, that her new acquaintance was at least as much embarrassed as herself. Since her being at Lambton, she had heard that Miss Darcy was exceedingly proud; but the observation of a very few minutes convinced her, that she was only exceedingly shy. She found it difficult to obtain even a word from her beyond a monosyllable.

Miss Darcy was tall, and on a larger scale than Elizabeth; and, though little more than sixteen, her figure was formed, and her appearance womanly and graceful. She was less handsome than her brother, but there was sense and good humour in her face, and her manners were perfectly unassuming and gentle. Elizabeth, who had expected to find in her as acute and unembarrassed an observer as ever Mr Darcy had been, was much relieved by discerning such different feelings.

They had not been long together, before Darcy told her that Bingley was also coming to wait on her; and she had barely time to express her satisfaction, and prepare for such a visitor, when Bingley's quick step was heard on the stairs, and in a moment he entered the room. All Elizabeth's anger against him had been long done away; but, had she still felt any, it could hardly have stood its ground against the unaffected cordiality with which he expressed himself, on seeing her again. He enquired in a friendly, though general way, after her family, and looked and spoke with the same good-humoured ease that he had ever done.

To Mr and Mrs Gardiner he was scarcely a less interesting personage than to herself. They had long wished to see him. The whole party before them, indeed, excited a lively attention. The suspicions which had just arisen of Mr Darcy and their niece, directed their observation towards each with an earnest, though guarded, enquiry; and they soon drew from those enquiries the full conviction that one of them at least knew what it was to love. Of the lady's sensations they remained a little in doubt; but that the gentleman was overflowing with admiration was evident enough.

Elizabeth, on her side, had much to do. She wanted to ascertain the feelings of each of her visitors, she wanted to compose her own, and to make herself agreeable to all; and in the latter object, where she feared most to fail, she was most sure of success, for those to whom she endeavoured to give pleasure were prepossessed in her favour. Bingley was ready, Georgiana was eager, and Darcy determined, to be pleased.

In seeing Bingley, her thoughts naturally flew to her sister; and oh! how ardently did she long to know, whether any of his were directed in a like manner. Sometimes she could fancy, that he talked less than on former occasions, and once or twice pleased herself with the notion that as he looked at her, he was trying to trace a resemblance. But, though this might be imaginary, she could not be deceived as to his behaviour to Miss Darcy, who had been set up as a rival of Jane. No look appeared on either side that spoke particular regard. Nothing occurred between them that could justify the hopes of his sister. On this point she was soon satisfied; and two or three little circumstances occurred ere they parted, which, in her anxious inter-pretation, denoted a recollection of Jane, not untinctured by tenderness, and a wish of saying more that might lead to the mention of her, had he dared. He observed to her, at a moment when the others were talking together, and in a tone which had something of real regret, that it 'was a very long time since he had had the pleasure of seeing her;' and, before she could reply, he added, 'It is above eight months. We have not met since the 26th of November, when we were all dancing together at Netherfield.'

Elizabeth was pleased to find his memory so exact; and he afterwards took occasion to ask her, when unattended to by any of the rest, whether *all* her sisters were at Longbourn. There was not much in the question, nor in the preceding remark, but there was a look and a manner which gave them meaning.

It was not often that she could turn her eyes on Mr Darcy himself; but, whenever she did catch a glimpse, she saw an expression of general com-plaisance, and in all that he said, she heard an accent so far removed from hauteur or disdain of his companions, as convinced her that the improvement of manners which she had yesterday witnessed, however temporary its existence might prove, had at least outlived one day. When she saw him thus seeking the acquaintance, and courting the good opinion of people, with whom any intercourse a few months ago would have been a disgrace; when she saw him thus civil, not only to herself, but to the very relations whom he had openly disdained, and recollected their last lively scene in Hunsford Parsonage, the difference, the change was so great, and struck so forcibly on her mind, that she could hardly restrain her astonishment from being visible. Never, even in the company of his dear friends at Netherfield, or his dignified relations at Rosings, had she seen him so desirous to please, so free from self-consequence, or unbending reserve as now, when no importance could result from the success of his endeavours, and when even the acquaintance of those to whom his attentions were addressed, would draw down the ridicule and censure of the ladies both of Netherfield and Rosings.

Their visitors staid with them above half an hour, and when they arose to depart, Mr Darcy called on his sister to join him in expressing their wish of seeing Mr and Mrs Gardiner, and Miss Bennet, to dinner at Pemberley, before they left the country. Miss Darcy, though with a diffidence which marked her little in the habit of giving invitations, readily obeyed. Mrs

Gardiner looked at her niece, desirous of knowing how *she*, whom the invitation most concerned, felt disposed as to its acceptance, but Elizabeth had turned away her head. Presuming, however, that this studied avoidance spoke rather a momentary embarrassment, than any dislike of the proposal, and seeing in her husband, who was fond of society, a perfect willingness to accept it, she ventured to engage for her attendance, and the day after the next was fixed on.

Bingley expressed great pleasure in the certainty of seeing Elizabeth again, having still a great deal to say to her, and many enquiries to make after all their Hertfordshire friends. Elizabeth, construing all this into a wish of hearing her speak of her sister, was pleased; and on this account, as well as some others, found herself, when their visitors left them, capable of considering the last half hour with some satisfaction, though while it was passing, the enjoyment of it had been little. Eager to be alone, and fearful of enquiries or hints from her uncle and aunt, she staid with them only long enough to hear their favourable opinion of Bingley, and then hurried away to dress.

But she had no reason to fear Mr and Mrs Gardiner's curiosity; it was not their wish to force her communication. It was evident that she was much better acquainted with Mr Darcy than they had before any idea of; it was evident that he was very much in love with her. They saw much to interest, but nothing to justify enquiry.

Of Mr Darcy it was now a matter of anxiety to think well; and, as far as their acquaintance reached, there was no fault to find. They could not be untouched by his politeness, and had they drawn his character from their own feelings, and his servant's report, without any reference to any other account, the circle in Hertfordshire to which he was known, would not have recognised it for Mr Darcy. There was now an interest, however, in believing the housekeeper; and they soon became sensible, that the authority of a servant who had known him since he was four years old, and whose own manners indicated respectability, was not to be hastily rejected. Neither had any thing occurred in the intelligence of their Lambton friends, that could materially lessen its weight. They had nothing to accuse him of but pride; pride he probably had, and if not, it would certainly be imputed by the inhabitants of a small market-town, where the family did not visit. It was acknowledged, however, that he was a liberal man, and did much good among the poor.

With respect to Wickham, the travellers soon found that he was not held there in much estimation; for though the chief of his concerns, with the son of his patron, were imperfectly understood, it was yet a well known fact that, on his quitting Derbyshire, he had left many debts behind him, which Mr Darcy afterwards discharged.

As for Elizabeth, her thoughts were at Pemberley this evening more than the last; and the evening, though as it passed it seemed long, was not long enough to determine her feelings towards *one* in that mansion; and she lay awake two whole hours, endeavouring to make them out. She certainly did not hate him. No; hatred had vanished long ago, and she had almost as long been ashamed of ever feeling a dislike against him, that could be so called. The respect created by the conviction of his valuable qualities, though at first unwillingly admitted, had for some time ceased to be repugnant to her feelings; and it was now heightened into somewhat of a friendlier nature, by the testimony so highly in his favour, and bringing forward his disposition in so amiable a light, which yesterday had produced. But above all, above respect and esteem, there was a motive within her of good will which could not be overlooked. It was gratitude. – Gratitude, not merely for having once loved her, but for loving her still well enough, to forgive all the petulance and acrimony of her manner in rejecting him, and all the unjust accusations accompanying her rejection. He who, she had been persuaded, would avoid her as his greatest enemy, seemed, on this accidental meeting, most eager to preserve the acquaintance, and without any indelicate display of regard, or any peculiarity of manner, where their two selves only were concerned, was soliciting the good opinion of her friends, and bent on making her known to his sister. Such a change in a man of so much pride, excited not only astonishment but gratitude – for to love, ardent love, it must be attributed; and as such its impression on her was of a sort to be encouraged, as by no means unpleasing, though it could not be exactly defined. She respected, she esteemed, she was grateful to him, she felt a real interest in his welfare; and she only wanted to know how far she wished that welfare to depend upon herself, and how far it would be for the happiness of both that she should employ the power, which her fancy told her she still possessed, of bringing on the renewal of his addresses.

It had been settled in the evening, between the aunt and niece, that such a striking civility as Miss Darcy's, in coming to them on the very day of her arrival at Pemberley, for she had reached it only to a late breakfast, ought to be imitated, though it could not be equalled, by some exertion of politeness on their side; and, consequently, that it would be highly expedient to wait on her at Pemberley the following morning. They were, therefore, to go. – Elizabeth was pleased, though, when she asked herself the reason, she had very little to say in reply.

Mr Gardiner left them soon after breakfast. The fishing scheme had been renewed the day before, and a positive engagement made of his meeting some of the gentlemen at Pemberley by noon.

Chapter Forty Five

CONVINCED AS ELIZABETH NOW WAS that Miss Bingley's dislike of her had origi-nated in jealousy, she could not help feeling how very unwelcome her appearance at Pemberley must be to her, and was curious to know with how much civility on that lady's side, the acquaintance would now be renewed.

On reaching the house, they were shewn through the hall into the saloon, whose northern aspect rendered it delightful for summer. Its windows opening to the ground, admitted a most refreshing view of the high woody hills behind the house, and of the beautiful oaks and Spanish chesnuts which were scattered over the intermediate lawn.

In this room they were received by Miss Darcy, who was sitting there with Mrs Hurst and Miss Bingley, and the lady with whom she lived in London. Georgiana's reception of them was very civil; but attended with all that embarrassment which, though proceeding from shyness and the fear of doing wrong, would easily give to those who felt themselves inferior, the belief of her being proud and reserved. Mrs Gardiner and her niece, however, did her justice, and pitied her.

By Mrs Hurst and Miss Bingley, they were noticed only by a curtsey; and on their being seated, a pause, awkward as such pauses must always be, succeeded for a few moments. It was first broken by Mrs Annesley, a genteel, agreeable-looking woman, whose endeavour to introduce some kind of discourse, proved her to be more truly well bred than either of the others; and between her and Mrs Gardiner, with occasional help from Elizabeth, the conversation was carried on. Miss Darcy looked as if she wished for courage enough to join in it; and sometimes did venture a short sentence, when there was least danger of its being heard.

Elizabeth soon saw that she was herself closely watched by Miss Bingley, and that she could not speak a word, especially to Miss Darcy, without calling her attention. This observation would not have prevented her from trying to talk to the latter, had they not been seated at an inconvenient distance; but she was not sorry to be spared the necessity of saying much. Her own thoughts were employing her. She expected every moment that some of the gentlemen would enter the room. She wished, she feared that the master of the house might be amongst them; and whether she wished or feared it most, she could scarcely determine. After sitting in this manner a quarter of an hour, without hearing Miss Bingley's voice, Elizabeth was roused by receiving from her a cold enquiry after the health of her family. She answered with equal indifference and brevity, and the other said no more.

The next variation which their visit afforded was produced by the entrance of servants with cold meat, cake, and a variety of all the finest fruits in season; but this did not take place till after many a significant look and smile from Mrs Annesley to Miss Darcy had been given, to remind her of her post. There was now employment for the whole party; for though they could not all talk, they could all eat; and the beautiful pyramids of grapes, nectarines, and peaches, soon collected them round the table.

While thus engaged, Elizabeth had a fair opportunity of deciding whether she most feared or wished for the appearance of Mr Darcy, by the feelings which prevailed on his entering the room; and then, though but a moment before she had believed her wishes to predominate, she began to regret that he came.

He had been some time with Mr Gardiner, who, with two or three other gentlemen from the house, was engaged by the river, and had left him only on learning that the ladies of the family intended a visit to Georgiana that morning. No sooner did he appear, than Elizabeth wisely resolved to be perfectly easy and unembarrassed; – a resolution the more necessary to be made, but perhaps not the more easily kept, because she saw that the suspicions of the whole party were awakened against them, and that there was scarcely an eye which did not watch his behaviour when he first came into the room. In no countenance was attentive curiosity so strongly marked as in Miss Bingley's, in spite of the smiles which overspread her face whenever she spoke to one of its objects; for jealousy had not yet made her desperate, and her attentions to Mr Darcy were by no means over. Miss Darcy, on her brother's entrance, exerted herself much more to talk; and

Elizabeth saw that he was anxious for his sister and herself to get acquainted, and forwarded, as much as possible, every attempt at conversation on either side. Miss Bingley saw all this likewise; and, in the imprudence of anger, took the first opportunity of saying, with sneering civility,

'Pray, Miss Eliza, are not the —shire militia removed from Meryton? They must be a great loss to *your* family.'

In Darcy's presence she dared not mention Wickham's name; but Elizabeth instantly comprehended that he was uppermost in her thoughts; and the various recollections connected with him gave her a moment's distress; but, exerting herself vigorously to repel the ill-natured attack, she presently answered the question in a tolerably disengaged tone. While she spoke, an involuntary glance shewed her Darcy with an heightened complexion, earnestly looking at her, and his sister overcome with confusion, and unable to lift up her eyes. Had Miss Bingley known what pain she was then giving her beloved friend, she undoubtedly would have refrained from the hint; but she had merely intended to discompose Elizabeth, by bringing forward the idea of a man to whom she believed her partial, to make her betray a sensibility which might injure her in Darcy's opinion, and perhaps to remind the latter of all the follies and absurdities, by which some part of her family were connected with that corps. Not a syllable had ever reached her of Miss Darcy's meditated elopement. To no creature had it been revealed, where secrecy was possible, except to Elizabeth; and from all Bingley's connections her brother was particularly anxious to conceal it, from that very wish which Elizabeth had long ago attributed to him, of their becoming hereafter her own. He had certainly formed such a plan, and without meaning that it should affect his endeavour to separate him from Miss Bennet, it is probable that it might add something to his lively concern for the welfare of his friend.

Elizabeth's collected behaviour, however, soon quieted his emotion; and as Miss Bingley, vexed and disappointed, dared not approach nearer to Wickham, Georgiana also recovered in time, though not enough to be able to speak any more. Her brother, whose eye she feared to meet, scarcely recollected her interest in the affair, and the very circumstance which had been designed to turn his thoughts from Elizabeth, seemed to have fixed them on her more, and more cheerfully.

Their visit did not continue long after the question and answer above-mentioned; and while Mr Darcy was attending them to their carriage, Miss Bingley was venting her feelings in criticisms on Elizabeth's person, behaviour, and dress. But Georgiana would not join her. Her brother's recommendation was enough to ensure her favour; his judgment could not err, and he had spoken in such terms of Elizabeth, as to leave Georgiana without the power of finding her otherwise than lovely and amiable. When Darcy returned to the saloon, Miss Bingley could not help repeating to him some part of what she had been saying to his sister.

'How very ill Eliza Bennet looks this morning, Mr Darcy,' she cried; 'I never in my life saw any one so much altered as she is since the winter. She is grown so brown and coarse! Louisa and I were agreeing that we should not have known her again.'

However little Mr Darcy might have liked such an address, he contented himself with coolly replying, that he perceived no other alteration than her being rather tanned, – no miraculous consequence of travelling in the summer.

'For my own part,' she rejoined, 'I must confess that I never could see any beauty in her. Her face is too thin; her complexion has no brilliancy; and her features are not at all handsome. Her nose wants character; there is nothing marked in its lines. Her teeth are tolerable, but not out of the common way; and as for her eyes, which have sometimes been called so fine, I never could perceive any thing extraordinary in them. They have a sharp, shrewish look, which I do not like at all; and in her air altogether, there is a self-sufficiency without fashion, which is intolerable.'

Persuaded as Miss Bingley was that Darcy admired Elizabeth, this was not the best method of recommending herself; but angry people are not always wise; and in seeing him at last look somewhat nettled, she had all the success she expected. He was resolutely silent however; and, from a determination of making him speak, she continued,

'I remember, when we first knew her in Hertfordshire, how amazed we all were to find that she was a reputed beauty; and I particularly recollect your saying one night, after they had been dining at Netherfield, "She a beauty! – I should as soon call her mother a wit." But afterwards she seemed to improve on you, and I believe you thought her rather pretty at one time.'

'Yes,' replied Darcy, who could contain himself no longer, 'but that was only when I first knew her, for it is many months since I have considered her as one of the handsomest women of my acquaintance.'

He then went away, and Miss Bingley was left to all the satisfaction of having forced him to say what gave no one any pain but herself.

Mrs Gardiner and Elizabeth talked of all that had occurred, during their visit, as they returned, except what had particularly interested them both. The looks and behaviour of every body they had seen were discussed, except of the person who had mostly engaged their attention. They talked of his sister, his friends, his house, his fruit, of every thing but himself; yet Elizabeth was longing to know what Mrs Gardiner thought of him, and Mrs Gardiner would have been highly gratified by her niece's beginning the subject.

Chapter Forty Six

ELIZABETH HAD BEEN A GOOD DEAL DISAPPOINTED in not finding a letter from Jane, on their first arrival at Lambton; and this disappointment had been renewed on each of the mornings that had now been spent there; but on the third, her repining was over, and her sister justified by the receipt of two letters from her at once, on one of which was marked that it had been missent elsewhere. Elizabeth was not surprised at it, as Jane had written the direction remarkably ill.

They had just been preparing to walk as the letters came in; and her uncle and aunt, leaving her to enjoy them in quiet, set off by themselves. The one missent must be first attended to; it had been written five days ago.

The beginning contained an account of all their little parties and engagements, with such news as the country afforded; but the latter half, which was dated a day later, and written in evident agitation, gave more important intelligence. It was to this effect:

'Since writing the above, dearest Lizzy, something has occurred of a most unexpected and serious nature; but I am afraid of alarming you – be assured that we are all well. What I have to say relates to poor Lydia. An express came at twelve last night, just as we were all gone to bed, from Colonel Forster, to inform us that she was gone off to Scotland with one of his officers; to own the truth, with Wickham! – Imagine our surprise. To Kitty, however, it does not seem so wholly unexpected. I am very, very sorry. So imprudent a match on both sides! – But I am willing to hope the best, and that his character has been misunderstood. Thoughtless and indiscreet I can easily believe him, but this step (and let us rejoice over it) marks nothing bad at heart. His choice is disinterested at least, for he must know my father can give her nothing. Our poor mother is sadly grieved. My father bears it better. How thankful am I, that we never let them know what has been said against him; we must forget it ourselves. They were off Saturday night about twelve, as is conjectured, but were not missed till yesterday morning at eight. The express was sent off directly. My dear Lizzy, they must have passed within ten miles of us. Colonel Forster gives us reason to expect him here soon. Lydia left a few lines for his wife, informing her of their intention. I must conclude, for I cannot be long from my poor mother. I am afraid you will not be able to make it out, but I hardly know what I have written.'

Without allowing herself time for consideration, and scarcely knowing what she felt, Elizabeth on finishing this letter, instantly seized the other, and opening it with the utmost impatience, read as follows: it had been written a day later than the conclusion of the first.

'By this time, my dearest sister, you have received my hurried letter; I wish this may be more intelligible, but though not confined for time, my head is so bewildered that I cannot answer for being coherent. Dearest Lizzy, I hardly know what I would write, but I have bad news for you, and it cannot be delayed. Imprudent as a marriage between Mr Wickham and our poor Lydia would be, we are now anxious to be assured it has taken place, for there is but too much reason to fear they are not gone to Scotland. Colonel Forster came yesterday, having left Brighton the day before, not many hours after the express. Though Lydia's short letter to Mrs F. gave them to understand that they were going to Gretna Green, something was dropped by Denny expressing his belief that W. never intended to go there, or to marry Lydia at all, which was repeated to Colonel F. who instantly taking the alarm, set off from B. intending to trace their route. He did trace them easily to Clapham, but no farther; for on entering that place they removed into a hackney-coach and dismissed the chaise that brought them from Epsom. All that is known after this is, that they were seen to continue the London road. I know not what to think. After making every possible enquiry on that side London, Colonel F. came on into Hertfordshire, anxiously renewing them at all the turnpikes, and at the inns in Barnet and Hatfield, but without any success, no such people had been seen to pass through. With the kindest concern he came on to Longbourn, and broke his apprehensions to us in a manner most creditable to his heart. I am sincerely grieved for him and Mrs F. but no one can throw any blame on them. Our distress, my dear

Lizzy, is very great. My father and mother believe the worst, but I cannot think so ill of him. Many circumstances might make it more eligible for them to be married privately in town than to pursue their first plan; and even if *he* could form such a design against a young woman of Lydia's connections, which is not likely, can I suppose her so lost to every thing? – Impossible. I grieve to find, however, that Colonel F. is not disposed to depend upon their marriage; he shook his head when I expressed my hopes, and said he feared W. was not a man to be trusted. My poor mother is really ill and keeps her room. Could she exert herself it would be better, but this is not to be expected; and as to my father, I never in my life saw him so affected. Poor Kitty has anger for having concealed their attachment; but as it was a matter of confidence one cannot wonder. I am truly glad, dearest Lizzy, that you have been spared something of these distressing scenes; but now as the first shock is over, shall I own that I long for your return? I am not so selfish, however, as to press for it, if inconvenient. Adieu. I take up my pen again to do, what I have just told you I would not, but circumstances are such, that I cannot help earnestly begging you all to come here, as soon as possible. I know my dear uncle and aunt so well, that I am not afraid of requesting it, though I have still something more to ask of the former. My father is going to London with Colonel Forster instantly, to try to discover her. What he means to do, I am sure I know not; but his excessive distress will not allow him to pursue any measure in the best and safest way, and Colonel Forster is obliged to be at Brighton again to-morrow evening. In such an exigence my uncle's advice and assistance would be every thing in the world; he will immediately comprehend what I must feel, and I rely upon his goodness.'

'Oh! where, where is my uncle?' cried Elizabeth, darting from her seat as she finished the letter, in eagerness to follow him, without losing a moment of the time so precious; but as she reached the door, it was opened by a servant, and Mr Darcy appeared. Her pale face and impetuous manner made him start, and before he could recover himself enough to speak, she, in whose mind every idea was superseded by Lydia's situation, hastily exlaimed, 'I beg your pardon, but I must leave you. I must find Mr Gardiner this moment, on business that cannot be delayed; I have not an instant to lose.'

'Good God! what is the matter?' cried he, with more feeling than politeness; then recollecting himself, 'I will not detain you a minute, but let me, or let the servant, go after Mr and Mrs Gardiner. You are not well enough; – you cannot go yourself.'

Elizabeth hesitated, but her knees trembled under her, and she felt how little would be gained by her attempting to pursue them. Calling back the servant, therefore, she commissioned him, though in so breathless an accent as made her almost unintelligible, to fetch his master and mistress home, instantly.

On his quitting the room, she sat down, unable to support herself, and looking so miserably ill, that it was impossible for Darcy to leave her, or to refrain from saying, in a tone of gentleness and commiseration, 'Let me call your maid. Is there nothing you could take, to give you present relief? – A glass of wine; – shall I get you one? – You are very ill.'

'No, I thank you;' she replied, endeavouring to recover herself. 'There is nothing the matter with me. I am quite well. I am only distressed by some dreadful news which I have just received from Longbourn.'

She burst into tears as she alluded to it, and for a few minutes could not speak another word. Darcy, in wretched suspense, could only say something indistinctly of his concern, and observe her in compassionate silence. At length, she spoke again. 'I have just had a letter from Jane, with such dreadful news. It cannot be concealed from any one. My youngest sister has left all her friends – has eloped; – has thrown herself into the power of – of Mr Wickham. They are gone off together from Brighton. You know him too well to doubt the rest. She has no money, no connections, nothing that can tempt him to – she is lost for ever.'

Darcy was fixed in astonishment. 'When I consider,' she added, in a yet more agitated voice, 'that *I* might have prevented it! – *I* who knew what he was. Had I but explained some part of it only – some part of what I learnt, to my own family! Had his character been known, this could not have happened. But it is all, all too late now.'

'I am grieved, indeed,' cried Darcy; 'grieved – shocked. But is it certain, absolutely certain?'

'Oh yes! – They left Brighton together on Sunday night, and were traced almost to London, but not beyond; they are certainly not gone to Scotland.'

'And what has been done, what has been attempted, to recover her?'

'My father is gone to London, and Jane has written to beg my uncle's immediate assistance, and we shall be off, I hope, in half an hour. But nothing can be done; I know very well that nothing can be done. How is such a man to be worked on? How are they even to be discovered? I have not the smallest hope. It is every way horrible!'

Darcy shook his head in silent acquiesence.

'When *my* eyes were opened to his real character. – Oh! had I known what I ought, what I dared, to do! But I knew not – I was afraid of doing too much. Wretched, wretched, mistake!'

Darcy made no answer. He seemed scarcely to hear her, and was walking up and down the room in earnest meditation; his brow contracted, his air gloomy. Elizabeth soon observed, and instantly understood it. Her power was sinking; every thing *must* sink under such a proof of family weakness, such an assurance of the deepest disgrace. She could neither wonder nor condemn, but the belief of his self-conquest brought nothing consolatory to her bosom, afforded no palliation of her distress. It was, on the contrary, exactly calculated to make her understand her own wishes; and never had she so honestly felt that she could have loved him, as now, when all love must be vain.

But self, though it would intrude, could not engross her, Lydia – the humiliation, the misery, she was bringing on them all, soon swallowed up every private care; and covering her face with her handkerchief, Elizabeth was soon lost to every thing else; and, after a pause of several minutes, was only recalled to a sense of her situation by the voice of her companion, who, in a manner, which though it spoke compassion, spoke likewise restraint, said, 'I am afraid you have been long desiring my absence, nor have I any thing to plead in excuse of my stay, but real, though unavailing, concern. Would to heaven that any thing could be either said or done on my part, that might offer consolation to such distress. – But I will not torment you with vain wishes, which may seem purposely to ask for your thanks. This unfortunate affair will, I fear, prevent my sister's having the pleasure of seeing you at Pemberley to day.'

'Oh, yes. Be so kind as to apologize for us to Miss Darcy. Say that urgent business calls us home immediately. Conceal the unhappy truth as long as it is possible. – I know it cannot be long.'

He readily assured her of his secrecy – again expressed his sorrow for her distress, wished it a happier conclusion than there was at present reason to hope, and leaving his compliments for her relations, with only one serious, parting, look, went away.

As he quitted the room, Elizabeth felt how improbable it was that they should ever see each other again on such terms of cordiality as had marked their several meetings in Derbyshire; and as she threw a retrospective glance over the whole of their acquaintance, so full of contradictions and varieties, sighed at the perverseness of those feelings which would now have promoted its continuance, and would formerly have rejoiced in its termination.

If gratitude and esteem are good foundations of affection, Elizabeth's change of sentiment will be neither improbable nor faulty. But if otherwise, if the regard springing from such sources is unreasonable or unnatural, in comparison of what is so often described as arising on a first interview with its object, and even before two words have been exchanged, nothing can be said in her defence, except that she had given somewhat of a trial to the latter method, in her partiality for Wickham, and that its ill-success might perhaps authorize her to seek the other less interesting mode of attachment. Be that as it may, she saw him go with regret; and in this early example of what Lydia's infamy must produce, found additional anguish as she reflected on that wretched business. Never, since reading Jane's second letter, had she entertained a hope of Wickham's meaning to marry her. No one but Jane, she thought, could flatter herself with such an expectation. Surprise was the least of her feelings on this development. While the contents of the first letter remained on her mind, she was all surprise – all astonishment that Wickham should marry a girl, whom it was impossible he could marry for money; and how Lydia could ever have attached him, had appeared incomprehensible. But now it was all too natural. For such an attachment as this, she might have sufficient charms; and though she did not suppose Lydia to be deliberately engaging in an elopement, without the intention of marriage, she had no difficulty in believing that neither her virtue nor her understanding would preserve her from falling an easy prey.

She had never perceived, while the regiment was in Hertfordshire, that Lydia had any partiality for him, but she was convinced that Lydia had wanted only encouragement to attach herself to any body. Sometimes one officer, sometimes another had been her favourite, as their attentions raised them in her opinion. Her affections had been continually fluctuating, but never without an object. The mischief of neglect and mistaken indulgence towards such a girl. – Oh! how acutely did she now feel it.

She was wild to be at home – to hear, to see, to be upon the spot, to share with Jane in the cares that must now fall wholly upon her, in a family so deranged; a father absent, a mother incapable of exertion, and requiring constant attendance; and though almost persuaded that nothing could be done for Lydia, her uncle's interference seemed of the utmost importance, and till he entered the room, the misery of her impatience was severe. Mr and Mrs Gardiner had hurried back in alarm, supposing, by the servant's account, that their niece was taken suddenly ill; – but satisfying them instantly on that head, she eagerly communicated the cause of their summons, reading the two letters aloud, and dwelling on the postscript of the last, with trembling energy. – Though Lydia had never been a favourite with them, Mr and Mrs Gardiner could not but be deeply affected. Not Lydia only, but all were concerned in it; and after the first exclamations of surprise and horror, Mr Gardiner readily promised every assistance in his power. – Elizabeth, though expecting no less, thanked him with tears of gratitude; and all three being actuated by one spirit, every thing relating to their journey was speedily settled. They were to be off as soon as possible. 'But what is to be done about Pemberley?' cried Mrs Gardiner, 'John told us Mr Darcy was here when you sent for us; – was it so?'

'Yes; and I told him we should not be able to keep our engagement. *That* is all settled.'

'That is all settled;' repeated the other, as she ran into her room to prepare. 'And are they upon such terms as for her to disclose the real truth! Oh, that I knew how it was!'

But wishes were vain; or at best could serve only to amuse her in the hurry and confusion of the following hour. Had Elizabeth been at leisure to be idle, she would have remained certain that all employment was impossible to one so wretched as herself; but she had her share of husiness as well as her aunt, and amongst the rest there were notes to be written to all their friends in Lambton, with false excuses for their sudden departure. An hour, however, saw the whole completed; and Mr Gardiner meanwhile having settled his account at the inn, nothing remained to be done but to go; and Elizabeth, after all the misery of the morning, found herself, in a shorter space of time than she could have supposed, seated in the carriage, and on the road to Longbourn.

Chapter Forty Seven

'I HAVE BEEN THINKING IT OVER AGAIN, Elizabeth,' said her uncle, as they drove from the town; 'and really, upon serious consideration, I am much more inclined than I was to judge as your eldest sister does of the matter. It appears to me so very unlikely, that any young man should form such a design against a girl who is by no means unprotected or friendless and who was actually staying in his colonel's family, that I am strongly inclined to hope the best. Could he expect that her friends would not step forward? Could he expect to be noticed again by the regiment, after such an affront to Colonel Forster? His temptation is not adequate to the risk.'

'Do you really think so?' cried Elizabeth, brightening up for a moment.

'Upon my word,' said Mrs Gardiner, 'I begin to be of your uncle's opinion. It is really too great a violation of decency, honour, and interest, for him to be guilty of it. I cannot think so very ill of Wickham. Can you, yourself, Lizzy, so wholly give him up, as to believe him capable of it?'

'Not perhaps of neglecting his own interest. But of every other neglect I can believe him capable. If, indeed, it should be so! But I dare not hope it. Why should they not go on to Scotland, if that had been the case?'

'In the first place,' replied Mr Gardiner, 'there is no absolute proof that they are not gone to Scotland.'

'Oh! but their removing from the chaise into an hackney coach is such a presumption! And, besides, no traces of them were to be found on the Barnet road.'

'Well, then – supposing them to be in London. They may be there, though for the purpose of concealment, for no more exceptionable purpose. It is not likely that money should be very abundant on either side; and it might strike them that they could be more economically, though less expeditiously, married in London, than in Scotland.'

'But why all this secrecy? Why any fear of detection? Why must their marriage be private? Oh! no, no, this it not likely. His most particular friend, you see by Jane's account, was persuaded of his never intending to marry her. Wickham will never marry a woman without some money. He cannot afford it. And what claims has Lydia, what attractions has she beyond youth, health, and good humour, that could make him for her sake, forego every chance of benefiting himself by marrying well? As to what restraint the apprehension of disgrace in the corps might throw on a dishonourable elopement with her, I am not able to judge; for I know nothing of the effects that such a step might produce. But as to your other objection, I am afraid it will hardly hold good. Lydia has no brothers to step forward; and he might imagine, from my father's behaviour, from his indolence and the little attention he has ever seemed to give to what was going forward in his family, that *he* would do as little, and think as little about it, as any father could do, in such a matter.'

'But can you think that Lydia is so lost to every thing but love of him, as to consent to live with him on any other terms than marriage?'

'It does seem, and it is most shocking indeed,' replied Elizabeth, with tears in her eyes, 'that a sister's sense of decency and virtue in such a point should admit of doubt. But, really, I know not what to say. Perhaps I am not doing her justice. But she is very young; she has never been taught to think on serious subjects; and for the last half year, nay, for a twelvemonth, she has been given up to nothing but amusement and vanity. She has been allowed to dispose of her time in the most idle and frivolous manner, and to adopt any opinions that came in her way. Since the —shire were first quartered in Meryton, nothing but love, flirtation, and officers, have been in her head. She has been doing every thing in her power by thinking and talking on the subject, to give greater – what shall I call it? susceptibility to her feelings; which are naturally lively enough. And we all know that Wickham has every charm of person and address than can captivate a woman.'

'But you see that Jane,' said her aunt, 'does not think so ill of Wickham, as to believe him capable of the attempt.'

'Of whom does Jane ever think ill? And who is there, whatever might be their former conduct, that she would believe capable of such an attempt, till it were proved against them? But Jane knows, as well as I do, what Wickham really is. We both know that he has been profligate in every sense of the word. That he has neither integrity nor honour. That he is as false and deceitful, as he is insinuating.'

'And do you really know all this?' cried Mrs Gardiner, whose curiosity as to the mode of her intelligence was all alive.

'I do, indeed,' replied Elizabeth, colouring. 'I told you the other day, of his infamous behaviour to Mr Darcy; and you, yourself, when last at Longbourn, heard in what manner he spoke of the man, who had behaved with such forbearance and liberality towards him. And there are other circumstances which I am not at liberty – which it is not worth while to relate; but his lies about the whole Pemberley family are endless. From what he said of Miss Darcy, I was thoroughly prepared to see a proud, reserved, disagreeable girl. Yet he knew to the contrary himself. He must know that she was as amiable and unpretending as we have found her.'

'But does Lydia know nothing of this? Can she be ignorant of what you and Jane seem so well to understand?'

'Oh, yes! – that, that is the worst of all. Till I was in Kent, and saw so much both of Mr Darcy and his relation, Colonel Fitzwilliam, I was ignorant of the truth myself. And when I returned home, the —shire was to leave Meryton in a week or fortnight's time. As that was the case, neither Jane, to whom I related the whole, nor I, thought it necessary to make our knowledge public; for of what use could it apparently be to any one, that the good opinion which all the neighbourhood had of him, should be overthrown? And even when it was settled that Lydia should go with Mrs Forster, the necessity of opening her eyes to his character never occurred to me. That *she* could be in any danger from the deception never entered my head. That such a consequence as *this* should ensue, you may easily believe was far enough from my thoughts.'

'When they all removed to Brighton, therefore, you had no reason, I suppose, to believe them fond of each other.'

'Not the slightest. I can remember no symptom of affection on either side; and had any thing of the kind been perceptible, you must be aware that ours is not a family, on which it could be thrown away. When first he entered the corps, she was ready enough to admire him; but so we all were. Every girl in, or near Meryton, was out of her senses about him for the first two months; but he never distinguished *her* by any particular attention, and, consequently, after a moderate period of extravagant and wild admiration, her fancy for him gave way, and others of the regiment, who treated her with more distinction, again became her favourites.'

It may be easily believed, that however little of novelty could be added to their fears, hopes, and conjectures, on this interesting subject, by its repeated discussion, no other could detain them from it long, during the whole of the journey. From Elizabeth's thoughts it was never absent. Fixed there by the keenest of all anguish, self reproach, she could find no interval of ease or forgetfulness.

They travelled as expeditiously as possible; and sleeping one night on the road, reached Longbourn by dinner-time the next day. It was a comfort to Elizabeth to consider that Jane could not have been wearied by long expectations.

The little Gardiners, attracted by the sight of a chaise, were standing on the steps of the house, as they entered the paddock; and when the carriage drove up to the door, the joyful surprise that lighted up their faces, and displayed itself over their whole bodies, in a variety of capers and frisks, was the first pleasing earnest of their welcome.

Elizabeth jumped out; and, after giving each of them an hasty kiss, hurried into the vestibule, where Jane, who came running down stairs from her mother's apartment, immediately met her.

Elizabeth, as she affectionately embraced her, whilst tears filled the eyes of both, lost not a moment in asking whether any thing had been heard of the fugitives.

'Not yet,' replied Jane. 'But now that my dear uncle is come, I hope everything will be well.'

'Is my father in town?'

'Yes, he went on Tuesday as I wrote you word.'

'And have you heard from him often?'

'We have heard only once. He wrote me a few lines on Wednesday, to say that he arrived in safety, and to give me his directions, which I particularly begged him to do. He merely added, that he should not write again, till he had something of importance to mention.'

'And my mother – How is she? How are you all?'

'My mother is tolerably well, I trust; though her spirits are greatly shaken. She is up stairs, and will have great satisfaction in seeing you all. She does not yet leave her dressing-room. Mary and Kitty, thank Heaven! are quite well.'

'But you – How are you?' cried Elizabeth, 'You look pale. How much you must have gone through!'

Her sister, however, assured her, of her being perfectly well; and their conversation, which had been passing while Mr and Mrs Gardiner were engaged with their children, was now put an end to, by the approach of the whole party. Jane ran to her uncle and aunt, and welcomed and thanked them both, with alternate smiles and tears.

When they were all in the drawing room, the questions which Elizabeth had already asked, were of course repeated by the others, and they soon found that Jane had no intelligence to give. The sanguine hope of good, however, which the benevolence of her heart suggested, had not yet deserted her; she still expected that it would all end well, and that every morning would bring some letter, either from Lydia or her father, to explain their proceedings, and perhaps announce the marriage.

Mrs Bennet, to whose apartment they all repaired, after a few minutes conversation together, received them exactly as might be expected; with tears and lamentations of regret, invectives against the villainous conduct of Wickham, and complaints of her own sufferings and ill usage; blaming every body but the person to whose ill judging indulgence the errors of her daughter must be principally owing.

'If I had been able,' said she, 'to carry my point of going to Brighton, with all my family, *this* would not have happened; but poor dear Lydia had nobody to take care of her. Why did the Forsters ever let her go out of their sight? I am sure there was some great neglect or other on their side, for she is not the kind of girl to do such a thing, if she had been well looked after. I always thought they were very unfit to have the charge of her; but I was over-ruled, as I always am. Poor dear child! And now here's Mr Bennet gone away, and I know he will fight Wickham, wherever he meets him, and then he will be killed, and what is to become of us all? The Collinses will turn us out, before he is cold in his grave; and if you are not kind to us, brother, I do not know what we shall do.'

They all exclaimed against such terrific ideas; and Mr Gardiner, after general assurances of his affection for her and all her family, told her that he meant to be in London the very next day, and would assist Mr Bennet in every endeavour for recovering Lydia.

'Do not give way to useless alarm,' added he, 'though it is right to be prepared for the worst, there is no occasion to look on it as certain. It is not quite a week since they left Brighton. In a few days more, we may gain some news of them, and till we know that they are not married, and have no design of marrying, do not let us give the matter over as lost. As soon as I get to town, I shall go to my brother, and make him come home with me to Gracechurch Street, and then we may consult together as to what is to be done.'

'Oh my dear brother,' replied Mrs Bennet, 'that is exactly what I could most wish for. And now do, when you get to town, find them out, wherever they may be; and if they are not married already, *make* them marry. And as for wedding clothes, do not let them wait for that, but tell Lydia she shall have as much money as she chuses, to buy them, after they are married. And, above all things, keep Mr Bennet from fighting. Tell him what a dreadful state I am in, – that I am frightened out of my wits; and have such tremblings, such flutterings all over me, such spasms in my side, and pains in my head, and such beatings at heart, that I can get no rest by night nor by day. And tell my dear Lydia, not to give any directions about her clothes, till she has seen me, for she does not know which are the best warehouses. Oh, brother, how kind you are! I know you will contrive it all.'

But Mr Gardiner, though he assured her again of his earnest endeavours in the cause, could not avoid recommending moderation to her, as well as in her hopes as her fears; and, after talking with her in this manner till dinner was on table, they left her to vent all her feelings on the housekeeper, who attended, in the absence of her daughters.

Though her brother and sister were persuaded that there was no real occasion for such a seclusion from the family, they did not attempt to oppose it, for they knew that she had not prudence enough to hold her tongue before the servants, while they waited at table, and judged it better that *one* only of the household, and the one whom they could most trust, should comprehend all her fears and solicitude on the subject.

In the dining-room they were soon joined by Mary and Kitty, who had been too busily engaged in their separate apartments, to make their appearance before. One came from her books, and the other from her toilette. The faces of both, however, were tolerably calm; and no change was visible in either, except that the loss of her favourite sister, or the anger which she had herself incurred in the business, had given something more of fretfulness than usual, to the accents of Kitty. As for Mary, she was mistress enough of herself to whisper to Elizabeth with a countenance of grave reflection, soon after they were seated at table,

'This is a most unfortunate affair; and will probably be much talked of. But we must stem the tide of malice, and pour into the wounded bosoms of each other, the balm of sisterly consolation.'

Then, perceiving in Elizabeth no inclination of replying, she added, 'Unhappy as the event must be for Lydia, we may draw from it this useful lesson; that loss of virtue in a female is irretrievable – that one false step involves her in endless ruin – that her reputation is no less brittle than it is beautiful, – and that she cannot be too much guarded in her behaviour towards the undeserving of the other sex.'

Elizabeth lifted up her eyes in amazement, but was too much oppressed to make any reply. Mary, however, continued to console herself with such kind of moral extractions from the evil before them.

In the afternoon, the two elder Miss Bennets were able to be for half an hour by themselves; and Elizabeth instantly availed herself of the opportunity of making many enquiries, which Jane was equally eager to satisfy. After joining in general lamentations over the dreadful sequel of this event, which Elizabeth considered as all but certain, and Miss Bennet could not assert to be wholly impossible; the former continued the subject, by saying,'But tell me all and every thing about it, which I have not already heard. Give me farther particulars. What did Colonel Forster say? Had they no apprehension of any thing before the elopement took place? They must have seen them together for ever.'

'Colonel Forster did own that he had often suspected some partiality, especially on Lydia's side, but nothing to give him any alarm. I am so grieved for him. His behaviour was attentive and kind to the utmost. He *was* coming to us, in order to assure us of his concern, before he had any idea of their now being gone to Scotland: when that apprehension first got abroad, it hastened his journey.'

'And was Denny convinced that Wickham would not marry? Did he know of their intending to go off? Had Colonel Forster seen Denny himself?'

'Yes; but when questioned by *him* Denny denied knowing any thing of their plan, and would not give his real opinion about it. He did not repeat his persuasion of their not marrying – and from *that*, I am inclined to hope, he might have been misunderstood before.'

'And till Colonel Forster came himself, not one of you entertained a doubt, I suppose, of their being really married?'

'How was it possible that such an idea should enter our brains! I felt a little uneasy – a little fearful of my sister's happiness with him in marriage, because I knew that his conduct had not been always quite right. My father and mother knew nothing of that, they only felt how imprudent a match it must be. Kitty then owned, with a very natural triumph on knowing more than the rest of us, that in Lydia's last letter, she had prepared her for such a step. She had known, it seems, of their being in love with each other, many weeks.'

'But not before they went to Brighton?'

'No, I believe not.'

'And did Colonel Forster appear to think ill of Wickham himself? Does he know his real character?'

'I must confess that he did not speak so well of Wickham as he formerly did. He believed him to be imprudent and extravagant. And since this sad affair has taken place, it is said, that he left Meryton greatly in debt; but I hope this may be false.'

'Oh, Jane, had we been less secret, had we told what we knew of him, this could not have happened!'

'Perhaps it would have been better,' replied her sister. 'But to expose the former faults of any person, without knowing what their present feelings were, seemed unjustifiable. We acted with the best intentions.'

'Could Colonel Forster repeat the particulars of Lydia's note to his wife?'

'He brought it with him for us to see.'

Jane then took it from her pocket-book, and gave it to Elizabeth. There were the contents:

MY DEAR HARRIET,

You will laugh when you know where I am gone, and I cannot help laughing myself at your surprise tomorrow morning, as soon as I am missed. I am going to Gretna Green, and if you cannot guess with who, I shall think you a simpleton, for there is but one man in the world I love, so think it no harm to be off. You need not send them word at Longbourn of my going, if you do not like it, for it will make the surprise the greater, when I write to them, and sign my name Lydia Wickham. What a good joke it will be! I can hardly write for laughing. Pray make my excuses to Pratt, for not keeping my engagement, and dancing with him to night. Tell him I hope he will excuse me when he knows all, and tell him I will dance with him at the next ball we meet, with great pleasure. I shall send for my clothes when I get to Longbourn; but I wish you would tell Sally to mend a great slit in my working muslin gown, before they are packed up. Good bye. Give my love to Colonel Forster, I hope you will drink to our good journey.

Your affectionate friend,

LYDIA BENNET.

'Oh! thoughtless, thoughtless Lydia!' cried Elizabeth when she had finished it. 'What a letter is this, to be written at such a moment. But at least it shews, that *she* was serious in the object of her journey. Whatever he might afterwards persuade her to, it was not on her side a *scheme* of infamy. My poor father! how he must have felt it!'

'I never saw any one so shocked. He could not speak a word for full ten minutes. My mother was taken ill immediately, and the whole house in such confusion!'

'Oh! Jane,' cried Elizabeth, 'was there a servant belonging to it, who did not know the whole story before the end of the day?'

'I do not know. – I hope there was. – But to be guarded at such a time, is very difficult. My mother was in hysterics, and though I endeavoured to give her every assistance in my power, I am afraid I did not do so much as I might have done! But the horror of what might possibly happen, almost took from me my faculties.'

'Your attendance upon her, has been too much for you. You do not look well. Oh! that I had been with you, you have had every care and anxiety upon yourself alone.'

'Mary and Kitty have been very kind, and would have shared in every fatigue, I am sure, but I did not think it right for either of them. Kitty is slight and delicate, and Mary studies so much, that her hours of repose should not be broken in on. My aunt Philips came to Longbourn on Tuesday, after my father went away; and was so good as to stay until Thursday with me. She was of great use and comfort to us all, and Lady Lucas has been very kind; she walked here on Wednesday morning to condole with us, and offered her services, or any of her daughters, if they could be of use to us.'

'She had better have stayed at home,' cried Elizabeth; 'perhaps she *meant* well, but, under such a misfortune as this, one cannot see too little of one's neighbours. Assistance is impossible; condolence, insufferable. Let them triumph over us at a distance, and be satisfied.'

She then proceeded to enquire into the measures which her father had intended to pursue, while in town, for the recovery of his daughter.

'He meant, I believe,' replied Jane, 'to go to Epsom, the place where they last changed horses, see the postilions, and try if any thing could be made out from them. His principal object must be, to discover the number of the hackney coach which took them from Clapham. It had come with a fare from London; and as he thought the circumstance of a gentleman and lady's removing from one carriage into another, might be remarked, he meant to make enquiries at Clapham. If he could any how discover at what house the coachman had before set down his fare, he determined to make enquiries there, and hoped it might not be impossible to find out the stand and number of the coach. I do not know of any other designs that he had formed; but he was in such a hurry to be gone, and his spirits so greatly discomposed, that I had difficulty in finding out even so much as this.'

Chapter Forty Eight

THE WHOLE PARTY WERE IN HOPES OF a letter from Mr Bennet the next morning, but the post came in without bringing a single line from him. His family knew him to be on all common occasions, a most negligent and dilatory correspondent, but at such a time, they had hoped for exertion. They were forced to conclude, that he had no pleasing intelligence to send, but even of *that* they would have been glad to be certain. Mr Gardiner had waited only for the letters before he set off.

When he was gone, they were certain at least of receiving constant information of what was going on, and their uncle promised, at parting, to prevail on Mr Bennet to return to Longbourn, as soon as he could, to the great consolation of his sister, who considered it as the only security for her husband's not being killed in a duel.

Mrs Gardiner and the children were to remain in Hertfordshire a few days longer, as the former thought her presence might be serviceable to her nieces. She shared in their attendance on Mrs Bennet, and was a great comfort to them, in their hours of freedom. Their other aunt also visited them frequently, and always, as she said, with the design of cheering and heartening them up, though as she never came without reporting some fresh instance of Wickham's extravagance or irregularity, she seldom went away without leaving them more dispirited than she found them.

All Meryton seemed striving to blacken the man, who, but three months before, had been almost an angel of light. He was declared to be in debt to every tradesman in the place, and his intrigues, all honoured with the title of seduction, had been extended into every tradesman's family. Every body declared that he was the wickedest young man in the world; and every body began to find out, that they had always distrusted the appearance of his goodness. Elizabeth, though she did not credit above half of what was said, believed enough to make her former assurance of her sister's ruin still more certain; and even Jane, who believed still less of it, became almost hopeless, more especially as the time was now come, when if they had gone to Scotland, which she had never come before entirely despaired of, they must in all probability have gained some news of them.

Mr Gardiner left Longbourn on Sunday; on Tuesday, his wife received a letter from him; it told them, that on his arrival, he had immediately found out his brother, and persuaded him to come to Gracechurch street. That Mr Bennet had been to Epsom and Clapham, before his arrival, but without gaining any satisfactory information; and that he was now determined to enquire at all the principal hotels in town, as Mr Bennet thought it possible they might have gone to one of them, on their first coming to London, before they procured lodgings. Mr Gardiner himself did not expect any success from this measure, but as his brother was eager in it, he meant to assist him in pursuing it. He added, that Mr Bennet seemed wholly disinclined at present, to leave London, and promised to write again very soon. There was also a postcript to this effect.

'I have written to Colonel Forster to desire him to find out, if possible, from some of the young man's intimates in the regiment, whether Wickham has any relations or connections, who would be likely to know in what part of the town he has now concealed himself. If there were any one, that one could apply to, with a probability of gaining such a clue as that, it might be of essential consequence. At present we have nothing to guide us. Colonel Forster will, I dare say, do every thing in his power to satisfy us on this head. But, on second thoughts, perhaps Lizzy could tell us, what relations he has now living, better than any other person.'

Elizabeth was at no loss to understand from whence this deference for her authority proceeded; but it was not in her power to give any information of so satisfactory a nature, as the compliment deserved.

She had never heard of his having had any relations, except a father and mother, both of whom had been dead many years. It was possible, however, that some of his companions in the —shire, might be able to give more information; and, though she was not very sanguine in expecting it, the application was a something to look forward to.

Every day at Longbourn was now a day of anxiety; but the most anxious part of each was when the post was expected. The arrival of letters was the first grand object of every morning's impatience. Through letters, whatever of good or bad was to be told, would be communicated, and every succeeding day was expected to bring some news of importance.

But before they heard again from Mr Gardiner, a letter arrived for their father, from a different quarter, from Mr Collins; which, as Jane had received directions to open all that came for him in his absence, she accordingly read; and Elizabeth, who knew what curiosities his letters always were, looked over her, and read it likewise. It was as follows:

MY DEAR SIR,

I feel myself called upon by our relationship, and my situation in life, to condole with you on the grievous affliction you are now suffering under, of which we were yesterday informed by a letter from Hertfordshire. Be assured, my dear Sir, that Mrs Collins and myself sincerely sympathise with you, and all your respectable family, in your present distress, which must be of the bitterest kind, because proceeding from a cause which no time can remove. No arguments shall be wanting on my part, that can alleviate so severe a misfortune; or that may comfort you, under a circumstance that must be of all others most afflicting to a parent's mind. The death of your daughter would have been a blessing in comparison of this. And it is the more to be lamented, because there is reason to suppose, as my dear Charlotte informs me, that this licentiousness of behaviour in your daughter, has proceeded from a faulty degree of indulgence, though, at the same time, for the consolation of yourself and Mrs Bennet, I am inclined to think that her own disposition must be naturally bad, or she could not be guilty of such an enormity, at so early an age. Howsoever that may be, you are grievously to be pitied, in which opinion I am not only joined by Mrs Collins, but likewise by lady Catherine and her daughter, to whom I have related the affair. They agree with me in apprehending that this false step in one daughter, will be injurious to the fortunes of all the others, for who, as lady Catherine herself condescendingly says, will connect themselves with such a family. And this consideration leads me moreover to reflect with augmented satisfaction on a certain event of last November, for had it been otherwise, I must have been involved in all your sorrow and disgrace. Let me advise you then, my dear Sir, to console yourself as much as possible, to throw off your unworthy child from your affection for ever, and leave her to reap the fruits of her own henious offence.

I am, dear Sir, &c. &c.

Mr Gardiner did not write again, till he had received an answer from Colonel Forster; and then he had nothing of a pleasant nature to send. It was not known that Wickham had a single relation, with whom he kept up any connection, and it was certain that he had no near one living. His former acquaintances had been numerous; but since he had been in the militia, it did not appear that he was on terms of particular friendship with any of them. There was no one therefore who could be pointed out, as likely to give any news of him. And in the wretched state of his own finances, there was a very powerful motive for secrecy, in addition to his fear of discovery by Lydia's relations, for it had just transpired that he had left gaming debts behind him, to a very considerable amount. Colonel Forster believed that more than a thousand pounds would be necessary to clear his expences at Brighton. He owed a good deal in the town, but his debts of honour were still more formidable. Mr Gardiner did not attempt to conceal these particulars from the Longbourn family; Jane heard them with horror. 'A gamester!' she cried. 'This is wholly unexpected. I had not an idea of it.'

Mr Gardiner added in his letter, that they might expect to see their father at home on the following day, which was Saturday. Rendered spiritless by the ill-success of all their endeavours, he had yielded to his brother-in-law's intreaty that he would return to his family, and leave it to him to do, whatever occasion might suggest to be advisable for continuing their pursuit. When Mrs Bennet was told of this, she did not express so much satisfaction as her children expected, considering what her anxiety for his life had been before.

'What, is he coming home, and without poor Lydia!' she cried. 'Sure he will not leave London before he has found them. Who is to fight Wickham, and make him marry her, if he comes away?'

As Mrs Gardiner began to wish to be at home, it was settled that she and her children should go to London, at the same time that Mr Bennet came from it. The coach, therefore, took them the first stage of their journey, and brought its master back to Longbourn.

Mrs Gardiner went away in all the perplexity about Elizabeth and her Derbyshire friend, that had attended her from that part of the world. His name had never been voluntarily mentioned before them by her niece; and the kind of half-expectation which Mrs Gardiner had formed, of their being followed by a letter from him, had ended in nothing. Elizabeth had received none since her return, that could come from Pemberley.

The present unhappy state of the family, rendered any other excuse for the lowness of her spirits unnecessary; nothing, therefore, could be fairly conjectured from *that*, though Elizabeth, who was by this time tolerably well acquainted with her own feelings, was perfectly aware, that, had she known nothing of Darcy, she could have borne the dread of Lydia's infamy somewhat better. It would have spared her, she thought, one sleepless night out of two.

When Mr Bennet arrived, he had all the appearance of his usual philosophic composure. He said as little as he had ever been in the habit of saying; made no mention of the business that had taken him away, and it was some time before his daughters had courage to speak of it.

It was not till the afternoon, when he joined them at tea, that Elizabeth ventured to introduce the subject; and then, on her briefly expressing her sorrow for what he must have endured, he replied, 'Say nothing of that. Who should suffer but myself? It has been my own doing, and I ought to feel it.'

'You must not be too severe upon yourself,' replied Elizabeth.

'You may well warn me against such an evil. Human nature is so prone to fall into it! No, Lizzy, let me once in my life feel how much I have been to blame. I am not afraid of being overpowered by the impression. It will pass away soon enough.'

'Do you suppose them to be in London?'

'Yes; where else can they be so well concealed?'

'And Lydia used to want to go to London,' added Kitty.

'She is happy, then,' said her father, drily; 'and her residence there will probably be of some duration.'

Then, after a short silence, he continued, 'Lizzy, I bear you no ill-will for being justified in your advice to me last May, which, considering the event, shews some greatness of mind.'

They were interrupted by Miss Bennet, who came to fetch her mother's tea.

'This is a parade,' cried he, 'which does one good; it gives such an elegance to misfortune! Another day I will do the same; I will sit in my library, in my night cap and powdering gown, and give as much trouble as I can, – or, perhaps, I may defer it, till Kitty runs away.'

'I am not going to run away, Papa,' said Kitty, fretfully; 'if *I* should ever go to Brighton, I would behave better than Lydia.'

'*You* go to Brighton! – I would not trust you so near it as East Bourne, for fifty pounds! No, Kitty, I have at last learnt to be cautious, and you will feel the effects of it. No officer is ever to enter my house again, nor even to pass through the village. Balls will be absolutely prohibited, unless you stand up with one of your sisters. And you are never to stir out of doors, till you can prove, that you have spent ten minutes of every day in a rational manner.'

Kitty, who took all these threats in a serious light, began to cry.

'Well, well,' said he, 'do not make yourself unhappy. If you are a good girl for the next ten years, I will take you to a review at the end of them.'

Chapter Forty Nine

TWO DAYS AFTER MR BENNET'S RETURN, as Jane and Elizabeth were walking together in the shrubbery behind the house, they saw the housekeeper coming towards them, and, concluding that she came to call them to their mother, went forward to meet her; but, instead of the expected summons, when they approached her, she said to Miss Bennet, 'I beg your pardon, madam, for interrupting you, but I was in hopes you might have got some good news from town, so I took the liberty of coming to ask.'

'What do you mean, Hill? We have heard nothing from town.'

'Dear madam,' cried Mrs Hill, in great astonishment, 'don't you know there is an express come for master from Mr Gardiner? He has been here this half hour, and master has had a letter.'

Away ran the girls, too eager to get in to have time for speech. They ran through the vestibule into the breakfast room; from thence to the library; – their father was in neither; and they were on the point of seeking him up stairs with their mother, when they were met by the butler, who said,

'If you are looking for my master, ma'am, he is walking towards the little copse.'

Upon this information, they instantly passed through the hall once more, and ran across the lawn after their father, who was deliberately pursuing his way towards a small wood on one side of the paddock.

Jane, who was not so light, nor so much in the habit of running as Elizabeth, soon lagged behind, while her sister, panting for breath, came up with him, and eagerly cried out,

'Oh, Papa, what news? what news? have you heard from my uncle?'

'Yes, I have had a letter from him by express.'

'Well, and what news does it bring? good or bad?'

'What is there of good to be expected?' said he, taking the letter from his pocket; 'but perhaps you would like to read it.'

Elizabeth impatiently caught it from his hand. Jane now came up.

'Read it aloud,' said their father, 'for I hardly know myself what it is about.'

Gracechurch-street, Monday,
August 2.

MY DEAR BROTHER,

At last I am able to send you some tidings of my niece, and such as, upon the whole, I hope will give you satisfaction. Soon after you left me on Saturday, I was fortunate enough to find out in what part of London they

*were. The particulars, I reserve till we meet. It is enough to know they are
discovered. I have seen them both —*

'Then it is, as I always hoped,' cried Jane: 'they are married!'
Elizabeth read on:

*I have seen them both. They are not married, nor can I find there was any
intention of being so; but if you are willing to perform the engagements
which I have ventured to make on your side, I hope it will not be long before
they are. All that is required of you is, to assure to your daughter, by
settlement, her equal share of the five thousand pounds, secured among your
children after the decease of yourself and my sister; and, moreover, to enter
into an engagement of allowing her, during your life, one hundred pounds
per annum. These are conditions, which, considering every thing, I had no
hesitation in complying with, as far as I thought myself privileged, for you.
I shall send this by express, that no time may be lost in bringing me your
answer. You will easily comprehend, from these particulars, that Mr Wickham's circumstances are not so hopeless as they are generally believed to be.
The world has been deceived in that respect; and I am happy to say, there
will be some little money, even when all his debts are discharged, to settle on
my niece, in addition to her own fortune. If, as I conclude will be the case,
you send me full powers to act in your name, throughout the whole of this
business, I will immediately give directions to Haggerston for preparing a
proper settlement. There will not be the smallest occasion for your coming
to town again; therefore, stay quietly at Longbourn, and depend on my
diligence and care. Send back your answer as soon as you can, and be careful
to write explicitly. We have judged it best, that my niece should be married
from this house, of which I hope you will approve. She comes to us to-day.
I shall write again as soon as any thing more is determined on. Your's, &c.*

EDW. GARDINER.

'Is it possible!' cried Elizabeth, when she had finished. 'Can it be possible
that he will marry her?'

'Wickham is not so undeserving, then, as we have thought him;' said
her sister. 'My dear father, I congratulate you.'

'And have you answered the letter?' said Elizabeth.

'No; but it must be done soon.'

Most earnestly did she then intreat him to lose no more time before he
wrote.

'Oh! my dear father,' she cried, 'come back, and write immediately.
Consider how important every moment is, in such a case.'

'Let me write for you,' said Jane, 'if you dislike the trouble yourself.'

'I dislike it very much,' he replied; 'but it must be done.'

And so saying, he turned back with them, and walked towards the
house.

'And may I ask?' said Elizabeth, 'but the terms, I suppose, must be
complied with.'

'Complied with! I am only ashamed of his asking so little.'

'And they *must* marry! Yet he is *such* a man!'

'Yes, yes, they must marry. There is nothing else to be done. But there
are two things that I want very much to know: – one is, how much money

your uncle has laid down, to bring it about; and the other, how I am ever to pay him.'

'Money! my uncle!' cried Jane, 'what do you mean, Sir?'

'I mean, that no man in his senses, would marry Lydia on so slight a temptation as one hundred a-year during my life, and fifty after I am gone.'

'That is very true,' said Elizabeth; 'though it had not occurred to me before. His debts to be discharged, and something still to remain! Oh! it must be my uncle's doings! Generous, good man, I am afraid he has distressed himself. A small sum would not do all this.'

'No,' said her father, 'Wickham's a fool, if he takes her with a farthing less than ten thousand pounds. I should be sorry to think so ill of him, in the very beginning of our relationship.'

'Ten thousand pounds! Heaven forbid! How is half such a sum to be repaid?'

Mr Bennet made no answer, and each of them, deep in thought, continued silent till they reached the house. Their father then went to the library to write, and the girls walked into the breakfast-room.

'And they are really to be married!' cried Elizabeth, as soon as they were by themselves. 'How strange this is! And for *this* we are to be thankful. That they should marry, small as is their chance of happiness, and wretched as is his character, we are forced to rejoice! Oh, Lydia!'

'I comfort myself with thinking,' replied Jane, 'that he certainly would not marry Lydia, if he had not a real regard for her. Though our kind uncle has done something towards clearing him, I cannot believe that ten thousand pounds, or any thing like it, has been advanced. He has children of his own, and may have more. How could he spare half ten thousand pounds?'

'If we are ever able to learn what Wickham's debts have been,' said Elizabeth, 'and how much is settled on his side on our sister, we shall exactly know what Mr Gardiner has done for them, because Wickham has not sixpence of his own. The kindness of my uncle and aunt can never be requited. Their taking her home, and affording her their personal protection and countenance, is such a sacrifice to her advantage, as years of gratitude cannot enough acknowledge. By this time she is actually with them! If such goodness does not make her miserable now, she will never deserve to be happy! What a meeting for her, when she first sees my aunt!'

'We must endeavour to forget all that has passed on either side,' said Jane: 'I hope and trust they will yet be happy. His consenting to marry her is a proof, I will believe, that he is come to a right way of thinking. Their mutual affection will steady them; and I flatter myself they will settle so quietly, and live in so rational a manner, as may in time make their past imprudence forgotten.'

'Their conduct has been such,' replied Elizabeth, 'as neither you, nor I, nor any body, can ever forget. It is useless to talk of it.'

It now occurred to the girls that their mother was in all likelihood perfectly ignorant of what had happened. They went to the library, therefore, and asked their father, whether he would not wish them to make it known to her. He was writing, and, without raising his head, coolly replied,

'Just as you please.'

'May we take my uncle's letter to read to her?'

'Take whatever you like, and get away.'

Elizabeth took the letter from his writing table, and they went up stairs together. Mary and Kitty were both with Mrs Bennet: one communication would, therefore, do for all. After a slight preparation for good news, the letter was read aloud. Mrs Bennet could hardly contain herself. As soon as Jane had read Mr Gardiner's hope of Lydia's being soon married, her joy burst forth, and every following sentence added to its exuberance. She was now in an irritation as violent from delight, as she had ever been fidgetty from alarm and vexation. To know that her daughter would be married was enough. She was disturbed by no fear for her felicity, nor humbled by any remembrance of her misconduct.

'My dear, dear Lydia!' she cried: 'This is delightful indeed! – She will' be married – I shall see her again! – She will be married at sixteen! – My good, kind brother! – I knew how it would be – I knew he would manage every thing. How I long to see her! and to see dear Wickham too! But the clothes, the wedding clothes! I will write to my sister Gardiner about them directly. Lizzy, my dear, run down to your father, and ask him how much he will give her. Stay, stay, I will go myself. Ring the bell, Kitty, for Hill. I will put on my things in a moment. My dear, dear Lydia! – How merry we shall be together when we meet!'

Her eldest daughter endeavoured to give some relief to the violence of these transports, by leading her thoughts to the obligations which Mr Gardiner's behaviour laid them all under.

'For we must attribute this happy conclusion,' she added, 'in a great measure, to his kindness. We are persuaded that he has pledged himself to assist Mr Wickham with money.'

'Well,' cried her mother, 'it is all very right; who should do it but her own uncle? If he had not had a family of his own, I and my children must have had all his money you know, and it is the first time we have ever had any thing from him, except a few presents. Well! I am so happy. In a short time, I shall have a daughter married. Mrs Wickham! How well it sounds. And she was only sixteen last June. My dear Jane, I am in such a flutter, that I am sure I can't write; so I will dictate, and you write for me. We will settle with your father about the money afterwards; but the things should be ordered immediately.'

She was then proceeding to all the particulars of calico, muslin, and cambric, and would shortly have dictated some very plentiful orders, had not Jane, though with some difficulty, persuaded her to wait, till her father was at leisure to be consulted. One day's delay she observed, would be of small importance; and her mother was too happy, to be quite so obstinate as usual. Other schemes too came into her head.

'I will go to Meryton,' said she, 'as soon as I am dressed, and tell the good, good news to my sister Philips. And as I come back, I can call on Lady Lucas and Mrs Long. Kitty, run down and order the carriage. An airing would do me a great deal of good, I am sure. Girls, can I do any thing for you in Meryton? Oh! here comes Hill. My dear Hill, have you heard the good news? Miss Lydia is going to be married; and you shall all have a bowl of punch, to make merry at her wedding.'

Mrs Hill began instantly to express her joy. Elizabeth received her congratulations amongst the rest, and then, sick of this folly, took refuge in her own room, that she might think with freedom.

Poor Lydia's situation must, at best, be bad enough; but that it was no worse, she had need to be thankful. She felt it so; and though, in looking forward, neither rational happiness nor worldly prosperity, could be justly expected for her sister; in looking back to what they had feared, only two hours ago, she felt all the advantages of what they had gained.

Chapter Fifty

MR BENNET HAD VERY OFTEN WISHED, before this period of his life, that, instead of spending his whole income, he had laid by an annual sum, for the better provision of his children, and of his wife, if she survived him. He now wished it more than ever. Had he done his duty in that respect, Lydia need not have been indebted to her uncle, for whatever of honour or credit could now be purchased for her. The satisfaction of prevailing on one of the most worthless young men in Great Britain to be her husband, might then have rested in its proper place.

He was seriously concerned, that a cause of so little advantage to any one, should be forwarded at the sole expence of his brother-in-law, and he was determined, if possible, to find out the extent of his assistance, and to discharge the obligation as soon as he could.

When first Mr Bennet had married, economy was held to be perfectly useless; for, of course, they were to have a son. This son was to join in cutting off the entail, as soon as he should be of age, and the widow and younger children would by that means be provided for. Five daughters successively entered the world, but yet the son was to come; and Mrs Bennet, for many years after Lydia's birth, had been certain that he would. This event had at last been despaired of, but it was then too late to be saving. Mrs Bennet had no turn for economy, and her husband's love of independence had alone prevented their exceeding their income.

Five thousand pounds was settled by marriage articles on Mrs Bennet and the children. But in what proportions it should be divided amongst the latter, depended on the will of the parents. This was one point, with regard to Lydia at least, which was now to be settled, and Mr Bennet could have no hesitation in acceding to the proposal before him. In terms of grateful acknowledgment for the kindness of his brother, though expressed most concisely, he then delivered on paper his perfect approbation of all that was done, and his willingness to fulfil the engagements that had been made for him. He had never before supposed that, could Wickham be prevailed on to marry his daughter, it would be done with so little inconvenience to himself, as by the present arrangement. He would scarcely be ten pounds a-year the loser, by the hundred that was to be paid them; for what with her board and pocket allowance, and the continual presents in money, which passed to her, through her mother's hands, Lydia's expences had been very little within that sum.

That it should be done with such trifling exertion on his side, too, was another very welcome surprise; for his chief wish at present, was to have as little trouble in the business as possible. When the first transports of rage which had produced his activity in seeking her were over, he naturally returned to all his former indolence. His letter was soon dispatched; for though dilatory in undertaking business, he was quick in its execution. He begged to know farther particulars of what he was indebted to his brother; but was too angry with Lydia, to send any message to her.

The good news quickly spread through the house; and with proportionate speed through the neighbourhood. It was borne in the latter with decent philosophy. To be sure it would have been more for the advantage of conversation, had Miss Lydia Bennet come upon the town; or, as the happiest alternative, been secluded from the world, in some distant farm house. But there was much to be talked of, in marrying her; and the good-natured wishes for her well-doing, which had proceeded before, from all the spiteful old ladies in Meryton, lost but little of their spirit in this change of circumstances, because with such an husband, her misery was considered certain.

It was a fortnight since Mrs Bennet had been down stairs, but on this happy day, she again took her seat at the head of her table, and in spirits oppressively high. No sentiment of shame gave a damp to her triumph. The marriage of a daughter, which had been the first object of her wishes, since Jane was sixteen, was now on the point of accomplishment, and her thoughts and her words ran wholly on those attendants of elegant nuptials, fine muslins, new carriages, and servants. She was busily searching through the neighbourhood for a proper situation for her daughter, and, without knowing or considering what their income might be, rejected many as deficient in size and importance.

'Haye-Park might do,' said she, 'if the Gouldings would quit it, or the great house at Stoke, if the drawing-room were larger; but Ashworth is too far off! I could not bear to have her ten miles from me; and as for Purvis Lodge, the attics are dreadful.'

Her husband allowed her to talk on without interruption, while the servants remained. But when they had withdrawn, he said to her, 'Mrs Bennet, before you take any, or all of these houses, for your son and daughter, let us come to a right understanding. Into *one* house in this neighbourhood, they shall never have admittance. I will not encourage the impudence of either, by receiving them at Longbourn.'

A long dispute followed this declaration; but Mr Bennet was firm: it soon led to another; and Mrs Bennet found, with amazement and horror, that her husband would not advance a guinea to buy clothes for his daughter. He protested that she should receive from him no mark of affection whatever, on the occasion. Mrs Bennet could hardly comprehend it. That his anger could be carried to such a point of inconceivable resentment, as to refuse his daughter a privilege, without which her marriage would scarcely seem valid, exceeded all that she could believe possible. She was more alive to the disgrace, which the want of new clothes must reflect on her daughter's nuptials, than to any sense of shame at her eloping and living with Wickham, a fortnight before they took place.

Elizabeth was now most heartily sorry that she had, from the distress of the moment, been led to make Mr Darcy acquainted with their fears for her sister; for since her marriage would so shortly give the proper termination to the elopement, they might hope to conceal its unfavourable beginning, from all those who were not immediately on the spot.

She had no fear of its spreading farther, through his means. There were few people on whose secrecy she would have more confidently depended; but at the same time, there was no one, whose knowledge of a sister's frailty would have moritifed her so much. Not, however, from any fear of disadvantage from it, individually to herself; for at any rate, there seemed a gulf impassable between them. Had Lydia's marriage been concluded on the most honourable terms, it was not to be supposed that Mr Darcy would connect himself with a family, where to every other objection would now be added, an alliance and relationship of the nearest kind with the man whom he so justly scorned.

From such a connection she could not wonder that he should shrink. The wish of procuring her regard, which she had assured herself of his feeling in Derbyshire, could not in rational expectation survive such a blow as this. She was humbled, she was grieved; she repented, though she hardly knew of what. She became jealous of his esteem, when she could no longer hope to be benefited by it. She wanted to hear of him, when there seemed the least chance of gaining intelligence. She was convinced that she could have been happy with him; when it was no longer likely they should meet.

What a triumph for him, as she often thought, could he know that the proposals which she had proudly spurned only four months ago, would now have been gladly and gratefully received! He was as generous, she doubted not, as the most generous of his sex. But while he was mortal, there must be a triumph.

She began now to comprehend that he was exactly the man, who, in disposition and talents, would most suit her. His understanding and temper, though unlike her own, would have answered all her wishes. It was an union that must have been to the advantage of both; by her ease and liveliness, his mind might have been softened, his manners improved, and from his judgment, information, and knowledge of the world, she must have received benefit of greater importance.

But no such happy marriage could now teach the admiring multitude what connubial felicity really was. An union of a different tendency, and precluding the possibility of the other, was soon to be formed in their family.

How Wickham and Lydia were to be supported in tolerable independence, she could not imagine. But how little of permanent happiness could belong to a couple who were only brought together because their passions were stronger than their virtue, she could easily conjecture.

Mr Gardiner soon wrote again to his brother. To Mr Bennet's acknowledgments he briefly replied, with assurances of his eagerness to promote the welfare of any of his family; and concluded with intreaties that the subject might never be mentioned to him again. The principal purport of his letter was to inform them, that Mr Wickham had resolved on quitting the Militia.

'It was greatly my wish that he should do so,' he added,

as soon as his marriage was fixed on. And I think you will agree with me, in considering a removal from the corps as highly desirable, both on his account and my niece's. It is Mr Wickham's intention to go into the regulars; and, among his former friends, there are still some who are able and willing to assist him in the army. He has the promise of an ensigncy in General —'s regiment, now quartered in the North. It is an advantage to have it so far from this part of the kingdom. He promises fairly, and I hope among different people, where they may each have a character to preserve, they will both be more prudent. I have written to Colonel Forster, to inform him of our present arrangements, and to request that he will satisfy the various creditors of Mr Wickham in and near Brighton, with assurances of speedy payment, for which I have pledged myself. And will you give yourself the trouble of carrying similar assurances to his creditors in Meryton, of whom I shall subjoin a list, according to his information. He has given in all his debts; I hope at least he has not deceived us. Haggerston has our directions, and all will be completed in a week. They will then join his regiment, unless they are first invited to Longbourn; and I understand from Mrs Gardiner, that my niece is very desirous of seeing you all, before she leaves the South. She is well, and begs to be dutifully remembered to you and her mother. - Your's, &c.

E. GARDINER.

Mr Bennet and his daughters saw all the advantages of Wickham's removal from the —shire, as clearly as Mr Gardiner could do. But Mrs Bennet, was not so well pleased with it. Lydia's being settled in the North, just when she had expected most pleasure and pride in her company, for she had by no means given up her plan of their residing in Hertfordshire, was a severe disappointment; and besides, it was such a pity that Lydia should be taken from a regiment where she was acquainted with every body, and had so many favourites.

'She is so fond of Mrs Forster,' said she, 'it will be quite shocking to send her away! And there are several of the young men, too, that she likes very much. The officers may not be so pleasant in General —'s regiment.'

His daughter's request, for such it might be considered, of being admitted into her family again, before she set off for the North, received at first an absolute negative. But Jane and Elizabeth, who agreed in wishing, for the sake of their sister's feelings and consequence, that she should be noticed on her marriage by her parents, urged him so earnestly, yet so rationally and so mildly, to receive her and her husband at Longbourn, as soon as they were married, that he was prevailed on to think as they thought, and act as they wished. And their mother had the satisfaction of knowing, that she should be able to shew her married daughter in the neighbourhood, before she was banished to the North. When Mr Bennet wrote again to his brother, therefore, he sent his permission for them to come; and it was settled, that as soon as the ceremony was over, they should proceed to Longbourn. Elizabeth was surprised, however, that Wickham should consent to such a scheme, and, had she consulted only her own inclination, any meeting with him would have been the last object of her wishes.

Chapter Fifty One

THEIR SISTER'S WEDDING DAY ARRIVED; and Jane and Elizabeth felt for her probably more than she felt for herself. The carriage was sent to meet them at —, and they were to return in it, by dinner-time. Their arrival was dreaded by the elder Miss Bennets; and Jane more especially, who gave Lydia the feelings which would have attended herself, had *she* been the culprit, was wretched in the thought of what her sister must endure.

They came. The family were assembled in the breakfast room, to receive them. Smiles decked the face of Mrs Bennet, as the carriage drove up to the door; her husband looked impenetrably grave; her daughters, alarmed, anxious, uneasy.

Lydia's voice was heard in the vestibule; the door was thrown open, and she ran into the room. Her mother stepped forwards, embraced her, and welcomed her with rapture; gave her hand with an affectionate smile to Wickham, who followed his lady, and wished them both joy, with an alacrity which shewed no doubt of their happiness.

Their reception from Mr Bennet, to whom they then turned, was not quite so cordial. His countenance rather gained in austerity; and he scarcely opened his lips. The easy assurance of the young couple, indeed, was enough to provoke him. Elizabeth was disgusted, and even Miss Bennet was shocked. Lydia was Lydia still; untamed, unabashed, wild, noisy, and fearless. She turned from sister to sister, demanding their congratulations, and when at length they all sat down, looked eagerly round the room, took notice of some little alteration in it, and observed, with a laugh, that it was a great while since she had been there.

Wickham was not at all more distressed than herself, but his manners were always so pleasing, that had his character and his marriage been exactly what they ought, his smiles and his easy address, while he claimed their relationship, would have delighted them all. Elizabeth had not before believed him quite equal to such assurance; but she sat down, resolving within herself, to draw no limits in future to the impudence of an impudent man. *She* blushed, and Jane blushed; but the cheeks of the two who caused their confusion, suffered no variation of colour.

There was no want of discourse. The bride and her mother could neither of them talk fast enough; and Wickham, who happened to sit near Elizabeth, began enquiring after his acquaintance in that neighbourhood, with a good humoured ease, which she felt very unable to equal in her replies. They seemed each of them to have the happiest memories in the world. Nothing of the past was recollected with pain; and Lydia led voluntarily to subjects, which her sisters would not have alluded to for the world.

'Only think of its being three months,' she cried, 'since I went away; it seems but a fortnight I declare; and yet there have been things enough happened in the time. Good gracious! when I went away, I am sure I had no more idea of being married till I came back again! though I thought it would be very good fun if I was.'

Her father lifted up his eyes. Jane was distressed. Elizabeth looked expressively at Lydia; but she, who never heard nor saw any thing of which she chose to be insensible, gaily continued, 'Oh! mamma, do the people here abouts know I am married to-day? I was afraid they might not; and we overtook William Goulding in his curricle, so I was determined he should know it, and so I let down the side glass next to him, and took off my glove, and let my hand just rest upon the window frame, so that he might see the ring, and then I bowed and smiled like any thing.'

Elizabeth could bear it no longer. She got up, and ran out of the room; and returned no more, till she heard them passing through the hall to the dining parlour. She then joined them soon enough to see Lydia, with anxious parade, walk up to her mother's right hand, and hear her say to her eldest sister, 'Ah! Jane, I take your place now, and you must go lower, because I am a married woman.'

It was not to be supposed that time would give Lydia that embarrassment, from which she had been so wholly free at first. Her ease and good spirits increased. She longed to see Mrs Philips, the Lucasses, and all their other neighbours, and to hear herself called 'Mrs Wickham,' by each of them; and in the mean time, she went after dinner to shew her ring and boast of being married, to Mrs Hill and the two housemaids.

'Well, mamma,' said she, when they were all returned to the breakfast room, 'and what do you think of my husband? Is not he a charming man? I am sure my sisters must all envy me. I only hope they may have half my good luck. They must all go to Brighton. That is the place to get husbands. What a pity it is, mamma, we did not all go.'

'Very true; and if I had my will, we should. But my dear Lydia, I don't at all like your going such a way off. Must it be so?'

'Oh, lord! yes; – there is nothing in that. I shall like it of all things. You and papa, and my sisters, must come down and see us. We shall be at Newcastle all the winter, and I dare say there will be some balls, and I will take care to get good partners for them all.'

'I should like it beyond any thing!' said her mother.

'And then when you go away, you may leave one or two of my sisters behind you; and I dare say I shall get husbands for them before the winter is over.'

'I thank you for my share of the favour,' said Elizabeth; 'but I do not particularly like your way of getting husbands.'

Their visitors were not to remain above ten days with them. Mr Wickham had received his commission before he left London, and he was to join his regiment at the end of a fortnight.

No one but Mrs Bennet, regretted that their stay would be so short; and she made the most of the time, by visiting about with her daughter, and having very frequent parties at home. These parties were acceptable to all; to avoid a family circle was even more desirable to such as did think, than such as did not.

Wickham's affection for Lydia, was just what Elizabeth had expected to find it; not equal to Lydia's for him. She had scarcely needed her present observation to be satisfied, from the reason of things, that their elopement had been brought on by the strength of her love, rather than by his; and she would have wondered why, without violently caring for her, he chose to elope with her at all, had she not felt certain that his flight was rendered necessary by distress of circumstances; and if that were the case, he was not the young man to resist an opportunity of having a companion.

Lydia was exceedingly fond of him. He was her dear Wickham on every occasion; no one was to be put in competition with him. He did every thing best in the world; and she was sure he would kill more birds on the first of September, than any body else in the country.

One morning, soon after their arrival, as she was sitting with her two elder sisters, she said to Elizabeth,

'Lizzy, I never gave *you* an account of my wedding, I believe. You were not by, when I told mamma, and the others, all about it. Are not you curious to hear how it was managed?'

'No really,' replied Elizabeth; 'I think there cannot be too little said on the subject.'

'La! You are so strange! But I must tell you how it went off. We were married, you know, at St Clement's, because Wickham's lodgings were in that parish. And it was settled that we should all be there by eleven o'clock. My uncle and aunt and I were to go together; and the others were to meet us at the church. Well, Monday morning came, and I was in such a fuss! I was so afraid you know that something would happen to put it off, and then I should have gone quite distracted. And there was my aunt, all the time I was dressing, preaching and talking away just as if she was reading a sermon. However, I did not hear above one word in ten, for I was thinking, you may suppose, of my dear Wickham. I longed to know whether he would be married in his blue coat.

'Well, and so we breakfasted at ten as usual; I thought it would never be over; for, by the bye, you are to understand, that my uncle and aunt were horrid unpleasant all the time I was with them. If you'll believe me, I did not once put my foot out of doors, though I was there a fortnight. Not one party, or scheme, or any thing. To be sure London was rather thin, but however the little Theatre was open. Well, and so just as the carriage came to the door, my uncle was called away upon business to that horrid man Mr Stone. And then, you know, when once they get together, there is no end of it. Well, I was so frightened I did not know what to do, for my uncle was to give me away; and if we were beyond the hour, we could not be married all day. But, luckily, he came back again in ten minutes time, and then we all set out. However, I recollected afterwards, that if he *had* been prevented going, the wedding need not be put off, for Mr Darcy might have done as well.'

'Mr Darcy!' repeated Elizabeth, in utter amazement.

'Oh, yes! – he was to come there with Wickham, you know. But gracious me! I quite forgot! I ought not to have said a word about it. I promised them so faithfully! What will Wickham say? It was to be such a secret!'

'If it was to be secret,' said Jane, 'say not another word on the subject. You may depend upon my seeking no further.'

'Oh! certainly,' said Elizabeth, though burning with curiosity; 'we will ask you no questions.'

'Thank you,' said Lydia, 'for if you did, I should certainly tell you all, and then Wickham would be angry.'

On such encouragement to ask, Elizabeth was forced to put it out of her power, by running away.

But to live in ignorance on such a point was impossible; or at least it was impossible not to try for information. Mr Darcy had been at her sister's wedding. It was exactly a scene, and exactly among people, where he had apparently least to do, and least temptation to go. Conjectures as to the meaning of it, rapid and wild, hurried into her brain; but she was satisfied with none. Those that best pleased her, as placing his conduct in the noblest light, seemed most improbable. She could not bear such suspense; and hastily seizing a sheet of paper, wrote a short letter to her aunt, to request an explanation of what Lydia had dropt, if it were compatible with the secrecy which had been intended.

'You may readily comprehend,' she added, 'what my curiosity must be to know how a person unconnected with any of us, and (comparatively speaking) a stranger to our family, should have been amongst you at such a time. Pray write instantly, and let me understand it – unless it is, for very cogent reasons, to remain in the secrecy which Lydia seems to think necessary; and then I must endeavour to be satisfied with ignorance.'

'Not that I *shall* though,' she added to herself, as she finished the letter; 'and my dear aunt, if you do not tell me in an honourable manner, I shall certainly be reduced to tricks and stratagems to find it out.'

Jane's delicate sense of honour would not allow her to speak to Elizabeth privately of what Lydia had let fall; Elizabeth was glad of it; – till it appeared whether her enquiries would receive any satisfaction, she had rather be without a confidante.

Chapter Fifty Two

ELIZABETH HAD THE SATISFACTION OF receiving an answer to her letter, as soon as she possibly could. She was no sooner in possession of it, than hurrying into the little copse, where she was least likely to be interrupted, she sat down on one of the benches, and prepared to be happy; for the length of the letter convinced her that it did not contain a denial.

Gracechurch-street, Sept. 6.

MY DEAR NIECE,

I have just received your letter, and shall devote this whole morning to answering it, as I foresee that a little writing will not comprise what I have to tell you. I must confess myself surprised by your application; I did not expect it from you. Don't think me angry, however, for I only mean to let you know, that I had not imagined such enquiries to be necessary on your side. If you do not choose to understand me, forgive my impertinence. Your uncle is as much surprised as I am – and nothing but the belief of your being a party concerned, would have allowed him to act as he has done. But if you are really innocent and ignorant, I must be more explicit. On the very day of my coming home from Longbourn, your uncle had a most unexpected visitor. Mr Darcy called, and was shut up with him several hours. It was all over before I arrived; so my curiosity was not so dreadfully racked as your's seems to have been. He came to tell Mr Gardiner that he had found out where your sister and Mr Wickham were, and that he had seen and talked with them both. Wickham repeatedly, Lydia once. From what I can collect, he left Derbyshire only one day after ourselves, and came to town with the resolution of hunting for them. The motive professed, was his conviction of its being owing to himself that Wickham's worthlessness had not been so well known, as to make it impossible for any young woman of character, to love or confide in him. He generously imputed the whole to his mistaken pride, and confessed that he had before thought it beneath him, to lay his private actions open to the world. His character was to speak for itself. He called it, therefore, his duty to step forward, and endeavour to remedy an evil, which had been brought on by himself. If he had another motive, I am sure it would never disgrace him. He had been some days in town, before he was able to discover them; but he had something to direct his search, which was more than we had; and the consciousness of this, was another reason for his resolving to follow us. There is a lady, it seems, a Mrs Younge, who was some time ago governess to Miss Darcy, and was dismissed from her charge on some cause of disapprobation, though he did not say what. She then took a large house in Edward-street, and has since maintained herself by letting lodgings. This Mrs Younge was, he knew, intimately acquainted with Wickham; and he went to her for intelligence of him, as soon as he got to town. But it was two or three days before he could get from her what he wanted. She would not betray her trust, I suppose, without bribery and corruption, for she really did know where her friend was to be found. Wickham indeed had gone to her, on their first arrival in London, and had she been able to receive them into her house, they would have taken up their abode with her. At length, however, our kind friend procured the wished-for direction. They were in — street. He saw Wickham, and afterwards insisted on seeing Lydia. His first object with her, he acknowledged, had been to persuade her to quit her present disgraceful situation, and return to her friends as soon as they could be prevailed on to receive her, offering his assistance, as far as it would go. But he found Lydia absolutely resolved on remaining where she was. She cared for none of her friends, she wanted no help of his, she would not hear of leaving Wickham. She was sure they should be married some time or other, and it did not much signify when. Since such were her feelings, it only remained, he thought, to secure and expedite a marriage, which, in his very first conversation with Wickham, he easily learnt, had never been his design. He confessed himself obliged to leave the regiment, on account of some debts of honour, which were very pressing; and scrupled not to lay all the ill-consequence of Lydia's flight, on her own folly alone. He meant to resign his commission immediately; and as to his future situation, he could conjure very little about it. He must go somewhere, but he did not know where, and he knew he should have nothing to live on. Mr Darcy asked him why he had not married your sister at once. Though Mr Bennet was not imagined to be very rich, he would have been able to do something for him, and his situation must have been benefited by marriage. But he found, in reply to this question, that Wickham still cherished the hope of more effectually making his fortune by marriage, in some other country. Under such circumstances, however, he was not likely to be proof against the temptation of immediate relief. They

met several times, for there was much to be discussed. Wickham of course
wanted more than he could get; but at length was reduced to be reasonable.
Every thing being settled between them, Mr Darcy's next step was to make
your uncle acquainted with it, and he first called in Gracechurch-street the
evening before I came home. But Mr Gardiner could not be seen, and Mr
Darcy found, on further enquiry, that your father was still with him, but
would quit town the next morning. He did not judge your father to be a
person whom he could so properly consult as your uncle, and therefore readily
postponed seeing him, till after the departure of the former. He did not leave
his name, and till the next day, it was only known that a gentleman had
called on business. On Saturday he came again. Your father was gone, your
uncle at home, and, as I said before, they had a great deal of talk together.
They met again on Sunday, and then I saw him too. It was not all settled
before Monday: as soon as it was, the express was sent off to Longbourn. But
our visitor was very obstinate. I fancy, Lizzy, that obstinacy is the real defect
of his character after all. He has been accused of many faults at different
times; but this is the true one. Nothing was to be done that he did not do
himself; though I am sure (and I do not speak it to be thanked, therefore say
nothing about it,) your uncle would most readily have settled the whole.
They battled it together for a long time, which was more than either the
gentleman or lady concerned in it deserved. But at last your uncle was forced
to yield, and instead of being allowed to be of use to his niece, was forced to
put up with only having the probable credit of it, which went sorely against
the grain; and I really believe your letter this morning gave him great pleasure,
because it required an explanation that would rob him of his borrowed
feathers, and give the praise where it was due. But, Lizzy, this must go no
farther than yourself, or Jane at most. You know pretty well, I suppose, what
has been done for the young people. His debts are to be paid, amounting, I
believe, to considerably more than a thousand pounds, another thousand in
addition to her own settled upon her, and his commission purchased. The
reason why all this was to be done by him alone, was such as I have given
above. It was owing to him, to his reserve, and want of proper consideration,
that Wickham's character had been so misunderstood, and consequently that
he had been received and noticed as he was. Perhaps there was some truth in
this; though I doubt whether his reserve, or anybody's reserve, can be
answerable for the event. But in spite of all this fine talking, my dear Lizzy,
you may rest perfectly assured, that your uncle would never have yielded, if
we had not given him credit for another interest in the affair. When all this
was resolved on, he returned again to his friends, who were still staying at
Pemberley; but it was agreed that he should be in London once more when
the wedding took place, and all money matters were then to receive the last
finish. I believe I have now told you every thing. It is a relation which you
tell me is to give you great surprise; I hope at least it will not afford you any
displeasure. Lydia came to us; and Wickham had constant admission to the
house. He was exactly what he had been, when I knew him in Hertfordshire;
but I would not tell you how little I was satisfied with her behaviour while
she staid with us, if I had not perceived, by Jane's letter last Wednesday, that
her conduct on coming home was exactly of a piece with it, and therefore
what I now tell you, can give you no fresh pain. I talked to her repeatedly
in the most serious manner, representing to her all the wickedness of what
she had done, and all the unhappiness she had brought on her family. If she

heard me, it was by good luck, for I am sure she did not listen. I was sometimes
quite provoked, but then I recollected my dear Elizabeth and Jane, and for
their sakes had patience with her. Mr Darcy was punctual in his return, and
as Lydia informed you, attended the wedding. He dined with us the next day,
and was to leave town again on Wednesday or Thursday. Will you be very
angry with me, my dear Lizzy, if I take this opportunity of saying (what I
was never bold enough to say before) how much I like him. His behaviour to
us has, in every respect, been as pleasing as when we were in Derbyshire. His
understanding and opinions all please me; he wants nothing but a little more
liveliness, and that, *if he marry* prudently, *his wife may teach him. I thought*
him very sly; – he hardly ever mentioned your name. But slyness seems the
fashion. Pray forgive me, if I have been very presuming, or at least do not
punish me so far, as to exclude me from P. I shall never be quite happy till
I have been all round the park. A low phaeton, with a nice little pair of
ponies, would be the very thing. But I must write no more. The children have
been wanting me this half hour. Your's, very sincerely,

M. GARDINER.

The contents of this letter threw Elizabeth into a flutter of spirits, in
which it was difficult to determine whether pleasure or pain bore the greatest
share. The vague and unsettled suspicions which uncertainty had produced
of what Mr Darcy might have been doing to forward her sister's match,
which she had feared to encourage, as an exertion of goodness too great to
be probable, and at the same time dreaded to be just, from the pain of
obligation, were proved beyond their greatest extent to be true! He had
followed them purposely to town, he had taken on himself all the trouble
and mortification attendant on such a research; in which supplication had
been necessary to a woman whom he must abominate and despise, and where
he was reduced to meet, frequently meet, reason with, persuade, and finally
bribe, the man whom he always most wished to avoid, and whose very name
it was punishment to him to pronounce. He had done all this for a girl
whom he could neither regard nor esteem. Her heart did whisper, that he
had done it for her. But it was a hope shortly checked by other considerations,
and she soon felt that even her vanity was insufficient, when required to
depend on his affection for her, for a woman who had already refused him,
as able to overcome a sentiment so natural as abhorrence against relationship
with Wickham. Brother-in-law of Wickham! Every kind of pride must revolt
from the connection. He had to be sure done much. She was ashamed to
think how much. But he had given a reason for his interference, which
asked no extraordinary stretch of belief. It was reasonable that he should feel
he had been wrong; he had liberality, and he had the means of exercising
it; and though she would not place herself as his principal inducement, she
could, perhaps, believe, that remaining partiality to her, might assist his
endeavours in a cause where her peace of mind must be materially concerned.
It was painful, exceedingly painful, to know that they were under obligations
to a person who could never receive a return. They owed the restoration of
Lydia, her character, every thing to him. Oh! how heartily did she grieve
over every ungracious sensation she had ever encouraged, every saucy speech
she had ever directed towards him. For herself she was humbled; but she
was proud of him. Proud that in a cause of compassion and honour, he had
been able to get the better of himself. She read over her aunt's commendation

of him again and again. It was hardly enough; but it pleased her. She was even sensible of some pleasure, though mixed with regret, on finding how steadfastly both she and her uncle had been persuaded that affection and confidence subsisted between Mr Darcy and herself.

She was roused from her seat, and her reflections, by someone's approach; and before she could strike into another path, she was overtaken by Wickham.

'I am afraid I interrupt your solitary ramble, my dear sister?' said he, as he joined her.

'You certainly do,' she replied with a smile; 'but it does not follow that the interruption must be unwelcome.'

'I should be sorry indeed, if it were. *We* were always good friends; and now we are better.'

'True. Are the others coming out?'

'I do not know. Mrs Bennet and Lydia are going in the carriage to Meryton. And so, my dear sister, I find from our uncle and aunt, that you have actually seen Pemberley.'

She replied in the affirmative.

'I almost envy you the pleasure, and yet I believe it would be too much for me, or else I could take it in my way to Newcastle. And you saw the old housekeeper, I suppose? Poor Reynolds, she was always very fond of me. But of course she did not mention my name to you.'

'Yes, she did.'

'And what did she say?'

'That you were gone into the army, and she was afraid had – not turned out well. At such a distance as *that*, you know, things are strangely misrepresented.'

'Certainly,' he replied, biting his lips. Elizabeth hoped she had silenced him; but he soon afterwards said,

'I was surprised to see Darcy in town last month. We passed each other several times. I wonder what he can be doing there.'

'Perhaps preparing for his marriage with Miss de Bourgh,' said Elizabeth. 'It must be something particular, to take him there at this time of year.'

'Undoubtedly. Did you see him while you were at Lambton? I thought I understood from the Gardiners that you had.'

'Yes; he introduced us to his sister.'

'And do you like her?'

'Very much.'

'I have heard, indeed, that she is uncommonly improved within this year or two. When I last saw her, she was not very promising. I am very glad you liked her. I hope she will turn out well.'

'I dare say she will; she has got over the most trying age.'

'Did you go by the village of Kympton?'

'I do not recollect that we did.'

'I mention it, because it is the living which I ought to have had. A most delightful place! – Excellent Parsonage House! It would have suited me in every respect.'

'How should you have liked making sermons?'

'Exceedingly well. I should have considered it as part of my duty, and the exertion would soon have been nothing. One ought not to repine; – but, to be sure, it would have been such a thing for me! The quiet, the retirement of such a life, would have answered all my ideas of happiness! But it was not to be. Did you ever hear Darcy mention the circumstance, when you were in Kent?'

'I *have* heard from authority, which I thought *as good*, that it was left you conditionally only, and at the will of the present patron.'

'You have. Yes, there was something in *that*; I told you so from the first, you may remember.'

'I *did* hear, too, that there was a time, when sermon-making was not so palatable to you as it seems to be at present; that you actually declared your resolution of never taking orders, and that the business had been compromised accordingly.'

'You did! and it was not wholly without foundation. You may remember what I told you on that point, when first we talked of it.'

They were now almost at the door of the house, for she had walked fast to get rid of him; and unwilling for her sister's sake, to provoke him, she only said in reply, with a good-humoured smile.

'Come, Mr Wickham, we are brother and sister, you know. Do not let us quarrel about the past. In future, I hope we shall be always of one mind.'

She held out her hand; he kissed it with affectionate gallantry, though he hardly knew how to look, and they entered the house.

Chapter Fifty Three

MR WICKHAM WAS SO PERFECTLY SATISFIED with this conversation, that he never again distressed himself, or provoked his dear sister Elizabeth, by introducing the subject of it; and she was pleased to find that she had said enough to keep him quiet.

The day of his and Lydia's departure soon came; and Mrs Bennet was forced to submit to a separation, which, as her husband by no means entered into her scheme of their all going to Newcastle, was likely to continue at least a twelvemonth.

'Oh! my dear Lydia,' she cried, 'when shall we meet again?'

'Oh, lord! I don't know. Not these two or three years perhaps.'

'Write to me very often, my dear.'

'As often as I can. But you know married women have never much time for writing. My sisters may write to *me*. They will have nothing else to do.'

Mr Wickham's adieus were much more affectionate than his wife's. He smiled, looked handsome, and said many pretty things.

'He is as fine a fellow,' said Mr Bennet, as soon as they were out of the house, 'as ever I saw. He simpers, and smirks, and makes love to us all. I am prodigiously proud of him. I defy even Sir William Lucas himself, to produce a more valuable son-in-law.'

The loss of her daughter made Mrs Bennet very dull for several days.

'I often think,' said she, 'that there is nothing so bad as parting with one's friends. One seems so forlorn without them.'

'This is the consequence you see, Madam, of marrying a daughter,' said Elizabeth. 'It must make you better satisfied that your other four are single.'

'It is no such thing. Lydia does not leave me because she is married; but only because her husband's regiment happens to be so far off. If that had been nearer, she would not have gone so soon.'

But the spiritless condition which this event threw her into, was shortly relieved, and her mind opened again to the agitation of hope, by an article of news, which then began to be in circulation. The housekeeper at Netherfield had received orders to prepare for the arrival of her master, who was coming down in a day or two, to shoot there for several weeks. Mrs Bennet was quite in the fidgets. She looked at Jane, and smiled, and shook her head by turns.

'Well, well, and so Mr Bingley is coming down, sister,' (for Mrs Philips first brought her the news.) 'Well, so much the better. Not that I care about it, though. He is nothing to us, you know, and I am sure I never want to see him again. But, however, he is very welcome to come to Netherfield, if he likes it. And who knows what *may* happen? But that is nothing to us. You know, sister, we agreed long ago never to mention a word about it. And so, it is quite certain he is coming?'

'You may depend on it,' replied the other, 'for Mrs Nicholls was in Meryton last night; I saw her passing by, and went out myself on purpose to know the truth of it; and she told me that it was certain true. He comes down on Thursday at the latest, very likely on Wednesday. She was going to the butcher's, she told me, on purpose to order in some meat on Wednesday, and she has got three couple of ducks, just fit to be killed.'

Miss Bennet had not been able to hear of his coming, without changing colour. It was many months since she had mentioned his name to Elizabeth; but now, as soon as they were alone together, she said,

'I saw you look at me to day, Lizzy, when my aunt told us of the present report; and I know I appeared distressed. But don't imagine it was from any silly cause. I was only confused for the moment, because I felt that I *should* be looked at. I do assure you, that the news does not affect me either with pleasure or pain. I am glad of one thing, that he comes alone; because we shall see the less of him. Not that I am afraid of *myself*, but I dread other people's remarks.'

Elizabeth did not know what to make of it. Had she not seen him in Derbyshire, she might have supposed him capable of coming there, with no other view than what was acknowledged; but she still thought him partial to Jane, and she wavered as to the greater probability of his coming there *with* his friend's permission, or being bold enough to come without it.

'Yet it is hard,' she sometimes thought, 'that this poor man cannot come to a house, which he has legally hired, without raising all this speculation! I *will* leave him to himself.'

In spite of what her sister declared, and really believed to be her feelings, in the expectation of his arrival, Elizabeth could easily perceive that her spirits were affected by it. They were more disturbed, more unequal, than she had often seen them.

The subject which had been so warmly canvassed between their parents, about a twelvemonth ago, was now brought forward again.

'As soon as ever Mr Bingley comes, my dear,' said Mrs Bennet, 'you will wait on him of course.'

'No, no. You forced me into visiting him last year, and promised if I went to see him, he should marry one of my daughters. But it ended in nòthing, and I will not be sent on a fool's errand again.'

His wife represented to him how absolutely necessary such an attention would be from all the neighbouring gentlemen, on his returning to Netherfield.

''Tis an etiquette I despise,' said he. 'If he wants our society, let him seek it. He knows where we live. I will not spend *my* hours in running after my neighbours every time they go away, and come back again.'

'Well, all I know is, that it will be abominably rude if you do not wait on him. But, however, that shan't prevent my asking him to dine here, I am determined. We must have Mrs Long and the Gouldings soon. That will make thirteen with ourselves, so there will be just room at table for him.'

Consoled by this resolution, she was the better able to bear her husband's incivility; though it was very mortifying to know that her neighbours might all see Mr Bingley in consequence of it, before *they* did. As the day of his arrival drew near,

'I begin to be sorry that he comes at all,' said Jane to her sister. 'It would be nothing; I could see him with perfect indifference, but I can hardly bear to hear it thus perpetually talked of. My mother means well; but she does not know, no one can know how much I suffer from what she says. Happy shall I be, when his stay at Netherfield is over!'

'I wish I could say any thing to comfort you,' replied Elizabeth; 'but it is wholly out of my power. You must feel it; and the usual satisfaction of preaching patience to a sufferer is denied me, because you have always so much.'

Mr Bingley arrived. Mrs Bennet, through the assistance of servants, contrived to have the earliest tidings of it, that the period of anxiety and fretfulness on her side, might be as long as it could. She counted the days that must intervene before their invitation could be sent; hopeless of seeing him before. But on the third morning after his arrival in Hertfordshire, she saw him from her dressing-room window, enter the paddock, and ride towards the house.

Her daughters were eagerly called to partake of her joy. Jane resolutely kept her place at the table; but Elizabeth, to satisfy her mother, went to the window – she looked, – she saw Mr Darcy with him, and sat down again by her sister.

'There is a gentleman with him, mamma,' said Kitty; 'who can it be?'

'Some acquaintance or other, my dear, I suppose; I am sure I do not know.'

'La!' replied Kitty, 'it looks just like that man that used to be with him before. Mr what's his name. That tall, proud man.'

'Good gracious! Mr Darcy! – and so it does I vow. Well, any friend of Mr Bingley's will always be welcome here to be sure; but else I must say that I hate the very sight of him.'

Jane looked at Elizabeth with surprise and concern. She knew but little of their meeting in Derbyshire, and therefore felt for the awkwardness which must attend her sister, in seeing him almost for the first time after receiving his explanatory letter. Both sisters were uncomfortable enough. Each felt for the other, and of course for themselves; and their mother talked on, of her dislike of Mr Darcy, and her resolution to be civil to him only as Mr Bingley's friend, without being heard by either of them. But Elizabeth had sources of uneasiness which could not be suspected by Jane, to whom she had never yet had courage to shew Mrs Gardiner's letter, or to relate her own change of sentiment towards him. To Jane, he could be only a man whose proposals she had refused, and whose merit she had undervalued; but to her own more extensive information, he was the person, to whom the whole family were indebted for the first of benefits, and whom she regarded herself with an interest, if not quite so tender, at least as reasonable and just, as what Jane felt for Bingley. Her astonishment at his coming – at his coming to Netherfield, to Longbourn, and voluntarily seeking her again, was almost equal to what she had known on first witnessing his altered behaviour in Derbyshire.

The colour which had been driven from her face, returned for half a minute with an additional glow, and a smile of delight added lustre to her eyes, as she thought for that space of time, that his affection and wishes must still be unshaken. But she would not be secure.

'Let me first see how he behaves,' said she; 'it will then be early enough for expectation.'

She sat intently at work, striving to be composed, and without daring to lift up her eyes, till anxious curiosity carried them to the face of her sister, as the servant was approaching the door. Jane looked a little paler than usual, but more sedate than Elizabeth had expected. On the gentlemen's appearing, her colour increased; yet she received them with tolerable ease, and with a propriety of behaviour equally free from any symptom of resentment, or any unnecessary complaisance.

Elizabeth said as little either as civility would allow, and sat down again to her work, with an eagerness which it did not often command. She had ventured only one glance at Darcy. He looked serious as usual; and she thought, more as he had been used to look in Hertfordshire, than as she had seen him at Pemberley. But, perhaps he could not in her mother's presence be what he was before her uncle and aunt. It was a painful, but not an improbable, conjecture.

Bingley, she had likewise seen for an instant, and in that short period saw him looking both pleased and embarrassed. He was received by Mrs Bennet with a degree of civility, which made her two daughters ashamed, especially when contrasted with the cold and ceremonious politeness of her curtsey and address to his friend.

Elizabeth particularly, who knew that her mother owed to the latter the preservation of her favourite daughter from irremediable infamy, was hurt and distressed to a most painful degree by a distinction, so ill applied.

Darcy, after enquiring of her how Mr and Mrs Gardiner did, a question which she could not answer without confusion, said scarcely any thing. He was not seated by her; perhaps that was the reason of his silence; but it had not been so in Derbyshire. There he had talked to her friends, when he could not to herself. But now several minutes elapsed, without bringing the sound of his voice; and when occasionally, unable to resist the impulse of curiosity, she raised her eyes to his face, she as often found him looking at Jane, as at herself, and frequently on no object but the ground. More thoughtfulness, and less anxiety to please than when they last met, were plainly expressed. She was disappointed, and angry with herself for being so.

'Could I expect it to be otherwise!' said she. 'Yet why did he come?'

She was in no humour for conversation with anyone but himself; and to him she had hardly courage to speak.

She enquired after his sister, but could do no more.

'It is a long time, Mr Bingley, since you went away,' said Mrs Bennet. He readily agreed to it.

'I began to be afraid you would never come back again. People *did* say, you meant to quit the place entirely at Michaelmas; but, however, I hope it is not true. A great many changes have happened in the neighbourhood, since you went away. Miss Lucas is married and settled. And one of my own daughters. I suppose you have heard of it; indeed, you must have seen it in the papers. It was in the Times and the Courier, I know; though it was not put in as it ought to be. It was only said, "Lately, George Wickham, Esq. to Miss Lydia Bennet," without there being a syllable said of her father, or the place where she lived, or any thing. It was my brother Gardiner's drawing up too, and I wonder how he came to make such an awkward business of it. Did you see it?'

Bingley replied that he did, and made his congratulations. Elizabeth dared not lift up her eyes. How Mr Darcy looked, therefore, she could not tell.

'It is a delightful thing, to be sure, to have a daughter well married,' continued her mother, 'but at the same time, Mr Bingley, it is very hard to have her taken such a way from me. They are gone down to Newcastle, a place quite northward, it seems, and there they are to stay. I do not know how long. His regiment is there; for I suppose you have heard of his leaving the —shire, and of his being gone into the regulars. Thank Heaven! he has *some* friends, though perhaps not so many as he deserves.'

Elizabeth, who knew this to be levelled at Mr Darcy, was in such misery of shame, that she could hardly keep her seat. It drew from her, however, the exertion of speaking, which nothing else had so effectually done before; and she asked Bingley, whether he meant to make any stay in the country at present. A few weeks, he believed.

'When you have killed all your own birds, Mr Bingley,' said her mother, 'I beg you will come here, and shoot as many as you please, on Mr Bennet's manor. I am sure he will be vastly happy to oblige you, and will save all the best of the covies for you.'

Elizabeth's misery increased, at such unnecessary, such officious attention! Were the same fair prospect to arise at present, as had flattered them a year ago, every thing, she was persuaded, would be hastening to the same vexatious conclusion. At that instant she felt, that years of happiness could not make Jane or herself amends, for moments of such painful confusion.

'The first wish of my heart,' said she to herself, 'is never more to be in company with either of them. Their society can afford no pleasure, that will atone for such wretchedness as this! Let me never see either one or the other again!'

Yet the misery, for which years of happiness were to offer no compensation, received soon afterwards material relief, from observing how much the beauty of her sister re-kindled the admiration of her former lover. When first he came in, he had spoken to her but little; but every five minutes seemed to be giving her more of his attention. He found her as handsome as she had been last year; as good natured, and as unaffected, though not quite so chatty. Jane was anxious that no difference should be perceived in her at all, and was really persuaded that she talked as much as ever. But her mind was so busily engaged, that she did not always know when she was silent.

When the gentlemen rose to go away, Mrs Bennet was mindful of her intended civility, and they were invited and engaged to dine at Longbourn in a few days time.

'You are quite a visit in my debt, Mr Bingley,' she added, 'for when you went to town last winter, you promised to take a family dinner with us, as soon as you returned. I have not forgot, you see; and I assure you, I was very much disappointed that you did not come back and keep your engagement.'

Bingley looked a little silly at this reflection, and said something of his concern, at having been prevented by business. They then went away.

Mrs Bennet had been strongly inclined to ask them to stay and dine there, that day; but, though she always kept a very good table, she did not think any thing less than two courses, could be good enough for a man, on whom she had such anxious designs, or satisfy the appetite and pride of one who had ten thousand a year.

Chapter Fifty Four

AS SOON AS THEY WERE GONE, ELIZABETH walked out to recover her spirits; or in other words, to dwell without interruption on those subjects that must deaden them more. Mr Darcy's behaviour astonished and vexed her.

'Why, if he came only to be silent, grave, and indifferent,' said she, 'did he come at all?'

She could settle it in no way that gave her pleasure.

'He could be still amiable, still pleasing, to my uncle and aunt, when he was in town; and why not to me? If he fears me, why come hither? If he no longer cares for me, why silent? Teazing, teazing, man! I will think no more about him.'

Her resolution was for a short time involuntarily kept by the approach of her sister, who joined her with a cheerful look, which shewed her better satisfied with their visitors, than Elizabeth.

'Now,' said she, 'that this first meeting is over, I feel perfectly easy. I know my own strength, and I shall never be embarrassed again by his coming. I am glad he dines here on Tuesday. It will then be publicly seen, that on both sides, we meet only as common and indifferent acquaintance.'

'Yes, very indifferent indeed,' said Elizabeth, laughingly. 'Oh, Jane, take care.'

'My dear Lizzy, you cannot think me so weak, as to be in danger now.'

'I think you are in very great danger of making him as much in love with you as ever.'

They did not see the gentlemen again till Tuesday; and Mrs Bennet, in the meanwhile, was giving way to all the happy schemes, which the good humour, and common politeness of Bingley, in half an hour's visit, had revived.

On Tuesday there was a large party assembled at Longbourn; and the two, who were most anxiously expected, to the credit of their punctuality as sportsmen, were in very good time. When they repaired to the dining-room, Elizabeth eagerly watched to see whether Bingley would take the place, which, in all their former parties, had belonged to him, by her sister. Her prudent mother, occupied by the same ideas, forbore to invite him to sit by herself. On entering the room, he seemed to hesitate; but Jane happened to look round, and happened to smile: it was decided. He placed himself by her.

Elizabeth, with a triumphant sensation, looked towards his friend. He bore it with noble indifference, and she would have imagined that Bingley had received his sanction to be happy, had she not seen his eyes likewise turned towards Mr Darcy, with an expression of half-laughing alarm.

His behaviour to her sister was such, during dinner time, as shewed an admiration of her, which, though more guarded than formerly, persuaded Elizabeth, that if left wholly to himself, Jane's happiness, and his own, would be speedily secured. Though she dared not depend upon the consequence, she yet received pleasure from observing his behaviour. It gave her all the animation that her spirits could boast; for she was in no cheerful humour. Mr Darcy was almost as far from her, as the table could divide them. He was on one side of her mother. She knew how little such a situation would give pleasure to either, or make either appear to advantage. She was not near enough to hear any of their discourse, but she could see how seldom they spoke to each other, and how formal and cold was their manner, whenever they did. Her mother's ungraciousness, made the sense of what they owed him more painful to Elizabeth's mind; and she would, at times, have given any thing to be privileged to tell him, that his kindness was neither unknown nor unfelt by the whole of the family.

She was in hopes that the evening would afford some opportunity of bringing them together; that the whole of the visit would not pass away without enabling them to enter into something more of conversation, than the mere ceremonious salutation attending his entrance. Anxious and uneasy, the period which passed in the drawing-room, before the gentlemen came, was wearisome and dull to a degree, that almost made her uncivil. She looked forward to their entrance, as the point on which all her chance of pleasure for the evening must depend.

'If he does not come to me, *then*,' said she, 'I shall give him up for ever.'

The gentlemen came; and she thought he looked as if he would have answered her hopes; but, alas! the ladies had crowded round the table, where Miss Bennet was making tea, and Elizabeth pouring out the coffee, in so close a confederacy, that there was not a single vacancy near her, which would admit of a chair. And on the gentlemen's approaching, one of the girls moved closer to her than ever, and said, in a whisper,

'The men shan't come and part us, I am determined. We want none of them; do we?'

Darcy had walked away to another part of the room. She followed him with her eyes, envied every one to whom he spoke, had scarcely patience enough to help anybody to coffee; and then was enraged against herself for being so silly!

'A man who has once been refused! How could I ever be foolish enough to expect a renewal of his love? Is there one among the sex, who would not protest against such a weakness as a second proposal to the same woman? There is no indignity so abhorrent to their feelings!'

She was a little revived, however, by his bringing back his coffee cup himself; and she seized the opportunity of saying,

'Is your sister at Pemberley still?'

'Yes, she will remain there till Christmas.'

'And quite alone? Have all her friends left her?'

'Mrs Annesley is with her. The others have been gone on to Scarborough, these three weeks.'

She could think of nothing more to say; but if he wished to converse with her, he might have better success. He stood by her, however, for some minutes, in silence; and, at last, on the young lady's whispering to Elizabeth again, he walked away.

When the tea-things were removed, and the card tables placed, the ladies all rose, and Elizabeth was then hoping to be soon joined by him, when all her views were overthrown, by seeing him fall a victim to her mother's rapacity for whist players, and in a few moments after seated with the rest of the party. She now lost every expectation of pleasure. They were confined for the evening at different tables, and she had nothing to hope, but that his eyes were so often turned towards her side of the room, as to make him play as unsuccessfully as herself.

Mrs Bennet had designed to keep the two Netherfield gentlemen to supper; but their carriage was unluckily ordered before any of the others, and she had no opportunity of detaining them.

'Well girls,' said she, as soon as they were left to themselves, 'What say you to the day? I think every thing has passed off uncommonly well, I assure you. The dinner was as well dressed as any I ever saw. The venison was roasted to a turn – and everybody said, they never saw so fat a haunch. The soup was fifty times better than what we had at the Lucas's last week; and even Mr Darcy acknowledged, that the partridges were remarkably well done; and I suppose he has two or three French cooks at least. And, my dear Jane, I never saw you look in greater beauty. Mrs Long said so too, for I asked her whether you did not. And what do you think she said besides? "Ah! Mrs Bennet, we shall have her at Netherfield at last." She did indeed. I do think Mrs Long is as good a creature as ever lived – and her nieces are very pretty behaved girls, and not at all handsome: I like them prodigiously.'

Mrs Bennet, in short, was in very great spirits; she had seen enough of Bingley's behaviour to Jane, to be convinced that she would get him at last; and her expectations of advantage to her family, when in a happy humour, were so far beyond reason, that she was quite disappointed at not seeing him there again the next day, to make his proposals.

'It has been a very agreeable day,' said Miss Bennet to Elizabeth. 'The party seemed so well selected, so suitable one with the other. I hope we may often meet again.'

Elizabeth smiled.

'Lizzy, you must not do so. You must not suspect me. It mortifies me. I assure you that I have now learnt to enjoy his conversation as an agreeable and sensible young man, without having a wish beyond it. I am perfectly satisfied from what his manners now are, that he never had any design of engaging my affection. It is only that he is blessed with greater sweetness of address, and a stronger desire of generally pleasing than any other man.'

'You are very cruel,' said her sister, 'you will not let me smile, and are provoking me to it every moment.'

'How hard it is in some cases to be believed!'

'And how impossible in others!'

'But why should you wish to persuade me that I feel more than I acknowledge?'

'That is a question which I hardly know how to answer. We all love to instruct, though we can teach only what is not worth knowing. Forgive me; and if you persist in indifference, do not make *me* your confidante.'

Chapter Fifty Five

A FEW DAYS AFTER THIS VISIT, Mr Bingley called again, and alone. His friend had left him that morning for London, but was to return home in ten days time. He sat with them above an hour, and was in remarkably good spirits. Mrs Bennet invited him to dine with them; but, with many expressions of concern, he confessed himself engaged elsewhere.

'Next time you call,' said she, 'I hope we shall be more lucky.'

He should be particularly happy at any time, &c. &c.; and if she would give him leave, would take an early opportunity of waiting on them.

'Can you come to-morrow?'

Yes, he had no engagement at all for to-morrow; and her invitation was accepted with alacrity.

He came, and in such very good time, that the ladies were none of them dressed. In ran Mrs Bennet to her daughter's room, in her dressing gown, and with her hair half finished, crying out,

'My dear Jane, make haste and hurry down. He is come – Mr Bingley is come. – He is, indeed. Make haste, make haste. Here, Sarah, come to Miss Bennet this moment, and help her on with her gown. Never mind Miss Lizzy's hair.'

'We will be down as soon as we can,' said Jane; 'but I dare say Kitty is forwarder than either of us, for she went up stairs half an hour ago.'

'Oh! hang Kitty! what has she to do with it? Come be quick, be quick! where is your sash my dear?'

But when her mother was gone, Jane would not be prevailed on to go down without one of her sisters.

The same anxiety to get them by themselves, was visible again in the evening. After tea, Mr Bennet retired to the library, as was his custom, and Mary went up stairs to her instrument. Two obstacles of the five being thus removed, Mrs Bennet sat looking and winking at Elizabeth and Catherine for a considerable time, without making any impression on them. Elizabeth would not observe her; and when at last Kitty did, she very innocently said 'What is the matter mamma? What do you keep winking at me for? What am I to do?'

'Nothing child, nothing. I did not wink at you.' She then sat still five minutes longer; but unable to waste such a precious occasion, she suddenly got up, and saying to Kitty,

'Come here, my love, I want to speak to you,' took her out of the room. Jane instantly gave a look at Elizabeth, which spoke her distress at such premeditation, and her intreaty that *she* would not give into it. In a few minutes, Mrs Bennet half opened the door and called out,

'Lizzy, my dear, I want to speak with you.'

Elizabeth was forced to go.

'We may as well leave them by themselves you know;' said her mother as soon as she was in the hall. 'Kitty and I are going up stairs to sit in my dressing room.'

Elizabeth made no attempt to reason with her mother, but remained quietly in the hall, till she and Kitty were out of sight, then returned into the drawing room.

Mrs Bennet's schemes for this day were ineffectual. Bingley was every thing that was charming, except the professed lover of her daughter. His ease and cheerfulness rendered him a most agreeable addition to their evening party; and he bore with the ill-judged officiousness of the mother, and heard all her silly remarks with a forbearance and command of countenance, particularly grateful to the daughter.

He scarcely needed an invitation to stay to supper; and before he went away, an engagement was formed, chiefly through his own and Mrs Bennet's means, for his coming next morning to shoot with her husband.

After this day, Jane said no more of her indifference. Not a word passed between the sisters concerning Bingley; but Elizabeth went to bed in the happy belief that all must speedily be concluded, unless Mr Darcy returned within the stated time. Seriously, however, she felt tolerably persuaded that all this must have taken place with that gentleman's concurrence.

Bingley was punctual to his appointment; and he and Mr Bennet spent the morning together, as had been agreed on. The latter was much more agreeable than his companion expected. There was nothing of presumption or folly in Bingley, that could provoke his ridicule, or disgust him into silence; and he was more communicative, and less eccentric than the other had ever seen him. Bingley of course returned with him to dinner; and in the evening Mrs Bennet's invitation was again at work to get every body away from him and her daughter. Elizabeth, who had a letter to write, went into the breakfast room for that purpose soon after tea; for as the others were all going to sit down to cards, she could not be wanted to counteract her mother's schemes.

But on returning to the drawing room, when her letter was finished, she saw, to her infinite surprise, there was reason to fear that her mother had been too ingenious for her. On opening the door, she perceived her sister and Bingley standing together over the hearth, as if engaged in earnest conversation; and had this led to no suspicion, the faces of both as they hastily turned round, and moved away from each other, would have told it all. *Their* situation was awkward enough; but *her's* she thought was still worse. Not a syllable was uttered by either; and Elizabeth was on the point of going away again, when Bingley, who as well as the other had sat down, suddenly rose, and whispering a few words to her sister, ran out of the room.

Jane could have no reserves from Elizabeth, where confidence would give pleasure; and instantly embracing her, acknowledged, with the liveliest emotion, that she was the happiest creature in the world.

"'Tis too much!' she added, 'by far too much. I do not deserve it. Oh! why is not every body as happy?'

Elizabeth's congratulations were given with a sincerity, a warmth, a delight, which words could but poorly express. Every sentence of kindness was a fresh source of happiness to Jane. But she would not allow herself to stay with her sister, or say half that remained to be said, for the present.

'I must go instantly to my mother;' she cried. 'I would not on any account trifle with her affectionate solicitude; or allow her to hear it from any one but myself. He is gone to my father already. Oh! Lizzy, to know that what I have to relate will give such pleasure to all my dear family! how shall I bear so much happiness!'

She then hastened away to her mother, who had purposely broken up the card party, and was sitting up stairs with Kitty.

Elizabeth, who was left by herself, now smiled at the rapidity and ease with which an affair was finally settled, that had given them so many previous months of suspense and vexation.

'And this,' said she, 'is the end of all his friend's anxious circumspection! of all his sister's falsehood and contrivance! the happiest, wisest, most reasonable end!'

In a few minutes she was joined by Bingley, whose conference with her father had been short and to the purpose.

'Where is your sister?' said he hastily, as he opened the door.

'With my mother up stairs. She will be down in a moment I dare say.'

He then shut the door, and coming up to her, claimed the good wishes and affection of a sister. Elizabeth honestly and heartily expressed her delight in the prospect of their relationship. They shook hands with great cordiality; and then till her sister came down, she had to listen to all he had to say, of his own happiness, and of Jane's perfections; and in spite of his being a lover, Elizabeth really believed all his expectations of felicity, to be rationally founded, because they had for basis the excellent understanding, and super-excellent disposition of Jane, and a general similarity of feeling and taste between her and himself.

It was an evening of no common delight to them all; the satisfaction of Miss Bennet's mind gave a glow of such sweet animation to her face, as made her look handsomer than ever. Kitty simpered and smiled, and hoped her turn was coming soon. Mrs Bennet could not give her consent, or speak her approbation in terms warm enough to satisfy her feelings, though she talked to Bingley of nothing else, for half an hour; and when Mr Bennet joined them at supper, his voice and manner plainly shewed how really happy he was.

Not a word, however, passed his lips in allusion to it, till their visitor took his leave for the night; but as soon as he was gone, he turned to his daughter and said,

'Jane, I congratulate you. You will be a very happy woman.'

Jane went to him instantly, kissed him, and thanked him for his goodness.

'You are a good girl;' he replied, 'and I have great pleasure in thinking you will be so happily settled. I have not a doubt of your doing very well together. Your tempers are by no means unlike. You are each of you so complying, that nothing will ever be resolved on; so easy, that every servant will cheat you; and so generous, that you will always exceed your income.'

'I hope not so. Imprudence or thoughtlessness in money matters, would be unpardonable in *me*.'

'Exceed their income! My dear Mr Bennet,' cried his wife, 'what are you talking of? Why, he has four or five thousand a-year, and very likely more.' Then addressing her daughter, 'Oh, my dear, dear Jane, I am so happy! I am sure I sha'nt get a wink of sleep all night. I knew how it would be. I always said it must be so, at last. I was sure you could not be so beautiful for nothing! I remember, as soon as ever I saw him, when he first came into Hertfordshire last year, I thought how likely it was that you should come together. Oh! he is the handsomest young man that ever was seen!'

Wickham, Lydia, were all forgotten. Jane was beyond competition her favourite child. At that moment, she cared for no other. Her younger sisters soon began to make interest with her for objects of happiness which she might in future be able to dispense.

Mary petitioned for the use of the library at Netherfield; and Kitty begged very hard for a few balls there every winter.

Bingley, from this time, was of course a daily visitor at Longbourn; coming frequently before breakfast, and always remaining till after supper; unless when some barbarous neighbour, who could not be enough detested, had given him an invitation to dinner, which he thought himself obliged to accept.

Elizabeth had now but little time for conversation with her sister; for while he was present, Jane had no attention to bestow on any one else; but she found herself considerably useful to both of them, in those hours of separation that must sometimes occur. In the absence of Jane, he always attached himself to Elizabeth, for the pleasure of talking of her; and when Bingley was gone, Jane constantly sought the same means of relief.

'He has made me so happy,' said she, one evening, 'by telling me, that he was totally ignorant of my being in town last spring! I had not believed it possible.'

'I suspected as much,' replied Elizabeth. 'But how did he account for it?'

'It must have been his sister's doing. They were certainly no friends to his acquaintance with me, which I cannot wonder at, since he might have chosen so much more advantageously in many respects. But when they see, as I trust they will, that their brother is happy with me, they will learn to be contented, and we shall be on good terms again; though we can never be what we once were to each other.'

'That is the most unforgiving speech,' said Elizabeth, 'that I ever heard you utter. Good girl! It would vex me, indeed, to see you again the dupe of Miss Bingley's pretended regard.'

'Would you believe it, Lizzy, that when he went to town last November, he really loved me, and nothing but a persuasion of *my* being indifferent, would have prevented his coming down again!'

'He made a little mistake to be sure; but it is to the credit of his modesty.'

This naturally introduced a panegyric from Jane on his diffidence, and the little value he put on his own good qualities.

Elizabeth was pleased to find, that he had not betrayed the interference of his friend, for, though Jane had the most generous and forgiving heart in the world, she knew it was a circumstance which must prejudice her against him.

'I am certainly the most fortunate creature that ever existed!' cried Jane. 'Oh! Lizzy, why am I thus singled from my family, and blessed above them all! If I could but see *you* as happy! If there *were* but such another man for you!'

'If you were to give me forty such men, I never could be so happy as you. Till I have your disposition, your goodness, I never can have your happiness. No, no, let me shift for myself; and, perhaps, if I have very good luck, I may meet with another Mr Collins in time.'

The situation of affairs in the Longbourn family could not be long a secret. Mrs Bennet was privileged to whisper it to Mrs Philips, and *she* ventured, without any permission, to do the same by all her neighbours in Meryton.

The Bennets were speedily pronounced to be the luckiest family in the world, though only a few weeks before, when Lydia had first run away, they had been generally proved to be marked out for misfortune.

Chapter Fifty Six

ONE MORNING, ABOUT A WEEK AFTER Bingley's engagement with Jane had been formed, as he and the females of the family were sitting together in the dining room, their attention was suddenly drawn to the window, by the sound of a carriage; and they perceived a chaise and four driving up the lawn. It was too early in the morning for visitors, and besides, the equipage did not answer to that of any of their neighbours. The horses were post; and neither the carriage, nor the livery of the servant who preceded it, were familiar to them. As it was certain, however, that somebody was coming, Bingley instantly prevailed on Miss Bennet to avoid the confinement of such an intrusion, and walk away with him into the shrubbery. They both set off, and the conjectures of the remaining three continued, though with little satisfaction, till the door was thrown open, and their visitor entered. It was Lady Catherine de Bourgh.

They were of course all intending to be surprised; but their astonishment was beyond their expectation; and on the part of Mrs Bennet and Kitty, though she was perfectly unknown to them, even inferior to what Elizabeth felt.

She entered the room with an air more than usually ungracious, made no other reply to Elizabeth's salutation, than a slight inclination of the head, and sat down without saying a word. Elizabeth had mentioned her name to her mother, on her ladyship's entrance, though no request of introduction had been made.

Mrs Bennet all amazement, though flattered by having a guest of such high importance, received her with the utmost politeness. After sitting for a moment in silence, she said very stiffly to Elizabeth,

'I hope you are well, Miss Bennet. That lady I suppose is your mother.'

Elizabeth replied very concisely that she was.

'And *that* I suppose is one of your sisters.'

'Yes, madam,' said Mrs Bennet, delighted to speak to lady Catherine. 'She is my youngest girl but one. My youngest of all, is lately married, and my eldest is some-where about the grounds, walking with a young man, who I believe will soon become a part of the family.'

'You have a very small park here,' returned lady Catherine after a short silence.

'It is nothing in comparison of Rosings, my lady, I dare say; but I assure you it is much larger than Sir William Lucas's.'

'This must be a most inconvenient sitting room for the evening, in summer; the windows are full west.'

Mrs Bennet assured her that they never sat there after dinner; and then added,

'May I take the liberty of asking your ladyship whether you left Mr and Mrs Collins well.'

'Yes, very well. I saw them the night before last.'

Elizabeth now expected that she would produce a letter for her from Charlotte, as it seemed the only probable motive for her calling. But no letter appeared, and she was completely puzzled.

Mrs. Bennet, with great civility, begged her ladyship to take some refreshment; but Lady Catherine very resolutely, and not very politely, declined eating any thing; and then rising up, said to Elizabeth,

'Miss Bennet, there seemed to be a prettyish kind of a little wilderness on one side of your lawn. I should be glad to take a turn in it, if you will favour me with your company.'

'Go, my dear,' cried her mother, 'and shew her ladyship about the different walks. I think she will be pleased with the hermitage.'

Elizabeth obeyed, and running into her own room for her parasol, attended her noble guest down stairs. As they passed through the hall, Lady Catherine opened the doors into the dining-parlour and drawing-room, and pronouncing them, after a short survey, to be decent looking rooms, walked on.

Her carriage remained at the door, and Elizabeth saw that her waiting-woman was in it. They proceeded in silence along the gravel walk that led to the copse; Elizabeth was determined to make no effort for conversation with a woman, who was now more than usually insolent and disagreeable.

'How could I ever think her like her nephew?' said she, as she looked in her face.

As soon as they entered the copse, Lady Catherine began in the following manner: –

'You can be at no loss, Miss Bennet, to understand the reason of my journey hither. Your own heart, your own conscience, must tell you why I come.'

Elizabeth looked with unaffected astonishment.

'Indeed, you are mistaken, Madam. I have not been at all able to account for the honour of seeing you here.'

'Miss Bennet,' replied her ladyship, in an angry tone, 'you ought to know, that I am not to be trifled with. But however insincere you may choose to be, you shall not find *me* so. My character has ever been celebrated for its sincerity and frankness, and in a cause of such moment as this, I shall certainly not depart from it. A report of a most alarming nature, reached me two days ago. I was told, that not only your sister was on the point of being most advantageously married, but that *you*, that Miss Elizabeth Bennet, would, in all likelihood, be soon afterwards united to my nephew, my own nephew, Mr Darcy. Though I *know* it must be a scandalous falsehood; though I would not injure him so much as to suppose the truth of it possible, I instantly resolved on setting off for this place, that I might make my sentiments known to you.'

'If you believed it impossible to be true,' said Elizabeth, colouring with astonishment and disdain, 'I wonder you took the trouble of coming so far. What would your ladyship propose by it?'

'At once to insist upon having such a report universally contradicted.'

'Your coming to Longbourn, to see me and my family,' said Elizabeth, coolly, 'will be rather a confirmation of it; if, indeed, such a report is in existence.'

'If! do you then pretend to be ignorant of it? Has it not been industriously circulated by yourselves? Do you not know that such a report is spread abroad?'

'I never heard that it was.'

'And can you likewise declare, that there is no *foundation* for it?'

'I do not pretend to possess equal frankness with your ladyship. *You* may ask questions which *I* shall not choose to answer.'

'This is not to be borne. Miss Bennet, I insist on being satisfied. Has he, has my nephew, made you an offer of marriage?'

'Your ladyship has declared it to be impossible.'

'It ought to be so; it must be so, while he retains the use of his reason. But *your* arts and allurements may, in a moment of infatuation, have made him forget what he owes to himself and to all his family. You may have drawn him in.'

'If I had, I shall be the last person to confess it.'

'Miss Bennet, do you know who I am? I have not been accustomed to such language as this. I am almost the nearest relation he has in the world, and am entitled to know all his dearest concerns.'

'But you are not entitled to know *mine*; nor will such behaviour as this, ever induce me to be explicit.'

'Let me be rightly understood. This match, to which you have the presumption to aspire, can never take place. No, never. Mr Darcy is engaged to *my daughter*. Now what have you to say?'

'Only this; that if he is so, you can have no reason to suppose he will make an offer to me.'

Lady Catherine hesitated for a moment, and then replied,

'The engagement between them is of a peculiar kind. From their infancy, they have been intended for each other. It was the favourite wish of *his* mother, as well as of her's. While in their cradles, we planned the union: and now, at the moment when the wishes of both sisters would be accomplished, in their marriage, to be prevented by a young woman of inferior birth, of no importance in the world, and wholly unallied to the family! Do you pay no regard to the wishes of his friends? To his tacit engagement with Miss de Bourgh? Are you lost to every feeling of propriety and delicacy? Have you not heard me say, that from his earliest hours he was destined for his cousin?'

'Yes, and I had heard it before. But what is that to me? If there is no other objection to my marrying your nephew, I shall certainly not be kept from it, by knowing that his mother and aunt wished him to marry Miss de Bourgh. You both did as much as you could, in planning the marriage. Its completion depended on others. If Mr Darcy is neither by honour nor inclination confined to his cousin, why is not he to make another choice? And if I am that choice, why may not I accept him?'

'Because honour, decorum, prudence, nay, interest, forbid it. Yes, Miss Bennet, interest; for do not expect to be noticed by his family or friends, if you wilfully act against the inclinations of all. You will be censured, slighted, and despised, by every one connected with him. Your alliance will be a disgrace; your name will never even be mentioned by any of us.'

'These are heavy misfortunes,' replied Elizabeth. 'But the wife of Mr Darcy must have such extraordinary sources of happiness necessarily attached to her situation, that she could, upon the whole, have no cause to repine.'

'Obstinate, headstrong girl! I am ashamed of you! Is this your gratitude for my attentions to you last spring? Is nothing due to me on that score?

'Let us sit down. You are to understand, Miss Bennet, that I came here with the determined resolution of carrying my purpose; nor will I be dissuaded from it. I have not been used to submit to any person's whims. I have not been in the habit of brooking disappointment.'

'*That* will make your ladyship's situation at present more pitiable; but it will have no effect on *me*.'

'I will not be interrupted. Hear me in silence. My daughter and my nephew are formed for each other. They are descended on the maternal side, from the same noble line; and, on the father's, from respectable, honourable, and ancient, though untitled families. Their fortune on both sides is splendid. They are destined for each other by the voice of every member of their respective houses; and what is to divide them? The upstart pretensions of a young woman without family, connections, or fortune. Is this to be endured! But it must not, shall not be. If you were sensible of your own good, you would not wish to quit the sphere, in which you have been brought up.'

'In marrying your nephew, I should not consider myself as quitting that sphere. He is a gentleman; I am a gentleman's daughter; so far we are equal.'

'True. You *are* a gentleman's daughter. But who was your mother? Who are your uncles and aunts? Do not imagine me ignorant of their condition.'

'Whatever my connections may be,' said Elizabeth, 'if your nephew does not object to them, they can be nothing to *you*.'

'Tell me once for all, are you engaged to him?'

Though Elizabeth would not, for the mere purpose of obliging Lady Catherine, have answered this question; she could not but say, after a moment's deliberation,

'I am not.'

Lady Catherine seemed pleased.

'And will you promise me, never to enter into such an engagement?'

'I will make no promise of the kind.'

'Miss Bennet I am shocked and astonished. I expected to find a more reasonable young woman. But do not deceive yourself into a belief that I will ever recede. I shall not go away, till you have given me the assurance I require.'

'And I certainly *never* give it. I am not to be intimidated into anything so wholly unreasonable. Your ladyship wants Mr Darcy to marry your daughter; but would my giving you the wished-for promise, make *their* marriage at all more probable? Supposing him to be attached to me, would *my* refusing to accept his hand, make him wish to bestow it on his cousin? Allow me to say, Lady Catherine, that the arguments with which you have supported this extraordinary application, have been as frivolous as the application was ill-judged. You have widely mistaken my character, if you think I can be worked on by such persuasions as these. How far your nephew might approve of your interference in *his* affairs, I cannot tell; but you have certainly no right to concern yourself in mine. I must beg, therefore, to be importuned no farther on the subject.'

'Not so hasty, if you please. I have by no means done. To all the objections I have already urged, I have still another to add. I am no stranger to the particulars of your youngest sister's infamous elopement. I know it all; that the young man's marrying her, was a patched-up business, at the expence of your father and uncles. And is *such* a girl to be my nephew's sister? Is *her* husband, is the son of his late father's steward, to be his brother? Heaven and earth! – of what are you thinking? Are the shades of Pemberley to be thus polluted?'

'You can *now* have nothing farther to say,' she resentfully answered. 'You have insulted me, in every possible method. I must beg to return to the house.'

And she rose as she spoke. Lady Catherine rose also, and they turned back. Her ladyship was highly incensed.

'You have no regard, then, for the honour and credit of my nephew! Unfeeling, selfish girl! Do you not consider that a connection with you, must disgrace him in the eyes of everybody?'

'Lady Catherine, I have nothing farther to say. You know my sentiments.'

'You are then resolved to have him?'

'I have said no such thing. I am only resolved to act in that manner, which will, in my own opinion, constitute my happiness, without reference to *you*, or to any person so wholly unconnected with me.'

'It is well. You refuse, then, to oblige me. You refuse to obey the claims of duty, honour, and gratitude. You are determined to ruin him in the opinion of all his friends, and make him the contempt of the world.'

'Neither duty, nor honour, nor gratitude,' replied Elizabeth, 'have any possible claim on me, in the present instance. No principle of either, would be violated by my marriage with Mr Darcy. And with regard to the resentment of his family, or the indignation of the world, if the former *were* excited by his marrying me, it would not give me one moment's concern – and the world in general would have too much sense to join in the scorn.'

'And this is your real opinion! This is your final resolve! Very well. I shall now know how to act. Do not imagine, Miss Bennet, that your ambition will ever be gratified. I came to try you. I hoped to find you reasonable; but depend upon it I will carry my point.'

In this manner Lady Catherine talked on, till they were at the door of the carriage, when turning hastily round, she added,

'I take no leave of you, Miss Bennet. I send no compliments to your mother. You deserve no such attention. I am most seriously displeased.'

Elizabeth made no answer; and without attempting to persuade her ladyship to return into the house, walked quietly into it herself. She heard the carriage drive away as she proceeded up stairs. Her mother impatiently met her at the door of the dressing-room, to ask why Lady Catherine would not come in again and rest herself.

'She did not choose it,' said her daughter, 'she would go.'

'She is a very fine-looking woman! and her calling here was prodigiously civil! for she only came, I suppose, to tell us the Collinses were well. She is on her road somewhere, I dare say, and so passing through Meryton, thought she might as well call on you. I suppose she had nothing particular to say to you, Lizzy?'

Elizabeth was forced to give into a little falsehood here; for to acknowledge the substance of their conversation was impossible.

Chapter Fifty Seven

THE DISCOMPOSURE OF SPIRITS, WHICH this extraordinary visit threw Elizabeth into, could not be easily overcome; nor could she for many hours, learn to think of it less than incessantly. Lady Catherine it appeared, had actually taken the trouble of this journey from Rosings, for the sole purpose of breaking off her supposed engagement with Mr Darcy. It was a rational scheme to be sure! but from what the report of their engagement could originate, Elizabeth was at a loss to imagine; till she recollected that *his* being the intimate friend of Bingley, and *her* being the sister of Jane, was enough, at a time when the expectation of one wedding, made every body eager for another, to supply the idea. She had not herself forgotten to feel that the marriage of her sister must bring them more frequently together. And her neighbours at Lucas lodge, therefore, (for through their communication with the Collinses, the report she concluded had reached Lady Catherine) had only set *that* down, as almost certain and immediate, which *she* had looked forward to as possible, at some future time.

In revolving Lady Catherine's expressions, however, she could not help feeling some uneasiness as to the possible consequence of her persisting in this interference. From what she had said of her resolution to prevent their marriage, it occurred to Elizabeth that she must meditate an application to her nephew; and how *he* might take a similar representation of the evils attached to a connection with her, she dared not pronounce. She knew not the exact degree of his affection for his aunt, or his dependence on her judgment, but it was natural to suppose that he thought much higher of her ladyship than *she* could do; and it was certain, that in enumerating the miseries of a marriage with *one*, whose immediate connections were so unequal to his own, his aunt would address him on his weakest side. With his notions of dignity, he would probably feel that the arguments, which to Elizabeth had appeared weak and ridiculous, contained much good sense and solid reasoning.

If he had been wavering before, as to what he should do, which had often seemed likely, the advice and intreaty of so near a relation might settle every doubt, and determine him at once to be as happy, as dignity unblemished could make him. In that case he would return no more. Lady Catherine might see him in her way through town; and his engagement to Bingley of coming again to Netherfield must give way.

'If, therefore, an excuse for not keeping his promise, should come to his friend within a few days,' she added, 'I shall know how to understand it. I shall then give over every expectation, every wish of his constancy. If he is satisfied with only regretting me, when he might have obtained my affections and hand, I shall soon cease to regret him at all.'

The surprise of the rest of the family, on hearing who their visitor had been, was very great; but they obligingly satisfied it, with the same kind of supposition, which had appeased Mrs Bennet's curiosity; and Elizabeth was spared from much teazing on the subject.

The next morning, as she was going down stairs, she was met by her father, who came out of his library with a letter in his hand.

'Lizzy,' said he, 'I was going to look for you; come into my room.'

She followed him thither; and her curiosity to know what he had to tell her, was heightened by the supposition of its being in some manner connected with the letter he held. It suddenly struck her that it might be from Lady Catherine; and she anticipated with dismay all the consequent explanations.

She followed her father to the fire place, and they both sat down. He then said,

'I have received a letter this morning that has astonished me exceedingly. As it principally concerns yourself, you ought to know its contents. I did not know before, that I had two daughters on the brink of matrimony. Let me congratulate you, on a very important conquest.'

The colour now rushed into Elizabeth's cheeks in the instantaneous conviction of its being a letter from the nephew, instead of the aunt; and she was undetermined whether most to be pleased that he explained himself at all, or offended that this letter was not rather addressed to herself; when her father continued,

'You look conscious. Young ladies have great penetration in such matters as these; but I think I may defy even your sagacity, to discover the name of your admirer. This letter is from Mr Collins.'

'From Mr Collins! and what can he have to say?'

'Something very much to the purpose of course. He begins with congratulations on the approaching nuptials of my eldest daughter, of which it seems he has been told, by some of the good-natured, gossiping Lucases. I shall not sport with your impatience, by reading what he says on that point. What relates to yourself, is as follows. 'Having thus offered you the sincere congratulations of Mrs Collins and myself on this happy event, let me now add a short hint on the subject of another: of which we have been advertised by the same authority. Your daughter Elizabeth, it is presumed, will not long bear the name of Bennet, after her elder sister has resigned it, and the chosen partner of her fate, may be reasonably looked up to, as one of the most illustrious personages in this land.'

'Can you possibly guess Lizzy, who is meant by this?' 'This young gentleman is blessed in a peculiar way, with every thing the heart of mortal can most desire, – splendid property, noble kindred, and extensive patronage. Yet in spite of all these temptations, let me warn my cousin Elizabeth, and yourself, of what evils you may incur, by a precipitate closure with this gentleman's proposals, which, of course, you will be inclined to take immediate advantage of.'

'Have you any idea, Lizzy, who this gentleman is? But now it comes out.'

'My motive for cautioning you, is as follows. We have reason to imagine that his aunt, Lady Catherine de Bourgh, does not look on the match with a friendly eye.'

'*Mr Darcy*, you see, is the man! Now, Lizzy, I think I *have* surprised you. Could he, or the Lucases, have pitched on any man, within the circle of our acquaintance, whose name would have given the lie more effectually to what they related? Mr Darcy, who never looks at any woman but to see a blemish, and who probably never looked at *you* in his life! It is admirable!'

Elizabeth tried to join in her father's pleasantry, but could only force one most reluctant smile. Never had his wit been directed in a manner so little agreeable to her.

'Are you not diverted?'

'Oh! yes. Pray read on.'

'After mentioning the likelihood of this marriage to her ladyship last night, she immediately, with her usual condescension, expressed what she felt on the occasion; when it became apparent, that on the score of some family objections on the part of my cousin, she would never give her consent to what she termed so disgraceful a match. I thought it my duty to give the speediest intelligence of this to my cousin, that she and her noble admirer may be aware of what they are about, and not run hastily into a marriage which has not been properly sanctioned.' 'Mr Collins moreover adds,' 'I am truly rejoiced that my cousin Lydia's sad business has been so well hushed up, and am only concerned that their living together before the marriage took place, should be so generally known. I must not, however, neglect the duties of my station, or refrain from declaring my amazement, at hearing that you received the young couple into your house as soon as they were married. It was an encouragement of vice; and had I been the rector of Longbourn, I should very strenuously have opposed it. You ought certainly to forgive them as christians, but never to admit them in your sight, or allow their names to be mentioned in your hearing.' '*That* is his notion of christian forgiveness! The rest of his letter is only about his dear Charlotte's situation, and his expectation of a young olive-branch. But, Lizzy, you look as if you did not enjoy it. You are not going to be *Missish*, I hope, and pretend to be affronted at an idle report. For what do we live, but to make sport for our neighbours, and laugh at them in our turn?'

'Oh!' cried Elizabeth, 'I am excessively diverted. But it is so strange!'

'Yes – *that* is what makes it amusing. Had they fixed on any other man it would have been nothing; but *his* perfect indifference, and *your* pointed dislike, make it so delightfully absurd! Much as I abominate writing, I would not give up Mr Collins's correspondence for any consideration. Nay, when I read a letter of his, I cannot help giving him the preference even over Wickham, much as I value the impudence and hypocrisy of my son-in-law. And pray, Lizzie, what said Lady Catherine about this report? Did she call to refuse her consent?'

To this question his daughter replied only with a laugh; and as it had been asked without the least suspicion, she was not distressed by his repeating it. Elizabeth had never been more at a loss to make her feelings appear what they were not. It was necessary to laugh, when she would rather have cried. Her father had most cruelly mortified her, by what he said of Mr Darcy's indifference, and she could do nothing but wonder at such a want of penetration, or fear that perhaps, instead of his seeing too *little*, she might have fancied too *much*.

Chapter Fifty Eight

INSTEAD OF RECEIVING ANY SUCH letter of excuse from his friend, as Elizabeth half expected Mr Bingley to do, he was able to bring Darcy with him to Longbourn before many days had passed after Lady Catherine's visit. The gentlemen arrived early; and, before Mrs Bennet had time to tell him of their having seen his aunt, of which her daughter sat in momentary dread, Bingley, who wanted to be alone with Jane, proposed their all walking out. It was agreed to. Mrs Bennet was not in the habit of walking, Mary could never spare time, but the remaining five set off together. Bingley and Jane, however, soon allowed the others to outstrip them. They lagged behind, while Elizabeth, Kitty, and Darcy, were to entertain each other. Very little was said by either; Kitty was too much afraid of him to talk; Elizabeth was secretly forming a desperate resolution; and perhaps he might be doing the same.

They walked towards the Lucases, because Kitty wished to call upon Maria; and as Elizabeth saw no occasion for making it a general concern, when Kitty left them, she went boldly on with him alone. Now was the moment for her resolution to be executed, and, while her courage was high, she immediately said,

'Mr Darcy, I am a very selfish creature; and, for the sake of giving relief to my own feelings, care not how much I may be wounding your's. I can no longer help thanking you for your unexampled kindness to my poor sister. Ever since I have known it, I have been most anxious to acknowledge to you how gratefully I feel it. Were it known to the rest of my family, I should not have merely my own gratitude to express.'

'I am sorry, exceedingly sorry,' replied Darcy, in a tone of surprise and emotion, 'that you have ever been informed of what may, in a mistaken light, have given you uneasiness. I did not think Mrs Gardiner was so little to be trusted.'

'You must not blame my aunt. Lydia's thoughtlessness first betrayed to me that you had been concerned in the matter; and, of course, I could not rest till I knew the particulars. Let me thank you again and again, in the name of all my family, for that generous compassion which induced you to take so much trouble, and bear so many mortifications, for the sake of discovering them.'

'If you *will* thank me,' he replied, 'let it be for yourself alone. That the wish of giving happiness to you, might add force to the other inducements which led me on, I shall not attempt to deny. But your *family* owe me nothing. Much as I respect them, I believe, I thought only of *you*.'

Elizabeth was too much embarrassed to say a word. After a short pause, her companion added, 'You are too generous to trifle with me. If your feelings are still what they were last April, tell me so at once. *My* affections and wishes are unchanged, but one word from you will silence me on this subject for ever.'

Elizabeth feeling all the more than common awkwardness and anxiety of his situation, now forced herself to speak; and immediately, though not very fluently, gave him to understand, that her sentiments had undergone so material a change, since the period to which he alluded, as to make her receive with gratitude and pleasure, his present assurances. The happiness which this reply produced, was such as he had probably never felt before; and he expressed himself on the occasion as sensibly and as warmly as a man violently in love can be supposed to do. Had Elizabeth been able to encounter his eye, she might have seen how well the expression of heart-felt delight, diffused over his face, became him; but, though she could not look, she could listen, and he told her of feelings, which, in proving of what importance she was to him, made his affection every moment more valuable.

They walked on, without knowing in what direction. There was too much to be thought, and felt, and said, for attention to any other objects. She soon learnt that they were indebted for their present good understanding to the efforts of his aunt, who *did* call on him in her return through London, and there relate her journey to Longbourn, its motive, and the substance of her conversation with Elizabeth; dwelling emphatically on every expression of the latter, which, in her ladyship's apprehension, peculiarly denoted her perverseness and assurance, in the belief that such a relation must assist her endeavours to obtain that promise from her nephew, which *she* had refused to give. But, unluckily for her ladyship, its effect had been exactly contrariwise.

'It taught me to hope,' said he, 'as I had scarcely ever allowed myself to hope before. I knew enough of your disposition to be certain, that, had you been absolutely, irrevocably decided against me, you would have acknowledged it to Lady Catherine, frankly and openly.'

Elizabeth coloured and laughed as she replied. 'Yes, you know enough of my *frankness* to believe me capable of *that*. After abusing you so abominably to your face, I could have no scruple in abusing you to all your relations.'

'What did you say of me, that I did not deserve? For, though your accusations were ill-founded, formed on mistaken premises, my behaviour to you at the time, had merited the severest reproof. It was unpardonable. I cannot think of it without abhorrence.'

'We will not quarrel for the greater share of blame annexed to that evening,' said Elizabeth. 'The conduct of neither, if strictly examined, will be irreproachable; but since then, we have both, I hope, improved in civility.'

'I cannot be so easily reconciled to myself. The recollection of what I then said, of my conduct, my manners, my expressions during the whole of it, is now, and has been many months, inexpressibly painful to me. Your reproof, so well applied, I shall never forget: "had you behaved in a more gentleman-like manner." Those were your words. You know not, you can scarcely conceive, how they have tortured me; – though it was some time, I confess, before I was reasonable enough to allow their justice.'

'I was certainly very far from expecting them to make so strong an impression. I had not the smallest idea of their being ever felt in such a way.'

'I can easily believe it. You thought me then devoid of every proper feeling, I am sure you did. The turn of your countenance I shall never forget, as you said that I could not have addressed you in any possible way, that would induce you to accept me.'

'Oh! do not repeat what I then said. These recollections will not do at all. I assure you, that I have long been most heartily ashamed of it.'

Darcy mentioned his letter. 'Did it,' said he, 'did it *soon* make you think better of me? Did you, on reading it, give any credit to its contents?'

She explained what its effect on her had been, and how gradually all her former prejudices had been removed.

'I knew,' said he, 'that what I wrote must give you pain, but it was necessary. I hope you have destroyed the letter. There was one part especially, the opening of it, which I should dread your having the power of reading again. I can remember some expressions which might justly make you hate me.'

'The letter shall certainly be burnt, if you believe it essential to the preservation of my regard; but, though we have both reason to think my opinions not entirely unalterable, they are not, I hope, quite so easily changed as that implies.'

'When I wrote that letter,' replied Darcy, 'I believed myself perfectly calm and cool, but I am since convinced that it was written in a dreadful bitterness of spirit.'

'The letter, perhaps, began in bitterness, but it did not end so. The adieu is charity itself. But think no more of the letter. The feelings of the person who wrote, and the person who received it, are now so widely different from what they were then, that every unpleasant circumstance attending it, ought to be forgotten. You must learn some of my philosophy. Think only of the past as its remembrance gives you pleasure.'

'I cannot give you credit for any philosophy of the kind. *Your* retrospections must be so totally void of reproach, that the contentment arising from them, is not of philosophy, but what is much better, of ignorance. But with *me*, it is not so. Painful recollections will intrude, which cannot, which ought not to be repelled. I have been a selfish being all my life, in practice, though not in principle. As a child I was taught what was *right*, but I was not taught to correct my temper. I was given good principles, but left to follow them in pride and conceit. Unfortunately an only son, (for many years an only *child*) I was spoilt by my parents, who though good themselves, (my father particularly, all that was benevolent and amiable,) allowed, encouraged, almost taught me to be selfish and overbearing, to care for none beyond my own family circle, to think meanly of all the rest of the world, to *wish* at least to think meanly of their sense and worth compared with my own. Such I was, from eight to eight and twenty; and such I might still have been but for you, dearest, loveliest Elizabeth! What do I not owe you! You taught me a lesson, hard indeed at first, but most advantageous. By you, I was properly humbled. I came to you without a doubt of my reception. You shewed me how insufficient were all my pretensions to please a woman worthy of being pleased.'

'Had you then persuaded yourself that I should?'

'Indeed I had. What will you think of my vanity? I believed you to be wishing, expecting my addresses.'

'My manners must have been in fault, but not intentionally I assure you. I never meant to deceive you, but my spirits might often lead me wrong. How you must have hated me after *that* evening?'

'Hate you! I was angry perhaps at first, but my anger soon began to take a proper direction.'

'I am almost afraid of asking what you thought of me; when we met at Pemberley. You blamed me for coming?'

'No indeed; I felt nothing but surprise.'

'Your surprise could not be greater than *mine* in being noticed by you. My conscience told me that I deserved no extraordinary politeness, and I confess that I did not expect to receive *more* than my due.'

'My object *then*,' replied Darcy, 'was to shew you, by every civility in my power, that I was not so mean as to resent the past; and I hoped to obtain your forgiveness, to lessen your ill opinion, by letting you see that your reproofs had been attended to. How soon any other wishes introduced themselves I can hardly tell, but I believe in about half an hour after I had seen you.'

He then told her of Georgiana's delight in her acquaintance, and of her disappointment at its sudden interruption; which naturally leading to the cause of that interruption, she soon learnt that his resolution of following her from Derbyshire in quest of her sister, had been formed before he quitted the inn, and that his gravity and thoughtfulness there, had arisen from no other struggles than what such a purpose must comprehend.

She expressed her gratitude again, but it was too painful a subject to each, to be dwelt on farther.

After walking several miles in a leisurely manner, and too busy to know any thing about it, they found at last, on examining their watches, that it was time to be at home.

'What could become of Mr Bingley and Jane!' was a wonder which introduced the discussion of *their* affairs. Darcy was delighted with their engagement; his friend had given him the earliest information of it.

'I must ask whether you were surprised?' said Elizabeth.

'Not at all. When I went away, I felt that it would soon happen.'

'That is to say, you had given your permission. I guessed as much.' And though he exclaimed at the term, she found that it had been pretty much the case.

'On the evening before my going to London,' said he, 'I made a confession to him, which I believe I ought to have made long ago. I told him of all that had occurred to make my former interference in his affairs, absurd and impertinent. His surprise was great. He had never had the slightest suspicion. I told him, moreover, that I believed myself mistaken in supposing, as I had done, that your sister was indifferent to him; and as I could easily perceive that his attachment to her was unabated, I felt no doubt of their happiness together.'

Elizabeth could not help smiling at his easy manner of directing his friend.

'Did you speak from your own observation,' said she, 'when you told him that my sister loved him, or merely from my information last spring?'

'From the former. I had narrowly observed her during the two visits which I had lately made her here; and I was convinced of her affection.'

'And your assurance of it, I suppose, carried immediate conviction to him.'

'It did. Bingley is most unaffectedly modest. His diffidence had prevented his depending on his own judgment in so anxious a case, but his reliance on mine, made every thing easy. I was obliged to confess one thing, which for a time, and not unjustly, offended him. I could not allow myself to conceal that your sister had been in town three months last winter, that I had known it, and purposely kept it from him. He was angry. But his anger, I am persuaded, lasted no longer than he remained in any doubt of your sister's sentiments. He has heartily forgiven me now.'

Elizabeth longed to observe that Mr Bingley had been a most delightful friend; so easily guided that his worth was invaluable; but she checked herself. She remembered that he had yet to learn to be laught at, and it was rather too early to begin. In anticipating the happiness of Bingley, which of course was to be inferior only to his own, he continued the conversation till they reached the house. In the hall they parted.

Chapter Fifty Nine

'MY DEAR LIZZY, WHERE CAN YOU have been walking to?' was a question which Elizabeth received from Jane as soon as she entered the room, and from all the others when they sat down to table. She had only to say in reply, that they had wandered about, till she was beyond her own knowledge. She coloured as she spoke; but neither that, nor any thing else, awakened a suspicion of the truth.

The evening passed quietly, unmarked by any thing extraordinary. The acknowledged lovers talked and laughed, the unacknowledged were silent. Darcy was not of a disposition in which happiness overflows in mirth; and Elizabeth, agitated and confused, rather *knew* that she was happy, than *felt* herself to be so; for, besides the immediate embarrassment, there were other evils before her. She anticipated what would be felt in the family when her situation became known; she was aware that no one liked him but Jane; and even feared that with the others it was a *dislike* which not all his fortune and consequence might do away.

At night she opened her heart to Jane. Though suspicion was very far from Miss Bennet's general habits, she was absolutely incredulous here.

'You are joking, Lizzy. This cannot be! – engaged to Mr Darcy! No, no, you shall not deceive me. I know it to be impossible.'

'This is a wretched beginning indeed! My sole dependence was on you; and I am sure nobody else will believe me, if you do not. Yet, indeed, I am in earnest. I speak nothing but the truth. He still loves me, and we are engaged.'

Jane looked at her doubtingly. 'Oh, Lizzy! it cannot be. I know how much you dislike him.'

'You know nothing of the matter. *That* is all to be forgot. Perhaps I did not always love him so well as I do now. But in such cases as these, a good memory is unpardonable. This is the last time I shall ever remember it myself.'

Miss Bennet still looked all amazement. Elizabeth again, and more seriously assured her of its truth.

'Good Heaven! can it be really so! Yet now I must believe you,' cried Jane. 'My dear, dear Lizzy, I would – I do congratulate you – but are you certain? forgive the question – are you quite certain that you can be happy with him?'

'There can be no doubt of that. It is settled beween us already, that we are to be the happiest couple in the world. But are you pleased, Jane? Shall you like to have such a brother?'

'Very, very much. Nothing could give either Bingley or myself more delight. But we considered it, we talked of it as impossible. And do you really love him quite well enough? Oh, Lizzy! do any thing rather than marry without affection. Are you quite sure that you feel what you ought to do?'

'Oh, yes! You will only think I feel *more* than I ought to do, when I tell you all.'

'What do you mean?'

'Why, I must confess, that I love him better than I do Bingley. I am afraid you will be angry.'

'My dearest sister, now *be* serious. I want to talk very seriously. Let me know every thing that I am to know, without delay. Will you tell me how long you have loved him?'

'It has been coming on so gradually, that I hardly know when it began. But I believe I must date it from my first seeing his beautiful grounds at Pemberley.'

Another intreaty that she would be serious, however, produced the desired effect; and she soon satisfied Jane by her solemn assurances of attachment. When convinced on that article, Miss Bennet had nothing farther to wish.

'Now I am quite happy,' she said, 'for you will be as happy as myself. I always had a value for him. Were it for nothing but his love of you, I must always have esteemed him; but now, as Bingley's friend and your husband, there can be only Bingley and yourself more dear to me. But Lizzy, you have been very sly, very reserved with me. How little did you tell me of what passed at Pemberley and Lambton! I owe all that I know of it, to another, not to you.'

Elizabeth told her the motives of her secrecy. She had been unwilling to mention Bingley; and the unsettled state of her own feelings had made her equally avoid the name of his friend. But now she would no longer conceal from her, his share in Lydia's marriage. All was acknowledged, and half the night spent in conversation.

'Good gracious!' cried Mrs Bennet, as she stood at a window the next morning, 'if that disagreeable Mr Darcy is not coming here again with our dear Bingley! What can he mean by being so tiresome as to be always coming here? I had no notion but he would go a shooting, or something or other, and not disturb us with his company. What shall we do with him? Lizzy, you must walk out with him again, that he may not be in Bingley's way.'

Elizabeth could hardly help laughing at so convenient a proposal; yet was really vexed that her mother should be always giving him such an epithet.

As soon as they entered, Bingley looked at her so expressively, and shook hands with such warmth, as left no doubt of his good information; and he soon afterwards said aloud, 'Mr Bennet, have you no more lanes hereabouts in which Lizzy may lose her way again to-day?'

'I advise Mr Darcy, and Lizzy, and Kitty,' said Mrs Bennet, 'to walk to Oakham Mount this morning. It is a nice long walk, and Mr Darcy has never seen the view.'

'It may do very well for the others,' replied Mr Bingley; 'but I am sure it will be too much for Kitty. Won't it, Kitty?'

Kitty owned that she had rather stay at home. Darcy professed a great curiosity to see the view from the Mount, and Elizabeth silently consented. As she went up stairs to get ready, Mrs Bennet followed her, saying,

'I am quite sorry, Lizzy, that you should be forced to have that disagreeable man all to yourself. But I hope you will not mind it: it is all for Jane's sake, you know; and there is no occasion for talking to him, except just now and then. So, do not put yourself to inconvenience.'

During their walk, it was resolved that Mr Bennet's consent should be asked in the course of the evening. Elizabeth reserved to herself the application for her mother's. She could not determine how her mother would take it; sometimes doubting whether all his wealth and grandeur would be enough to overcome her abhorrence of the man. But whether she were violently set against the match, or violently delighted with it, it was certain that her manner would be equally ill adapted to do credit to her sense; and she could no more bear that Mr Darcy should hear the first raptures of her joy, than the first vehemence of her disapprobation.

In the evening, soon after Mr Bennet withdrew to the library, she saw Mr Darcy rise also and follow him, and her agitation on seeing it was extreme. She did not fear her father's opposition, but he was going to be made unhappy, and that it should be through her means, that *she*, his favourite child, should be distressing him by her choice, should be filling him with fears and regrets in disposing of her, was a wretched reflection, and she sat in misery till Mr Darcy appeared again, when, looking at him, she was a little relieved by his smile. In a few minutes he approached the table where she was sitting with Kitty; and, while pretending to admire her work, said in a whisper, 'Go to your father, he wants you in the library.' She was gone directly.

Her father was walking about the room, looking grave and anxious. 'Lizzy,' said he, 'what are you doing? Are you out of your senses, to be accepting this man? Have not you always hated him?'

How earnestly did she then wish that her former opinions had been more reasonable, her expressions more moderate! It would have spared her from explanations and professions which it was exceedingly awkward to give; but they were now necessary, and she assured him with some confusion, of her attachment to Mr Darcy.

'Or in other words, you are determined to have him. He is rich, to be sure, and you may have more fine clothes and fine carriages than Jane. But will they make you happy?'

'Have you any other objection,' said Elizabeth, 'than your belief of my indifference?'

'None at all. We all know him to be a proud, unpleasant sort of man; but this would be nothing if you really liked him.'

'I do, I do like him,' she replied, with tears in her eyes, 'I love him. Indeed he has no improper pride. He is perfectly amiable. You do not know what he really is; then pray do not pain me by speaking of him in such terms.'

'Lizzy,' said her father, 'I have given him my consent. He is the kind of man, indeed, to whom I should never dare refuse any thing, which he condescended to ask. I now give it to *you*, if you are resolved on having him. But let me advise you to think better of it. I know your disposition, Lizzy. I know that you could be neither happy nor respectable, unless you truly esteemed your husband; unless you looked up to him as a superior. Your lively talents would place you in the greatest danger in an unequal marriage. You could scarcely escape discredit and misery. My child, let me not have the grief of seeing *you* unable to respect your partner in life. You know not what you are about.'

Elizabeth, still more affected, was earnest and solemn in her reply; and at length, by repeated assurances that Mr Darcy was really the object of her choice, by explaining the gradual change which her estimation of him had undergone, relating her absolute certainty that his affection was not the work of a day, but had stood the test of many months suspense, and enumerating with energy all his good qualities, she did conquer her father's incredulity, and reconcile him to the match.

'Well, my dear,' said he, when she ceased speaking, 'I have no more to say. If this be the case, he deserves you. I could not have parted with you, my Lizzy, to any one less worthy.'

To complete the favourable impression, she then told him what Mr Darcy had voluntarily done for Lydia. He heard her with astonishment.

'This is an evening of wonders, indeed! And so, Darcy did every thing; made up the match, gave the money, paid the fellow's debts, and got him his commission! So much the better. It will save me a world of trouble and economy. Had it been your uncle's doing, I must and *would* have paid him; but these violent young lovers carry every thing their own way. I shall offer to pay him to-morrow; he will rant and storm about his love for you, and there will be an end of the matter.'

He then recollected her embarrassment a few days before, on his reading Mr Collins's letter; and after laughing at her some time, allowed her at last to go – saying, as she quitted the room, 'If any young men come for Mary or Kitty, send them in, for I am quite at leisure.'

Elizabeth's mind was now relieved from a very heavy weight; and, after half an hour's quiet reflection in her own room, she was able to join the others with tolerable composure. Every thing was too recent for gaiety, but the evening passed tranquilly away; there was no longer any thing material to be dreaded, and the comfort of ease and familiarity would come in time.

When her mother went up to her dressing-room at night, she followed her, and made the important communication. Its effect was most extraordinary; for on first hearing it, Mrs Bennet sat quite still, and unable to utter a syllable. Nor was it under many, many minutes, that she could comprehend what she heard; though not in general backward to credit what was for the advantage of her family, or that came in the shape of a lover to any of them. She began at length to recover, to fidget about in her chair, get up, sit down again, wonder, and bless herself.

'Good gracious! Lord bless me! only think! dear me! Mr Darcy! Who would have thought it! And is it really true? Oh! my sweetest Lizzy! how rich and how great you will be! What pin-money, what jewels, what carriages you will have! Jane's is nothing to it – nothing at all. I am so pleased – so happy. Such a charming man! – so handsome! so tall! – Oh, my dear Lizzy! pray apologise for my having disliked him so much before. I hope he will overlook it. Dear, dear Lizzy. A house in town! Every thing that is charming! Three daughters married! Ten thousand a year! Oh, Lord! What will become of me. I shall go distracted.'

This was enough to prove that her approbation need not be doubted: and Elizabeth, rejoicing that such an effusion was heard only by herself, soon went away. But before she had been three minutes in her own room, her mother followed her.

'My dearest child,' she cried, 'I can think of nothing else! Ten thousand a year, and very likely more! 'Tis as good as a Lord! And a special licence. You must and shall be married by a special licence. But my dearest love, tell me what dish Mr Darcy is particularly fond of, that I may have it to-morrow.'

This was a sad omen of what her mother's behaviour to the gentleman himself might be; and Elizabeth found, that though in the certain possession of his warmest affection, and secure of her relations' consent, there was still something to be wished for. But the morrow passed off much better than she expected; for Mrs Bennet luckily stood in such awe of her intended son-in-law, that she ventured not to speak to him, unless it was in her power to offer him any attention, or mark her deference for his opinion.

Elizabeth had the satisfaction of seeing her father taking pains to get acquainted with him; and Mr Bennet soon assured her that he was rising every hour in his esteem.

'I admire all my three sons-in-law highly,' said he. 'Wickham, perhaps, is my favourite; but I think I shall like *your* husband quite as well as Jane's.'

Chapter Sixty

ELIZABETH'S SPIRITS SOON RISING to playfulness again, she wanted Mr Darcy to account for his having ever fallen in love with her. 'How could you begin? said she. 'I can comprehend your going on charmingly, when you had once made a beginning; but what could set you off in the first place?'

'I cannot fix on the hour, or the spot, or the look, or the words, which laid the foundation. It is too long ago. I was in the middle before I knew that I *had* begun.'

'My beauty you had early withstood, and as for my manners – my behaviour to *you* was at least always bordering on the uncivil, and I never spoke to you without rather wishing to give you pain than not. Now be sincere; did you admire me for my impertinence?'

'For the liveliness of your mind, I did.'

'You may as well call it impertinence at once. It was very little less. The fact is, that you were sick of civility, of deference, of officious attention. You were disgusted with the women who were always speaking and looking, and thinking for *your* approbation alone. I roused, and interested you, because I was so unlike *them*. Had you not been really amiable you would have hated me for it; but in spite of the pains you took to disguise yourself, your feelings were always noble and just; and in your heart, you thoroughly despised the persons who so assiduously courted you. There – I have saved you the trouble of accounting for it; and really, all things considered, I begin to think it perfectly reasonable. To be sure, you knew no actual good of me – but nobody thinks of *that* when they fall in love.'

'Was there no good in your affectionate behaviour to Jane, while she was ill at Netherfield?'

'Dearest Jane! who could have done less for her? But make a virtue of it by all means. My good qualities are under your protection, and you are to exaggerate them as much as possible; and, in return, it belongs to me to find occasions for teazing and quarrelling with you as often as may be; and I shall begin directly by asking you what made you so unwilling to come to the point at last. What made you so shy of me, when you first called, and afterwards dined here? Why, especially, when you called, did you look as if you did not care about me?'

'Because you were grave and silent, and gave me no encouragement.'

'But I was embarrassed.'

'And so was I'.

'You might have talked to me more when you came to dinner.'

'A man who had felt less, might.'

'How unlucky that you should have a reasonable answer to give, and that I should be so reasonable as to admit it! But I wonder how long you *would* have gone on, if you had been left to yourself. I wonder when you *would* have spoken, if I had not asked you! My resolution of thanking you for your kindness to Lydia had certainly great effect. *Too much*, I am afraid; for what becomes of the moral, if our comfort springs from a breach of promise, for I ought not to have mentioned the subject? This will never do.'

'You need not distress yourself. The moral will be perfectly fair. Lady Catherine's unjustifiable endeavours to separate us, were the means of removing all my doubts. I am not indebted for my present happiness to your eager desire of expressing your gratitude. I was not in a humour to wait for any opening of your's. My aunt's intelligence had given me hope, and I was determined at once to know every thing.'

'Lady Catherine has been of infinite use, which ought to make her happy, for she loves to be of use. But tell me, what did you come down to Netherfield for? Was it merely to ride to Longbourn and be embarrassed? or had you intended any more serious consequence?'

'My real purpose was to see *you*, and to judge, if I could, whether I might ever hope to make you love me. My avowed one, or what I avowed to myself, was to see whether your sister were still partial to Bingley, and if she were, to make the confession to him which I have since made.'

'Shall you ever have courage to announce to Lady Catherine, what is to befall her?'

'I am more likely to want time than courage, Elizabeth. But it ought to be done, and if you will give me a sheet of paper, it shall be done directly.'

'And if I had not a letter to write myself, I might sit by you, and admire the evenness of your writing, as another young lady once did. But I have an aunt, too, who must not be longer neglected.'

From an unwillingness to confess how much her intimacy with Mr Darcy had been over-rated, Elizabeth had never yet answered Mrs Gardiner's long letter, but now, having *that* to communicate which she knew would be most welcome, she was almost ashamed to find, that her uncle and aunt had already lost three days of happiness, and immediately wrote as follows:

I would have thanked you before, my dear aunt, as I ought to have done, for your long, kind, satisfactory, detail of particulars; but to say the truth, I was too cross to write. You supposed more than really existed. But now suppose as much as you chuse; give a loose to your fancy, indulge your imagination in every possible flight which the subject will afford, and unless you believe me actually married, you cannot greatly err. You must write again very soon, and praise him a great deal more than you did in your last. I thank you, again and again, for not going to the Lakes. How could I be so silly as to wish it! Your idea of the ponies is delightful. We will go round the Park every day. I am the happiest creature in the world. Perhaps other people have said so before, but not one with such justice. I am happier even than Jane; she only smiles, I laugh. Mr Darcy sends you all the love in the world, that he can spare from me. You are all to come to Pemberley at Christmas. Your's &c.

Mr Darcy's letter to Lady Catherine, was in a different style; and still different from either, was what Mr Bennet sent to Mr Collins, in reply to his last.

Dear Sir,

I must trouble you once more for congratulations. Elizabeth will soon be the wife of Mr Darcy. Console Lady Catherine as well as you can. But, if I were you, I would stand by the nephew. He has more to give.

Your's sincerely, &c.

Miss Bingley's congratulations to her brother, on his approaching marriage, were all that was affectionate and insincere. She wrote even to Jane on the occasion, to express her delight, and repeat all her former professions of regard. Jane was not deceived, but she was affected; and though feeling no reliance on her, could not help writing her a much kinder answer than she knew was deserved.

The joy which Miss Darcy expressed on receiving similar information, was as sincere as her brother's in sending it. Four sides of paper were insufficient to contain all her delight, and all her earnest desire of being loved by her sister.

Before any answer could arrive from Mr Collins, or any congratulations to Elizabeth, from his wife, the Longbourn family heard that the Collinses were come themselves to Lucas lodge. The reason of this sudden removal was soon evident. Lady Catherine had been rendered so exceedingly angry by the contents of her nephew's letter, that Charlotte, really rejoicing in the match, was anxious to get away till the storm was blown over. At such a moment, the arrival of her friend was a sincere pleasure to Elizabeth, though in the course of their meeting she must sometimes think the pleasure dearly bought, when she saw Mr Darcy exposed to all the parading and obsequious civility of her husband. He bore it however with admirable calmness. he could even listen to Sir William Lucas, when he complimented him on carrying away the brightest jewel of the country, and expressed his hopes of their all meeting frequently at St James's, with very decent composure. If he did shrug his shoulders, it was not till Sir William was out of sight.

Mrs Philips's vulgarity was another, and perhaps a greater tax on his forbearance; and though Mrs Philips, as well as her sister, stood in too much awe of him to speak with the familiarity which Bingley's good humour encouraged, yet, whenever she *did* speak, she must be vulgar. Nor was her respect for him, though it made her more quiet, at all likely to make her more elegant. Elizabeth did all she could, to shield him from the frequent notice of either, and was ever anxious to keep him to herself, and to those of her family with whom he might converse without mortification; and though the uncomfortable feelings arising from all this took from the season of courtship much of its pleasure, it added to the hope of the future; and she looked forward with delight to the time when they should be removed from society so little pleasing to either, to all the comfort and elegance of their family party at Pemberley.

Chapter Sixty One

HAPPY FOR ALL HER MATERNAL FEELINGS was the day on which Mrs Bennet got rid of her two most deserving daughters. With what delighted pride she afterwards visited Mrs Bingley and talked of Mrs Darcy may be guessed. I wish I could say, for the sake of her family, that the accomplishment of her earnest desire in the establishment of so many of her children, produced so happy an effect as to make her a sensible, amiable, well-informed woman for the rest of her life; though perhaps it was lucky for her husband, who might not have relished domestic felicity in so unusual a form, that she still was occasionally nervous and invariably silly.

Mr Bennet missed his second daughter exceedingly; his affection for her drew him oftener from home than any thing else could do. He delighted in going to Pemberley, especially when he was least expected.

Mr Bingley and Jane remained at Netherfield only a twelve-month. So near a vicinity to her mother and Meryton relations was not desirable even to *his* easy temper, or *her* affectionate heart. The darling wish of his sisters was then gratified; he bought an estate in a neighbouring county to Derbyshire, and Jane and Elizabeth, in addition to every other source of happiness, were within thirty miles of each other.

Kitty, to her very material advantage, spent the chief of her time with her two elder sisters. In society so superior to what she had generally known, her improvement was great. She was not of so ungovernable a temper as

Lydia, and, removed from the influence of Lydia's example, she became, by proper attention and management, less irritable, less ignorant, and less insipid. From the farther disadvantage of Lydia's society she was of course carefully kept, and though Mrs Wickham frequently invited her to come and stay with her, with the promise of balls and young men, her father would never consent to her going.

Mary was the only daughter who remained at home; and she was necessarily drawn from the pursuit of accomplishments by Mrs Bennet's being quite unable to sit alone. Mary was obliged to mix more with the world, but she could still moralize over every morning visit; and as she was no longer mortified by comparisons between her sisters' beauty and her own, it was suspected by her father that she submitted to the change without much reluctance.

As for Wickham and Lydia, their characters suffered no revolution from the marriage of her sisters. He bore with philosophy the conviction that Elizabeth must now become acquainted with whatever of his ingratitude and falsehood had before been unknown to her; and in spite of every thing, was not wholly without hope that Darcy might yet be prevailed on to make his fortune. The congratulatory letter which Elizabeth received from Lydia on her marriage, explained to her that, by his wife at least, if not by himself, such a hope was cherished. The letter was to this effect:

MY DEAR LIZZY,

I wish you joy. If you love Mr Darcy half as well as I do my dear Wickham, you must be very happy. It is a great comfort to have you so rich, and when you have nothing else to do, I hope you will think of us. I am sure Wickham would like a place at court very much, and I do not think we shall have quite money enough to live upon without some help. Any place would do, of about three or four hundred a year; but, however, do not speak to Mr Darcy about it, if you had rather not.

Your's, &c.

As it happened that Elizabeth had *much* rather not, she endeavoured in her answer to put an end to every intreaty and expectation of the kind. Such relief, however, as it was in her power to afford, by the practice of what might be called economy in her own private expences, she frequently sent them. It had always been evident to her that such an income as theirs, under the direction of two persons so extravagant in their wants, and heedless of the future, must be very insufficient to their support; and whenever they changed their quarters, either Jane or herself were sure of being applied to, for some little assistance towards discharging their bills. Their manner of living, even when the restoration of peace dismissed them to a home, was unsettled in the extreme. They were always moving from place to place in quest of a cheap situation, and always spending more than they ought. His affection for her soon sunk into indifference; her's lasted a little longer; and in spite of her youth and her manners, she retained all the claims to reputation which her marriage had given her.

Though Darcy could never receive *him* at Pemberley, yet, for Elizabeth's sake, he assisted him farther in his profession. Lydia was occasionally a visitor there, when her husband was gone to enjoy himself in London or Bath; and with the Bingleys they both of them frequently staid so long, that even

Bingley's good humour was overcome, and he proceeded so far as to *talk* of giving them a hint to be gone.

Miss Bingley was very deeply mortified by Darcy's marriage; but as she thought it advisable to retain the right of visiting at Pemberley, she dropt all her resentment; was fonder than ever of Georgiana, almost as attentive to Darcy as heretofore, and paid off every arrear of civility to Elizabeth.

Pemberley was now Georgiana's home; and the attachment of the sisters was exactly what Darcy had hoped to see. They were able to love each other, even as well as they intended. Georgiana had the highest opinion in the world of Elizabeth; though at first she often listened with an astonishment bordering on alarm, at her lively, sportive, manner of talking to her brother. He, who had always inspired in herself a respect which almost overcame her affection, she now saw the object of open pleasantry. Her mind received knowledge which had never before fallen in her way. By Elizabeth's instructions she began to comprehend that a woman may take liberties with her husband, which a brother will not always allow in a sister more than ten years younger than himself.

Lady Catherine was extremely indignant on the marriage of her nephew; and as she gave way to all the genuine frankness of her character, in her reply to the letter which announced its arrangement, she sent him language so very abusive, especially of Elizabeth, that for some time all intercourse was at an end. But at length, by Elizabeth's persuasion, he was prevailed on to overlook the offence, and seek a reconciliation; and, after a little farther resistance on the part of his aunt, her resentment gave way, either to her affection for him, or her curiosity to see how his wife conducted herself; and she condescended to wait on them at Pemberley, in spite of that pollution which its woods had received, not merely from the presence of such a mistress, but the visits of her uncle and aunt from the city.

With the Gardiners, they were always on the most intimate terms. Darcy, as well as Elizabeth, really loved them; and they were both ever sensible of the warmest gratitude towards the persons who, by bringing her into Derbyshire, had been the means of uniting them.

Sense and Sensibility

Chapter One

THE FAMILY OF DASHWOOD HAD BEEN long settled in Sussex. Their estate was large, and their residence was at Norland Park, in the centre of their property, where, for many generations, they had lived in so respectable a manner, as to engage the general good opinion of their surrounding acquaintance. The late owner of this estate was a single man, who lived to a very advanced age, and who for many years of his life, had a constant companion and housekeeper in his sister. But her death, which happened ten years before his own, produced a great alteration in his home; for to supply her loss, he invited and received into his house the family of his nephew Mr Henry Dashwood, the legal inheritor of the Norland estate, and the person to whom he intended to bequeath it. In the society of his nephew and niece, and their children, the old Gentleman's days were comfortably spent. His attachment to them all increased. The constant attention of Mr and Mrs Henry Dashwood to his wishes, which proceeded not merely from interest, but from goodness of heart, gave him every degree of solid comfort which his age could receive; and the cheerfulness of the children added a relish to his existence.

By a former marriage, Mr Henry Dashwood had one son: by his present lady, three daughters. The son, a steady respectable young man, was amply provided for by the fortune of his mother, which had been large, and half of which devolved on him on his coming of age. By his own marriage, likewise, which happened soon afterwards, he added to his wealth. To him therefore the succession to the Norland estate was not so really important as to his sisters; for their fortune, independent of what might arise to them from their father's inheriting that property, could be but small. Their mother had nothing, and their father only seven thousand pounds in his own disposal; for the remaining moiety of his first wife's fortune was also secured to her child, and he had only a life interest in it.

The old Gentleman died; his will was read, and like almost every other will, gave as much disappointment as pleasure. He was neither so unjust, nor so ungrateful, as to leave his estate from his nephew; – but he left it to him on such terms as destroyed half the value of the bequest. Mr Dashwood had wished for it more for the sake of his wife and daughters than for himself or his son: – but to his son, and his son's son, a child of four years old, it was secured, in such a way, as to leave to himself no power of providing for those who were most dear to him, and who most needed a provision, by any charge on the estate, or by any sale of its valuable woods. The whole was tied up for the benefit of this child, who, in occasional visits with his father and mother at Norland, had so far gained on the affections of his uncle, by such attractions as are by no means unusual in children of two or three years old; an imperfect articulation, an earnest desire of having his own way, many cunning tricks, and a great deal of noise, as to outweigh all the value of all the attention which, for years, he had received from his neice and her daughters. He meant not to be unkind however, and, as a mark of his affection for the three girls, he left them a thousand pounds a-piece.

Mr Dashwood's disappointment was, at first, severe; but his temper was cheerful and sanguine, and he might reasonably hope to live many years, and by living economically, lay by a considerable sum from the produce of an estate already large, and capable of almost immediate improvement. But the fortune, which had been so tardy in coming, was his only one twelve-month. He survived his uncle no longer; and ten thousand pounds, including the late legacies, was all that remained for his widow and daughters.

His son was sent for, as soon as his danger was known, and to him Mr Dashwood recommended, with all the strength and urgency which illness could command, the interest of his mother-in-law and sisters.

Mr John Dashwood had not the strong feelings of the rest of the family; but he was affected by a recommendation of such a nature at such a time, and he promised to do every thing in his power to make them comfortable. His father was rendered easy by such an assurance, and Mr John Dashwood had then leisure to consider how much there might prudently be in his power to do for them.

He was not an ill-disposed young man, unless to be rather cold hearted, and rather selfish, is to be ill-disposed: but he was, in general, well respected; for he conducted himself with propriety in the discharge of his ordinary duties. Had he married a more amiable woman, he might have been made still more respectable than he was: – he might even have been made amiable himself; for he was very young when he married, and very fond of his wife. But Mrs John Dashwood was a strong caricature of himself; – more narrow-minded and selfish.

When he gave his promise to his father, he meditated within himself to increase the fortunes of his sisters by the present of a thousand pounds a-piece. He then really thought himself equal to it. The prospect of four thousand a-year, in addition to his present income, besides the remaining half of his own mother's fortune, warmed his heart and made him feel capable of generosity. – 'Yes, he would give them three thousand pounds: it would be liberal and handsome! It would be enough to make them completely easy. Three thousand pounds! he could spare so considerable a sum with little inconvenience.' – He thought of it all day long, and for many days successively, and he did not repent.

No sooner was his father's funeral over, than Mrs John Dashwood, without sending any notice of her intention to her mother-in-law, arrived with her child and their attendants. No one could dispute her right to come; the house was her husband's from the moment of his father's decease; but the indelicacy of her conduct was so much the greater, and to a woman in Mrs Dashwood's situation, with only common feelings, must have been highly unpleasing: – but in *her* mind there was a sense of honour so keen, a generosity so romantic, that any offence of the kind, by whomsoever given or received, was to her a source of immoveable disgust. Mrs John Dashwood had never been a favourite with any of her husband's family; but she had had no opportunity, till the present, of shewing them with how little attention to the comfort of other people she could act when occasion required it.

So acutely did Mrs Dashwood feel this ungracious behaviour, and so earnestly did she despise her daughter-in-law for it, that, on the arrival of the latter, she would have quitted the house for ever, had not the entreaty of her eldest girl induced her first to reflect on the propriety of going, and her own tender love for all her three children determined her afterwards to stay, and for their sakes avoid a breach with their brother.

Elinor, this eldest daughter whose advice was so effectual, possessed a strength of understanding, and coolness of judgment, which qualified her, though only nineteen, to be the counsellor of her mother, and enabled her frequently to counteract, to the advantage of them all, that eagerness of mind in Mrs Dashwood which must generally have led to imprudence. She had an excellent heart; – her disposition was affectionate, and her feelings were strong; but she knew how to govern them: it was a knowledge which her mother had yet to learn, and which one of her sisters had resolved never to be taught.

Marianne's abilities were, in many respects, quite equal to Elinor's. She was sensible and clever; but eager in every thing; her sorrows, her joys, could have no moderation. She was generous, amiable, interesting: she was every thing but prudent. The resemblance between her and her mother was strikingly great.

Elinor saw, with concern, the excess of her sister's sensibility; but by Mrs Dashwood it was valued and cherished. They encouraged each other now in the violence of their affliction. The agony of grief which overpowered them at first, was voluntarily renewed, was sought for, was created again and again. They gave themselves up wholly to their sorrow, seeking increase of wretchedness in every reflection that could afford it, and resolved against ever admitting consolation in future. Elinor, too, was deeply afflicted; but still she could struggle, she could exert herself. She could consult with her brother, could receive her sister-in-law on her arrival, and treat her with proper attention; and could strive to rouse her mother to similar exertion, and encourage her to similar forbearance.

Margaret, the other sister, was a good-humoured well-disposed girl; but as she had already imbibed a good deal of Marianne's romance, without having much of her sense, she did not, at thirteen, bid fair to equal her sisters at a more advanced period of life.

Chapter Two

MRS JOHN DASHWOOD NOW INSTALLED herself mistress of Norland; and her mother and sisters-in-law were degraded to the condition of visitors. As such, however, they were treated by her with quiet civility: and by her husband with as much kindness as he could feel towards any body beyond himself, his wife, and their child. He really pressed them, with some earnestness, to consider Norland as their home; and, as no plan appeared so eligible to Mrs Dashwood as remaining there till she could accommodate herself with a house in the neighbourhood, his invitation was accepted.

A continuance in a place where every thing reminded her of former delight, was exactly what suited her mind. In seasons of cheerfulness, no temper could be more cheerful than hers, or possess, in a greater degree, that sanguine expectation of happiness which is happiness itself. But in sorrow she must be equally carried away by her fancy, and as far beyond consolation as in pleasure she was beyond alloy.

Mrs John Dashwood did not at all approve of what her husband intended to do for his sisters. To take three thousand pounds from the fortune of their dear little boy, would be impoverishing him to the most dreadful degree. She begged him to think again on the subject. How could he answer it to himself to rob his child, and his only child too, of so large a sum? And what possible claim could the Miss Dashwoods, who were related to him only by half blood, which she considered as no relationship at all, have on his generosity to so large an amount. It was very well known that no affection was ever supposed to exist between the children of any man by different marriages; and why was he to ruin himself, and their poor little Harry, by giving away all his money to his half sisters?

'It was my father's last request to me,' replied her husband, 'that I should assist his widow and daughters.'

'He did not know what he was talking of, I dare say; ten to one but he was light-headed at the time. Had he been in his right senses, he could not have thought of such a thing as begging you to give away half your fortune from your own child.'

'He did not stipulate for any particular sum, my dear Fanny; he only requested me, in general terms, to assist them, and make their situation more comfortable than it was in his power to do. Perhaps it would have been as well if he had left it wholly to myself. He could hardly suppose I should neglect them. But as he required the promise, I could not do less than give it: at least I thought so at the time. The promise, therefore, was given, and must be performed. Something must be done for them whenever they leave Norland and settle in a new home.'

'Well, then, *let* something be done for them; but *that* something need not be three thousand pounds. Consider,' she added, 'that when the money is once parted with, it never can return. Your sisters will marry, and it will be gone for ever. If, indeed, it could ever be restored to our poor little boy –'

'Why, to be sure,' said her husband, very gravely, 'that would make a great difference. The time may come when Harry will regret that so large a sum was parted with. If he should have a numerous family, for instance, it would be a very convenient addition.'

'To be sure it would.'

'Perhaps, then, it would be better for all parties if the sum were diminished one half. – Five hundred pounds would be a prodigious increase to their fortunes!'

'Oh! beyond any thing great! What brother on earth would do half so much for his sisters, even if *really* his sisters! And as it is – only half blood! – But you have such a generous spirit!'

'I would not wish to do any thing mean,' he replied, 'One had rather, on such occasions, do too much than too little. No one, at least, can think I have not done enough for them: even themselves, they can hardly expect more.'

'There is no knowing what *they* may expect,' said the lady, 'but we are not to think of their expectations: the question is, what you can afford to do.'

'Certainly – and I think I may afford to give them five hundred pounds a-piece. As it is, without any addition of mine, they will each have above three thousand pounds on their mother's death – a very comfortable fortune for any young woman.'

'To be sure it is; and, indeed, it strikes me that they can want no addition at all. They will have ten thousand pounds divided amongst them. If they marry, they will be sure of doing well, and if they do not, they may all live very comfortably together on the interest of ten thousand pounds.'

'That is very true, and, therefore, I do not know whether, upon the whole, it would not be more advisable to do something for their mother while she lives rather than for them – something of the annuity kind I mean. – My sisters would feel the good effects of it as well as herself. A hundred a year would make them all perfectly comfortable.'

His wife hesitated a little, however, in giving her consent to this plan.

'To be sure,' said she, 'it is better than parting with fifteen hundred pounds at once. But then if Mrs Dashwood should live fifteen years we shall be completely taken in.'

'Fifteen years! my dear Fanny; her life cannot be worth half that purchase.'

'Certainly not; but if you observe, people always live for ever when there is any annuity to be paid them; and she is very stout and healthy, and hardly forty. An annuity is a very serious business; it comes over and over every year, and there is no getting rid of it. You are not aware of what you are doing. I have known a great deal of the trouble of annuities; for my mother was clogged with the payment of three to old superannuated servants by my father's will, and it is amazing how disagreeable she found it. Twice every year these annuities were to be paid; and then there was the trouble of getting it to them; and then one of them was said to have died, and afterwards it turned out to be no such thing. My mother was quite sick of it. Her income was not her own, she said, with such perpetual claims on it; and it was the more unkind in my father, because, otherwise, the money would have been entirely at my mother's disposal, without any restriction whatever. It has given me such an abhorrence of annuities, that I am sure I would not pin myself down to the payment of one for all the world.'

'It is certainly an unpleasant thing,' replied Mr Dashwood, 'to have those kind of yearly drains on one's income. One's fortune, as your mother justly says, is *not* one's own. To be tied down to the regular payment of such a sum, on every rent day, is by no means desirable: it takes away one's independence.'

'Undoubtedly; and after all you have no thanks for it. They think themselves secure, you do no more than what is expected, and it raises no gratitude at all. If I were you, whatever I did should be done at my own discretion entirely. I would not bind myself to allow them any thing yearly. It may be very inconvenient some years to spare a hundred, or even fifty pounds from our own expences.'

'I believe you are right, my love; it will be better that there should be no annuity in the case; whatever I may give them occasionally will be of far greater assistance than a yearly allowance, because they would only enlarge their style of living if they felt sure of a larger income, and would not be sixpence the richer for it at the end of the year. It will certainly be much the best way. A present of fifty pounds, now and then, will prevent their ever being distressed for money, and will, I think, be amply discharging my promise to my father.'

'To be sure it will. Indeed, to say the truth, I am convinced within myself that your father had no idea of your giving them any money at all. The assistance he thought of, I dare say, was only such as might be reasonably expected of you; for instance, such as looking out for a comfortable small house for them, helping them to move their things, and sending them presents of fish and game, and so forth, whenever they are in season. I'll lay my life that he meant nothing farther; indeed, it would be very strange and unreasonable if he did. Do but consider, my dear Mr Dashwood, how excessively comfortable your mother-in-law and her daughters may live on the interest of seven thousand pounds, besides the thousand pounds belonging to each of the girls, which brings them in fifty pounds a-year a-piece, and, of course, they will pay their mother for their board out of it. Altogether, they will have five hundred a-year amongst them, and what on earth can four women want for more than that? – They will live so cheap! Their housekeeping will be nothing at all. They will have no carriage, no horses, and hardly any servants; they will keep no company, and can have no expences of any kind! Only conceive how comfortable they will be! Five hundred a-year! I am sure I cannot imagine how they will spend half of it; and as to your giving them more, it is quite absurd to think of it. They will be much more able to give *you* something.'

'Upon my word,' said Mr Dashwood, 'I believe you are perfectly right. My father certainly could mean nothing more by his request to me than what you say. I clearly understand it now, and I will strictly fulfil my engagement by such acts of assistance and kindness to them as you have described. When my mother removes into another house my services shall be readily given to accommodate her as far as I can. Some little present of furniture too may be acceptable then.'

'Certainly,' returned Mrs John Dashwood, 'But however, *one* thing must be considered. When your father and mother moved to Norland, though the furniture of Stanhill was sold, all the china, plate, and linen was saved, and is now left to your mother. Her house will therefore be almost completely fitted up as soon as she takes it.'

'That is a material consideration undoubtedly. A valuable legacy indeed! And yet some of the plate would have been a very pleasant addition to our own stock here.'

'Yes; and the set of breakfast china is twice as handsome as what belongs to this house. A great deal too handsome, in my opinion, for any place *they* can ever afford to live in. But, however, so it is. Your father thought only of *them*. And I must say this: that you owe no particular gratitude to him, nor attention to his wishes, for we very well know that if he could, he would have left almost every thing in the world to *them*.'

This argument was irresistible. It gave to his intentions whatever of decision was wanting before; and he finally resolved, that it would be absolutely unnecessary, if not highly indecorous, to do more for the widow and children of his father, than such kind of neighbourly acts as his own wife pointed out.

Chapter Three

MRS DASHWOOD REMAINED AT NORLAND several months; not from any disinclination to move when the sight of every well known spot ceased to raise the violent emotion which it produced for a while; for when her spirits began to revive, and her mind became capable of some other exertion than that of heightening its affliction by melancholy remembrances, she was impatient to be gone, and indefatigable in her inquiries for a suitable dwelling in the neighbourhood of Norland; for to remove far from that beloved spot was impossible. But she could hear of no situation that at once answered her notions of comfort and ease, and suited the prudence of her eldest daughter, whose steadier judgment rejected several houses as too large for their income, which her mother would have approved.

Mrs Dashwood had been informed by her husband of the solemn promise on the part of his son in their favour, which gave comfort to his last earthly reflections. She doubted the sincerity of this assurance no more than he had doubted it himself, and she thought of it for her daughters' sake with satisfaction, though as for herself she was persuaded that a much smaller provision than 7000l. would support her in affluence. For their brother's sake too, for the sake of her own heart she rejoiced; and she reproached herself for being unjust to his merit before, in believing him incapable of generosity. His attentive behaviour to herself and his sisters convinced her that their welfare was dear to him, and, for a long time, she firmly relied on the liberality of his intentions.

The contempt which she had, very early in their acquaintance, felt for her daughter-in-law, was very much increased by the farther knowledge of her character, which half a year's residence in her family afforded; and perhaps in spite of every consideration of politeness or maternal affection on the side of the former, the two ladies might have found it impossible to have lived together so long, had not a particular circumstance occurred to give still greater eligibility, according to the opinions of Mrs Dashwood, to her daughters' continuance at Norland.

This circumstance was a growing attachment between her eldest girl and the brother of Mrs John Dashwood, a gentlemanlike and pleasing young man, who was introduced to their acquaintance soon after his sister's establishment at Norland, and who had since spent the greatest part of his time there.

Some mothers might have encouraged the intimacy from motives of interest, for Edward Ferrars was the eldest son of a man who had died very rich; and some might have repressed it from motives of prudence, for, except a trifling sum, the whole of his fortune depended on the will of his mother. But Mrs Dashwood was alike uninfluenced by either consideration. It was enough for her that he appeared to be amiable, that he loved her daughter, and that Elinor returned the partiality. It was contrary to every doctrine of her's that difference of fortune should keep any couple asunder who were attracted by resemblance of disposition; and that Elinor's merit should not be acknowledged by every one who knew her, was to her comprehension impossible.

Edward Ferrars was not recommended to their good opinion by any peculiar graces of person or address. He was not handsome, and his manners required intimacy to make them pleasing. He was too diffident to do justice to himself; but when his natural shyness was overcome, his behaviour gave every indication of an open affectionate heart. His understanding was good, and his education had given it solid improvement. But he was neither fitted by abilities nor disposition to answer the wishes of his mother and sister, who longed to see him distinguished – as – they hardly knew what. They wanted him to make a fine figure in the world in some manner or other. His mother wished to interest him in political concerns, to get him into parliament, or to see him connected with some of the great men of the day. Mrs John Dashwood wished it likewise; but in the mean while, till one of these superior blessings could be attained, it would have quieted her ambition to see him driving a barouche. But Edward had no turn for great men or barouches. All his wishes centered in domestic comfort and the quiet of private life. Fortunately he had a younger brother who was more promising.

Edward had been staying several weeks in the house before he engaged much of Mrs Dashwood's attention; for she was, at that time, in such affliction as rendered her careless of surrounding objects. She saw only that he was quiet and unobtrusive, and she liked him for it. He did not disturb the wretchedness of her mind by ill-timed conversation. She was first called to observe and approve him farther, by a reflection which Elinor chanced one day to make on the difference between him and his sister. It was a contrast which recommended him most forcibly to her mother.

'It is enough,' said she; 'to say that he is unlike Fanny is enough. It implies every thing amiable. I love him already.'

'I think you will like him,' said Elinor, 'when you know more of him.'

'Like him!' replied her mother with a smile. 'I can feel no sentiment of approbation inferior to love.'

'You may esteem him.'

'I have never yet known what it was to separate esteem and love.'

Mrs Dashwood now took pains to get acquainted with him. Her manners were attaching and soon banished his reserve. She speedily comprehended all his merits; the persuasion of his regard for Elinor perhaps assisted her penetration; but she really felt assured of his worth: and even that quietness of manner which militated against all her established ideas of what a young man's address ought to be, was no longer uninteresting when she knew his heart to be warm and his temper affectionate.

No sooner did she perceive any symptom of love in his behaviour to Elinor, than she considered their serious attachment as certain, and looked forward to their marriage as rapidly approaching.

'In a few months, my dear Marianne,' said she, 'Elinor will in all probability be settled for life. We shall miss her; but *she* will be happy.'

'Oh! mama, how shall we do without her?'

'My love, it will be scarcely a separation. We shall live within a few miles of each other, and shall meet every day of our lives. You will gain a brother, a real affectionate brother. I have the highest opinion in the world of Edward's heart. But you look grave, Marianne; do you disapprove your sister's choice?'

'Perhaps,' said Marianne, 'I may consider it with some surprise. Edward is very amiable, and I love him tenderly. But yet – he is not the kind of young man – there is a something wanting – his figure is not striking; it has none of that grace which I should expect in the man who could seriously attach my sister. His eyes want all that spirit, that fire, which at once announce virtue and intelligence. And besides all this, I am afraid, mama, he has no real taste. Music seems scarcely to attract him, and though he admires Elinor's drawings very much, it is not the admiration of a person who can understand their worth. It is evident, in spite of his frequent attention to her while she draws, that in fact he knows nothing of the matter. He admires as a lover, not as a connoisseur. To satisfy me, those characters must be united. I could not be happy with a man whose taste did not in every point coincide with my own. He must enter into all my feelings; the same books, the same music must charm us both. Oh! mama, how spiritless, how tame was Edward's manner in reading to us last night! I felt for my sister most severely. Yet she bore it with so much composure, she seemed scarcely to notice it. I could hardly keep my seat. To hear those beautiful lines which have frequently almost driven me wild, pronounced with such impenetrable calmness, such dreadful indifference!' –

'He would certainly have done more justice to simple and elegant prose. I thought so at the time; but you *would* give him Cowper.'

'Nay, mama, if he is not to be animated by Cowper! – but we must allow for difference of taste. Elinor has not my feelings, and therefore she may overlook it, and be happy with him. But it would have broke *my* heart had I loved him, to hear him read with so little sensibility. Mama, the more I know of the world, the more am I convinced that I shall never see a man whom I can really love. I require so much! He must have all Edward's virtues, and his person and manners must ornament his goodness with every possible charm.'

'Remember, my love, that you are not seventeen. It is yet too early in life to despair of such an happiness. Why should you be less fortunate than your mother? In one circumstance only, my Marianne, may your destiny be different from her's!'

Chapter Four

'WHAT A PITY IT IS, ELINOR,' said Marianne, 'that Edward should have no taste for drawing.'

'No taste for drawing,' replied Elinor; 'why should you think so? He does not draw himself, indeed, but he has great pleasure in seeing the performances of other people, and I assure you he is by no means deficient in natural taste, though he has not had opportunities of improving it. Had he ever been in the way of learning, I think he would have drawn very well. He distrusts his own judgment in such matters so much, that he is always unwilling to give his opinion on any picture; but he has an innate propriety and simplicity of taste, which in general direct him perfectly right.'

Marianne was afraid of offending, and said no more on the subject; but the kind of approbation which Elinor described as excited in him by the drawings of other people, was very far from that rapturous delight, which, in her opinion, could alone be called taste. Yet, though smiling within herself at the mistake, she honoured her sister for that blind partiality to Edward which produced it.

'I hope, Marianne,' continued Elinor, 'you do not consider him as deficient in general taste. Indeed, I think I may say that you cannot, for your behaviour to him is perfectly cordial, and if *that* were your opinion, I am sure you could never be civil to him.'

Marianne hardly knew what to say. She would not wound the feelings of her sister on any account, and yet to say what she did not believe was impossible. At length she replied:

'Do not be offended, Elinor, if my praise of him is not in every thing equal to your sense of his merits. I have not had so many opportunities of estimating the minuter propensities of his mind, his inclinations and tastes as you have; but I have the highest opinion in the world of his goodness and sense. I think him every thing that is worthy and amiable.'

'I am sure,' replied Elinor with a smile, 'that his dearest friends could not be dissatisfied with such a commendation as that. I do not perceive how you could express yourself more warmly.'

Marianne was rejoiced to find her sister so easily pleased.

'Of his sense and his goodness,' continued Elinor, 'no one can, I think, be in doubt, who has seen him often enough to engage him in unreserved conversation. The excellence of his understanding and his principles can be concealed only by that shyness which too often keeps him silent. You know enough of him to do justice to his solid worth. But of his minuter propensities as you call them you have from peculiar circumstances been kept more ignorant than myself. He and I have been at times thrown a good deal together, while you have been wholly engrossed on the most affectionate principle by my mother. I have seen a great deal of him, have studied his sentiments and heard his opinion on subjects of literature and taste; and, upon the whole, I venture to pronounce that his mind is well-informed, his enjoyment of books exceedingly great, his imagination lively, his observation just and correct, and his taste delicate and pure. His abilities in every respect improve as much upon acquaintance as his manners and person. At first sight, his address is certainly not striking; and his person can hardly be called handsome, till the expression of his eyes, which are uncommonly good, and the general sweetness of his countenance, is perceived. At present, I know him so well, that I think him really handsome; or, at least, almost so. What say you, Marianne?'

'I shall very soon think him handsome, Elinor, if I do not now. When you tell me to love him as a brother, I shall no more see imperfection in his face, than I now do in his heart.'

Elinor started at this declaration, and was sorry for the warmth she had been betrayed into, in speaking of him. She felt that Edward stood very high in her opinion. She believed the regard to be mutual; but she required greater certainty of it to make Marianne's conviction of their attachment agreeable to her. She knew that what Marianne and her mother conjectured one moment, they believed the next – that with them, to wish was to hope, and to hope was to expect. She tried to explain the real state of the case to her sister.

'I do not attempt to deny,' said she, 'that I think very highly of him –
that I greatly esteem, that I like him.'

Marianne here burst forth with indignation –

'Esteem him! Like him! Cold-hearted Elinor! Oh! worse than cold-hearted!
Ashamed of being otherwise. Use those words again and I will leave the
room this moment.'

Elinor could not help laughing. 'Excuse me,' said she, 'and be assured
that I meant no offence to you, by speaking, in so quiet a way, of my own
feelings. Believe them to be stronger than I have declared; believe them, in
short, to be such as his merit, and the suspicion – the hope of his affection
for me may warrant, without imprudence or folly. But farther than this you
must not believe. I am by no means assured of his regard for me. There are
moments when the extent of it seems doubtful; and till his sentiments are
fully known, you cannot wonder at my wishing to avoid any encouragement
of my own partiality, by believing or calling it more than it is. In my heart
I feel little – scarcely any doubt of his preference. But there are other points
to be considered besides his inclination. He is very far from being independent.
What his mother really is we cannot know; but, from Fanny's occasional
mention of her conduct and opinions, we have never been disposed to think
her amiable; and I am very much mistaken if Edward is not himself aware
that there would be many difficulties in his way, if he were to wish to marry
a woman who had not either a great fortune or high rank.'

Marianne was astonished to find how much the imagination of her
mother and herself had outstripped the truth.

'And you really are not engaged to him!' said she. 'Yet it certainly soon
will happen. But two advantages will proceed from this delay. I shall not lose
you so soon, and Edward will have greater opportunity of improving that
natural taste for your favourite pursuit which must be so indispensably
necessary to your future felicity. Oh! if he should be so far stimulated by
your genius as to learn to draw himself, how delightful it would be!'

Elinor had given her real opinion to her sister. She could not consider
her partiality for Edward in so prosperous a state as Marianne had believed
it. There was, at times, a want of spirits about him which, if it did not
denote indifference, spoke a something almost as unpromising. A doubt of
her regard, supposing him to feel it, need not give him more than inquietude.
It would not be likely to produce that dejection of mind which frequently
attended him. A more reasonable cause might be found in the dependent
situation which forbad the indulgence of his affection. She knew that his
mother neither behaved to him so as to make his home comfortable at
present, nor to give him any assurance that he might form a home for
himself, without strictly attending to her views for his aggrandizement.
With such a knowledge as this, it was impossible for Elinor to feel easy on
the subject. She was far from depending on that result of his preference of
her, which her mother and sister still considered as certain. Nay, the longer
they were together the more doubtful seemed the nature of his regard; and
sometimes, for a few painful minutes, she believed it to be no more than
friendship.

But, whatever might really be its limits, it was enough, when perceived
by his sister, to make her uneasy; and at the same time, (which was still
more common,) to make her uncivil. She took the first opportunity of
affronting her mother-in-law on the occasion, talking to her so expressively

of her brother's great expectations, of Mrs Ferrars's resolution that both her sons should marry well, and of the danger attending any young woman who attempted to *draw him in*; that Mrs Dashwood could neither pretend to be unconscious, nor endeavour to be calm. She gave her an answer which marked her contempt, and instantly left the room, resolving that, whatever might be the inconvenience or expense of so sudden a removal, her beloved Elinor should not be exposed another week to such insinuations.

In this state of her spirits, a letter was delivered to her from the post, which contained a proposal particularly well timed. It was the offer of a small house, on very easy terms, belonging to a relation of her own, a gentleman of consequence and property in Devonshire. The letter was from this gentleman himself, and written in the true spirit of friendly accommodation. He understood that she was in need of a dwelling, and though the house he offered her was merely a cottage, he assured her that every thing should be done to it which she might think necessary, if the situation pleased her. He earnestly pressed her, after giving the particulars of the house and garden, to come with her daughters to Barton Park, the place of his own residence, from whence she might judge, herself, whether Barton Cottage, for the houses were in the same parish, could, by any alteration, be made comfortable to her. He seemed really anxious to accommodate them and the whole of his letter was written in so friendly a style as could not fail of giving pleasure to his cousin; more especially at a moment when she was suffering under the cold and unfeeling behaviour of her nearer connections. She needed no time for deliberation or inquiry. Her resolution was formed as she read. The situation of Barton, in a county so far distant from Sussex as Devonshire, which, but a few hours before, would have been a sufficient objection to outweigh every possible advantage belonging to the place, was now its first recommendation. To quit the neighbourhood of Norland was no longer an evil; it was an object of desire; it was a blessing, in comparison of the misery of continuing her daughter-in-law's guest: and to remove for ever from that beloved place would be less painful than to inhabit or visit it while such a woman was its mistress. She instantly wrote Sir John Middleton her acknowledgments of his kindness, and her acceptance of his proposal; and then hastened to shew both letters to her daughters, that she might be secure of their approbation before her answer were sent.

Elinor had always thought it would be more prudent for them to settle at some distance from Norland than immediately amongst their present acquaintance. On *that* head, therefore, it was not for her to oppose her mother's intention of removing into Devonshire. The house, too, as described by Sir John, was on so simple a scale, and the rent so uncommonly moderate, as to leave her no right of objection on either point; and, therefore, though it was not a plan which brought any charm to her fancy, though it was a removal from the vicinity of Norland beyond her wishes, she made no attempt to dissuade her mother from sending her letter of acquiescence.

Chapter Five

NO SOONER WAS HER ANSWER dispatched, than Mrs Dashwood indulged herself in the pleasure of announcing to her son-in-law and his wife that she was provided with an house, and should incommode them no longer than till every thing were ready for her inhabiting it. They heard her with surprise. Mrs John Dashwood said nothing; but her husband civilly hoped that she would not be settled far from Norland. She had great satisfaction in replying that she was going into Devonshire. – Edward turned hastily towards her, on hearing this, and, in a voice of surprise and concern, which required no explanation to her, repeated, 'Devonshire! Are you, indeed, going there? So far from hence! And to what part of it?' She explained the situation. It was within four miles northward of Exeter.

'It is but a cottage,' she continued, 'but I hope to see many of my friends in it. A room or two can easily be added; and if my friends find no difficulty in travelling so far to see me, I am sure I will find none in accommodating them.'

She concluded with a very kind invitation to Mr and Mrs John Dashwood to visit her at Barton; and to Edward she gave one with still greater affection. Though her late conversation with her daughter-in-law had made her resolve on remaining at Norland no longer than was unavoidable, it had not produced the smallest effect on her in that point to which it principally tended. To separate Edward and Elinor was as far from being her object as ever; and she wished to shew Mrs John Dashwood by this pointed invitation to her brother, how totally she disregarded her disapprobation of the match.

Mr John Dashwood told his mother again and again how exceedingly sorry he was that she had taken an house at such a distance from Norland as to prevent his being of any service to her in removing her furniture. He really felt conscientiously vexed on the occasion; for the very exertion to which he had limited the performance of his promise to his father was by this arrangement rendered impracticable. – The furniture was all sent round by water. It chiefly consisted of household linen, plate, china, and books, with an handsome pianoforte of Marianne's. Mrs John Dashwood saw the packages depart with a sigh: she could not help feeling it hard that as Mrs Dashwood's income would be so trifling in comparison with their own, she should have any handsome article of furniture.

Mrs Dashwood took the house for a twelvemonth; it was ready furnished, and she might have immediate possession. No difficulty arose on either side in the agreement; and she waited only for the disposal of her effects at Norland, and to determine her future household, before she set off for the west; and this, as she was exceedingly rapid in the performance of every thing that interested her, was soon done. – The horses which were left her by her husband, had been sold soon after his death, and an opportunity now offering of disposing of her carriage, she agreed to sell that likewise at the earnest advice of her eldest daughter. For the comfort of her children, had she consulted only her own wishes, she would have kept it; but the discretion of Elinor prevailed. *Her* wisdom too limited the number of their servants to three; two maids and a man, with whom they were speedily provided from amongst those who had formed their establishment at Norland.

The man and one of the maids were sent off immediately into Devonshire, to prepare the house for their mistress's arrival; for as Lady Middleton was entirely unknown to Mrs Dashwood, she preferred going directly to the cottage to being a visitor at Barton Park; and she relied so undoubtingly on Sir John's description of the house, as to feel no curiosity to examine it herself till she entered it as her own. Her eagerness to be gone from Norland was preserved from diminution by the evident satisfaction of her daughter-in-law in the prospect of her removal; a satisfaction which was but feebly attempted to be concealed under a cold invitation to her to defer her departure. Now was the time when her son-in-law's promise to his father might with particular propriety be fulfilled. Since he had neglected to do it on first coming to the estate, their quitting his house might be looked on as the most suitable period for its accomplishment. But Mrs Dashwood began shortly to give over every hope of the kind, and to be convinced, from the general drift of his discourse, that his assistance extended no farther than their maintenance for six months at Norland. He so frequently talked of the increasing expenses of housekeeping, and of the perpetual demands upon his purse, which a man of any consequence in the world was beyond calculation exposed to, that he seemed rather to stand in need of more money himself than to have any design of giving money away.

In a very few weeks from the day which brought Sir John Middleton's first letter to Norland, every thing was so far settled in their future abode as to enable Mrs Dashwood and her daughters to begin their journey.

Many were the tears shed by them in their last adieus to a place so much beloved. 'Dear, dear Norland!' said Marianne, as she wandered alone before the house, on the last evening of their being there; 'when shall I cease to regret you! – when learn to feel a home elsewhere! – Oh! happy house, could you know what I suffer in now viewing you from this spot, from whence perhaps I may view you no more! – And you, ye well-known trees! – but you will continue the same. – No leaf will decay because we are removed, nor any branch become motionless although we can observe you no longer! – No; you will continue the same; unconscious of the pleasure or the regret you occasion, and insensible of any change in those who walk under your shade! – But who will remain to enjoy you?'

Chapter Six

THE FIRST PART OF THEIR JOURNEY was performed in too melancholy a disposition to be otherwise than tedious and unpleasant. But as they drew towards the end of it, their interest in the appearance of a country which they were to inhabit overcame their dejection, and a view of Barton Valley as they entered it gave them cheerfulness. It was a pleasant fertile spot, well wooded, and rich in pasture. After winding along it for more than a mile, they reached their own house. A small green court was the whole of its demesne in front; and a neat wicket gate admitted them into it.

As a house, Barton Cottage, though small, was comfortable and compact; but as a cottage it was defective, for the building was regular, the roof was tiled, the window shutters were not painted green, nor were the walls covered with honeysuckles. A narrow passage led directly through the house into the garden behind. On each side of the entrance was a sitting room, about sixteen feet square; and beyond them were the offices and the stairs. Four bed-rooms and two garrets formed the rest of the house. It had not been built many years and was in good repair. In comparison of Norland, it was poor and small indeed! – but the tears which recollection called forth as they entered the house were soon dried away. They were cheered by the joy of the servants on their arrival, and each for the sake of the others resolved to appear happy. It was very early in September; the season was fine, and from first seeing the place under the advantage of good weather, they received an impression in its favour which was of material service in recommending it to their lasting approbation.

The situation of the house was good. High hills rose immediately behind, and at no great distance on each side; some of which were open downs, the others cultivated and woody. The village of Barton was chiefly on one of these hills, and formed a pleasant view from the cottage windows. The prospect in front was more extensive; it commanded the whole of the valley, and reached into the country beyond. The hills which surrounded the cottage terminated the valley in that direction; under another name, and in another course, it branched out again between two of the steepest of them.

With the size and furniture of the house Mrs Dashwood was upon the whole well satisfied; for though her former style of life rendered many additions to the latter indispensable, yet to add and improve was a delight to her; and she had at this time ready money enough to supply all that was wanted of greater elegance to the apartments. 'As for the house itself, to be sure,' said she, 'it is too small for our family, but we will make ourselves tolerably comfortable for the present, as it is too late in the year for improvements. Perhaps in the spring, if I have plenty of money, as I dare say I shall, we may think about building. These parlours are both too small for such parties of our friends as I hope to see often collected here; and I have some thoughts of throwing the passage into one of them with perhaps a part of the other, and so leave the remainder of that other for an entrance; this, with a new drawing room which may be easily added, and a bed-chamber and garret above, will make it a very snug little cottage. I could wish the stairs were handsome. But one must not expect every thing; though I suppose it would be no difficult matter to widen them. I shall see how much I am before-hand with the world in the spring, and we will plan our improvements accordingly.'

In the mean time, till all these alterations could be made from the savings of an income of five hundred a-year by a woman who never saved in her life, they were wise enough to be contented with the house as it was; and each of them was busy in arranging their particular concerns, and endeavouring, by placing around them their books and other possessions, to form themselves a home. Marianne's pianoforte was unpacked and properly disposed of; and Elinor's drawings were affixed to the walls of their sitting room.

In such employments as these they were interrupted soon after breakfast the next day by the entrance of their landlord, who called to welcome them to Barton, and to offer them every accommodation from his own house and garden in which their's might at present be deficient. Sir John Middleton was a good looking man about forty. He had formerly visited at Stanhill, but it was too long ago for his young cousins to remember him. His countenance was thoroughly good-humoured; and his manners were as·friendly as the style of his letter. Their arrival seemed to afford him real satisfaction, and their comfort to be an object of real solicitude to him. He said much of his earnest desire of their living in the most sociable terms with his family, and pressed them so cordially to dine at Barton Park every day till they were better settled at home, that, though his entreaties were carried to a point of perseverance beyond civility, they could not give offence. His kindness was not confined to words; for within an hour after he left them, a large basket full of garden stuff and fruit arrived from the park, which was followed before the end of the day by a present of game. He insisted moreover on conveying all their letters to and from the post for them, and would not be denied the satisfaction of sending them his newspaper every day.

Lady Middleton had sent a very civil message by him, denoting her intention of waiting on Mrs Dashwood as soon as she could be assured that her visit would be no inconvenience; and as this message was answered by an invitation equally polite, her ladyship was introduced to them the next day.

They were of course very anxious to see a person on whom so much of their comfort at Barton must depend; and the elegance of her appearance was favourable to their wishes. Lady Middleton was not more than six or seven and twenty; her face was handsome, her figure tall and striking, and her address graceful. Her manners had all the elegance which her husband's wanted. But they would have been improved by some share of his frankness and warmth; and her visit was long enough to detract something from their first admiration, by shewing that though perfectly well-bred, she was reserved, cold, and had nothing to say for herself beyond the most common-place inquiry or remark.

Conversation however was not wanted, for Sir John was very chatty, and Lady Middleton had taken the wise precaution of bringing with her their eldest child, a fine little boy about six years old, by which means there was one subject always to be recurred to by the ladies in case of extremity, for they had to enquire his name and age, admire his beauty, and ask him questions which his mother answered for him, while he hung about her and held down his head, to the great surprise of her ladyship, who wondered at his being so shy before company as he could make noise enough at home. On every formal visit a child ought to be of the party, by way of provision for discourse. In the present case it took up ten minutes to determine whether the boy were most like his father or mother, and in what particular he resembled either, for of course every body differed, and every body was astonished at the opinion of the others.

An opportunity was soon to be given to the Dashwoods of debating on the rest of the children, as Sir John would not leave the house without securing their promise of dining at the park the next day.

Chapter Seven

BARTON PARK WAS ABOUT HALF A MILE from the cottage. The ladies had passed near it in their way along the valley, but it was screened from their view at home by the projection of an hill. The house was large and handsome; and the Middletons lived in a style of equal hospitality and elegance. The former was for Sir John's gratification, the latter for that of his lady. They were scarcely ever without some friends staying with them in the house, and they kept more company of every kind than any other family in the neighbourhood. It was necessary to the happiness of both; for however dissimilar in temper and outward behaviour, they strongly resembled each other in that total want of talent and taste which confined their employments, unconnected with such as society produced, within a very narrow compass. Sir John was a sportsman, Lady Middleton a mother. He hunted and shot, and she humoured her children; and these were their only resources. Lady Middleton had the advantage of being able to spoil her children all the year round, while Sir John's independent employments were in existence only half the time. Continual engagements at home and abroad, however, supplied all the deficiencies of nature and education; supported the good spirits of Sir John, and gave exercise to the good-breeding of his wife.

Lady Middleton piqued herself upon the elegance of her table, and of all her domestic arrangements; and from this kind of vanity was her greatest enjoyment in any of their parties. But Sir John's satisfaction in society was much more real; he delighted in collecting about him more young people than his house would hold, and the noisier they were the better was he pleased. He was a blessing to all the juvenile part of the neighbourhood, for in summer he was for ever forming parties to eat cold ham and chicken out of doors, and in winter his private balls were numerous enough for any young lady who was not suffering under the insatiable appetite of fifteen.

The arrival of a new family in the country was always a matter of joy to him, and in every point of view he was charmed with the inhabitants he had now procured for his cottage at Barton. The Miss Dashwoods were young, pretty, and unaffected. It was enough to secure his good opinion; for to be unaffected was all that a pretty girl could want to make her mind as captivating as her person. The friendliness of his disposition made him happy in accommodating those, whose situation might be considered, in comparison with the past, as unfortunate. In shewing kindness to his cousins therefore he had the real satisfaction of a good heart; and in settling a family of females only in his cottage, he had all the satisfaction of a sportsman; for a sportsman, though he esteems only those of his sex who are sportsmen likewise, is not often desirous of encouraging their taste by admitting them to a residence within his own manor.

Mrs Dashwood and her daughters were met at the door of the house by Sir John, who welcomed them to Barton Park with unaffected sincerity; and as he attended them to the drawing room repeated to the young ladies the concern which the same subject had drawn from him the day before, at being unable to get any smart young men to meet them. They would see, he said, only one gentleman there besides himself; a particular friend who was staying at the park, but who was neither very young nor very gay. He hoped they would all excuse the smallness of the party, and could assure them it should never happen so again. He had been to several families that morning in hopes of procuring some addition to their number, but it was moonlight and every body was full of engagements. Luckily Lady Middleton's mother had arrived at Barton within the last hour, and as she was a very cheerful agreeable woman, he hoped the young ladies would not find it so very dull as they might imagine. The young ladies, as well as their mother, were perfectly satisfied with having two entire strangers of the party, and wished for no more.

Mrs Jennings, Lady Middleton's mother, was a good-humoured, merry, fat, elderly woman, who talked a great deal, seemed very happy, and rather vulgar. She was full of jokes and laughter, and before dinner was over had said many witty things on the subject of lovers and husbands; hoped they had not left their hearts behind them in Sussex, and pretended to see them blush whether they did or not. Marianne was vexed at it for her sister's sake, and turned her eyes towards Elinor to see how she bore these attacks, with an earnestness which gave Elinor far more pain than could arise from such common-place raillery as Mrs Jennings's.

Colonel Brandon, the friend of Sir John, seemed no more adapted by resemblance of manner to be his friend, than Lady Middleton was to be his wife, or Mrs Jennings to be Lady Middleton's mother. He was silent and grave. His appearance however was not unpleasing, in spite of his being in the opinion of Marianne and Margaret an absolute old bachelor, for he was on the wrong side of five and thirty; but though his face was not handsome his countenance was sensible, and his address was particularly gentlemanlike.

There was nothing in any of the party which could recommend them as companions to the Dashwoods; but the cold insipidity of Lady Middleton was so particularly repulsive, that in comparison of it the gravity of Colonel Brandon, and even the boisterous mirth of Sir John and his mother-in-law was interesting. Lady Middleton seemed to be roused to enjoyment only by the entrance of her four noisy children after dinner, who pulled her about, tore her clothes, and put an end to every kind of discourse except what related to themselves.

In the evening, as Marianne was discovered to be musical, she was invited to play. The instrument was unlocked, every body prepared to be charmed, and Marianne, who sang very well, at their request went through the chief of the songs which Lady Middleton had brought into the family on her marriage, and which perhaps had lain ever since in the same position on the pianoforté, for her ladyship had celebrated that event by giving up music, although by her mother's account she had played extremely well, and by her own was very fond of it.

Marianne's performance was highly applauded. Sir John was loud in his admiration at the end of every song, and as loud in his conversation with the others while every song lasted. Lady Middleton frequently called him to order, wondered how any one's attention could be diverted from music for a moment, and asked Marianne to sing a particular song which Marianne had just finished. Colonel Brandon alone, of all the party, heard her without being in raptures. He paid her only the compliment of attention; and she felt a respect for him on the occasion, which the others had reasonably forfeited by their shameless want of taste. His pleasure in music, though it amounted not to that extatic delight which alone could sympathize with her own, was estimable when contrasted against the horrible insensibility of the others; and she was reasonable enough to allow that a man of five and thirty might well have outlived all acuteness of feeling and every exquisite power of enjoyment. She was perfectly disposed to make every allowance for the colonel's advanced state of life which humanity required.

Chapter Eight

MRS JENNINGS WAS A WIDOW, with an ample jointure. She had only two daughters, both of whom she had lived to see respectably married, and she had now therefore nothing to do but to marry all the rest of the world. In the promotion of this object she was zealously active, as far as her ability reached; and missed no opportunity of projecting weddings among all the young people of her acquaintance. She was remarkably quick in the discovery of attachments, and had enjoyed the advantage of raising the blushes and the vanity of many a young lady by insinuations of her power over such a young man; and this kind of discernment enabled her soon after her arrival at Barton decisively to pronounce that Colonel Brandon was very much in love with Marianne Dashwood. She rather suspected it to be so, on the very first evening of their being together, from his listening so attentively while she sang to them; and when the visit was returned by the Middletons' dining at the cottage, the fact was ascertained by his listening to her again. It must be so. She was perfectly convinced of it. It would be an excellent match, for *he* was rich and *she* was handsome. Mrs Jennings had been anxious to see Colonel Brandon well married, ever since her connection with Sir John first brought him to her knowledge; and she was always anxious to get a good husband for every pretty girl.

The immediate advantage to herself was by no means inconsiderable, for it supplied her with endless jokes against them both. At the park she laughed at the colonel, and in the cottage at Marianne. To the former her raillery was probably, as far as it regarded only himself, perfectly indifferent; but to the latter it was at first incomprehensible; and when its object was understood, she hardly knew whether most to laugh at its absurdity, or censure its impertinence, for she considered it as an unfeeling reflection on the colonel's advanced years, and on his forlorn condition as an old bachelor.

Mrs Dashwood, who could not think a man five years younger than herself, so exceedingly ancient as he appeared to the youthful fancy of her daughter, ventured to clear Mrs Jennings from the probability of wishing to throw ridicule on his age.

'But at least, mama, you cannot deny the absurdity of the accusation, though you may not think it intentionally illnatured. Colonel Brandon is certainly younger than Mrs Jennings, but he is old enough to be *my* father; and if he were ever animated enough to be in love, must have long outlived every sensation of the kind. It is too ridiculous! When is a man to be safe from such wit, if age and infirmity will not protect him?'

'Infirmity!' said Elinor, 'do you call Colonel Brandon infirm? I can easily suppose that his age may appear much greater to you than to my mother; but you can hardly deceive yourself as to his having the use of his limbs!'

'Did not you hear him complain of the rheumatism? and is not that the commonest infirmity of declining life?'

'My dearest child,' said her mother laughing, 'at this rate you must be in continual terror of *my* decay; and it must seem to you a miracle that my life has been extended to the advanced age of forty.'

'Mama, you are not doing me justice. I know very well that Colonel Brandon is not old enough to make his friends yet apprehensive of losing him in the course of nature. He may live twenty years longer. But thirty-five has nothing to do with matrimony.'

'Perhaps,' said Elinor, 'thirty-five and seventeen had better not have any thing to do with matrimony together. But if there should by any chance happen to be a woman who is single at seven and twenty, I should not think Colonel Brandon's being thirty-five any objection to his marrying *her*.'

'A woman of seven and twenty,' said Marianne, after pausing a moment, 'can never hope to feel or inspire affection again, and if her home be uncomfortable, or her fortune small, I can suppose that she might bring herself to submit to the offices of a nurse, for the sake of the provision and security of a wife. In his marrying such a woman therefore there would be nothing unsuitable. It would be a compact of convenience, and the world would be satisfied. In my eyes it would be no marriage at all, but that would be nothing. To me it would seem only a commercial exchange, in which each wished to be benefited at the expense of the other.'

'It would be impossible, I know,' replied Elinor, 'to convince you that a woman of seven and twenty could feel for a man of thirty-five any thing near enough to love, to make him a desirable companion for her. But I must object to your dooming Colonel Brandon and his wife to the constant confinement of a sick chamber, merely because he chanced to complain yesterday (a very cold damp day) of a slight rheumatic feel in one of his shoulders.'

'But he talked of flannel waistcoats,' said Marianne; 'and with me a flannel waistcoat is invariably connected with aches, cramps, rheumatisms, and every species of ailment that can afflict the old and the feeble.'

'Had he been only in a violent fever, you would not have despised him half so much. Confess, Marianne, is not there something interesting to you in the flushed cheek, hollow eye, and quick pulse of a fever?'

Soon after this, upon Elinor's leaving the room, 'Mama,' said Marianne, 'I have an alarm on the subject of illness, which I cannot conceal from you. I am sure Edward Ferrars is not well. We have now been here almost a fortnight, and yet he does not come. Nothing but real indisposition could occasion this extraordinary delay. What else can detain him at Norland?'

'Had you any idea of his coming so soon?' said Mrs Dashwood. '*I* had none. On the contrary, if I have felt any anxiety at all on the subject, it has been in recollecting that he sometimes shewed a want of pleasure and readiness in accepting my invitation, when I talked of his coming to Barton. Does Elinor expect him already?'

'I have never mentioned it to her, but of course she must.'

'I rather think you are mistaken, for when I was talking to her yesterday of getting a new grate for the spare bedchamber, she observed that there was no immediate hurry for it, as it was not likely that the room would be wanted for some time.'

'How strange this is! what can be the meaning of it! But the whole of their behaviour to each other has been unaccountable! How cold, how composed were their last adieus! How languid their conversation the last evening of their being together! In Edward's farewell there was no distinction between Elinor and me: it was the good wishes of an affectionate brother to both. Twice did I leave them purposely together in the course of the last morning, and each time did he most unaccountably follow me out of the room. And Elinor, in quitting Norland and Edward, cried not as I did. Even now her self-command is invariable. When is she dejected or melancholy? When does she try to avoid society, or appear restless and dissatisfied in it?'

Chapter Nine

THE DASHWOODS WERE NOW SETTLED at Barton with tolerable comfort to themselves. The house and the garden, with all the objects surrounding them, were now become familiar, and the ordinary pursuits which had given to Norland half its charms, were engaged in again with far greater enjoyment than Norland had been able to afford, since the loss of their father. Sir John Middleton, who called on them every day for the first fortnight, and who was not in the habit of seeing much occupation at home, could not conceal his amazement on finding them always employed.

Their visitors, except those from Barton Park, were not many; for, in spite of Sir John's urgent entreaties that they would mix more in the neighbourhood, and repeated assurances of his carriage being always at their service, the independence of Mrs Dashwood's spirit overcame the wish of society for her children; and she was resolute in declining to visit any family beyond the distance of a walk. There were but few who could be so classed; and it was not all of them that were attainable. About a mile and a half from the cottage, along the narrow winding valley of Allenham, which issued from that of Barton, as formerly described, the girls had, in one of their earliest walks, discovered an ancient respectable looking mansion which, by reminding them a little of Norland, interested their imagination and made them wish to be better acquainted with it. But they learnt, on inquiry, that its possessor, an elderly lady of very good character, was unfortunately too infirm to mix with the world, and never stirred from home.

The whole country about them abounded in beautiful walks. The high downs which invited them from almost every window of the cottage to seek the exquisite enjoyment of air on their summits, were an happy alternative when the dirt of the valleys beneath shut up their superior beauties; and towards one of these hills did Marianne and Margaret one memorable morning direct their steps, attracted by the partial sunshine of a showery sky, and unable longer to bear the confinement which the settled rain of the two preceding days had occasioned. The weather was not tempting enough to draw the two others from their pencil and their book, in spite of Marianne's declaration that the day would be lastingly fair, and that every threatening cloud would be drawn off from their hills; and the two girls set off together.

They gaily ascended the downs, rejoicing in their own penetration at every glimpse of blue sky; and when they caught in their faces the animating gales of an high south-westerly wind, they pitied the fears which had prevented their mother and Elinor from sharing such delightful sensations. 'Is there a felicity in the world,' said Marianne, 'superior to this? – Margaret, we will walk here at least two hours.'

Margaret agreed, and they pursued their way against the wind, resisting it with laughing delight for about twenty minutes longer, when suddenly the clouds united over their heads, and a driving rain set full in their face. – Chagrined and surprised, they were obliged, though unwillingly, to turn back, for no shelter was nearer than their own house. One consolation however remained for them, to which the exigence of the moment gave more than usual propriety; it was that of running with all possible speed down the steep side of the hill which led immediately to their garden gate.

They set off. Marianne had at first the advantage, but a false step brought her suddenly to the ground, and Margaret, unable to stop herself to assist her, was involuntarily hurried along, and reached the bottom in safety.

A gentleman carrying a gun, with two pointers playing round him, was passing up the hill and within a few yards of Marianne, when her accident happened. He put down his gun and ran to her assistance. She had raised herself from the ground, but her foot had been twisted in the fall, and she was scarcely able to stand. The gentleman offered his services, and perceiving that her modesty declined what her situation rendered necessary, took her up in his arms without farther delay, and carried her down the hill. Then passing through the garden, the gate of which had been left open by Margaret, he bore her directly into the house, whither Margaret was just arrived, and quitted not his hold till he had seated her in a chair in the parlour.

Elinor and her mother rose up in amazement at their entrance, and while the eyes of both were fixed on him with an evident wonder and a secret admiration which equally sprung from his appearance, he apologized for his intrusion by relating its cause, in a manner so frank and so graceful, that his person, which was uncommonly handsome, received additional charms from his voice and expression. Had he been even old, ugly, and vulgar, the gratitude and kindness of Mrs Dashwood would have been secured by any act of attention to her child; but the influence of youth, beauty, and elegance, gave an interest to the action which came home to her feelings.

She thanked him again and again; and with a sweetness of address which always attended her, invited him to be seated. But this he declined, as he was dirty and wet. Mrs Dashwood then begged to know to whom she was obliged. His name, he replied, was Willoughby, and his present home was at Allenham, from whence he hoped she would allow him the honour of calling tomorrow to inquire after Miss Dashwood. The honour was readily granted, and he then departed, to make himself still more interesting, in the midst of an heavy rain.

His manly beauty and more than common gracefulness were instantly the theme of general admiration, and the laugh which his gallantry raised against Marianne, received particular spirit from his exterior attractions. – Marianne herself had seen less of his person than the rest, for the confusion which crimsoned over her face, on his lifting her up, had robbed her of the power of regarding him after their entering the house. But she had seen enough of him to join in all the admiration of the others, and with an energy which always adorned her praise. His person and air were equal to what her fancy had ever drawn for the hero of a favourite story; and in his carrying her into the house with so little previous formality, there was a rapidity of thought which particularly recommended the action to her. Every circumstance belonging to him was interesting. His name was good, his residence was in their favourite village, and she soon found out that of all manly dresses a shooting-jacket was the most becoming. Her imagination was busy, her reflections were pleasant, and the pain of a sprained ancle was disregarded.

Sir John called on them as soon as the next interval of fair weather that morning allowed him to get out of doors; and Marianne's accident being related to him, he was eagerly asked whether he knew any gentleman of the name of Willoughby at Allenham.

'Willoughby!' cried Sir John; 'what, is *he* in the country? That is good news however; I will ride over tomorrow, and ask him to dinner on Thursday.'

'You know him then,' said Mrs Dashwood.

'Know him! to be sure I do. Why, he is down here every year.'

'And what sort of a young man is he?'

'As good a kind of fellow as ever lived, I assure you. A very decent shot, and there is not a bolder rider in England.'

'And is *that* all you can say for him?' cried Marianne, indignantly. 'But what are his manners on more intimate acquaintance? What his pursuits, his talents and genius?'

Sir John was rather puzzled.

'Upon my soul,' said he, 'I do not know much about him as to all *that*. But he is a pleasant, good humoured fellow, and has got the nicest little black bitch of a pointer I ever saw. Was she out with him today?'

But Marianne could no more satisfy him as to the colour of Mr Willoughby's pointer, than he could describe to her the shades of his mind.

'But who is he?' said Elinor. 'Where does he come from? Has he a house at Allenham?'

On this point Sir John could give more certain intelligence; and he told them that Mr Willoughby had no property of his own in the country; that he resided there only while he was visiting the old lady at Allenham Court, to whom he was related, and whose possessions he was to inherit; adding, 'Yes, yes, he is very well worth catching, I can tell you, Miss Dashwood; he has a pretty little estate of his own in Somersetshire besides; and if I were you, I would not give him up to my younger sister in spite of all this tumbling down hills. Miss Marianne must not expect to have all the men to herself. Brandon will be jealous, if she does not take care.'

'I do not believe,' said Mrs Dashwood, with a good humoured smile, 'that Mr Willoughby will be incommoded by the attempts of either of *my* daughters towards what you call *catching* him. It is not an employment to which they have been brought up. Men are very safe with us, let them be ever so rich. I am glad to find, however, from what you say, that he is a respectable young man, and one whose acquaintance will not be ineligible.'

'He is as good a sort of fellow, I believe, as ever lived,' repeated Sir John. 'I remember last Christmas at a little hop at the park, he danced from eight o'clock till four, without once sitting down.'

'Did he indeed?' cried Marianne with sparkling eyes, 'and with elegance, with spirit?'

'Yes; and he was up again at eight to ride to covert.'

'That is what I like; that is what a young man ought to be. Whatever be his pursuits, his eagerness in them should know no moderation, and leave him no sense of fatigue.'

'Aye, aye, I see how it will be,' said Sir John, 'I see how it will be. You will be setting your cap at him now, and never think of poor Brandon.'

'That is an expression, Sir John,' said Marianne, warmly, 'which I particularly dislike. I abhor every common-place phrase by which wit is intended; and "setting one's cap at a man," or "making a conquest," are the most odious of all. Their tendency is gross and illiberal; and if their construction could ever be deemed clever, time has long ago destroyed all its ingenuity.'

Sir John did not much understand this reproof; but he laughed as heartily as if he did, and then replied,

'Aye, you will make conquests enough, I dare say, one way or other. Poor Brandon! he is quite smitten already, and he is very well worth setting your cap at, I can tell you, in spite of all this tumbling about and spraining of ancles.'

Chapter Ten

MARIANNE'S PRESERVER, AS MARGARET, with more elegance than precision, stiled Willoughby, called at the cottage early the next morning to make his personal inquiries. He was received by Mrs Dashwood with more than politeness; with a kindness which Sir John's account of him and her own gratitude prompted; and every thing that passed during the visit, tended to assure him of the sense, elegance, mutual affection, and domestic comfort of the family to whom accident had now introduced him. Of their personal charms he had not required a second interview to be convinced.

Miss Dashwood had a delicate complexion, regular features and a remarkably pretty figure. Marianne was still handsomer. Her form, though not so correct as her sister's, in having the advantage of height, was more striking; and her face was so lovely, that when in the common cant of praise she was called a beautiful girl, truth was less violently outraged than usually happens. Her skin was very brown, but from its transparency, her complexion was uncommonly brilliant; her features were all good; her smile was sweet and attractive, and in her eyes, which were very dark, there was a life, a spirit, an eagerness which could hardly be seen without delight. From Willoughby their expression was at first held back, by the embarrassment which the remembrance of his assistance created. But when this passed away, when her spirits became collected, when she saw that to the perfect good-breeding of the gentleman, he united frankness and vivacity, and above all, when she heard him declare that of music and dancing he was passionately fond, she gave him such a look of approbation as secured the largest share of his discourse to herself for the rest of his stay.

It was only necessary to mention any favourite amusement to engage her to talk. She could not be silent when such points were introduced, and she had neither shyness nor reserve in their discussion. They speedily discovered that their enjoyment of dancing and music was mutual, and that it arose from a general conformity of judgment in all that related to either. Encouraged by this to a further examination of his opinions, she proceeded to question him on the subject of books; her favourite authors were brought forward and dwelt upon with so rapturous a delight, that any young man of five and twenty must have been insensible indeed, not to become an immediate convert to the excellence of such works, however disregarded before. Their taste was strikingly alike. The same books, the same passages were idolized by each – or if any difference appeared, any objection arose, it lasted no longer than till the force of her arguments and the brightness of her eyes could be displayed. He acquiesced in all her decisions, caught all her enthusiasm; and long before his visit concluded, they conversed with the familiarity of a long-established acquaintance.

'Well, Marianne,' said Elinor, as soon as he had left them, 'for one morning I think you have done pretty well. You have already ascertained Mr Willoughby's opinion in almost every matter of importance. You know what he thinks of Cowper and Scott; you are certain of his estimating their beauties as he ought, and you have received every assurance of his admiring Pope no more than is proper. But how is your acquaintance to be long supported, under such extraordinary dispatch of every subject for discourse? You will soon have exhausted each favourite topic. Another meeting will suffice to explain his sentiments on picturesque beauty, and second marriages, and then you can have nothing farther to ask.' –

'Elinor,' cried Marianne, 'is this fair? is this just? are my ideas so scanty? But I see what you mean. I have been too much at my ease, too happy, too frank. I have erred against every common-place notion of decorum; I have been open and sincere where I ought to have been reserved, spiritless, dull, and deceitful: – had I talked only of the weather and the roads, and had I spoken only once in ten minutes, this reproach would have been spared.'

'My love,' said her mother, 'you must not be offended with Elinor – she was only in jest. I should scold her myself, if she were capable of wishing to check the delight of your conversation with our new friend.' – Marianne was softened in a moment.

Willoughby, on his side, gave every proof of his pleasure in their acquaintance, which an evident wish of improving it could offer. He came to them every day. To inquiry after Marianne was at first his excuse; but the encouragement of his reception, to which every day gave greater kindness, made such an excuse unnecessary before it had ceased to be possible, by Marianne's perfect recovery. She was confined for some days to the house; but never had any confinement been less irksome. Willoughby was a young man of good abilities, quick imagination, lively spirits, and open, affectionate manners. He was exactly formed to engage Marianne's heart, for with all this, he joined not only a captivating person, but a natural ardour of mind which was now roused and increased by the example of her own, and which recommended him to her affection beyond every thing else.

His society became gradually her most exquisite enjoyment. They read, they talked, they sang together; his musical talents were considerable; and he read with all the sensibility and spirit which Edward had unfortunately wanted.

In Mrs Dashwood's estimation, he was as faultless as in Marianne's; and Elinor saw nothing to censure in him but a propensity, in which he strongly resembled and peculiarly delighted her sister, of saying too much what he thought on every occasion, without attention to persons or circumstances. In hastily forming and giving his opinion of other people, in sacrificing general politeness to the enjoyment of undivided attention where his heart was engaged, and in slighting too easily the forms of worldly propriety, he displayed a want of caution which Elinor could not approve, in spite of all that he and Marianne could say in its support.

Marianne began now to perceive that the desperation which had seized her at sixteen and a half, of ever seeing a man who could satisfy her ideas of perfection, had been rash and unjustifiable. Willoughby was all that her fancy had delineated in that unhappy hour and in every brighter period, as capable of attaching her; and his behaviour declared his wishes to be in that respect as earnest, as his abilities were strong.

Her mother too, in whose mind not one speculative thought of their marriage had been raised, by his prospect of riches, was led before the end of a week to hope and expect it; and secretly to congratulate herself on having gained two such sons-in-law as Edward and Willoughby.

Colonel Brandon's partiality for Marianne, which had so early been discovered by his friends, now first became perceptible to Elinor, when it ceased to be noticed by them. Their attention and wit were drawn off to his more fortunate rival; and the raillery which the other had incurred before any partiality arose, was removed when his feelings began really to call for the ridicule so justly annexed to sensibility. Elinor was obliged, though unwillingly, to believe that the sentiments which Mrs Jennings had assigned him for her own satisfaction, were now actually excited by her sister; and that however a general resemblance of disposition between the parties might forward the affection of Mr Willoughby, an equally striking opposition of character was no hindrance to the regard of Colonel Brandon. She was it with concern; for what could a silent man of five and thirty hope, when opposed by a very lively one of five and twenty? and as she could not even wish him successful, she heartily wished him indifferent. She liked him – in spite of his gravity and reserve, she beheld in him an object of interest. His manners, though serious, were mild; and his reserve appeared rather the result of some oppression of spirits, than of any natural gloominess of temper. Sir John had dropt hints of past injuries and disappointments, which justified her belief of his being an unfortunate man, and she regarded him with respect and compassion.

Perhaps she pitied and esteemed him the more because he was slighted by Willoughby and Marianne, who, prejudiced against him for being neither lively nor young, seemed resolved to undervalue his merits.

'Brandon is just the kind of man,' said Willoughby one day, when they were talking of him together, 'whom every body speaks well of, and nobody cares about; whom all are delighted to see, and nobody remembers to talk to.'

'That is exactly what I think of him,' cried Marianne.

'Do not boast of it, however,' said Elinor, 'for it is injustice in both of you. He is highly esteemed by all the family at the park, and I never see him myself without taking pains to converse with him.'

'That he is patronized by *you*,' replied Willoughby, 'is certainly in his favour; but as for the esteem of the others, it is a reproach in itself. Who would submit to the indignity of being approved by such women as Lady Middleton and Mrs Jennings, that could command the indifference of any body else?'

'But perhaps the abuse of such people as yourself and Marianne, will make amends for the regard of Lady Middleton and her mother. If their praise is censure, your censure may be praise, for they are not more undiscerning, than you are prejudiced and unjust.'

'In defence of your protégé you can even be saucy.'

'My protégé, as you call him, is a sensible man; and sense will always have attractions for me. Yes, Marianne, even in a man between thirty and forty. He has seen a great deal of the world; has been abroad; has read, and has a thinking mind. I have found him capable of giving me much information on various subjects, and he has always answered my inquiries with the readiness of good-breeding and good nature.'

'That is to say,' cried Marianne contemptuously, 'he has told you that in the East Indies the climate is hot, and the mosquitoes are troublesome.'

'He *would* have told me so, I doubt not, had I made any such inquiries, but they happened to be points on which I had been previously informed.'

'Perhaps,' said Willoughby, 'his observations may have extended to the existence of nabobs, gold mohrs, and palanquins.'

'I may venture to say that *his* observations have stretched much farther than your candour. But why should you dislike him?'

'I do not dislike him. I consider him, on the contrary, as a very respectable man, who has every body's good word and nobody's notice; who has more money than he can spend, more time than he knows how to employ, and two new coats every year.'

'Add to which,' cried Marianne, 'that he has neither genius, taste, nor spirit. That his understanding has no brilliancy, his feelings no ardour, and his voice no expression.'

'You decide on his imperfections so much in the mass,' replied Elinor, 'and so much on the strength of your own imagination, that the commendation I am able to give of him is comparatively cold and insipid. I can only pronounce him to be a sensible man, well-bred, well-informed, of gentle address, and I believe possessing an amiable heart.'

'Miss Dashwood,' cried Willoughby, 'you are now using me unkindly. You are endeavouring to disarm me by reason, and to convince me against my will. But it will not do. You shall find me as stubborn as you can be artful. I have three unanswerable reasons for disliking Colonel Brandon: he has threatened me with rain when I wanted it to be fine; he has found fault with the hanging of my curricle, and I cannot persuade him to buy my brown mare. If it will be any satisfaction to you, however, to be told, that I believe his character to be in other respects irreproachable, I am ready to confess it. And in return for an acknowledgment, which must give me some pain, you cannot deny me the privilege of disliking him as much as ever.'

Chapter Eleven

LITTLE HAD MRS DASHWOOD or her daughters imagined when they first came into Devonshire, that so many engagements would arise to occupy their time as shortly presented themselves, or that they should have such frequent invitations and such constant visitors as to leave them little leisure for serious employment. Yet such was the case. When Marianne was recovered, the schemes of amusement at home and abroad, which Sir John had been previously forming, were put in execution. The private balls at the park then began; and parties on the water were made and accomplished as often as a showery October would allow. In every meeting of the kind Willoughby was included; and the ease and familiarity which naturally attended these parties were exactly calculated to give increasing intimacy to his acquaintance with the Dashwoods, to afford him opportunity of witnessing the excellencies of Marianne, of marking his animated admiration of her, and of receiving, in her behaviour to himself, the most pointed assurance of her affection.

Elinor could not be surprised at their attachment. She only wished that it were less openly shewn; and once or twice did venture to suggest the propriety of some self-command to Marianne. But Marianne abhorred all concealment where no real disgrace could attend unreserve; and to aim at the restraint of sentiments which were not in themselves illaudable, appeared to her not merely an unnecessary effort, but a disgraceful subjection of reason to common-place and mistaken notions. Willoughby thought the same; and their behaviour, at all times, was an illustration of their opinions.

When he was present she had no eyes for any one else. Every thing he did, was right. Every thing he said, was clever. If their evenings at the park were concluded with cards, he cheated himself and all the rest of the party to get her a good hand. If dancing formed the amusement of the night, they were partners for half the time; and when obliged to separate for a couple of dances, were careful to stand together and scarcely spoke a word to any body else. Such conduct made them of course most exceedingly laughed at; but ridicule could not shame, and seemed hardly to provoke them.

Mrs Dashwood entered into all their feelings with a warmth which left her no inclination for checking this excessive display of them. To her it was but the natural consequence of a strong affection in a young and ardent mind.

This was the season of happiness to Marianne. Her heart was devoted to Willoughby, and the fond attachment to Norland, which she brought with her from Sussex, was more likely to be softened than she had thought it possible before, by the charms which his society bestowed on her present home.

Elinor's happiness was not so great. Her heart was not so much at ease, nor her satisfaction in their amusements so pure. They afforded her no companion that could make amends for what she had left behind, nor that could teach her to think of Norland with less regret than ever. Neither Lady Middleton nor Mrs Jennings could supply to her the conversation she missed; although the latter was an everlasting talker, and from the first had regarded her with a kindness which ensured her a large share of her discourse. She had already repeated her own history to Elinor three or four times; and had Elinor's memory been equal to her means of improvement, she might have known very early in their acquaintance all the particulars of Mr Jennings's last illness, and what he said to his wife a few minutes before he died. Lady Middleton was more agreeable than her mother, only in being more silent. Elinor needed little observation to perceive that her reserve was a mere calmness of manner with which sense had nothing to do. Towards her husband and mother she was the same as to them; and intimacy was therefore neither to be looked for nor desired. She had nothing to say one day that she had not said the day before. Her insipidity was invariable, for even her spirits were always the same; and though she did not oppose the parties arranged by her husband, provided every thing were conducted in style and her two eldest children attended her, she never appeared to receive more enjoyment from them, than she might have experienced in sitting at home; – and so little did her presence add to the pleasure of the others, by any share in their conversation, that they were sometimes only reminded of her being amongst them by her solicitude about her troublesome boys.

In Colonel Brandon alone, of all her new acquaintance, did Elinor find a person who could in any degree claim the respect of abilities, excite the interest of friendship, or give pleasure as a companion. Willoughby was out of the question. Her admiration and regard, even her sisterly regard, was all his own; but he was a lover; his attentions were wholly Marianne's, and a far less agreeable man might have been more generally pleasing. Colonel Brandon, unfortunately for himself, had no such encouragement to think only of Marianne, and in conversing with Elinor he found the greatest consolation for the total indifference of her sister.

Elinor's compassion for him increased, as she had reason to suspect that the misery of disappointed love had already been known by him. This suspicion was given by some words which accidentally dropt from him one evening at the park, when they were sitting down together by mutual consent, while the others were dancing. His eyes were fixed on Marianne, and, after a silence of some minutes, he said with a faint smile. 'Your sister, I understand, does not approve of second attachments.'

'No,' replied Elinor, 'her opinions are all romantic.'

'Or rather, as I believe, she considers them impossible to exist.'

'I believe she does. But how she contrives it without reflecting on the character of her own father, who had himself two wives, I know not. A few years however will settle her opinions on the reasonable basis of common sense and observation; and then they may be more easy to define and to justify than they now are, by any body but herself.'

'This will probably be the case,' he replied; 'and yet there is something so amiable in the prejudices of a young mind, that one is sorry to see them give way to the reception of more general opinions.'

'I cannot agree with you there,' said Elinor. 'There are inconveniences attending such feelings as Marianne's, which all the charms of enthusiasm and ignorance of the world cannot atone for. Her systems have all the unfortunate tendency of setting propriety at nought; and a better acquaintance with the world is what I look forward to as her greatest possible advantage.'

After a short pause he resumed the conversation by saying –

'Does your sister make no distinction in her objections against a second attachment? or is it equally criminal in every body? Are those who have been disappointed in their first choice, whether from the inconstancy of its object, or the perverseness of circumstances, to be equally indifferent during the rest of their lives?'

'Upon my word, I am not acquainted with the minutia of her principles. I only know that I never yet heard her admit any instance of a second attachment's being pardonable.'

'This,' said he, 'cannot hold; but a change, a total change of sentiments – No, no, do not desire it, – for when the romantic refinements of a young mind are obliged to give way, how frequently are they succeeded by such opinions as are but too common, and too dangerous! I speak from experience. I once knew a lady who in temper and mind greatly resembled your sister, who thought and judged like her, but who from an inforced change – from a series of unfortunate circumstances' – Here he stopt suddenly; appeared to think that he had said too much, and by his countenance gave rise to conjectures, which might not otherwise have entered Elinor's head. The lady would probably have passed without suspicion, had he not convinced Miss Dashwood that what concerned her ought not to escape his lips. As it was, it required but a slight effort of fancy to connect his emotion with the tender recollection of past regard. Elinor attempted no more. But Marianne, in her place, would not have done so little. The whole story would have been speedily formed under her active imagination; and every thing established in the most melancholy order of disastrous love.

Chapter Twelve

AS ELINOR AND MARIANNE WERE walking together the next morning the latter communicated a piece of news to her sister, which in spite of all that she knew before of Marianne's imprudence and want of thought, surprised her by its extravagant testimony of both. Marianne told her, with the greatest delight, that Willoughby had given her a horse, one that he had bred himself on his estate in Somersetshire, and which was exactly calculated to carry a woman. Without considering that it was not in her mother's plan to keep any horse, that if she were to alter her resolution in favour of this gift, she must buy another for the servant, and keep a servant to ride it, and after all, build a stable to receive them, she had accepted the present without hesitation, and told her sister of it in raptures.

'He intends to send his groom into Somersetshire immediately for it,' she added, 'and when it arrives, we will ride every day. You shall share its use with me. Imagine to yourself, my dear Elinor, the delight of a gallop on some of these downs.'

Most unwilling was she to awaken from such a dream of felicity, to comprehend all the unhappy truths which attended the affair; and for some time she refused to submit to them. As to an additional servant, the expence would be a trifle; mama she was sure would never object to it; and any horse would do for *him*; he might always get one at the park; as to a stable, the merest shed would be sufficient. Elinor then ventured to doubt the propriety of her receiving such a present from a man so little, or at least so lately known to her. This was too much.

'You are mistaken, Elinor,' said she warmly, 'in supposing I know very little of Willoughby. I have not known him long indeed, but I am much better acquainted with him, than with any other creature in the world, except yourself and mama. It is not time or opportunity that is to determine intimacy; – it is disposition alone. Seven years would be insufficient to make some people acquainted with each other, and seven days are more than enough for others. I should hold myself guilty of greater impropriety in accepting a horse from my brother, than from Willoughby. Of John I know very little, though we have lived together for years; but of Willoughby my judgment has long been formed.'

Elinor thought it wisest to touch that point no more. She knew her sister's temper. Opposition on so tender a subject would only attach her the more to her own opinion. But by an appeal to her affection for her mother, by representing the inconveniences which that indulgent mother must draw on herself, if (as would probably be the case) she consented to this increase of establishment, Marianne was shortly subdued; and she promised not to tempt her mother to such imprudent kindness by mentioning the offer, and to tell Willoughby when she saw him next, that it must be declined.

She was faithful to her word; and when Willoughby called at the cottage, the same day, Elinor heard her express her disappointment to him in a low voice, on being obliged to forego the acceptance of his present. The reasons for this alteration were at the same time related, and they were such as to make further entreaty on his side impossible. His concern however was very apparent; and after expressing it with earnestness, he added in the same low voice – 'But, Marianne, the horse is still yours, though you cannot use it now. I shall keep it only till you can claim it. When you leave Barton to form your own establishment in a more lasting home, Queen Mab shall receive you.'

This was all overheard by Miss Dashwood; and in the whole of the sentence, in his manner of pronouncing it, and in his addressing her sister by her christian name alone, she instantly saw an intimacy so decided, a meaning so direct, as marked a perfect agreement between them. From that moment she doubted not of their being engaged to each other; and the belief of it created no other surprise, than that she, or any of their friends, should be left by tempers so frank, to discover it by accident.

Margaret related something to her the next day, which placed this matter in a still clearer light. Willoughby had spent the preceding evening with them, and Margaret, by being left some time in the parlour with only him and Marianne, had had opportunity for observations, which, with a most important face, she communicated to her eldest sister, when they were next by themselves.

'Oh! Elinor,' she cried, 'I have such a secret to tell you about Marianne. I am sure she will be married to Mr Willoughby very soon.'

'You have said so,' replied Elinor, 'almost every day since they first met on High-church Down; and they had not known each other a week, I believe, before you were certain that Marianne wore his picture round her neck; but it turned out to be only the miniature of our great uncle.'

'But indeed this is quite another thing. I am sure they will be married very soon, for he has got a lock of her hair.'

'Take care, Margaret. It may be only the hair of some great uncle of *his*.'

'But indeed, Elinor, it is Marianne's. I am almost sure it is, for I saw him cut it off. Last night after tea, when you and mama went out of the room, they were whispering and talking together as fast as could be, and he seemed to be begging something of her, and presently he took up her scissors and cut off a long lock of her hair, for it was all tumbled down her back; and he kissed it, and folded it up in a piece of white paper, and put it into his pocket-book.'

From such particulars, stated on such authority, Elinor could not with-hold her credit: nor was she disposed to it, for the circumstance was in perfect unison with what she had heard and seen herself.

Margaret's sagacity was not always displayed in a way so satisfactory to her sister. When Mrs Jennings attacked her one evening at the park, to give the name of the young man who was Elinor's particular favourite, which had been long a matter of great curiosity to her, Margaret answered by looking at her sister, and saying, 'I must not tell, may I, Elinor?'

This of course made every body laugh; and Elinor tried to laugh too. But the effort was painful. She was convinced that Margaret had fixed on a person, whose name she could not bear with composure to become a standing joke with Mrs Jennings.

Marianne felt for her most sincerely; but she did more harm than good to the cause, by turning very red, and saying in an angry manner to Margaret,

'Remember that whatever your conjectures may be, you have no right to repeat them.'

'I never had any conjectures about it,' replied Margaret; 'it was you who told me of it yourself.'

This increased the mirth of the company, and Margaret was eagerly pressed to say something more.

'Oh! pray, Miss Margaret, let us know all about it,' said Mrs Jennings. 'What is the gentleman's name?'

'I must not tell, ma'am. But I know very well what it is; and I know where he is too.'

'Yes, yes, we can guess where he is; at his own house at Norland to be sure. He is the curate of the parish I dare say.'

'No, *that* he is not. He is of no profession at all.'

'Margaret,' said Marianne with great warmth, 'you know that all this is an invention of your own, and that there is no such person in existence.'

'Well then he is lately dead, Marianne, for I am sure there was such a man once, and his name begins with an F.'

Most grateful did Elinor feel to Lady Middleton for observing at this moment, 'that it rained very hard,' though she believed the interruption to proceed less from any attention to her than from her ladyship's great dislike of all such inelegant subjects of raillery as delighted her husband and mother. The idea however started by her, was immediately pursued by Colonel Brandon, who was on every occasion mindful of the feelings of others; and much was said on the subject of rain by both of them. Willoughby opened the piano-forte, and asked Marianne to sit down to it; and thus amidst the various endeavours of different people to quit the topic, it fell to the ground. But not so easily did Elinor recover from the alarm into which it had thrown her.

A party was formed this evening for going on the following day to see a very fine place about twelve miles from Barton, belonging to a brother-in-law of Colonel Brandon, without whose interest it could not be seen, as the proprietor, who was then abroad, had left strict orders on that head. The grounds were declared to be highly beautiful, and Sir John, who was particularly warm in their praise, might be allowed to be a tolerable judge, for he had formed parties to visit them, at least, twice every summer for the last ten years. They contained a noble piece of water; a sail on which was to form a great part of the morning's amusement; cold provisions were to be taken, open carriages only to be employed, and every thing conducted in the usual style of a complete party of pleasure.

To some few of the company, it appeared rather a bold undertaking, considering the time of year, and that it had rained every day for the last fortnight; – and Mrs Dashwood, who had already a cold, was persuaded by Elinor to stay at home.

Chapter Thirteen

THEIR INTENDED EXCURSION to Whitwell turned out very different from what Elinor had expected. She was prepared to be wet through, fatigued, and frightened; but the event was still more unfortunate, for they did not go at all.

By ten o'clock the whole party were assembled at the park, where they were to breakfast. The morning was rather favourable, though it had rained all night, as the clouds were then dispersing across the sky, and the sun frequently appeared. They were all in high spirits and good humour, eager to be happy, and determined to submit to the greatest inconveniences and hardships rather than be otherwise.

While they were at breakfast the letters were brought in. Among the rest there was one for Colonel Brandon; – he took it, looked at the direction, changed colour, and immediately left the room.

'What is the matter with Brandon?' said Sir John.

Nobody could tell.

'I hope he has had no bad news,' said Lady Middleton. 'It must be something extraordinary that could make Colonel Brandon leave my breakfast table so suddenly.'

In about five minutes he returned.

'No bad news, Colonel, I hope;' said Mrs Jennings, as soon as he entered the room.

'None at all, ma'am, I thank you.'

'Was it from Avignon? I hope it is not to say that your sister is worse.'

'No, ma'am. It came from town, and is merely a letter of business.'

'But how came the hand to discompose you so much, if it was only a letter of business? Come, come, this won't do, Colonel; so let us hear the truth of it.'

'My dear Madam,' said Lady Middleton, 'recollect what you are saying.'

'Perhaps it is to tell you that your cousin Fanny is married?' said Mrs Jennings, without attending to her daughter's reproof.

'No, indeed, it is not.'

'Well, then, I know who it is from, Colonel. And I hope she is well.'

'Whom do you mean, ma'am?' said he, colouring a little.

'Oh! you know who I mean.'

'I am particularly sorry, ma'am,' said he, addressing Lady Middleton, 'that I should receive this letter today, for it is on business which requires my immediate attendance in town.'

'In town!' cried Mrs Jennings. 'What can you have to do in town at this time of year?'

'My own loss is great,' he continued, 'in being obliged to leave so agreeable a party; but I am the more concerned, as I fear my presence is necessary to gain your admittance at Whitwell.'

What a blow upon them all was this!

'But if you write a note to the housekeeper, Mr Brandon,' said Marianne eagerly, 'will it not be sufficient?'

He shook his head.

'We must go,' said Sir John. – 'It shall not be put off when we are so near it. You cannot go to town till tomorrow, Brandon, that is all.'

'I wish it could be so easily settled. But it is not in my power to delay my journey for one day!'

'If you would but let us know what your business is,' said Mrs Jennings, 'we might see whether it could be put off or not.'

'You would not be six hours later,' said Willoughby, 'if you were to defer your journey till our return.'

'I cannot afford to lose *one* hour.' –

Elinor then heard Willoughby say in a low voice to Marianne, 'There are some people who cannot bear a party of pleasure. Brandon is one of them. He was afraid of catching cold I dare say, and invented this trick for getting out of it. I would lay fifty guineas the letter was of his own writing.'

'I have no doubt of it,' replied Marianne.

'There is no persuading you to change your mind, Brandon, I know of old,' said Sir John, 'when once you are determined on any thing. But, however, I hope you will think better of it. Consider, here are the two Miss Careys come over from Newton, the three Miss Dashwoods walked up from the cottage, and Mr Willoughby got up two hours before his usual time, on purpose to go to Whitwell.'

Colonel Brandon again repeated his sorrow at being the cause of disappointing the party; but at the same time declared it to be unavoidable.

'Well then, when will you come back again?'

'I hope we shall see you at Barton,' added her ladyship, 'as soon as you can conveniently leave town; and we must put off the party to Whitwell till you return.'

'You are very obliging. But it is so uncertain, when I may have it in my power to return, that I dare not engage for it at all.'

'Oh! he must and shall come back,' cried Sir John. 'If he is not here by the end of the week, I shall go after him.'

'Aye, so do, Sir John,' cried Mrs Jennings, 'and then perhaps you may find out what his business is.'

'I do not want to pry into other men's concerns. I suppose it is something he is ashamed of.'

Colonel Brandon's horses were announced.

'You do not go to town on horseback, do you?' added Sir John.

'No. Only to Honiton. I shall then go post.'

'Well, as you are resolved to go, I wish you a good journey. But you had better change your mind.'

'I assure you it is not in my power.'

He then took leave of the whole party.

'Is there no chance of my seeing you and your sisters in town this winter, Miss Dashwood?'

'I am afraid, none at all.'

'Then I must bid you farewell for a longer time than I should wish to do.'

To Marianne, he merely bowed and said nothing.

'Come, Colonel,' said Mrs Jennings, 'before you go, do let us know what you are going about.'

He wished her a good morning, and attended by Sir John, left the room.

The complaints and lamentations which politeness had hitherto restrained, now burst forth universally; and they all agreed again and again how provoking it was to be so disappointed.

'I can guess what his business is, however,' said Mrs Jennings exultingly.

'Can you ma'am?' said almost every body.

'Yes; it is about Miss Williams, I am sure.'

'And who is Miss Williams?' asked Marianne.

'What! do not you know who Miss Williams is? I am sure you must have heard of her before. She is a relation of the Colonel's, my dear; a very near relation. We will not say how near, for fear of shocking the young ladies.' Then lowering her voice a little, she said to Elinor, 'She is his natural daughter.'

'Indeed!'

'Oh! yes; and as like him as she can stare. I dare say the Colonel will leave her all his fortune.'

When Sir John returned, he joined most heartily in the general regret on so unfortunate an event; concluding however by observing, that as they were all got together, they must do something by way of being happy; and after some consultation it was agreed, that although happiness could only be enjoyed at Whitwell, they might procure a tolerable composure of mind by driving about the country. The carriages were then ordered; Willoughby's was first, and Marianne never looked happier than when she got into it. He drove through the park very fast, and they were soon out of sight; and nothing more of them was seen till their return, which did not happen till after the return of all the rest. They both seemed delighted with their drive, but said only in general terms that they had kept in the lanes, while the others went on the downs.

It was settled that there should be a dance in the evening, and that every body should be extremely merry all day long. Some more of the Careys came to dinner, and they had the pleasure of sitting down nearly twenty to table, which Sir John observed with great contentment. Willoughby took his usual place between the two elder Miss Dashwoods. Mrs Jennings sat on Elinor's right hand; and they had not been long seated, before she leant behind her and Willoughby and said to Marianne, loud enough for them both to hear, 'I have found you out in spite of all your tricks. I know where you spent the morning.'

Marianne coloured, and replied very hastily, 'Where, pray?' –

'Did not you know,' said Willoughby, 'that we had been out in my curricle?'

'Yes, yes, Mr Impudence, I know that very well, and I was determined to find out *where* you had been to. – I hope you like your house, Miss Marianne. It is a very large one I know, and when I come to see you, I hope you will have new-furnished it, for it wanted it very much, when I was there six years ago.'

Marianne turned away in great confusion. Mrs Jennings laughed heartily; and Elinor found that in her resolution to know where they had been, she had actually made her own woman enquire of Mr Willoughby's groom, and that she had by that method been informed that they had gone to Allenham, and spent a considerable time there in walking about the garden and going all over the house.

Elinor could hardly believe this to be true, as it seemed very unlikely that Willoughby should propose, or Marianne consent, to enter the house while Mrs Smith was in it, with whom Marianne had not the smallest acquaintance.

As soon as they left the dining-room, Elinor enquired of her about it; and great was her surprise when she found that every circumstance related by Mrs Jennings was perfectly true. Marianne was quite angry with her for doubting it.

'Why should you imagine, Elinor, that we did not go there, or that we did not see the house? Is not it what you have often wished to do yourself?'

'Yes, Marianne, but I would not go while Mrs Smith was there, and with no other companion than Mr Willoughby.'

'Mr Willoughby however is the only person who can have a right to shew that house; and as we went in an open carriage, it was impossible to have any other companion. I never spent a pleasanter morning in my life.'

'I am afraid,' replied Elinor, 'that the pleasantness of an employment does not always evince its propriety.'

'On the contrary, nothing can be stronger proof of it, Elinor; for if there had been any real impropriety in what I did, I should have been sensible of it at the time, for we always know when we are acting wrong, and with such a conviction I could have had no pleasure.'

'But, my dear Marianne, as it has already exposed you to some very impertinent remarks, do you not now begin to doubt the discretion of your own conduct?'

'If the impertinent remarks of Mrs Jennings are to be the proof of impropriety in conduct, we are all offending every moment of all our lives. I value not her censure any more than I should do her commendation. I am not sensible of having done any thing wrong in walking over Mrs Smith's grounds, or in seeing her house. They will one day be Mr Willoughby's, and . . .'

'If they were one day to be your own, Marianne, you would not be justified in what you have done.'

She blushed at this hint; but it was even visibly gratifying to her; and after a ten minutes' interval of earnest thought, she came to her sister again, and said with great good humour, 'Perhaps, Elinor, it *was* rather ill-judged in me to go to Allenham; but Mr Willoughby wanted particularly to shew me the place; and it is a charming house I assure you. – There is one remarkably pretty sitting room up stairs; of a nice comfortable size for constant use, and with modern furniture it would be delightful. It is a corner room, and has windows on two sides. On one side you look across the bowling-green, behind the house, to a beautiful hanging wood, and on the other you have a view of the church and village, and, beyond them, of those fine bold hills that we have so often admired. I did not see it to advantage, for nothing could be more forlorn than the furniture, – but if it were newly fitted up – a couple of hundred pounds, Willoughby says, would make it one of the pleasantest summer-rooms in England.'

Could Elinor have listened to her without interruption from the others, she would have described every room in the house with equal delight.

Chapter Fourteen

THE SUDDEN TERMINATION of Colonel Brandon's visit at the park, with his steadiness in concealing its cause, filled the mind and raised the wonder of Mrs Jennings for two or three days; she was a great wonderer, as every one must be who takes a very lively interest in all the comings and goings of all their acquaintance. She wondered with little intermission what could be the reason of it; was sure there must be some bad news, and thought over every kind of distress that could have befallen him, with a fixed determination that he should not escape them all.

'Something very melancholy must be the matter, I am sure,' said she. 'I could see it in his face. Poor man! I am afraid his circumstances may be bad. The estate at Delaford was never reckoned more than two thousand a year, and his brother left every thing sadly involved. I do think he must have been sent for about money matters, for what else can it be? I wonder whether it is so. I would give any thing to know the truth of it. Perhaps it is about Miss Williams and, by the bye, I dare say it is, because he looked so conscious when I mentioned her. May be she is ill in town; nothing in the world more likely, for I have a notion she is always rather sickly. I would lay any wager it is about Miss Williams. It is not so very likely he should be distressed in his circumstances *now*, for he is a very prudent man, and to be sure must have cleared the estate by this time. I wonder what it can be! May be his sister is worse at Avignon, and has sent for him over. His setting off in such a hurry seems very like it. Well, I wish him out of all his trouble with all my heart, and a good wife into the bargain.'

So wondered, so talked Mrs Jennings. Her opinion varying with every fresh conjecture, and all seeming equally probable as they arose. Elinor, though she felt really interested in the welfare of Colonel Brandon, could not bestow all the wonder of his going so suddenly away, which Mrs Jennings was desirous of her feeling; for besides that the circumstance did not in her opinion justify such lasting amazement or variety of speculation, her wonder was otherwise disposed of. It was engrossed by the extraordinary silence of her sister and Willoughby on the subject, which they must know to be peculiarly interesting to them all. As this silence continued, every day made it appear more strange and more incompatible with the disposition of both.

Why they should not openly acknowledge to her mother and herself, what their constant behaviour to each other declared to have taken place, Elinor could not imagine.

She could easily conceive that marriage might not be immediately in their power; for though Willoughby was independent, there was no reason to believe him rich. His estate had been rated by Sir John at about six or seven hundred a year; but he lived at an expense to which that income could hardly be equal, and he had himself often complained of his poverty. But for this strange kind of secrecy maintained by them relative to their engagement, which in fact concealed nothing at all, she could not account; and it was so wholly contradictory to their general opinions and practice, that a doubt sometimes entered her mind of their being really engaged, and this doubt was enough to prevent her making any inquiry of Marianne.

Nothing could be more expressive of attachment to them all, than Willoughby's behaviour. To Marianne it had all the distinguishing tenderness which a lover's heart could give, and to the rest of the family it was the affectionate attention of a son and a brother. The cottage seemed to be considered and loved by him as his home; many more of his hours were spent there than at Allenham; and if no general engagement collected them at the park, the exercise which called him out in the morning was almost certain of ending there, where the rest of the day was spent by himself at the side of Marianne, and by his favourite pointer at her feet.

One evening in particular, about a week after Colonel Brandon had left the country, his heart seemed more than usually open to every feeling of attachment to the objects around him; and on Mrs Dashwood's happening to mention her design of improving the cottage in the spring, he warmly opposed every alteration of a place which affection had established as perfect with him.

'What!' he exclaimed – 'Improve this dear cottage! No. *That* I will never consent to. Not a stone must be added to its walls, not an inch to its size, if my feelings are regarded.'

'Do not be alarmed,' said Miss Dashwood, 'nothing of the kind will be done; for my mother will never have money enough to attempt it.'

'I am heartily glad of it,' he cried. 'May she always be poor, if she can employ her riches no better.'

'Thank you, Willoughby. But you may be assured that I would not sacrifice one sentiment of local attachment of yours, or of any one whom I loved, for all the improvements in the world. Depend upon it that whatever unemployed sum may remain, when I make up my accounts in the spring, I would even rather lay it uselessly by than dispose of it in a manner so painful to you. But are you really so attached to this place as to see no defect in it?'

'I am,' said he. 'To me it is faultless. Nay, more, I consider it as the only form of building in which happiness is attainable, and were I rich enough, I would instantly pull Combe down, and build it up again in the exact plan of this cottage.'

'With dark narrow stairs, and a kitchen that smokes, I suppose,' said Elinor.

'Yes,' cried he in the same eager tone, 'with all and every thing belonging to it; – in no one convenience or *in*convenience about it, should the least variation be perceptible. Then, and then only, under such a roof, I might perhaps be as happy at Combe as I have been at Barton.'

'I flatter myself,' replied Elinor, 'that even under the disadvantage of better rooms and a broader staircase, you will hereafter find your own house as faultless as you now do this.'

'There certainly are circumstances,' said Willoughby, 'which might greatly endear it to me; but this place will always have one claim on my affection, which no other can possibly share.'

Mrs Dashwood looked with pleasure at Marianne, whose fine eyes were fixed so expressively on Willoughby, as plainly denoted how well she understood him.

'How often did I wish,' added he, 'when I was at Allenham this time twelvemonth, that Barton cottage was inhabited! I never passed within view of it without admiring its situation, and grieving that no one should live in it. How little did I then think that the very first news I should hear from Mrs Smith, when I next came into the country, would be that Barton cottage was taken: and I felt an immediate satisfaction and interest in the event, which nothing but a kind of prescience of what happiness I should experience from it, can account for. Must it not have been so, Marianne?' speaking to her in a lowered voice. Then continuing his former tone, he said, 'And yet this house you would spoil, Mrs Dashwood? You would rob it of its simplicity by imaginary improvement! and this dear parlour, in which our acquaintance first began, and in which so many happy hours have been since spent by us together, you would degrade to the condition of a common entrance, and every body would be eager to pass through the room which has hitherto contained within itself, more real accommodation and comfort than any other apartment of the handsomest dimensions in the world could possibly afford.'

Mrs Dashwood again assured him that no alteration of the kind should be attempted.

'You are a good woman,' he warmly replied. 'Your promise makes me easy. Extend it a littler farther, and it will make me happy. Tell me that not only your house will remain the same, but that I shall ever find you and yours as unchanged as your dwelling; and that you will always consider me with the kindness which has made every thing belonging to you so dear to me.'

The promise was readily given, and Willoughby's behaviour during the whole of the evening declared at once his affection and happiness.

'Shall we see you tomorrow to dinner?' said Mrs Dashwood when he was leaving them. 'I do not ask you to come in the morning, for we must walk to the park, to call on Lady Middleton.'

He engaged to be with them by four o'clock.

Chapter Fifteen

MRS DASHWOOD'S VISIT to Lady Middleton took place the next day, and two of her daughters went with her; but Marianne excused herself from being of the party under some trifling pretext of employment; and her mother, who

concluded that a promise had been made by Willoughby the night before of
calling on her while they were absent, was perfectly satisfied with her
remaining at home.

On their return from the park they found Willoughby's curricle and
servant in waiting at the cottage, and Mrs Dashwood was convinced that her
conjecture had been just. So far it was all as she had foreseen; but on entering
the house she beheld what no foresight had taught her to expect. They were
no sooner in the passage than Marianne came hastily out of the parlour
apparently in violent affliction, with her handkerchief at her eyes; and
without noticing them ran up stairs. Surprised and alarmed they proceeded
directly into the room she had just quitted, where they found only Willoughby, who was leaning against the mantle-piece with his back towards
them. He turned round on their coming in, and his countenance shewed
that he strongly partook of the emotion which overpowered Marianne.

'Is any thing the matter with her?' cried Mrs Dashwood as she entered
– 'is she ill?'

'I hope not,' he replied, trying to look cheerful; and with a forced smile
presently added, 'It is I who may rather expect to be ill – for I am now
suffering under a very heavy disappointment!'

'Disappointment!'

'Yes, for I am unable to keep my engagement with you. Mrs Smith has
this morning exercised the privilege of riches upon a poor dependant cousin,
by sending me on business to London. I have just received my dispatches,
and taken my farewel of Allenham; and by way of exhilaration I am now
come to take my farewel of you.'

'To London! – and are you going this morning?'

'Almost this moment.'

'This is very unfortunate. But Mrs Smith must be obliged; – and her
business will not detain you from us long I hope.'

He coloured as he replied, 'You are very kind, but I have no idea of
returning into Devonshire immediately. My visits to Mrs Smith are never
repeated within the twelvemonth.'

'And is Mrs Smith your only friend? Is Allenham the only house in the
neighbourhood to which you will be welcome? For shame, Willoughby. Can
you wait for an invitation here?'

His colour increased; and with his eyes fixed on the ground he only
replied, 'You are too good.'

Mrs Dashwood looked at Elinor with surprise. Elinor felt equal amazement. For a few moments every one was silent. Mrs Dashwood first spoke.

'I have only to add, my dear Willoughby, that at Barton cottage you will
always be welcome; for I will not press you to return here immediately,
because you only can judge how far that might be pleasing to Mrs Smith;
and on this head I shall be no more disposed to question your judgment than
to doubt your inclination.'

'My engagements at present,' replied Willoughby confusedly, 'are of
such a nature – that – I dare not flatter myself – '

He stopt. Mrs Dashwood was too much astonished to speak, and another
pause succeeded. This was broken by Willoughby, who said with a faint
smile, 'It is folly to linger in this manner. I will not torment myself any
longer by remaining among friends whose society it is impossible for me
now to enjoy.'

He then hastily took leave of them all and left the room. They saw him step into his carriage, and in a minute it was out of sight.

Mrs Dashwood felt too much for speech, and instantly quitted the parlour to give way in solitude to the concern and alarm which this sudden departure occasioned.

Elinor's uneasiness was at least equal to her mother's. She thought of what had just passed with anxiety and distrust. Willoughby's behaviour in taking leave of them, his embarrassment, and affection of cheerfulness, and, above all, his unwillingness to accept her mother's invitation, a backwardness so unlike a lover, so unlike himself, greatly disturbed her. One moment she feared that no serious design had ever been formed on his side; and the next that some unfortunate quarrel had taken place between him and her sister; – the distress in which Marianne had quitted the room was such as a serious quarrel could most reasonably account for, though when she considered what Marianne's love for him was, a quarrel seemed almost impossible.

But whatever might be the particulars of their separation, her sister's affliction was indubitable; and she thought with the tenderest compassion of that violent sorrow which Marianne was in all probability not merely giving way to as a relief, but feeding and encouraging as a duty.

In about half an hour her mother returned, and though her eyes were red, her countenance was not uncheerful.

'Our dear Willoughby is now some miles from Barton, Elinor,' said she, as she sat down to work, 'and with how heavy a heart does he travel?'

'It is all very strange. So suddenly to be gone! It seems but the work of a moment. And last night he was with us so happy, so cheerful, so affectionate? And now after only ten minutes notice – Gone too without intending to return! – Something more than what he owned to us must have happened. He did not speak, he did not behave like himself. You must have seen the difference as well as I. What can it be? Can they have quarrelled? Why else should he have shewn such unwillingness to accept your invitation here?' –

'It was not inclination that he wanted, Elinor; I could plainly see *that*. He had not the power of accepting it. I have thought it all over I assure you, and I can perfectly account for every thing that at first seemed strange to me as well as to you.'

'Can you indeed?'

'Yes. I have explained it to myself in the most satisfactory way; – but you, Elinor, who love to doubt where you can – It will not satisfy *you*, I know; but you shall not talk *me* out of my trust in it. I am persuaded that Mrs Smith suspects his regard for Marianne, disapproves of it, (perhaps because she has other views for him,) and on that account is eager to get him away; – and that the business which she sends him off to transact, is invented as an excuse to dismiss him. This is what I believe to have happened. He is moreover aware that she *does* disapprove the connection, he dares not therefore at present confess to her his engagement with Marianne, and he feels himself obliged, from his dependent situation, to give into her schemes, and absent himself from Devonshire for a while. You will tell me, I know, that this may, or may *not* have happened; but I will listen to no cavil, unless you can point out any other method of understanding the affair as satisfactory as this. And now, Elinor, what have you to say?'

'Nothing, for you have anticipated my answer.'

'Then you would have told me, that it might or might not have happened. Oh! Elinor, how incomprehensible are your feelings! You had rather take evil upon credit than good. You had rather look out for misery for Marianne and guilt for poor Willoughby, than an apology for the latter. You are resolved to think him blameable, because he took leave of us with less affection than his usual behaviour has shewn. And is no allowance to be made for inadvertence, or for spirits depressed by recent disappointment? Are no probabilities to be accepted, merely because they are not certainties? Is nothing due to the man whom we have all so much reason to love, and no reason in the world to think ill of? To the possibility of motives unanswerable in themselves, though unavoidably secret for a while? And, after all, what is it you suspect him of?'

'I can hardly tell you myself. – But suspicion of something unpleasant is the inevitable consequence of such an alteration as we have just witnessed in him. There is great truth, however, in what you have now urged of the allowances which ought to be made for him, and it is my wish to be candid in my judgment of every body. Willoughby may undoubtedly have very sufficient reasons for his conduct, and I will hope that he has. But it would have been more like Willoughby to acknowledge them at once. Secrecy may be advisable; but still I cannot help wondering at its being practised by him.'

'Do not blame him, however, for departing from his character, where the deviation is necessary. But you really do admit the justice of what I have said in his defence? – I am happy – and he is acquitted.'

'Not entirely. It may be proper to conceal their engagement (if they *are* engaged) from Mrs Smith – and if that is the case, it must be highly expedient for Willoughby to be but little in Devonshire at present. But this is no excuse for their concealing it from us.'

'Concealing it from us! my dear child, do you accuse Willoughby and Marianne of concealment? This is strange indeed, when your eyes have been reproaching them every day for incautiousness.'

'I want no proof of their affection,' said Elinor; 'but of their engagement I do.'

'I am perfectly satisfied of both.'

'Yet not a syllable has been said to you on the subject, by either of them.'

'I have not wanted syllables where actions have spoken so plainly. Has not his behaviour to Marianne and to all of us, for at least the last fortnight, declared that he loved and considered her as his future wife, and that he felt for us the attachment of the nearest relation? Have we not perfectly understood each other? Has not my consent been daily asked by his looks, his manner, his attentive and affectionate respect? My Elinor, is it possible to doubt their engagement? How could such a thought occur to you? How is it to be supposed that Willoughby, persuaded as he must be of your sister's love, should leave her, and leave her perhaps for months, without telling her of his affection; – that they should part without a mutual exchange of confidence?'

'I confess,' replied Elinor, 'that every circumstance except *one* is in favour of their engagement; but that *one* is the total silence of both on the subject, and with me it almost outweighs every other.'

'How strange this is! You must think wretchedly indeed of Willoughby, if after all that has openly passed between them, you can doubt the nature of the terms on which they are together. Has he been acting a part in his behaviour to your sister all this time? Do you suppose him really indifferent to her?'

'No, I cannot think that. He must and does love her I am sure.'

'But with a strange kind of tenderness, if he can leave her with such indifference, such carelessness of the future, as you attribute to him.'

'You must remember, my dear mother, that I have never considered this matter as certain. I have had my doubts, I confess; but they are fainter than they were, and they may soon be entirely done away. If we find they correspond, every fear of mine will be removed.'

'A mighty concession indeed! If you were to see them at the altar, you would suppose they were going to be married. Ungracious girl! But I require no such proof. Nothing in my opinion has ever passed to justify doubt; no secrecy has been attempted; all has been uniformly open and unreserved. You cannot doubt your sister's wishes. It must be Willoughby therefore who you suspect. But why? Is he not a man of honour and feeling? Has there been any inconsistency on his side to create alarm? can he be deceitful?'

'I hope not, I believe not,' cried Elinor. 'I love Willoughby, sincerely love him; and suspicion of his integrity cannot be more painful to yourself than to me. It has been involuntary, and I will not encourage it. I was startled, I confess, by the alteration in his manners this morning; – he did not speak like himself, and did not return your kindness with any cordiality. But all this may be explained by such a situation of his affairs as you have supposed. He had just parted from my sister, had seen her leave him in the greatest affliction; and if he felt obliged, from a fear of offending Mrs Smith, to resist the temptation of returning here soon, and yet aware that by declining your invitation, by saying that he was going away for some time, he should seem to act an ungenerous, a suspicious part by our family, he might well be embarrassed and disturbed. In such a case, a plain and open avowal of his difficulties would have been more to his honour I think, as well as more consistent with his general character; – but I will not raise objections against any one's conduct on so illiberal a foundation, as a difference in judgment from myself, or a deviation from what I may think right and consistent.'

'You speak very properly. Willoughby certainly does not deserve to be suspected. Though we have not known him long, he is no stranger in this part of the world; and who has ever spoken to his disadvantage? Had he been in a situation to act independently and marry immediately, it might have been odd that he should leave us without acknowledging every thing to me at once: but this is not the case. It is an engagement in some respects not prosperously begun, for their marriage must be at a very uncertain distance; and even secrecy, as far as it can be observed, may now be very advisable.'

They were interrupted by the entrance of Margaret; and Elinor was then at liberty to think over the representations of her mother, to acknowledge the probability of many, and hope for the justice of all.

They saw nothing of Marianne till dinner time, when she entered the room and took her place at the table without saying a word. Her eyes were red and swollen; and it seemed as if her tears were even then restrained with difficulty. She avoided the looks of them all, could neither eat nor speak, and after some time, on her mother's silently pressing her hand with tender compassion, her small degree of fortitude was quite overcome, she burst into tears and left the room.

This violent oppression of spirits continued the whole evening. She was without any power, because she was without any desire of command over herself. The slightest mention of any thing relative to Willoughby overpowered her in an instant; and though her family were most anxiously attentive to her comfort, it was impossible for them, if they spoke at all, to keep clear of every subject which her feelings connected with him.

Chapter Sixteen

MARIANNE WOULD HAVE THOUGHT herself very inexcusable had she been able to sleep at all the first night after parting from Willoughby. She would have been ashamed to look her family in the face the next morning, had she not risen from her bed in more need of repose than when she lay down in it. But the feelings which made such composure a disgrace, left her in no danger of incurring it. She was awake the whole night, and she wept the greatest part of it. She got up with an headache, was unable to talk, and unwilling to take any nourishment; giving pain every moment to her mother and sisters, and forbidding all attempt at consolation from either. Her sensibility was potent enough!

When breakfast was over she walked out by herself, and wandered about the village of Allenham, indulging the recollection of past enjoyment and crying over the present reverse for the chief of the morning.

The evening passed off in the equal indulgence of feeling. She played over every favourite song that she had been used to play to Willoughby, every air in which their voices had been oftenest joined, and sat at the instrument gazing on every line of music that he had written out for her, till her heart was so heavy that no farther sadness could be gained; and this nourishment of grief was every day applied. She spent whole hours at the pianoforté alternately singing and crying; her voice often totally suspended by her tears. In books too, as well as in music, she courted the misery which a contrast between the past and present was certain of giving. She read nothing but what they had been used to read together.

Such violence of affliction indeed could not be supported for ever; it sunk within a few days into a calmer melancholy; but these employments, to which she daily recurred, her solitary walks and silent meditations, still produced occasional effusions of sorrow as lively as ever.

No letter from Willoughby came; and none seemed expected by Marianne. Her mother was surprised, and Elinor again became uneasy. But Mrs Dashwood could find explanations whenever she wanted them, which at least satisfied herself.

'Remember, Elinor,' said she, 'how very often Sir John fetches our letters himself from the post, and carries them to it. We have already agreed that secrecy may be necessary, and we must acknowledge that it could not be maintained if their correspondence were to pass through Sir John's hands.'

Elinor could not deny the truth of this, and she tried to find in it a motive sufficient for their silence. But there was one method so direct, so simple, and in her opinion so eligible of knowing the real state of the affair, and of instantly removing all mystery, that she could not help suggesting it to her mother.

'Why do you not ask Marianne at once,' said she, 'whether she is or is not engaged to Willoughby? From you, her mother, and so kind, so indulgent a mother, the question could not give offence. It would be the natural result of your affection for her. She used to be all unreserve, and to you more especially.'

'I would not ask such a question for the world. Supposing it possible that they are not engaged, what distress would not such an inquiry inflict! At any rate it would be most ungenerous. I should never deserve her confidence again, after forcing from her a confession of what is meant at present to be unacknowledged to any one. I know Marianne's heart: I know that she dearly loves me, and that I shall not be the last to whom the affair is made known, when circumstances make the revealment of it eligible. I would not attempt to force the confidence of any one; of a child much less; because a sense of duty would prevent the denial which her wishes might direct.'

Elinor thought this generosity overstrained, considering her sister's youth, and urged the matter farther, but in vain; common sense, common care, common prudence, were all sunk in Mrs Dashwood's romantic delicacy.

It was several days before Willoughby's name was mentioned before Marianne by any of her family; Sir John and Mrs Jennings, indeed, were not so nice; their witticisms added pain to many a painful hour; – but one evening, Mrs Dashwood, accidentally taking up a volume of Shakespeare, exclaimed,

'We have never finished Hamlet, Marianne; our dear Willoughby went away before we could get through it. We will put it by, and when he comes again ... But it may be months, perhaps, before *that* happens.'

'Months!' cried Marianne, with strong surprise. 'No – nor many weeks.'

Mrs Dashwood was sorry for what she had said; but it gave Elinor pleasure, as it produced a reply from Marianne so expressive of confidence in Willoughby and knowledge of his intentions.

One morning, about a week after his leaving the country, Marianne was prevailed on to join her sisters in their usual walk, instead of wandering away by herself. Hitherto she had carefully avoided every companion in her rambles. If her sisters intended to walk on the downs, she directly stole away towards the lanes; if they talked of the valley, she was as speedy in climbing the hills, and could never be found when the others set off. But at length she was secured by the exertions of Elinor, who greatly disapproved such continual seclusion. They walked along the road through the valley, and chiefly in silence, for Marianne's *mind* could not be controlled, and Elinor, satisfied with gaining one point, would not then attempt more. Beyond the entrance of the valley, where the country, though still rich, was less wild and more open, a long stretch of the road which they had travelled on first coming to Barton, lay before them; and on reaching that point, they stopped to look around them, and examine a prospect which formed the distance of their view from the cottage, from a spot which they had never happened to reach in any of their walks before.

Amongst the objects in the scene, they soon discovered an animated one; it was a man on horseback riding towards them. In a few minutes they could distinguish him to be a gentleman; and in a moment afterwards Marianne rapturously exclaimed,

'It is he; it is indeed; – I know it is!' – And was hastening to meet him, when Elinor cried out,

'Indeed, Marianne, I think you are mistaken. It is not Willoughby. The person is not tall enough for him, and has not his air.'

'He has, he has,' cried Marianne, 'I am sure he has. His air, his coat, his horse. I knew how soon he would come.'

She walked eagerly on as she spoke; and Elinor, to screen Marianne from particularity, as she felt almost certain of its not being Willoughby, quickened her pace and kept up with her. They were soon within thirty yards of the gentleman. Marianne looked again; her heart sunk within her; and abruptly turning round, she was hurrying back, when the voices of both her sisters were raised to detain her, a third, almost as well known as Willoughby's, joined them in begging her to stop, and she turned round with surprise to see and welcome Edward Ferrars.

He was the only person in the world who could at that moment be forgiven for not being Willoughby; the only one who could have gained a smile from her; but she dispersed her tears to smile on *him*, and in her sister's happiness forgot for a time her own disappointment.

He dismounted, and giving his horse to his servant, walked back with them to Barton, whither he was purposely coming to visit them.

He was welcomed by them all with great cordiality, but especially by Marianne, who shewed more warmth of regard in her reception of him than even Elinor herself. To Marianne, indeed, the meeting between Edward and her sister was but a continuation of that unaccountable coldness which she had often observed at Norland in their mutual behaviour. On Edward's side, more particularly, there was a deficiency of all that a lover ought to look and say on such an occasion. He was confused, seemed scarcely sensible of pleasure in seeing them, looked neither rapturous nor gay, said little but what was forced from him by questions, and distinguished Elinor by no mark of affection. Marianne saw and listened with increasing surprise. She began almost to feel a dislike of Edward; and it ended, as every feeling must end with her, by carrying back her thoughts to Willoughby, whose manners formed a contrast sufficiently striking to those of his brother elect.

After a short silence which succeeded the first surprise and inquiries of meeting, Marianne asked Edward if he came directly from London. No, he had been in Devonshire a fortnight.

'A fortnight!' she repeated, surprised at his being so long in the same county with Elinor without seeing her before.

He looked rather distressed as he added, that he had been staying with some friends near Plymouth.

'Have you been lately in Sussex?' said Elinor.

'I was at Norland about a month ago.'

'And how does dear, dear Norland look?' cried Marianne.

'Dear, dear Norland,' said Elinor, 'probably looks much as it always does at this time of year. The woods and walks thickly covered with dead leaves.'

'Oh!' cried Marianne, 'with what transporting sensations have I formerly seen them fall! How have I delighted, as I walked, to see them driven in showers about me by the wind! What feelings have they, the season, the air altogether inspired! Now there is no one to regard them. They are seen only as a nuisance, swept hastily off, and driven as much as possible from the sight.'

'It is not every one,' said Elinor, 'who has your passion for dead leaves.'

'No; my feelings are not often shared, not often understood. But *sometimes* they are.' – As she said this, she sunk into a reverie for a few moments; – but rousing herself again, 'Now, Edward,' said she, calling his attention to the prospect, 'here is Barton valley. Look up to it, and be tranquil if you can. Look at those hills! Did you ever see their equals? To the left is Barton park, amongst those woods and plantations. You may see one end of the house. And there, beneath that farthest hill, which rises with such grandeur, is our cottage.'

'It is a beautiful country,' he replied; 'but these bottoms must be dirty in winter.'

'How can you think of dirt, with such objects before you?'

'Because,' replied he, smiling, 'among the rest of the objects before me, I see a very dirty lane.'

'How strange!' said Marianne to herself as she walked on.

'Have you an agreeable neighbourhood here? Are the Middletons pleasant people?'

'No, not at all,' answered Marianne, 'we could not be more unfortunately situated.'

'Marianne,' cried her sister, 'how can you say so? How can you be so unjust? They are a very respectable family, Mr Ferrars; and towards us have behaved in the friendliest manner. Have you forgot, Marianne, how many pleasant days we have owed to them?'

'No,' said Marianne in a low voice, 'nor how many painful moments.'

Elinor took no notice of this, and directing her attention to their visitor, endeavoured to support something like discourse with him by talking of their present residence, its conveniences, &c. extorting from him occasional questions and remarks. His coldness and reserve mortified her severely; she was vexed and half angry; but resolving to regulate her behaviour to him by the past rather than the present, she avoided every appearance of resentment or displeasure, and treated him as she thought he ought to be treated from the family connection.

Chapter Seventeen

MRS DASHWOOD WAS SURPRISED only for a moment at seeing him; for his coming to Barton was, in her opinon, of all things the most natural. Her joy and expressions of regard long outlived her wonder. He received the kindest welcome from her; and shyness, coldness, reserve could not stand against such a reception. They had begun to fail him before he entered the house, and they were quite overcome by the captivating manners of Mrs Dashwood. Indeed a man could not very well be in love with either of her daughters, without extending the passion to her; and Elinor had the satisfaction of seeing him soon become more like himself. His affections seemed to reanimate towards them all, and his interest in their welfare again became perceptible.

He was not in spirits however; he praised their house, admired its prospects, was attentive, and kind; but still he was not in spirits. The whole family perceived it, and Mrs Dashwood, attributing it to some want of liberality in his mother, sat down to table indignant against all selfish parents.

'What are Mrs Ferrars's views for you at present, Edward?' said she, when dinner was over and they had drawn round the fire; 'are you still to be a great orator in spite of yourself?'

'No. I hope my mother is now convinced that I have no more talents than inclination for a public life!'

'But how is your fame to be established? for famous you must be to satisfy all your family; and with no inclination for expense, no affection for strangers, no profession, and no assurance, you may find it a difficult matter.'

'I shall not attempt it. I have no wish to be distinguished; and I have every reason to hope I never shall. Thank Heaven! I cannot be forced into genius and eloquence.'

'You have no ambition, I well know. Your wishes are all moderate.'

'As moderate as those of the rest of the world, I believe. I wish as well as every body else to be perfectly happy; but like every body else it must be in my own way. Greatness will not make me so.'

'Strange if it would!' cried Marianne. 'What have wealth or grandeur to do with happiness?'

'Grandeur has but little,' said Elinor, 'but wealth has much to do with it.'

'Elinor, for shame!' said Marianne; 'money can only give happiness where there is nothing else to give it. Beyond a competence, it can afford no real satisfaction, as far as mere self is concerned.'

'Perhaps,' said Elinor, smiling, 'we may come to the same point. *Your* competence and *my* wealth are very much alike, I dare say; and without them, as the world goes now, we shall both agree that every kind of external comfort must be wanting. Your ideas are only more noble than mine. Come, what is your competence?'

'About eighteen hundred or two thousand a-year; not more than *that*.'

Elinor laughed. '*Two* thousand a-year! *One* is my wealth! I guessed how it would end.'

'And yet two thousand a-year is a very moderate income,' said Marianne. 'A family cannot well be maintained on a smaller. I am sure I am not extravagant in my demands. A proper establishment of servants, a carriage, perhaps two, and hunters, cannot be supported on less.'

Elinor smiled again, to hear her sister describing so accurately their future expenses at Combe Magna.

'Hunters' repeated Edward – 'But why must you have hunters? Every body does not hunt.'

Marianne coloured as she replied, 'But most people do.'

'I wish,' said Margaret, striking out a novel thought, 'that somebody would give us all a large fortune apiece!'

'Oh that they would!' cried Marianne, her eyes sparkling with animation, and her cheeks glowing with the delight of such imaginary happiness.

'We are all unanimous in that wish, I suppose,' said Elinor, 'in spite of the insufficiency of wealth.'

'Oh dear!' cried Margaret, 'how happy I should be! I wonder what I should do with it!'

Marianne looked as if she had no doubt on that point.

'I should be puzzled to spend a large fortune myself,' said Mrs Dashwood, 'if my children were all to be rich without my help.'

'You must begin your improvements on this house,' observed Elinor, 'and your difficulties will soon vanish.'

'What magnificent orders would travel from this family to London,' said Edward, 'in such an event! What a happy day for booksellers, music-sellers, and print-shops! You, Miss Dashwood, would give a general commission for every new print of merit to be sent you – and as for Marianne, I know her greatness of soul, there would not be music enough in London to content her. And books! – Thomson, Cowper, Scott – she would buy them all over and over again; she would buy up every copy, I believe, to prevent their falling into unworthy hands; and she would have every book that tells her how to admire an old twisted tree. Should not you, Marianne? Forgive me, if I am very saucy. But I was willing to shew you that I had not forgot our old disputes.'

'I love to be reminded of the past, Edward – whether it be melancholy or gay, I love to recall it – and you will never offend me by talking of former times. You are very right in supposing how my money would be spent – some of it, at least – my loose cash would certainly be employed in improving my collection of music and books.'

'And the bulk of your fortune would be laid out in annuities on the authors or their heirs.'

'No, Edward, I should have something else to do with it.'

'Perhaps then you would bestow it as a reward on that person who wrote the ablest defence of your favourite maxim, that no one can ever be in love more than once in their life – for your opinion on that point is unchanged, I presume?'

'Undoubtedly. At my time of life opinions are tolerably fixed. It is not likely that I should now see or hear anything to change them.'

'Marianne is as steadfast as ever, you see,' said Elinor, 'she is not at all altered.'

'She is only grown a little more grave than she was.'

'Nay, Edward,' said Marianne, '*you* need not reproach me. You are not very gay yourself.'

'Why should you think so!' replied he, with a sigh. 'But gaiety never was a part of *my* character.'

'Nor do I think it a part of Marianne's,' said Elinor; 'I should hardly call her a lively girl – she is very earnest, very eager in all she does – sometimes talks a great deal and always with animation – but she is not often really merry.'

'I believe you are right,' he replied, 'and yet I have always set her down as a lively girl.'

'I have frequently detected myself in such kind of mistakes,' said Elinor, 'in a total misapprehension of character in some point or other: fancying people so much more gay or grave, or ingenious or stupid than they really are, and I can hardly tell why or in what the deception originated. Sometimes one is guided by what they say of themselves, and very frequently by what other people say of them, without giving oneself time to deliberate and judge.'

'But I thought it was right, Elinor,' said Marianne, 'to be guided wholly by the opinion of other people. I thought our judgments were given us merely to be subservient to those of our neighbours. This has always been your doctrine, I am sure.'

'No, Marianne, never. My doctrine has never aimed at the subjection of the understanding. All I have ever attempted to influence has been the behaviour. You must not confound my meaning. I am guilty, I confess, of having often wished you to treat our acquaintance in general with greater attention; but when have I advised you to adopt their sentiments or conform to their judgment in serious matters?'

'You have not been able to bring your sister over to your plan of general civility,' said Edward to Elinor. 'Do you gain no ground'?

'Quite the contrary,' replied Elinor, looking expressively at Marianne.

'My judgment,' he returned, 'is all on your side of the question; but I am afraid my practice is much more on your sister's. I never wish to offend, but I am so foolishly shy, that I often seem negligent, when I am only kept back by my natural awkwardness. I have frequently thought that I must have been intended by nature to be fond of low company, I am so little at my ease among strangers of gentility!'

'Marianne has not shyness to excuse any inattention of hers,' said Elinor.

'She knows her own worth too well for false shame,' replied Edward. 'Shyness is only the effect of a sense of inferiority in some way or other. If I could persuade myself that my manners were perfectly easy and graceful, I should not be shy.'

'But you would still be reserved,' said Marianne, 'and that is worse.'

Edward stared – 'Reserved! Am I reserved, Marianne?'

'Yes, very.'

'I do not understand you,' replied he, colouring. 'Reserved! – how, in what manner? What am I to tell you? What can you suppose?'

Elinor looked surprised at his emotion, but trying to laugh off the subject, she said to him, 'Do not you know my sister well enough to understand what she means? Do not you know she calls every one reserved who does not talk as fast, and admire what she admires as rapturously as herself?'

Edward made no answer. His gravity and thoughtfulness returned on him in their fullest extent – and he sat for some time silent and dull.

Chapter Eighteen

ELINOR SAW, WITH GREAT uneasiness, the low spirits of her friend. His visit afforded her but a very partial satisfaction, while his own enjoyment in it appeared so imperfect. If was evident that he was unhappy; she wished it were equally evident that he still distinguished her by the same affection which once she had felt no doubt of inspiring; but hitherto the continuance of his preference seemed very uncertain; and the reservedness of his manner towards her contradicted one moment what a more animated look had intimated the preceding one.

He joined her and Marianne in the breakfast-room the next morning before the others were down; and Marianne, who was always eager to promote their happiness as far as she could, soon left them to themselves. But before she was half way upstairs she heard the parlour door open, and, turning round, was astonished to see Edward himself come out.

'I am going into the village to see my horses,' said he, 'as you are not yet ready for breakfast; I shall be back again presently.'

Edward returned to them with fresh admiration of the surrounding country; in his walk to the village, he had seen many parts of the valley to advantage; and the village itself, in a much higher situation than the cottage, afforded a general view of the whole, which had exceedingly pleased him. This was a subject which ensured Marianne's attention, and she was beginning to describe her own admiration of these scenes, and to question him more minutely on the objects that had particularly struck him, when Edward interrupted her by saying, 'You must not inquire too far, Marianne – remember I have no knowledge in the picturesque, and I shall offend you by my ignorance and want of taste if we come to particulars. I shall call hills steep, which ought to be bold; surfaces strange and uncouth, which ought to be irregular and rugged; and distant objects out of sight, which ought only to be indistinct through the soft medium of a hazy atmosphere. You must be satisfied with such admiration as I can honestly give. I call it a very fine country – the hills are steep, the woods seem full of fine timber, and the valley looks comfortable and snug – with rich meadows and several neat farm houses scattered here and there. It exactly answers my idea of a fine country, because it unites beauty with utility – and I dare say it is a picturesque one too, because you admire it; I can easily believe it to be full of rocks and promontories, grey moss and brush wood, but these are all lost on me. I know nothing of the picturesque.'

'I am afraid it is but too true,' said Marianne; 'but why should you boast of it?'

'I suspect,' said Elinor, 'that to avoid one kind of affectation, Edward here falls into another. Because he believes many people pretend to more admiration of the beauties of nature than they really feel, and is disgusted with such pretensions, he affects greater indifference and less discrimination in viewing them himself than he possesses. He is fastidious and will have an affectation of his own.'

'It is very true,' said Marianne, 'that admiration of landscape scenery is become a mere jargon. Every body pretends to feel and tries to describe with the taste and elegance of him who first defined what picturesque beauty was. I detest jargon of every kind, and sometimes I have kept my feelings to myself, because I could find no language to describe them in but what was worn and hackneyed out of all sense and meaning.'

'I am convinced,' said Edward, 'that you really feel all the delight in a fine prospect which you profess to feel. But, in return, your sister must allow me to feel no more than I profess. I like a fine prospect, but not on picturesque principles. I do not like crooked, twisted, blasted trees. I admire them much more if they are tall, straight and flourishing. I do not like ruined, tattered cottages. I am not fond of nettles, or thistles, or heath blossoms. I have more pleasure in a snug farm-house than a watch-tower – and a troop of tidy, happy villagers please me better than the finest banditti in the world.'

Marianne looked with amazement at Edward, with compassion at her sister. Elinor only laughed.

The subject was continued no farther; and Marianne remained thoughtfully silent, till a new object suddenly engaged her attention. She was sitting by Edward, and in taking his tea from Mrs Dashwood, his hand passed so directly before her, as to make a ring, with a plait of hair in the centre, very conspicuous on one of his fingers.

'I never saw you wear a ring before, Edward,' she cried. 'Is that Fanny's hair? I remember her promising to give you some. But I should have thought her hair had been darker.'

Marianne spoke inconsiderately what she really felt – but when she saw how much she had pained Edward, her own vexation at her want of thought could not be surpassed by his. He coloured very deeply, and giving a momentary glance at Elinor, replied, 'Yes; it is my sister's hair. The setting always casts a different shade on it you know.'

Elinor had met his eye, and looked conscious likewise. That the hair was her own, she instantaneously felt as well satisfied as Marianne; the only difference in their conclusions was, that what Marianne considered as a free gift from her sister, Elinor was conscious must have been procured by some theft or contrivance unknown to herself. She was not in a humour, however, to regard it as an affront, and affecting to take no notice of what passed, by instantly talking of something else, she internally resolved henceforward to catch every opportunity of eyeing the hair and of satisfying herself, beyond all doubt, that it was exactly the shade of her own.

Edward's embarrassment lasted some time, and it ended in an absence of mind still more settled. He was particularly grave the whole morning. Marianne severely censured herself for what she had said; but her own forgiveness might have been more speedy, had she known how little offence it had given her sister.

Before the middle of the day, they were visited by Sir John and Mrs Jennings, who, having heard of the arrival of a gentleman at the cottage, came to take a survey of the guest. With the assistance of his mother-in-law, Sir John was not long in discovering that the name of Ferrars began with an F. and this prepared a future mine of raillery against the devoted Elinor, which nothing but the newness of their acquaintance with Edward could have prevented from being immediately sprung. But, as it was, she only learned from some very significant looks, how far their penetration, founded on Margaret's instructions, extended.

Sir John never came to the Dashwoods without either inviting them to dine at the park the next day, or to drink tea with them that evening. On the present occasion, for the better entertainment of their visitor, towards whose amusement he felt himself bound to contribute, he wished to engage them for both.

'You *must* drink tea with us tonight,' said he, 'for we shall be quite alone – and tomorrow you must absolutely dine with us, for we shall be a large party.'

Mrs Jennings enforced the necessity. 'And who knows but you may raise a dance,' said she. 'And that will tempt *you*, Miss Marianne.'

'A dance!' cried Marianne. 'Impossible! Who is to dance?'

'Who! why yourselves, and the Careys, and Whitakers to be sure. –

What! you thought nobody could dance because a certain person that shall be nameless is gone!'

'I wish with all my soul,' cried Sir John, 'that Willoughby were among us again.'

This, and Marianne's blushing, gave new suspicions to Edward. 'And who is Willoughby?' said he, in a low voice, to Miss Dashwood, by whom he was sitting.

She gave him a brief reply. Marianne's countenance was more communicative. Edward saw enough to comprehend, not only the meaning of others, but such of Marianne's expressions as had puzzled him before; and when their visitors left them, he went immediately round to her and said, in a whisper, 'I have been guessing. Shall I tell you my guess?'

'What do you mean?'

'Shall I tell you?'

'Certainly.'

'Well then; I guess that Mr Willoughby hunts.'

Marianne was surprised and confused, yet she could not help smiling at the quiet archness of his manner, and, after a moment's silence, said, ·

'Oh! Edward! How can you? – But the time will come I hope . . . I am sure you will like him.'

'I do not doubt it,' replied he, rather astonished at her earnestness and warmth; for had he not imagined it to be a joke for the good of her acquaintance in general, founded only on a something or a nothing between Mr Willoughby and herself, he would not have ventured to mention it.

Chapter Nineteen

EDWARD REMAINED A WEEK at the cottage; he was earnestly pressed by Mrs Dashwood to stay longer; but as if he were bent only on self-mortification, he seemed resolved to be gone when his enjoyment among his friends was at the height. His spirits, during the last two or three days, though still very unequal, were greatly improved – he grew more and more partial to the house and environs – never spoke of going away without a sigh – declared his time to be wholly disengaged – even doubted to what place he should go when he left them – but still, go he must. Never had any week passed so quickly – he could hardly believe it to be gone. He said so repeatedly; other things he said too, which marked the turn of his feelings and gave the lie to his actions. He had no pleasure at Norland; he detested being in town; but either to Norland or London, he must go. He valued their kindness beyond any thing, and his greatest happiness was in being with them. Yet he must leave them at the end of a week, in spite of their wishes and his own, and without any restraint on his time.

Elinor placed all that was astonishing in this way of acting to his mother's account; and it was happy for her that he had a mother whose character was so imperfectly known to her, as to be the general excuse for every thing strange on the part of her son. Disappointed, however, and vexed as she was, and sometimes displeased with his uncertain behaviour to herself, she was very well disposed on the whole to regard his actions with all the candid allowances and generous qualifications, which had been rather more painfully extorted from her, for Willoughby's service, by her mother. His want of spirits, of openness, and of consistency, were most usually attributed to his want of independence, and his better knowledge of Mrs Ferrars's disposition and designs. The shortness of his visit, the steadiness of his purpose in leaving them, originated in the same fettered inclination, the same inevitable necessity of temporizing with his mother. The old, well-established grievance of duty against will, parent against child, was the cause of all. She would have been glad to know when these difficulties were to cease, this opposition was to yield, – when Mrs Ferrars would be reformed, and her son be at liberty to be happy. But from such vain wishes, she was forced to turn for comfort to the renewal of her confidence in Edward's affection, to the remembrance of every mark of regard in look or word which fell from him while at Barton, and above all to that flattering proof of it which he constantly wore round his finger.

'I think, Edward,' said Mrs Dashwood, as they were at breakfast the last morning, 'you would be a happier man if you had any profession to engage your time and give an interest to your plans and actions. Some inconvenience to your friends, indeed, might result from it – you would not be able to give them so much of your time. But (with a smile) you would be materially benefited in one particular at least – you would know where to go when you left them.'

'I do assure you,' he replied, 'that I have long thought on this point, as you think now. It has been, and is, and probably will always be a heavy misfortune to me, that I have had no necessary business to engage me, no profession to give me employment, or afford me any thing like independence. But unfortunately my own nicety, and the nicety of my friends, have made me what I am, an idle, helpless being. We never could agree in our choice of a profession. I always preferred the church, as I still do. But that was not smart enough for my family. They recommended the army. That was a great deal too smart for me. The law was allowed to be genteel enough; many young men, who had chambers in the Temple, made a very good appearance in the first circles, and drove about town in very knowing gigs. But I had no inclination for the law, even in this less abstruse study of it, which my family approved. As for the navy, it had fashion on its side, but I was too old when the subject was first started to enter it – and, at length, as there was no necessity for my having any profession at all, as I might be as dashing and expensive without a red coat on my back as with one, idleness was pronounced on the whole to be the most advantageous and honourable, and a young man of eighteen is not in general so earnestly bent on being busy as to resist the solicitations of his friends to do nothing. I was therefore entered at Oxford and have been properly idle ever since.'

'The consequence of which, I suppose, will be,' said Mrs Dashwood, 'since leisure has not promoted your own happiness, that your sons will be brought up to as many pursuits, employments, professions, and trades as Columella's.'

'They will be brought up,' said he, in a serious accent, 'to be as unlike myself as is possible. In feeling, in action, in condition, in every thing.'

'Come, come; this is all an effusion of immediate want of spirits, Edward. You are in a melancholy humour, and fancy that any one unlike yourself must be happy. But remember that the pain of parting from friends will be felt by every body at times, whatever be their education or state. Know your own happiness. You want nothing but patience – or give it a more fascinating name, call it hope. Your mother will secure to you, in time, that independence you are so anxious for; it is her duty, and it will, it must ere long become her happiness to prevent your whole youth from being wasted in discontent. How much may not a few months do?'

'I think,' replied Edward, 'that I may defy many months to produce any good to me.'

This desponding turn of mind, though it could not be communicated to Mrs Dashwood, gave additional pain to them all in the parting, which shortly took place, and left an uncomfortable impression on Elinor's feelings especially, which required some trouble and time to subdue. But as it was her determination to subdue it, and to prevent herself from appearing to suffer more than what all her family suffered on his going away, she did not adopt the method so judiciously employed by Marianne, on a similar occasion, to augment and fix her sorrow, by seeking silence, solitude and idleness. Their means were as different as their objects, and equally suited to the advancement of each.

Elinor sat down to her drawing-table as soon as he was out of the house, busily employed herself the whole day, neither sought nor avoided the mention of his name, appeared to interest herself almost as much as ever in the general concerns of the family, and if, by this conduct, she did not lessen her own grief, it was at least prevented from unnecessary increase, and her mother and sisters were spared much solicitude on her account.

Such behaviour as this, so exactly the reverse of her own, appeared no more meritorious to Marianne, than her own had seemed faulty to her. The business of self-command she settled very easily; – with strong affections it was impossible, with calm ones it could have no merit. That her sister's affections *were* calm, she dared not deny, though she blushed to acknowledge it; and of the strength of her own, she gave a very striking proof, by still loving and respecting that sister, in spite of this mortifying conviction.

Without shutting herself up from her family, or leaving the house in determined solitude to avoid them, or laying awake the whole night to indulge meditation, Elinor found every day afforded her leisure enough to think of Edward, and of Edward's behaviour, in every possible variety which the different state of her spirits at different times could produce; – with tenderness, pity, approbation, censure and doubt. There were moments in abundance, when, if not by the absence of her mother and sisters, at least by the nature of their employments, conversation was forbidden among them, and every effect of solitude was produced. Her mind was inevitably at liberty; her thoughts could not be chained elsewhere; and the past and the future, on a subject so interesting, must be before her, must force her attention, and engross her memory, her reflection, and her fancy.

From a reverie of this kind, as she sat at her drawing-table, she was roused one morning, soon after Edward's leaving them, by the arrival of company. She happened to be quite alone. The closing of the little gate, at the entrance of the green court in front of the house, drew her eyes to the window, and she saw a large party walking up to the door. Amongst them were Sir John and Lady Middleton and Mrs Jennings, but there were two others, a gentleman and lady, who were quite unknown to her. She was sitting near the window, and as soon as Sir John perceived her, he left the rest of the party to the ceremony of knocking at the door, and stepping across the turf, obliged her to open the casement to speak to him, though the space was so short between the door and the window, as to make it hardly possible to speak at one without being heard at the other.

'Well,' said he, 'we have brought you some strangers. How do you like them?'

'Hush! they will hear you.'

'Never mind if they do. It is only the Palmers. Charlotte is very pretty, I can tell you. You may see her if you look this way.'

As Elinor was certain of seeing her in a couple of minutes, without taking that liberty, she begged to be excused.

'Where is Marianne? Has she run away because we are come? I see her instrument is open.'

'She is walking, I believe.'

They were now joined by Mrs Jennings, who had not patience enough to wait till the door was opened before she told *her* story. She came hallooing to the window, 'How do you do, my dear? How does Mrs Dashwood do? And where are your sisters? What! all alone! you will be glad of a little company to sit with you. I have brought my other son and daughter to see you. Only think of their coming so suddenly! I thought I heard a carriage last night, while we were drinking our tea, but it never entered my head that it could be them. I thought of nothing but whether it might not be Colonel Brandon come back again; so I said to Sir John, I do think I hear a carriage; perhaps it is Colonel Brandon come back again' –

Elinor was obliged to turn from her, in the middle of her story, to receive the rest of the party; Lady Middleton introduced the two strangers; Mrs Dashwood and Margaret came down stairs at the same time, and they all sat down to look at one another, while Mrs Jennings continued her story as she walked through the passage into the parlour, attended by Sir John.

Mrs Palmer was several years younger than Lady Middleton, and totally unlike her in every respect. She was short and plump, had a very pretty face, and the finest expression of good humour in it that could possibly be. Her manners were by no means so elegant as her sister's, but they were much more prepossessing. She came in with a smile, smiled all the time of her visit, except when she laughed, and smiled when she went away. Her husband was a grave looking young man of five or six and twenty, with an air of more fashion and sense than his wife, but of less willingness to please or be pleased. He entered the room with a look of self-consequence, slightly bowed to the ladies, without speaking a word, and, after briefly surveying them and their apartments, took up a newspaper from the table and continued to read it as long as he stayed.

Mrs Palmer, on the contrary, who was strongly endowed by nature with a turn for being uniformly civil and happy, was hardly seated before her admiration of the parlour and every thing in it burst forth.

'Well! what a delightful room this is! I never saw anything so charming! Only think, mama, how it is improved since I was here last! I always thought it such a sweet place, ma'am! (turning to Mrs Dashwood,) but you have made it so charming! Only look, sister, how delightful every thing is! How I should like such a house for myself! Should not you, Mr Palmer?'

Mr Palmer made her no answer, and did not even raise his eyes from the newspaper.

'Mr Palmer does not hear me,' said she, laughing, 'he never does sometimes. It is so ridiculous!'

This was quite a new idea to Mrs Dashwood, she had never been used to find wit in the inattention of any one, and could not help looking with surprise at them both.

Mrs Jennings in the mean time, talked on as loud as she could, and continued her account of their surprise, the evening before, on seeing their friends, without ceasing till every thing was told. Mrs Palmer laughed heartily at the recollection of their astonishment, and every body agreed, two or three times over, that it had been quite an agreeable surprise.

'You may believe how glad we all were to see them,' added Mrs Jennings, leaning forwards towards Elinor, and speaking in a low voice as if she meant to be heard by no one else, though they were seated on different sides of the room; 'but, however, I can't help wishing they had not travelled quite so fast, nor made such a long journey of it, for they came all round by London upon account of some business, for you know (nodding significantly and pointing to her daughter) it was wrong in her situation. I wanted her to stay at home and rest this morning, but she would come with us; she longed so much to see you all!'

Mrs Palmer laughed, and said it would not do her any harm.

'She expects to be confined in February,' continued Mrs Jennings.

Lady Middleton could no longer endure such a conversation, and therefore exerted herself to ask Mr Palmer if there was any news in the paper.

'No, none at all,' he replied, and read on.

'Here comes Marianne,' cried Sir John. 'Now, Palmer, you shall see a monstrous pretty girl.'

He immediately went into the passage, opened the front door, and ushered her in himself. Mrs Jennings asked her, as soon as she appeared, if she had not been to Allenham; and Mrs Palmer laughed so heartily at the question, as to shew she understood it. Mr Palmer looked up on her entering the room, stared at her some minutes, and then returned to his newspaper. Mrs Palmer's eye was now caught by the drawings which hung round the room. She got up to examine them.

'Oh! dear, how beautiful these are! Well! how delightful! Do but look, mama, how sweet! I declare they are quite charming; I could look at them for ever.' And then sitting down again, she very soon forgot that there were any such things in the room.

When Lady Middleton rose to go away, Mr Palmer rose also, laid down the newspaper, stretched himself, and looked at them all round.

'My love, have you been asleep?' said his wife, laughing.

He made her no answer; and only observed, after again examining the room, that it was very low pitched, and that the ceiling was crooked. He then made his bow and departed with the rest.

Sir John had been very urgent with them all to spend the next day at the park. Mrs Dashwood, who did not chuse to dine with them oftener than they dined at the cottage, absolutely refused on her own account; her daughters might do as they pleased. But they had no curiosity to see how Mr and Mrs Palmer ate their dinner, and no expectation of pleasure from them in any other way. They attempted, therefore, likewise to excuse themselves; the weather was uncertain and not likely to be good. But Sir John would not be satisfied – the carriage should be sent for them and they must come. Lady Middleton too, though she did not press their mother, pressed them. Mrs Jennings and Mrs Palmer joined their entreaties, all seemed equally anxious to avoid a family party; and the young ladies were obliged to yield.

'Why should they ask us?' said Marianne, as soon as they were gone. 'The rent of this cottage is said to be low; but we have it on very hard terms, if we are to dine at the park whenever any one is staying either with them, or with us.'

'They mean no less to be civil and kind to us now,' said Elinor, 'by these frequent invitations than by those which we received from them a few weeks ago. The alteration is not in them, if their parties are grown tedious and dull. We must look for the change elsewhere.'

Chapter Twenty

AS THE MISS DASHWOODS entered the drawing-room of the park the next day, at one door, Mrs Palmer came running in at the other, looking as good humoured and merry as before. She took them all most affectionately by the hand, and expressed great delight in seeing them again.

'I am so glad to see you!' said she, seating herself between Elinor and Marianne, 'for it is so bad a day I was afraid you might not come, which would be a shocking thing, as we go away again tomorrow. We must go, for the Westons come to us next week you know. It was quite a sudden thing our coming at all, and I knew nothing of it till the carriage was coming to the door, and then Mr Palmer asked me if I would go with him to Barton. He is so droll! He never tells me any thing! I am so sorry we cannot stay longer; however we shall meet again in town very soon, I hope.'

They were obliged to put an end to such an expectation.

'Not go to town!' cried Mrs Palmer, with a laugh, 'I shall be quite disappointed if you do not. I could get the nicest house in the world for you, next door to our's, in Hanover-square. You must come, indeed. I am sure I shall be very happy to chaperon you at any time till I am confined, if Mrs Dashwood should not like to go into public.'

They thanked her; but were obliged to resist all her entreaties.

'Oh! my love,' cried Mrs Palmer to her husband, who just then entered the room – 'You must help me persuade the Miss Dashwoods to go to town this winter.'

Her love made no answer; and after slightly bowing to the ladies, began complaining of the weather.

'How horrid all this is!' said he. 'Such weather makes every thing and every body disgusting. Dulness is as much produced within doors as without, by rain. It makes one detest all one's acquaintance. What the devil does Sir John mean by not having a billiards room in his house? How few people know what comfort is! Sir John is as stupid as the weather.'

The rest of the company soon dropt in.

'I am afraid, Miss Marianne,' said Sir John, 'you have not been able to take your usual walk to Allenham today.'

Marianne looked very grave and said nothing.

'Oh! don't be so sly before us,' said Mrs Palmer; 'for we know all about it, I assure you; and I admire your taste very much, for I think he is extremely handsome. We do not live a great way from him in the country, you know. Not above ten miles, I dare say.'

'Much nearer thirty,' said her husband.

'Ah! well! there is not much difference. I never was at his house; but they say it is a sweet pretty place.'

'As vile a spot as I ever saw in my life,' said Mr Palmer.

Marianne remained perfectly silent, though her countenance betrayed her interest in what was said.

'Is it very ugly?' continued Mrs Palmer – 'then it must be some other place that is so pretty I suppose.'

When they were seated in the dining room, Sir John observed with regret that they were only eight altogether.

'My dear,' said he to his lady, 'it is very provoking that we should be so few. Why did you not ask the Gilberts to come to us today?'

'Did not I tell you, Sir John, when you spoke to me about it before, that it could not be done? They dined with us last.'

'You and I, Sir John,' said Mrs Jennings, 'should not stand upon such ceremony.'

'Then you would be very ill-bred,' cried Mr Palmer.

'My love, you contradict every body,' – said his wife with her usual laugh. 'Do you know that you are quite rude?'

'I did not know I contradicted any body in calling your mother ill-bred.'

'Aye, you may abuse me as you please,' said the good-natured old lady, 'you have taken Charlotte off my hands, and cannot give her back again. So there I have the whip hand of you.'

Charlotte laughed heartily to think that her husband could not get rid of her; and exultingly said, she did not care how cross he was to her, as they must live together. It was impossible for any one to be more thoroughly good-natured, or more determined to be happy than Mrs Palmer. The studied indifference, insolence, and discontent of her husband gave her no pain; and when he scolded or abused her, she was highly diverted.

'Mr Palmer is so droll!' said she, in a whisper, to Elinor. 'He is always out of humour.'

Elinor was not inclined, after a little observation, to give him credit for being so genuinely and unaffectedly ill-natured or ill-bred as he wished to appear. His temper might perhaps be a little soured by finding, like many others of his sex, that through some unaccountable bias in favour of beauty, he was the husband of a very silly woman, – but she knew that this kind of blunder was too common for any sensible man to be lastingly hurt by it. – It was rather a wish of distinction she believed, which produced his contemptuous treatment of every body, and his general abuse of every thing before him. It was the desire of appearing superior to other people. The motive was too common to be wondered at; but the means, however they might succeed by establishing his superiority in ill-breeding, were not likely to attach any one to him except his wife.

'Oh! my dear Miss Dashwood,' said Mrs Palmer soon afterwards, 'I have got such a favour to ask of you and your sister. Will you come and spend some time at Cleveland this Christmas? Now, pray do, – and come while the Westons are with us. You cannot think how happy I shall be! It will be quite delightful! – My love,' applying to her husband, 'don't you long to have the Miss Dashwoods come to Cleveland?'

'Certainly,' – he replied with a sneer – 'I came into Devonshire with no other view.'

'There now' – said his lady, 'you see Mr Palmer expects you; so you cannot refuse to come.'

They both eagerly and resolutely declined her invitation.

'But indeed you must and shall come. I am sure you will like it of all things. The Westons will be with us, and it will be quite delightful. You cannot think what a sweet place Cleveland is; and we are so gay now, for Mr Palmer is always going about the country canvassing against the election; and so many people come to dine with us that I never saw before, it is quite charming! But, poor fellow! it is very fatiguing to him! for he is forced to make every body like him.'

Elinor could hardly keep her countenance as she assented to the hardship of such an obligation.

'How charming it will be,' said Charlotte, 'when he is in Parliament! – won't it? How I shall laugh! It will be so ridiculous to see all his letters directed to him with an M.P. – But do you know, he says, he will never frank for me? He declares he won't. Don't you, Mr Palmer?'

Mr Palmer took no notice of her.

'He cannot bear writing, you know,' she continued – 'he says it is quite shocking.'

'No,' said he, 'I never said any thing so irrational. Don't palm all your abuses of language upon me.'

'There now; you see how droll he is. This is always the way with him! Sometimes he won't speak to me for half a day together, and then he comes out with something so droll – all about any thing in the world.'

She surprised Elinor very much as they returned into the drawing-room by asking her whether she did not like Mr Palmer excessively.

'Certainly;' said Elinor, 'he seems very agreeable.'

'Well – I am so glad you do. I thought you would, he is so pleasant; and Mr Palmer is excessively pleased with you and your sisters I can tell you, and you can't think how disappointed he will be if you don't come to Cleveland. – I can't imagine why you should object to it.'

Elinor was again obliged to decline her invitation; and by changing the subject, put a stop to her entreaties. She thought it probable that as they lived in the same county, Mrs Palmer might be able to give some more particular account of Willoughby's general character, than could be gathered from the Middletons' partial acquaintance with him; and she was eager to gain from any one, such a confirmation of his merits as might remove the possibility of fear for Marianne. She began by inquiring if they saw much of Mr Willoughby at Cleveland, and whether they were intimately acquainted with him.

'Oh! dear, yes; I know him extremely well,' replied Mrs Palmer – 'Not that I ever spoke to him indeed; but I have seen him for ever in town. Somehow or other I never happened to be staying at Barton while he was at Allenham. Mama saw him here once before; – but I was with my uncle at

Weymouth. However, I dare say we should have seen a great deal of him in Somersetshire, if it had not happened very unluckily that we should never have been in the country together. He is very little at Combe, I believe; but if he were ever so much there, I do not think Mr Palmer would visit him, for he is in the opposition you know, and besides it is such a way off. I know why you inquire about him, very well; your sister is to marry him. I am monstrous glad of it, for then I shall have her for a neighbour you know.'

'Upon my word,' replied Elinor, 'you know much more of the matter than I do, if you have any reason to expect such a match.'

'Don't pretend to deny it, because you know it is what every body talks of. I assure you I heard of it in my way through town.'

'My dear Mrs Palmer!'

'Upon my honour I did. – I met Colonel Brandon Monday morning in Bond-street, just before we left town, and he told me of it directly.'

'You surprise me very much. Colonel Brandon tell you of it! Surely you must be mistaken. To give such intelligence to a person who could not be interested in it, even if it were true, is not what I should expect Colonel Brandon to do.'

'But I do assure you it was so, for all that, and I will tell you how it happened. When we met him, he turned back and walked with us; and so we began talking of my brother and sister, and one thing and another, and I said to him, "So, Colonel, there is a new family come to Barton cottage, I hear, and mama sends me word they are very pretty, and that one of them is going to be married to Mr Willoughby of Combe Magna. Is it true, pray? for of course you must know, as you have been in Devonshire so lately.'

'And what did the Colonel say?'

'Oh! – he did not say much; but he looked as if he knew it to be true, so from that moment I set it down as certain. It will be quite delightful, I declare! When is it to take place?'

'Mr Brandon was very well I hope.'

'Oh! yes, quite well; and so full of your praises, he did nothing but say fine things of you.'

'I am flattered by his commendation. He seems an excellent man; and I think him uncommonly pleasing.'

'So do I. – He is such a charming man, that it is quite a pity he should be so grave and so dull. Mama says *he* was in love with your sister too. – I assure you it was a great compliment if he was, for he hardly ever falls in love with any body.'

'Is Mr Willoughby much known in your part of Somersetshire?' said Elinor.

'Oh! yes, extremely well; that is, I do not believe many people are acquainted with him, because Combe Magna is so far off; but they all think him extremely agreeable I assure you. Nobody is more liked than Mr Willoughby wherever he goes, and so you may tell your sister. She is a monstrous lucky girl to get him, upon my honour; not but that he is much more lucky in getting her, because she is so very handsome and agreeable, that nothing can be good enough for her. However I don't think her hardly at all handsomer than you, I assure you; for I think you both excessively pretty, and so does Mr Palmer too I am sure, though we could not get him to own it last night.'

Mrs Palmer's information respecting Willoughby was not very material; but any testimony in his favour, however small, was pleasing to her.

'I am so glad we are got acquainted at last,' continued Charlotte. – 'And now I hope we shall always be great friends. You can't think how much I longed to see you! It is so delightful that you should live at the cottage! Nothing can be like it to be sure! And I am so glad your sister is going to be well married! I hope you will be a great deal at Combe Magna. It is a sweet place by all accounts.'

'You have been long acquainted with Colonel Brandon, have not you?'

'Yes, a great while; ever since my sister married. – He was a particular friend of Sir John's. I believe,' she added in a low voice, 'he would have been very glad to have had me, if he could. Sir John and Lady Middleton wished it very much. But mama did not think the match good enough for me, otherwise Sir John would have mentioned it to the Colonel, and we should have been married immediately.'

'Did not Colonel Brandon know of Sir John's proposal to your mother before it was made? Had he never owned his affection to yourself?'

'Oh! no; but if mama had not objected to it, I dare say he would have liked it of all things. He had not seen me then above twice, for it was before I left school. However I am much happier as I am. Mr Palmer is just the kind of man I like.'

Chapter Twenty One

THE PALMERS RETURNED to Cleveland the next day, and the two families at Barton were again left to entertain each other. But this did not last long; Elinor had hardly got their last visitors out of her head, had hardly done wondering at Charlotte's being so happy without a cause, at Mr Palmer's acting so simply, with good abilities, and at the strange unsuitableness which often existed between husband and wife, before Sir John's and Mrs Jennings's active zeal in the cause of society, procured her some other new acquaintance to see and observe.

In a morning's excursion to Exeter, they had met with two young ladies, whom Mrs Jennings had the satisfaction of discovering to be her relations, and this was enough for Sir John to invite them directly to the park, as soon as their present engagements at Exeter were over. Their engagements at Exeter instantly gave way before such an invitation, and Lady Middleton was thrown into no little alarm on the return of Sir John, by hearing that she was very soon to receive a visit from two girls whom she had never seen in her life, and of whose elegance, – whose tolerable gentility even, she could have no proof; for the assurances of her husband and mother on that subject went for nothing at all. Their being her relations too made it so much the worse; and Mrs Jennings's attempts at consolation were therefore unfortunately founded, when she advised her daughter not to care about their being so fashionable; because they were all cousins and must put up with one another. As it was impossible however now to prevent their coming, Lady Middleton resigned herself to the idea of it, with all the philosophy of a well-bred woman, contenting herself with merely giving her husband a gentle reprimand on the subject five or six times every day.

The young ladies arrived, their appearance was by no means ungenteel or unfashionable. Their dress was very smart, their manners very civil, they were delighted with the house, and in raptures with the furniture, and they happened to be so doatingly fond of children that Lady Middleton's good opinion was engaged in their favour before they had been an hour at the Park. She declared them to be very agreeable girls indeed, which for her ladyship was enthusiastic admiration. Sir John's confidence in his own judgment rose with this animated praise, and he set off directly for the cottage to tell the Miss Dashwoods of the Miss Steeles' arrival, and to assure them of their being the sweetest girls in the world. From such commendation as this, however, there was not much to be learned; Elinor well knew that the sweetest girls in the world were to be met with in every part of England, under every possible variation of form, face, temper and understanding. Sir John wanted the whole family to walk to the Park directly and look at his guests. Benevolent, philanthropic man! It was painful to him even to keep a third cousin to himself.

'Do come now said he – pray come – you must come – I declare you shall come – You can't think how you will like them. Lucy is monstrous pretty, and so good humoured and agreeable! The children are all hanging about her already, as if she was an old acquaintance. And they both long to see you of all things, for they have heard at Exeter that you are the most beautiful creatures in the world; and I have told them it is all very true, and a great deal more. You will be delighted with them I am sure. They have brought the whole coach full of playthings for the children. How can you be so cross as not to come? Why they are your cousins, you know, after a fashion. You are my cousins, and they are my wife's, so you must be related.'

But Sir John could not prevail. He could only obtain a promise of their calling at the Park within a day or two, and then left them in amazement at their indifference, to walk home and boast anew of their attractions to the Miss Steeles, as he had been already boasting of the Miss Steeles to them.

When their promised visit to the Park and consequent introduction to these young ladies took place, they found in the appearance of the eldest, who was nearly thirty, with a very plain and not a sensible face, nothing to admire; but in the other, who was not more than two or three and twenty, they acknowledged considerable beauty; her features were pretty, and she had a sharp quick eye, and a smartness of air, which though it did not give actual elegance or grace, gave distinction to her person. – Their manners were particularly civil, and Elinor soon allowed them credit for some kind of sense, when she saw with what constant and judicious attentions they were making themselves agreeable to Lady Middleton. With her children they were in continual raptures, extolling their beauty, courting their notice, and humouring all their whims; and such of their time as could be spared from the importunate demands which this politeness made on it, was spent in admiration of whatever her ladyship was doing, if she happened to be doing any thing, or in taking patterns of some elegant new dress, in which her appearance the day before had thrown them into unceasing delight. Fortunately for those who pay their court through such foibles, a fond mother, though, in pursuit of praise for her children, the most rapacious of human beings, is likewise the most credulous; her demands are exorbitant; but she will swallow any thing; and the excessive affection and endurance of the Miss Steeles towards her offspring, were viewed therefore by Lady Middleton without the smallest surprise or distrust. She saw with maternal complacency all the impertinent incroachments and mischievous tricks to which her cousins submitted. She saw their sashes untied, their hair pulled about their ears, their work-bags searched, and their knives and scissors stolen away, and felt no doubt of its being a reciprocal enjoyment. It suggested no other surprise than that Elinor and Marianne should sit so composedly by, without claiming a share in what was passing.

'John is in such spirits today!' said she, on his taking Miss Steele's pocket handkerchief, and throwing it out of the window – 'He is full of monkey tricks.'

And soon afterwards, on the second boy's violently pinching one of the same lady's fingers, she fondly observed, 'How playful William is!'

'And here is my sweet little Annamaria,' she added, tenderly caressing a little girl of three years old, who had not made a noise for the last two minutes; 'And she is always so gentle and quiet – Never was there such a quiet little thing!'

But unfortunately in bestowing these embraces, a pin in her ladyship's head dress slightly scratching the child's neck, produced from this pattern of gentleness, such violent screams, as could hardly be outdone by any creature professedly noisy. The mother's consternation was excessive; but it could not surpass the alarm of the Miss Steeles, and every thing was done by all three, in so critical an emergency, which affection could suggest as likely to assuage the agonies of the little sufferer. She was seated in her mother's lap, covered with kisses, her wound bathed with lavender-water, by one of the Miss Steeles, who was on her knees to attend her, and her mouth stuffed with sugar plums by the other. With such a reward for her tears, the child was too wise to cease crying. She still screamed and sobbed lustily, kicked her two brothers for offering to touch her, and all their united soothings were ineffectual till Lady Middleton luckily remembering that in a scene of similar distress last week, some apricot marmalade had been successfully applied for a bruised temple, the same remedy was eagerly proposed for this unfortunate scratch, and a slight intermission of screams in the young lady on hearing it, gave them reason to hope that it would not be rejected. – She was carried out of the room therefore in her mother's arms, in quest of this medicine, and as the two boys chose to follow, though earnestly entreated by their mother to stay behind, the four young ladies were left in a quietness which the room had not known for many hours.

'Poor little creature!' said Miss Steele, as soon as they were gone. 'It might have been a very sad accident.'

'Yet I hardly know how,' cried Marianne, 'unless it had been under totally different circumstances. But this is the usual way of heightening alarm, where there is nothing to be alarmed at in reality.'

'What a sweet woman Lady Middleton is!' said Lucy Steele.

Marianne was silent; it was impossible for her to say what she did not feel, however trivial the occasion; and upon Elinor therefore the whole task of telling lies when politeness required it, always fell. She did her best when thus called on, by speaking of Lady Middleton with more warmth than she felt, though with far less than Miss Lucy.

'And Sir John too,' cried the elder sister, 'what a charming man he is!'

Here too, Miss Dashwood's commendation, being only simple and just, came in without any éclat. She merely observed that he was perfectly good humoured and friendly.

'And what a charming little family they have! I never saw such fine children in my life – I declare I quite doat upon them already, and indeed I am always distractedly fond of children.'

'I should guess so,' said Elinor with a smile, 'from what I have witnessed this morning.'   .

'I have a notion,' said Lucy, 'you think the little Middletons rather too much indulged; perhaps they may be the outside of enough; but it is so natural in Lady Middleton; and for my part, I love to see children full of life and spirits; I cannot bear them if they are tame and quiet.'

'I confess,' replied Elinor, 'that while I am at Barton Park, I never think of tame and quiet children with any abhorrence.'

A short pause succeeded this speech, which was first broken by Miss Steele, who seemed very much disposed for conversation, and who now said rather abruptly, 'And how do you like Devonshire, Miss Dashwood? I suppose you were very sorry to leave Sussex.'

In some surprise at the familiarity of this question, or at least of the manner in which it was spoken, Elinor replied that she was.

'Norland is a prodigious beautiful place, is not it?' added Miss Steele.

'We have heard Sir John admire it excessively,' said Lucy, who seemed to think some apology necessary for the freedom of her sister.

'I think every one *must* admire it,' replied Elinor, 'who ever saw the place; though it is not to be supposed that any one can estimate its beauties as we do.'

'And had you a great many smart beaux there? I suppose you have not so many in this part of the world; for my part, I think they are a vast addition always.'

'But why should you think,' said Lucy, looking ashamed of her sister, 'that there are not as many genteel young men in Devonshire as Sussex?'

'Nay, my dear, I'm sure I don't pretend to say that there an't. I'm sure there's a vast many smart beaux in Exeter; but you know, how could I tell what smart beaux there might be about Norland; and I was only afraid the Miss Dashwoods might find it dull at Barton, if they had not so many as they used to have. But perhaps you young ladies may not care about the beaux, and had as lief be without them as with them. For my part, I think they are vastly agreeable, provided they dress smart and behave civil. But I can't bear to see them dirty and nasty. Now there's Mr Rose at Exeter, a prodigious smart young man, quite a beau, clerk to Mr Simpson you know, and yet if you do but meet him of a morning, he is not fit to be seen. – I suppose your brother was quite a beau, Miss Dashwood, before he married, as he was so rich?'

'Upon my word,' replied Elinor, 'I cannot tell you, for I do not perfectly comprehend the meaning of the word. But this I can say, that if he ever was a beau before he married, he is one still, for there is not the smallest alteration in him.'

'Oh! dear! one never thinks of married mens' being beaux – they have something else to do.'

'Lord! Anne,' cried her sister, 'you can talk of nothing but beaux; – you will make Miss Dashwood believe you think of nothing else.' And then to turn the discourse, she began admiring the house and the furniture.

This specimen of the Miss Steeles was enough. The vulgar freedom and folly of the eldest left her no recommendation, and as Elinor was not blinded by the beauty, or the shrewd look of the youngest, to her want of real elegance and artlessness, she left the house without any wish of knowing them better.

Not so, the Miss Steeles. – They came from Exeter, well provided with admiration for the use of Sir John Middleton, his family, and all his relations, and no niggardly proportion was now dealt out to his fair cousins, whom they declared to be the most beautiful, elegant, accomplished, and agreeable girls they had ever beheld, and with whom they were particularly anxious to be better acquainted. – And to be better acquainted therefore, Elinor soon found was their inevitable lot, for as Sir John was entirely on the side of the Miss Steeles, their party would be too strong for opposition, and that kind of intimacy must be submitted to, which consists of sitting an hour or two together in the same room almost every day. Sir John could do no more; but he did not know that any more was required; to be together was, in his opinion, to be intimate, and while his continual schemes for their meeting were effectual, he had not a doubt of their being established friends.

To do him justice, he did every thing in his power to promote their unreserve, by making the Miss Steeles acquainted with whatever he knew or supposed of his cousins' situations in the most delicate particulars, – and Elinor had not seen them more than twice, before the eldest of them wished her joy on her sister's having been so lucky as to make a conquest of a very smart beau since she came to Barton.

' 'Twill be a fine thing to have her married so young to be sure,' said she, 'and I hear he is quite a beau, and prodigious handsome. And I hope you may have as good luck yourself soon, – but perhaps you may have a friend in the corner already.'

Elinor could not suppose that Sir John would be more nice in proclaiming his suspicions of her regard for Edward, than he had been with respect to Marianne; indeed it was rather his favourite joke of the two, as being somewhat newer and more conjectural; and since Edward's visit, they had never dined together, without his drinking to her best affections with so much significancy and so many nods and winks, as to excite general attention. The letter F— had been likewise invariably brought forward, and found productive of such countless jokes, that its character as the wittiest letter in the alphabet had been long established with Elinor.

The Miss Steeles, as she expected, had now all the benefit of these jokes, and in the eldest of them they raised a curiosity to know the name of the gentleman alluded to, which, though often impertinently expressed, was perfectly of a piece with her general inquisitiveness into the concerns of their family. But Sir John did not sport long with the curiosity which he delighted to raise, for he had at least as much pleasure in telling the name, as Miss Steele had in hearing it.

'His name is Ferrars,' said he, in a very audible whisper; 'but pray do not tell it, for it's a great secret.'

'Ferrars!' repeated Miss Steele; 'Mr Ferrars is the happy man, is he? What! your sister-in-law's brother, Miss Dashwood? a very agreeable young man to be sure; I know him very well.'

'How can you say so, Anne?' cried Lucy, who generally made an amendment to all her sister's assertions. 'Though we have seen him once or twice at my uncle's, it is rather too much to pretend to know him very well.'

Elinor heard all this with attention and surprise. 'And who was this uncle? Where did he live? How came they acquainted?' She wished very much to have the subject continued, though she did not chuse to join in it herself; but nothing more of it was said, and for the first time in her life, she thought Mrs Jennings deficient either in curiosity after petty information, or in a disposition to communicate it. The manner in which Miss Steele had spoken of Edward, increased her curiosity; for it struck her as being rather ill-natured and suggested the suspicion of that lady's knowing, or fancying herself to know something to his disadvantage. – But her curiosity was unavailing, for no farther notice was taken of Mr Ferrars's name by Miss Steele when alluded to, or even openly mentioned by Sir John.

Chapter Twenty Two

MARIANNE, WHO HAD NEVER much toleration for any thing like impertinence, vulgarity, inferiority of parts, or even difference of taste from herself, was at this time particularly ill-disposed, from the state of her spirits, to be pleased with the Miss Steeles, or to encourage their advances; and to the invariable coldness of her behaviour towards them, which checked every endeavour at intimacy on their side, Elinor principally attributed that preference of herself which soon became evident in the manners of both, but especially of Lucy, who missed no opportunity of engaging her in conversation, or of striving to improve their acquaintance by an easy and frank communication of her sentiments.

Lucy was naturally clever; her remarks were often just and amusing; and as a companion for half an hour Elinor frequently found her agreeable; but her powers had received no aid from education, she was ignorant and illiterate, and her deficiency of all mental improvement, her want of information in the most common particulars, could not be concealed from Miss Dashwood, in spite of her constant endeavour to appear to advantage. Elinor saw, and pitied her for, the neglect of abilities which education might have rendered so respectable; but she saw, with less tenderness of feeling, the thorough want of delicacy, of rectitude, and integrity of mind, which her attentions, her assiduities, her flatteries at the Park betrayed; and she could have no lasting satisfaction in the company of a person who joined insincerity with ignorance; whose want of instruction prevented their meeting in conversation on terms of equality, and whose conduct towards others, made every shew of attention and deference towards herself perfectly valueless.

'You will think my question an odd one, I dare say,' said Lucy to her one day as they were walking together from the park to the cottage – 'but pray, are you personally acquainted with your sister-in-law's mother, Mrs Ferrars?'

Elinor *did* think the question a very odd one, and her countenance expressed it, as she answered that she had never seen Mrs Ferrars.

'Indeed!' replied Lucy; 'I wonder at that, for I thought you must have seen her at Norland sometimes. Then perhaps you cannot tell me what sort of a woman she is?'

'No,' returned Elinor, cautious of giving her real opinion of Edward's mother, and not very desirous of satisfying, what seemed impertinent curiosity – 'I know nothing of her.'

'I am sure you think me very strange, for inquiring about her in such a way,' said Lucy, eyeing Elinor attentively as she spoke; 'but perhaps there may be reasons – I wish I might venture; but however I hope you will do me the justice of believing that I do not mean to be impertinent.'

Elinor made her a civil reply, and they walked on for a few minutes in silence. It was broken by Lucy, who renewed the subject again by saying with some hesitation,

'I cannot bear to have you think me impertinently curious. I am sure I would rather do any thing in the world than be thought so by a person whose good opinion is so well worth having as yours. And I am sure I should not have the smallest fear of trusting *you*; indeed I should be very glad of your advice how to manage in such an uncomfortable situation as I am; but however there is no occasion to trouble *you*. I am sorry you do not happen to know Mrs Ferrars.'

'I am sorry I do *not*,' said Elinor, in great astonishment, 'if it could be of any use to *you* to know my opinion of her. But really, I never understood that you were at all connected with that family, and therefore I am a little surprised, I confess, at so serious an inquiry into her character.'

'I dare say you are, and I am sure I do not at all wonder at it. But if I dared tell you all, you would not be so much surprised. Mrs Ferrars is certainly nothing to me at present, – but the time *may* come – how soon it will come must depend upon herself – when we may be very intimately connected.'

She looked down as she said this, amiably bashful, with only one side glance at her companion to observe its effect on her.

'Good heavens!' cried Elinor, 'what do you mean? Are you acquainted with Mr Robert Ferrars? Can you be?' And she did not feel much delighted with the idea of such a sister-in-law.

'No,' replied Lucy, 'not to Mr *Robert* Ferrars – I never saw him in my life; but,' fixing her eyes upon Elinor, 'to his elder brother.'

What felt Elinor at that moment? Astonishment, that would have been as painful as it was strong, had not an immediate disbelief of the assertion attended it. She turned towards Lucy in silent amazement, unable to divine the reason or object of such a declaration, and though her complexion varied, she stood firm in incredulity and felt in no danger of an hysterical fit, or a swoon.

'You may well be surprised,' continued Lucy; 'for to be sure you could have had no idea of it before; for I dare say he never dropped the smallest hint of it to you or any of your family; because it was always meant to be a great secret, and I am sure has been faithfully kept so by me to this hour. Not a soul of all my relations know of it but Anne, and I never should have mentioned it to you, if I had not felt the greatest dependance in the world upon your secrecy; and I really thought my behaviour in asking so many questions about Mrs Ferrars, must seem so odd, that it ought to be explained. And I do not think Mr Ferrars can be displeased, when he knows I have trusted you, because I know he has the highest opinion in the world of all your family, and looks upon yourself and the other Miss Dashwoods, quite as his own sisters.' – She paused.

Elinor for a few moments remained silent. Her astonishment at what she heard was at first too great for words; but at length forcing herself to speak, and to speak cautiously, she said with a calmness of manner, which tolerably well concealed her surprise and solicitude – 'May I ask if your engagement is of long standing?'

'We have been engaged these four years.'

'Four years!'

'Yes.'

Elinor, though greatly shocked, still felt unable to believe it.

'I did not know,' said she, 'that you were even acquainted till the other day.'

'Our acquaintance, however, is of many years date. He was under my uncle's care, you know, a considerable while.'

'Your uncle!'

'Yes; Mr Pratt. Did you never hear him talk of Mr Pratt?'

'I think I have,' replied Elinor, with an exertion of spirits, which increased with her increase of emotion.

'He was four years with my uncle, who lives at Longstaple, near Plymouth. It was there our acquaintance begun, for my sister and me was often staying with my uncle, and it was there our engagement was formed, though not till a year after he had quitted as a pupil; but he was almost always with us afterwards. I was very unwilling to enter into it, as you may imagine, without the knowledge and approbation of his mother; but I was too young and loved him too well to be so prudent as I ought to have been. – Though you do not know him so well as me, Miss Dashwood, you must have seen enough of him to be sensible he is very capable of making a woman sincerely attached to him.'

'Certainly,' answered Elinor, without knowing what she said; but after a moment's reflection, she added with revived security of Edward's honour and love, and her companion's falsehood – 'Engaged to Mr Edward Ferrars! – I confess myself so totally surprised at what you tell me, that really – I beg your pardon; but surely there must be some mistake of person or name. We cannot mean the same Mr Ferrars.'

'We can mean no other,' cried Lucy smiling. 'Mr Edward Ferrars, the eldest son of Mrs Ferrars of Park-street, and brother of your sister-in-law, Mrs John Dashwood, is the person I mean; you must allow that I am not likely to be deceived, as to the name of the man on who all my happiness depends.'

'It is strange,' replied Elinor in a most painful perplexity, 'that I should never have heard him even mention your name.'

'No; considering our situation, it was not strange. Our first care has been to keep the matter secret. – You knew nothing of me, or my family, and therefore there could be no occasion for ever mentioning my name to you, and as he was always particularly afraid of his sister's suspecting any thing, that was reason enough for his not mentioning it.'

She was silent. – Elinor's security sunk; but her self-command did not sink with it.

'Four years you have been engaged,' said she with a firm voice.

'Yes; and heaven knows how much longer we may have to wait. Poor Edward! It puts him quite out of heart.' Then taking a small miniature from her pocket, she added, 'To prevent the possibility of mistake, be so good as to look at this face. It does not do him justice to be sure, but yet I think you cannot be deceived as to the person it was drew for. – I have had it above these three years.'

She put it into her hands as she spoke, and when Elinor saw the painting, whatever other doubts her fear of a too hasty decision, or her wish of detecting falsehood might suffer to linger in her mind, she could have none of its being Edward's face. She returned it almost instantly, acknowledging the likeness.

'I have never been able,' continued Lucy, 'to give him my picture in return, which I am very much vexed at, for he has been always so anxious to get it! But I am determined to set for it the very first opportunity.'

'You are quite in the right,' replied Elinor calmly. They then proceeded a few paces in silence. Lucy spoke first.

'I am sure,' said she, 'I have no doubt in the world of your faithfully keeping this secret, because you must know of what importance it is to us, not to have it reach his mother; for she would never approve of it, I dare say. I shall have no fortune, and I fancy she is an exceeding proud woman.'

'I certainly did not seek your confidence,' said Elinor; 'but you do me no more than justice in imagining that I may be depended on. Your secret is safe with me; but pardon me if I express some surprise at so unnecessary a communication. You must at least have felt that my being acquainted with it could not add to its safety.'

As she said this, she looked earnestly at Lucy, hoping to discover something in her countenance; perhaps the falsehood of the greatest part of what she had been saying; but Lucy's countenance suffered no change.

'I was afraid you would think I was taking a great liberty with you,' said she, 'in telling you all this. I have not known you long to be sure, personally at least, but I have known you and all your family by description a great while; and as soon as I saw you, I felt almost as if you was an old acquaintance. Besides in the present case, I really thought some explanation was due to you after my making such particular inquiries about Edward's mother; and I am so unfortunate, that I have not a creature whose advice I can ask. Anne is the only person that knows of it, and she has no judgment at all; indeed she does me a great deal more harm than good, for I am in constant fear of her betraying me. She does not know how to hold her tongue, as you must perceive, and I am sure I was in the greatest fright in the world t'other day, when Edward's name was mentioned by Sir John, lest she should out with it all. You can't think how much I go through in my mind from it altogether. I only wonder that I am alive after what I have suffered for Edward's sake these last four years. Every thing in such suspense and uncertainty; and seeing him so seldom – we can hardly meet above twice a-year. I am sure I wonder my heart is not quite broke.'

Here she took out her handkerchief; but Elinor did not feel very compassionate.

'Sometimes,' continued Lucy, after wiping her eyes, 'I think whether it would not be better for us both, to break off the matter entirely.' As she said this, she looked directly at her companion. 'But then at other times I have not resolution enough for it. – I cannot bear the thoughts of making him so miserable, as I know the very mention of such a thing would do. And on my own account too – so dear as he is to me – I don't think I could be equal to it. What would you advise me to do in such a case, Miss Dashwood? What would you do yourself?'

'Pardon me,' replied Elinor, startled by the question; 'but I can give you no advice under such circumstances. Your own judgment must direct you.'

'To be sure,' continued Lucy, after a few minutes silence on both sides, 'his mother must provide for him sometime or other; but poor Edward is *so* cast down about it! Did not you think him dreadful low-spirited when he was at Barton? He was so miserable when he left us at Longstaple, to go to you, that I was afraid you would think him quite ill.'

'Did he come from your uncle's then, when he visited us?'

'Oh! yes; he had been staying a fortnight with us. Did you think he came directly from town?'

'No,' replied Elinor, most feelingly sensible of every fresh circumstance in favour of Lucy's veracity; 'I remember he told us, that he had been staying a fortnight with some friends near Plymouth.' She remembered too, her own surprise at the time, at his mentioning nothing farther of those friends, at his total silence with respect even to their names.

'Did not you think him sadly out of spirits?' repeated Lucy.

'We did indeed, particularly so when he first arrived.'

'I begged him to exert himself for fear you should suspect what was the matter; but it made him so melancholy, not being able to stay more than a fortnight with us, and seeing me so much affected. – Poor fellow! – I am afraid it is just the same with him now; for he writes in wretched spirits. I heard from him just before I left Exeter;' taking a letter from her pocket and carelessly showing the direction to Elinor. 'You know his hand, I dare say, a charming one it is; but that is not written so well as usual. – He was tired, I dare say, for he had just filled the sheet to me as full as possible.'

Elinor saw that it *was* his hand, and she could doubt no longer. The picture, she had allowed herself to believe, might have been accidentally obtained; it might not have been Edward's gift; but a correspondence between them by letter, could subsist only under a positive engagement, could be authorized by nothing else; for a few moments, she was almost overcome – her heart sunk within her, and she could hardly stand; but exertion was indispensably necessary, and she struggled so resolutely against the oppression of her feelings, that her success was speedy, and for the time complete.

'Writing to each other,' said Lucy, returning the letter into her pocket, 'is the only comfort we have in such long separations. Yes, *I* have one other comfort in his picture; but poor Edward has not even *that*. If he had but my picture, he says he should be easy. I gave him a lock of my hair set in a ring when he was at Longstaple last, and that was some comfort to him, he said, but not equal to a picture. Perhaps you might notice the ring when you saw him?'

'I did,' said Elinor, with a composure of voice, under which was concealed an emotion and distress beyond any thing she had ever felt before. She was mortified, shocked, confounded.

Fortunately for her, they had now reached the cottage, and the conversation could be continued no farther. After sitting with them a few minutes, the Miss Steeles returned to the Park, and Elinor was then at liberty to think and be wretched.

[*At this point in the first and
second editions, Volume I ended.*]

Chapter Twenty Three

HOWEVER SMALL ELINOR'S GENERAL dependance on Lucy's veracity might be, it was impossible for her on serious reflection to suspect it in the present case, where no temptation could be answerable to the folly of inventing a falsehood of such a description. What Lucy had asserted to be true, therefore, Elinor could not, dared not longer doubt; supported as it was too on every side by such probabilities and proofs, and contradicted by nothing but her own wishes. Their opportunity of acquaintance in the house of Mr Pratt was a foundation for the rest, at once indisputable and alarming; and Edward's visit near Plymouth, his melancholy state of mind, his dissatisfaction at his own prospects, his uncertain behaviour towards herself, the intimate knowledge of the Miss Steeles as to Norland and their family connections, which had often surprised her, the picture, the letter, the ring, formed altogether such a body of evidence, as overcame every fear of condemning him unfairly, and established as a fact, which no partiality could set aside, his ill-treatment of herself. – Her resentment of such behaviour, her indignation at having been its dupe, for a short time made her feel only for herself; but other ideas, other considerations soon arose. Had Edward been intentionally deceiving her? Had he feigned a regard for her which he did not feel? Was his engagement to Lucy, an engagement of the heart? No; whatever it might once have been, she could not believe it such at present. His affection was all her own. She could not be deceived in that. Her mother, sisters, Fanny, all had been conscious of his regard for her at Norland; it was not an illusion of her own vanity. He certainly loved her. What a softener of the heart was this persuasion! How much could it not tempt her to forgive! He had been blameable, highly blameable, in remaining at Norland after he first felt her influence over him to be more than it ought to be. In that, he could not be defended; but if he had injured her, how much more had he injured himself; if her case were pitiable, his was hopeless. His imprudence had made her miserable for a while; but it seemed to have deprived himself of all chance of ever being otherwise. She might in time regain tranquillity, but *he*, what had he to look forward to? Could he ever be tolerably happy with Lucy Steele; could he, were his affection for herself out of the question, with his integrity, his delicacy, and well-informed mind, be satisfied with a wife like her – illiterate, artful, and selfish?

The youthful infatuation of nineteen would naturally blind him to every thing but her beauty and good nature; but the four succeeding years – years, which if rationally spent, give such improvement to the understanding, must have opened his eyes to her defects of education, while the same period of time, spent on her side in inferior society and more frivolous pursuits, had perhaps robbed her of that simplicity, which might once have given an interesting character to her beauty.

If in the supposition of his seeking to marry herself, his difficulties from his mother had seemed great, how much greater were they now likely to be, when the object of his engagement was undoubtedly inferior in connections, and probably inferior in fortune to herself. These difficulties, indeed, with an heart so alienated from Lucy, might not press very hard upon his patience; but melancholy was the state of the person, by whom the expectation of family opposition and unkindness, could be felt as a relief!

As these considerations occurred to her in painful succession, she wept for him, more than for herself. Supported by the conviction of having done nothing to merit her present unhappiness, and consoled by the belief that Edward had done nothing to forfeit her esteem, she thought she could even now, under the first smart of the heavy blow, command herself enough to guard every suspicion of the truth from her mother and sisters. And so well was she able to answer her own expectations, that when she joined them at dinner only two hours after she had first suffered the extinction of all her dearest hopes, no one would have supposed from the appearance of the sisters, that Elinor was mourning in secret over obstacles which must divide her for ever from the object of her love, and that Marianne was internally dwelling on the perfections of a man, of whose whole heart she felt thoroughly possessed, and whom she expected to see in every carriage which drove near their house.

The necessity of concealing from her mother and Marianne, what had been entrusted in confidence to herself, though it obliged her to unceasing exertion, was no aggravation of Elinor's distress. On the contrary it was a relief to her, to be spared the communication of what would give such affliction to them, and to be saved likewise from hearing that condemnation of Edward, which would probably flow from the excess of their partial affection for herself, and which was more than she felt equal to support.

From their counsel, or their conversation she knew she could receive no assistance, their tenderness and sorrow must add to her distress, while her self-command would neither receive encouragement from their example nor from their praise. She was stronger alone, and her own good sense so well supported her, that her firmness was as unshaken, her appearance of cheerfulness as invariable, as with regrets so poignant and so fresh, it was possible for them to be.

Much as she had suffered from her first conversation with Lucy on the subject, she soon felt an earnest wish of renewing it; and this for more reasons than one. She wanted to hear many particulars of their engagement repeated again, she wanted more clearly to understand what Lucy really felt for Edward, whether there were any sincerity in her declaration of tender regard for him, and she particularly wanted to convince Lucy, by her readiness to enter on the matter again, and her calmness in conversing on it, that she was no otherwise interested in it than as a friend, which she very much feared her involuntary agitation, in their morning discourse, must have left at least doubtful. That Lucy was disposed to be jealous of her, appeared very probable; it was plain that Edward had always spoken highly in her praise, not merely from Lucy's assertion, but from her venturing to trust her on so short a personal acquaintance, with a secret, so confessedly and evidently important. And even Sir John's joking intelligence must have had some weight. But indeed, while Elinor remained so well assured within herself of being really beloved by Edward, it required no other consideration of probabilities to make it natural that Lucy should be jealous; and that she was so, her very confidence was a proof. What other reason for the disclosure of the affair could there be, but that Elinor might be informed by it of Lucy's superior claims on Edward, and be taught to avoid him in future? She had little difficulty in understanding thus much of her rival's intentions, and while she was firmly resolved to act by her as every principle of honour and honesty directed, to combat her own affection for Edward and to see him as little as possible ; she could not deny herself the comfort of endeavouring to convince Lucy that her heart was unwounded. And as she could now have nothing more painful to hear on the subject than had already been told, she did not mistrust her own ability of going through a repetition of particulars with composure.

But it was not immediately that an opportunity of doing so could be commanded, though Lucy was as well disposed as herself to take advantage of any that occurred; for the weather was not often fine enough to allow of their joining in a walk, where they might most easily separate themselves from the others; and though they met at least every other evening either at the park or cottage, and chiefly at the former, they could not be supposed to meet for the sake of conversation. Such a thought would never enter either Sir John or Lady Middleton's head, and therefore very little leisure was ever given for general chat, and none at all for particular discourse. They met for the sake of eating, drinking, and laughing together, playing at cards, or consequences, or any other game that was sufficiently noisy.

One or two meetings of this kind had taken place, without affording Elinor any chance of engaging Lucy in private, when Sir John called at the cottage one morning, to beg in the name of charity, that they would all dine with Lady Middleton that day, as he was obliged to attend the club at Exeter, and she would otherwise be quite alone, except her mother and the two Miss Steeles. Elinor, who foresaw a fairer opening for the point she had in view, in such a party as this was likely to be, more at liberty among themselves under the tranquil and well-bred direction of Lady Middleton than when her husband united them together in one noisy purpose, immediately accepted the invitation; Margaret, with her mother's permission, was equally compliant, and Marianne, though always unwilling to join any of their parties, was persuaded by her mother, who could not bear to have her seclude herself from any chance of amusement, to go likewise.

The young ladies went, and Lady Middleton was happily preserved from the frightful solitude which had threatened her. The insipidity of the meeting was exactly such as Elinor had expected; it produced not one novelty of thought or expression, and nothing could be less interesting than the whole of their discourse both in the dining parlour and the drawing room: to the latter, the children accompanied them, and while they remained there, she was too well convinced of the impossibility of engaging Lucy's attention to attempt it. They quitted it only with the removal of the tea-things. The card-table was then placed, and Elinor began to wonder at herself for having ever entertained a hope of finding time for conversation at the park. They all rose up in preparation for a round game.

'I am glad,' said Lady Middleton to Lucy, 'you are not going to finish poor little Annamaria's basket this evening; for I am sure it must hurt your eyes to work fillagree by candlelight. And we will make the dear little love some amends for her disappointment to-morrow, and then I hope she will not much mind it.'

This hint was enough, Lucy recollected herself instantly and replied, 'Indeed you are very much mistaken, Lady Middleton; I am only waiting to know whether you can make your party without me, or I should have been at my fillagree already. I would not disappoint the little angel for all the world, and if you want me at the card-table now, I am resolved to finish the basket after supper.'

'You are very good, I hope it won't hurt your eyes – will you ring the bell for some working candles? My poor little girl would be sadly disappointed, I know, if the basket was not finished tomorrow, for though I told her it certainly would not, I am sure she depends upon having it done.'

Lucy directly drew her work table near her and reseated herself with an alacrity and cheerfulness which seemed to infer that she could taste no greater delight than in making a fillagree basket for a spoilt child.

Lady Middleton proposed a rubber of Casino to the others. No one made any objection but Marianne, who, with her usual inattention to the forms of general civility, exclaimed, 'Your ladyship will have the goodness to excuse *me* – you know I detest cards. I shall go to the piano-forté; I have not touched it since it was tuned.' And without farther ceremony, she turned away and walked to the instrument.

Lady Middleton looked as if she thanked heaven that *she* had never made so rude a speech.

'Marianne can never keep long from that instrument you know, ma'am,' said Elinor, endeavouring to smooth away the offence; 'and I do not much wonder at it; for it is the very best toned piano-forté I ever heard.'

The remaining five were now to draw their cards.

'Perhaps,' continued Elinor, 'if I should happen to cut out, I may be of some use to Miss Lucy Steele, in rolling her papers for her; and there is so much still to be done to the basket, that it must be impossible I think for her labour singly, to finish it this evening. I should like the work exceedingly, if she would allow me a share in it.'

'Indeed I shall be very much obliged to you for your help,' cried Lucy, 'for I find there is more to be done to it than I thought there was; and it would be a shocking thing to disappoint dear Annamaria after all.'

'Oh! that would be terrible indeed,' said Miss Steele – 'Dear little soul, how I do love her!'

'You are very kind' said Lady Middleton to Elinor: 'and as you really like the work, perhaps you will be as well pleased not to cut in till another rubber, or will you take your chance now?'

Elinor joyfully profited by the first of these proposals, and thus by a little of that address, which Marianne could never condescend to practise, gained her own end, and pleased Lady Middleton at the same time. Lucy made room for her with ready attention, and the two fair rivals were thus seated side by side at the same table, and with the utmost harmony engaged in forwarding the same work. The piano-forté, at which Marianne, wrapt up in her own music and her own thoughts, had by this time forgotten that any body was in the room besides herself, was luckily so near them that Miss Dashwood now judged, she might safely, under the shelter of its noise, introduce the interesting subject, without any risk of being heard at the card-table.

Chapter Twenty Four

IN A FIRM, THOUGH CAUTIOUS tone, Elinor thus began.

'I should be undeserving of the confidence you have honoured me with, if I felt no desire for its continuance, or no farther curiosity on its subject. I will not apologize therefore for bringing it forward again.'

'Thank you,' cried Lucy warmly, 'for breaking the ice; you have set my heart at ease by it; for I was somehow or other afraid I had offended you by what I told you that Monday.'

'Offended me! How could you suppose so? Believe me,' and Elinor spoke it with the truest sincerity, 'nothing could be farther from my intention, than to give you such an idea. Could you have a motive for the trust, that was not honourable and flattering to me?'

'And yet I do assure you,' replied Lucy, her little sharp eyes full of meaning, 'there seemed to me to be a coldness and displeasure in your manner, that made me quite uncomfortable. I felt sure that you was angry with me; and have been quarrelling with myself ever since, for having took such a liberty as to trouble you with my affairs. But I am very glad to find it was only my own fancy, and that you do not really blame me. If you knew what a consolation it was to me to relieve my heart by speaking to you of what I am always thinking of every moment of my life, your compassion would make you overlook every thing else I am sure.'

'Indeed I can easily believe that it was a very great relief to you, to acknowledge your situation to me, and be assured that you shall never have reason to repent it. Your case is a very unfortunate one; you seem to me to be surrounded with difficulties, and you will have need of all your mutual affection to support you under them. Mr Ferrars, I believe, is entirely dependent on his mother.'

'He has only two thousand pounds of his own; it would be madness to marry upon that, though for my own part, I could give up every prospect of more without a sigh. I have been always used to a very small income, and could struggle with any poverty for him; but I love him too well to be the selfish means of robbing him, perhaps, of all that his mother might give him if he married to please her. We must wait, it may be for many years. With almost every other man in the world, it would be an alarming prospect; but Edward's affection and constancy nothing can deprive me of I know.'

'That conviction must be every thing to you; and he is undoubtedly supported by the same trust in your's. If the strength of your reciprocal attachment had failed, as between many people and under many circumstances it naturally would during a four years' engagement, your situation would have been pitiable indeed.'

Lucy here looked up; but Elinor was careful in guarding her countenance from every expression that could give her words a suspicious tendency.

'Edward's love for me,' said Lucy, 'has been pretty well put to the test, by our long, very long absence since we were first engaged, and it has stood the trial so well, that I should be unpardonable to doubt it now. I can safely say that he has never gave me one moment's alarm on that account from the first.'

Elinor hardly knew whether to smile or sigh at this assertion.

Lucy went on. 'I am rather of a jealous temper too by nature, and from our different situations in life, from his being so much more in the world than me, and our continual separation, I was enough inclined for suspicion, to have found out the truth in an instant, if there had been the slightest alteration in his behaviour to me when we met, or any lowness of spirits that I could not account for, or if he had talked more of one lady than another, or seemed in any respect less happy at Longstaple than he used to be. I do not mean to say that I am particularly observant or quick-sighted in general, but in such a case I am sure I could not be deceived.'

'All this,' thought Elinor, 'is very pretty; but it can impose upon neither of us.'

'But what,' said she after a short silence, 'are your views? or have you none but that of waiting for Mrs Ferrars' death, which is a melancholy and shocking extremity? – Is her son determined to submit to this, and to all the tediousness of the many years of suspense in which it may involve you, rather than run the risk of her displeasure for a while by owning the truth?'

'If we could be certain that it would be only for a while! But Mrs Ferrars is a very headstrong proud woman, and in her first fit of anger upon hearing it, would very likely secure every thing to Robert, and the idea of that, for Edward's sake, frightens away all my inclination for hasty measures.'

'And for your own sake too, or you are carrying your disinterestedness beyond reason.'

Lucy looked at Elinor again, and was silent.

'Do you know Mr Robert Ferrars?' asked Elinor.

'Not at all – I never saw him; but I fancy he is very unlike his brother – silly and a great coxcomb.'

'A great coxcomb!' repeated Miss Steele, whose ear had caught those words by a sudden pause in Marianne's music. – 'Oh! they are talking of their favourite beaux, I dare say.'

'No, sister,' cried Lucy, 'you are mistaken there, our favourite beaux are *not* great coxcombs.'

'I can answer for it that Miss Dashwood's is not,' said Mrs Jennings, laughing heartily; 'for he is one of the modestest, prettiest behaved young men I ever saw; but as for Lucy, she is such a sly little creature, there is no finding out who *she* likes.'

'Oh!' cried Miss Steele, looking significantly round at them, 'I dare say Lucy's beau is quite as modest and pretty behaved as Miss Dashwood's.'

Elinor blushed in spite of herself. Lucy bit her lip, and looked angrily at her sister. A mutual silence took place for some time. Lucy first put an end to it by saying in a lower tone, though Marianne was then giving them the powerful protection of a very magnificent concerto –

'I will honestly tell you of one scheme which has lately come into my head, for bringing matters to bear; indeed I am bound to let you into the secret, for you are a party concerned. I dare say you have seen enough of Edward to know that he would prefer the church to every other profession; now my plan is that he should take orders as soon as he can, and then through your interest, which I am sure you would be kind enough to use out of friendship for him, and I hope out of some regard to me, your brother might be persuaded to give him Norland living; which I understand is a very good one, and the present incumbent not likely to live a great while. That would be enough for us to marry upon, and we might trust to time and chance for the rest.'

'I should be always happy,' replied Elinor, 'to shew any mark of my esteem and friendship for Mr Ferrars; but do not you perceive that my interest on such an occasion would be perfectly unnecessary? He is brother to Mrs John Dashwood – *that* must be recommendation enough to her husband.'

'But Mrs John Dashwood would not much approve of Edward's going into orders.'

'Then I rather suspect that my interest would do very little.'

They were again silent for many minutes. At length Lucy exclaimed with a deep sigh,

'I believe it would be the wisest way to put an end to the business at once by dissolving the engagement. We seem so beset with difficulties on every side, that though it would make us miserable for a time, we should be happier perhaps in the end. But you will not give me your advice, Miss Dashwood?'

'No;' answered Elinor, with a smile, which concealed very agitated feelings, 'on such a subject I certainly will not. You know very well that my opinion would have no weight with you, unless it were on the side of your wishes.'

'Indeed you wrong me,' replied Lucy with great solemnity; 'I know nobody of whose judgment I think so highly as I do of yours; and I do really believe, that if you was to say to me, "I advise you by all means to put an end to your engagement with Edward Ferrars, it will be more for the happiness of both of you," I should resolve upon doing it immediately.'

Elinor blushed for the insincerity of Edward's future wife, and replied, 'This compliment would effectually frighten me from giving any opinion on the subject had I formed one. It raises my influence much too high; the power of dividing two people so tenderly attached is too much for an indifferent person.'

' 'Tis because you are an indifferent person,' said Lucy, with some pique, and laying a particular stress on those words, 'that your judgment might justly have such weight with me. If you could be supposed to be biassed in any respect by your own feelings, your opinion would not be worth having.'

Elinor thought it wisest to make no answer to this, lest they might provoke each other to an unsuitable increase of ease and unreserve; and was even partly determined never to mention the subject again. Another pause therefore of many minutes' duration, succeeded this speech, and Lucy was still the first to end it.

'Shall you be in town this winter, Miss Dashwood?' said she with all her accustomary complacency.

'Certainly not.'

'I am sorry for that,' returned the other, while her eyes brightened at the information, 'it would have gave me such pleasure to meet you there! But I dare say you will go for all that. To be sure, your brother and sister will ask you to come to them.'

'It will not be in my power to accept their invitation if they do.'

'How unlucky that is! I had quite depended upon meeting you there.

Anne and me are to go the latter end of January to some relations who have been wanting us to visit them these several years! But I only go for the sake of seeing Edward. He will be there in February, otherwise London would have no charms for me; I have not spirits for it.'

Elinor was soon called to the card-table by the conclusion of the first rubber, and the confidential discourse of the two ladies was therefore at an end, to which both of them submitted without any reluctance, for nothing had been said on either side, to make them dislike each other less than they had done before; and Elinor sat down to the card-table with the melancholy persuasion that Edward was not only without affection for the person who was to be his wife; but that he had not even the chance of being tolerably happy in marriage, which sincere affection on *her* side would have given, for self-interest alone could induce a woman to keep a man to an engagement, of which she seemed so thoroughly aware that he was weary.

From this time the subject was never revived by Elinor, and when entered on by Lucy, who seldom missed an opportunity of introducing it, and was particularly careful to inform her confidante, of her happiness whenever she received a letter from Edward, it was treated by the former with calmness and caution, and dismissed as soon as civility would allow; for she felt such conversations to be an indulgence which Lucy did not deserve, and which were dangerous to herself.

The visit of the Miss Steeles at Barton Park was lengthened far beyond what the first invitation implied. Their favour increased, they could not be spared; Sir John would not hear of their going; and in spite of their numerous and long arranged engagements in Exeter, in spite of the absolute necessity of their returning to fulfil them immediately, which was in full force at the end of every week, they were prevailed on to stay nearly two months at the park, and to assist in the due celebration of that festival which requires a more than ordinary share of private balls and large dinners to proclaim its importance.

Chapter Twenty Five

THOUGH MRS JENNINGS WAS IN the habit of spending a large portion of the year at the houses of her children and friends, she was not without a settled habitation of her own. Since the death of her husband, who had traded with success in a less elegant part of the town, she had resided every winter in a house in one of the streets near Portman-square. Towards this home, she began on the approach of January to turn her thoughts, and thither she one day abruptly, and very unexpectedly by them, asked the elder Miss Dashwoods to accompany her. Elinor, without observing the varying complexion of her sister, and the animated look which spoke no indifference to the plan, immediately gave a grateful but absolute denial for both, in which she believed herself to be speaking their united inclinations. The reason alleged was their determined resolution of not leaving their mother at that time of the year. Mrs Jennings received the refusal with some surprise, and repeated her invitation immediately.

'Oh! Lord, I am sure your mother can spare you very well, and I *do* beg you will favour me with your company, for I've quite set my heart upon it. Don't fancy that you will be any inconvenience to me, for I shan't put myself at all out of my way for you. It will only be sending Betty by the coach, and I hope I can afford *that*. We three shall be able to go very well in my chaise; and when we are in town, if you do not like to go wherever I do, well and good, you may always go with one of my daughters. I am sure your mother will not object to it; for I have had such good luck in getting my own children off my hands, that she will think me a very fit person to have the charge of you; and if I don't get one of you at least well married before I have done with you, it shall not be my fault. I shall speak a good word for you to all the young men, you may depend upon it.'

'I have a notion,' said Sir John, 'that Miss Marianne would not object to such a scheme, if her elder sister would come into it. It is very hard indeed that she should not have a little pleasure, because Miss Dashwood does not wish it. So I would advise you two, to set off for town, when you are tired of Barton, without saying a word to Miss Dashwood about it.'

'Nay,' cried Mrs Jennings, 'I am sure I shall be monstrous glad of Miss Marianne's company, whether Miss Dashwood will go or not, only the more the merrier say I, and I thought it would be more comfortable for them to be together; because if they got tired of me, they might talk to one another, and laugh at my odd ways behind my back. But one or the other, if not both of them, I must have. Lord bless me! how do you think I can live poking by myself, I who have been always used till this winter to have Charlotte with me. Come, Miss Marianne, let us strike hands upon the bargain, and if Miss Dashwood will change her mind by and bye, why so much the better.'

'I thank you, ma'am, sincerely thank you,' said Marianne, with warmth; 'your invitation has insured my gratitude for ever, and it would give me such happiness, yes almost the greatest happiness I am capable of, to be able to accept it. But my mother, my dearest, kindest mother, – I feel the justice of what Elinor has urged, and if she were to be made less happy, less comfortable by our absence – Oh! no nothing should tempt me to leave her. It should not, must not be a struggle.'

Mrs Jennings repeated her assurance that Mrs Dashwood could spare them perfectly well; and Elinor, who now understood her sister, and saw to what indifference to almost every thing else, she was carried by her eagerness to be with Willoughby again, made no farther direct opposition to the plan, and merely referred it to her mother's decision, from whom however she scarcely expected to receive any support in her endeavour to prevent a visit, which she could not approve of for Marianne, and which on her own account she had particular reasons to avoid. Whatever Marianne was desirous of, her mother would be eager to promote – she could not expect to influence the latter to cautiousness of conduct in an affair, respecting which she had never been able to inspire her with distrust; and she dared not explain the motive of her own disinclination for going to London. That Marianne, fastidious as she was, thoroughly acquainted with Mrs Jennings' manners, and invariably disgusted by them, should overlook every inconvenience of that kind, should disregard whatever must be most wounding to her irritable feelings, in her pursuit of one object, was such a proof, so strong, so full, of the importance of that object to her, as Elinor, in spite of all that had passed, was not prepared to witness.

On being informed of the invitation, Mrs Dashwood, persuaded that such an excursion would be productive of much amusement to both her daughters, and perceiving through all her affectionate attention to herself, how much the heart of Marianne was in it, would not hear of their declining the offer upon *her* account; insisted on their both accepting it directly, and then began to foresee with her usual cheerfulness, a variety of advantages that would accrue to them all, from this separation.

'I am delighted with the plan,' she cried, 'it is exactly what I could wish. Margaret and I shall be as much benefited by it as yourselves. When you and the Middletons are gone, we shall go on so quietly and happily together with our books and our music! You will find Margaret so improved when you come back again! And I have a little plan of alteration for your bedrooms too, which may now be performed without inconvenience to any one. It is very right that you *should* go to town; I would have every young woman of your condition in life, acquainted with the manners and amusements of London. You will be under the care of a motherly good sort of woman, of whose kindness to you I can have no doubt. And in all probability you will *see* your brother, and whatever may be his faults, or the faults of his wife, when I consider whose son he is, I cannot bear to have you so wholly estranged from each other.'

'Though with your usual anxiety for our happiness,' said Elinor, 'you have been obviating every impediment to the present scheme which occurred to you, there is still one objection which, in my opinion, cannot be so easily removed.'

Marianne's countenance sunk.

'And what,' said Mrs Dashwood, 'is my dear prudent Elinor going to suggest? What formidable obstacle is she now to bring forward? Do not let me hear a word about the expense of it.'

'My objection is this; though I think very well of Mrs Jennings's heart, she is not a woman whose society can afford us pleasure, or whose protection will give us consequence.'

'That is very true,' replied her mother; 'but of her society, separately from that of other people, you will scarcely have any thing at all, and you will almost always appear in public with Lady Middleton.'

'If Elinor is frightened away by her dislike of Mrs Jennings,' said Marianne, 'at least it need not prevent *my* accepting her invitation. I have no such scruples, and I am sure, I could put up with every unpleasantness of that kind with very little effort.'

Elinor could not help smiling at this display of indifference towards the manners of a person, to whom she had often had difficulty in persuading Marianne to behave with tolerable politeness; and resolved within herself, that if her sister persisted in going, she would go likewise, as she did not think it proper that Marianne should be left to the sole guidance of her own judgment, or that Mrs Jennings should be abandoned to the mercy of Marianne for all the comfort of her domestic hours. To this determination she was the more easily reconciled, by recollecting, that Edward Ferrars, by Lucy's account, was not to be in town before February; and that their visit, without any unreasonable abridgment, might be previously finished.

'I will have you *both* go,' said Mrs Dashwood; 'these objections are nonsensical. You will have much pleasure in being in London, and especially in being together; and if Elinor would ever condescend to anticipate enjoyment, she would foresee it there from a variety of sources; she would perhaps expect some from improving her acquaintance with her sister-in-law's family.'

Elinor had often wished for an opportunity of attempting to weaken her mother's dependence on the attachment of Edward and herself, that the shock might be the less when the whole truth were revealed, and now on this attack, though almost hopeless of success, she forced herself to begin her design by saying, as calmly as she could, 'I like Edward Ferrars very much, and shall always be glad to see him; but as to the rest of the family, it is a matter of perfect indifference to me, whether I am ever known to them or not.'

Mrs Dashwood smiled and said nothing. Marianne lifted up her eyes in astonishment, and Elinor conjectured that she might as well have held her tongue.

After very little farther discourse, it was finally settled that the invitation should be fully accepted. Mrs Jennings received the information with a great deal of joy, and many assurances of kindness and care; nor was it a matter of pleasure merely to her. Sir John was delighted; for to a man, whose prevailing anxiety was the dread of being alone, the acquisition of two, to the number of inhabitants in London, was something. Even Lady Middleton took the trouble of being delighted, which was putting herself rather out of her way; and as for the Miss Steeles, especially Lucy, they had never been so happy in their lives as this intelligence made them.

Elinor submitted to the arrangement which counter-acted her wishes, with less reluctance than she had expected to feel. With regard to herself, it was now a matter of unconcern whether she went to town or not, and when she saw her mother so thoroughly pleased with the plan, and her sister exhilarated by it in look, voice, and manner, restored to all her usual animation, and elevated to more than her usual gaiety, she could not be dissatisfied with the cause, and would hardly allow herself to distrust the consequence.

Marianne's joy was almost a degree beyond happiness, so great was the perturbation of her spirits and her impatience to be gone. Her unwillingness to quit her mother was her only restorative to calmness; and at the moment of parting, her grief on that score was excessive. Her mother's affliction was hardly less, and Elinor was the only one of the three, who seemed to consider the separation as any thing short of eternal.

Their departure took place in the first week in January. The Middletons were to follow in about a week. The Miss Steeles kept their station at the park, and were to quit it only with the rest of the family.

Chapter Twenty Six

ELINOR COULD NOT FIND HERSELF in the carriage with Mrs Jennings, and beginning a journey to London under her protection, and as her guest, without wondering at her own situation, so short had their acquaintance with that lady been, so wholly unsuited were they in age and disposition, and so many had been her objections against such a measure only a few days before! But these objections had all, with that happy ardour of youth which Marianne and her mother equally shared, been overcome or overlooked; and Elinor, in spite of every occasional doubt of Willoughby's constancy, could not witness the rapture of delightful expectation which filled the whole soul and beamed in the eyes of Marianne, without feeling how blank was her own prospect, how cheerless her own state of mind in the comparison, and how gladly she would engage in the solicitude of Marianne's situation to have the same animating object in view, the same possibility of hope. A short, a very short time however must now decide what Willoughby's intentions were; in all probability he was already in town. Marianne's eagerness to be gone declared her dependance on finding him there; and Elinor was resolved not only upon gaining every new light as to his character which her own observation or the intelligence of others could give her, but likewise upon watching his behaviour to her sister with such zealous attention, as to ascertain what he was and what he meant, before many meetings had taken place. Should the result of her observations be unfavourable, she was determined at all events to open the eyes of her sister; should it be otherwise, her exertions would be of a different nature – she must then learn to avoid every selfish comparison, and banish every regret which might lessen her satisfaction in the happiness of Marianne.

They were three days on their journey, and Marianne's behaviour as they travelled was a happy specimen of what her future complaisance and companionableness to Mrs Jennings might be expected to be. She sat in silence almost all the way, wrapt in her own meditations, and scarcely ever voluntarily speaking, except when any object of picturesque beauty within their view drew from her an exclamation of delight exclusively addressed to her sister. To atone for this conduct therefore, Elinor took immediate possession of the post of civility which she had assigned herself, behaved with the greatest attention to Mrs Jennings, talked with her, laughed with her, and listened to her whenever she could; and Mrs Jennings on her side treated them both with all possible kindness, was solicitous on every occasion for their ease and enjoyment, and only disturbed that she could not make them choose their own dinners at the inn, nor extort a confession of their preferring salmon to cod, or boiled fowls to veal cutlets. They reached town by three o'clock the third day, glad to be released, after such a journey, from the confinement of a carriage, and ready to enjoy all the luxury of a good fire.

The house was handsome and handsomely fitted up, and the young ladies were immediately put in possession of a very comfortable apartment. It had formerly been Charlotte's, and over the mantlepiece still hung a landscape in coloured silks of her performance, in proof of her having spent seven years at a great school in town to some effect.

As dinner was not to be ready in less than two hours from their arrival, Elinor determined to employ the interval in writing to her mother, and sat down for that purpose. In a few moments Marianne did the same. 'I am writing home, Marianne,' said Elinor; 'had not you better defer your letter for a day or two?'

'I am *not* going to write to my mother,' replied Marianne hastily, and as if wishing to avoid any farther inquiry. Elinor said no more; it immediately struck her that she must then be writing to Willoughby, and the conclusion which as instantly followed was, that however mysteriously they might wish to conduct the affair, they must be engaged. This conviction, though not entirely satisfactory, gave her pleasure, and she continued her letter with greater alacrity. Marianne's was finished in a very few minutes; in length it could be no more than a note: it was then folded up, sealed and directed with eager rapidity. Elinor thought she could distinguish a large W. in the direction, and no sooner was it complete than Marianne, ringing the bell, requested the footman who answered it, to get that letter conveyed for her to the two-penny post. This decided the matter at once.

Her spirits still continued very high, but there was a flutter in them which prevented their giving much pleasure to her sister, and this agitation increased as the evening drew on. She could scarcely eat any dinner, and when they afterwards returned to the drawing room, seemed anxiously listening to the sound of every carriage.

It was a great satisfaction to Elinor that Mrs Jennings, by being much engaged in her own room, could see little of what was passing. The tea things were brought in, and already had Marianne been disappointed more than once by a rap at a neighbouring door, when a loud one was suddenly heard which could not be mistaken for one at any other house, Elinor felt secure of its announcing Willoughby's approach, and Marianne starting up moved towards the door. Every thing was silent; this could not be borne many seconds, she opened the door, advanced a few steps towards the stairs, and after listening half a minute, returned into the room in all the agitation which a conviction of having heard him would naturally produce; in the extasy of her feelings at that instant she could not help exclaiming, 'Oh! Elinor, it is Willoughby, indeed it is!' and seemed almost ready to throw herself into his arms, when Colonel Brandon appeared.

It was too great a shock to be borne with calmness, and she immediately left the room. Elinor was disappointed too; but at the same time her regard for Colonel Brandon ensured his welcome with her, and she felt particularly hurt that a man so partial to her sister should perceive that she experienced nothing but grief and disappointment in seeing him. She instantly saw that it was not unnoticed by him, that he even observed Marianne as she quitted the room, with such astonishment and concern, as hardly left him the recollection of what civility demanded towards herself.

'Is your sister ill?' said he.

Elinor answered in some distress that she was, and then talked of head-aches, low spirits, and over fatigues; and of every thing to which she could decently attribute her sister's behaviour.

He heard her with the most earnest attention, but seeming to recollect himself, said no more on the subject, and began directly to speak of his pleasure at seeing them in London, making the usual inquiries about their journey and the friends they had left behind.

In this calm kind of way, with very little interest on either side, they continued to talk, both of them out of spirits, and the thoughts of both engaged elsewhere. Elinor wished very much to ask whether Willoughby were then in town, but she was afraid of giving him pain by any inquiry after his rival; and at length by way of saying something, she asked if he had been in London ever since she had seen him last. 'Yes,' he replied, with some embarrassment, 'almost ever since; I have been once or twice at Delaford for a few days, but it has never been in my power to return to Barton.'

This, and the manner in which it was said, immediately brought back to her remembrance, all the circumstances of his quitting that place, with the uneasiness and suspicions they had caused to Mrs Jennings, and she was fearful that her question had implied much more curiosity on the subject than she had ever felt.

Mrs Jennings soon came in. 'Oh! Colonel,' said she, with her usual noisy cheerfulness, 'I am monstrous glad to see you – sorry I could not come before – beg your pardon, but I have been forced to look about me a little, and settle my matters; for it is a long while since I have been at home, and you know one has always a world of little odd things to do after one has been away for any time; and then I have had Cartwright to settle with – Lord, I have been as busy as a bee ever since dinner! But pray, Colonel, how came you to conjure out that I should be in town today?'

'I had the pleasure of hearing it at Mr Palmer's, where I have been dining.'

'Oh! you did; well, and how do they all do at their house? How does Charlotte do? I warrant you she is a fine size by this time.'

'Mrs Palmer appeared quite well, and I am commissioned to tell you, that you will certainly see her to-morrow.'

'Aye, to be sure, I thought as much. Well, Colonel, I have brought two young ladies with me, you see – that is, you see but one of them now, but there is another somewhere. Your friend Miss Marianne, too – which you will not be sorry to hear. I do not know what you and Mr Willoughby will do between you about her. Aye, it is a fine thing to be young and handsome. Well! I was young once, but I never was very handsome – worse luck for me. However I got a very good husband, and I don't know what the greatest beauty can do more. Ah! poor man! he has been dead these eight years and better. But Colonel, where have you been to since we parted? And how does your business go on? Come, come, let's have no secrets among friends.'

He replied with his accustomary mildness to all her inquiries, but without satisfying her in any. Elinor now began to make the tea, and Marianne was obliged to appear again.

After her entrance, Colonel Brandon became more thoughtful and silent than he had been before, and Mrs Jennings could not prevail on him to stay long. No other visitor appeared that evening, and the ladies were unanimous in agreeing to go early to bed.

Marianne rose the next morning with recovered spirits and happy looks. The disappointment of the evening before seemed forgotten in the expectation of what was to happen that day. They had not long finished their breakfast before Mrs Palmer's barouche stopt at the door, and in a few minutes she came laughing into the room; so delighted to see them all, that it was hard to say whether she received most pleasure from meeting her mother or the Miss Dashwoods again. So surprised at their coming to town, though it was what she had rather expected all along; so angry at their accepting her mother's invitation after having declined her own, though at the same time she would never have forgiven them if they had not come!

'Mr Palmer will be so happy to see you,' said she; 'what do you think he said when he heard of your coming with mama? I forget what it was now, but it was something so droll!'

After an hour or two spent in what her mother called comfortable chat, or in other words, in every variety of inquiry concerning all their acquaintance on Mrs Jennings's side, and in laughter without cause on Mrs Palmer's, it was proposed by the latter that they should all accompany her to some shops where she had business that morning, to which Mrs Jennings and Elinor readily consented, as having likewise some purchases to make themselves; and Marianne, though declining it at first, was induced to go likewise.

Wherever they went, she was evidently always on the watch. In Bond-street especially, where much of their business lay, her eyes were in constant inquiry; and in whatever shop the party were engaged, her mind was equally abstracted from every thing actually before them, from all that interested and occupied the others. Restless and dissatisfied every where, her sister could never obtain her opinion of any article of purchase, however it might equally concern them both; she received no pleasure from any thing; was only impatient to be at home again, and could with difficulty govern her vexation at the tediousness of Mrs Palmer, whose eye was caught by every thing pretty, expensive, or new; who was wild to buy all, could determine on none, and dawdled away her time in rapture and indecision.

It was late in the morning before they returned home; and no sooner had they entered the house than Marianne flew eagerly up stairs, and when Elinor followed, she found her turning from the table with a sorrowful countenance, which declared that no Willoughby had been there.

'Has no letter been left here for me since we went out?' said she to the footman who then entered with the parcels. She was answered in the negative. 'Are you quite sure of it?' she replied. 'Are you certain that no servant, no porter has left any letter or note?'

The man replied that none had.

'How very odd!' said she in a low and disappointed voice, as she turned away to the window.

'How odd indeed!' repeated Elinor within herself, regarding her sister with uneasiness. 'If she had not known him to be in town she would not have written to him, as she did; she would have written to Combe Magna; and if he is in town, how odd that he should neither come nor write! Oh! my dear mother, you must be wrong in permitting an engagement between a daughter so young, a man so little known, to be carried on in so doubtful, so mysterious a manner! *I* long to inquire; but how will *my* interference be borne!'

She determined after some consideration, that if appearances continued many days longer, as unpleasant as they now were, she would represent in the strongest manner to her mother the necessity of some serious inquiry into the affair.

Mrs Palmer and two elderly ladies of Mrs Jennings's intimate acquaintance, whom she had met and invited in the morning, dined with them. The former left them soon after tea to fulfil her evening engagements; and Elinor was obliged to assist in making a whist table for the others. Marianne was of no use on these occasions, as she would never learn the game, but though her time was therefore at her own disposal, the evening was by no means more productive of pleasure to her than to Elinor, for it was spent in all the anxiety of expectation and the pain of disappointment. She sometimes endeavoured for a few minutes to read; but the book was soon thrown aside, and she returned to the more interesting employment of walking backwards and forwards across the room, pausing for a moment whenever she came to the window, in hopes of distinguishing the long-expected rap.

Chapter Twenty Seven

'IF THIS OPEN WEATHER HOLDS much longer,' said Mrs Jennings, when they met at breakfast the following morning, 'Sir John will not like leaving Barton next week; 'tis a sad thing for sportsmen to lose a day's pleasure. Poor souls! I always pity them when they do; they seem to take it so much to heart.'

'That is true,' cried Marianne in a cheerful voice, and walking to the window as she spoke, to examine the day. 'I had not thought of *that*. This weather will keep many sportsmen in the country.'

It was a lucky recollection, all her good spirits were restored by it. 'It is charming weather for *them* indeed,' she continued, as she sat down to the breakfast table with a happy countenance. 'How much they must enjoy it! But' (with a little return of anxiety) 'it cannot be expected to last long. At this time of year, and after such a series of rain, we shall certainly have very little more of it. Frosts will soon set in, and in all probability with severity. In another day or two perhaps; this extreme mildness can hardly last longer – nay, perhaps it may freeze tonight!'

'At any rate,' said Elinor, wishing to prevent Mrs Jennings from seeing her sister's thoughts as clearly as she did, 'I dare say we shall have Sir John and Lady Middleton in town by the end of next week.'

'Aye, my dear, I'll warrant you we do. Mary always has her own way.'

'And now,' silently conjectured Elinor, 'she will write to Combe by this day's post.'

But if she *did*, the letter was written and sent away with a privacy which eluded all her watchfulness to ascertain the fact. Whatever the truth of it might be, and far as Elinor was from feeling thorough contentment about it, yet while she saw Marianne in spirits, she could not be very uncomfortable herself. And Marianne was in spirits; happy in the mildness of the weather, and still happier in her expectation of a frost.

The morning was chiefly spent in leaving cards at the houses of Mrs Jennings's acquaintance to inform them of her being in town; and Marianne was all the time busy in observing the direction of the wind, watching the variations of the sky and imagining an alteration in the air.

'Don't you find it colder than it was in the morning, Elinor? There seems to me a very decided difference. I can hardly keep my hands warm even in my muff. It was not so yesterday, I think. The clouds seem parting too, the sun will be out in a moment; and we shall have a clear afternoon.'

Elinor was alternately diverted and pained; but Marianne persevered, and saw every night in the brightness of the fire, and every morning in the appearance of the atmosphere, the certain symptoms of approaching frost.

The Miss Dashwoods had no greater reason to be dissatisfied with Mrs Jennings's style of living, and set of acquaintance, than with her behaviour to themselves, which was invariably kind. Every thing in her household arrangements was conducted on the most liberal plan, and excepting a few old city friends, whom, to Lady Middleton's regret, she had never dropped, she visited no one, to whom an introduction could at all discompose the feelings of her young companions. Pleased to find herself more comfortably situated in that particular than she had expected, Elinor was very willing to compound for the want of much real enjoyment from any of their evening parties, which, whether at home or abroad, formed only for cards, could have little to amuse her.

Colonel Brandon, who had a general invitation to the house, was with them almost every day; he came to look at Marianne and talk to Elinor, who often derived more satisfaction from conversing with him than from any other daily occurrence, but who saw at the same time with much concern his continued regard for her sister. She feared it was a strengthening regard. It grieved her to see the earnestness with which he often watched Marianne, and his spirits were certainly worse than when at Barton.

About a week after their arrival it became certain that Willoughby was also arrived. His card was on the table, when they came in from the morning's drive.

'Good God!' said Marianne, 'he has been here while we were out.' Elinor, rejoiced to be assured of his being in London, now ventured to say, 'depend upon it he will call again tomorrow.' But Marianne seemed hardly to hear her, and on Mrs Jennings's entrance, escaped with the precious card.

This event, while it raised the spirits of Elinor, restored to those of her sister, all, and more than all, their former agitation. From this moment her mind was never quiet; the expectation of seeing him every hour of the day, made her unfit for anything. She insisted on being left behind, the next morning, when the others went out.

Elinor's thoughts were full of what might be passing in Berkeley-street during their absence; but a moment's glance at her sister when they returned was enough to inform her, that Willoughby had paid no second visit there. A note was just then brought in, and laid on the table.

'For me!' cried Marianne, stepping hastily forward.

'No, ma'am, for my mistress.'

But Marianne, not convinced, took it instantly up.

'It is indeed for Mrs Jennings; how provoking!'

'You are expecting a letter then?' said Elinor, unable to be longer silent.

'Yes, a little – not much.'

After a short pause, 'You have no confidence in me, Marianne.'

'Nay, Elinor, this reproach from you – you who have confidence in no one!'

'Me!' returned Elinor in some confusion; 'indeed, Marianne, I have nothing to tell.'

'Nor I,' answered Marianne with energy, 'our situations then are alike. We have neither of us any thing to tell; you, because you do not communicate, and I, because I conceal nothing.'

Elinor, distressed by this charge of reserve in herself, which she was not at liberty to do away, knew not how, under such circumstances, to press for greater openness in Marianne.

Mrs Jennings soon appeared, and the note being given her, she read it aloud. It was from Lady Middleton, announcing their arrival in Conduit-street the night before, and requesting the company of her mother and cousins the following evening. Business on Sir John's part, and a violent cold on her own, prevented their calling in Berkeley-street. The invitation was accepted: but when the hour of appointment drew near, necessary as it was in common civility to Mrs Jennings, that they should both attend her on such a visit, Elinor had some difficulty in persuading her sister to go, for still she had seen nothing of Willoughby; and therefore was not more indisposed for amusement abroad, than unwilling to run the risk of his calling again in her absence.

Elinor found, when the evening was over, that disposition is not materially altered by a change of abode, for although scarcely settled in town, Sir John had contrived to collect around him, nearly twenty young people, and to amuse them with a ball. This was an affair, however, of which Lady Middleton did not approve. In the country, an unpremeditated dance was very allowable; but in London, where the reputation of elegance was more important and less easily attained, it was risking too much for the gratification of a few girls, to have it known that Lady Middleton had given a small dance of eight or nine couple, with two violins, and a mere side-board collation.

Mr and Mrs Palmer were of the party; from the former, whom they had not seen before since their arrival in town, as he was careful to avoid the appearance of any attention to his mother-in-law, and therefore never came near her, they received no mark of recognition on their entrance. He looked at them slightly, without seeming to know who they were, and merely nodded to Mrs Jennings from the other side of the room. Marianne gave one glance round the apartment as she entered; it was enough, *he* was not there – and she sat down, equally ill-disposed to receive or communicate pleasure. After they had been assembled about an hour, Mr Palmer sauntered towards the Miss Dashwoods to express his surprise on seeing them in town, though Colonel Brandon had been first informed of their arrival at his house, and he had himself said something very droll on hearing that they were to come.

'I thought you were both in Devonshire,' said he.

'Did you?' replied Elinor.

'When do you go back again?'

'I do not know.' And thus ended their discourse.

Never had Marianne been so unwilling to dance in her life, as she was that evening, and never so much fatigued by the exercise. She complained of it as they returned to Berkeley-street.

'Aye, aye,' said Mrs Jennings, 'we know the reason of all that very well; if a certain person who shall be nameless, had been there, you would not have been a bit tired; and to say the truth it was not very pretty of him not to give you the meeting when he was invited.'

'Invited!' cried Marianne.

'So my daughter Middleton told me, for it seems Sir John met him somewhere in the street this morning.'

Marianne said no more, but looked exceedingly hurt. Impatient in this situation to be doing something that might lead to her sister's relief, Elinor resolved to write the next morning to her mother, and hoped by awakening her fears for the health of Marianne, to procure those inquiries which had been so long delayed; and she was still more eagerly bent on this measure by perceiving after breakfast on the morrow, that Marianne was again writing to Willoughby, for she could not suppose it to be to any other person.

About the middle of the day, Mrs Jennings went out by herself on business, and Elinor began her letter directly, while Marianne, too restless for employment, too anxious for conversation, walked from one window to the other, or sat down by the fire in melancholy meditation. Elinor was very earnest in her application to her mother, relating all that had passed, her suspicions of Willoughby's inconstancy, urging her by every plea of duty and affection to demand from Marianne, an account of her real situation with respect to him.

Her letter was scarcely finished, when a rap foretold a visitor, and Colonel Brandon was announced. Marianne, who had seen him from the window, and who hated company of any kind, left the room before he entered it. He looked more than usually grave, and though expressing satisfaction at finding Miss Dashwood alone, as if he had somewhat in particular to tell her, sat for some time without saying a word. Elinor, persuaded that he had some communication to make in which her sister was concerned, impatiently expected its opening. It was not the first time of her feeling the same kind of conviction; for more than once before, beginning with the observation of 'your sister looks unwell today,' or 'your sister seems out of spirits,' he had appeared on the point, either of disclosing, or of inquiring, something particular about her. After a pause of several minutes, their silence was broken, by his asking her in a voice of some agitation, when he was to congratulate her on the acquisition of a brother? Elinor was not prepared for such a question, and having no answer ready, was obliged to adopt the simple and common expedient, of asking what he meant? He tried to smile as he replied, 'your sister's engagement to Mr Willoughby is very generally known.'

'It cannot be generally known,' returned Elinor, 'for her own family do not know it.'

He looked surprised and said, 'I beg your pardon, I am afraid my inquiry has been impertinent; but I had not supposed any secrecy intended, as they openly correspond, and their marriage is universally talked of.'

'How can that be? By whom can you have heard it mentioned?'

'By many – by some of whom you know nothing, by others with whom you are most intimate, Mrs Jennings, Mrs Palmer, and the Middletons. But still I might not have believed it, for where the mind is perhaps rather unwilling to be convinced, it will always find something to support its doubts, if I had not, when the servant let me in today, accidentally seen a letter in his hand, directed to Mr Willoughby in your sister's writing. I came to inquire, but I was convinced before I could ask the question. Is every thing finally settled? Is it impossible to –? But I have no right, and I could have no chance of succeeding. Excuse me, Miss Dashwood. I believe I have been wrong in saying so much, but I hardly know what to do, and on your prudence I have the strongest dependence. Tell me that it is all absolutely resolved on, that any attempt, that in short concealment, if concealment be possible, is all that remains.'

These words, which conveyed to Elinor a direct avowal of his love for her sister, affected her very much. She was not immediately able to say any thing, and even when her spirits were recovered, she debated for a short time, on the answer it would be most proper to give. The real state of things between Willoughby and her sister was so little known to herself, that in endeavouring to explain it, she might be as liable to say too much as too little. Yet as she was convinced that Marianne's affection for Willoughby, could leave no hope of Colonel Brandon's success, whatever the event of that affection might be, and at the same time wished to shield her conduct from censure, she thought it most prudent and kind, after some consideration, to say more than she really knew or believed. She acknowledged, therefore, that though she had never been informed by themselves of the terms on which they stood with each other, of their mutual affection she had no doubt, and of their correspondence she was not astonished to hear.

He listened to her with silent attention, and on her ceasing to speak, rose directly from his seat, and after saying in a voice of emotion, 'to your sister I wish all imaginable happiness; to Willoughby that he may endeavour to deserve her,' – took leave, and went away.

Elinor derived no comfortable feelings from this conversation, to lessen the uneasiness of her mind on other points; she was left, on the contrary, with a melancholy impression of Colonel Brandon's unhappiness, and was prevented even from wishing it removed, by her anxiety for the very event that must confirm it.

Chapter Twenty Eight

NOTHING OCCURRED DURING THE NEXT three or four days, to make Elinor regret what she had done, in applying to her mother; for Willoughby neither came nor wrote. They were engaged about the end of that time to attend Lady Middleton to a party, from which Mrs Jennings was kept away by the indisposition of her youngest daughter; and for this party, Marianne, wholly dispirited, careless of her appearance, and seeming equally indifferent whether she went or staid, prepared, without one look of hope, or one expression of pleasure. She sat by the drawing-room fire after tea, till the moment of Lady Middleton's arrival, without once stirring from her seat, or altering her attitude, lost in her own thoughts and insensible of her sister's presence; and when at last they were told that Lady Middleton waited for them at the door, she started as if she had forgotten that any one was expected.

They arrived in due time at the place of destination, and as soon as the string of carriages before them would allow, alighted, ascended the stairs, heard their names announced from one landing-place to another in an audible voice, and entered a room splendidly lit up, quite full of company, and insufferably hot. When they had paid their tribute of politeness by curtsying to the lady of the house, they were permitted to mingle in the crowd, and take their share of the heat and inconvenience, to which their arrival must necessarily add. After some time spent in saying little and doing less, Lady Middleton sat down to Casino, and as Marianne was not in spirits for moving about, she and Elinor luckily succeeding to chairs, placed themselves at no great distance from the table.

They had not remained in this manner long, before Elinor perceived Willoughby, standing within a few yards of them, in earnest conversation with a very fashionable looking young woman. She soon caught his eye, and he immediately bowed, but without attempting to speak to her, or to approach Marianne, though he could not but see her; and then continued his discourse with the same lady. Elinor turned involuntarily to Marianne, to see whether it could be unobserved by her. At that moment she first perceived him, and her whole countenance glowing with sudden delight, she would have moved towards him instantly, had not her sister caught hold of her.

'Good heavens!' she exclaimed, 'he is there – he is there – Oh! why does he not look at me? why cannot I speak to him?'

'Pray, pray be composed,' cried Elinor, 'and do not betray what you feel to every body present. Perhaps he has not observed you yet.'

This however was more than she could believe herself; and to be composed at such a moment was not only beyond the reach of Marianne, it was beyond her wish. She sat in an agony of impatience, which affected every feature.

At last he turned round again, and regarded them both; she started up, and pronouncing his name in a tone of affection, held out her hand to him. He approached, and addressing himself rather to Elinor than Marianne, as if wishing to avoid her eye, and determined not to observe her attitude, inquired in a hurried manner after Mrs Dashwood, and asked how long they had been in town. Elinor was robbed of all presence of mind by such an address, and was unable to say a word. But the feelings of her sister were instantly expressed. Her face was crimsoned over, and she exclaimed in a voice of the greatest emotion, 'Good God! Willoughby, what is the meaning of this? Have you not received my letters? Will you not shake hands with me?'

He could not then avoid it, but her touch seemed painful to him, and he held her hand only for a moment. During all this time he was evidently struggling for composure. Elinor watched his countenance and saw its expression becoming more tranquil. After a moment's pause, he spoke with calmness.

'I did myself the honour of calling in Berkeley-street last Tuesday, and very much regretted that I was not fortunate enough to find yourselves and Mrs Jennings at home. My card was not lost, I hope.'

'But have you not received my notes?' cried Marianne in the wildest anxiety. 'Here is some mistake I am sure – some dreadful mistake. What can be the meaning of it? Tell me, Willoughby; for heaven's sake tell me, what is the matter?'

He made no reply; his complexion changed and all his embarrassment returned; but as if, on catching the eye of the young lady with whom he had been previously talking, he felt the necessity of instant exertion, he recovered himself again, and after saying, 'Yes, I had the pleasure of receiving the information of your arrival in town, which you were so good as to send me,' turned hastily away with a slight bow and joined his friend.

Marianne, now looking dreadfully white, and unable to stand, sunk into her chair, and Elinor, expecting every moment to see her faint, tried to screen her from the observation of others, while reviving her with lavender water.

'Go to him, Elinor,' she cried, as soon as she could speak, 'and force him to come to me. Tell him I must see him again – must speak to him instantly. – I cannot rest – I shall not have a moment's peace till this is explained – some dreadful misapprehension or other. – Oh go to him this moment.'

'How can that be done? No, my dearest Marianne, you must wait. This is not a place for explanations. Wait only till to-morrow.'

With difficulty however could she prevent her from following him herself; and to persuade her to check her agitation, to wait, at least, with the appearance of composure, till she might speak to him with more privacy and more effect, was impossible; for Marianne continued incessantly to give way in a low voice to the misery of her feelings, by exclamations of wretchedness. In a short time Elinor saw Willoughby quit the room by the door towards the staircase, and telling Marianne that he was gone, urged the impossibility of speaking to him again that evening, as a fresh argument for her to be calm. She instantly begged her sister would entreat Lady Middleton to take them home, as she was too miserable to stay a minute longer.

Lady Middleton, though in the middle of a rubber, on being informed that Marianne was unwell, was too polite to object for a moment to her wish of going away, and making over her cards to a friend, they departed as soon as the carriage could be found. Scarcely a word was spoken during their return to Berkeley-street. Marianne was in a silent agony, too much oppressed even for tears; but as Mrs Jennings was luckily not come home, they could go directly to their own room, where hartshorn restored her a little to herself. She was soon undressed and in bed, and as she seemed desirous of being alone, her sister then left her, and while she waited the return of Mrs Jennings, had leisure enough for thinking over the past.

That some kind of engagement had subsisted between Willoughby and Marianne she could not doubt; and that Willoughby was weary of it, seemed equally clear; for however Marianne might still feed her own wishes, *she* could not attribute such behaviour to mistake or misapprehension of any kind. Nothing but a thorough change of sentiment could account for it. Her indignation would have been still stronger than it was, had she not witnessed that embarrassment which seemed to speak a consciousness of his own misconduct, and prevented her from believing him so unprincipled as to have been sporting with the affections of her sister from the first, without any design that would bear investigation. Absence might have weakened his regard, and convenience might have determined him to overcome it, but that such a regard had formerly existed she could not bring herself to doubt.

As for Marianne, on the pangs which so unhappy a meeting must already have given her, and on those still more severe which might await her in its probable consequence, she could not reflect without the deepest concern. Her own situation gained in the comparison; for while she could *esteem* Edward as much as ever, however they might be divided in future, her mind might be always supported. But every circumstance that could embitter such an evil seemed uniting to heighten the misery of Marianne in a final separation from Willoughby – in an immediate and irreconcilable rupture with him.

Chapter Twenty Nine

BEFORE THE HOUSE-MAID had lit their fire the next day, or the sun gained any power over a cold, gloomy morning in January, Marianne, only half-dressed, was kneeling against one of the window-seats for the sake of all the little light she could command from it, and writing as fast as a continual flow of tears would permit her. In this situation, Elinor, roused from sleep by her agitation and sobs, first perceived her; and after observing her for a few moments with silent anxiety, said, in a tone of the most considerate gentleness,

'Marianne, may I ask?' –

'No, Elinor,' she replied, 'ask nothing; you will soon know all.'

The sort of desperate calmness with which this was said, lasted no longer than while she spoke, and was immediately followed by a return of the same excessive affliction. It was some minutes before she could go on with her letter, and the frequent bursts of grief which still obliged her, at intervals, to withhold her pen, were proofs enough of her feeling how more than probable it was that she was writing for the last time to Willoughby.

Elinor paid her every quiet and unobtrusive attention in her power; and she would have tried to soothe and tranquillize her still more, had not Marianne entreated her, with all the eagerness of the most nervous irritability, not to speak to her for the world. In such circumstances, it was better for both that they should not be long together; and the restless state of Marianne's mind not only prevented her from remaining in the room a moment after she was dressed, but requiring at once solitude and continual change of place, made her wander about the house till breakfast time, avoiding the sight of every body.

At breakfast she neither ate, nor attempted to eat any thing; and Elinor's attention was then all employed, not in urging her, not in pitying her, nor in appearing to regard her, but in endeavouring to engage Mrs Jennings's notice entirely to herself.

As this was a favourite meal with Mrs Jennings, it lasted a considerable time, and they were just setting themselves, after it, round the common working table, when a letter was delivered to Marianne, which she eagerly caught from the servant, and, turning of a death-like paleness, instantly ran out of the room. Elinor, who saw as plainly by this, as if she had seen the direction, that it must come from Willoughby, felt immediately such a sickness at heart as made her hardly able to hold up her head, and sat in such a general tremor as made her fear it impossible to escape Mrs Jennings's notice. That good lady, however, saw only that Marianne had received a letter from Willoughby, which appeared to her a very good joke, and which she treated accordingly, by hoping, with a laugh, that she would find it to her liking. Of Elinor's distress, she was too busily employed in measuring lengths of worsted for her rug, to see any thing at all; and calmly continuing her talk, as soon as Marianne disappeared, she said,

'Upon my word I never saw a young woman so desperately in love in my life! *My* girls were nothing to her, and yet they used to be foolish enough; but as for Miss Marianne, she is quite an altered creature. I hope, from the bottom of my heart, he won't keep her waiting much longer, for it is quite grievous to see her look so ill and forlorn. Pray, when are they to be married?'

Elinor, though never less disposed to speak than at that moment, obliged herself to answer such an attack as this, and, therefore, trying to smile, replied, 'And have you really, ma'am, talked yourself into a persuasion of my sister's being engaged to Mr Willoughby? I thought it had been only a joke, but so serious a question seems to imply more; and I must beg, therefore, that you will not deceive yourself any longer. I do assure you that nothing would surprise me more than to hear of their being going to be married.'

'For shame, for shame, Miss Dashwood! how can you talk so! Don't we all know that it must be a match, that they were over head and ears in love with each other from the first moment they met? Did not I see them together in Devonshire every day, and all day long; and did not I know that your sister came to town with me on purpose to buy wedding clothes? Come, come, this won't do. Because you are so sly about it yourself, you think nobody else has any senses; but it is no such thing, I can tell you, for it has been known all over town this ever so long. I tell every body of it and so does Charlotte.'

'Indeed, ma'am,' said Elinor, very seriously, 'you are mistaken. Indeed, you are doing a very unkind thing in spreading the report, and you will find that you have, though you will not believe me now.'

Mrs Jennings laughed again, but Elinor had not spirits to say more, and eager at all events to know what Willoughby had written, hurried away to their room, where, on opening the door, she saw Marianne stretched on the bed, almost choked by grief, one letter in her hand, and two or three others lying by her. Elinor drew near, but without saying a word; and seating herself on the bed, took her hand, kissed her affectionately several times, and then gave way to a burst of tears, which at first was scarcely less violent than Marianne's. The latter, though unable to speak, seemed to feel all the tenderness of this behaviour, and after some time thus spent in joint affliction, she put all the letters into Elinor's hands; and then covering her face with her handkerchief, almost screamed with agony. Elinor, who knew that such grief, shocking as it was to witness it, must have its course, watched by her till this excess of suffering had somewhat spent itself, and then turning eagerly to Willoughby's letter, read as follows:

Bond-street, January.

My DEAR MADAM,

I have just had the honour of receiving your letter, for which I beg to return my sincere acknowledgments. I am much concerned to find there was any thing in my behaviour last night that did not meet your approbation; and though I am quite at a loss to discover in what point I could be so unfortunate as to offend you, I entreat your forgiveness of what I can assure you to have been perfectly unintentional. I shall never reflect on my former acquaintance with your family in Devonshire without the most grateful pleasure, and flatter myself it will not be broken by any mistake or misapprehension of my actions. My esteem for your whole family is very sincere; but if I have been so unfortunate as to give rise to a belief of more than I felt, or meant to express, I shall reproach myself for not having been more guarded in my professions of that esteem. That I should ever have meant more you will allow to be impossible, when you understand that my affections have been long engaged elsewhere, and it will not be many weeks, I believe, before this engagement is fulfilled. It is with great regret that I obey your commands of returning the letters, with which I have been honoured from you, and the lock of hair, which you so obligingly bestowed on me.

I am, dear Madam,
Your most obedient
humble Servant,
JOHN WILLOUGHBY.

With what indignation such a letter as this must be read by Miss Dashwood, may be imagined. Though aware, before she began it, that it must bring a confession of his inconstancy, and confirm their separation for ever, she was not aware that such language could be suffered to announce it; nor could she have supposed Willoughby capable of departing so far from the appearance of every honourable and delicate feeling – so far from the common decorum of a gentleman, as to send a letter so impudently cruel: a letter which, instead of bringing with his desire of a release any professions of regret, acknowledged no breach of faith, denied all peculiar affection whatever – a letter of which every line was an insult, and which proclaimed its writer to be deep in hardened villany.

She paused over it for some time with indignant astonishment; then read it again and again; but every perusal only served to increase her abhorrence of the man, and so bitter were her feelings against him, that she dared not trust herself to speak, lest she might wound Marianne still deeper by treating their disengagement, not as a loss to her of any possible good but as an escape from the worst and most irremediable of all evils, a connection, for life, with an unprincipled man, as a deliverance the most real, a blessing the most important.

In her earnest meditations on the contents of the letter, on the depravity of that mind which could dictate it, and, probably, on the very different mind of a very different person, who had no other connection whatever with the affair than what her heart gave him with every thing that passed, Elinor forgot the immediate distress of her sister, forgot that she had three letters on her lap yet unread, and so entirely forgot how long she had been in the room, that when on hearing a carriage drive up to the door, she went to the window to see who could be coming so unreasonably early, she was all astonishment to perceive Mrs Jennings's chariot, which she knew had not been ordered till one. Determined not to quit Marianne, though hopeless of contributing, at present, to her ease, she hurried away to excuse herself from attending Mrs Jennings, on account of her sister being indisposed. Mrs Jennings, with a thoroughly good-humoured concern for its cause, admitted the excuse most readily, and Elinor, after seeing her safe off, returned to Marianne, whom she found attempting to rise from the bed, and whom she reached just in time to prevent her from falling on the floor, faint and giddy from a long want of proper rest and food; for it was many days since she had any appetite, and many nights since she had really slept; and now, when her mind was no longer supported by the fever of suspense, the consequence of all this was felt in an aching head, a weakened stomach, and a general nervous faintness. A glass of wine, which Elinor procured for her directly, made her more comfortable, and she was at last able to express some sense of her kindness, by saying,

'Poor Elinor! how unhappy I make you!'

'I only wish,' replied her sister, 'there were any thing I *could* do, which might be of comfort to you.'

This, as every thing else would have been, was too much for Marianne, who could only exclaim, in the anguish of her heart, 'Oh! Elinor, I am miserable indeed,' before her voice was entirely lost in sobs.

Elinor could no longer witness this torrent of unresisted grief in silence.

'Exert yourself, dear Marianne,' she cried, 'if you would not kill yourself and all who love you. Think of your mother; think of her misery while *you* suffer; for her sake you must exert yourself.'

'I cannot, I cannot,' cried Marianne; 'leave me, leave me, if I distress you; leave me, hate me, forget me! but do not torture me so. Oh! how easy for those who have no sorrow of their own to talk of exertion! Happy, happy Elinor, you cannot have an idea of what I suffer.'

'Do you call me happy, Marianne? Ah! if you knew! – And can you believe me to be so, while I see you so wretched!'

'Forgive me, forgive me,' throwing her arms round her sister's neck; I know you feel for me; I know what a heart you have; but yet you are – you must be happy; Edward loves you – what, oh! what can do away such happiness as that?'

'Many, many circumstances,' said Elinor, solemnly.

'No, no, no,' cried Marianne wildly, 'he loves you, and only you. You can have no grief.'

'I can have no pleasure while I see you in this state.'

'And you will never see me otherwise. Mine is a misery which nothing can do away.'

'You must not talk so, Marianne. Have you no comforts? no friends? Is your loss such as leaves no opening for consolation? Much as you suffer now, think of what you would have suffered if the discovery of his character had been delayed to a later period – if your engagement had been carried on for months and months, as it might have been, before he chose to put an end to it. Every additional day of unhappy confidence, on your side, would have made the blow more dreadful.'

'Engagement!' cried Marianne, 'there has been no engagement.'

'No engagement?'

'No, he is not so unworthy as you believe him. He has broken no faith with me.'

'But he told you that he loved you?'

'Yes – no – never absolutely. It was every day implied, but never professedly declared. Sometimes I thought it had been – but it never was.'

'Yet you wrote to him?' –

'Yes – could that be wrong after all that had passed? – But I cannot talk.'

Elinor said no more, and turning again to the three letters which now raised a much stronger curiosity than before, directly ran over the contents of all. The first, which was what her sister had sent him on their arrival in town, was to this effect.

> *Berkeley-street, January.*
>
> *How surprised you will be, Willoughby, on receiving this; and I think you will feel something more than surprise, when you know that I am in town. An opportunity of coming hither, though with Mrs Jennings, was a temptation we could not resist. I wish you may receive this in time to come here to-night, but I will not depend on it. At any rate I shall expect you to-morrow. For the present, adieu.*
>
> *M.D.*

Her second note, which had been written on the morning after the dance at the Middletons', was in these words:–

> *I cannot express my disappointment in having missed you the day before yesterday, nor my astonishment at not having received any answer to a note which I sent you above a week ago. I have been expecting to hear from you, and still more to see you, every hour of the day. Pray call again as soon as possible, and explain the reason of my having expected this in vain. You had*

better come earlier another time, because we are generally out by one. We were last night at Lady Middleton's, where there was a dance. I have been told that you were asked to be one of the party. But could it be so? You must be very much altered indeed since we parted, if that could be the case, and you not there. But I will not suppose this possible, and I hope very soon to receive your personal assurance of its being otherwise.

M.D.

The contents of her last note to him were these:–

What am I to imagine, Willoughby, by your behaviour last night? Again I demand an explanation of it. I was prepared to meet you with the pleasure which our separation naturally produced, with the familiarity which our intimacy at Barton appeared to me to justify. I was repulsed indeed! I have passed a wretched night in endeavouring to excuse a conduct which can scarcely be called less than insulting; but though I have not yet been able to form any reasonable apology for your behaviour, I am perfectly ready to hear your justification of it. You have perhaps been misinformed, or purposely deceived, in something concerning me, which may have lowered me in your opinion. Tell me what it is, explain the grounds on which you acted, and I shall be satisfied, in being able to satisfy you. It would grieve me indeed to be obliged to think ill of you; but if I am to do it, if I am to learn that you are not what we have hitherto believed you, that your regard for us all was insincere, that your behaviour to me was intended only to deceive, let it be told as soon as possible. My feelings are at present in a state of dreadful indecision; I wish to acquit you, but certainty on either side will be ease to what I now suffer. If your sentiments are no longer what they were, you will return my notes, and the lock of my hair which is in your possession.

M.D.

That such letters, so full of affection and confidence, could have been so answered, Elinor, for Willoughby's sake, would have been unwilling to believe. But her condemnation of him did not blind her to the impropriety of their having been written at all; and she was silently grieving over the imprudence which had hazarded such unsolicited proofs of tenderness, not warranted by anything preceding, and most severely condemned by the event, when Marianne, perceiving that she had finished the letters, observed to her that they contained nothing but what any one would have written in the same situation.

'I felt myself,' she added, 'to be as solemnly engaged to him, as if the strictest legal covenant had bound us to each other.'

'I can believe it,' said Elinor; 'but unfortunately he did not feel the same.'

'He *did* feel the same, Elinor – for weeks and weeks he felt it. I know he did. Whatever may have changed him now, (and nothing but the blackest art employed against me can have done it,) I was once as dear to him as my own soul could wish. This lock of hair, which now he can so readily give up, was begged of me with the most earnest supplication. Had you seen his look, his manner, had you heard his voice at that moment! Have you forgot the last evening of our being together at Barton? The morning that we parted too! When he told me that it might be many weeks before we meet again – his distress – can I ever forget his distress!'

For a moment or two she could say no more; but when this emotion had passed away, she added, in a firmer tone,

'Elinor, I have been cruelly used; but not by Willoughby.'

'Dearest Marianne, who but himself? By whom can he have been instigated?'

'By all the world, rather than by his own heart. I could rather believe every creature of my acquaintance leagued together to ruin me in his opinion, than believe his nature capable of such cruelty. This woman of whom he writes – whoever she be – or any one, in short, but your own dear self, mama, and Edward, may have been so barbarous to belie me. Beyond you three, is there a creature in the world whom I would not rather suspect of evil than Willoughby, whose heart I know so well?'

Elinor would not contend, and only replied, 'Whoever may have been so detestably your enemy, let them be cheated of their malignant triumph, my dear sister, by seeing how nobly the consciousness of your own innocence and good intentions supports your spirits. It is a reasonable and laudable pride which resists such malevolence.'

'No, no,' cried Marianne, 'misery such as mine has no pride. I care not who knows that I am wretched. The triumph of seeing me so may be open to all the world. Elinor, Elinor, they who suffer little may be proud and independent as they like – may resist insult, or return mortification – but I cannot, I must feel – I must be wretched – and they are welcome to enjoy the consciousness of it that can.'

'But for my mother's sake and mine' –

'I would do more than for my own. But to appear happy when I am so miserable – Oh! who can require it?'

Again they were both silent. Elinor was employed in walking thoughtfully from the fire to the window, from the window to the fire, without knowing that she received warmth from one, or discerning objects through the other; and Marianne, seated at the foot of the bed, with her head leaning against one of its posts, again took up Willoughby's letter, and after shuddering over every sentence, exclaimed –

'It is too much! Oh! Willoughby, Willoughby, could this be yours! Cruel, cruel – nothing can acquit you. Elinor, nothing can. Whatever he might have heard against me – ought he not to have suspended his belief? ought he not to have told me of it, to have given me the power of clearing myself? "The lock of hair, (repeating it from the letter,) which you so obligingly bestowed on me" – That is unpardonable. Willoughby, where was your heart, when you wrote those words? Oh! barbarously insolent! – Elinor, can he be justified?'

'No, Marianne, in no possible way.'

'And yet this woman – who knows what her art may have been – how long it may have been premeditated, and how deeply contrived by her! – Who is she? – Who can she be? – Whom did I ever hear him talk of as young and attractive among his female acquaintance? – Oh! no one, no one – he talked to me only of myself.'

Another pause ensued; Marianne was greatly agitated, and it ended thus.

'Elinor, I must go home. I must go and comfort mama. Cannot we be gone to-morrow?'

'To-morrow, Marianne!'

'Yes; why should I stay here? I came only for Willoughby's sake – and now who cares for me? Who regards me?'

'It would be impossible to go to-morrow. We owe Mrs Jennings much more than civility; and civility of the commonest kind must prevent such a hasty removal as that.'

'Well, then, another day or two, perhaps; but I cannot stay here long, I cannot stay to endure the questions and remarks of all these people. The Middletons and Palmers – how am I to bear their pity? The pity of such a woman as Lady Middleton! Oh! what would *he* say to that!'

Elinor advised her to lie down again, and for a moment she did so; but no attitude could give her ease; and in restless pain of mind and body she moved from one posture to another, till growing more and more hysterical, her sister could with difficulty keep her on the bed at all, and for some time was fearful of being constrained to call for assistance. Some lavender drops, however, which she was at length persuaded to take, were of use; and from that time till Mrs Jennings returned, she continued on the bed quiet and motionless.

Chapter Thirty

MRS JENNINGS CAME IMMEDIATELY to their room on her return, and without waiting to have her request of admittance answered, opened the door and walked in with a look of real concern.

'How do you do my dear?' – said she in a voice of great compassion to Marianne, who turned away her face without attempting to answer.

'How is she, Miss Dashwood? – Poor thing! she looks very bad. – No wonder. Aye, it is but too true. He is to be married very soon – a good-for-nothing fellow! I have no patience with him. Mrs Taylor told me of it half an hour ago, and she was told it by a particular friend of Miss Grey herself, else I am sure I should not have believed it; and I was almost ready to sink as it was. Well, said I, all I can say is, that if it is true, he has used a young lady of my acquaintance abominably ill, and I wish with all my soul his wife may plague his heart out. And so I shall always say, my dear, you may depend on it. I have no notion of men's going on in this way; and if ever I meet him again, I will give him such a dressing as he has not had this many a day. But there is one comfort, my dear Miss Marianne; he is not the only young man in the world worth having; and with your pretty face you will never want admirers. Well, poor thing! I won't disturb her any longer, for she had better have her cry out at once and have done with it. The Parrys and Sandersons luckily are coming tonight you know, and that will amuse her.'

She then went away, walking on tiptoe out of the room, as if she supposed her young friend's affliction could be increased by noise.

Marianne, to the surprise of her sister, determined on dining with them. Elinor even advised her against it. But 'no, she would go down; she could bear it very well, and the bustle about her would be less.' Elinor, pleased to have her governed for a moment by such a motive, though believing it hardly possible that she could sit out the dinner, said no more; and adjusting her dress for her as well as she could, while Marianne still remained on the bed, was ready to assist her into the dining room as soon as they were summoned to it.

When there, though looking most wretchedly, she ate more and was calmer than her sister had expected. Had she tried to speak, or had she been conscious of half Mrs Jennings's well-meant but ill-judged attentions to her, this calmness could not have been maintained; but not a syllable escaped her lips, and the abstraction of her thoughts preserved her in ignorance of every thing that was passing before her.

Elinor, who did justice to Mrs Jennings's kindness, though its effusions were often distressing, and sometimes almost ridiculous, made her those acknowledgments, and returned her those civilities, which her sister could not make or return for herself. Their good friend saw that Marianne was unhappy, and felt that every thing was due to her which might make her at all less so. She treated her therefore, with all the indulgent fondness of a parent towards a favourite child on the last day of its holidays. Marianne was to have the best place by the fire, was to be tempted to eat by every delicacy in the house, and to be amused by the relation of all the news of the day. Had not Elinor, in the sad countenance of her sister, seen a check to all mirth, she could have been entertained by Mrs Jennings's endeavours to cure a disappointment in love, by a variety of sweetmeats and olives, and a good fire. As soon, however, as the consciousness of all this was forced by continual repetition on Marianne, she could stay no longer. With an hasty exclamation of misery, and a sign to her sister not to follow her, she directly got up and hurried out of the room.

'Poor soul!' cried Mrs Jennings, as soon as she was gone, 'how it grieves me to see her! And I declare if she is not gone away without finishing her wine! And the dried cherries too! Lord! nothing seems to do her any good. I am sure if I knew of any thing she would like, I would send all over the town for it. Well, it is the oddest thing to me, that a man should use such a pretty girl so ill! But when there is plenty of money on one side, and next to none on the other, Lord bless you! they care no more about such things! –'

'The lady then – Miss Grey I think you called her – is very rich?'

'Fifty thousand pounds, my dear. Did you ever see her? a smart, stilish girl they say, but not handsome. I remember her aunt very well, Biddy Henshawe; she married a very wealthy man. But the family are all rich together. Fifty thousand pounds! and by all accounts it won't come before it's wanted; for they say he is all to pieces. No wonder! dashing about with his curricle and hunters! Well, it don't signify talking, but when a young man, be he who he will, comes and makes love to a pretty girl, and promises marriage, he has no business to fly off from his word only because he grows poor, and a richer girl is ready to have him. Why don't he, in such a case, sell his horses, let his house, turn off his servants, and make a thorough reform at once? I warrant you, Miss Marianne would have been ready to wait till matters came round. But that won't do, now-a-days; nothing in the way of pleasure can ever be given up by the young men of this age.'

'Do you know what kind of a girl Miss Grey is? Is she said to be amiable?'

'I never heard any harm of her; indeed I hardly ever heard her mentioned;

except that Mrs Taylor did say this morning, that one day Miss Walker hinted to her, that she believed Mr and Mrs Ellison would not be sorry to have Miss Grey married, for she and Mrs Ellison could never agree.' –

'And who are the Ellisons?'

'Her guardians, my dear. But now she is of age and may choose for herself; and a pretty choice she has made! – What now,' after pausing a moment – 'your poor sister is gone to her own room I suppose to moan by herself. Is there nothing one can get to comfort her? Poor dear, it seems quite cruel to let her be alone. Well, by-an-by we shall have a few friends, and that will amuse her a little. What shall we play at? She hates whist I know; but is there no round game she cares for?'

'Dear ma'am, this kindness is quite unnecessary. Marianne I dare say will not leave her room again this evening. I shall persuade her if I can to go early to bed, for I am sure she wants rest.'

'Aye, I believe that will be best for her. Let her name her own supper, and go to bed. Lord! no wonder she has been looking so bad and so cast down this last week or two, for this matter I suppose has been hanging over her head as long as that. And so the letter that came today finished it! Poor soul! I am sure if I had had a notion of it, I would not have joked her about it for all my money. But then you know, how should I guess such a thing? I made sure of its being nothing but a common love letter, and you know young people like to be laughed at about them. Lord! how concerned Sir John and my daughters will be when they hear it! If I had had my senses about me I might have called in Conduit-street in my way home, and told them of it. But I shall see them tomorrow.'

'It would be unnecessary I am sure, for you to caution Mrs Palmer and Sir John against ever naming Mr Willoughby, or making the slightest allusion to what has passed, before my sister. Their own good-nature must point out to them the real cruelty of appearing to know any thing about it when she is present; and the less that may ever be said to myself on the subject, the more my feelings will be spared, as you my dear madam will easily believe.'

'Oh! Lord! yes, that I do indeed. It must be terrible for you to hear it talked of; and as for your sister, I am sure I would not mention a word about it to her for the world. You saw I did not all dinner time. No more would Sir John nor my daughters, for they are all very thoughtful and considerate; especially if I give them a hint, as I certainly will. For my part, I think the less that is said about such things, the better, the sooner 'tis blown over and forgot. And what good does talking ever do you know?'

'In this affair it can only do harm; more so perhaps than in many cases of a similar kind, for it has been attended by circumstances which, for the sake of every one concerned in it, make it unfit to become the public conversation. I must do this justice to Mr Willoughby – he has broken no positive engagement with my sister.'

'Law, my dear! Don't pretend to defend him. No positive engagement indeed! after taking her all over Allenham House, and fixing on the very rooms they were to live in hereafter!'

Elinor, for her sister's sake, could not press the subject farther, and she hoped it was not required of her for Willoughby's; since, though Marianne might lose much, he could gain very little by the enforcement of the real truth. After a short silence on both sides, Mrs Jennings, with all her natural hilarity, burst forth again.

'Well, my dear, 'tis a true saying about an ill wind, for it will be all the better for Colonel Brandon. He will have her at last; aye, that he will. Mind me, now, if they an't married by Midsummer. Lord! how he'll chuckle over this news! I hope he will come tonight. It will be all to one a better match for your sister. Two thousand a year without debt or drawback – except the little love-child, indeed; aye, I had forgot her; but she may be 'prenticed out at small cost, and then what does it signify? Delaford is a nice place, I can tell you; exactly what I call a nice old fashioned place, full of comforts and conveniences; quite shut in with great garden walls that are covered with the best fruit-trees in the country: and such a mulberry tree in one corner! Lord! how Charlotte and I did stuff the only time we were there! Then, there is a dove-cote, some delightful stewponds, and a very pretty canal; and every thing, in short, that one could wish for: and, moreover, it is close to the church, and only a quarter of a mile from the turnpike-road, so 'tis never dull, for if you only go and sit up in an old yew arbour behind the house, you may see all the carriages that pass along. Oh! 'tis a nice place! A butcher hard by in the village, and the parsonage-house within a stone's throw. To my fancy, a thousand times prettier than Barton Park, where they are forced to send three miles for their meat, and have not a neighbour nearer than your mother. Well, I shall spirit up the Colonel as soon as I can. One shoulder of mutton, you know, drives another down. If we *can* but put Willoughby out of her head!'

'Aye, if we can do *that*, Ma'am,' said Elinor, 'we shall do very well with or without Colonel Brandon.' And then rising, she went away to join Marianne, whom she found, as she expected, in her own room, leaning, in silent misery, over the small remains of a fire, which, till Elinor's entrance, had been her only light.

'You had better leave me,' was all the notice that her sister received from her.

'I will leave you,' said Elinor 'if you will go to bed.' But this, from the momentary perverseness of impatient suffering, she at first refused to do. Her sister's earnest, though gentle persuasion, however, soon softened her to compliance, and Elinor saw her lay her aching head on the pillow, and saw her, as she hoped, in a way to get some quiet rest before she left her.

In the drawing-room, whither she then repaired, she was soon joined by Mrs Jennings, with a wine-glass, full of something, in her hand.

'My dear,' said she, entering, 'I have just recollected that I have some of the finest old Constantia wine in the house, that ever was tasted, so I have brought a glass of it for your sister. My poor husband! how fond he was of it! Whenever he had a touch of his old cholicky gout, he said it did him more good than any thing else in the world. Do take it to your sister.'

'Dear ma'am,' replied Elinor, smiling at the difference of the complaints for which it was recommended, 'how good you are! But I have just left Marianne in bed, and, I hope, almost asleep; and as I think nothing will be of so much service to her as rest, if you will give me leave, I will drink the wine myself.'

Mrs Jennings, though regretting that she had not been five minutes earlier, was satisfied with the compromise; and Elinor, as she swallowed the chief of it, reflected that, though its good effects on a cholicky gout were, at present, of little importance to her, its healing powers on a disappointed heart might be as reasonably tried on herself as on her sister.

Colonel Brandon came in while the party were at tea, and by his manner of looking round the room for Marianne, Elinor immediately fancied that he neither expected, nor wished to see her there, and, in short, that he was already aware of what occasioned her absence. Mrs Jennings was not struck by the same thought; for, soon after his entrance, she walked across the room to the tea-table where Elinor presided, and whispered – 'The Colonel looks as grave as ever you see. He knows nothing of it; do tell him, my dear.'

He shortly afterwards drew a chair close to her's, and, with a look which perfectly assured her of his good information, inquired after her sister.

'Marianne is not well,' said she. 'She has been indisposed all day, and we have persuaded her to go to bed.'

'Perhaps, then,' he hesitatingly replied, 'what I heard this morning may be – there may be more truth in it than I could believe possible at first.'

'What did you hear?'

'That a gentleman, whom I had reason to think – in short, that a man, whom I *knew* to be engaged – but how shall I tell you? If you know it already, as surely you must, I may be spared.'

'You mean,' answered Elinor with forced calmness, 'Mr Willoughby's marriage with Miss Grey. Yes, we *do* know it all. This seems to have been a day of general elucidation, for this very morning first unfolded it to us. Mr Willoughby is unfathomable! Where did you hear it?'

'In a stationer's shop in Pall Mall, where I had business. Two ladies were waiting for their carriage, and one of them was giving the other an account of the intended match, in a voice so little attempting concealment, that it was impossible for me not to hear all. The name of Willoughby, John Willoughby, frequently repeated, first caught my attention, and what followed was a positive assertion that every thing was now finally settled respecting his marriage with Miss Grey – it was no longer to be a secret – it would take place even within a few weeks, with many particulars of preparations and other matters. One thing, especially, I remember, because it served to identify the man still more: – as soon as the ceremony was over, they were to go to Combe Magna, his seat in Somersetshire. My astonishment! – but it would be impossible to describe what I felt. The communicative lady I learnt, on inquiry, for I staid in the shop till they were gone, was a Mrs Ellison, and that, as I have been since informed, is the name of Miss Grey's guardian.'

'It is. But have you likewise heard that Miss Grey has fifty thousand pounds? In that, if in anything, we may find an explanation.'

'It may be so; but Willoughby is capable – at least I think' – he stopped a moment; then added in a voice which seemed to distrust itself, 'And your sister – how did she –'

'Her sufferings have been very severe. I have only to hope that they may be proportionately short. It has been, it is a most cruel affliction. Till yesterday, I believe, she never doubted his regard; and even now, perhaps – but I am almost convinced that he never was really attached to her. He has been very deceitful! and, in some points, there seems a hardness of heart about him.'

'Ah!' said Colonel Brandon, 'there is, indeed! But your sister does not – I think you said so – she does not consider it quite as you do?'

'You know her disposition, and may believe how eagerly she would still justify him if she could.'

He made no answer; and soon afterwards, by the removal of the tea-things, and the arrangement of the card parties, the subject was necessarily dropped. Mrs Jennings, who had watched them with pleasure while they were talking, and who expected to see the effect of Miss Dashwood's communication, in such an instantaneous gaiety on Colonel Brandon's side, as might have become a man in the bloom of youth, of hope and happiness, saw him, with amazement, remain the whole evening more serious and thoughtful than usual.

Chapter Thirty One

FROM A NIGHT OF MORE SLEEP than she had expected, Marianne awoke the next morning to the same consciousness of misery in which she had closed her eyes.

Elinor encouraged her as much as possible to talk of what she felt; and before breakfast was ready, they had gone through the subject again and again; with the same steady conviction and affectionate counsel on Elinor's side, the same impetuous feelings and varying opinions on Marianne's, as before. Sometimes she could believe Willoughby to be as unfortunate and as innocent as herself, and at others, lost every consolation in the impossibility of acquitting him. At one moment she was absolutely indifferent to the observation of all the world, at another she would seclude herself from it for ever, and at a third could resist it with energy. In one thing, however, she was uniform, when it came to the point, in avoiding, where it was possible, the presence of Mrs Jennings, and in a determined silence when obliged to endure it. Her heart was hardened against the belief of Mrs Jennings's entering into her sorrows with any compassion.

'No, no, no, it cannot be,' she cried; 'she cannot feel. Her kindness is not sympathy; her good nature is not tenderness. All that she wants is gossip, and she only likes me now because I supply it.'

Elinor had not needed this to be assured of the injustice to which her sister was often led in her opinion of others, by the irritable refinement of her own mind, and the too great importance placed by her on the delicacies of a strong sensibility, and the graces of a polished manner. Like half the rest of the world, if more than half there be that are clever and good, Marianne, with excellent abilities and an excellent disposition, was neither reasonable nor candid. She expected from other people the same opinions and feelings as her own, and she judged of their motives by the immediate effect of their actions on herself. Thus a circumstance occurred, while the sisters were together in their own room after breakfast, which sunk the heart of Mrs Jennings still lower in her estimation; because, through her own weakness, it chanced to prove a source of fresh pain to herself, though Mrs Jennings was governed in it by an impulse of the utmost goodwill.

With a letter in her outstretched hand, and countenance gaily smiling, from the persuasion of bringing comfort, she entered their room, saying,

'Now, my dear, I bring you something that I am sure will do you good.'

Marianne heard enough. In one moment her imagination placed before her a letter from Willoughby, full of tenderness and contrition, explanatory of all that had passed, satisfactory, convincing; and instantly followed by Willoughby himself, rushing eagerly into the room to inforce, at her feet, by the eloquence of his eyes, the assurances of his letter. The work of one moment was destroyed by the next. The hand writing of her mother, never till then unwelcome, was before her; and, in the acuteness of the disappoint- ment which followed such an extasy of more than hope, she felt as if, till that instant, she had never suffered.

The cruelty of Mrs Jennings no language, within her reach in her moments of happiest eloquence, could have expressed; and now she could reproach her only by the tears which streamed from her eyes with passionate violence – a reproach, however, so entirely lost on its object, that after many expressions of pity, she withdrew, still referring her to the letter for comfort. But the letter, when she was calm enough to read it, brought little comfort. Willoughby filled every page. Her mother, still confident of their engagement, and relying as warmly as ever on his constancy, had only been roused by Elinor's application, to intreat from Marianne greater openness towards them both; and this, with such tenderness towards her, such affection for Wil- loughby, and such a conviction of their future happiness in each other, that she wept with agony through the whole it.

All her impatience to be at home again now returned; her mother was dearer to her than ever; dearer through the very excess of her mistaken confidence in Willoughby, and she was wildly urgent to be gone. Elinor, unable herself to determine whether it were better for Marianne to be in London or at Barton, offered no counsel of her own except of patience till their mother's wishes could be known; and at length she obtained her sister's consent to wait for that knowledge.

Mrs Jennings left them earlier than usual; for she could not be easy till the Middletons and Palmers were able to grieve as much as herself; and positively refusing Elinor's offered attendance, went out alone for the rest of the morning. Elinor, with a very heavy heart, aware of the pain she was going to communicate, and perceiving by Marianne's letter how ill she had succeeded in laying any foundation for it, then sat down to write her mother an account of what had passed, and intreat her directions for the future; while Marianne, who came into the drawing-room on Mrs Jennings's going away, remained fixed at the table where Elinor wrote, watching the advance- ment of her pen, grieving over her for the hardship of such a task, and grieving still more fondly over its effect on her mother.

In this manner they had continued about a quarter of an hour, when Marianne, whose nerves could not then bear any sudden noise, was startled by a rap at the door.

'Who can this be?' cried Elinor. 'So early too! I thought we *had* been safe.'

Marianne moved to the window –

'It is Colonel Brandon!' said she, with vexation. 'We are never safe from *him*.'

'He will not come in, as Mrs Jennings is from home.'

'I will not trust to *that*,' retreating to her own room. 'A man who has nothing to do with his own time has no conscience in his intrusion on that of others.'

The event proved her conjecture right, though it was founded on injustice and error; for Colonel Brandon *did* come in; and Elinor, who was convinced that solicitude for Marianne brought him thither, and who saw *that* solicitude in his disturbed and melancholy look, and in his anxious though brief enquiry after her, could not forgive her sister for esteeming him so lightly.

'I met Mrs Jennings in Bond-street,' said he, after the first salutation, 'and she encouraged me to come on; and I was the more easily encouraged, because I thought it probable that I might find you alone, which. I was very desirious of doing. My object – my wish – my sole wish in desiring it – I hope, I believe it is – is to be a means of giving comfort; – no, I must not say comfort – not present comfort – but conviction, lasting conviction to your sister's mind. My regard for her, for yourself, for your mother – will you allow me to prove it, by relating some circumstances, which nothing but a *very* sincere regard – nothing but an earnest desire of being useful – I think I am justified – though where so many hours have been spent in convincing myself that I am right, is there not some reason to fear I may be wrong?' He stopped.

'I understand you,' said Elinor, 'You have something to tell me of Mr Willoughby, that will open his character farther. Your telling it will be the greatest act of friendship that can be shewn Marianne. *My* gratitude will be insured immediately by any information tending to that end, and *her's* must be granted by it in time. Pray, pray let me hear it.'

'You shall; and, to be brief, when I quitted Barton last October, – but this will give you no idea – I must go farther back. You will find me a very awkward narrator, Miss Dashwood; I hardly know where to begin. A short account of myself, I believe, will be necessary, and it *shall* be a short one. On such a subject,' sighing heavily, 'I can have little temptation to be diffuse.'

He stopt a moment for recollection, and then, with another sigh, went on.

'You have probably entirely forgotten a conversation – (it is not to be supposed that it could make any impression on you) – a conversation between us one evening at Barton Park – it was the evening of a dance – in which I alluded to a lady I had once known, as resembling, in some measure, your sister Marianne.'

'Indeed,' answered Elinor, 'I have *not* forgotten it.' He looked pleased by this remembrance, and added,

'If I am not deceived by the uncertainty, the partiality of tender recollection, there is a very strong resemblance between them, as well in mind as person. The same warmth of heart, the same eagerness of fancy and spirits. This lady was one of my nearest relations, an orphan from her infancy, and under the guardianship of my father. Our ages were nearly the same, and from our earliest years we were playfellows and friends. I cannot remember the time when I did not love Eliza; and my affection for her, as we grew up, was such, as perhaps, judging from my present forlorn and cheerless gravity, you might think me incapable of having ever felt. Her's, for me, was, I believe, fervent as the attachment of your sister to Mr Willoughby and it was, though from a different cause, no less unfortunate. At seventeen, she was lost to me for ever. She was married – married against her inclination to my brother. Her fortune was large, and our family estate much encumbered. And this, I fear, is all that can be said for the conduct of one, who was at once her uncle and guardian. My brother did not deserve her; he did not even love her. I had hoped that her regard for me would support her under any difficulty, and for some time it did; but at last the misery of her situation, for she experienced great unkindness, overcame all her resolution, and though she had promised me that nothing – but how blindly I relate! I have never told you how this was brought on. We were within a few hours of eloping together for Scotland. The treachery, or the folly, of my cousin's maid betrayed us. I was banished to the house of a relation far distant, and she was allowed no liberty, no society, no amusement, till my father's point was gained. I had depended on her fortitude too far, and the blow was a severe one – but had her marriage been happy, so young as I then was, a few months must have reconciled me to it, or at least I should not have now to lament it. This however was not the case. My brother had no regard for her; his pleasures were not what they ought to have been, and from the first he treated her unkindly. The consequence of this, upon a mind so young, so lively, so inexperienced as Mrs Brandon's, was but too natural. She resigned herself at first to all the misery of her situation; and happy had it been if she had not lived to overcome those regrets which the remembrance of me occasioned. But can we wonder that with such a husband to provoke inconstancy, and without a friend to advise or restrain her, (for my father lived only a few months after their marriage, and I was with my regiment in the East Indies) she should fall? Had I remained in England, perhaps – but I meant to promote the happiness of both by removing from her for years, and for that purpose had procured my exchange. The shock which her marriage had given me,' he continued, in a voice of great agitation, 'was of trifling weight – was nothing – to what I felt when I heard, about two years afterwards, of her divorce. It was *that* which threw this gloom, – even now the recollection of what I suffered –'

He could say no more, and rising hastily walked for a few minutes about the room. Elinor, affected by his relation, and still more by his distress, could not speak. He saw her concern, and coming to her, took her hand, pressed it, and kissed it with grateful respect. A few minutes more of silent exertion enabled him to proceed with composure.

'It was nearly three years after this unhappy period before I returned to England. My first care, when I *did* arrive, was of course to seek for her; but the search was as fruitless as it was melancholy. I could not trace her beyond her first seducer, and there was every reason to fear that she had removed from him only to sink deeper in a life of sin. Her legal allowance was not adequate to her fortune, nor sufficient for her comfortable maintenance, and I learnt from my brother, that the power of receiving it had been made over some months before to another person. He imagined, and calmly could he imagine it, that her extravagance and consequent distress had obliged her to dispose of it for some immediate relief. At last, however, and after I had been six months in England, I *did* find her. Regard for a former servant of my own, who had since fallen into misfortune, carried me to visit him in a spunging-house, where he was confined for debt; and there, in the same house, under a similar confinement, was my unfortunate sister. So altered – so faded – worn down by acute suffering of every kind! hardly could I believe the melancholy and sickly figure before me, to be the remains of the lovely, blooming, healthful girl, on whom I had once doated. What I endured in so beholding her – but I have no right to wound your feelings by attempting to describe it – I have pained you too much already. That she was, to all appearance, in the last stage of consumption, was – yes, in such a situation it was my greatest comfort. Life could do nothing for her, beyond giving time for a better preparation for death; and that was given. I saw her placed in comfortable lodgings, and under proper attendants; I visited her every day during the rest of her short life; I was with her in her last moments.'

Again he stopped to recover himself; and Elinor spoke her feelings in an exclamation of tender concern, at the fate of his unfortunate friend.

'Your sister, I hope, cannot be offended,' said he, 'by the resemblance I have fancied between her and my poor disgraced relation. Their fates, their fortunes cannot be the same; and had the natural sweet disposition of the one been guarded by a firmer mind, or an happier marriage, she might have been all that you will live to see the other be. But to what does all this lead? I seem to have been distressing you for nothing. Ah! Miss Dashwood – a subject such as this – untouched for fourteen years – it is dangerous to handle it at all! I will be more collected – more concise. She left to my care her only child, a little girl, the offspring of her first guilty connection, who was then about three years old. She loved the child, and had always kept it with her. It was a valued, a precious trust to me; and gladly would I have discharged it in the strictest sense, by watching over her education myself, had the nature of our situations allowed it; but I had no family, no home; and my little Eliza was therefore placed at school. I saw her there whenever I could, and after the death of my brother, (which happened about five years ago, and which left to me the possession of the family property,) she frequently visited me at Delaford. I called her a distant relation; but I am well aware that I have in general been suspected of a much nearer connection with her. It is now three years ago, (she had just reached her fourteenth year,) that I removed her from school, to place her under the care of a very respectable woman, residing in Dorsetshire, who had the charge of four or five other girls of about the same time of life; and for two years I had every reason to be pleased with her situation. But last February, almost a twelvemonth back, she suddenly disappeared. I had allowed her, (imprudently, as it has since turned out,) at her earnest desire, to go to Bath with one of her young friends, who was attending her father there for his health. I knew him to be a very good sort of man, and I thought well of his daughter – better than she deserved, for, with a most obstinate and ill-judged secrecy, she would tell nothing, would give no clue, though she certainly knew all. He, her father, a well-meaning, but not a quick-sighted man, could really, I believe, give no information; for he had been generally confined to the house, while the girls were ranging over the town and making what acquaintance they chose; and he tried to convince me, as thoroughly as he was convinced himself, of his daughter's being entirely unconcerned in the business. In short, I could learn nothing but that she was gone; all the rest, for eight long months, was left to conjecture. What I thought, what I feared, may be imagined; and what I suffered too.'

'Good heavens!' cried Elinor, 'could it be – could Willoughby!' –

'The first news that reached me of her,' he continued, 'came in a letter from herself, last October. It was forwarded to me from Delaford, and I received it on the very morning of our intended party to Whitwell; and this was the reason of my leaving Barton so suddenly, which I am sure must at the time have appeared strange to every body, and which I believe gave offence to some. Little did Mr Willoughby imagine, I suppose, when his looks censured me for incivility in breaking up the party, that I was called away to the relief of one, whom he had made poor and miserable; but *had* he known it, what would it have availed? Would he have been less gay or less happy in the smiles of your sister? No, he had already done that, which no man who *can* feel for another, would do. He had left the girl whose youth and innocence he had seduced, in a situation of the utmost distress, with no creditable home, no help, no friends, ignorant of his address! He had left her promising to return; he neither returned, nor wrote, nor relieved her.'

'This is beyond every thing!' exclaimed Elinor.

'His character is now before you; expensive, dissipated, and worse than both. Knowing all this, as I have now known it many weeks, guess what I must have felt on seeing your sister as fond of him as ever, and on being assured that she was to marry him; guess what I must have felt for all your sakes. When I came to you last week and found you alone, I came determined to know the truth; though irresolute what to do when it *was* known. My behaviour must have seemed strange to you then; but now you will com-prehend it. To suffer you all to be so deceived; to see your sister – but what could I do? I had no hope of interfering with success; and sometimes I thought your sister's influence might yet reclaim him. But now, after such dishonourable usage, who can tell what were his designs on her? Whatever they may have been, however, she may now, and hereafter doubtless *will*, turn with gratitude towards her own condition, when she compares it with that of my poor Eliza, when she considers the wretched and hopeless situation of this poor girl, and pictures her to herself, with an affection for him as strong, still as strong as her own, and with a mind tormented by self-reproach, which must attend her through life. Surely this comparison must have its use with her. She will feel her own sufferings to be nothing. They proceed from no misconduct, and can bring no disgrace. On the contrary, every friend must be made still more her friend by them. Concern for her unhappiness, and respect for her fortitude under it, must strengthen every attachment. Use your own discretion, however, in communicating to her what I have told you. You must know best what will be its effect; but had I not seriously, and from my heart believed it might be of service, might lessen her regrets, I would not have suffered myself to trouble you with this account of my family afflictions, with a recital which may seem to have been intended to raise myself at the expense of others.'

Elinor's thanks followed this speech with grateful earnestness; attended too with the assurance of her expecting material advantage to Marianne, from the communication of what had passed.

'I have been more pained,' said she, 'by her endeavours to acquit him than by all the rest; for it irritates her mind more than the most perfect conviction of his unworthiness can do. Now, though at first she will suffer much, I am sure she will soon become easier. Have you,' she continued, after a short silence, 'ever seen Mr Willoughby since you left him at Barton?'

'Yes,' he replied gravely, 'once I have. One meeting was unavoidable.'

Elinor, startled by his manner, looked at him anxiously, saying,

'What? have you met him to –'

'I could meet him in no other way. Eliza confessed to me, though most reluctantly, the name of her lover; and when he returned to town, which was within a fortnight after myself, we met by appointment, he to defend, I to punish his conduct. We returned unwounded, and the meeting, therefore, never got abroad.'

Elinor sighed over the fancied necessity of this; but to a man and a soldier, she presumed not to censure it.

'Such,' said Colonel Brandon, after a pause, 'has been the unhappy resemblance between the fate of mother and daughter! and so imperfectly have I discharged my trust!'

'Is she still in town?'

'No; as soon as she recovered from her lying-in, for I found her near her delivery, I removed her and her child into the country, and there she remains.'

Recollecting, soon afterwards, that he was probably dividing Elinor from her sister, he put an end to his visit, receiving from her again the same grateful acknowledgments, and leaving her full of compassion and esteem for him.

Chapter Thirty Two

WHEN THE PARTICULARS OF THIS conversation were repeated by Miss Dashwood to her sister, as they very soon were, the effect on her was not entirely such as the former had hoped to see. Not that Marianne appeared to distrust the truth of any part of it, for she listened to it all with the most steady and submissive attention, made neither objection nor remark, attempted no vindication of Willoughby, and seemed to shew by her tears that she felt it to be impossible. But though this behaviour assured Elinor that the conviction of his guilt *was* carried home to her mind, though she saw with satisfaction the effect of it, in her no longer avoiding Colonel Brandon when he called, in her speaking to him, even voluntarily speaking, with a kind of compassionate respect, and though she saw her spirits less violently irritated than before, she did not see her less wretched. Her mind did become settled, but it was settled in a gloomy dejection. She felt the loss of Willoughby's character yet more heavily than she had felt the loss of his heart; his seduction and desertion of Miss Williams, the misery of that poor girl, and the doubt of what his designs might *once* have been on herself, preyed altogether so much on her spirits, that she could not bring herself to speak of what she felt even to Elinor; and brooding over her sorrows in silence, gave more pain to her sister than could have been communicated by the most open and most frequent confession of them.

To give the feelings or the language of Mrs Dashwood on receiving and answering Elinor's letter, would be only to give a repetition of what her daughters had already felt and said; of a disappointment hardly less painful than Marianne's, and an indignation even greater than Elinor's. Long letters from her, quickly succeeding each other, arrived to tell all that she suffered and thought; to express her anxious solicitude for Marianne, and entreat she would bear up with fortitude under this misfortune. Bad indeed must the nature of Marianne's affliction be, when her mother could talk of fortitude!

mortifying and humiliating must be the origin of those regrets, which *she* could wish her not to indulge!

Against the interest of her own individual comfort, Mrs Dashwood had determined that it would be better for Marianne to be anywhere, at that time, than at Barton, where every thing within her view would be bringing back the past in the strongest and most afflicting manner, by constantly placing Willoughby before her, such as she had always seen him there. She recommended it to her daughters, therefore, by all means not to shorten their visit to Mrs Jennings; the length of which, though never exactly fixed, had been expected by all to comprise at least five or six weeks. A variety of occupations, of objects, and of company, which could not be procured at Barton, would be inevitable there, and might yet, she hoped, cheat Marianne, at times, into some interest beyond herself, and even into some amusement, much as the idea of both might now be spurned by her.

From all danger of seeing Willoughby again, her mother considered her to be at least equally safe in town as in the country, since his acquaintance must now be dropped by all who called themselves her friends. Design could never bring them in each other's way: negligence could never leave them exposed to a surprise; and chance had less in its favour in the crowd of London than even in the retirement of Barton, where it might force him before her while paying that visit at Allenham on his marriage, which Mrs Dashwood, from foreseeing at first as a probable event, had brought herself to expect as a certain one.

She had yet another reason for wishing her children to remain where they were; a letter from her son-in-law had told her that he and his wife were to be in town before the middle of February, and she judged it right that they should sometimes see their brother.

Marianne had promised to be guided by her mother's opinion, and she submitted to it therefore without opposition, though it proved perfectly different from what she wished and expected, though she felt it to be entirely wrong, formed on mistaken grounds; and that by requiring her longer continuance in London it deprived her of the only possible alleviation of her wretchedness, the personal sympathy of her mother, and doomed her to such society and such scenes as must prevent her ever knowing a moment's rest.

But it was a matter of great consolation to her, that what brought evil to herself would bring good to her sister; and Elinor, on the other hand, suspecting that it would not be in her power to avoid Edward entirely, comforted herself by thinking, that though their long stay would therefore militate against her own happiness, it would be better for Marianne than an immediate return into Devonshire.

Her carefulness in guarding her sister from ever hearing Willoughby's name mentioned, was not thrown away. Marianne, though without knowing it herself, reaped all its advantage; for neither Mrs Jennings, nor Sir John, nor even Mrs Palmer herself, ever spoke of him before her. Elinor wished that the same forbearance could have extended towards herself, but that was impossible, and she was obliged to listen day after day to the indignation of them all.

Sir John could not have thought it possible. 'A man of whom he had always had such reason to think well! Such a good natured fellow! He did not believe there was a bolder rider in England! It was an unaccountable business. He wished him at the devil with all his heart. He would not speak another word to him, meet him where he might, for all the world! No, not if it were to be by the side of Barton covert, and they were kept waiting for two hours together. Such a scoundrel of a fellow! such a deceitful dog! It was only the last time they met that he had offered him one of Folly's puppies! and this was the end of it!'

Mrs Palmer, in her way, was equally angry. 'She was determined to drop his acquaintance immediately, and she was very thankful that she had never been acquainted with him at all. She wished with all her heart Combe Magna was not so near Cleveland; but it did not signify, for it was a great deal too far off to visit; she hated him so much that she was resolved never to mention his name again, and she should tell everybody she saw, how good-for-nothing he was.'

The rest of Mrs Palmer's sympathy was shewn in procuring all the particulars in her power of the approaching marriage, and communicating them to Elinor. She could soon tell at what coachmaker's the new carriage was building, bv what painter Mr Willoughby's portrait was drawn, and at what warehouse Miss Grey's clothes might be seen.

The calm and polite unconcern of Lady Middleton on the occasion was an happy relief to Elinor's spirits, oppressed as they often were by the clamorous kindness of the others. It was a great comfort to her, to be sure of exciting no interest in *one* person at least among their circle of friends; a great comfort to know that there was *one* who would meet her without feeling any curiosity after particulars, or any anxiety for her sister's health.

Every qualification is raised at times, by the circumstances of the moment, to more than its real value; and she was sometimes worried down by officious condolence to rate good-breeding as more indispensable to comfort than good-nature.

Lady Middleton expressed her sense of the affair about once every day, or twice, if the subject occurred very often, by saying, 'It is very shocking indeed!' and by the means of this continual though gentle vent, was able not only to see the Miss Dashwoods from the first without the smallest emotion, but very soon to see them without recollecting a word of the matter; and having thus supported the dignity of her own sex, and spoken her decided censure of what was wrong in the other, she thought herself at liberty to attend to the interest of her own assemblies, and therefore determined (though rather against the opinion of Sir John) that as Mrs Willoughby would at once be a woman of elegance and fortune, to leave her card with her as soon as she married.

Colonel Brandon's delicate unobtrusive inquiries were never unwelcome to Miss Dashwood. He had abundantly earned the privilege of intimate discussion of her sister's disappointment, by the friendly zeal with which he had endeavoured to soften it, and they always conversed with confidence. His chief reward for the painful exertion of disclosing past sorrows and present humiliations, was given in the pitying eye with which Marianne sometimes observed him, and the gentleness of her voice when ever (though it did not often happen) she was obliged, or could oblige herself to speak to him. *These* assured him that his exertion had produced an increase of good-will towards himself, and *these* gave Elinor hopes of its being farther augmented hereafter; but Mrs Jennings, who knew nothing of all this, who knew only that the Colonel continued as grave as ever, and that she could neither prevail on him to make the offer himself, nor commission her to make it for him, began, at the end of two days, to think that, instead of Midsummer, they would not be married till Michaelmas, and by the end of a week that it would not be a match at all. The good understanding between the Colonel and Miss Dashwood seemed rather to declare that the honours of the mulberry-tree, the canal, and the yew arbour, would all be made over to *her*; and Mrs Jennings had for some time ceased to think at all of Mr Ferrars.

Early in February, within a fortnight from the receipt of Willoughby's letter, Elinor had the painful office of informing her sister that he was married. She had taken care to have the intelligence conveyed to herself, as soon as it was known that the ceremony was over, as she was desirous that Marianne should not receive the first notice of it from the public papers, which she saw her eagerly examining every morning.

She received the news with resolute composure; made no observation on it, and at first shed no tears; but after a short time they would burst out, and for the rest of the day, she was in a state hardly less pitiable than when she first learnt to expect the event.

The Willoughbys left town as soon as they were married; and Elinor now hoped, as there could be no danger of her seeing either of them, to prevail on her sister, who had never yet left the house since the blow first fell, to go out again by degrees as she had done before.

About this time, the two Miss Steeles, lately arrived at their cousin's house in Bartlett's Buildings, Holborn, presented themselves again before their more grand relations in Conduit and Berkeley-street; and were welcomed by them all with great cordiality.

Elinor only was sorry to see them. Their presence always gave her pain, and she hardly knew how to make a very gracious return to the overpowering delight of Lucy in finding her *still* in town.

'I should have been quite disappointed if I had not found you here *still*,' said she repeatedly, with a strong emphasis on the word. 'But I always thought I *should*. I was almost sure you would not leave London yet awhile; though you *told* me, you know, at Barton, that you should not stay above a *month*. But I thought, at the time, that you would most likely change your mind when it came to the point. It would have been such a great pity to have went away before your brother and sister came. And now to be sure you will be in no hurry to be gone. I am amazingly glad you did not keep to *your word*'.

Elinor perfectly understood her, and was forced to use all her self-command to make it appear that she did *not*.

'Well, my dear,' said Mrs Jennings, 'and how did you travel?'

'Not in the stage, I assure you,' replied Miss Steele, with quick exultation; 'we came post all the way and had a very smart beau to attend us. Dr Davies was coming to town, and so we thought we'd join him in a post-chaise; and he behaved very genteelly, and paid ten or twelve shillings more than we did.'

'Oh, oh!' cried Mrs Jennings; 'very pretty, indeed! and the Doctor is a single man, I warrant you.'

'There now,' said Miss Steele, affectedly simpering, 'everybody laughs at me so about the Doctor, and I cannot think why. My cousins say they are sure I have made a conquest; but for my part I declare I never think about him from one hour's end to another. "Lord! here comes your beau, Nancy," my cousin said t'other day, when she saw him crossing the street to the house. My beau, indeed! said I – I cannot think who you mean. The Doctor is no beau of mine.'

'Aye, aye, that is very pretty talking – but it won't do – the Doctor is the man, I see.'

'No, indeed!' replied her cousin, with affected earnestness, 'and I beg you will contradict it, if you ever hear it talked of.'

Mrs Jennings directly gave her the gratifying assurance that she certainly would *not*, and Miss Steele was made completely happy.

'I suppose you will go and stay with your brother and sister, Miss Dashwood, when they come to town,' said Lucy, returning, after a cessation of hostile hints, to the charge.

'No, I do not think we shall.'

'Oh, yes, I dare say you will.'

Elinor would not humour her by farther opposition.

'What a charming thing it is that Mrs Dashwood can spare you both for so long a time together!'

'Long a time, indeed!' interposed Mrs Jennings. 'Why, their visit is but just begun!'

Lucy was silenced.

'I am sorry we cannot see your sister, Miss Dashwood,' said Miss Steele. 'I am sorry she is not well;' for Marianne had left the room on their arrival.

'You are very good. My sister will be equally sorry to miss the pleasure of seeing you; but she has been very much plagued lately with nervous head-aches, which make her unfit for company or conversation.'

'Oh, dear, that is a great pity! but such old friends as Lucy and me! – I think she might see *us*; and I am sure we would not speak a word.'

Elinor, with great civility, declined the proposal. Her sister was perhaps laid down upon the bed, or in her dressing gown, and therefore not able to come to them.

'Oh, if that's all,' cried Miss Steele, 'we can just as well go and see *her*.'

Elinor began to find this impertinence too much for her temper; but she was saved the trouble of checking it, by Lucy's sharp reprimand, which now, as on many occasions, though it did not give much sweetness to the manners of one sister, was of advantage in governing those of the other.

Chapter Thirty Three

AFTER SOME OPPOSITION, Marianne yielded to her sister's entreaties, and consented to go out with her and Mrs Jennings one morning for half an hour. She expressly conditioned, however, for paying no visits, and would do no more than accompany them to Gray's in Sackville-street, where Elinor was carrying on a negociation for the exchange of a few old-fashioned jewels of her mother.

When they stopped at the door, Mrs Jennings recollected that there was a lady at the other end of the street, on whom she ought to call; and as she had no business at Gray's, it was resolved, that while her young friends transacted their's, she should pay her visit and return for them.

On ascending the stairs, the Miss Dashwoods found so many people before them in the room, that there was not a person at liberty to attend to their orders; and they were obliged to wait. All that could be done was, to sit down at that end of the counter which seemed to promise the quickest succession; one gentleman only was standing there, and it is probable that Elinor was not without hope of exciting his politeness to a quicker dispatch. But the correctness of his eye, and the delicacy of his taste, proved to be beyond his politeness. He was giving orders for a toothpick-case for himself, and till its size, shape, and ornaments were determined, all of which, after examining and debating for a quarter of an hour over every toothpick-case in the shop, were finally arranged by his own inventive fancy, he had no leisure to bestow any other attention on the two ladies, than what was comprised in three or four very broad stares; a kind of notice which served to imprint on Elinor the remembrance of a person and face, of strong, natural, sterling insignificance, though adorned in the first style of fashion.

Marianne was spared from the troublesome feelings of contempt and resentment, on this impertinent examination of their features, and on the puppyism of his manner in deciding on all the different horrors of the different toothpick-cases presented to his inspection, by remaining unconscious of it all; for she was as well able to collect her thoughts within herself, and be as ignorant of what was passing around her, in Mr Gray's shop, as in her own bed-room.

At last the affair was decided. The ivory, the gold, and the pearls all received their appointment, and the gentleman having named the last day on which his existence could be continued without the possession of the toothpick-case, drew on his gloves with leisurely care, and bestowing another glance on the Miss Dashwoods, but such a one as seemed rather to demand than express admiration, walked off with an happy air of real conceit and affected indifference.

Elinor lost no time in bringing her business forward, and was on the point of concluding it, when another gentleman presented himself at her side. She turned her eyes towards his face, and found him with some surprise to be her brother.

Their affection and pleasure in meeting, was just enough to make a very creditable appearance in Mr Gray's shop. John Dashwood was really far from being sorry to see his sisters again; it rather gave him satisfaction; and his inquiries after their mother were respectful and attentive.

Elinor found that he and Fanny had been in town two days.

'I wished very much to call upon you yesterday,' said he, 'but it was impossible, for we were obliged to take Harry to see the wild beasts at Exeter Exchange: and we spent the rest of the day with Mrs Ferrars. Harry was vastly pleased. *This* morning I had fully intended to call on you, if I could possibly find a spare half hour, but one has always so much to do on first coming to town. I am come here to bespeak Fanny a seal. But tomorrow I think I shall certainly be able to call in Berkeley-street, and be introduced to your friend Mrs Jennings. I understand she is a woman of very good fortune. And the Middletons too, you must introduce me to *them*. As my mother-in-law's relations, I shall be happy to shew them every respect. They are excellent neighbours to you in the country, I understand.'

'Excellent indeed. Their attention to our comfort, their friendliness in every particular, is more than I can express.'

'I am extremely glad to hear it, upon my word; extremely glad indeed. But so it ought to be; they are people of large fortune, they are related to you, and every civility, and accommodation that can serve to make your situation pleasant, might be reasonably expected. And so you are most comfortably settled in your little cottage and want for nothing! Edward brought us a most charming account of the place; the most complete thing of its kind, he said, that ever was, and you all seemed to enjoy it beyond any thing. It was a great satisfaction to us to hear it, I assure you.'

Elinor did feel a little ashamed of her brother; and was not sorry to be spared the necessity of answering him, by the arrival of Mrs Jennings's servant, who came to tell her that his mistress waited for them at the door.

Mr Dashwood attended them down stairs, was introduced to Mrs Jennings at the door of her carriage, and repeating his hope of being able to call on them the next day, took leave.

His visit was duly paid. He came with a pretence at an apology from their sister-in-law, for not coming too; 'but she was so much engaged with her mother, that really she had no leisure for going any where.' Mrs Jennings, however, assured him directly, that she should not stand upon ceremony, for they were all cousins, or something like it, and she should certainly wait on Mrs John Dashwood very soon, and bring her sisters to see her. His manners to *them*, though calm, were perfectly kind; to Mrs Jennings most attentively civil; and on Colonel Brandon's coming in soon after himself, he eyed him with a curiosity which seemed to say, that he only wanted to know him to be rich, to be equally civil to *him*.

After staying with them half an hour, he asked Elinor to walk with him to Conduit-street, and introduce him to Sir John and Lady Middleton. The weather was remarkably fine, and she readily consented. As soon as they were out of the house, his enquiries began.

'Who is Colonel Brandon? Is he a man of fortune?'

'Yes; he has a very good property in Dorsetshire.'

'I am glad of it. He seems a most gentlemanlike man; and I think Elinor, I may congratulate you on the prospect of a very respectable establishment in life.'

'Me, brother! what do you mean?'

'He likes you. I observed him narrowly, and am convinced of it. What is the amount of his fortune?'

'I believe about two thousand a-year.'

'Two thousand a-year;' and then working himself up to a pitch of enthusiastic generosity, he added, 'Elinor, I wish, with all my heart, it were *twice* as much, for your sake.'

'Indeed I believe you,' replied Elinor; 'but I am very sure that Colonel Brandon has not the smallest wish of marrying *me*.'

'You are mistaken, Elinor; you are very much mistaken. A very little trouble on your side secures him. Perhaps just at present he may be undecided; the smallness of your fortune may make him hang back; his friends may all advise him against it. But some of those little attentions and encouragements which ladies can so easily give, will fix him, in spite of himself. And there can be no reason why you should not try for him. It is not to be supposed that any prior attachment on your side – in short, you know as to an attachment of that kind, it is quite out of the question, the objections are insurmountable – you have too much sense not to see all that. Colonel Brandon must be the man; and no civility shall be wanting on mv part, to make him pleased with you and your family. It is a match that must give universal satisfaction. In short, it is a kind of thing that' – lowering his voice to an important whisper – 'will be exceedingly welcome to *all parties.*' Recollecting himself, however, he added, 'That is, I mean to say – your friends are all truly anxious to see you well settled; Fanny particularly, for she has your interest very much at heart, I assure you. And her mother too, Mrs Ferrars, a very good-natured woman, I am sure it would give her great pleasure; she said as much the other day.'

Elinor would not vouchsafe any answer.

'It would be something remarkable now,' he continued, 'something droll, if Fanny should have a brother and I a sister settling at the same time. And yet it is not very unlikely.'

'Is Mr Edward Ferrars,' said Elinor, with resolution, 'going to be married?'

'It is not actually settled, but there is such a thing in agitation. He has a most excellent mother. Mrs Ferrars, with the utmost liberality, will come forward, and settle on him a thousand a year, if the match takes place. The lady is the Hon. Miss Morton, only daughter of the late Lord Morton, with thirty thousand pounds. A very desirable connection on both sides, and I have not a doubt of its taking place in time. A thousand a-year is a great deal for a mother to give away, to make over for ever; but Mrs Ferrars has a noble spirit. To give you another instance of her liberality: – The other day, as soon as we came to town, aware that money could not be very plenty with us just now, she put bank-notes into Fanny's hands to the amount of two hundred pounds. And extremely acceptable it is, for we must live at a great expense while we are here.'

He paused for her assent and compassion; and she forced herself to say,

'Your expenses both in town and country must certainly be considerable, but your income is a large one.'

'Not so large, I dare say, as many people suppose. I do not mean to complain, however; it is undoubtedly a comfortable one, and I hope will in time be better. The inclosure of Norland Common, now carrving on, is a most serious drain. And then I have made a little purchase within this half year; East Kingham Farm, you must remember the place, where old Gibson used to live. The land was so very desirable for me in every respect, so immediately adjoining my own property, that I felt it my duty to buy it. I could not have answered it to my conscience to let it fall into any other hands. A man must pay for his convenience; and it *has* cost me a vast deal of money.'

'More than you think it really and intrinsically worth.'

'Why, I hope not that. I might have sold it again the next day, for more than I gave; but with regard to the purchase-money, I might have been very unfortunate indeed; for the stocks were at that time so low, that if I had not happened to have the necessary sum in my banker's hands, I must have sold out to very great loss.'

Elinor could only smile.

'Other great and inevitable expenses too we have had on first coming to Norland. Our respected father, as you well know, bequeathed all the Stanhill effects that remained at Norland (and very valuable they were) to your mother. Far be it from me to repine at his doing so; he had an undoubted right to dispose of his own property as he chose, but, in consequence of it, we have been obliged to make large purchases of linen, china, &c. to supply the place of what was taken away. You may guess, after all these expenses, how very far we must be from being rich, and how acceptable Mrs Ferrar's kindness is.'

'Certainly,' said Elinor; 'and assisted by her liberality, I hope you may yet live to be in easy circumstances.'

'Another year or two may do much towards it,' he gravely replied; 'but however there is still a great deal to be done. There is not a stone laid of Fanny's greenhouse, and nothing but the plan of the flower-garden marked out.'

'Where is the green-house to be?'

'Upon the knoll behind the house. The old walnut trees are all come down to make room for it. It will be a very fine object from many parts of the park, and the flower-garden will slope down just before it, and be exceedingly pretty. We have cleared away all the old thorns that grew in patches over the brow.'

Elinor kept her concern and her censure to herself; and was very thankful that Marianne was not present, to share the provocation.

Having now said enough to make his poverty clear, and to do away the necessity of buying a pair of ear-rings for each of his sisters, in his next visit at Gray's, his thoughts took a cheerfuller turn, and he began to congratulate Elinor on having such a friend as Mrs Jennings.

'She seems a most valuable woman indeed – Her house, her style of living, all bespeak an exceeding good income; and it is an acquaintance that has not only been of great use to you hitherto, but in the end may prove materially advantageous. – Her inviting you to town is certainly a vast thing in your favour; and indeed, it speaks altogether so great a regard for you, that in all probability when she dies you will not be forgotten. – She must have a great deal to leave.'

'Nothing at all, I should rather suppose; for she has only her jointure, which will descend to her children.'

'But it is not to be imagined that she lives up to her income. Few people of common prudence will do *that*; and whatever she saves, she will be able to dispose of.'

'And do you not think it more likely that she should leave it to her daughters, than to us?'

'Her daughters are both exceedingly well married, and therefore I cannot perceive the necessity of her remembering them farther. Whereas, in my opinion, by her taking so much notice of you, and treating you in this kind of way, she has given you a sort of claim on her future consideration, which a conscientious woman would not disregard. Nothing can be kinder than her behaviour; and she can hardly do all this, without being aware of the expectation she raises.'

'But she raises none in those most concerned. Indeed, brother, your anxiety for our welfare and prosperity carries you too far.'

'Why to be sure,' said he, seeming to recollect himself, 'people who have little, have very little in their power. But, my dear Elinor, what is the matter with Marianne? – she looks very unwell, has lost her colour, and is grown quite thin. Is she ill?'

'She is not well, she has had a nervous complaint on her for several weeks.'

'I am sorry for that. At her time of life, any thing of an illness destroys the bloom for ever! Her's has been a very short one! She was as handsome a girl last September, as any I ever saw; and as likely to attract the men. There was something in her style of beauty, to please them particularly. I remember Fanny used to say that she would marry sooner and better than you did; not but what she is exceedingly fond of *you*, but so it happened to strike her. She will be mistaken, however. I question whether Marianne *now*, will marry a man worth more than five or six hundred a-year, at the utmost, and I am very much deceived if *you* do not do better. Dorsetshire! I know very little of Dorsetshire; but, my dear Elinor, I shall be exceedingly glad to know more of it; and think I can answer for your having Fanny and myself among the earliest and best pleased of your visitors.'

Elinor tried very seriously to convince him that there was no likelihood of her marrying Colonel Brandon; but it was an expectation of too much pleasure to himself to be relinquished, and he was really resolved on seeking an intimacy with that gentleman, and promoting the marriage by every possible attention. He had just compunction enough for having done nothing for his sisters himself, to be exceedingly anxious that everybody else should do a great deal; and an offer from Colonel Brandon, or a legacy from Mrs Jennings, was the easiest means of atoning for his own neglect.

They were lucky enough to find Lady Middleton at home, and Sir John came in before their visit ended. Abundance of civilities passed on all sides. Sir John was ready to like anybody, and though Mr Dashwood did not seem to know much about horses, he soon set him down as a very good-natured fellow: while Lady Middleton saw enough of fashion in his appearance, to think his acquaintance worth having; and Mr Dashwood went away delighted with both.

'I shall have a charming account to carry to Fanny,' said he, as he walked back with his sister. 'Lady Middleton is really a most elegant woman! Such a woman as I am sure Fanny will be glad to know. And Mrs Jennings too, an exceedingly well-behaved woman, though not so elegant as her daughter. Your sister need not have any scruple even of visiting *her*, which, to say the truth, has been a little the case, and very naturally; for we only knew that Mrs Jennings was the widow of a man who had got all his money in a low way; and Fanny and Mrs Ferrars were both strongly prepossessed that neither she nor her daughters were such kind of women as Fanny would like to associate with. But now I can carry her a most satisfactory account of both.'

Chapter Thirty Four

MRS JOHN DASHWOOD HAD SO much confidence in her husband's judgment that she waited the very next day both on Mrs Jennings and her daughter; and her confidence was rewarded by finding even the former, even the woman with whom her sisters were staying, by no means unworthy her notice; and as for Lady Middleton, she found her one of the most charming women in the world!

Lady Middleton was equally pleased with Mrs Dashwood. There was a kind of cold hearted selfishness on both sides, which mutually attracted them; and they sympathised with each other in an insipid propriety of demeanour, and a general want of understanding.

The same manners however, which recommended Mrs John Dashwood to the good opinion of Lady Middleton, did not suit the fancy of Mrs Jennings, and to *her* she appeared nothing more than a little proud-looking woman of uncordial address, who met her husband's sisters without any affection and almost without having any thing to say to them; for of the quarter of an hour bestowed on Berkeley-street, she sat at least seven minutes and a half in silence.

Elinor wanted very much to know, though she did not chuse to ask, whether Edward was then in town; but nothing would have induced Fanny voluntarily to mention his name before her, till able to tell her that his marriage with Miss Morton was resolved on, or till her husband's expectations on Colonel Brandon were answered; because she believed them still so very much attached to each other, that they could not be too sedulously divided in word and deed on every occasion. The intelligence however, which *she* would not give, soon flowed from another quarter. Lucy came very shortly to claim Elinor's compassion on being unable to see Edward, though he had arrived in town with Mr and Mrs Dashwood. He dared not come to Bartlett's Buildings for fear of detection, and though their mutual impatience to meet, was not to be told, they could do nothing at present but write.

Edward assured them himself of his being in town, within a very short time, by twice calling in Berkeley-street. Twice was his card found on the table, when they returned from their morning's engagements. Elinor was pleased that he had called; and still more pleased that she had missed him.

The Dashwoods were so prodigiously delighted with the Middletons, that though not much in the habit of giving any thing, they determined to give them – a dinner; and soon after their acquaintance began, invited them to dine in Harley-street, where they had taken a very good house for three months. Their sisters and Mrs Jennings were invited likewise, and John Dashwood was careful to secure Colonel Brandon, who, always glad to be where the Miss Dashwoods were, received his eager civilities with some surprise, but much more pleasure. They were to meet Mrs Ferrars; but Elinor could not learn whether her sons were to be of the party. The expectation of seeing *her*, however, was enough to make her interested in the engagement; for though she could not meet Edward's mother without that strong anxiety which had once promised to attend such an introduction, though she could now see her with perfect indifference as to her opinion of herself, her desire of being in company with Mrs Ferrars, her curiosity to know what she was like, was as lively as ever.

The interest with which she thus anticipated the party, was soon afterwards increased, more powerfully than pleasantly, by her hearing that the Miss Steeles were also to be at it.

So well had they recommended themselves to Lady Middleton, so agreeable had their assiduities made them to her, that though Lucy was certainly not elegant, and her sister not even genteel, she was as ready as Sir John to ask them to spend a week or two in Conduit-street: and it happened to be particularly convenient to the Miss Steeles, as soon as the Dashwoods' invitation was known, that their visit should begin a few days before the party took place.

Their claims to the notice of Mrs John Dashwood, as the nieces of the gentleman who for many years had had the care of her brother, might not have done much, however, towards procuring them seats at her table; but as Lady Middleton's guests they must be welcome; and Lucy, who had long wanted to be personally known to the family, to have a nearer view of their characters and her own difficulties, and to have an opportunity of endeavouring to please them, had seldom been happier in her life than she was on receiving Mrs John Dashwood's card.

On Elinor its effect was very different. She began immediately to determine that Edward who lived with his mother, must be asked as his mother was, to a party given by his sister; and to see him for the first time after all that passed, in the company of Lucy! – she hardly knew how she could bear it!

These apprehensions perhaps were not founded entirely on reason, and certainly not at all on truth. They were relieved however, not by her own recollection, but by the good will of Lucy, who believed herself to be inflicting a severe disappointment when she told her that Edward certainly would not be in Harley-street on Tuesday, and even hoped to be carrying the pain still farther by persuading her, that he was kept away by that extreme affection for herself, which he could not conceal when they were together.

The important Tuesday came that was to introduce the two young ladies to this formidable mother-in-law.

'Pity me, dear Miss Dashwood!' said Lucy, as they walked up the stairs together – for the Middletons arrived so directly after Mrs Jennings, that they all followed the servant at the same time – 'There is nobody here but you, that can feel for me. – I declare I can hardly stand. Good gracious! – In a moment I shall see the person that all my happiness depends on – that is to be my mother!' –

Elinor could have given her immediate relief by suggesting the possibility of its being Miss Morton's mother, rather than her own, whom they were about to behold; but instead of doing that, she assured her, and with great sincerity, that she did pity her, – to the utter amazement of Lucy, who, though really uncomfortable herself, hoped at least to be an object of irrepressible envy to Elinor.

Mrs Ferrars was a little, thin woman, upright, even to formality, in her figure, and serious, even to sourness, in her aspect. Her complexion was sallow; and her features small, without beauty, and naturally without expression; but a lucky contraction of the brow had rescued her countenance from the disgrace of insipidity, by giving it the strong characters of pride and ill nature. She was not a woman of many words: for, unlike people in general, she proportioned them to the number of her ideas; and of the few syllables that did escape her, not one fell to the share of Miss Dashwood, whom she eyed with the spirited determination of disliking her at all events.

Elinor could not *now* be made unhappy by this behaviour. – A few months ago it would have hurt her exceedingly; but it was not in Mrs Ferrar's power to distress her by it now; – and the difference of her manners to the Miss Steeles, a difference which seemed purposely made to humble her more, only amused her. She could not but smile to see the graciousness of both mother and daughter towards the very person – for Lucy was particularly distinguished – whom of all others, had they known as much as she did, they would have been most anxious to mortify; while she herself, who had comparatively no power to wound them, sat pointedly slighted by both. But while she smiled at a graciousness so misapplied, she could not reflect on the mean-spirited folly from which it sprung, nor observe the studied attentions with which the Miss Steeles courted its continuance, without thoroughly despising them all four.

Lucy was all exultation on being so honourably distinguished; and Miss Steele wanted only to be teazed about Dr Davis to be perfectly happy.

The dinner was a grand one, the servants were numerous, and every thing bespoke the Mistress's inclination for shew, and the Master's ability to support it. In spite of the improvements and additions which were making to the Norland estate, and in spite of its owner having once been within some thousand pounds of being obliged to sell out at a loss, nothing gave any symptom of that indigence which he had tried to infer from it; – no poverty of any kind, except of conversation, appeared – but there, the deficiency was considerable. John Dashwood had not much to say for himself that was worth hearing, and his wife had still less. But there was no peculiar disgrace in this, for it was very much the case with the chief of their visitors, who almost all laboured under one or other of these disqualifications for being agreeable – Want of sense, either natural or improved – want of elegance – want of spirits – or want of temper.

When the ladies withdrew to the drawing-room after dinner, this poverty was particularly evident, for the gentlemen *had* supplied the discourse with some variety – the variety of politics, inclosing land, and breaking horses – but then it was all over; and one subject only engaged the ladies till coffee came in, which was the comparative heights of Harry Dashwood, and Lady Middleton's second son William, who were nearly of the same age.

Had both the children been there, the affair might have been determined too easily by measuring them at once; but as Harry only was present, it was all conjectural assertion on both sides, and every body had a right to be equally positive in their opinion, and to repeat it over and over again as often as they liked.

The parties stood thus:

The two mothers, though each really convinced that her own son was the tallest, politely decided in favour of the other.

The two grandmothers, with not less partiality, but more sincerity, were equally earnest in support of their own descendant.

Lucy, who was hardly less anxious to please one parent than the other, thought the boys were both remarkably tall for their age, and could not conceive that there could be the smallest difference in the world between them; and Miss Steele, with yet greater address gave it, as fast as she could, in favour of each.

Elinor, having once delivered her opinion on William's side, by which she offended Mrs Ferrars and Fanny still more, did not see the necessity of enforcing it by any farther assertion; and Marianne, when called on for her's, offended them all, by declaring that she had no opinion to give, as she had never thought about it.

Before her removing from Norland, Elinor had painted a very pretty pair of screens for her sister-in-law, which being now just mounted and brought home, ornamented her present drawing room; and these screens, catching the eye of John Dashwood on his following the other gentlemen into the room, were officiously handed by him to Colonel Brandon for his admiration.

'These are done by my eldest sister,' said he; 'and you, as a man of taste, will, I dare say, be pleased with them. I do not know whether you ever happened to see any of her performances before, but she is in general reckoned to draw extremely well.'

The Colonel, though disclaiming all pretensions to connoisseurship, warmly admired the screens, as he would have done any thing painted by Miss Dashwood; and the curiosity of the others being of course excited, they were handed round for general inspection. Mrs Ferrars, not aware of their being Elinor's work, particularly requested to look at them; and after they had received the gratifying testimony of Lady Middleton's approbation, Fanny presented them to her mother, considerately informing her at the same time, that they were done by Miss Dashwood.

'Hum' - said Mrs Ferrars - 'very pretty,' - and without regarding them at all, returned them to her daughter.

Perhaps Fanny thought for a moment that her mother had been quite rude enough, - for, colouring a little, she immediately said,

'They are very pretty, ma'am - an't they?' But then again, the dread of having been too civil, too encouraging herself, probably came over her, for she presently added,

'Do you not think they are something in Miss Morton's style of painting, ma'am? - *She does* paint most delightfully! - How beautifully her last landscape is done!'

'Beautifully indeed! But *she* does every thing well.'

Marianne could not bear this. - She was already greatly displeased with Mrs Ferrars; and such ill-timed praise of another, at Elinor's expense, though she had not any notion of what was principally meant by it, provoked her immediately to say with warmth,

'This is admiration of a very particular kind! - what is Miss Morton to us? - who knows, or who cares, for her? - it is Elinor of whom *we* think and speak.'

And so saying, she took the screens out of her sister-in-law's hands, to admire them herself as they ought to be admired.

Mrs Ferrars looked exceedingly angry, and drawing herself up more stiffly than ever, pronounced in retort this bitter phillippic; 'Miss Morton is Lord Morton's daughter.'

Fanny looked very angry too, and her husband was all in a fright at his sister's audacity. Elinor was much more hurt by Marianne's warmth, than she had been by what produced it; but Colonel Brandon's eyes, as they were fixed on Marianne, declared that he noticed only what was amiable in it, the affectionate heart which could not bear to see a sister slighted in the smallest point.

Marianne's feelings did not stop here. The cold insolence of Mrs Ferrars's general behaviour to her sister, seemed, to her, to foretel such difficulties and distresses to Elinor, as her own wounded heart taught her to think of with horror; and urged by a strong impulse of affectionate sensibility, she moved, after a moment, to her sister's chair, and putting one arm round her neck, and one cheek close to hers, said in a low, but eager, voice,

'Dear, dear Elinor, don't mind them. Don't let them make *you* unhappy.'

She could say no more; her spirits were quite overcome, and hiding her face on Elinor's shoulder, she burst into tears. – Every body's attention was called, and almost every body was concerned. – Colonel Brandon rose up and went to them without knowing what he did. – Mrs Jennings, with a very intelligent 'Ah! poor dear,' immediately gave her, her salts; and Sir John felt so desperately enraged against the author of this nervous distress, that he instantly changed his seat to one close by Lucy Steele, and gave her, in a whisper, a brief account of the whole shocking affair.

In a few minutes, however, Marianne was recovered enough to put an end to the bustle, and sit down among the rest; though her spirits retained the impression of what had passed, the whole evening.

'Poor Marianne!' said her brother to Colonel Brandon in a low voice, as soon as he could secure his attention, – 'She has not such good health as her sister, – she is very nervous, – she has not Elinor's constitution; – and one must allow that there is something very trying to a young woman who *has been* a beauty, in the loss of her personal attractions. You would not think it perhaps, but Marianne *was* remarkably handsome a few months ago; quite as handsome as Elinor. – Now you see it is all gone.'

Chapter Thirty Five

ELINOR'S CURIOSITY TO SEE Mrs Ferrars was satisfied. – She had found in her every thing that could tend to make a farther connection between the families, undesirable. – She had seen enough of her pride, her meanness, and her determined prejudice against herself, to comprehend all the difficulties that must have perplexed the engagement, and retarded the marriage, of Edward and herself, had he been otherwise free; – and she had seen almost enough to be thankful for her *own* sake, that one greater obstacle preserved her from suffering under any other of Mrs Ferrars's creation, preserved her from all dependence upon her caprice, or any solicitude for her good opinion. Or at least, if she did not bring herself quite to rejoice in Edward's being fettered to Lucy, she determined, that had Lucy been more amiable, she *ought* to have rejoiced.

She wondered that Lucy's spirits could be so very much elevated by the civility of Mrs Ferrars; – that her interest and her vanity should so very much blind her, as to make the attention which seemed only paid her because she was *not Elinor*, appear a compliment to herself – or to allow her to derive encouragement from a preference only given her, because her real situation was unknown. But that it was so, had not only been declared by Lucy's eyes at the time, but was declared over again the next morning more openly, for at her particular desire, Lady Middleton set her down in Berkeley-street on the chance of seeing Elinor alone, to tell her how happy she was.

The chance proved a lucky one, for a message from Mrs Palmer soon after she arrived, carried Mrs Jennings away.

'My dear friend,' cried Lucy as soon as they were by themselves, 'I come to talk to you of my happiness. Could any thing be so flattering as Mrs Ferrars's way of treating me yesterday? So exceeding affable as she was! – You know how I dreaded the thoughts of seeing her; – but the very moment I was introduced, there was such an affability in her behaviour as really should seem to say, she had quite took a fancy to me. Now was not it so? – You saw it all; and was not you quite struck with it?'

'She was certainly very civil to you.'

'Civil! – Did you see nothing but only civility? – I saw a vast deal more. Such kindness as fell to the share of nobody but me! – No pride, no hauteur, and your sister just the same – all sweetness and affability!'

Elinor wished to talk of something else, but Lucy still pressed her to own that she had reason for her happiness; and Elinor was obliged to go on.–

'Undoubtedly, if they had known your engagement,' said she, 'nothing could be more flattering than their treatment of you; – but as that was not the case' –

'I guessed you would say so' – replied Lucy quickly – 'but there was no reason in the world why Mrs Ferrars should seem to like me, if she did not, and her liking me is every thing. You shan't talk me out of my satisfaction. I am sure it will all end well, and there will be no difficulties at all, to what I used to think. Mrs Ferrars is a charming woman, and so is your sister. They are both delightful women indeed! – I wonder I should never hear you say how agreeable Mrs Dashwood was!'

To this, Elinor had no answer to make, and did not attempt any.

'Are you ill, Miss Dashwood? – you seem low – you don't speak; – sure you an't well.'

'I never was in better health.'

'I am glad of it with all my heart, but really you did not look it. I should be so sorry to have you ill; you, that have been the greatest comfort to me in the world! – Heaven knows what I should have done without your friendship.' –

Elinor tried to make a civil answer, though doubting her own success. But it seemed to satisfy Lucy, for she directly replied.

'Indeed I am perfectly convinced of your regard for me, and next to Edward's love, it is the greatest comfort I have. – Poor Edward! – But now, there is one good thing, we shall be able to meet, and meet pretty often, for Lady Middleton's delighted with Mrs Dashwood, so we shall be a good deal in Harley-street, I dare say, and Edward spends half his time with his sister – besides, Lady Middleton and Mrs Ferrars will visit now; – and Mrs Ferrars and your sister were both so good to say more than once, they should always be glad to see me. – They are such charming women! – I am sure if ever you tell your sister what I think of her, you cannot speak too high.'

But Elinor would not give her any encouragement to hope that she *should* tell her sister. Lucy continued.

'I am sure I should have seen it in a moment, if Mrs Ferrars had took a dislike to me. If she had only made me a formal curtsey, for instance, without saying a word, and never after had took any notice of me, and never looked at me in a pleasant way – you know what I mean, – if I had been treated in that forbidding sort of way, I should have gave it all up in despair. I could not have stood it. For where she *does* dislike, I know it is most violent.'

Elinor was prevented from making any reply to this civil triumph, by the door's being thrown open, the servant's announcing Mr Ferrars, and Edward's immediately walking in.

It was a very awkward moment; and the countenance of each shewed that it was so. They all looked exceedingly foolish; and Edward seemed to have as great an inclination to walk out of the room again, as to advance further into it. The very circumstance, in its unpleasantest form, which they would each have been most anxious to avoid, had fallen on them – They were not only all three together, but were together without the relief of any other person. The ladies recovered themselves first. It was not Lucy's business to put herself forward, and the appearance of secrecy must still be kept up. She could therefore only *look* her tenderness, and after slightly addressing him, said no more.

But Elinor had more to do; and so anxious was she, for his sake and her own, to do it well, that she forced herself, after a moment's recollection, to welcome him, with a look and manner that were almost easy, and almost open; and another struggle, another effort still improved them. She would not allow the presence of Lucy, nor the consciousness of some injustice towards herself, to deter her from saying that she was happy to see him, and that she had very much regretted being from home, when he called before in Berkeley-street. She would not be frightened from paying him those attentions which, as a friend and almost a relation, were his due, by the observant eyes of Lucy, though she soon perceived them to be narrowly watching her.

Her manners gave some re-assurance to Edward, and he had courage enough to sit down; but his embarrassment still exceeded that of the ladies in a proportion, which the case rendered reasonable, though his sex might make it rare; for his heart had not the indifference of Lucy's, nor could his conscience have quite the ease of Elinor's.

Lucy, with a demure and settled air, seemed determined to make no contribution to the comfort of the others, and would not say a word; and almost every thing that *was* said, proceeded from Elinor, who was obliged to volunteer all the information about her mother's health, their coming to town, &c. which Edward ought to have inquired about, but never did.

Her exertions did not stop here; for she soon afterwards felt herself so heroically disposed as to determine, under pretence of fetching Marianne, to leave the others by themselves: and she really did it, and *that* in the handsomest manner, for she loitered away several minutes on the landing-place, with the most highminded fortitude, before she went to her sister. When that was once done, however, it was time for the raptures of Edward to cease; for Marianne's joy hurried her into the drawing-room immediately. Her pleasure in seeing him was like every other of her feelings, strong in itself, and strongly spoken. She met him with a hand that would be taken, and a voice that expressed the affection of a sister.

'Dear Edward!' she cried, 'this is a moment of great happiness! – This would almost make amends for every thing!'

Edward tried to return her kindness as it deserved, but before such witnesses he dared not say half what he really felt. Again they all sat down, and for a moment or two all were silent; while Marianne was looking with the most speaking tenderness, sometimes at Edward and sometimes at Elinor, regretting only that their delight in each other should be checked by Lucy's unwelcome presence. Edward was the first to speak, and it was to notice

Marianne's altered looks, and express his fear of her not finding London agree with her.

'Oh! don't think of me!' she replied, with spirited earnestness, though her eyes were filled with tears as she spoke, 'don't think of *my* health. Elinor is well, you see. That must be enough for us both.'

This remark was not calculated to make Edward or Elinor more easy, nor to conciliate the good will of Lucy, who looked up at Marianne with no very benignant expression.

'Do you like London?' said Edward, willing to say any thing that might introduce another subject.

'Not at all. I expected much pleasure in it, but I have found none. The sight of you, Edward, is the only comfort it has afforded; and thank Heaven! you are what you always were!'

She paused – no one spoke.

'I think, Elinor,' she presently added, 'we must employ Edward to take care of us in our return to Barton. In a week or two, I suppose, we shall be going; and, I trust, Edward will not be very unwilling to accept the charge.'

Poor Edward muttered something, but what it was, nobody knew, not even himself. But Marianne, who saw his agitation, and could easily trace it to whatever cause best pleased herself, was perfectly satisfied, and soon talked of something else.

'We spent such a day, Edward, in Harley-street yesterday! So dull, so wretchedly dull! – But I have much to say to you on that head, which cannot be said now.'

And with this admirable discretion did she defer the assurance of her finding their mutual relatives more disagreeable than ever, and of her being particularly disgusted with his mother, till they were more in private.

'But why were you not there, Edward? – Why did you not come?'

'I was engaged elsewhere.'

'Engaged! But what was that, when such friends were to be met?'

'Perhaps, Miss Marianne,' cried Lucy, eager to take some revenge on her, 'you think young men never stand upon engagements, if they have no mind to keep them, little as well as great.'

Elinor was very angry, but Marianne seemed entirely insensible of the sting; for she calmly replied,

'Not so, indeed; for seriously speaking, I am very sure that conscience only kept Edward from Harley-street. And I really believe he *has* the most delicate conscience in the world; the most scrupulous in performing every engagement however minute, and however it may make against his interest or pleasure. He is the most fearful of giving pain, of wounding expectation, and the most incapable of being selfish, of any body I ever saw. Edward, it is so and I will say it. What! are you never to hear yourself praised! – Then, you must be no friend of mine; for those who will accept of my love and esteem, must submit to my open commendation.'

The nature of her commendation, in the present case, however, happened to be particularly ill-suited to the feelings of two thirds of her auditors, and was so very unexhilarating to Edward, that he very soon got up to go away.

'Going so soon!' said Marianne; 'my dear Edward, this must not be.'

And drawing him a little aside, she whispered her persuasion that Lucy could not stay much longer. But even this encouragement failed, for he would go; and Lucy, who would have outstaid him had his visit lasted two hours, soon afterwards went away.

'What can bring her here so often!' said Marianne, on her leaving them. 'Could she not see that we wanted her gone! – how teazing to Edward!'

'Why so? – we were all his friends, and Lucy has been the longest known to him of any. It is but natural that he should like to see her as well as ourselves.'

Marianne looked at her steadily, and said, 'You know, Elinor, that this is a kind of talking which I cannot bear. If you only hope to have your assertion contradicted, as I must suppose to be the case, you ought to recollect that I am the last person in the world to do it. I cannot descend to be tricked out of assurances, that are not really wanted.'

She then left the room; and Elinor dared not follow her to say more, for bound as she was by her promise of secrecy to Lucy, she could give no information that would convince Marianne; and painful as the consequences of her still continuing in an error might be, she was obliged to submit to it. All that she could hope, was that Edward would not often expose her or himself to the distress of hearing Marianne's mistaken warmth, nor to the repetition of any other part of the pain that had attended their recent meeting – and this she had every reason to expect.

Chapter Thirty Six

WITHIN A FEW DAYS AFTER THIS MEETING, the newspapers announced to the world, that the Lady of Thomas Palmer, Esq. was safely delivered of a son and heir; a very interesting and satisfactory paragraph, at least to all those intimate connections who knew it before.

This event, highly important to Mrs Jennings's happiness, produced a temporary alteration in the disposal of her time, and influenced, in a like degree, the engagements of her young friends; for as she wished to be as much as possible with Charlotte, she went thither every morning as soon as she was dressed, and did not return till late in the evening; and the Miss Dashwoods, at the particular request of the Middletons, spent the whole of every day in Conduit-street. For their own comfort, they would much rather have remained, at least all the morning, in Mrs Jennings's house; but it was not a thing to be urged against the wishes of everybody. Their hours were therefore made over to Lady Middleton and the two Miss Steeles, by whom their company was in fact as little valued, as it was professedly sought.

They had too much sense to be desirable companions to the former; and by the latter they were considered with a jealous eye, as intruding on *their* ground, and sharing the kindness which they wanted to monopolize. Though nothing could be more polite than Lady Middleton's behaviour to Elinor and Marianne, she did not really like them at all. Because they neither flattered herself nor her children, she could not believe them good-natured; and because they were fond of reading, she fancied them satirical: perhaps without exactly knowing what it was to be satirical; but *that* did not signify. It was censure in common use, and easily given.

Their presence was a restraint both on her and on Lucy. It checked the idleness of one, and the business of the other. Lady Middleton was ashamed of doing nothing before them, and the flattery which Lucy was proud to think of and administer at other times, she feared they would despise her for offering. Miss Steele was the least discomposed of the three, by their presence; and it was in their power to reconcile her to it entirely. Would either of them, only have given her a full and minute account of the whole affair between Marianne and Mr Willoughby, she would have thought herself amply rewarded for the sacrifice of the best place by the fire after dinner, which their arrival occasioned. But this conciliation was not granted; for though she often threw out expressions of pity for her sister to Elinor, and more than once dropt a reflection on the inconstancy of beaux before Marianne, no effect was produced, but a look of indifference from the former, or of disgust in the latter. An effort even yet lighter might have made her their friend. Would they only have laughed at her about the Doctor! But so little were they, anymore than the others, inclined to oblige her, that if Sir John dined from home, she might spend a whole day without hearing any other raillery on the subject, than what she was kind enough to bestow on herself.

All these jealousies and discontents, however, were so totally unsuspected by Mrs Jennings, that she thought it a delightful thing for the girls to be together; and generally congratulated her young friends every night, on having escaped the company of a stupid old woman so long. She joined them sometimes at Sir John's, and sometimes at her own house; but wherever it was, she always came in excellent spirits, full of delight and importance, attributing Charlotte's well doing to her own care, and ready to give so exact, so minute a detail of her situation, as only Miss Steele had curiosity enough to desire. One thing *did* disturb her; and of that she made her daily complaint. Mr Palmer maintained the common, but unfatherly opinion among his sex, of all infants being alike; and though she could plainly perceive at different times, the most striking resemblance between this baby and every one of his relations on both sides, there was no convincing his father of it; no persuading him to believe that it was not exactly like every other baby of the same age; nor could he even be brought to acknowledge the simple proposition of its being the finest child in the world.

I come now to the relation of a misfortune, which about this time befell Mrs John Dashwood. It so happened that while her two sisters with Mrs Jennings were first calling on her in Harley-street, another of her acquaintance had dropt in – a circumstance in itself not apparently likely to produce evil to her. But while the imaginations of other people will carry them away to form wrong judgments of our conduct, and to decide on it by slight appearances, one's happiness must in some measure be always at the mercy of chance. In the present instance, this last-arrived lady allowed her fancy so far to outrun truth and probability, that on merely hearing the name of the Miss Dashwoods, and understanding them to be Mr Dashwood's sisters, she immediately concluded them to be staying in Harley-street; and this misconstruction produced within a day or two afterwards, cards of invitation for them as well as for their brother and sister, to a small musical party at her house. The consequence of which was, that Mrs John Dashwood was obliged to submit not only to the exceedingly great inconvenience of sending her carriage for the Miss Dashwoods; but, what was still worse, must be subject to all the unpleasantness of appearing to treat them with attention; and who could tell that they might not expect to go out with her a second time? The power of disappointing them, it was true, must always be her's. But that was not enough; for when people are determined on a mode of conduct which they know to be wrong, they feel injured by the expectation of any thing better from them.

Marianne had now been brought by degrees, so much into the habit of going out every day, that it was become a matter of indifference to her, whether she went or not; and she prepared quietly and mechanically for every evening's engagement, though without expecting the smallest amusement from any, and very often without knowing till the last moment, where it was to take her.

To her dress and appearance she was grown so perfectly indifferent, as not to bestow half the consideration on it, during the whole of her toilette, which it received from Miss Steele in the first five minutes of their being together, when it was finished. Nothing escaped *her* minute observation and general curiosity; she saw every thing, and asked every thing; was never easy till she knew the price of every part of Marianne's dress; could have guessed the number of her gowns altogether with better judgment than Marianne herself, and was not without hopes of finding out before they parted, how much her washing cost per week, and how much she had every year to spend upon herself. The impertinence of these kind of scrutinies, moreover, was generally concluded with a compliment, which though meant as its douceur, was considered by Marianne as the greatest impertinence of all; for after undergoing an examination into the value and make of her gown, the colour of her shoes, and the arrangement of her hair, she was almost sure of being told that upon 'her word she looked vastly smart, and she dared to say would make a great many conquests.'

With such encouragement as this, was she dismissed on the present occasion to her brother's carriage; which they were ready to enter five minutes after it stopped at the door, a punctuality not very agreeable to their sister-in-law, who had preceded them to the house of her acquaintance, and was there hoping for some delay on their part that might inconvenience either herself or her coachman.

The events of the evening were not very remarkable. The party, like other musical parties, comprehended a great many people who had real taste for the performance, and a great many more who had none at all; and the performers themselves were, as usual, in their own estimation, and that of their immediate friends, the first private performers in England.

As Elinor was neither musical, nor affecting to be so, she made no scruple of turning away her eyes from the grand pianoforté, whenever it suited her, and unrestrained even by the presence of a harp, and a violoncello, would fix them at pleasure on any other object in the room. In one of these excursive glances she perceived among a group of young men, the very he, who had given them a lecture on toothpick-cases at Gray's. She perceived him soon afterwards looking at herself, and speaking familiarly to her brother; and had just determined to find out his name from the latter, when they both came towards her, and Mr Dashwood introduced him to her as Mr Robert Ferrars.

He addressed her with easy civility, and twisted his head into a bow which assured her as plainly as words could have done, that he was exactly the coxcomb she had heard him described to be by Lucy. Happy had it been for her, if her regard for Edward had depended less on his own merit, than on the merit of his nearest relations! For then his brother's bow must have given the finishing stroke to what the ill-humour of his mother and sister would have begun. But while she wondered at the difference of the two young men, she did not find that the emptiness and conceit of the one, put her at all out of charity with the modesty and worth of the other. Why they *were* different, Robert exclaimed to her himself in the course of a quarter of an hour's conversation; for, talking of his brother, and lamenting the extreme *gaucherie* which he really believed kept him from mixing in proper society, he candidly and generously attributed it much less to any natural deficiency, than to the misfortune of a private education; while he himself, though probably without any particular, any material superiority by nature, merely from the advantage of a public school, was as well fitted to mix in the world as any other man.

'Upon my soul,' he added, 'I believe it is nothing more; and so I often tell my mother, when she is grieving about it. "My dear Madam," I always say to her, "you must make yourself easy. The evil is now irremediable, and it has been entirely your own doing. Why would you be persuaded by my uncle, Sir Robert, against your own judgment, to place Edward under private tuition, at the most critical time of his life? If you had only sent him to Westminster as well as myself, instead of sending him to Mr Pratt's, all this would have been prevented." This is the way in which I always consider the matter, and my mother is perfectly convinced of her error.'

Elinor would not oppose his opinion, because, whatever might be her general estimation of the advantage of a public school, she could not think of Edward's abode in Mr Pratt's family, with any satisfaction.

'You reside in Devonshire, I think' – was his next observation, 'in a cottage near Dawlish.'

Elinor set him right as to its situation, and it seemed rather surprising to him that anybody could live in Devonshire, without living near Dawlish. He bestowed his hearty approbation however on their species of house.

'For my own part,' said he, 'I am excessively fond of a cottage; there is always so much comfort, so much elegance about them. And I protest, if I had any money to spare, I should buy a little land and build one myself, within a short distance of London, where I might drive myself down at any time, and collect a few friends about me, and be happy. I advise every body who is going to build, to build a cottage. My friend Lord Courtland came to me the other day on purpose to ask my advice, and laid before me three different plans of Bonomi's. I was to decide on the best of them. "My dear Courtland," said I, immediately throwing them all into the fire, "do not adopt either of them, but by all means build a cottage." And that, I fancy, will be the end of it.'

'Some people imagine that there can be no accommodations, no space in a cottage; but this is all a mistake. I was last month at my friend Elliott's near Dartford. Lady Elliott wished to give a dance. "But how can it be done?" said she; "my dear Ferrars, do tell me how it is to be managed. There is not a room in this cottage that will hold ten couple, and where can the supper be?" I immediately saw that there could be no difficulty in it, so I said, "My dear Lady Elliott, do not be uneasy. The dining parlour will admit eighteen couple with ease; card-tables may be placed in the drawing-room; the library may be open for tea and other refreshments; and let the supper be set out in the saloon." Lady Elliott was delighted with the thought. We measured the dining-room, and found it would hold exactly eighteen couple, and the affair was arranged precisely after my plan. So that, in fact, you see, if people do but know how to set about it, every comfort may be as well enjoyed in a cottage as in the most spacious dwelling.'

Elinor agreed to it all, for she did not think he deserved the compliment of rational opposition.

As John Dashwood had no more pleasure in music than his eldest sister, his mind was equally at liberty to fix on any thing else; and a thought struck him during the evening, which he communicated to his wife, for her approbation, when they got home. The consideration of Mrs Dennison's mistake, in supposing his sisters their guests, had suggested the propriety of their being really invited to become such, while Mrs Jennings's engagements kept her from home. The expense would be nothing, the inconvenience not more; and it was altogether an attention, which the delicacy of his conscience pointed out to be requisite to its complete enfranchisement from his promise to his father. Fanny was startled at the proposal.

'I do not see how it can be done,' said she, 'without affronting Lady Middleton, for they spend every day with her; otherwise I should be exceedingly glad to do it. You know I am always ready to pay them any attention in my power, as my taking them out this evening shews. But they are Lady Middleton's visitors. How can I ask them away from her?'

Her husband, but with great humility, did not see the force of her objection. 'They had already spent a week in this manner in Conduit-street, and Lady Middleton could not be displeased at their giving the same number of days to such near relations.'

Fanny paused a moment, and then, with fresh vigour, said,

'My love, I would ask them with all my heart, if it was in my power. But I had just settled within myself to ask the Miss Steeles to spend a few days with us. They are very well behaved, good kind of girls; and I think the attention is due to them, as their uncle did so very well by Edward. We can ask your sisters some other year, you know; but the Miss Steeles may not be in town any more. I am sure you will like them; indeed, you *do* like them, you know, very much already, and so does my mother; and they are such favourites with Harry!'

Mr Dashwood was convinced. He saw the necessity of inviting the Miss Steeles immediately, and his conscience was pacified by the resolution of inviting his sisters another year; at the same time, however, slyly suspecting that another year would make the invitation needless, by bringing Elinor to town as Colonel Brandon's wife, and Marianne as *their* visitor.

Fanny, rejoicing in her escape, and proud of the ready wit that had procured it, wrote the next morning to Lucy, to request her company and her sister's, for some days, in Harley-street, as soon as Lady Middleton could spare them. This was enough to make Lucy really and reasonably happy. Mrs Dashwood seemed actually working for her, herself; cherishing all her hopes, and promoting all her views! Such an opportunity of being with Edward and his family was, above all things, the most material to her interest, and such an invitation the most gratifying to her feelings! It was an advantage that could not be too gratefully acknowledged, nor too speedily made use of; and the visit to Lady Middleton, which had not before had any precise limits, was instantly discovered to have been always meant to end in two days' time.

When the note was shewn to Elinor, as it was within ten minutes after its arrival, it gave her, for the first time, some share in the expectations of Lucy; for such a mark of uncommon kindness, vouchsafed on so short an acquaintance, seemed to declare that the good will towards her arose from something more than merely malice against herself; and might be brought, by time and address, to do every thing that Lucy wished. Her flattery had already subdued the pride of Lady Middleton, and made an entry into the close heart of Mrs John Dashwood; and these were effects that laid open the probability of greater.

The Miss Steeles removed to Harley-street, and all that reached Elinor of their influence there, strengthened her expectation of the event. Sir John, who called on them more than once, brought home such accounts of the favour that they were in, as must be universally striking. Mrs Dashwood had never been so much pleased with any young women in her life, as she was with them; had given each of them a needle book, made by some emigrant; called Lucy by her Christian name; and did not know whether she should ever be able to part with them.

*[At this point in the first and
second editions, Volume II ended.]*

Chapter Thirty Seven

MRS PALMER WAS SO WELL AT the end of a fortnight, that her mother felt it no longer necessary to give up the whole of her time to her; and contenting herself with visiting her once or twice a day, returned from that period to her own home, and her own habits, in which she found the Miss Dashwoods very ready to reassume their former share.

About the third or fourth morning after their being thus resettled in Berkeley-street, Mrs Jennings, on returning from her ordinary visit to Mrs Palmer, entered the drawing-room, where Elinor was sitting by herself, with an air of such hurrying importance as prepared her to hear something wonderful; and giving her time only to form that idea, began directly to justify it by saying,

'Lord! my dear Miss Dashwood! have you heard the news!'

'No, ma'am. What is it?'

'Something so strange! But you shall hear it all. – When I got to Mr Palmer's, I found Charlotte quite in a fuss about the child. She was sure it was very ill – it cried, and fretted, and was all over pimples. So I looked at it directly, and, "Lord! my dear," says I, "it is nothing in the world but the red-gum;" and nurse said just the same. But Charlotte, she would not be satisfied, so Mr Donavan was sent for; and luckily he happened to be just come in from Harley-street, so he stepped over directly, and as soon as ever he saw the child, he said just as we did, that it was nothing in the world but the red-gum, and then Charlotte was easy. And so, just as he was going away again, it came into my head, I am sure I do not know how I happened to think of it, but it came into my head to ask him if there was any news. So upon that, he smirked, and simpered, and looked grave, and seemed to know something or other, and at last he said in a whisper, "For fear any unpleasant report should reach the young ladies under your care as to their sister's indisposition, I think it advisable to say, that I believe there is no great reason for alarm; I hope Mrs Dashwood will do very well." '

'What! is Fanny ill?'

'That is exactly what I said, my dear. "Lord!" says I, "is Mrs Dashwood ill?" So then it all came out; and the long and the short of the matter, by all I can learn, seems to be this. Mr Edward Ferrars, the very young man I used to joke with you about (but however, as it turns out, I am monstrous glad there never was any thing in it), Mr Edward Ferrars, it seems, has been engaged above this twelvemonth to my cousin Lucy! – There's for you, my dear! – And not a creature knowing a syllable of the matter except Nancy! – Could you have believed such a thing possible? – There is no great wonder in their liking one another; but that matters should be brought so forward between them, and nobody suspect it! *That* is strange! – I never happened to see them together, or I am sure I should have found it out directly. Well, and so this was kept a great secret, for fear of Mrs Ferrars, and neither she nor your brother or sister suspected a word of the matter; – till this very morning, poor Nancy, who, you know, is a well-meaning creature, but no conjurer, popt it all out. "Lord!" thinks she to herself, "they are all so fond of Lucy, to be sure they will make no difficulty about it;" and so, away she went to your sister, who was sitting all alone at her carpet-work, little suspecting what was to come – for she had just been saying to your brother, only five minutes before, that she thought to make a match between Edward and some Lord's daughter or other, I forget who. So you may think what a blow it was to all her vanity and pride. She fell into violent hysterics immediately, with such screams as reached your brother's ears, as he was sitting in his own dressing-room down stairs, thinking about writing a letter to his steward in the country. So up he flew directly, and a terrible scene took place, for Lucy was come to them by that time, little dreaming what was going on. Poor soul! I pity *her*. And I must say, I think she was used very hardly; for your sister scolded like any fury, and soon drove her into a fainting fit. Nancy, she fell upon her knees, and cried bitterly; and your brother, he walked about the room, and said he did not know what to do. Mrs Dashwood declared they should not stay a minute longer in the house, and your brother was forced to go down upon *his* knees too, to persuade her to let them stay till they had packed up their clothes. *Then* she fell into hysterics again, and he was so frightened that he would send for Mr Donavan, and Mr Donavan found the house in all this uproar. The carriage was at the door ready to take my poor cousins away, and they were just stepping in as he came off; poor Lucy in such a condition, he says, she could hardly walk; and Nancy, she was almost as bad. I declare, I have no patience with your sister; and I hope, with all my heart, it will be a match in spite of her. Lord! what a taking poor Mr Edward will be in when he hears of it! To have his love used so scornfully! for they say he is monstrous fond of her, as well he may. I should not wonder, if he was to be in the greatest of a passion! – and

Mr Donavan thinks just the same. He and I had a great deal of talk about it; and the best of all is, that he is gone back again to Harley-street, that he may be within call when Mrs Ferrars is told of it, for she was sent for as soon as ever my cousin left the house, for your sister was sure *she* would be in hysterics too; and so she may, for what I care. I have no pity for either of them. I have no notion of people's making such a to-do about money and greatness. There is no reason on earth why Mr Edward and Lucy should not marry; for I am sure Mrs Ferrars may afford to do very well by her son, and though Lucy has next to nothing herself, she knows better than any body how to make the most of every thing; and I dare say, if Mrs Ferrars would only allow him five hundred a-year, she would make as good an appearance with it as any body else would with eight. Lord! how snug they might live in such another cottage as yours – or a little bigger – with two maids and two men; and I believe I could help them to a housemaid, for my Betty has a sister out of place, that would fit them exactly.'

Here Mrs Jennings ceased, and as Elinor had had time enough to collect her thoughts, she was able to give such an answer, and make such observations, as the subject might naturally be supposed to produce. Happy to find that she was not suspected of any extraordinary interest in it; that Mrs Jennings (as she had of late often hoped might be the case) had ceased to imagine her at all attached to Edward; and happy above all the rest, in the absence of Marianne, she felt very well able to speak of the affair without embarrassment, and to give her judgment, as she believed, with impartiality on the conduct of every one concerned in it.

She could hardly determine what her own expectation of its event really was; though she earnestly tried to drive away the notion of its being possible to end otherwise at last, than in the marriage of Edward and Lucy. What Mrs Ferrars would say and do, though there could not be a doubt of its nature, she was anxious to hear; and still more anxious to know how Edward would conduct himself. For *him* she felt much compassion; – for Lucy very little – and it cost her some pains to procure that little; – for the rest of the party none at all.

As Mrs Jennings could talk on no other subject, Elinor soon saw the necessity of preparing Marianne for its discussion. No time was to be lost in undeceiving her, in making her acquainted with the real truth, and in endeavouring to bring her to hear it talked of by others, without betraying that she felt any uneasiness for her sister, or any resentment against Edward.

Elinor's office was a painful one. – She was going to remove what she really believed to be her sister's chief consolation, – to give such particulars of Edward, as she feared would ruin him for ever in her good opinion, – and to make Marianne, by a resemblance in their situations, which to *her* fancy would seem strong, feel all her own disappointment over again. But unwelcome as such a task must be, it was necessary to be done, and Elinor therefore hastened to perform it.

She was very far from wishing to dwell on her own feelings, or to represent herself as suffering much, any otherwise than as the self-command she had practised since her first knowledge of Edward's engagement, might suggest a hint of what was practicable to Marianne. Her narration was clear and simple; and though it could not be given without emotion, it was not accompanied by violent agitation, nor impetuous grief. – *That* belonged rather to the hearer, for Marianne listened with horror, and cried excessively.

Elinor was to be the comforter of others in her own distresses, no less than in theirs; and all the comfort that could be given by assurances of her own composure of mind, and a very earnest vindication of Edward from every charge but of imprudence, was readily offered.

But Marianne for some time would give credit to neither. Edward seemed a second Willoughby; and acknowledging as Elinor did, that she *had* loved him most sincerely, could she feel less than herself! As for Lucy Steele, she considered her so totally unamiable, so absolutely incapable of attaching a sensible man, that she could not be persuaded at first to believe, and afterwards to pardon, any former affection of Edward for her. She would not even admit it to have been natural; and Elinor left her to be convinced that it was so, by that which only could convince her, a better knowledge of mankind.

Her first communication had reached no farther than to state the fact of the engagement, and the length of time it had existed. – Marianne's feelings had then broken in, and put an end to all regularity of detail; and for some time all that could be done was to sooth her distress, lessen her alarms, and combat her resentment. The first question on her side, which led to farther particulars, was,

'How long has this been known to you, Elinor? has he written to you?'

'I have known it these four months. When Lucy first came to Barton Park last November, she told me in confidence of her engagement.'

At these words, Marianne's eyes expressed the astonishment, which her lips could not utter. After a pause of wonder, she exclaimed,

'Four months! – Have you known of this four months?' –

Elinor confirmed it.

'What! – while attending me in all my misery, has this been on your heart? – and I have reproached you for being happy!' –

'It was not fit that you should then know how much I was the reverse!' –

'Four months!' – cried Marianne again. – 'So calm! – so cheerful! – how have you been supported?' –

'By feeling that I was doing my duty. – My promise to Lucy, obliged me to be secret. I owed it to her, therefore, to avoid giving any hint of the truth; and I owed it to my family and friends, not to create in them a solicitude about me, which it could not be in my power to satisfy.'

Marianne seemed much struck. –

'I have very often wished to undeceive yourself and my mother,' added Elinor; 'and once or twice I have attempted it; – but without betraying my trust, I never could have convinced you.'

'Four months! – and yet you loved him!' –

'Yes. But I did not love only him; – and while the comfort of others was dear to me, I was glad to spare them from knowing how much I felt. Now, I can think and speak of it with little emotion. I would not have you suffer on my account; for I assure you I no longer suffer materially myself. I have many things to support me. I am not conscious of having provoked the disappointment by any imprudence of my own, and I have borne it as much as possible without spreading it farther. I acquit Edward of all essential misconduct. I wish him very happy; and I am so sure of his always doing his duty, that though now he may harbour some regret, in the end he must become so. Lucy does not want sense, and that is the foundation on which every thing good may be built. – And after all, Marianne, after all that is bewitching in the idea of a single and constant attachment, and all that can be said of one's happiness depending entirely on any particular person, it is not meant – it is not fit – it is not possible that it should be so. – Edward will marry Lucy; he will marry a woman superior in person and understanding to half her sex; and time and habit will teach him to forget that he ever thought another superior to *her*.' –

'If such is your way of thinking,' said Marianne, 'if the loss of what is most valued is so easily to be made up by something else, your resolution, your self-command, are, perhaps, a little less to be wondered at. – They are brought more within my comprehension.'

'I understand you. – You do not suppose that I have ever felt much. – For four months, Marianne, I have had all this hanging on my mind, without being at liberty to speak of it to a single creature; knowing that it would make you and my mother most unhappy whenever it were explained to you, yet unable to prepare you for it in the least. – It was told me, – it was in a manner forced on me by the very person herself, whose prior engagement ruined all my prospects; and told me, as I thought, with triumph. – This person's suspicions, therefore, I have had to oppose, by endeavouring to appear indifferent where I have been most deeply interested; – and it has not been only once; – I have had her hopes and exultation to listen to again and again. – I have known myself to be divided from Edward for ever, without hearing one circumstance that could make me less desire the connection. – Nothing has proved him unworthy; nor has any thing declared him indifferent to me. – I have had to contend against the unkindness of his sister, and the insolence of his mother; and have suffered the punishment of an attachment, without enjoying its advantages. – And all this has been going on at a time, when, as you too well know, it has not been my only unhappiness. – If you can think me capable of ever feeling – surely you may suppose that I have suffered *now*. The composure of mind with which I have brought myself at present to consider the matter, the consolation that I have been willing to admit, have been the effect of constant and painful exertion; – they did not spring up of themselves; – they did not occur to relieve my spirits at first – No, Marianne. – *Then*, if I had not been bound to silence, perhaps nothing could have kept me entirely – not even what I owed to my dearest friends – from openly shewing that I was *very* unhappy.' –

Marianne was quite subdued. –

'Oh! Elinor,' she cried, 'you have made me hate myself for ever. – How barbarous have I been to you! – you, who have been my only comfort, who have borne with me in all my misery, who have seemed to be only suffering for me! – Is this my gratitude! – Is this the only return I can make you? – Because your merit cries out upon myself, I have been trying to do it away.'

The tenderest caresses followed this confession. In such a frame of mind as she was now in, Elinor had no difficulty in obtaining from her whatever promise she required; and at her request, Marianne engaged never to speak of the affair to any one with the least appearance of bitterness; – to meet Lucy without betraying the smallest increase of dislike to her; – and even to see Edward himself, if chance should bring them together, without any diminution of her usual cordiality. – These were great concessions; – but where Marianne felt that she had injured, no reparation could be too much for her to make.

She performed her promise of being discreet, to admiration. – She attended to all that Mrs Jennings had to say upon the subject, with an unchanging complexion, dissented from her in nothing, and was heard three times to say, 'Yes, ma'am.' – She listened to her praise of Lucy with only moving from one chair to another, and when Mrs Jennings talked of Edward's affection, it cost her only a spasm in her throat. – Such advances towards heroism in her sister, made Elinor feel equal to any thing herself.

The next morning brought a farther trial of it, in a visit from their brother, who came with a most serious aspect to talk over the dreadful affair, and bring them news of his wife.

'You have heard, I suppose,' said he with great solemnity, as soon as he was seated, 'of the very shocking discovery that took place under our roof yesterday.'

They all looked their assent; it seemed too awful a moment for speech.

'Your sister,' he continued, 'has suffered dreadfully. Mrs Ferrars too – in short it has been a scene of such complicated distress – but I will hope that the storm may be weathered without our being any of us quite overcome. Poor Fanny! she was in hysterics all yesterday. But I would not alarm you too much. Donavan says there is nothing materially to be apprehended; her constitution is a good one, and her resolution equal to any thing. She has borne it all, with the fortitude of an angel! She says she never shall think well of anybody again; and one cannot wonder at it, after being so deceived! – meeting with such ingratitude, where so much kindness had been shewn, so much confidence had been placed! It was quite out of the benevolence of her heart, that she had asked these young women to her house; merely because she thought they deserved some attention, were harmless, well-behaved girls, and would be pleasant companions; for otherwise we both wished very much to have invited you and Marianne to be with us, while your kind friend there, was attending her daughter. And now to be so rewarded! "I wish with all my heart," says poor Fanny in her affectionate way, "that we had asked your sisters instead of them." '

Here he stopped to be thanked; which being done, he went on.

'What poor Mrs Ferrars suffered, when first Fanny broke it to her, is not to be described. While she with the truest affection had been planning a most eligible connection for him, was it to be supposed that he could be all the time secretly engaged to another person! – such a suspicion could never have entered her head! If she suspected *any* prepossession elsewhere, it could not be in *that* quarter. "*There*, to be sure," said she, "I might have thought myself safe." She was quite in an agony. We consulted together, however, as to what should be done, and at last she determined to send for Edward. He came. But I am sorry to relate what ensued. All that Mrs Ferrars could say to make him put an end to the engagement, assisted too as you may well suppose by my arguments, and Fanny's entreaties, was of no avail. Duty, affection, every thing was disregarded. I never thought Edward so stubborn, so unfeeling before. His mother explained to him her liberal designs, in case of his marrying Miss Morton; told him she would settle on him the Norfolk estate, which, clear of land-tax, brings in a good thousand a-year; offered even, when matters grew desperate, to make it twelve hundred; and in opposition to this, if he still persisted in this low connection, represented to him the certain penury that must attend the match. His own two thousand pounds she protested should be his all; she would never see him again; and so far would she be from affording him the smallest assistance, that if he were to enter into any profession with a view of better support, she would do all in her power to prevent his advancing in it.'

Here Marianne, in an ecstacy of indignation, clapped her hands together, and cried, 'Gracious God! can this be possible!'

'Well may you wonder, Marianne,' replied her brother, 'at the obstinacy which could resist such arguments as these. Your exclamation is very natural.'

Marianne was going to retort, but she remembered her promises, and forbore.

'All this, however,' he continued, 'was urged in vain. Edward said very little; but what he did say, was in the most determined manner. Nothing should prevail on him to give up his engagement. He would stand to it, cost him what it might.'

'Then,' cried Mrs Jennings with blunt sincerity, no longer able to be silent, 'he has acted like an honest man! I beg your pardon, Mr Dashwood, but if he had done otherwise, I should have thought him a rascal. I have some little concern in the business, as well as yourself, for Lucy Steele is my cousin, and I believe there is not a better kind of girl in the world, nor one who more deserves a good husband.'

John Dashwood was greatly astonished; but his nature was calm, not open to provocation, and he never wished to offend anybody, especially anybody of good fortune. He therefore replied, without any resentment,

'I would by no means speak disrespectfully of any relation of yours, madam. Miss Lucy Steele is, I dare say, a very deserving young woman, but in the present case you know, the connection must be impossible. And to have entered into a secret engagement with a young man under her uncle's care, the son of a woman especially of such very large fortune as Mrs Ferrars, is perhaps altogether a little extraordinary. In short, I do not mean to reflect upon the behaviour of any person whom you have a regard for, Mrs Jennings. We all wish her extremely happy, and Mrs Ferrars's conduct throughout the whole, has been such as every conscientious, good mother, in like circumstances, would adopt. It has been dignified and liberal. Edward has drawn his own lot, and I fear it will be a bad one.'

Marianne sighed out her similar apprehension; and Elinor's heart wrung for the feelings of Edward, while braving his mother's threats, for a woman who could not reward him.

'Well, sir,' said Mrs Jennings, 'and how did it end?'

'I am sorry to say, ma'am, in a most unhappy rupture: – Edward is dismissed for ever from his mother's notice. He left her house yesterday, but where he is gone, or whether he is still in town, I do not know; for we of course can make no inquiry.'

'Poor young man! – and what is to become of him?'

'What, indeed, ma'am! It is a melancholy consideration. Born to the prospect of such affluence! I cannot conceive a situation more deplorable. The interest of two thousand pounds – how can a man live on it! – and when to that is added the recollection, that he might, but for his own folly, within three months have been in the receipt of two thousand, five hundred a-year, (for Miss Morton has thirty thousand pounds,) I cannot picture to myself a more wretched condition. We must all feel for him; and the more so, because it is totally out of our power to assist him.'

'Poor young man!' cried Mrs Jennings, 'I am sure he should be very welcome to bed and board at my house; and so I would tell him if I could see him. It is not fit that he should be living about at his own charge now, at lodgings and taverns.'

Elinor's heart thanked her for such kindness towards Edward, though she could not forbear smiling at the form of it.

'If he would only have done as well by himself,' said John Dashwood, 'as all his friends were disposed to do by him, he might now have been in his proper situation, and would have wanted for nothing. But as it is, it must be out of anybody's power to assist him. And there is one thing more preparing against him, which must be worse than all – his mother has determined, with a very natural kind of spirit, to settle *that* estate upon Robert immediately, which might have been Edward's, on proper conditions. I left her this morning with her lawyer, talking over the business.'

'Well!' said Mrs Jennings, 'that is *her* revenge. Everybody has a way of their own. But I don't think mine would be, to make one son independent, because another had plagued me.'

Marianne got up, and walked about the room.

'Can any thing be more galling to the spirit of a man,' continued John, 'than to see his younger brother in possession of an estate which might have been his own? Poor Edward! I feel for him sincerely.'

A few minutes more spent in the same kind of effusion, concluded his visit; and with repeated assurances to his sisters that he really believed there was no material danger in Fanny's indisposition, and that they need not therefore be very uneasy about it, he went away; leaving the three ladies unanimous in their sentiments on the present occasion, as far at least as it regarded Mrs Ferrars's conduct, the Dashwoods' and Edward's.

Marianne's indignation burst forth as soon as he quitted the room; and as her vehemence made reserve impossible in Elinor, and unnecessary in Mrs Jennings, they all joined in a very spirited critique upon the party.

Chapter Thirty Eight

MRS JENNINGS WAS VERY WARM in her praise of Edward's conduct, but only Elinor and Marianne understood its true merit. *They* only knew how little he had had to tempt him to be disobedient, and how small was the consolation, beyond the consciousness of doing right, that could remain to him in the loss of friends and fortune. Elinor gloried in his integrity; and Marianne forgave all his offences in compassion for his punishment. But though confidence between them was, by this public discovery, restored to its proper state, it was not a subject on which either of them were fond of dwelling when alone. Elinor avoided it upon principle, as tending to fix still more upon her thoughts, by the too warm, too positive assurances of Marianne, that belief of Edward's continued affection for herself which she rather wished to do away; and Marianne's courage soon failed her, in trying to converse upon a topic which always left her more dissatisfied with herself than ever, by the comparision it necessarily produced between Elinor's conduct and her own.

She felt all the force of that comparison; but not as her sister had hoped, to urge her to exertion now; she felt it with all the pain of continual self-reproach, regretted most bitterly that she had never exerted herself before; but it brought only the torture of penitence, without the hope of amendment. Her mind was so much weakened that she still fancied present exertion impossible, and therefore it only dispirited her more.

Nothing new was heard by them, for a day or two afterwards, of affairs in Harley-street, or Bartlett's Buildings. But though so much of the matter was known to them already, that Mrs Jennings might have had enough to do in spreading that knowledge farther, without seeking after more, she had resolved from the first to pay a visit of comfort and inquiry to her cousins as soon as she could; and nothing but the hindrance of more visitors than usual, had prevented her going to them within that time.

The third day succeeding their knowledge of the particulars, was so fine, so beautiful a Sunday as to draw many to Kensington Gardens, though it was only the second week in March. Mrs Jennings and Elinor were of the number; but Marianne, who knew that the Willoughbys were again in town, and had a constant dread of meeting them, chose rather to stay at home, than venture into so public a place.

An intimate acquaintance of Mrs Jennings joined them soon after they entered the Gardens, and Elinor was not sorry that by her continuing with them, and engaging all Mrs Jennings's conversation, she was herself left to quiet reflection. She saw nothing of the Willoughbys, nothing of Edward, and for some time nothing of anybody who by any chance whether grave or gay, be interesting to her. But at last she found herself with some surprise, accosted by Miss Steele, who, though looking rather shy, expressed great satisfaction in meeting them, and on receiving encouragement from the particular kindness of Mrs Jennings, left her own party for a short time, to join their's. Mrs Jennings immediately whispered to Elinor,

'Get it all out of her, my dear. She will tell you any thing if you ask. You see I cannot leave Mrs Clarke.'

It was lucky, however for Mrs Jennings's curiosity and Elinor's too, that she would tell any thing *without* being asked, for nothing would otherwise have been learnt.

'I am so glad to meet you;' said Miss Steele, taking her familiarly by the arm – 'for I wanted to see you of all things in the world.' And then lowering her voice, 'I suppose Mrs Jennings has heard all about it. Is she angry?'

'Not at all, I believe, with you.'

'That is a good thing. And Lady Middleton, is *she* angry?'

'I cannot suppose it possible that she should.'

'I am monstrous glad of it. Good gracious! I have had such a time of it! I never saw Lucy in such a rage in my life. She vowed at first she would never trim me up a new bonnet, nor do any thing else for me again, so long as she lived; but now she is quite come to, and we are as good friends as ever. Look, she made me this bow to my hat, and put in the feather last night. There now, *you* are going to laugh at me too. But why should not I wear pink ribbons? I do not care it is *is* the Doctor's favourite colour. I am sure, for my part, I should never have known he *did* like it better than any other colour, if he had not happened to say so. My cousins have been so plaguing me! – I declare sometimes I do not know which way to look before them.'

She had wandered away to a subject on which Elinor had nothing to say, and therefore soon judged it expedient to find her way back again to the first.

'Well, but Miss Dashwood,' speaking triumphantly. 'people may say what they chuse about Mr Ferrars's declaring he would not have Lucy, for it's no such a thing I can tell you; and it's quite a shame for such ill-natured reports to be spread abroad. Whatever Lucy might think about it herself, you know, it was no business of other people to set it down for certain.'

'I never heard anything of the kind hinted at before, I assure you,' said Elinor.

'Oh! did not you? But it *was* said, I know, very well, and by more than one; for Miss Godby told Miss Sparks, that nobody in their senses could expect Mr Ferrars to give up a woman like Miss Morton, with thirty thousand pounds to her fortune, for Lucy Steele that had nothing at all; and I had it from Miss Sparks myself. And besides that, my cousin Richard said himself, that when it came to the point, he was afraid Mr Ferrars would be off; and when Edward did not come near us for three days, I could not tell what to think myself; and I believe in my heart Lucy gave it up all for lost; for we came away from your brother's Wednesday, and we saw nothing of him not all Thursday, Friday, and Saturday, and did not know what to become with him. Once Lucy thought to write to him, but then her spirit rose against that. However this morning he came just as we came home from church; and then it all came out, how he had been sent for Wednesday to Harley-street, and been talked to by his mother and all of them, and how he had declared before them all that he loved nobody but Lucy, and nobody but Lucy would he have. And how he had been so worried by what passed, that as soon as he had went away from his mother's house, he had got upon his horse, and rid into the country some where or other; and how he had staid about at an inn all Thursday and Friday, on purpose to get the better of it. And after thinking it all over and over again, he said, it seemed to him as if, now he had no fortune, and no nothing at all, it would be quite unkind to keep her on to the engagement, because it must be for her loss, for he had nothing but two thousand pounds, and no hope of any thing else; and if he was to go into orders, as he had some thoughts, he could get nothing but a curacy, and how was they to live upon that? – He could not bear to think of her doing no better, and so he begged, if she had the least mind for it, to put an end to the matter directly, and leave him to shift for himself. I heard him say all this as plain as could possibly be. And it was entirely for *her* sake, and upon *her* account, that he said a word about being off, and not upon his own. I will take my oath he never dropt a syllable of being tired of her, or of wishing to marry Miss Morton, or anything like it. But, to be sure, Lucy would not give ear to such kind of talking; so she told him directly (with a great deal about sweet and love, you know, and all that – Oh, la! one can't repeat such kind of things you know) – she told him directly, she had not the least mind in the world to be off, for she could live with him upon a trifle, and how little so ever he might have, she should be very glad to have it all, you know, or something of the kind. So then he was monstrous happy, and talked on some time about what they should do, and they agreed he should take orders directly, and they must wait to be married till he got a living. And just then I could not hear any more, for my cousin called from below to tell me Mrs Richardson was come in her coach, and would take one of us to Kensington Gardens; so I was forced to go into the room and interrupt them, to ask Lucy if she would like to go, but she did not care to leave

Edward; so I just run up stairs and put on a pair of silk stockings, and came off with the Richardsons.'

'I do not understand what you mean by interrupting them,' said Elinor; 'you were all in the same room together, were not you?'

'No, indeed, not us. La! Miss Dashwood, do you think people make love when any body else is by? Oh for shame! – To be sure you must know better than that. (Laughing affectedly.) – No, no; they were shut up in the drawing-room together, and all I heard was only by listening at the door.'

'How!' cried Elinor; 'have you been repeating to me what you only learnt yourself by listening at the door? I am sorry I did not know it before; for I certainly would not have suffered you to give me particulars of a conversation which you ought not to have known yourself. How could you behave so unfairly by your sister?'

'Oh, la! there is nothing in *that*. I only stood at the door, and heard what I could. And I am sure Lucy would have done just the same by me; for a year or two back, when Martha Sharpe and I had so many secrets together, she never made any bones of hiding in a closet, or behind a chimney-board, on purpose to hear what we said.'

Elinor tried to talk of something else; but Miss Steele could not be kept beyond a couple of minutes, from what was uppermost in her mind.

'Edward talks of going to Oxford soon,' said she, 'but now he is lodging at No. –, Pall Mall. What an ill-natured woman his mother is, an't she? And your brother and sister were not very kind! However, I shan't say anything against them to *you*; and to be sure they did send us home in their own chariot, which was more than I looked for. And for my part, I was all in a fright for fear your sister should ask us for the huswifes she had gave us a day or two before; but however, nothing was said about them, and I took care to keep mine out of sight. Edward have got some business at Oxford, he says; so he must go there for a time; and after *that*, as soon as he can light upon a Bishop, he will be ordained. I wonder what curacy he will get! – Good gracious! (giggling as she spoke) I'd lay my life I know what my cousins will say, when they hear of it. They will tell me I should write to the Doctor, to get Edward the curacy of his new living. I know they will; but I am sure I would not do such a thing for all the world. – "La!" I shall say directly, "I wonder how you could think of such a thing. *I* write to the Doctor, indeed!"'

'Well,' said Elinor, 'it is a comfort to be prepared against the worst. You have got your answer ready.'

Miss Steele was going to reply on the same subject but the approach of her own party made another more necessary.

'Oh, la! here come the Richardsons. I had a vast deal more to say to you, but I must not stay away from them not any longer. I assure you they are very genteel people. He makes a monstrous deal of money, and they keep their own coach. I have not time to speak to Mrs Jennings about it myself, but pray tell her I am quite happy to hear she is not in anger against us, and Lady Middleton the same; and if any thing should happen to take you and your sister away, and Mrs Jennings should want company, I am sure we should be very glad to come and stay with her for as long a time as she likes. I suppose Lady Middleton won't ask us any more this bout. Good bye; I am sorry Miss Marianne was not here. Remember me kindly to her. La! if you have not got your spotted muslin on! – I wonder you was not afraid of its being torn.'

Such was her parting concern; for after this, she had time only to pay her farewell compliments to Mrs Jennings, before her company was claimed by Mrs Richardson; and Elinor was left in possession of knowledge which might feed her powers of reflection some time, though she had learnt very little more than what had been already foreseen and foreplanned in her own mind. Edward's marriage with Lucy was as firmly determined on, and the time of its taking place remained as absolutely uncertain, as she had concluded it would be; – every thing depended, exactly after her expectation, on his getting that preferment, of which, at present, there seemed not the smallest chance.

As soon as they returned to the carriage, Mrs Jennings was eager for information; but as Elinor wished to spread as little as possible intelligence that had in the first place been so unfairly obtained, she confined herself to the brief repetition of such simple particulars, as she felt assured that Lucy, for the sake of her own consequence, would chuse to have known. The continuance of their engagement, and the means that were to be taken for promoting its end, was all her communication; and this produced from Mrs Jennings the following natural remark.

'Wait for his having a living! – aye, we all know how *that* will end; – they will wait a twelvemonth, and finding no good comes of it, will set down upon a curacy of fifty pounds a-year, with the interest of his two thousand pounds, and what little matter Mr Steele and Mr Pratt can give her. – Then they will have a child every year! and Lord help 'em! how poor they will be! – I must see what I can give them towards furnishing their house. Two maids and two men indeed! – as I talked of t'other day. – No, no, they must get a stout girl of all works. – Betty's sister would never do for them *now*.'

The next morning brought Elinor a letter by the two-penny post from Lucy herself. It was as follows:

Bartlett's Buildings, March.
I hope my dear Miss Dashwood will excuse the liberty I take of writing to her; but I know your friendship for me will make you pleased to hear such a good account of myself and my dear Edward, after all the troubles we have went through lately, therefore will make no more apologies, but proceed to say that, thank God! though we have suffered dreadfully, we are both quite well now, and as happy as we must always be in one another's love. We have had great trials, and great persecutions, but however, at the same time, gratefully acknowledge many friends, yourself not the least among them, whose great kindness I shall always thankfully remember, as will Edward too, who I have told of it. I am sure you will be glad to hear, as likewise dear Mrs Jennings, I spent two happy hours with him yesterday afternoon, he would not hear of our parting, though earnestly did I, as I thought my duty required, urge him to it for prudence sake, and would have parted for ever on the spot, would he consent to it; but he said it should never be, he did not regard his mother's anger, while he could have my affections; our prospects are not very bright, to be sure, but we must wait, and hope for the best; he will be ordained shortly, and should it ever be in your power to recommend him to any body that has a living to bestow, am very sure you will not forget us, and dear Mrs Jennings too, trust she will speak a good word for us to Sir John, or Mr Palmer,

*or any friend that may be able to assist us. - Poor Anne was much to blame
for what she did, but she did it for the best, so I say nothing; hope Mrs
Jennings won't think it too much trouble to give us a call, should she come
this way any morning, 'twould be a great kindness, and my cousins would be
proud to know her. - My paper reminds me to conclude, and begging to be
most gratefully and respectfully remembered to her, and to Sir John, and Lady
Middleton, and the dear children, when you chance to see them, and love to
Miss Marianne,*

I am, &c. &c.

As soon as Elinor finished it, she performed what she concluded to be
its writer's real design, by placing it in the hands of Mrs Jennings, who read
it aloud with many comments of satisfaction and praise.

'Very well indeed! – how prettily she writes! – aye, that was quite proper
to let him be off if he would. That was just like Lucy. – Poor soul! I wish I
could get him a living with all my heart. – She calls me dear Mrs Jennings,
you see. She is a good-hearted girl as ever lived. – Very well upon my word.
That sentence is very prettily turned. Yes, yes, I will go and see her, sure
enough. How attentive she is, to think of everybody! – Thank you, my dear,
for shewing it me. It is as pretty a letter as ever I saw, and does Lucy's head
and heart great credit.'

Chapter Thirty Nine

THE MISS DASHWOODS HAD NOW been rather more than two months in town, and
Marianne's impatience to be gone increased every day. She sighed for the air,
the liberty, the quiet of the country; and fancied that if any place could give
her ease, Barton must do it. Elinor was hardly less anxious than herself for
their removal, and only so much less bent on its being effected immediately,
as that she was conscious of the difficulties of so long a journey, which
Marianne could not be brought to acknowledge. She began, however, seriously
to turn her thoughts towards its accomplishment, and had already mentioned
their wishes to their kind hostess, who resisted them with all the eloquence
of her good-will, when a plan was suggested, which, though detaining them
from home yet a few weeks longer, appeared to Elinor altogether much more
eligible than any other. The Palmers were to remove to Cleveland about the
end of March, for the Easter holidays; and Mrs Jennings, with both her
friends, received a very warm invitation from Charlotte to go with them.
This would not, in itself, have been sufficient for the delicacy of Miss
Dashwood; – but it was inforced with so much real politeness by Mr Palmer
himself, as joined to the very great amendment of his manners towards them
since her sister had been known to be unhappy, induced her to accept it
with pleasure.

When she told Marianne what she had done, however, her first reply
was not very auspicious.

'Cleveland!' – she cried, with great agitation. 'No, I cannot go to
Cleveland.' –

'You forget,' said Elinor, gently, 'that its situation is not . . . that it is not in the neighbourhood of . . .'

'But it is in Somersetshire. – I cannot go into Somersetshire. – There, where I looked forward to going . . . No, Elinor, you cannot expect me to go there.'

Elinor would not argue upon the propriety of overcoming such feelings; – she only endeavoured to counteract them by working on others; – and represented it, therefore, as a measure which would fix the time of her returning to that dear mother, whom she so much wished to see, in a more eligible, more comfortable manner, than any other plan could do, and perhaps without any greater delay. From Cleveland, which was within a few miles of Bristol, the distance to Barton was not beyond one day, though a long day's journey; and their mother's servant might easily come there to attend them down; and as there could be no occasion for their staying above a week at Cleveland, they might now be at home in little more than three weeks' time. As Marianne's affection for her mother was sincere, it must triumph, with little difficulty, over the imaginary evils she had started.

Mrs Jennings was so far from being weary of her guests, that she pressed them very earnestly to return with her again from Cleveland. Elinor was grateful for the attention, but it could not alter their design; and their mother's concurrence being readily gained, every thing relative to their return was arranged as far as it could be; – and Marianne found some relief in drawing up a statement of the hours, that were yet to divide her from Barton.

'Ah! Colonel, I do not know what you and I shall do without the Miss Dashwoods;' – was Mrs Jennings's address to him when he first called on her, after their leaving her was settled – 'for they are quite resolved upon going home from the Palmers; – and how forlorn we shall be, when I come back! – Lord! we shall sit and gape at one another as dull as two cats.'

Perhaps Mrs Jennings was in hopes, by this vigorous sketch of their future ennui, to provoke him to make that offer, which might give himself an escape from it; – and if so, she had soon afterwards good reason to think her object gained; for, on Elinor's moving to the window to take more expeditiously the dimensions of a print, which she was going to copy for her friend, he followed her to it with a look of particular meaning, and conversed with her there for several minutes. The effect of his discourse on the lady too, could not escape her observation, for though she was too honourable to listen, and had even changed her seat, on purpose that she might *not* hear, to one close by the piano forté on which Marianne was playing, she could not keep herself from seeing that Elinor changed colour, attended with agitation, and was too intent on what he said, to pursue her employment. – Still farther in confirmation of her hopes, in the interval of Marianne's turning from one lesson to another, some words of the Colonel's inevitably reached her ear, in which he seemed to be apologizing for the badness of his house. This set the matter beyond a doubt. She wondered indeed at his thinking it necessary to do so; – but supposed it to be the proper etiquette. What Elinor said in reply she could not distinguish, but judged from the motion of her lips that she did not think *that* any material objection; – and Mrs Jennings commended her in her heart for being so honest. They then talked on for a few minutes longer without her catching a syllable, when

another lucky stop in Marianne's performance brought her these words in
the Colonel's calm voice,

'I am afraid it cannot take place very soon.'

Astonished and shocked at so unlover-like a speech, she was almost
ready to cry out, 'Lord! what should hinder it?' – but checking her desire,
confined herself to this silent ejaculation.

'This is very strange! – sure he need not wait to be older.' –

This delay on the Colonel's side, however, did not seem to offend or
mortify his fair companion in the least, for on their breaking up the
conference soon afterwards, and moving different ways, Mrs Jennings very
plainly heard Elinor say, and with a voice which shewed her to feel what
she said,

'I shall always think myself very much obliged to you.'

Mrs Jennings was delighted with her gratitude, and only wondered, that
after hearing such a sentence, the Colonel should be able to take leave of
them, as he immediately did, with the utmost sang-froid, and go away
without making her any reply! – She had not thought her old friend could
have made so indifferent a suitor.

What had really passed between them was to this effect.

'I have heard,' said he, with great compassion, 'of the injustice your
friend Mr Ferrars has suffered from his family; for if I understand the matter
right, he has been entirely cast off by them for persevering in his engagement
with a very deserving young woman – Have I been rightly informed? – Is it
so?' –

Elinor told him that it was.

'The cruelty, the impolitic cruelty,' – he replied, with great feeling –
'of dividing, or attempting to divide, two young people long attached to each
other, is terrible – Mrs Ferrars does not know what she may be doing – what
she may drive her son to. I have seen Mr Ferrars two or three times in
Harley-street, and am much pleased with him. He is not a young man with
whom one can be intimately acquainted in a short time, but I have seen
enough of him to wish him well for his own sake, and as a friend of yours,
I wish it still more. I understand that he intends to take orders. Will you be
so good as to tell him that the living of Delaford, now just vacant, as I am
informed by this day's post, is his, if he think it worth his acceptance – but
that, perhaps, so unfortunately circumstanced as he is now, it may be
nonsense to appear to doubt; I only wish it were more valuable. – It is a
rectory, but a small one; the late incumbent, I believe, did not make more
than 200*l*. per annum, and though it is certainly capable of improvement, I
fear, not to such an amount as to afford him a very comfortable income.
Such as it is, however, my pleasure in presenting him to it, will be very
great. Pray assure him of it.'

Elinor's astonishment at this commission could hardly have been greater,
had the Colonel been really making her an offer of his hand. The preferment,
which only two days before she had considered as hopeless for Edward, was
already provided to enable him to marry; – and *she*, of all people in the
world, was fixed on to bestow it! – Her emotion was such as Mrs Jennings
had attributed to a very different cause; – but whatever minor feelings less
pure, less pleasing, might have a share in that emotion, her esteem for the
general benevolence, and her gratitude for the particular friendship, which
together prompted Colonel Brandon to this act, were strongly felt, and

warmly expressed. She thanked him for it with all her heart, spoke of Edward's principles and disposition with that praise which she knew them to deserve; and promised to undertake the commission with pleasure, if it were really his wish to put off so agreeable an office to another. But at the same time, she could not help thinking that no one could so well perform it as himself. It was an office in short, from which, unwilling to give Edward the pain of receiving an obligation from *her*, she would have been very glad to be spared herself; – but Colonel Brandon, on motives of equal delicacy, declining it likewise, still seemed so desirous of its being given through her means, that she would not on any account make farther opposition. Edward, she believed, was still in town, and fortunately she had heard his address from Miss Steele. She could undertake therefore to inform him of it, in the course of the day. After this had been settled, Colonel Brandon began to talk of his own advantage in securing so respectable and agreeable a neighbour, and *then* it was that he mentioned with regret, that the house was small and indifferent; – an evil which Elinor, as Mrs Jennings had supposed her to do, made very light of, at least as far as regarded its size.

'The smallness of the house,' said she, 'I cannot imagine any inconvenience to them, for it will be in proportion to their family and income.'

By which the Colonel was surprised to find that *she* was considering Mr Ferrars's marriage as the certain consequence of the presentation; for he did not suppose it possible that Delaford living could supply such an income, as any body in his style of life would venture to settle on – and he said so.

'This little rectory *can* do no more than make Mr Ferrars comfortable as a bachelor; it cannot enable him to marry. I am sorry to say that my patronage ends with this; and my interest is hardly more extensive. If, however, by any unforseen chance it should be in my power to serve him farther, I must think very differently of him from what I now do, if I am not as ready to be useful to him then, as I sincerely wish I could be at present. What I am now doing indeed, seems nothing at all, since it can advance him so little towards what must be his principal, his only object of happiness. His marriage must still be a distant good; – at least, I am afraid it cannot take place very soon. –'

Such was the sentence which, when misunderstood, so justly offended the delicate feelings of Mrs Jennings; but after this narration of what really passed between Colonel Brandon and Elinor, while they stood at the window, the gratitude expressed by the latter on their parting, may perhaps appear in general, not less reasonably excited, nor less properly worded than if it had arisen from an offer of marriage.

Chapter Forty

'WELL, MISS DASHWOOD,' said Mrs Jennings, sagaciously smiling, as soon as the gentleman had withdrawn, 'I do not ask you what the Colonel has been saying to you; for though, upon my honour, I *tried* to keep out of hearing, I could not help catching enough to understand his business. And I assure you I never was better pleased in my life, and I wish you joy of it with all my heart.'

'Thank you, ma'am,' said Elinor, 'It is a matter of great joy to me; and I feel the goodness of Colonel Brandon most sensibly. There are not many men who would act as he has done. Few people who have so compassionate an heart! I never was more astonished in my life.'

'Lord! my dear, you are very modest! I an't the least astonished at it in the world, for I have often thought of late, there was nothing more likely to happen.'

'You judged from your knowledge of the Colonel's general benevolence; but at least you could not foresee that the opportunity would so very soon occur.'

'Opportunity!' repeated Mrs Jennings – 'Oh! as to that, when a man has once made up his mind to such a thing, somehow or other he will soon find an opportunity. Well, my dear, I wish you joy of it again and again; and if ever there was a happy couple in the world, I think I shall soon know where to look for them.'

'You mean to go to Delaford after them I suppose,' said Elinor, with a faint smile.

'Aye, my dear, that I do, indeed. And as to the house being a bad one, I do not know what the Colonel would be at, for it is as good a one as ever I saw.'

'He spoke of its being out of repair.'

'Well, and whose fault is that? why don't he repair it? – who should do it but himself?'

They were interrupted by the servant's coming in to announce the carriage being at the door; and Mrs Jennings immediately preparing to go, said –

'Well, my dear, I must be gone before I have had half my talk out. But, however, we may have it all over in the evening, for we shall be quite alone. I do not ask you to go with me, for I dare say your mind is too full of the matter to care for company; and besides, you must long to tell your sister all about it.'

Marianne had left the room before the conversation began.

'Certainly, ma'am, I shall tell Marianne of it; but I shall not mention it at present to anybody else.'

'Oh! very well,' said Mrs Jennings rather disappointed. 'Then you would not have me tell it Lucy, for I think of going as far as Holborn today.'

'No, ma'am, not even Lucy if you please. One day's delay will not be very material; and till I have written to Mr Ferrars, I think it ought not to be mentioned to any body else. I shall do *that* directly. It is of importance that no time should be lost with him, for he will of course have much to do relative to his ordination.'

This speech at first puzzled Mrs Jennings exceedingly. Why Mr Ferrars was to be written to about it in such a hurry, she could not immediately comprehend. A few moments' reflection, however, produced a very happy idea, and she exclaimed; –

'Oh ho! – I understand you. Mr Ferrars is to be the man. Well, so much the better for him. Aye, to be sure, he must be ordained in readiness; and I am very glad to find things are so forward between you. But, my dear, is not this rather out of character? Should not the Colonel write himself? – sure, he is the proper person.'

Elinor did not quite understand the beginning of Mrs Jennings's speech; neither did she think it worth inquiring into; and therefore only replied to its conclusion.

'Colonel Brandon is so delicate a man, that he rather wished any one to announce his intentions to Mr Ferrars than himself.'

'And so *you* are forced to do it. Well, *that* is an odd kind of delicacy! However, I will not disturb you (seeing her preparing to write.) You know your own concerns best. So good bye, my dear. I have not heard of any thing to please me so well since Charlotte was brought to bed.'

And away she went; but returning again in a moment,

'I have just been thinking of Betty's sister, my dear. I should be very glad to get her so good a mistress. But whether she would do for a lady's maid, I am sure I can't tell. She is an excellent housemaid, and works very well at her needle. However, you will think of all that at your leisure.'

'Certainly, ma'am,' replied Elinor, not hearing much of what she said, and more anxious to be alone, than to be mistress of the subject.

How she should begin – how she should express herself in her note to Edward, was now all her concern. The particular circumstances between them made a difficulty of that which to any other person would have been the easiest thing in the world; but she equally feared to say too much or too little, and sat deliberating over her paper, with the pen in her hand, till broken in on by the entrance of Edward himself.

He had met Mrs Jennings at the door in her way to the carriage, as he came to leave his farewell card; and she, after apologizing for not returning herself, had obliged him to enter, by saying that Miss Dashwood was above, and wanted to speak with him on very particular business.

Elinor had just been congratulating herself, in the midst of her perplexity, that however difficult it might be to express herself properly by letter, it was at least preferable to giving the information by word of mouth, when her visitor entered, to force her upon this greatest exertion of all. Her astonishment and confusion were very great on his so sudden appearance. She had not seen him before since his engagement became public, and therefore not since his knowing her to be acquainted with it; which, with the consciousness of what she had been thinking of, and what she had to tell him, made her feel particularly uncomfortable for some minutes. He too was much distressed, and they sat down together in a most promising state of embarrassment. – Whether he had asked her pardon for his intrustion on first coming into the room, he could not recollect; but determining to be on the safe side, he made his apology in form as soon as he could say any thing, after taking a chair.

'Mrs Jennings told me,' said he, 'that you wished to speak with me, at least I understood her so – or I certainly should not have intruded on you in such a manner; though at the same time, I should have been extremely sorry to leave London without seeing you and your sister; especially as it will most likely be some time – it is not probable that I should soon have the pleasure of meeting you again. I go to Oxford tomorrow.'

'You would not have gone, however,' said Elinor, recovering herself, and determined to get over what she so much dreaded as soon as possible, 'without receiving our good wishes, even if we had not been able to give them in person. Mrs Jennings was quite right in what she said. I have something of consequence to inform you of, which I was on the point of communicating by paper. I am charged with a most agreeable office, (breathing rather faster than usual as she spoke.) Colonel Brandon, who was here only ten minutes ago, has desired me to say that, understanding you mean to take orders, he has great pleasure in offering you the living of Delaford, now just vacant, and only wishes it were more valuable. Allow me to congratulate you on having so respectable and well-judging a friend, and to join in his wish that the living – it is about two hundred a-year – were much more considerable, and such as might better enable you to – as might be more than a temporary accommodation to yourself – such, in short, as might establish all your views of happiness.'

What Edward felt, as he could not say it himself, it cannot be expected that any one else should say for him. He *looked* all the astonishment which such unexpected, such unthought-of information could not fail of exciting; but he said only these two words.

'Colonel Brandon!'

'Yes,' continued Elinor, gathering more resolution, as some of the worst was over; 'Colonel Brandon means it as a testimony of his concern for what has lately passed – for the cruel situation in which the unjustifiable conduct of your family has placed you – a concern which I am sure Marianne, myself, and all your friends must share; and likewise as a proof of his high esteem for your general character, and his particular approbation of your behaviour on the present occasion.'

'Colonel Brandon give *me* a living! – Can it be possible?'

'The unkindness of your own relations has made you astonished to find friendship any where.'

'No,' replied he, with sudden consciousness, 'not to find it in *you*; for I cannot be ignorant that to you, to your goodness I owe it all. – I feel it – I would express it if I could – but, as you well know, I am no orator.'

'You are very much mistaken. I do assure you that you owe it entirely, at least almost entirely, to your own merit, and Colonel Brandon's discernment of it. I have had no hand in it. I did not even know, till I understood his design, that the living was vacant; nor had it ever occurred to me that he might have had such a living in his gift. As a friend of mine, of my family, he may perhaps – indeed I know he *has*, still greater pleasure in bestowing it; but, upon my word, you owe nothing to my solicitation.'

Truth obliged her to acknowledge some small share in the action, but she was at the same time so unwilling to appear as the benefactress of Edward, that she acknowledged it with hesitation; which probably contributed to fix that suspicion in his mind which had recently entered it. For a short time he sat deep in thought, after Elinor had ceased to speak; – at last, and as if it were rather an effort, he said,

'Colonel Brandon seems a man of great worth and respectability. I have always heard him spoken of as such, and your brother I know esteems him highly. He is undoubtedly a sensible man, and in his manners perfectly the gentleman.'

'Indeed,' replied Elinor, 'I believe that you will find him, on farther acquaintance, all that you have heard him to be, and as you will be such very near neighbours, (for I understand the parsonage is almost close to the mansion-house,) it is particularly important that he *should* be all this.'

Edward made no answer; but when she had turned away her head, gave her a look so serious, so earnest, so uncheerful, as seemed to say, that he might hereafter wish the distance between the parsonage and the mansion-house much greater.

'Colonel Brandon, I think, lodges in St James's-street,' said he, soon afterwards, rising from his chair.

Elinor told him the number of the house.

'I must hurry away then, to give him those thanks which you will not allow me to give *you*; to assure him that he has made me a very – an exceedingly happy man.'

Elinor did not offer to detain him; and they parted, with a very earnest assurance on *her* side of her unceasing good wishes for his happiness in every change of situation that might befal him; on *his*, with rather an attempt to return the same good will, than the power of expressing it.

'When I see him again,' said Elinor to herself, as the door shut him out, 'I shall see him the husband of Lucy.'

And with this pleasing anticipation, she sat down to re-consider the past, recal the words and endeavour to comprehend all the feelings of Edward; and, of course, to reflect on her own with discontent.

When Mrs Jennings came home, though she returned from seeing people whom she had never seen before, and of whom therefore she must have a great deal to say, her mind was so much more occupied by the important secret in her possession, than by anything else, that she reverted to it again as soon as Elinor appeared.

'Well, my dear,' she cried, 'I sent you up the young man. Did not I do right? – And I suppose you had no great difficulty – You did not find him very unwilling to accept your proposal?'

'No, ma'am; *that* was not very likely.'

'Well, and how soon will he be ready? – For it seems all to depend upon that.'

'Really,' said Elinor, 'I know so little of these kind of forms, that I can hardly even conjecture as to the time, or the preparation necessary; but I suppose two or three months will complete his ordination.'

'Two or three months!' cried Mrs Jennings; 'Lord! my dear, how calmly you talk of it; and can the Colonel wait two or three months! Lord bless me! – I am sure it would put *me* quite out of patience! – And though one would be very glad to do a kindness by poor Mr Ferrars, I do think it is not worth while to wait two or three months for him. Sure, somebody else might be found that would do as well; somebody that is in orders already.'

'My dear ma'am,' said Elinor, 'what can you be thinking of? – Why, Colonel Brandon's only object is to be of use to Mr Ferrars.'

'Lord bless you, my dear! – Sure you do not mean to persuade me that the Colonel only marries you for the sake of giving ten guineas to Mr Ferrars!'

The deception could not continue after this; and an explanation immediately took place, by which both gained considerable amusement for the moment, without any material loss of happiness to either, for Mrs Jennings only exchanged one form of delight for another, and still without forfeiting her expectation of the first.

'Aye, aye, the parsonage is but a small one,' said she, after the first ebullition of surprise and satisfaction was over, 'and very likely *may* be out of repair; but to hear a man apologising, as I thought, for a house that to my knowledge has five sitting rooms on the ground-floor, and I think the housekeeper told me, could make up fifteen beds! – and to you too, that had been used to live in Barton Cottage! – It seemed quite ridiculous. But, my dear, we must touch up the Colonel to do something to the parsonage, and make it comfortable for them, before Lucy goes to it.'

'But Colonel Brandon does not seem to have any idea of the living's being enough to allow them to marry.'

'The Colonel is a ninny, my dear; because he has two thousand a-year himself, he thinks that nobody else can marry on less. Take my word for it, that, if I am alive, I shall be paying a visit at Delaford Parsonage before Michaelmas; and I am sure I sha'nt go it Lucy an't there.'

Elinor was quite of her opinion, as to the probability of their not waiting for any thing more.

Chapter Forty One

EDWARD, HAVING CARRIED HIS thanks to Colonel Brandon, proceeded with his happiness to Lucy; and such was the excess of it by the time he reached Bartlett's Buildings, that she was able to assure Mrs Jennings, who called on her again the next day with her congratulations, that she had never seen him in such spirits before in her life.

Her own happiness, and her own spirits, were at least very certain; and she joined Mrs Jennings most heartily in her expectation of their being all comfortably together in Delaford Parsonage before Michaelmas. So far was she, at the same time, from any backwardness to give Elinor that credit which Edward *would* give her, that she spoke of her friendship for them both with the most grateful warmth, was ready to own all their obligation to her, and openly declared that no exertion for their good on Miss Dashwood's part, either present or future, would ever surprise her, for she believed her capable of doing anything in the world for those she really valued. As for Colonel Brandon, she was not only ready to worship him as a saint, but was moreover truly anxious that he should be treated as one in all worldly concerns; anxious that his tythes should be raised to the utmost; and secretly resolved to avail herself, at Delaford, as far as she possibly could, of his servants, his carriage, his cows, and his poultry.

It was now above a week since John Dashwood had called in Berkeley-street, and as since that time no notice had been taken by them of his wife's indisposition, beyond one verbal enquiry, Elinor began to feel it necessary to pay her a visit. – This was an obligation, however, which not only opposed her own inclination, but which had not the assistance of any encouragement from her companions. Marianne, not contented with absolutely refusing to go herself, was very urgent to prevent her sister's going at all; and Mrs Jennings, though her carriage was always at Elinor's service, so very much disliked Mrs John Dashwood, that not even her curiosity to see how she looked after the late discovery, nor her strong desire to affront her by taking Edward's part, could overcome her unwillingness to be in her company again. The consequence was, that Elinor set out by herself to pay a visit, for which no one could really have less inclination, and to run the risk of a tête-à-tête with a woman, whom neither of the others had so much reason to dislike.

Mrs Dashwood was denied; but before the carriage could turn from the house, her husband accidentally came out. He expressed great pleasure in meeting Elinor, told her that he had been just going to call in Berkeley-street, and assuring her that Fanny would be very glad to see her, invited her to come in.

They walked up stairs into the drawing-room. – Nobody was there.

'Fanny is in her own room, I suppose,' said he; – 'I will go to her presently, for I am sure she will not have the least objection in the world to seeing you. – Very far from it indeed. Now especially there cannot be – but however, you and Marianne were always great favourites. – Why would not Marianne come?' –

Elinor made what excuse she could for her.

'I am not sorry to see you alone,' he replied, 'for I have a good deal to say to you. This living of Colonel Brandon's – can it be true? – has he really given it to Edward? – I heard it yesterday by chance, and was coming to you on purpose to inquire farther about it.'

'It is perfectly true. – Colonel Brandon has given the living of Delaford to Edward.'

'Really! – Well, this is very astonishing! – no relationship! – no connection between them! – and now that livings fetch such a price! – what was the value of this?'

'About two hundred a-year.'

'Very well – and for the next presentation to a living of that value – supposing the late incumbent to have been old and sickly, and likely to vacate it soon – he might have got I dare say – fourteen hundred pounds. And how came he not to have settled that matter before this person's death? – Now indeed it would be too late to sell it, but a man of Colonel Brandon's sense! – I wonder he should be so improvident in a point of such common, such natural, concern! – Well, I am convinced that there is a vast deal of inconsistency in almost every human character. I suppose, however – on recollection – that the case may probably be this. Edward is only to hold the living till the person to whom the Colonel has really sold the presentation, is old enough to take it. – Aye, aye, that is the fact, depend upon it.'

Elinor contradicted it, however, very positively; and by relating that she had herself been employed in conveying the offer from Colonel Brandon to Edward, and therefore must understand the terms on which it was given, obliged him to submit to her authority.

'It is truly astonishing!' – he cried, after hearing what she said – 'what could be the Colonel's motive?'

'A very simple one – to be of use to Mr Ferrars.'

'Well, well; whatever Colonel Brandon may be, Edward is a very lucky man! – You will not mention the matter to Fanny, however, for though I have broke it to her, and she bears it vastly well – she will not like to hear it much talked of.'

Elinor had some difficulty here to refrain from observing, that she thought Fanny might have borne with composure, an acquisition of wealth to her brother, by which neither she nor her child could be possibly impoverished.

'Mrs Ferrars,' added he, lowering his voice to the tone becoming so important a subject, 'knows nothing about it at present, and I believe it will be best to keep it entirely concealed from her as long as may be. – When the marriage takes place, I fear she must hear of it all.'

'But why should such precaution be used? – Though it is not to be supposed that Mrs Ferrars can have the smallest satisfaction in knowing that her son has money enough to live upon, – for *that* must be quite out of the question; yet why, after her late behaviour, is she supposed to feel at all? – she has done with her son, she has cast him off for ever, and has made all those over whom she had any influence, cast him off likewise. Surely, after doing so, she cannot be imagined liable to any impression of sorrow or of joy on his account – she cannot be interested in any thing that befalls him. – She would not be so weak as to throw away the comfort of a child, and yet retain the anxiety of a parent!'

'Ah! Elinor,' said John, 'your reasoning is very good, but it is founded on ignorance of human nature. When Edward's unhappy match takes place, depend upon it his mother will feel as much as if she had never discarded him; and therefore every circumstance that may accelerate that dreadful event, must be concealed from her as much as possible. Mrs Ferrars can never forget that Edward is her son.'

'You surprise me; I should think it must nearly have escaped her memory by *this* time.'

'You wrong her exceedingly. Mrs Ferrars is one of the most affectionate mothers in the world.'

Elinor was silent.

'We think *now*' – said Mr Dashwood, after a short pause, 'of *Robert's* marrying Miss Morton.'

Elinor, smiling at the grave and decisive importance of her brother's tone, calmly replied,

'The lady, I suppose, has no choice in the affair.'

'Choice! – how do you mean?' –

'I only mean, that I suppose from your manner of speaking, it must be the same to Miss Morton whether she marry Edward or Robert.'

'Certainly, there can be no difference; for Robert will now to all intents and purposes be considered as the eldest son; – and as to any thing else, they are both very agreeable young men, I do not know that one is superior to the other.'

Elinor said no more, and John was also for a short time silent. – His reflections ended thus.

'Of *one* thing, my dear sister,' kindly taking her hand, and speaking in an awful whisper – 'I may assure you; – and I *will* do it, because I know it must gratify you. I have good reason to think – indeed I have it from the best authority, or I should not repeat it, for otherwise it would be very wrong to say any thing about it – but I have it from the very best authority – not that I ever precisely heard Mrs Ferrars say it herself – but her daughter *did*, and I have it from her – That in short, whatever objections there might be against a certain – a certain connection – you understand me – it would have been far preferable to her, it would not have given her half the vexation that *this* does. I was exceedingly pleased to hear that Mrs Ferrars considered it in that light – a very gratifying circumstance you know to us all. "It would have been beyond comparison," she said, "the least evil of the two, and she would be glad to compound *now* for nothing worse." But however, all that is quite out of the question – not to be thought of or mentioned – as to any attachment you know – it never could be – all that is gone by. But I thought I would just tell you of this, because I knew how much it must please you. Not that you have any reason to regret, my dear Elinor. There is no doubt of your doing exceedingly well – quite as well, or better, perhaps, all things considered. Has Colonel Brandon been with you lately?'

Elinor had heard enough, if not to gratify her vanity, and raise her self-importance, to agitate her nerves and fill her mind; – and she was therefore glad to be spared from the necessity of saying much in reply herself, and from the danger of hearing any thing more from her brother, by the entrance of Mr Robert Ferrars. After a few moments' chat, John Dashwood, recollecting that Fanny was yet uninformed of his sister's being there, quitted the room in quest of her; and Elinor was left to improve her acquaintance with Robert, who, by the gay unconcern, the happy self-complacency of his manner while enjoying so unfair a division of his mother's love and liberality, to the prejudice of his banished brother, earned only by his own dissipated course of life, and that brother's integrity, was confirming her most unfavourable opinion of his head and heart.

They had scarcely been two minutes by themselves, before he began to speak of Edward; for he too had heard of the living and was very inquisitve on the subject. Elinor repeated the particulars of it, as she had given them to John; and their effect on Robert, though very different, was not less striking than it had been on *him*. He laughed most immoderately. The idea of Edward's being a clergyman, and living in a small parsonage-house, diverted him beyond measure; – and when to that was added the fanciful imagery of Edward reading prayers in a white surplice, and publishing the banns of marriage between John Smith and Mary Brown, he could conceive nothing more ridiculous.

Elinor, while she waited in silence, ánd immovable gravity, the conclusion of such folly, could not restrain her eyes from being fixed on him with a look that spoke all the contempt it excited. It was a look, however, very well bestowed, for it relieved her own feelings, and gave no intelligence to him. He was recalled from wit to wisdom, not by any reproof of her's, but by his own sensibility.

'We may treat it as a joke,' said he at last, recovering from the affected laugh which had considerably lengthened out the genuine gaiety of the moment – 'but upon my soul, it is a most serious business. Poor Edward! he is ruined for ever. I am extremely sorry for it – for I know him to be a very good-hearted creature; as well-meaning a fellow perhaps, as any in the world. You must not judge of him, Miss Dashwood, from *your* slight acquaintance. – Poor Edward! – His manners are certainly not the happiest in nature. – But we are not all born, you know, with the same powers – the same address. – Poor fellow! – to see him in a circle of strangers! – to be sure it was pitiable enough! – but, upon my soul, I believe he has as good a heart as any in the kingdom; and I declare and protest to you I never was so shocked in my life, as when it all burst forth. I could not believe it. – My mother was the first person who told me of it, and I, feeling myself called on to act with resolution, immediately said to her, "My dear madam, I do not know what you may intend to do on the occasion, but as for myself, I must say, that if Edward does marry this young woman, *I* never will see him again." That was what I said immediately, – I was most uncommonly shocked indeed! – Poor

Edward! – he has done for himself completely – shut himself out for ever from all decent society! – but, as I directly said to my mother, I am not in the least surprised at it; from his style of education it was always to be expected. My poor mother was half frantic.'

'Have you ever seen the lady?'

'Yes; once, while she was staying in this house, I happened to drop in for ten minutes; and I saw quite enough of her. The merest awkward country girl, without style, or elegance, and almost without beauty. – I remember her perfectly. Just the kind of girl I should suppose likely to captivate poor Edward. I offered immediately, as soon as my mother related the affair to me, to talk to him myself, and dissuade him from the match; but it was too late *then*, I found, to do any thing, for unluckily, I was not in the way at first, and knew nothing of it till after the breach had taken place, when it was not for me, you know, to interfere. But had I been informed of it a few hours earlier – I think it is most probable – that something might have been hit on. I certainly should have represented it to Edward in a very strong light. "My dear fellow," I should have said, "consider what you are doing. You are making a most disgraceful connection, and such a one as your family are unanimous in disapproving," I cannot help thinking, in short, that means might have been found. But now it is all too late. He must be starved, you know; – that is certain; absolutely starved.'

He had just settled this point with great composure, when the entrance of Mrs John Dashwood put an end to the subject. But though *she* never spoke of it out of her own family, Elinor could see its influence on her mind, in the something like confusion of countenance with which she entered, and an attempt at cordiality in her behaviour to herself. She even proceeded so far as to be concerned to find that Elinor and her sister were so soon to leave town, as she had hoped to see more of them; – an exertion in which her husband, who attended her into the room, and hung enamoured over her accents, seemed to distinguish every thing that was most affectionate and graceful.

Chapter Forty Two

ONE OTHER SHORT CALL IN HARLEY-STREET, in which Elinor received her brother's congratulations on their travelling so far towards Barton without any expense, and on Colonel Brandon's being to follow them to Cleveland in a day or two, completed the intercourse of the brother and sisters in town; – and a faint invitation from Fanny, to come to Norland whenever it should happen to be in their way, which of all things was the most unlikely to occur, with a more warm, though less public, assurance, from John to Elinor, of the promptitude with which he should come to see her at Delaford, was all that foretold any meeting in the country.

It amused her to observe that all her friends seemed determined to send her to Delaford; – a place, in which, of all others, she would now least chuse to visit, or wish to reside; for not only was it considered as her future home by her brother and Mrs Jennings, but even Lucy, when they parted, gave her a pressing invitation to visit her there.

Very early in April, and tolerably early in the day, the two parties from Hanover-square and Berkeley-street set out from their respective homes, to meet, by appointment, on the road. For the convenience of Charlotte and her child, they were to be more than two days on their journey, and Mr Palmer, travelling more expeditiously with Colonel Brandon, was to join them at Cleveland soon after their arrival.

Marianne, few as had been her hours of comfort in London, and eager as she had long been to quit it, could not, when it came to the point, bid adieu to the house in which she had for the last time enjoyed those hopes, and that confidence, in Willoughby, which were now extinguished for ever, without great pain. Nor could she leave the place in which Willoughby remained, busy in new engagements, and new schemes, in which *she* could have no share, without shedding many tears.

Elinor's satisfaction at the moment of removal, was more positive. She had no such object for her lingering thoughts to fix on, she left no creature behind, from whom it would give her a moment's regret to be divided for ever, she was pleased to be free herself from the persecution of Lucy's friendship, she was grateful for bringing her sister away unseen by Willoughby since his marriage, and she looked forward with hope to what a few months of tranquillity at Barton might do towards restoring Marianne's peace of mind, and confirming her own.

Their journey was safely performed. The second day brought them into the cherished, or the prohibited, county of Somerset, for as such was it dwelt on by turns in Marianne's imagination; and in the forenoon of the third they drove up to Cleveland.

Cleveland was a spacious, modern-built house, situated on a sloping lawn. It had no park, but the pleasure-grounds were tolerably extensive; and like every other place of the same degree of importance, it had its open shrubbery, and closer wood walk, a road of smooth gravel winding round a plantation, led to the front, the lawn was dotted over with timber, the house itself was under the guardianship of the fir, the mountain-ash, and the acacia; and a thick screen of them altogether, interspersed with tall Lombardy poplars, shut out the offices.

Marianne entered the house with an heart swelling with emotion from the consciousness of being only eighty miles from Barton, and not thirty from Combe Magna; and before she had been five minutes within its walls, while the others were busily helping Charlotte shew her child to the housekeeper, she quitted it again, stealing away through the winding shrubberies, now just beginning to be in beauty, to gain a distant eminence; where, from its Grecian temple, here eye, wandering over a wide tract of country to the south-east, could fondly rest on the farthest ridge of hills in the horizon, and fancy that from their summits Combe Magna might be seen.

In such moments of precious, invaluable misery, she rejoiced in tears of agony to be at Cleveland; and as she returned by a different circuit to the house, feeling all the happy privilege of country liberty, of wandering from place to place in free and luxurious solitude, she resolved to spend almost every hour of every day while she remained with the Palmers, in the indulgence of such solitary rambles.

She returned just in time to join the others as they quitted the house, on an excursion through its more immediate premises; and the rest of the morning was easily whiled away, in lounging round the kitchen garden, examining the bloom upon its walls, and listening to the gardener's lamentations upon blights, – in dawdling through the green-house, where the loss of her favourite plants, unwarily exposed, and nipped by the lingering frost, raised the laughter of Charlotte, – and in visiting her poultry-yard, where, in the disappointed hopes of her dairy-maid, by hens forsaking their nests, or being stolen by a fox, or in the rapid decease of a promising young brood, she found fresh sources of merriment.

The morning was fine and dry, and Marianne, in her plan of enjoyment abroad, had not calculated for any change of weather during their stay at Cleveland. With great surprise therefore, did she find herself prevented by a settled rain from going out again after dinner. She had depended on a twilight walk to the Grecian temple, and perhaps all over the grounds, and an evening merely cold or damp would not have deterred her from it; but an heavy and settled rain even *she* could not fancy dry or pleasant weather for walking.

Their party was small, and the hours passed quietly away. Mrs Palmer had her child, and Mrs Jennings her carpet-work; they talked of the friends they had left behind, arranged Lady Middleton's engagements, and wondered whether Mr Palmer and Colonel Brandon would get farther than Reading that night. Elinor, however little concerned in it, joined in their discourse, and Marianne, who had the knack of finding her way in every house to the library, however it might be avoided by the family in general, soon procured herself a book.

Nothing was wanting on Mrs Palmer's side that constant and friendly good-humour could do, to make them feel themselves welcome. The openness and heartiness of her manner, more than atoned for that want of recollection and elegance, which made her often deficient in the forms of politeness; her kindness, recommended by so pretty a face, was engaging; her folly, though evident, was not disgusting, because it was not conceited; and Elinor could have forgiven every thing but her laugh.

The two gentlemen arrived the next day to a very late dinner, affording a pleasant enlargement of the party, and a very welcome variety to their conversation, which a long morning of the same continued rain had reduced very low.

Elinor had seen so little of Mr Palmer, and in that little had seen so much variety in his address to her sister and herself, that she knew not what to expect to find him in his own family. She found him, however, perfectly the gentleman in his behaviour to all his visitors, and only occasionally rude to his wife and her mother; she found him very capable of being a pleasant companion, and only prevented from being so always, by too great an aptitude to fancy himself as much superior to people in general, as he must feel himself to be to Mrs Jennings and Charlotte. For the rest of his character and habits, they were marked, as far as Elinor could perceive, with no traits at all unusual in his sex and time of life. He was nice in his eating, uncertain in his hours; fond of his child, though affecting to slight it; and idled away the mornings at billiards, which ought to have been devoted to business. She liked him, however, upon the whole much better than she had expected, and in her heart was not sorry that she could like him no more; – not sorry to be driven by the observation of his Epicurism, his selfishness, and his conceit, to rest with complacency on the remembrance of Edward's generous temper, simple taste, and diffident feelings.

Of Edward, or at least of some of his concerns, she now received intelligence from Colonel Brandon, who had been into Dorsetshire lately; and who, treating her at once as the disinterested friend of Mr Ferrars, and the kind confidante of himself, talked to her a great deal of the Parsonage at Delaford, described its deficiencies, and told her what he meant to do himself towards removing them. – His behaviour to her in this, as well as in every other particular, his open pleasure in meeting her after an absence of only ten days, his readiness to converse with her, and his deference for her opinion, might very well justify Mrs Jennings's persuasion of his attachment, and would have been enough, perhaps, had not Elinor still, as from the first, believed Marianne his real favourite, to make her suspect it herself. But as it was, such a notion had scarcely ever entered her head, except by Mrs Jennings's suggestion; and she could not help believing herself the nicest observer of the two; – she watched his eyes, while Mrs Jennings thought only of his behaviour; – and while his looks of anxious solicitude on Marianne's feeling, in her head and throat, the beginnings of an heavy cold, because unexpressed by words, entirely escaped the latter lady's observation; – *she* could discover in them the quick feelings, and needless alarm of a lover.

Two delightful twilight walks on the third and fourth evenings of her being there, not merely on the dry gravel of the shrubbery, but all over the grounds, and especially in the most distant parts of them, where there was something more of wildness than in the rest, where the trees were the oldest, and the grass was the longest and wettest, had – assisted by the still greater imprudence of sitting in her wet shoes and stockings – give Marianne a cold so violent, as, though for a day or two trifled with or denied, would force itself by increasing ailments, on the concern of every body, and the notice of herself. Prescriptions poured in from all quarters, and as usual, were all declined. Though heavy and feverish, with a pain in her limbs, a cough, and a sore throat, a good night's rest was to cure her entirely; and it was with difficulty that Elinor prevailed on her, when she went to bed, to try one or two of the simplest of the remedies.

Chapter Forty Three

MARIANNE GOT UP THE NEXT MORNING at her usual time; to every inquiry replied that she was better, and tried to prove herself so, by engaging in her accustomary employments. But a day spent in sitting shivering over the fire with a book in her hand, which she was unable to read, or in lying, weary and languid, on a sofa, did not speak much in favour of her amendment; and when, at last, she went early to bed, more and more indisposed, Colonel Brandon was only astonished at her sister's composure, who, though attending and nursing her the whole day, against Marianne's inclination, and forcing proper medicines on her at night, trusted, like Marianne, to the certainty and efficacy of sleep, and felt no real alarm.

A very restless and feverish night, however, disappointed the expectation of both; and when Marianne, after persisting in rising, confessed herself unable to sit up, and returned voluntarily to her bed, Elinor was very ready to adopt Mrs Jennings's advice, of sending for the Palmers' apothecary.

He came, examined his patient, and though encouraging Miss Dashwood to expect that a very few days would restore her sister to health, yet, by pronouncing her disorder to have a putrid tendency, and allowing the word 'infection' to pass his lips, gave instant alarm to Mrs Palmer on her baby's account. Mrs Jennings, who had been inclined from the first to think Marianne's complaint more serious than Elinor, now looked very grave on Mr Harris's report, and confirming Charlotte's fears and caution, urged the necessity of her immediate removal with her infant; and Mr Palmer, though treating their apprehensions as idle, found the anxiety and importunity of his wife too great to be withstood. Her departure therefore was fixed on; and, within an hour after Mr Harris's arrival, she set off, with her little boy and his nurse, for the house of a near relation of Mr Palmer's, who lived a few miles on the other side of Bath; whither her husband promised, at her earnest entreaty, to join her in a day or two; and whither she was almost equally urgent with her mother to accompany her. Mrs Jennings, however, with a kindness of heart which made Elinor really love her, declared her resolution of not stirring from Cleveland as long as Marianne remained ill, and of endeavouring, by her own attentive care, to supply to her the place of the mother she had taken her from; and Elinor found her on every occasion a most willing and active helpmate, desirous to share in all her fatigues, and often by her better experience in nursing, of material use.

Poor Marianne, languid and low from the nature of her malady, and feeling herself universally ill, could no longer hope that tomorrow would find her recovered; and the idea of what tomorrow would have produced, but for this unlucky illness, made every ailment more severe; for on that day they were to have begun their journey home; and, attended the whole way by a servant of Mrs Jennings, were to have taken their mother by surprise on the following forenoon. The little that she said, was all in lamentation of this inevitable delay; though Elinor tried to raise her spirits, and make her believe, as she then really believed herself, that it would be a very short one.

The next day produced little or no alteration in the state of the patient; she certainly was not better, and except that there was no amendment, did not appear worse. Their party was now farther reduced; for Mr Palmer, though very unwilling to go, as well from real humanity and good-nature, as from a dislike of appearing to be frightened away by his wife, was persuaded at last by Colonel Brandon to perform his promise of following her; and while he was preparing to go, Colonel Brandon himself, with a much greater exertion, began to talk of going likewise. – Here, however, the kindness of Mrs Jennings interposed most acceptably; for to send the Colonel away while his love was in so much uneasiness on her sister's account, would be to deprive them both, she thought, of every comfort; and therefore telling him at once that his stay at Cleveland was necessary to herself, that she should want him to play at piquet of an evening, while Miss Dashwood was above with her sister, &c. she urged him so strongly to remain, that he, who was gratifying the first wish of his own heart by a compliance, could not long even affect to demur; especially as Mrs Jennings's entreaty was warmly seconded by Mr Palmer, who seemed to feel a relief to himself, in leaving behind him a person so well able to assist or advise Miss Dashwood in any emergence.

Marianne was of course kept in ignorance of all these arrangements. She knew not that she had been the means of sending the owners of Cleveland away, in about seven days from the time of their arrival. It gave her no surprise that she saw nothing of Mrs Palmer; and as it gave her likewise no concern, she never mentioned her name.

Two days passed away from the time of Mr Palmer's departure, and her situation continued, with little variation, the same. Mr Harris, who attended her every day, still talked boldly of a speedy recovery, and Miss Dashwood was equally sanguine; but the expectation of the others was by no means so cheerful. Mrs Jennings had determined very early in the seisure that Marianne would never get over it, and Colonel Brandon, who was chiefly of use in listening to Mrs Jennings's forebodings, was not in a state of mind to resist their influence. He tried to reason himself out of fears, which the different judgment of the apothecary seemed to render absurd; but the many hours of each day in which he was left entirely alone, were but too favourable for the admission of every melancholy idea, and he could not expel from his mind the persuasion that he should see Marianne no more.

On the morning of the third day however, the gloomy anticipations of both were almost done away; for when Mr Harris arrived, he declared his patient materially better. Her pulse was much stronger, and every symptom more favourable than on the preceding visit. Elinor, confirmed in every pleasant hope, was all cheerfulness; rejoicing that in her letters to her mother, she had pursued her own judgment rather than her friend's, in making very light of the indisposition which delayed them at Cleveland; and almost fixing on the time when Marianne would be able to travel.

But the day did not close so auspiciously as it began. – Towards the evening, Marianne became ill again, growing more heavy, restless, and uncomfortable than before. Her sister, however, still sanguine, was willing to attribute the change to nothing more than the fatigue of having sat up to have her bed made; and carefully administering the cordials prescribed, saw her with satisfaction sink at last into a slumber, from which she expected the most beneficial effects. Her sleep, though not so quiet as Elinor wished to see it, lasted a considerable time; and anxious to observe the result of it herself, she resolved to sit with her during the whole of it. Mrs Jennings, knowing nothing of any change in the patient, went unusually early to bed; her maid, who was one of the principal nurses, was recreating herself in the housekeeper's room, and Elinor remained alone with Marianne.

The repose of the latter became more and more disturbed; and her sister, who watched with unremitting attention her continual change of posture, and heard the frequent but inarticulate sounds of complaint which passed her lips, was almost wishing to rouse her from so painful a slumber, when Marianne, suddenly awakened by some accidental noise in the house, started hastily up, and with feverish wildness, cried out –

'Is mama coming? –'

'Not yet,' replied the other, concealing her terror, and assisting Marianne to lie down again, 'but she will be here, I hope, before it is long. It is a great way, you know, from hence to Barton.'

'But she must not go round by London,' cried Marianne, in the same hurried manner, 'I shall never see her, if she goes by London.'

Elinor perceived with alarm that she was not quite herself, and while attempting to sooth her, eagerly felt her pulse. It was lower and quicker than ever! and Marianne, still talking wildly of mama, her alarm increased so rapidly, as to determine her on sending instantly for Mr Harris, and dispatching a messenger to Barton for her mother. To consult with Colonel Brandon on the best means of effecting the latter, was a thought which immediately followed the resolution of its performance; and as soon as she had rung up the maid to take her place by her sister, she hastened down to the drawing-room, where she knew he was generally to be found at a much later hour than the present.

It was no time for hesitation. Her fears and her difficulties were immediately before him. Her fears, he had no courage, no confidence to attempt the removal of; – he listened to them in silent despondence; – but her difficulties were instantly obviated, for with a readiness that seemed to speak the occasion, and the service pre-arranged in his mind, he offered himself as the messenger who should fetch Mrs Dashwood. Elinor made no resistance that was not easily overcome. She thanked him with brief, though fervent gratitude, and while he went to hurry off his servant with a message to Mr Harris, and an order for post-horses directly, she wrote a few lines to her mother.

The comfort of such a friend at that moment as Colonel Brandon – of such a companion for her mother, – how gratefully was it felt! – a companion whose judgment would guide, whose attendance must relieve, and whose friendship might sooth her! – as far as the shock of such a summons *could* be lessened to her, his presence, his manners, his assistance, would lessen it.

He, meanwhile, whatever he might feel, acted with all the firmness of a collected mind, made every necessary arrangement with the utmost dispatch, and calculated with exactness the time in which she might look for his return. Not a moment was lost in delay of any kind. The horses arrived, even before they were expected, and Colonel Brandon only pressing her hand with a look of solemnity, and a few words spoken too low to reach her ear, hurried into the carriage. It was then about twelve o'clock, and she returned to her sister's apartment to wait for the arrival of the apothecary, and to watch by her the rest of the night. It was a night of almost equal suffering to both. Hour after hour passed away in sleepless pain and delirium on Marianne's side, and in the most cruel anxiety on Elinor's, before Mr Harris appeared. Her apprehensions once raised, paid by their excess for all her former security; and the servant who sat up with her, for she would not allow Mrs Jennings to be called, only tortured her more, by hints of what her mistress had always thought.

Marianne's ideas were still, at intervals, fixed incoherently on her mother, and whenever she mentioned her name, it gave a pang to the heart of poor Elinor, who, reproaching herself for having trifled with so many days of illness, and wretched for some immediate relief, fancied that all relief might soon be in vain, that every thing had been delayed too long, and pictured to herself her suffering mother arriving too late to see this darling child, or to see her rational.

She was on the point of sending again for Mr Harris, or if *he* could not come, for some other advice, when the former – but not till after five o'clock – arrived. His opinion, however, made some little amends for his delay, for though acknowledging a very unexpected and unpleasant alteration in his patient, he would not allow the danger to be material, and talked of the relief which a fresh mode of treatment must procure, with a confidence which, in a lesser degree, was communicated to Elinor. He promised to call again in the course of three or four hours, and left both the patient and her anxious attendant more composed than he had found them.

With strong concern, and with many reproaches for not being called to their aid, did Mrs Jennings hear in the morning of what had passed. Her former apprehensions, now with greater reason restored, left her no doubt of the event; and though trying to speak comfort to Elinor, her conviction of her sister's danger would not allow her to offer the comfort of hope. Her heart was really grieved. The rapid decay, the early death of a girl so young, so lovely as Marianne, must have struck a less interested person with concern. On Mrs Jennings's compassion she had other claims. She had been for three months her companion, was still under her care, and she was known to have been greatly injured, and long unhappy. The distress of her sister too, particularly a favourite, was before her; – and as for their mother, when Mrs Jennings considered that Marianne might probably be to *her* what Charlotte was to herself, her sympathy in *her* sufferings was very sincere.

Mr Harris was punctual in his second visit; – but he came to be disappointed in his hopes of what the last would produce. His medicines had failed; – the fever was unabated; and Marianne only more quiet – not more herself – remained in an heavy stupor. Elinor, catching all, and more than all, his fears in a moment, proposed to call in farther advice. But he judged it unnecessary; he had still something more to try, some fresh application, of whose success he was almost as confident as the last, and his visit concluded with encouraging assurances which reached the ear, but could not enter the heart, of Miss Dashwood. She was calm, except when she thought of her mother, but she was almost hopeless; and in this state she continued till noon, scarcely stirring from her sister's bed, her thoughts wandering from one image of grief, one suffering friend to another, and her spirits oppressed to the utmost by the conversation of Mrs Jennings, who scrupled not to attribute the severity and danger of this attack, to the many weeks of previous indisposition which Marianne's disappointment had brought on. Elinor felt all the reasonableness of the idea, and it gave fresh misery to her reflections.

About noon, however, she began – but with a caution – a dread of disappointment, which for some time kept her silent, even to her friend – to fancy, to hope she could perceive a slight amendment in her sister's pulse; – she waited, watched, and examined it again and again; – and at last, with an agitation more difficult to bury under exterior calmness, than all her foregoing distress, ventured to communicate her hopes. Mrs Jennings, though forced, on examination, to acknowledge a temporary revival, tried to keep her young friend from indulging a thought of its continuance; – and Elinor, conning over every injunction of distrust, told herself likewise not to hope. But it was too late. Hope had already entered; and feeling all its anxious flutter, she bent over her sister to watch – she hardly knew for what. Half an hour passed away, and the favourable symptom yet blessed her. Others even arose to confirm it. Her breath, her skin, her lips, all flattered Elinor with signs of amendment, and Marianne fixed her eyes on her with a rational, though languid, gaze. Anxiety and hope now oppressed her in equal degrees, and left her no moment of tranquillity till the arrival of Mr Harris at four o'clock; – when his assurances, his felicitations on a recovery in her sister even surpassing his expectation, gave her confidence, comfort, and tears of joy.

Marianne was in every respect materially better, and he declared her entirely out of danger. Mrs Jennings, perhaps satisfied with the partial justification of her forebodings which had been found in their late alarm, allowed herself to trust in his judgment, and admitted with unfeigned joy, and soon with unequivocal cheerfulness, the probability of an entire recovery.

Elinor could not be cheerful. Her joy was of a different kind, and led to anything rather than to gaiety. Marianne restored to life, health, friends, and to her doating mother, was an idea to fill her heart with sensations of exquisite comfort, and expand it in fervent gratitude; – but it led to no outward demonstrations of joy, no words, no smiles. All within Elinor's breast was satisfaction, silent and strong.

She continued by the side of her sister with little intermission the whole afternoon, calming every fear, satisfying every enquiry of her enfeebled spirits, supplying every succour, and watching almost every look and every breath. The possibility of a relapse would of course, in some moments, occur to remind her of what anxiety was – but when she saw, on her frequent and minute examination, that every symptom of recovery continued, and saw Marianne at six o'clock sink into a quiet, steady, and to all appearance comfortable, sleep, she silenced every doubt.

The time was now drawing on, when Colonel Brandon might be expected back. At ten o'clock, she trusted, or at least not much later her mother would be relieved from the dreadful suspense in which she must now be travelling towards them. The Colonel too! – perhaps scarcely less an object of pity! – Oh! – how slow was the progress of time which yet kept them in ignorance!

At seven o'clock, leaving Marianne still sweetly asleep, she joined Mrs Jennings in the drawing-room to tea. Of breakfast she had been kept by her fears, and of dinner by their sudden reverse, from eating much; – and the present refreshment, therefore, with such feelings of content as she brought to it, was particularly welcome. Mrs Jennings would have persuaded her at its conclusion to take some rest before her mother's arrival, and allow *her* to take her place by Marianne; but Elinor had no sense of fatigue, no capability of sleep at that moment about her, and she was not to be kept away from her sister an unnecessary instant. Mrs Jennings therefore attending her up stairs into the sick chamber, to satisfy herself that all continued right, left her there again to her charge and her thoughts, and retired to her own room to write letters and sleep.

The night was cold and stormy. The wind roared round the house, and the rain beat against the windows; but Elinor, all happiness within, regarded it not. Marianne slept through every blast, and the travellers – they had a rich reward in store, for every present inconvenience.

The clock struck eight. Had it been ten, Elinor would have been convinced that at that moment she heard a carriage driving up to the house; and so strong was the persuasion that she *did*, in spite of the *almost* impossibility of their being already come, that she moved into the adjoining dressing-closet and opened a window-shutter, to be satisfied of the truth. She instantly saw that her ears had not deceived her. The flaring lamps of a carriage were immediately in view. By their uncertain light she thought she could discern it to be drawn by four horses; and this, while it told the excess of her poor mother's alarm, gave some explanation to such unexpected rapidity.

Never in her life had Elinor found it so difficult to be calm, as at that moment. The knowledge of what her mother must be feeling as the carriage stopt at the door, – of her doubt – her dread – perhaps her despair! – and of what *she* had to tell! – with such knowledge it was impossible to be calm. All that remained to be done, was to be speedy; and therefore staying only till she could leave Mrs Jennings's maid with her sister, she hurried down stairs.

The bustle in the vestibule, as she passed along an inner lobby, assured her that they were already in the house. She rushed forwards towards the drawing-room, – she entered it, – and saw only Willoughby.

Chapter Forty Four

ELINOR, STARTING BACK WITH A look of horror at the sight of him, obeyed the first impulse of her heart in turning instantly to quit the room, and her hand was already on the lock, when its action was suspended by his hastily advancing, and saying, in a voice rather of command than supplication,

'Miss Dashwood, for half an hour – for ten minutes – I entreat you to stay.'

'No, sir,' she replied with firmness, 'I shall *not* stay. Your business cannot be with *me*. The servants, I suppose, forgot to tell you that Mr Palmer was not in the house.'

'Had they told me,' he cried with vehemence, 'that Mr Palmer and all his relations were at the devil, it would not have turned me from the door. My business is with you, and only you.'

'With me!' – in the utmost amazement – 'well, sir – be quick – and if you can – less violent.'

'Sit down, and I will be both.'

She hesitated; she knew not what to do. The possibility of Colonel Brandon's arriving and finding him there, came across her. But she had promised to hear him, and her curiosity no less than her honour was engaged. After a moment's recollection, therefore, concluding that prudence required dispatch, and that her acquiescence would best promote it, she walked silently towards the table and sat down. He took the opposite chair, and for half a minute not a word was said by either.

'Pray be quick, sir' – said Elinor impatiently – 'I have no time to spare.'

He was sitting in an attitude of deep meditation, and seemed not to hear her.

'Your sister,' said he, with abruptness, a moment afterwards – 'is out of danger. I heard it from the servant. God be praised! – But is it true? is it really true?'

Elinor would not speak. He repeated the inquiry with yet greater eagerness.

'For God's sake tell me, is she out of danger, or is she not?'

'We hope she is.'

He rose up, and walked across the room.

'Had I known as much half an hour ago – But since I *am* here' – speaking with a forced vivacity as he returned to his seat – 'what does it signify? – For once, Miss Dashwood – it will be the last time, perhaps – let us be cheerful together. – I am in a fine mood for gaiety. – Tell me honestly' – a deeper glow overspreading his cheeks – 'do you think me most a knave or a fool?'

Elinor looked at him with greater astonishment than ever. She began to think that he must be in liquor; – the strangeness of such a visit, and of such manners, seemed no otherwise intelligible; and with this impression she immediately rose, saying,

'Mr Willoughby, I advise you at present to return to Combe – I am not at leisure to remain with you longer. – Whatever your business may be with me, it will be better recollected and explained to-morrow.'

'I understand you,' he replied, with an expressive smile, and a voice perfectly calm, 'yes, I am very drunk. – A pint of porter with my cold beef at Marlborough was enough to over-set me.'

'At Marlborough!' – cried Elinor, more and more at a loss to understand what he would be at.

'Yes – I left London this morning at eight o'clock, and the only ten minutes I have spent out of my chaise since that time, procured me a nuncheon at Marlborough.'

The steadiness of his manner, and the intelligence of his eye as he spoke, convincing Elinor, that whatever other unpardonable folly might bring him to Cleveland, he was not brought there by intoxication, she said, after a moment's recollection,

'Mr Willoughby, you *ought* to feel, and I certainly *do* – that after what has passed – your coming here in this manner, and forcing yourself upon my notice, requires a very particular excuse. – What is it, that you mean by it?' –

'I mean' – said he, with serious energy – 'if I can, to make you hate me one degree less than you do *now*. I mean to offer some kind of explanation, some kind of apology, for the past; to open my whole heart to you, and by convincing you, that though I have been always a blockhead, I have not been always a rascal, to obtain something like forgiveness from Ma – from your sister.'

'Is this the real reason of your coming?'

'Upon my soul it is,' – was his answer, with a warmth which brought all the former Willoughby to her remembrance, and in spite of herself made her think him sincere.

'If that is all, you may be satisfied already, – for Marianne *does* – she has *long* forgiven you.'

'Has she!' – he cried, in the same eager tone. – 'Then she has forgiven me before she ought to have done it. But she shall forgive me again, and on more reasonable grounds. – *Now* will you listen to me?'

Elinor bowed her assent.

'I do not know,' said he, after a pause of expectation on her side, and thoughtfulness on his own, – 'how *you* may have accounted for my behaviour to your sister, or what diabolical motive you may have imputed to me. – Perhaps you will hardly think the better of me, – it is worth the trial however, and you shall hear every thing. When I first became intimate in your family, I had no other intention, no other view in the acquaintance than to pass my time pleasantly while I was obliged to remain in Devonshire, more pleasantly than I had ever done before. Your sister's lovely person and interesting manners could not but please me; and her behaviour to me almost from the first, was of a kind – It is astonishing, when I reflect on what it was, and what *she* was, that my heart should have been so insensible! But at first I must confess, my vanity only was elevated by it. Careless of her happiness, thinking only of my own amusement, giving way to feelings which I had always been too much in the habit of indulging, I endeavoured, by every means in my power, to make myself pleasing to her, without any design of returning her affection.'

Miss Dashwood at this point, turning her eyes on him with the most angry contempt, stopped him, by saying,

'It is hardly worth while, Mr Willoughby, for you to relate, or for me to listen any longer. Such a beginning as this cannot be followed by any thing. – Do not let me be pained by hearing any thing more on the subject.'

'I insist on your hearing the whole of it,' he replied. 'My fortune was never large, and I had always been expensive, always in the habit of associating with people of better income than myself. Every year since my coming of age, or even before, I believe, had added to my debts; and though the death of my old cousin, Mrs Smith, was to set me free; yet that event being uncertain, and possibly far distant, it had been for some time my intention to re-establish my circumstances by marrying a woman of fortune. To attach myself to your sister, therefore, was not a thing to be thought of; – and with a meanness, selfishness, cruelty – which no indignant, no contemptuous look, even of yours, Miss Dashwood, can ever reprobate too much – I was acting in this manner, trying to engage her regard, without a thought of returning it. – But one thing may be said for me, even in that horrid state of selfish vanity, I did not know the extent of the injury I meditated, because I did not *then* know what it was to love. But have I ever known it? – Well may it be doubted; for, had I really loved, could I have sacrificed my feelings to vanity, to avarice? – or, what is more, could I have sacrificed her's? – But I have done it. To avoid a comparative poverty, which her affection and her society would have deprived of all its horrors, I have, by raising myself to affluence, lost every thing that could make it a blessing.'

'You did then,' said Elinor, a little softened, 'believe yourself at one time attached to her.'

'To have resisted such attractions, to have withstood such tenderness! – Is there a man on earth who could have done it! – Yes, I found myself, by insensible degrees, sincerely fond of her; and the happiest hours of my life were what I spent with her, when I felt my intentions were strictly honourable, and my feelings blameless. Even *then*, however, when fully determined on paying my addresses to her, I allowed myself most improperly to put off, from day to day, the moment of doing it, from an unwillingness to enter into an engagement while my circumstances were so greatly embarrassed. I will not reason here – nor will I stop for *you* to expatiate on the absurdity, and the worse than absurdity, of scrupling to engage my faith where my honour was already bound. The event has proved, that I was a cunning fool, providing with great circumspection for a possible opportunity of making myself contemptible and wretched for ever. At last, however, my resolution was taken, and I had determined, as soon as I could engage her alone, to justify the attentions I had so invariably paid her, and openly assure her of an affection which I had already taken such pains to display. But in the interim – in the interim of the very few hours that were to pass, before I could have an opportunity of speaking with her in private – a circumstance occurred – an unlucky circumstance, to ruin all my resolution, and with it all my comfort. A discovery took place, – here he hesitated and looked down. – 'Mrs Smith had somehow or other been informed, I imagine by some distant relation, whose interest it was to deprive me of her favour, of an affair, a connection – but I need not explain myself farther,' he added, looking at her with an heightened colour and an enquiring eye, – 'your particular intimacy – you have probably heard the whole story long ago.'

'I have,' returned Elinor, colouring likewise, and hardening her heart anew against any compassion for him, 'I have heard it all. And how you will explain away any part of your guilt in that dreadful business, I confess is beyond my comprehension.'

'Remember,' cried Willoughby, 'from whom you received the account. Could it be an impartial one? I acknowledge that her situation and her character ought to have been respected by me. I do not mean to justify myself, but at the same time cannot leave you to suppose that I have nothing to urge – that because she was injured she was irreproachable, and because I was a libertine, *she* must be a saint. If the violence of her passions, the weakness of her understanding – I do not mean, however, to defend myself. Her affection for me deserved better treatment, and I often, with great self-reproach, recal the tenderness which, for a very short time, had the power of creating any return. I wish – I heartily wish it had never been. But I have injured more than herself; and I have injured one, whose affection for me – (may I say it?) was scarcely less warm than her's; and whose mind – Oh! how infinitely superior!' –

'Your indifference, however, towards that unfortunate girl – I must say it, unpleasant to me as the discussion of such a subject may well be – your indifference is no apology for your cruel neglect of her. Do not think yourself excused by any weakness, any natural defect of understanding on her side, in the wanton cruelty so evident on yours. You must have known, that while you were enjoying yourself in Devonshire pursuing fresh schemes, always gay, always happy, she was reduced to the extremest indigence.'

'But, upon my soul, I did *not* know it,' he warmly replied; 'I did not recollect that I had omitted to give her my direction; and common sense might have told her how to find it out.'

'Well, sir, and what said Mrs Smith?'

'She taxed me with the offence at once, and my confusion may be guessed. The purity of her life, the formality of her notions, her ignorance of the world – every thing was against me. The matter itself I could not deny, and vain was every endeavour to soften it. She was previously disposed, I believe, to doubt the morality of my conduct in general, and was moreover discontented with the very little attention, the very little portion of my time that I had bestowed on her, in my present visit. In short, it ended in a total breach. By one measure I might have saved myself. In the height of her morality, good woman! she offered to forgive the past, if I would marry Eliza. That could not be – and I was formally dismissed from her favour and her house. The night following this affair – I was to go the next morning – was spent by me in deliberating on what my future conduct should be. The struggle was great – but it ended too soon. My affection for Marianne, my thorough conviction of her attachment to me – it was all insufficient to outweigh that dread of poverty, or get the better of those false ideas of the necessity of riches, which I was naturally inclined to feel, and expensive society had increased. I had reason to believe myself secure of my present wife, if I chose to address her, and I persuaded myself to think that nothing else in common prudence remained for me to do. An heavy scene however awaited me, before I could leave Devonshire; – I was engaged to dine with you on that very day; some apology was therefore necessary for my breaking the engagement. But whether I should write this apology, or deliver it in person, was a point of long debate. To see Marianne, I felt, would be dreadful, and I even doubted whether I could see her again, and keep to my resolution. In that point, however, I undervalued my own magnanimity, as the event declared; for I went, I saw her, and saw her miserable and left her miserable – and left her hoping never to see her again.'

'Why did you call, Mr Willoughby?' said Elinor, reproachfully; 'a note would have answered every purpose. – Why was it necessary to call?'

'It was necessary to my own pride. I could not bear to leave the country in a manner that might lead you, or the rest of the neighbourhood, to suspect any part of what had really passed between Mrs Smith and myself – and I resolved therefore on calling at the cottage, in my way to Honiton. The sight of your dear sister, however, was really dreadful; and to heighten the matter, I found her alone. You were all gone I do not know where. I had left her only the evening before, so fully, so firmly resolved within myself on doing right! A few hours were to have engaged her to me for ever; and I remember how happy, how gay were my spirits, as I walked from the cottage to Allenham, satisfied with myself, delighted with every body! But in this, our last interview of friendship, I approached her with a sense of guilt that almost took from me the power of dissembling. Her sorrow, her disappointment, her deep regret, when I told her that I was obliged to leave Devonshire so immediately – I never shall forget it – united too with such reliance, such confidence in me! – Oh, God! – what an hard-hearted rascal I was!'

They were both silent for a few moments. Elinor first spoke.

'Did you tell her that you should soon return?'

'I do not know what I told her,' he replied, impatiently; 'less than was due to the past, beyond a doubt, and in all likelihood much more than was justified by the future. I cannot think of it. – It won't do – Then came your dear mother to torture me farther, with all her kindness and confidence. Thank Heaven! it *did* torture me. I was miserable. Miss Dashwood, you cannot have an idea of the comfort it gives me to look back on my own misery. I owe such a grudge to myself for the stupid, rascally folly of my own heart, that all my past sufferings under it are only triumph and exultation to me now. Well, I went, left all that I loved, and went to those to whom, at best, I was only indifferent. My journey to town – travelling with my own horses, and therefore so tediously – no creature to speak to – my own reflections so cheerful – when I looked forward everything so inviting! – when I looked back at Barton, the picture so soothing! – oh! it was a blessed journey!'

He stopt.

'Well, sir,' said Elinor, who, though pitying him, grew impatient for his departure, 'and this is all?'

'All! – no, – have you forgot what passed in town? – That infamous letter – Did she shew it you?'

'Yes, I saw every note that passed.'

'When the first of her's reached me, (as it immediately did, for I was in town the whole time,) what I felt is – in the common phrase, not to be expressed; in a more simple one – perhaps too simple to raise any emotion – my feelings were very, very painful. – Every line, every word was – in the hackneyed metaphor which their dear writer, were she here, would forbid – a dagger to my heart. To know that Marianne was in town was – in the same language – a thunderbolt. – Thunderbolts and daggers! – what a reproof would she have given me! – her taste, her opinions – I believe they are better known to me than my own, – and I am sure they are dearer.'

Elinor's heart, which had undergone many changes in the course of this extraordinary conversation, was now softened again; – yet she felt it her duty to check such ideas in her companion as the last.

'This is not right, Mr Willoughby. – Remember that you are married. Relate only what in your conscience you think necessary for me to hear.'

'Marianne's note, by assuring me that I was still as dear to her as in former days, that in spite of the many, many weeks we had been separated, she was as constant in her own feelings, and as full of faith in the constancy of mine as ever, awakened all my remorse. I say awakened, because time and London, business and dissipation, had in some measure quieted it, and I had been growing a fine hardened villain, fancying myself indifferent to her, and chusing to fancy that she too must have become indifferent to me; talking to myself of our past attachment as a mere idle, trifling, business, shrugging up my shoulders in proof of its being so, and silencing every reproach, overcoming every scruple, by secretly saying now and then, "I shall be heartily glad to hear she is well married." – But this note made me know myself better. I felt that she was infinitely dearer to me than any other woman in the world, and that I was using her infamously. But everything was then just settled between Miss Grey and me. To retreat was impossible. All that I had to do, was to avoid you both. I sent no answer to Marianne, intending by that means to preserve myself from her farther notice; and for some time I was even determined not to call in Berkeley-street; – but at last, judging it wiser to affect the air of a cool, common acquaintance than anything else, I watched you all safely out of the house one morning, and left my name.'

'Watched us out of the house!'

'Even so. You would be surprised to hear how often I watched you, how often I was on the point of falling in with you. I have entered many a shop to avoid your sight, as the carriage drove by. Lodging as I did in Bond-street, there was hardly a day in which I did not catch a glimpse of one or other of you; and nothing but the most constant watchfulness on my side, a most invariably prevailing desire to keep out of your sight, could have separated us so long. I avoided the Middletons as much as possible, as well as everybody else who was likely to prove an acquaintance in common. Not aware of their being in town, however, I blundered on Sir John, I believe, the first day of his coming, and the day after I had called at Mrs Jennings's. He asked me to a party, a dance at his house in the evening. – Had he *not* told me as an inducement that you and your sister were to be there, I should have felt it too certain a thing, to trust myself near him. The next morning brought another short note from Marianne – still affectionate, open, artless, confiding – everything that could make *my* conduct most hateful. I could not answer

at Cleveland – a letter that morning received from Mrs Jennings declared her danger most imminent – the Palmers all gone off in a fright, &c. – I was too much shocked to be able to pass myself off as insensible even to the undiscerning Sir John. His heart was softened in seeing mine suffer; and so much of his ill-will was done away, that when we parted, he almost shook me by the hand while he reminded me of an old promise about a pointer puppy. What I felt on hearing that your sister was dying – and dying too, believing me the greatest villain upon earth, scorning, hating me in her latest moments – for how could I tell what horrid projects might not have been imputed? *One* person I was sure would represent me as capable of anything – What I felt was dreadful! – My resolution was soon made, and at eight o'clock this morning I was in my carriage. Now you know all.'

Elinor made no answer. Her thoughts were silently fixed on the irreparable injury which too early an independence and its consequent habits of idleness, dissipation, and luxury, had made in the mind, the character, the happiness, of a man who, to every advantage of person and talents, united a disposition naturally open and honest, and a feeling, affectionate temper. The world had made him extravagant and vain – Extravagance and vanity had made him cold-hearted and selfish. Vanity, while seeking its own guilty triumph at the expense of another, had involved him in a real attachment, which extravagance, or at least its offspring, necessity, had required to be sacrificed. Each faulty propensity in leading him to evil, had led him likewise to punishment. The attachment, from which against honour, against feeling, against every better interest he had outwardly torn himself, now, when no longer allowable, governed every thought; and the connection, for the sake of which he had, with little scruple, left her sister to misery, was likely to prove a source of unhappiness to himself of a far more incurable nature. From a reverie of this kind she was recalled at the end of some minutes by Willoughby, who, rousing himself from a reverie at least equally painful, started up in preparation for going, and said,

'There is no use in staying here; I must be off.'

'Are you going back to town?'

'No – to Combe Magna. I have business there; from thence to town in a day or two. Good bye.'

He held out his hand. She could not refuse to give him her's; – he pressed it with affection.

'And you *do* think something better of me than you did?' – said he, letting it fall, and leaning against the mantle-piece as if forgetting he was to go.

Elinor assured him that she did; – that she forgave, pitied, wished him well – was even interested in his happiness – and added some gentle counsel as to the behaviour most likely to promote it. His answer was not very encouraging.

'As to that,' said he, 'I must rub through the world as well as I can. Domestic happiness is out of the question. If, however, I am allowed to think that you and yours feel an interest in my fate and actions, it may be the means – it may put me on my guard – at least, it will be something to live for. Marianne to be sure is lost to me for ever. Were I even by any blessed chance at liberty again' –

Elinor stopped him with a reproof.

'Well' – he replied – 'once more good bye. I shall now go away and live in dread of one event.'

'What do you mean?'

'Your sister's marriage.'

'You are very wrong. She can never be more lost to you than she is now.'

'But she will be gained by some one else. And if that some one should be the very he whom, of all others, I could least bear – But I will not stay to rob myself of all your compassionate goodwill, by shewing that where I have most injured I can least forgive. Good bye, – God bless you!'

And with these words, he almost ran out of the room.

Chapter Forty Five

ELINOR, FOR SOME TIME AFTER he left her, for some time even after the sound of his carriage had died away, remained too much oppressed by a croud of ideas, widely differing in themselves, but of which sadness was the general result, to think even of her sister.

Willoughby, he, whom only half an hour ago she had abhorred as the most worthless of men, Willoughby, in spite of all his faults, excited a degree of commiseration for the sufferings produced by them, which made her think of him as now separated for ever from her family with a tenderness, a regret, rather in proportion, as she soon acknowledged within herself – to his wishes than to his merits. She felt that his influence over her mind was heightened by circumstances which ought not in reason to have weight; by that person of uncommon attraction, that open, affectionate, and lively manner which it was no merit to possess; and by that still ardent love for Marianne, which it was not even innocent to indulge. But she felt that it was so, long, long before she could feel his influence less.

When at last she returned to the unconscious Marianne, she found her just awaking, refreshed by so long and sweet a sleep to the extent of her hopes. Elinor's heart was full. The past, the present, the future, Willoughby's visit, Marianne's safety, and her mother's expected arrival, threw her altogether into an agitation of spirits which kept off every indication of fatigue, and made her only fearful of betraying herself to her sister. Short was the time, however, in which that fear could affect her, for within half an hour after Willoughby's leaving the house, she was again called down stairs by the sound of another carriage. – Eager to save her mother from every unnecessary moment's horrible suspense, she ran immediately into the hall, and reached the outward door just in time to receive and support her as she entered it.

Mrs Dashwood, whose terror as they drew near the house had produced almost the conviction of Marianne's being no more, had no voice to enquire after her, no voice even for Elinor; but *she*, waiting neither for salutation nor inquiry, instantly gave the joyful relief; – and her mother, catching it with all her usual warmth, was in a moment as much overcome by her happiness, as she had been before by her fears. She was supported into the drawing-room between her daughter and her friend; – and there, shedding tears of joy, though still unable to speak, embraced Elinor again and again, turning from her at intervals to press Colonel Brandon's hand, with a look which spoke at once her gratitude, and her conviction of his sharing with herself in the bliss of the moment. He shared it, however, in a silence even greater than her own.

As soon as Mrs Dashwood had recovered herself, to see Marianne was her first desire; and in two minutes she was with her beloved child, rendered dearer to her than ever by absence, unhappiness, and danger. Elinor's delight, as she saw what each felt in the meeting, was only checked by an apprehension of its robbing Marianne of farther sleep; – but Mrs Dashwood could be calm, could be even prudent, when the life of a child was at stake, and Marianne, satisfied in knowing her mother was near her, and conscious of being too weak for conversation, submitted readily to the silence and quiet prescribed by every nurse around her. Mrs Dashwood *would* sit up with her all night, and Elinor, in compliance with her mother's entreaty, went to bed. But the rest, which one night entirely sleepless, and many hours of the most wearing anxiety seemed to make requisite, was kept off by irritation of spirits. Willoughby, 'poor Willoughby,' as she now allowed herself to call him, was constantly in her thoughts; she would not but have heard his vindication for the world, and now blamed, now acquitted herself for having judged him so harshly before. But her promise of relating it to her sister was invariably painful. She dreaded the performance of it, dreaded what its effect on Marianne might be; doubted whether after such an explanation she could ever by happy with another; and for a moment wished Willoughby a widower. Then, remembering Colonel Brandon, reproved herself, felt that to *his* sufferings and his constancy far more than to his rival's, the reward of her sister was due, and wished any thing rather than Mrs Willoughby's death.

The shock of Colonel Brandon's errand at Barton had been much softened to Mrs Dashwood by her own previous alarm; for so great was her uneasiness about Marianne, that she had already determined to set out for Cleveland on that very day, without waiting for any farther intelligence, and had so far settled her journey before his arrival, that the Careys were then expected every moment to fetch Margaret away, as her mother was unwilling to take her where there might be infection.

Marianne continued to mend every day, and the brilliant cheerfulness of Mrs Dashwood's looks and spirits proved her to be, as she repeatedly declared herself, one of the happiest women in the world. Elinor could not hear the declaration, nor witness its proofs without sometimes wondering whether her mother ever recollected Edward. But Mrs Dashwood, trusting to the temperate account of her own disappointment which Elinor had sent her, was led away by the exuberance of her joy to think only of what would increase it. Marianne was restored to her from a danger in which, as she now began to feel, her own mistaken judgment in encouraging the unfortunate attachment to Willoughby, had contributed to place her; – and in her recovery she had yet another source of joy unthought of by Elinor. It was thus imparted to her, as soon as any opportunity of private conference between them occurred.

'At last we are alone. My Elinor, you do not yet know all my happiness. Colonel Brandon loves Marianne. He has told me so himself.'

Her daughter, feeling by turns both pleased and pained, surprised and not surprised, was all silent attention.

'You are never like me, dear Elinor, or I should wonder at your composure now. Had I sat down to wish for any possible good to my family, I should have fixed on Colonel Brandon's marrying one of you as the object most desirable. And I believe Marianne will be the most happy with him of the two.'

Elinor was half inclined to ask her reason for thinking so, because satisfied that none founded on an impartial consideration of their age, characters, or feelings, could be given; – but her mother must always be carried away by her imagination on any interesting subject, and therefore instead of an inquiry, she passed it off with a smile.

'He opened his whole heart to me yesterday as we travelled. It came out quite unawares, quite undesignedly. I, you may well believe, could talk of nothing but my child; – he could not conceal his distress; I saw that it equalled my own, and he perhaps, thinking that mere friendship, as the world now goes, would not justify so warm a sympathy – or rather not thinking at all, I suppose – giving way to irresistible feelings, made me acquainted with his earnest, tender, constant, affection for Marianne. He has loved her, my Elinor, ever since the first moment of seeing her.'

Here, however, Elinor perceived, – not the language, not the professions of Colonel Brandon, but the natural embellishments of her mother's active fancy, which fashioned every thing delightful to her, as it chose.

'His regard for her, infinitely surpassing anything that Willoughby ever felt or feigned, as much more warm, as more sincere or constant – which ever we are to call it – has subsisted through all the knowledge of dear Marianne's unhappy prepossession for that worthless young man! – and without selfishness – without encouraging a hope! – could he have seen her happy with another – Such a noble mind! – such openness, such sincerity! – no one can be deceived in *him*.'

'Colonel Brandon's character,' said Elinor, 'as an excellent man, is well established.'

'I know it is' – replied her mother seriously, 'or after such a warning, I should be the last to encourage such affection, or even to be pleased by it. But his coming for me as he did, with such active, such ready friendship, is enough to prove him one of the worthiest of men.'

'His character, however,' answered Elinor, 'does not rest on *one* act of kindness, to which his affection for Marianne, were humanity out of the case, would have prompted him. To Mrs Jennings, to the Middletons, he has been long and intimately known; they equally love and respect him; and even my own knowledge of him, though lately acquired, is very considerable; and so highly do *I* value and esteem him, that if Marianne can be happy with him, I shall be as ready as yourself to think our connection the greatest blessing to us in the world. What answer did you give him? – Did you allow him to hope?'

'Oh! my love, I could not then talk of hope to him or to myself. Marianne might at that moment be dying. But he did not ask for hope or encouragement. His was an involuntary confidence, an irrepressible effusion to a soothing friend – not an application to a parent. Yet after a time I *did* say, for at first I was quite overcome – that if she lived, as I trusted she might, my greatest happiness would lie in promoting their marriage; and since our arrival, since our delightful security I have repeated it to him more fully, have given him every encouragement in my power. Time, a very little time, I tell him, will do everything; – Marianne's heart is not to be wasted for ever on such a man as Willoughby. – His own merits must soon secure it.'

'To judge from the Colonel's spirits, however, you have not yet made him equally sanguine.'

'No. – He thinks Marianne's affection too deeply rooted for any change in it under a great length of time, and even supposing her heart again free, is too diffident of himself to believe, that with such a difference of age and disposition, he could ever attach her. There, however, he is quite mistaken. His age is only so much beyond her's, as to be an advantage, as to make his character and principles fixed; – and his disposition, I am well convinced, is exactly the very one to make your sister happy. And his person, his manners too, are all in his favour. My partiality does not blind me; he certainly is not so handsome as Willoughby – but at the same time, there is something much more pleasing in his countenance. – There was always a something, – if you remember, – in Willoughby's eyes at times, which I did not like.'

Elinor could *not* remember it; – but her mother, without waiting for her assent, continued,

'And his manners, the Colonel's manners are not only more pleasing to me than Willoughby's ever were, but they are of a kind I well know to be more solidly attaching to Marianne. Their gentleness, their genuine attention to other people, and their manly unstudied simplicity is much more accordant with her real disposition, than the liveliness – often artificial, and often ill-timed of the other. I am very sure myself, that had Willoughby turned out as really amiable, as he has proved himself the contrary, Marianne would yet never have been so happy with *him*, as she will be with Colonel Brandon.'

She paused. – Her daughter could not quite agree with her, but her dissent was not heard, and therefore gave no offence.

'At Delaford, she will be within an easy distance of me,' added Mrs Dashwood, 'even if I remain at Barton; and in all probability, – for I hear it is a large village, – indeed there certainly *must* be some small house or cottage close by, that would suit us quite as well as our present situation.'

Poor Elinor! – here was a new scheme for getting her to Delaford! – but her spirit was stubborn.

'His fortune too! – for at my time of life you know, everybody cares about *that*; – and though I neither know, nor desire to know, what it really is, I am sure it must be a good one.'

Here they were interrupted by the entrance of a third person, and Elinor withdrew to think it all over in private, to wish success to her friend, and yet in wishing it, to feel a pang for Willoughby.

Chapter Forty Six

MARIANNE'S ILLNESS, THOUGH weakening in its kind, had not been long enough to make her recovery slow; and with youth, natural strength, and her mother's presence in aid, it proceeded so smoothly as to enable her to remove, within four days after the arrival of the latter, into Mrs Palmer's dressing-room. When there, at her own particular request, for she was impatient to pour forth her thanks to him for fetching her mother, Colonel Brandon was invited to visit her.

His emotion in entering the room, in seeing her altered looks, and in receiving the pale hand which she immediately held out to him, was such, as, in Elinor's conjecture, must arise from something more than his affection for Marianne, or the consciousness of its being known to others; and she soon discovered in his melancholy eye and varying complexion as he looked at her sister, the probable recurrence of many past scenes of misery to his mind, brought back by that resemblance between Marianne and Eliza already acknowledged, and now strengthened by the hollow eye, the sickly skin, the posture of reclining weakness, and the warm acknowledgment of peculiar obligation.

Mrs Dashwood, not less watchful of what passed than her daughter, but with a mind very differently influenced, and therefore watching to very different effect, saw nothing in the Colonel's behaviour but what arose from the most simple and self-evident sensations, while in the actions and words of Marianne she persuaded herself to think that something more than gratitude already dawned.

At the end of another day or two, Marianne growing visibly stronger every twelve hours, Mrs Dashwood, urged equally by her own and her daughter's wishes, began to talk of removing to Barton. On *her* measures depended those of her two friends; Mrs Jennings could not quit Cleveland during the Dashwoods' stay, and Colonel Brandon was soon brought, by their united request, to consider his own abode there as equally determinate, if not equally indispensable. At his and Mrs Jennings's united request in return, Mrs Dashwood was prevailed on to accept the use of his carriage on her journey back, for the better accommodation of her sick child; and the Colonel, at the joint invitation of Mrs Dashwood and Mrs Jennings, whose active good-nature made her friendly and hospitable for other people as well as herself, engaged with pleasure to redeem it by a visit at the cottage, in the course of a few weeks.

The day of separation and departure arrived; and Marianne, after taking so particular and lengthened a leave of Mrs Jennings, one so earnestly grateful, so full of respect and kind wishes as seemed due to her own heart from a secret acknowledgment of past inattention, and bidding Colonel Brandon farewel with the cordiality of a friend, was carefully assisted by him into the carriage, of which he seemed anxious that she should engross at least half. Mrs Dashwood and Elinor then followed, and the others were left by themselves, to talk of the travellers, and feel their own dulness, till Mrs Jennings was summoned to her chaise to take comfort in the gossip of her maid for the loss of her two young companions; and Colonel Brandon immediately afterwards took his solitary way to Delaford.

The Dashwoods were two days on the road, and Marianne bore her journey on both, without essential fatigue. Every thing that the most zealous affection, the most solicitous care could do to render her comfortable, was the office of each watchful companion, and each found their reward in her bodily ease, and her calmness of spirits. To Elinor, the observation of the latter was particularly grateful. She, who had seen her week after week so constantly suffering, oppressed by anguish of heart which she had neither courage to speak of, nor fortitude to conceal, now saw with a joy, which no other could equally share, an apparent composure of mind, which, in being the result as she trusted of serious reflection, must eventually lead her to contentment and cheerfulness.

As they approached Barton, indeed, and entered on scenes, of which every field and every tree brought some peculiar, some painful recollection, she grew silent and thoughtful, and turning away her face from their notice, sat earnestly gazing through the window. But here, Elinor could neither wonder nor blame; and when she saw, as she assisted Marianne from the carriage, that she had been crying, she saw only an emotion too natural in itself to raise anything less tender than pity, and in its unobtrusiveness entitled to praise. In the whole of her subsequent manner, she traced the direction of a mind awakened to reasonable exertion; for no sooner had they entered their common sitting-room, than Marianne turned her eyes around it with a look of resolute firmness, as if determined at once to accustom herself to the sight of every object with which the remembrance of Willoughby could be connected. – She said little, but every sentence aimed at cheerfulness, and though a sigh sometimes escaped her, it never passed away without the atonement of a smile. After dinner she would try her pianoforté. She went to it; but the music on which her eye first rested was an opera, procured for her by Willoughby, containing some of their favourite duets, and bearing on its outward leaf her own name in his hand writing. – That would not do. – She shook her head, put the music aside, and after running over the keys for a minute complained of feebleness in her fingers, and closed the instrument again; declaring however with firmness as she did so, that she should in future practise much.

The next morning produced no abatement in these happy symptoms. On the contrary, with a mind and body alike strengthened by rest, she looked and spoke with more genuine spirit, anticipating the pleasure of Margaret's return, and talking of the dear family party which would then be restored, of their mutual pursuits and cheerful society as the only happiness worth a wish.

'When the weather is settled, and I have recovered my strength,' said she, 'we will take long walks together every day. We will walk to the farm at the edge of the down, and see how the children go on; we will walk to Sir John's new plantations at Barton-Cross, and the Abbeyland; and we will often go to the old ruins of the Priory, and try to trace its foundations as far as we are told they once reached. I know we shall be happy. I know the summer will pass happily away. I mean never to be later in rising than six, and from that time till dinner I shall divide every moment between music and reading. I have formed my plan, and am determined to enter on a course of serious study. Our own library is too well known to me, to be resorted to for anything beyond mere amusement. But there are many works well worth reading, at the Park; and there are others of more modern production which I know I can borrow of Colonel Brandon. By reading only six hours a-day, I shall gain in the course of a twelve-month a great deal of instruction which I now feel myself to want.'

Elinor honoured her for a plan which originated so nobly as this; though smiling to see the same eager fancy which had been leading her to the extreme of languid indolence and selfish repining, now at work in introducing excess into a scheme of such rational employment and virtuous self-control.

Her smile however changed to a sigh when she remembered that her promise to Willoughby was yet unfulfilled, and feared she had that to communicate which might again unsettle the mind of Marianne, and ruin at least for a time this fair prospect of busy tranquillity. Willing therefore to delay the evil hour, she resolved to wait till her sister's health were more secure, before she appointed it. But the resolution was made only to be broken.

Marianne had been two or three days at home, before the weather was fine enough for an invalid like herself to venture out. But at last a soft, genial morning appeared; such as might tempt the daughter's wishes and the mother's confidence; and Marianne, leaning on Elinor's arm, was authorised to walk as long as she could without fatigue, in the lane before the house.

The sisters set out at a pace, slow as the feebleness of Marianne in an exercise hitherto untried since her illness required; – and they had advanced only so far beyond the house as to admit a full view of the hill, the important hill behind, when pausing with her eyes turned towards it, Marianne calmly said,

'There, exactly there' – pointing with one hand, 'on that projecting mound, – there I fell; and there I first saw Willoughby.'

Her voice sunk with the word, but presently reviving she added,

'I am thankful to find that I can look with so little pain on the spot! – shall we ever talk on that subject, Elinor?' – hesitatingly it was said, – 'Or will it be wrong? – I *can* talk of it now, I hope, as I ought to do.' –

Elinor tenderly invited her to be open.

'As for regret,' said Marianne, 'I have done with that, as far as *he* is concerned. I do not mean to talk to you of what my feelings have been for him, but what they are *now*. – At present, if I could be satisfied on one point, if I could be allowed to think that he was not *always* acting a part, not *always* deceiving me; – but above all, if I could be assured that he never was so *very* wicked as my fears have sometimes fancied him, since the story of that unfortunate girl' –

She stopt. – Elinor joyfully treasured her words as she answered,

'If you could be assured of that, you think you should be easy.'

'Yes. My peace of mind is doubly involved in it; – for not only is it horrible to suspect a person, who has been what *he* has been to *me*, of such designs, – but what must it make me appear to myself? – What in a situation like mine, but a most shamefully unguarded affection could expose me to' –

'How then,' asked her sister, 'would you account for his behaviour?'

'I would suppose him, – Oh! how gladly would I suppose him, only fickle, very, very fickle.'

Elinor said no more. She was debating within herself on the eligibility of beginning her story directly, or postponing it till Marianne were in stronger health; – and they crept on for a few minutes in silence.

'I am not wishing him too much good,' said Marianne at last with a sigh, 'when I wish his secret reflections may be no more unpleasant than my own. He will suffer enough in them.'

'Do you compare your conduct with his?'

'No. I compare it with what it ought to have been; I compare it with yours.'

'Our situations have borne little resemblance.'

'They have borne more than our conduct. – Do not, my dearest Elinor, let your kindness defend what I know your judgment must censure. My illness has made me think – It has given me leisure and calmness for serious recollection. Long before I was enough recovered to talk, I was perfectly able to reflect. I considered the past; I saw in my own behaviour since the beginning of our acquaintance with him last autumn, nothing but a series of imprudence towards myself, and want of kindness to others. I saw that my own feelings had prepared my sufferings, and that my want of fortitude under them had almost led me to the grave. My illness, I well knew, had been entirely brought on by myself, by such negligence of my own health, as I had felt even at the time to be wrong. Had I died, – it would have been self-destruction. I did not know my danger till the danger was removed; but with such feelings as these reflections gave me, I wonder at my recovery, – wonder that the very eagerness of my desire to live, to have time for atonement to my God, and to you all, did not kill me at once. Had I died, – in what peculiar misery should I have left you, my nurse, my friend, my sister! – You, who had seen all the fretful selfishness of my latter days; who had known all the murmurings of my heart! – How should I have lived in your remembrance! – My mother too! How could you have consoled her! – I cannot express my own abhorrence of myself. Whenever I looked towards the past, I saw some duty neglected, or some failing indulged. Every body seemed injured by me. The kindness, the unceasing kindness of Mrs Jennings, I had repaid with ungrateful contempt. To the Middletons, the Palmers, the Steeles, to every common acquaintance even, I had been insolent and unjust; with an heart hardened against their merits, and a temper irritated by their very attention. – To John, to Fanny, – yes, even to them, little as they deserve, I had given less than their due. But you, – you above all, above my mother, had been wronged by me. I, and only I, knew your heart and its sorrows; yet, to what did it influence me? – not to any compassion that could benefit you or myself. – Your example was before me: but to what avail? – Was I more considerate of you and your comfort? Did I imitate your forbearance, or lessen your restraints, by taking any part in those offices of general complaisance or particular gratitude which you had hitherto been left to discharge alone? – No; – not less when I knew you to be unhappy, than when I had believed you at ease, did I turn away from every exertion of duty or friendship; scarcely allowing sorrow to exist but with me, regretting only that heart which had deserted and wronged me, and leaving you, for whom I professed an unbounded affection, to be miserable for my sake.'

Here ceased the rapid flow of her self-reproving spirit; and Elinor, impatient to sooth, though too honest to flatter, gave her instantly that praise and support which her frankness and her contrition so well deserved. Marianne pressed her hand and replied,

'You are very good. – The future must be my proof. I have laid down my plan, and if I am capable of adhering to it – my feelings shall be governed and my temper improved. They shall no longer worry others, nor torture myself. I shall now live solely for my family. You, my mother, and Margaret, must henceforth be all the world to me; you will share my affections entirely between you. From you, from my home, I shall never again have the smallest incitement to move; and if I do mix in other society it will be only to shew that my spirit is humbled, my heart amended, and that I can practise the civilities, the lesser duties of life, with gentleness, and forbearance. As for Willoughby – to say that I shall soon or that I shall ever forget him, would be idle. His remembrance can be overcome by no change of circumstances or opinions. But it shall be regulated, it shall be checked by religion, by reason, by constant employment.'

She paused – and added in a lower voice, 'If I could but know *his* heart, everything would become easy.'

Elinor, who had now been for some time reflecting on the propriety or impropriety of speedily hazarding her narration, without feeling at all nearer decision than at first, heard this; and perceiving that as reflection did nothing, resolution must do all, soon found herself leading to the fact.

She managed the recital, as she hoped, with address; prepared her anxious listener with caution; related simply and honestly the chief points on which Willoughby grounded his apology; did justice to his repentance, and softened only his protestations of present regard. Marianne said not a word. – She trembled, her eyes were fixed on the ground, and her lips became whiter than even sickness had left them. A thousand inquiries sprung up from her heart, but she dared not urge one. She caught every syllable with panting eagerness; her hand, unknowingly to herself, closely pressed her sister's, and tears covered her cheeks.

Elinor, dreading her being tired, led her towards home; and till they reached the door of the cottage, easily conjecturing what her curiosity must be though no question was suffered to speak it, talked of nothing but Willoughby, and their conversation together; and was carefully minute in every particular of speech and look, where minuteness could be safely indulged. As soon as they entered the house, Marianne with a kiss of gratitude and these two words just articulate through her tears, 'Tell mama,' withdrew from her sister and walked slowly up stairs. Elinor would not attempt to disturb a solitude so reasonable as what she now sought; and with a mind anxiously pre-arranging its result, and a resolution of reviving the subject again, should Marianne fail to do it, she turned into the parlour to fulfil her parting injunction.

Chapter Forty Seven

MRS DASHWOOD DID NOT HEAR unmoved the vindication of her former favourite. She rejoiced in his being cleared from some part of his imputed guilt; – she was sorry for him; – she wished him happy. But the feelings of the past could not be recalled. – Nothing could restore him with a faith unbroken – a character unblemished, to Marianne. Nothing could do away the knowledge of what the latter had suffered through his means, nor remove the guilt of his conduct towards Eliza. Nothing could replace him, therefore, in her former esteem, nor injure the interests of Colonel Brandon.

Had Mrs Dashwood, like her daughter, heard Willoughby's story from himself – had she witnessed his distress, and been under the influence of his countenance and his manner, it is probable that her compassion would have been greater. But it was neither in Elinor's power, nor in her wish, to rouse such feelings in another, by her retailed explanation, as had at first been called forth in herself. Reflection had given calmness to her judgment, and sobered her own opinion of Willoughby's deserts; – she wished, therefore, to declare only the simple truth, and lay open such facts as were really due to his character, without any embellishment of tenderness to lead the fancy astray.

In the evening, when they were all three together, Marianne began voluntarily to speak of him again; – but that it was not without an effort, the restless, unquiet thoughtfulness in which she had been for some time previously sitting – her rising colour, as she spoke – and her unsteady voice, plainly shewed.

'I wish to assure you both,' said she, 'that I see every thing – as you can desire me to do.'

Mrs Dashwood would have interrupted her instantly with soothing tenderness, had not Elinor, who really wished to hear her sister's unbiassed opinion, by an eager sign, engaged her silence. Marianne slowly continued –

'It is a great relief to me – what Elinor told me this morning – I have now heard exactly what I wished to hear.' – For some moments her voice was lost; but recovering herself, she added, and with greater calmness than before – 'I am now perfectly satisfied, I wish for no change. I never could have been happy with him, after knowing, as sooner or later I must have known, all this. – I should have had no confidence, no esteem. Nothing could have done it away to my feelings.'

'I know it – I know it,' cried her mother. 'Happy with a man of libertine practices! – With one who had so injured the peace of the dearest of our friends, and the best of men! – No – my Marianne has not a heart to be made happy with such a man! – Her conscience, her sensitive conscience, would have felt all that the conscience of her husband ought to have felt.'

Marianne sighed, and repeated – 'I wish for no change.'

'You consider the matter,' said Elinor, 'exactly as a good mind and a sound understanding must consider it; and I dare say, your perceive, as well as myself, not only in this, but in many other circumstances, reason enough to be convinced that your marriage must have involved you in many certain troubles and disappointments, in which you would have been poorly supported by an affection, on his side, much less certain. Had you married, you must have been always poor. His expensiveness is acknowledged even by himself, and his whole conduct declares that self-denial is a word hardly understood by him. His demands and your inexperience together on a small, very small income, must have brought on distress which would not be the *less* grievous to you, from having been entirely unknown and unthought of before. Your sense of honour and honesty would have led you I know, when aware of your situation, to attempt all the economy that would appear to you possible; and perhaps, as long as your frugality retrenched only on your own comfort, you might have been suffered to practise it, but beyond that – and how little could the utmost of your single management do to stop the ruin which had begun before your marriage? – Beyond *that*, had you endeavoured, however reasonably, to abridge *his* enjoyments, is it not to be feared, that instead of prevailing on feelings so selfish to consent to it, you would have lessened your own influence on his heart, and made him regret the connection which had involved him in such difficulties?'

Marianne's lips quivered, and she repeated the word 'Selfish?' in a tone that implied – 'do you really think him selfish?'

'The whole of his behaviour,' replied Elinor, 'from the beginning to the end of the affair, has been grounded on selfishness. It was selfishness which first made him sport with your affections; which afterwards, when his own were engaged, made him delay the confession of it, and which finally carried him from Barton. His own enjoyment, or his own ease, was, in every particular, his ruling principle.'

'It is very true. *My* happiness never was his object.'

'At present,' continued Elinor, 'he regrets what he has done. And why does he regret it? – Because he finds it has not answered towards himself. It has not made him happy. His circumstances are now unembarrassed – he suffers from no evil of that kind; and he thinks only that he has married a woman of a less amiable temper than yourself. But does it thence follow that had he married you, he would have been happy? – The inconveniences would have been different. He would then have suffered under the pecuniary distresses which, because they are removed, he now reckons as nothing. He would have had a wife of whose temper he could make no complaint, but he would have been always necessitous – always poor; and probably would soon have learnt to rank the innumerable comforts of a clear estate and good income as of far more importance, even to domestic happiness, than the mere temper of a wife.'

'I have not a doubt of it,' said Marianne; 'and I have nothing to regret – nothing but my own folly.'

'Rather say your mother's imprudence, my child,' said Mrs Dashwood; '*she* must be answerable.'

Marianne would not let her proceed; – and Elinor, satisfied that each felt their own error, wished to avoid any survey of the past that might weaken her sister's spirits; she therefore, pursuing the first subject, immediately continued,

'*One* observation may, I think, be fairly drawn from the whole of the story – that all Willoughby's difficulties have arisen from the first offence against virtue, in his behaviour to Eliza Williams. That crime has been the origin of every lesser one, and of all his present discontents.'

Marianne assented most feelingly to the remark; and her mother was led by it to an enumeration of Colonel Brandon's injuries and merits, warm as friendship and design could unitedly dictate. Her daughter did not look, however, as if much of it were heard by her.

Elinor, according to her expectation, saw on the two or three following days, that Marianne did not continue to gain strength as she had done; but while her resolution was unsubdued, and she still tried to appear cheerful and easy, her sister could safely trust to the effect of time upon her health.

Margaret returned, and the family were again all restored to each other, again quietly settled at the cottage, and if not pursuing their usual studies with quite so much vigour as when they first came to Barton, at least planning a vigorous prosecution of them in future.

Elinor grew impatient for some tidings of Edward. She had heard nothing of him since her leaving London, nothing new of his plans, nothing certain even of his present abode. Some letters had passed between her and her brother, in consequence of Marianne's illness; and in the first of John's, there had been this sentence: – 'We know nothing of our unfortunate Edward, and can make no enquiries on so prohibited a subject, but conclude him to be still at Oxford;' which was all the intelligence of Edward afforded her by the correspondence, for his name was not even mentioned in any of the succeeding letters. She was not doomed, however, to be long in ignorance of his measures.

Their man-servant had been sent one morning to Exeter on business; and when, as he waited at table, he had satisfied the enquiries of his mistress as to the event of his errand, this was his voluntary communication –

'I suppose you know, ma'am, that Mr Ferrars is married.'

Marianne gave a violent start, fixed her eyes upon Elinor, saw her turning pale, and fell back in her chair in hysterics. Mrs Dashwood, whose eyes, as she answered the servant's inquiry, had intuitively taken the same direction, was shocked to perceive by Elinor's countenance how much she really suffered, and in a moment afterwards, alike distressed by Marianne's situation, knew not on which child to bestow her principal attention.

The servant, who saw only that Miss Marianne was taken ill, had sense enough to call one of the maids, who, with Mrs Dashwood's assistance, supported her into the other room. By that time. Marianne was rather better, and her mother leaving her to the care of Margaret and the maid, returned to Elinor, who, though still much disordered, had so far recovered the use of her reason and voice as to be just beginning an inquiry of Thomas, as to the source of his intelligence. Mrs Dashwood immediately took all that trouble on herself; and Elinor had the benefit of the information without the exertion of seeking it.

'Who told you that Mr Ferrars was married, Thomas?'

'I see Mr Ferrars myself, ma'am this morning in Exeter, and his lady too, Miss Steele as was. They was shopping in a chaise at the door of the New London Inn, as I went there with a message from Sally at the Park to her brother, who is one of the post-boys. I happened to look up as I went by the chaise, and so I see directly it was the youngest Miss Steele; so I took off my hat, and she knew me and called to me, and inquired after you, ma'am, and the young ladies, especially Miss Marianne, and bid me I should give her compliments and Mr Ferrars's, their best compliments and service, and how sorry they was they had not time to come on and see you, but they was in a great hurry to go forwards, for they was going further down for a little while, but howsever, when they come back, they'd make sure to come and see you.'

'But did she tell you she was married, Thomas?'

'Yes, ma'am. She smiled, and said how she had changed her name since she was in these parts. She was always a very affable and free-spoken young lady, and very civil behaved. So, I made free to wish her joy.'

'Was Mr Ferrars in the carriage with her?'

'Yes, ma'am, I just see him leaning back in it, but he did not look up; – he never was a gentleman much for talking.'

Elinor's heart could easily account for his not putting himself forward; and Mrs Dashwood probably found the same explanation.

'Was there no one else in the carriage?'

'No, ma'am, only they two.'

'Do you know where they came from?'

'They come straight from town, as Miss Lucy – Mrs Ferrars told me.'

'And are going farther westward?'

'Yes, ma'am – but not to bide long. They will soon be back again, and then they'd be sure and call here.'

Mrs Dashwood now looked at her daughter; but Elinor knew better than to expect them. She recognised the whole of Lucy in the message, and was very confident that Edward would never come near them. She observed, in a low voice, to her mother, that they were probably going down to Mr Pratt's, near Plymouth.

Thomas's intelligence seemed over. Elinor looked as if she wished to hear more.

'Did you see them off, before you came away?'

'No, ma'am – the horses was just coming out, but I could not bide any longer; I was afraid of being late.'

'Did Mrs Ferrars look well?'

'Yes, ma'am, she said how she was very well; and to my mind she was always a very handsome young lady – and she seemed vastly contented.'

Mrs Dashwood could think of no other question, and Thomas and the table-cloth, now alike needless, were soon afterwards dismissed. Marianne had already sent to say that she should eat nothing more. Mrs Dashwood's and Elinor's appetites were equally lost, and Margaret might think herself very well off, that with so much uneasiness as both her sisters had lately experienced, so much reason as they had often had to be careless of their meals, she had never been obliged to go without her dinner before.

When the dessert and the wine were arranged, and Mrs Dashwood and Elinor were left by themselves, they remained long together in a similarity of thoughtfulness and silence. Mrs Dashwood feared to hazard any remark, and ventured not to offer consolation. She now found that she had erred in relying on Elinor's representation of herself; and justly concluded that every thing had been expressly softened at the time, to spare her from an increase of unhappiness, suffered as she then had suffered for Marianne. She found that she had been misled by the careful, the considerate attention of her daughter, to think the attachment, which once she had so well understood, much slighter in reality, than she had been wont to believe, or than it was now proved to be. She feared that under this persuasion she had been unjust, inattentive, nay, almost unkind, to her Elinor; – that Marianne's affliction, because more acknowledged, more immediately before her, had too much engrossed her tenderness, and led her away to forget than in Elinor she might have a daughter suffering almost as much, certainly with less self-provocation, and greater fortitude.

Chapter Forty Eight

ELINOR NOW FOUND THE DIFFERENCE between the expectation of an unpleasant event, however certain the mind may be told to consider it, and certainly itself. She now found, that in spite of herself, she had always admitted a hope, while Edward remained single, that something would occur to prevent his marrying Lucy; that some resolution of his own, some mediation of friends, or some more eligible opportunity of establishment for the lady, would arise to assist the happiness of all, but he was now married, and she condemned her heart for the lurking flattery, which so much heightened the pain of the intelligence.

That he should be married so soon, before (as she imagined) he could be in orders, and consequently before he could be in possession of the living, surprised her a little at first. But she soon saw how likely it was that Lucy, in her self-provident care, in her haste to secure him, should overlook every thing but the risk of delay. They were married, married in town, and now hastening down to her uncle's. What had Edward felt on being within four miles of Barton, on seeing her mother's servant, on hearing Lucy's message!

They would soon, she supposed, be settled at Delaford. – Delaford, – that place in which so much conspired to give her an interest; which she wished to be acquainted with, and yet desired to avoid. She saw them in an instant in their parsonage-house; saw in Lucy, the active, contriving manager, uniting at once a desire of smart appearance, with the utmost frugality, and ashamed to be suspected of half her economical practices; – pursuing her own interest in every thought, courting the favour of Colonel Brandon, of Mrs Jennings, and of every wealthy friend. In Edward – she knew not what she saw, nor what she wished to see; – happy or unhappy, – nothing pleased her; she turned away her head from every sketch of him.

Elinor flattered herself that some one of their connections in London would write to them to announce the event, and give farther particulars, – but day after day passed off, and brought no letter, no tidings. Though uncertain that any one were to blame, she found fault with every absent friend. They were all thoughtless or indolent.

'When do you write to Colonel Brandon, ma'am?' was an enquiry which sprung from the impatience of her mind to have something going on.

'I wrote to him, my love, last week, and rather expect to see, than to hear from him again. I earnestly pressed his coming to us, and should not be surprised to see him walk in today or tomorrow, or any day.'

This was gaining something, something to look forward to. Colonel Brandon *must* have some information to give.

Scarcely had she so determined it, when the figure of a man on horseback drew her eyes to the window. He stopt at their gate. It was a gentleman, it was Colonel Brandon himself. Now she should hear more; and she trembled in expectation of it. But – it was *not* Colonel Brandon – neither his air – nor his height. Were it possible, she should say it must be Edward. She looked again. He had just dismounted; – she could not be mistaken; – it *was* Edward. She moved away and sat down. 'He comes from Mr Pratt's purposely to see us. I *will* be calm; I *will* be mistress of myself.'

In a moment she perceived that the others were likewise aware of the mistake. She saw her mother and Marianne change colour; saw them look at herself, and whisper a few sentences to each other. She would have given the world to be able to speak – and to make them understand that she hoped no coolness, no slight, would appear in their behaviour to him; – but she had no utterance, and was obliged to leave all to their own discretion.

Not a syllable passed aloud. They all waited in silence for the appearance of their visitor. His footsteps were heard along the gravel path; in a moment he was in the passage; and in another, he was before them.

His countenance, as he entered the room, was not too happy, even for Elinor. His complexion was white with agitation, and he looked as if fearful of his reception, and conscious that he merited no kind one. Mrs Dashwood, however, conforming, as she trusted, to the wishes of that daughter, by whom she then meant in the warmth of her heart to be guided in everything, met him with a look of forced complacency, gave him her hand, and wished him joy.

He coloured, and stammered out an unintelligible reply. Elinor's lips had moved with her mother's, and when the moment of action was over, she wished that she had shaken hands with him too. But it was then too late, and with a countenance meaning to be open, she sat down again and talked of the weather.

Marianne had retreated as much as possible out of sight, to conceal her distress; and Margaret, understanding some part, but not the whole, of the case, thought it incumbent on her to be dignified, and therefore took a seat as far from him as she could, and maintained a strict silence.

When Elinor had ceased to rejoice in the dryness of the season, a very awful pause took place. It was put an end to by Mrs Dashwood, who felt obliged to hope that he had left Mrs Ferrars very well. In a hurried manner, he replied in the affirmative.

Another pause.

Elinor, resolving to exert herself, though fearing the sound of her own voice, now said,

'Is Mrs Ferrars at Longstaple?'

'At Longstaple!' he replied, with an air of surprise – 'No, my mother is in town.'

'I meant,' said Elinor, taking up some work from the table, 'to inquire after Mrs *Edward* Ferrars.'

She dared not look up; – but her mother and Marianne both turned their eyes on him. He coloured, seemed perplexed, looked doubtingly, and after some hesitation, said,

'Perhaps you mean – my brother – you mean Mrs – Mrs *Robert* Ferrars.'

'Mrs Robert Ferrars!' – was repeated by Marianne and her mother, in an accent of the utmost amazement; – and though Elinor could not speak, even *her* eyes were fixed on him with the same impatient wonder. He rose from his seat and walked to the window, apparently from not knowing what to do; took up a pair of scissars that lay there, and while spoiling both them and their sheath by cutting the latter to pieces as he spoke, said, in an hurried voice,

'Perhaps you do not know – you may not have heard that my brother is lately married to – to the youngest – to Miss Lucy Steele.'

His words were echoed with unspeakable astonishment by all but Elinor, who sat with her head leaning over her work, in a state of such agitation as made her hardly know where she was.

'Yes,' said he, 'they were married last week, and are now at Dawlish.'

Elinor could sit no longer. She almost ran out of the room, and as soon as the door was closed, burst into tears of joy, which at first she thought would never cease. Edward, who had till then looked any where, rather than at her, saw her hurry away, and perhaps saw – or even heard, her emotion; for immediately afterwards he fell into a reverie, which no remarks, no inquiries, no affectionate address of Mrs Dashwood could penetrate, and at last, without saying a word, quitted the room, and walked out towards the village – leaving the others in the greatest astonishment and perplexity on a change in his situation, so wonderful and so sudden; – a perplexity which they had no means of lessening but by their own conjectures.

Chapter Forty Nine

UNACCOUNTABLE, HOWEVER, AS the circumstances of his release might appear to the whole family, it was certain that Edward was free: and to what purpose that freedom would be employed was easily pre-determined by all; – for after experiencing the blessings of *one* imprudent engagement, contracted without his mother's consent, as he had already done for more than four years, nothing less could be expected of him in the failure of *that*, than the immediate contraction of another.

His errand at Barton, in fact, was a simple one. It was only to ask Elinor to marry him; – and considering that he was not altogether inexperienced in such a question, it might be strange that he should feel so uncomfortable in the present case as he really did, so much in need of encouragement and fresh air.

How soon he had walked himself into the proper resolution, however, how soon an opportunity of exercising it occurred, in what manner he expressed himself, and how he was received, need not be particularly told. This only need be said; – that when they all sat down to table at four o'clock, about three hours after his arrival, he had secured his lady, engaged her mother's consent, and was not only in the rapturous profession of the lover, but in the reality of reason and truth, one of the happiest of men. His situation indeed was more than commonly joyful. He had more than the ordinary triumph of accepted love to swell his heart, and raise his spirits. He was released without any reproach to himself, from an entanglement which had long formed his misery, from a woman whom he had long ceased to love; – and elevated at once to that security with another, which he must have thought of almost with despair, as soon as he had learnt to consider it with desire. He was brought, not from doubt or suspense, but from misery to happiness; – and the change was openly spoken in such a genuine, flowing, grateful cheerfulness, as his friends had never witnessed in him before.

His heart was now open to Elinor, all its weaknesses, all its errors confessed, and his first boyish attachment to Lucy treated with all the philosophic dignity of twenty-four.

'It was a foolish, idle inclination on my side,' said he, 'the consequence of ignorance of the world – and want of employment. Had my mother given me some active profession when I was removed at eighteen from the care of Mr Pratt, I think – nay, I am sure, it would never have happened; for though I left Longstaple with what I thought, at the time, a most unconquerable preference for his niece, yet had I then had any pursuit, any object to engage my time and keep me at a distance from her for a few months, I should very soon have outgrown the fancied attachment, especially by mixing more with the world, as in such a case I must have done. But instead of having anything to do, instead of having any profession chosen for me, or being allowed to chuse any myself, I returned home to be completely idle; and for the first twelvemonth afterwards, I had not even the nominal employment, which belonging to the university would have given me, for I was not entered at

Oxford till I was nineteen. I had therefore nothing in the world to do, but to fancy myself in love; and as my mother did not make my home in every respect comfortable, as I had no friend, no companion in my brother, and disliked new acquaintance, it was not unnatural for me to be very often at Longstaple, where I always felt myself at home, and was always sure of a welcome; and accordingly I spent the greatest part of my time there from eighteen to nineteen: Lucy appeared everything that was amiable and oblig-ing. She was pretty too – at least I thought so *then*, and I had seen so little of other women, that I could make no comparisons, and see no defects. Considering everything, therefore, I hope, foolish as our engagement was, foolish as it has since in every way been proved, it was not at the time an unnatural, or an inexcusable piece of folly.'

The change which a few hours had wrought in the minds and the happiness of the Dashwoods, was such – so great – as promised them all, the satisfaction of a sleepless night. Mrs Dashwood, too happy to be comfortable, knew not how to love Edward, nor praise Elinor enough, how to be enough thankful for his release without wounding his delicacy, nor how at once to give them leisure for unrestrained conversation together, and yet enjoy, as she wished, the sight and society of both.

Marianne could speak *her* happiness only by tears. Comparisons would occur – regrets would arise; – and her joy, though sincere as her love for her sister, was of a kind to give her neither spirits nor language.

But Elinor – How are *her* feelings to be described? – From the moment of learning that Lucy was married to another, that Edward was free, to the moment of his justifying the hopes which had so instantly followed, she was everything by turns but tranquil. But when the second moment had passed, when she found every doubt, every solicitude removed, compared her situation with what so lately it had been, – saw him honourably released from his former engagement, saw him instantly profiting by the release, to address herself and declare an affection as tender, as constant as she had ever supposed it to be, – she was oppressed, she was overcome by her own felicity; – and happily disposed as is the human mind to be easily familiarized with any change for the better, it required several hours to give sedateness to her spirits, or any degree of tranquillity to her heart.

Edward was now fixed at the cottage at least for a week, for whatever other claims might be made on him, it was impossible that less than a week should be given up to the enjoyment of Elinor's company, or suffice to say half that was to be said of the past, the present, and the future; – for though a very few hours spent in the hard labour of incessant talking will dispatch more subjects than can really be in common between any two rational creatures, yet with lovers it is different. Between *them* no subject is finished, no communication is even made, till it has been made at least twenty times over.

Lucy's marriage, the unceasing and reasonable wonder among them all, formed of course one of the earliest discussions of the lovers; – and Elinor's particular knowledge of each party made it appear to her in every view, as one of the most extraordinary and unaccountable circumstances she had ever heard. How they could be thrown together, and by what attraction Robert could be drawn on to marry a girl, of whose beauty she had herself heard him speak without any admiration, – a girl too already engaged to his brother, and on whose account that brother had been thrown off by his family – it was beyond her comprehension to make out. To her own heart it was a delightful affair, to her imagination it was even a ridiculous one, but to her reason, her judgment, it was completely a puzzle.

Edward could only attempt an explanation by supposing, that perhaps at first accidentally meeting, the vanity of the one had been so worked on by the flattery of the other, as to lead by degrees to all the rest. Elinor remembered what Robert had told her in Harley-street, of his opinion of what his own mediation in his brother's affairs might have done, if applied to in time. She repeated it to Edward.

'*That* was exactly like Robert,' – was his immediate observation. – 'And *that*,' he presently added, 'might perhaps be in *his* head when the acquaintance between them first began. And Lucy perhaps at first might think only of procuring his good offices in my favour. Other designs might afterwards arise.'

How long it had been carrying on between them, however, he was equally at a loss with herself to make out; for at Oxford, where he had remained by choice ever since his quitting London, he had had no means of hearing of her but from herself, and her letters to the very last were neither less frequent, nor less affectionate than usual. Not the smallest suspicion, therefore, had ever occurred to prepare him for what followed; – and when at last it burst on him in a letter from Lucy herself, he had been for some time, he believed, half stupified between the wonder, the horror, and the joy of such a deliverance. He put the letter into Elinor's hands.

DEAR SIR

Being very sure I have long lost your affections, I have thought myself at liberty to bestow my own on another, and have no doubt of being as happy with him as I once used to think I might be with you; but I scorn to accept a hand while the heart was another's. Sincerely wish you happy in your choice, and it shall not be my fault if we are not always good friends, as our near relationship now makes proper. I can safely say I owe you no ill-will, and am sure you will be too generous to do us any ill offices. Your brother has gained my affections entirely, and as we could not live without one another, we are just returned from the altar, and are now on our way to Dawlish for a few weeks, which place your dear brother has great curiosity to see, but thought I would first trouble you with these few lines, and shall always remain,

Your sincere well-wisher, friend, and sister,

LUCY FERRARS.

I have burnt all your letters, and will return your picture the first opportunity. Please to destroy my scrawls – but the ring with my hair you are very welcome to keep.

Elinor read and returned it without any comment.

'I will not ask your opinion of it as a composition,' said Edward. – 'For worlds would not I have had a letter of her's seen by *you* in former days. – In a sister it is bad enough, but in a wife! – how I have blushed over the pages of her writing! – and I believe I may say that since the first half year of our foolish – business – this is the only letter I ever received from her, of which the substance made me any amends for the defect of the style.'

'However it may have come about,' said Elinor, after a pause – 'they are certainly married. And your mother has brought on herself a most appropriate punishment. The independence she settled on Robert, through resentment against you, has put it in his power to make his own choice; and she has actually been bribing one son with a thousand a-year, to do the very deed which she disinherited the other for intending to do. She will hardly be less hurt, I suppose, by Robert's marrying Lucy, than she would have been by your marrying her.'

'She will be more hurt by it, for Robert always was her favourite. – She will be more hurt by it, and on the same principle will forgive him much sooner.'

In what state the affair stood at present between them, Edward knew not, for no communication with any of his family had yet been attempted by him. He had quitted Oxford within four and twenty hours after Lucy's letter arrived, and with only one object before him, the nearest road to Barton, had had no leisure to form any scheme of conduct, with which that road did not hold the most intimate connection. He could do nothing till he were assured of his fate with Miss Dashwood; and by his rapidity in seeking *that* fate, it is to be supposed, in spite of the jealousy with which he had once thought of Colonel Brandon, in spite of the modesty with which he rated his own deserts, and the politeness with which he talked of his doubts, he did not, upon the whole, expect a very cruel reception. It was his business, however, to say that he *did*, and he said it very prettily. What he might say on the subject a twelvemonth after, must be referred to the imagination of husbands and wives.

That Lucy had certainly meant to deceive, to go off with a flourish of malice against him in her message by Thomas, was perfectly clear to Elinor; and Edward himself, now thoroughly enlightened on her character, had no scruple in believing her capable of the utmost meanness of wanton ill-nature. Though his eyes had been long opened, even before his acquaintance with Elinor began, to her ignorance and a want of liberality in some of her opinions – they had been equally imputed, by him, to her want of education; and till her last letter reached him, he had always believed her to be a well-disposed, good-hearted girl, and thoroughly attached to himself. Nothing but such a persuasion could have prevented his putting an end to an engagement, which, long before the discovery of it laid him open to his mother's anger, had been a continual source of disquiet and regret to him.

'I thought it my duty,' said he, 'independent of my feelings, to give her the option of continuing the engagement or not, when I was renounced by my mother, and stood to all appearance without a friend in the world to assist me. In such a situation as that, where there seemed nothing to tempt the avarice or the vanity of any living creature, how could I suppose, when she so earnestly, so warmly insisted on sharing my fate, whatever it might be, that any thing but the most disinterested affection was her inducement? And even now, I cannot comprehend on what motive she acted, or what fancied advantage it could be to her, to be fettered to a man for whom she had not the smallest regard, and who had only two thousand pounds in the world. She could not foresee that Colonel Brandon would give me a living.'

'No, but she might suppose that something would occur in your favour; that your own family might in time relent. And at any rate, she lost nothing by continuing the engagement, for she has proved that it fettered neither her inclination nor her actions. The connection was certainly a respectable one, and probably gained her consideration among her friends; and, if nothing more advantageous occurred, it would be better for her to marry you than be single.'

Edward was of course immediately convinced that nothing could have been more natural than Lucy's conduct, nor more self-evident than the motive of it.

Elinor scolded him, harshly as ladies always scold the imprudence which compliments themselves, for having spent so much time with them at Norland, when he must have felt his own inconstancy.

'Your behaviour was certainly very wrong,' said she, 'because – to say nothing of my own conviction, our relations were all led away by it to fancy and expect what, as you were then situated, could never be.'

He could only plead an ignorance of his own heart, and a mistaken confidence in the force of his engagement.

'I was simple enough to think, that because my faith was plighted to another, there could be no danger in my being with you; and that the consciousness of my engagement was to keep my heart as safe and sacred as my honour. I felt that I admired you, but I told myself it was only friendship; and till I began to make comparisons between yourself and Lucy, I did not know how far I was got. After that, I suppose, I was wrong in remaining so much in Sussex, and the arguments with which I reconciled myself to the expediency of it, were no better than these: – The danger is my own; I am doing no injury to anybody but myself.'

Elinor smiled, and shook her head.

Edward heard with pleasure of Colonel Brandon's being expected at the Cottage, as he really wished not only to be better acquainted with him, but to have an opportunity of convincing him that he no longer resented his giving him the living of Delaford – 'Which, at present,' said he, 'after thanks so ungraciously delivered as mine were on the occasion, he must think I have never forgiven him for offering.'

Now he felt astonished himself that he had never yet been to the place. But so little interest had he taken in the matter, that he owed all his knowledge of the house, garden, and glebe, extent of the parish, condition of the land, and rate of the tythes, to Elinor herself, who had heard so much of it from Colonel Brandon, and heard it with so much attention, as to be entirely mistress of the subject.

One question after this only remained undecided, between them, one difficulty only was to be overcome. They were brought together by mutual affection, with the warmest approbation of their real friends, their intimate knowledge of each other seemed to make their happiness certain – and they only wanted something to live upon. Edward had two thousand pounds, and Elinor one, which, with Delaford living, was all that they could call their own; for it was impossible that Mrs Dashwood should advance anything, and they were neither of them quite enough in love to think that three hundred and fifty pounds a-year would supply them with the comforts of life.

Edward was not entirely without hopes of some favourable change in his mother towards him; and on that he rested for the residue of their income. But Elinor had no such dependance; for since Edward would still be unable to marry Miss Morton, and his chusing herself had been spoken of in Mrs Ferrars's flattering language as only a lesser evil than his chusing

Lucy Steele, she feared that Robert's offence would serve no other purpose than to enrich Fanny.

About four days after Edward's arrival, Colonel Brandon appeared, to complete Mrs Dashwood's satisfaction, and to give her the dignity of having, for the first time since her living at Barton, more company with her than the house would hold. Edward was allowed to retain the privilege of first comer, and Colonel Brandon therefore walked every night to his old quarters at the Park; from whence he usually returned in the morning, early enough to interrupt the lovers' first tête-à-tête before breakfast.

A three weeks' residence at Delaford, where, in his evening hours at least, he had little to do but to calculate the disproportion between thirty-six and seventeen, brought him to Barton in a temper of mind which needed all the improvement in Marianne's looks, all the kindness of her welcome, and all the encouragement of her mother's language, to make it cheerful. Among such friends, however, and such flattery, he did revive. No rumour of Lucy's marriage had yet reached him; – he knew nothing of what had passed; and the first hours of his visit were consequently spent in hearing and in wondering. Every thing was explained to him by Mrs Dashwood, and he found fresh reason to rejoice in what he had done for Mr Ferrars, since eventually it promoted the interest of Elinor.

It would be needless to say, that the gentlemen advanced in the good opinion of each other, as they advanced in each other's acquaintance, for it could not be otherwise. Their resemblance in good principles and good sense, in disposition and manner of thinking, would probably have been sufficient to unite them in friendship, without any other attraction; but their being in love with two sisters, and two sisters fond of each other, made that mutual regard inevitable and immediate, which might otherwise have waited the effect of time and judgment.

The letters from town, which a few days before would have made every nerve in Elinor's body thrill with transport, now arrived to be read with less emotion than mirth. Mrs Jennings wrote to tell the wonderful tale, to vent her honest indignation against the jilting girl, and pour forth her compassion towards poor Mr Edward, who, she was sure, had quite doted upon the worthless hussey, and was now, by all accounts, almost broken-hearted, at Oxford. – 'I do think,' she continued, 'nothing was ever carried on so sly; for it was but two days before Lucy called and sat a couple of hours with me. Not a soul suspected anything of the matter, not even Nancy, who, poor soul! came crying to me the day after, in a great fright for fear of Mrs Ferrars, as well as not knowing how to get to Plymouth; for Lucy it seems borrowed all her money before she went off to be married, on purpose we suppose to make a shew with, and poor Nancy had not seven shillings in the world; – so I was very glad to give her five guineas to take her down to Exeter, where she thinks of staying three or four weeks with Mrs Burgess, in hopes, as I tell her, to fall in with the Doctor again. And I must say that Lucy's crossness not to take her along with them in the chaise is worse than all. Poor Mr Edward! I cannot get him out of my head, but you must send for him to Barton, and Miss Marianne must try to comfort him.'

Mr Dashwood's strains were more solemn. Mrs Ferrars was the most unfortunate of women – poor Fanny had suffered agonies of sensibility – and he considered the existence of each, under such a blow, with grateful wonder. Robert's offence was unpardonable, but Lucy's was infinitely worse. Neither of them was ever again to be mentioned to Mrs Ferrars; and even, if she might hereafter be induced to forgive her son, his wife should never be acknowledged as her daughter, nor be permitted to appear in her presence. The secrecy with which every thing had been carried on between them, was rationally treated as enormously heightening the crime, because, had any suspicion of it occurred to the others, proper measures would have been taken to prevent the marriage; and he called on Elinor to join with him in regretting that Lucy's engagement with Edward had not rather been fulfilled, than that she should thus be the means of spreading misery farther in the family. – He thus continued:

'Mrs Ferrars has never yet mentioned Edward's name, which does not surprise us; but to our great astonishment, not a line has been received from him on the occasion. Perhaps, however, he is kept silent by his fear of offending, and I shall, therefore, give him a hint, by a line to Oxford, that his sister and I both think a letter of proper submission from him, addressed perhaps to Fanny, and by her shewn to her mother, might not be taken amiss; for we all know the tenderness of Mrs Ferrars's heart, and that she wishes for nothing so much as to be on good terms with her children.'

This paragraph was of some importance to the prospects and conduct of Edward. It determined him to attempt a reconciliation, though not exactly in the manner pointed out by their brother and sister.

'A letter of proper submission!' repeated he; 'would they have me beg my mother's pardon for Robert's ingratitude to *her*, and breach of honour to *me*? – I can make no submission – I am grown neither humble nor penitent by what has passed. – I am grown very happy, but that would not interest. – I know of no submission that *is* proper for me to make.'

'You may certainly ask to be forgiven,' said Elinor, 'because you have offended; – and I should think you might *now* venture so far as to profess some concern for having ever formed the engagement which drew on you your mother's anger.'

He agreed that he might.

'And when she has forgiven you, perhaps a little humility may be convenient while acknowledging a second engagement, almost as imprudent in *her* eyes, as the first.'

He had nothing to urge against it, but still resisted the idea of a letter of proper submission; and therefore, to make it easier to him, as he declared a much greater willingness to make mean concessions by word of mouth than on paper, it was resolved that, instead of writing to Fanny, he should go to London, and personally intreat her good offices in his favour. – 'And if they really *do* interest themselves,' said Marianne, in her new character of candour, 'in bringing about a reconciliation, I shall think that even John and Fanny are not entirely without merit.'

After a visit on Colonel Brandon's side of only three or four days, the two gentlemen quitted Barton together. – They were to go immediately to Delaford, that Edward might have some personal knowledge of his future home, and assist his patron and friend in deciding on what improvements were needed to it; and from thence, after staying there a couple of nights, he was to proceed on his journey to town.

Chapter Fifty

AFTER A PROPER RESISTANCE ON THE part of Mrs Ferrars, just so violent and so steady as to preserve her from that reproach which she always seemed fearful of incurring, the reproach of being too amiable, Edward was admitted to her presence, and pronounced to be again her son.

Her family had of late been exceedingly fluctuating. For many years of her life she had had two sons; but the crime and annihilation of Edward a few weeks ago, had robbed her of one; the similar annihilation of Robert had left her for a fortnight without any; and now, by the resuscitation of Edward, she had one again.

In spite of his being allowed once more to live, however, he did not feel the continuance of his existence secure, till he had revealed his present engagement; for the publication of that circumstance, he feared, might give a sudden turn to his constitution, and carry him off as rapidly as before. With apprehensive caution therefore it was revealed, and he was listened to with unexpected calmness. Mrs Ferrars at first reasonably endeavoured to dissuade him from marrying Miss Dashwood, by every argument in her power; – told him, that in Miss Morton he would have a woman of higher rank and larger fortune; – and enforced the assertion, by observing that Miss Morton was the daughter of a nobleman with thirty thousand pounds, while Miss Dashwood was only the daughter of a private gentleman, with no more than *three*; but when she found that, though perfectly admitting the truth of her representation, he was by no means inclined to be guided by it, she judged it wisest, from the experience of the past, to submit – and therefore, after such an ungracious delay as she owed to her own dignity, and as served to prevent every suspicion of good-will, she issued her decree of consent to the marriage of Edward and Elinor.

What she would engage to do towards augmenting their income, was next to be considered; and here it plainly appeared, that though Edward was now her only son, he was by no means her eldest; for while Robert was inevitably endowed with a thousand pounds a-year, not the smallest objection was made against Edward's taking orders for the sake of two hundred and fifty at the utmost; nor was anything promised either for the present or in future, beyond the ten thousand pounds, which had been given with Fanny.

It was as much, however, as was desired, and more than was expected by Edward and Elinor; and Mrs Ferrars herself, by her shuffling excuses, seemed the only person surprised at her not giving more.

With an income quite sufficient to their wants thus secured to them, they had nothing to wait for after Edward was in possession of the living, but the readiness of the house, to which Colonel Brandon, with an eager desire for the accommodation of Elinor, was making considerable improvements; and after waiting some time for their completion, after experiencing, as usual, a thousand disappointments and delays, from the unaccountable dilatoriness of the workmen, Elinor, as usual, broke through the first positive resolution of not marrying till every thing was ready, and the ceremony took place in Barton church early in the autumn.

The first month after their marriage was spent with their friend at the Mansion-house, from whence they could superintend the progress of the Parsonage, and direct every thing as they liked on the spot; – could chuse papers, project shrubberies, and invent a sweep. Mrs Jennings's prophecies, though rather jumbled together, were chiefly fulfilled; for she was able to visit Edward and his wife in their Parsonage by Michaelmas, and she found in Elinor and her husband, as she really believed, one of the happiest couple in the world. They had in fact nothing to wish for, but the marriage of Colonel Brandon and Marianne, and rather better pasturage for their cows.

They were visited on their first settling by almost all their relations and friends. Mrs Ferrars came to inspect the happiness which she was almost ashamed of having authorised; and even the Dashwoods were at the expense of a journey from Sussex to do them honour.

'I will not say that I am disappointed, my dear sister,' said John, as they were walking together one morning before the gates of Delaford House, 'that would be saying too much, for certainly you have been one of the most fortunate young women in the world, as it is. But, I confess, it would give me great pleasure to call Colonel Brandon brother. His property here, his place, his house, every thing in such respectable and excellent condition! – and his woods! – I have not seen such timber any where in Dorsetshire, as there is now standing in Delaford Hanger! – And though, perhaps, Marianne may not seem exactly the person to attract him – yet I think it would altogether be adviseable for you to have them now frequently staying with you, for as Colonel Brandon seems a great deal at home, nobody can tell what may happen – for, when people are much thrown together, and see little of anybody else – and it will always be in your power to set her off to advantage, and so forth; – in short, you may as well give her a chance – You understand me.' –

But though Mrs Ferrars *did* come to see them, and always treated them with the make-believe of decent affection, they were never insulted by her real favour and preference. *That* was due to the folly of Robert, and the cunning of his wife; and it was earned by them before many months had passed away. The selfish sagacity of the latter, which had at first drawn Robert into the scrape, was the principal instrument of his deliverance from it; for her respectful humility, assiduous attentions, and endless flatteries, as soon as the smallest opening was given for their exercise, reconciled Mrs Ferrars to his choice, and re-established him completely in her favour.

The whole of Lucy's behaviour in the affair, and the prosperity which crowned it, therefore, may be held forth as a most encouraging instance of what an earnest, an unceasing attention to self-interest, however its progress may be apparently obstructed, will do in securing every advantage of fortune, with no other sacrifice than that of time and conscience. When Robert first sought her acquaintance, and privately visited her in Bartlett's Buildings, it was only with the view imputed to him by his brother. He merely meant to persuade her to give up the engagement; and as there could be nothing to overcome but the affection of both, he naturally expected that one or two interviews would settle the matter. In that point, however, and that only, he erred; – for though Lucy soon gave him hopes that his eloquence would convince her in *time*, another visit, another conversation, was always wanted to produce this conviction. Some doubts always lingered in her mind when they parted, which could only be removed by another half hour's discourse with himself. His attendance was by this means secured, and the rest followed in course. Instead of talking of Edward, they came gradually to talk only of Robert, – a subject on which he had always more to say than on any other, and in which she soon betrayed an interest even equal to his own; and in short, it became speedily evident to both, that he had entirely supplanted his brother. He was proud of his conquest, proud of tricking Edward, and very proud of marrying privately without his mother's consent. What immediately followed is known. They passed some months in great happiness at Dawlish; for she had many relations and old acqaintance to cut – and he drew several plans for magnificent cottages; – and from thence returning to town, procured the forgiveness of Mrs Ferrars, by the simple expedient of asking it, which, at Lucy's instigation, was adopted. The forgiveness at first, indeed, as was reasonable, comprehended only Robert; and Lucy, who had owed his mother no duty, and therefore could have transgressed none, still remained some weeks longer unpardoned. But perseverance in humility of conduct and messages, in self-condemnation for Robert's offence, and gratitude for the unkindness she was treated with, procured her in time the haughty notice which overcame her by its graciousness, and led soon afterwards, by rapid degrees, to the highest state of affection and influence. Lucy became as necessary to Mrs Ferrars, as either Robert or Fanny; and while Edward was never cordially forgiven for having once intended to marry her, and Elinor, though superior to her in fortune and birth, was spoken of as an intruder, *she* was in every thing considered, and always openly acknowledged, to be a favourite child. They settled in town, received very liberal assistance from Mrs Ferrars, were on the best terms imaginable with the Dashwoods; and setting aside the jealousies and ill-will continually subsisting between Fanny and Lucy, in which their husbands of course took a part, as well as the frequent domestic disagreements between Robert and Lucy themselves, nothing could exceed the harmony in which they all lived together.

What Edward had done to forfeit the right of eldest son, might have puzzled many people to find out; and what Robert had done to succeed to it, might have puzzled them still more. It was an arrangement, however, justified in its effects, if not in its cause; for nothing ever appeared in Robert's style of living or of talking, to give a suspicion of his regretting the extent of his income, as either leaving his brother too little, or bringing himself too much; – and if Edward might be judged from the ready discharge of his duties in every particular, from an increasing attachment to his wife and his home, and from the regular cheerfulness of his spirits, he might be supposed no less contented with his lot, no less free from every wish of an exchange.

Elinor's marriage divided her as little from her family as could well be contrived, without rendering the cottage at Barton entirely useless, for her mother and sisters spent much more than half their time with her. Mrs Dashwood was acting on motives of policy as well as pleasure in the frequency of her visits at Delaford; for her wish of bringing Marianne and Colonel Brandon together was hardly less earnest, though rather more liberal than what John had expressed. It was now her darling object. Precious as was the company of her daughter to her, she desired nothing so much as to give up its constant enjoyment to her valued friend; and to see Marianne settled at the mansion-house was equally the wish of Edward and Elinor. They each felt his sorrows, and their own obligations, and Marianne, by general consent, was to be the reward of all.

With such a confederacy against her – with a knowledge so intimate of his goodness – with a conviction of his fond attachment to herself, which at last, though long after it was observable to everybody else – burst on her – what could she do?

Marianne Dashwood was born to an extraordinary fate. She was born to discover the falsehood of her own opinions, and to counteract, by her conduct, her most favourite maxims. She was born to overcome an affection formed so late in life as at seventeen, and with no sentiment superior to strong esteem and lively friendship, voluntarily to give her hand to another! – and *that* other, a man who had suffered no less than herself under the event of a former attachment, whom, two years before, she had considered too old to be married, – and who still sought the constitutional safeguard of a flannel waistcoat!

But so it was. Instead of falling a sacrifice to an irresistible passion, as once she had fondly flattered herself with expecting, – instead of remaining even for ever with her mother, and finding her only pleasures in retirement and study, as afterwards in her more calm and sober judgment she had determined on, – she found herself at nineteen, submitting to new attachments, entering on new duties, placed in a new home, a wife, the mistress of a family, and the patroness of a village.

Colonel Brandon was now as happy, as all those who best loved him, believed he deserved to be; – in Marianne he was consoled for every past affliction; – her regard and her society restored his mind to animation, and his spirits to cheerfulness; and that Marianne found her own happiness in forming his, was equally the persuasion and delight of each observing friend. Marianne could never love by halves; and her whole heart became, in time, as much devoted to her husband, as it had once been to Willoughby.

Willoughby could not hear of her marriage without a pang; and his punishment was soon afterwards complete in the voluntary forgiveness of Mrs Smith, who, by stating his marriage with a woman of character, as the source of her clemency, gave him reason for believing that had he behaved with honour towards Marianne, he might at once have been happy and rich. That his repentance of misconduct, which thus brought its own punishment, was sincere, need not be doubted; – nor that he long thought of Colonel Brandon with envy, and of Marianne with regret. But that he was for ever inconsolable, that he fled from society, or contracted an habitual gloom of temper, or died of a broken heart, must not be depended on – for he did neither. He lived to exert, and frequently to enjoy himself. His wife was not always out of humour, nor his home always uncomfortable; and in his breed of horses and dogs, and in sporting of every kind, he found no inconsiderable degree of domestic felicity.

For Marianne, however – in spite of his incivility in surviving her loss – he always retained that decided regard which interested him in everything that befell her, and made her his secret standard of perfection in woman; – and many a rising beauty would be slighted by him in after-days as bearing no comparison with Mrs Brandon.

Mrs Dashwood was prudent enough to remain at the cottage, without attempting a removal to Delaford; and fortunately for Sir John and Mrs Jennings, when Marianne was taken from them, Margaret had reached an age highly suitable for dancing, and not very ineligible for being supposed to have a lover.

Between Barton and Delaford, there was that constant communication which strong family affection would naturally dictate; – and among the merits and the happiness of Elinor and Marianne, let it not be ranked as the least considerable, that though sisters, and living almost within sight of each other, they could live without disagreement between themselves, or producing coolness between their husbands.